Nature and Necessity

Praise for *Nature and Necessity*

This is a wonderfully in-depth journey into the lives of a remarkable family led by Petula, the ultimate, ruthless matriarch. It is not just a journey in time, with family events leading to a compelling, affectionate and dramatic denouement, but a journey in prose, too. Because every sentence is a delight to read, crafted with an intricate yet intuitive design that makes the words themselves every bit as compelling as the plot. For this excellent reason, it is not an airport novel as every sentence deserves to be savored and many lingered over for their originality, inner meaning and insights into this wonderfully dysfunctional family. Its portrayal of country life has an enviable authenticity which means it is surely cut from real life. But it is sculpted to have a special significance and theme that raises it above ordinary reality. It is the story of a family, dark, deep, funny and, above all, likeable. I'm missing Petula and her children already.

Pat Mills, Creator of 2000AD.

A vast, immersive family saga, this book insists on the mud in blood, the wood in flesh – the astounding inextricability of the human animal from the earth in which it was formed. Goddard shows us that blood-relations are exactly that – bloody. This is nature writing at its most intensely observed, and ever mindful of our position within the colossal movements of the world. The 'necessity' of the title is inarguable.

Niall Griffiths, Author of Grits.

Tariq Goddard is good on houses and the people who inhabit them and the interplay between the inanimate and the humans who ascribe the inanimate with qualities that vary from the banal to the outré.

In this instance the humans are snobbish, social climbing Yorkshire bohemians, gruesome people whose mores, pretences and hierarchical delusions are pungently portrayed. Their children are unspeakable. Their aquaintances include a marvellous caricature of Ted Hughes and some deftly drawn theatre folk. The book is a stern warning not to venture north of the Humber – though it is of course possible that such monsters of self-preoccupation may be found in, say, Cranborne Chase.

Jonathan Meades, Author of An Encyclopaedia of Myself.

Also by Tariq Goddard

TARIQ GODDARD

Nature and Necessity

Published by Repeater Books
An imprint of Watkins Media Ltd

19-21 Cecil Court
London
WC2N 4EZ
UK

www.repeaterbooks.com
A Repeater Books paperback original 2017
1

Distributed in the United States by Random House, Inc., New York.

Cover design, snake vignette: Johnny Bull
Typography and typesetting: Jan Middendorp
Typefaces: Chaparral, Alegreya and AbsaraSans

ISBN: 978-1-910924-44-0
Ebook ISBN: 978-1-910924-45-7

Printed in the UK

For my children, Lola, Spike and Titus, and in memory of their grandfather, David John Goddard, 1926–2013.

In memory of Mark Fisher (1968–2017).

In memory of Sara Hammond (1975–2017).

The rat race is for rats.

    – Jimmy Reid

Necessity is the kingdom of nature; freedom is the kingdom of grace.

    – Arthur Schopenhauer

Prologue

Even though they were mother and daughter they were known mostly as 'the sisters'. It was a union that would lead them both into lives they wished they had not had. Petula, a divisive redhead and social titan, was their leader; Regan, the third of her children, and first in command, her mother's life project and puckish enforcer. Whether people embraced them or not depended on their daring, and the sisters' initiative, for they were tireless initiators. From the start, there were an elect few for whom they would perform, and countless extras who were expected to do the performing. Their criteria for deciding who fell where was unattainable by effort alone. What the performers thought of this depended on whether they were picked for the first team, or left on the bench to wonder and fade. For many it proved an elusive code to break; the sisters enjoyed mysteries and gave little away. Others remained tantalised to the end, waiting for the postcard, telephone call or text that would usher them up the hill for an audience at The Heights.

For over thirty-five years, the sisters could be found in the village of Mockery Gap, a setting too beautiful for most natives to be allowed to live out their days in. Though northern, the village shared many features with its southern siblings; young professionals and their families, a smattering of overdevelopment and a nest of millionaire residences where labourers' cottages once stood. The house the sisters lived in, The Heights, was saved from literary comparisons by being one of three attractive buildings on the same farm, the second and third dwellings demonstrating their inferiority by their state of evolving disrepair and inhabitants' vocations. Of these houses, the best that could be said was that their names, like cities swapping hands in a civil war, came to take meanings appropriate to the sisters' changing attitudes towards their inhabitants. The bigger of the two houses, Tianta, Celtic for 'Fighter' or 'Warrior' – there was confusion over which – was occupied by Jasper, son and brother to the sisters, and found halfway up the hill. When the sisters were unhappy with Jasper they called this house 'The Pimple'. Lower down the hill was Chudleigh, the home of the Hardfields, a family that came with the estate; theirs a smaller cottage that the sisters dubbed 'The Wart' whether they were happy with them or not.

Though it gave the appearance of being a working farm, The Heights was a front for the good life, despite Petula's insistence to the contrary. The facts were that the estate and its peacocks, guinea fowl, geese and free-range hens were largely decorative, the production of eggs and the making of money mostly incidental to their existence there. The same principle held for the prize-winning pigs that paraded yearly through the village every Bullrush Fair, never finding their way onto the breakfast table or butcher's counter, and the farm donkey, Caligula, who photographed well for the children's section of *Yorkshire Life*, garlands of orange peel and seashells hanging from his obliging mane. The oilseed rape and wheat fields snaking round The Heights were no different, merely the agricultural trimmings of a painting whose real subject matter lay elsewhere. Nearly all of the arable land was leased to local farmers. These quietly embittered men owned the grazing cattle and sheep that completed an atmosphere of rural industry. The real money for the lavish upkeep of The Heights came from factory-farms in the Philippines, owned by Petula's estranged husband, and the rest of her bucolic high jinks supplemented by warehouse complexes outside Sheffield and Leeds. All this left Petula free to publicly pursue the official business of the farm, a highly convoluted and inimitable form of flower arranging.

This highly visible, and largely unprofitable, occupation enjoyed a reputation and profile well in excess of its annual turnover, allowing Petula to compare it to opera, a similar loss-making but culturally necessary venture. Running her company seasonally, Petula specialised in pink and white tulips, purple iris and apple blossom in spring. With the arrival of summer, she turned to blue cornflowers, delicate cow parsley and bobbing cosmos, and in winter deep-red holly berries, trailing ivy and twisted twigs. Her clients were mostly local markets, a few ladies who made scents, and weddings, though Petula's reputation for wanting to control every aspect of these kept bookings to a trickle. For the most part the flowers died where they grew, were thrown away or donated to schools, churches and charity. Petula took it all in her formidable stride. Her real passion, she said, was the house; once a modest Arts and Crafts cottage, now arguably the most attractive dwelling in the county. The Heights had evolved into her calling, its changing interiors, paintings, sculpture and furnishings the equal of a museum, if not an interactive installation in its own right. It was her creation, so she felt, the product of rare taste and persistent endeavour, its aesthetic glory her triumph and how she wished the world to see her. It did not matter if this display failed to reflect truth, as even in her own company, Petula did not see things as they were but as she wished others to, the public self the only one she would acknowledge, even to Regan. And so the years passed as a reflection of what she thought they were, an unpreventable march towards what she preferred to call 'modest local success'.

As first witness to Petula, Regan saw it all. Fanaticism ran in the blood, and her early devotion to her mother bordered on the ideological. The imperative to remain loyal was inculcated into the children, though in Regan's case there was little need to go to such lengths; she was a natural disciple. The first eyes she saw life through were Petula's, and as her mother rooted for herself, it was natural for Regan to root for her too. For years it was impossible for her to separate her mother's interests and battles from her own. Conflict was the pillow Petula slept on, fluffing it up when it threatened to become too comfortable a fit. Because she was loud, opinionated and forthright, her children assumed she told the world what it did not want to hear, the heresy that she might be audacious and possessed by her own fictions rarely crossing their minds. It shocked Regan especially that Petula's construction of reality could be misconstrued as caprice, and those who thought so were isolated, demonised and set upon with relish. In the event, cruel whispers did little to dent the high regard Petula was held in, at least at the public events she policed, and disapproval was usually forced to take strange and subterranean forms.

Victory over her adversaries did not bring love. The difficulty with Petula's indefatigability was that little got close to it, and as people can only love what they enjoy true knowledge of, Petula had to make do with several approximations of the real thing. Love became shorthand for what her admirers really felt – intense esteem at the battling example she set, awe even, but never love. So far as that was concerned she remained an unknown object.

Perhaps this was why a shrill current of hurt was often noticeable in her voice, a primary wound she had no intention of closing. Without completely meaning to, she cultivated it, filling it with generous helpings of fresh pain, until the morning came when she awoke to find hurt installed as the organising principle of her life.

'Regan,' said Petula, tearing open the blinds, 'how long have you been up? I wish you wouldn't put the lights on when there's perfectly good sunshine *outside*, you know I hate artificial *light*, it makes me feel like I'm living in perennial winter. It's cold enough in here as it is.'

'It *is* November.'

'November my teeth, November's for sad old things to freeze

to death in. We're not sad old things, for us there's no such thing as autumn.'

Regan thumbed the switch leaving the room at the mercy of blinding, blazing sunlight. She was dressed in purple silk pyjamas, the kind worn by oriental courtesans or a pantomime Aladdin, and in spite of her slightly boyish attire, was a green-eyed thirty-two year-old woman in her prime. Her face was tight, pinched and angular; the skin stretched over a wrinkleless diamond consisting of a triangular chin, mountaintop cheekbones, and a skull worthy of donation to medicine, sitting on a neck of geometrical elegance. When Regan smiled, her expression grew so taut that her mother joked it could be steamed off with a whistling kettle, others finding it alluring, if not a little severe in construction.

'But my birthday is in November...'

'I wouldn't go on about that if I were you, *nothing* with a zero behind it is good news.'

'I'll be thirty-three, no, two.'

'Rubbish, you're twenty-nine, aren't you? We haven't had your thirtieth yet.'

'We put up a marquee for it Mum, there was lots of noise and people kept using your bathroom. It all definitely happened.'

'Is there something the matter with you?'

'I'm sorry?'

'You seem to be talking through your teeth, are you nervous about something?'

'No, no, I don't think so... why, are you?'

'How could I be in all this glorious sunshine?'

The kitchen they stood in was the throne room of The Heights. It sat at the closing stages of a long and broad corridor that connected the two wings of the house, Petula's half and Regan's end, two mounted stacks either side of a tunnel, the shape of the building resembling a double-headed arrow with weighted tips. Large windows ensured good views and little privacy from prying eyes, which was how Petula liked it, the world looking in to see the sisters looking back. With its exposed position on top of a hill, living in The Heights was akin to joining passengers on a great cruise liner, the upper deck battered by the wind and rain, while down below a party presided, with the two tiers, the storm and the supper, never quite reconciled.

'Has Brickwall moved those sheep yet? They can hardly *walk*, little wonder Vesey doesn't want them in the village where everyone can see the poor shape they're in.' Petula did not like silence, even if she did not care much about sheep.

'I can't remember, has he?'

'I wish you'd take more interest in the farm, I can't keep everything going on my own forever.'

'Oh you can.'

'Don't. If I didn't chase, harry and harangue, those poor animals would be crawling round on their chins, eating stumps. Call themselves farmers? It'd make me laugh if it didn't make me ill,' Petula winced, her bad ankle tense and swollen. 'They can't look after their own clothes, let alone livestock. I've already written to your father about it, fat lot of use, but he may as well know what's going on, it's *his* "farm" after all.'

It was a rare admission of reality and both women blanched at being reminded of the power relation that maintained them, for although they were separated and Petula exercised nominal control of The Heights on a vast allowance, she did not own the building – only a few of the newer objects in it. Most assumed she came from money, or was divorced and the house was hers, misconceptions she did nothing to discourage.

'To hell with the *man, he* only remembers us when it suits him.'

Petula was tall, full-breasted and heavier than she looked, without being in the slightest bit fat. Her shoulder-length hair was burnt-red, and her wide shoulders and long forearms exuded Amazonian fortitude, last tested pulling down the jodhpurs of the master of the local hunt a week earlier. Despite her immense strength of character, her body was failing her, the act of sitting painful for her lower back and knees; and avoiding the temptation to flop on a chair, having only been awake for ten minutes, she practically shouted:

'*And* I suppose nothing's been done about the hot water either?'

'He said Skinner will come next week.'

'Skinner! Next *week*, first as tragedy then as farce! I'd sooner knock the pipes down myself. It was his fault we're in this mess, I told your father not to hire him, they never listen. It's like the Hampton Court Maze up in that attic. You'd think they'd take some pride in their work. Heaven knows, I do in mine. As I get older I become more open about my faults and infinitely more forgiving about those of others,' she lied, 'but that man really does take the full St Michael.'

The habit of blaming others ran deep in Petula, starting with her father, moving on to her husbands, settling on her son, and always primed to affix itself to various tradesmen, farmers and lovers. There was no disguising that it was usually men who fulfilled this role, or that hers was a life (and family) a lot of men had run away from. Men were like children to Petula: it was not good to let them make decisions for themselves too early on, yet by the time they came of age they took them to spite her earlier care.

Petula squinted and pursed her flinty lips. '*Is* that Jazzy out there by the bird table?' The sky had tipped to one side, as if God was having trouble seeing straight, and in the bifurcating light Petula could make out a figure, its silhouette giving off an aura of agitation in defeat.

'It could be, he likes to feed the birds.'

'He's been saying that all year and I still end up doing it, I've learnt not to set my watch by hope with that boy.'

'He's having a hard time, I think.'

'He *is* a hard time.'

'He's unlucky.' Until quite recently, Regan had clung to the belief that her mother was a fair person given to an unfeasibly large number of unfair remarks. 'And he hasn't learnt to budget properly.'

'Life isn't fair on those of us whose backbones are made of self-pity. You can't confuse karma with morality. What you *deserve* isn't always *fair*. Morality is the stuff of judgement, but life is an energy. Jazzy is all one and none of the other.'

Regan nodded, 'In a way.' With all the goodwill she could scrape together, a condition and activity she was more troubled by than proficient in, she knew her brother's life stratagem was roughly predicated on her mother, her father or herself 'carking' it, preferably at one and the same time, and found that she could best love him on occasions, such as those that had existed for the past few years, when her mother did not.

Petula moved her long fingers over the Aga, their tips dancing nervously upon the heat. 'What time did you ask him to come over?'

'Two, the same time as everyone else, it was on the invites I thought. Did you want to get him on his own first?'

'Never mind him, are you *sure* they're all coming?'

'I think so, I rang around and asked like you said I should, and told them it was important, like you asked me to. They all said they would be here; at least, everyone I talked to did.'

'Do you think your insisting made the difference?'

'To their coming?'

'What else?'

'*Perhaps*, no, they would have come anyway. They love it here, you know that, it's their spiritual home, what was it Hall calls it, a "magical kingdom"?'

'That man is an obsequious creep, but happily not wrong about everything.'

Petula regulated her circle through large and frequent meals, the superlatives used to describe them as grandiloquent and

sticky as the marmalade-glazed hams consumed by the privileged attendees. For her family, rather than friends, these
occasions were somewhat less looked-forward-to. A few even
approached them with trepidation; a call from The Heights
taking on the role of a high-court summons. In the past few
months assorted relatives had done the hitherto unthinkable
and failed to show on demand. This fed into a perverse aspect
of Petula's statecraft. There was nothing more likely to rouse
her than someone she considered beneath her appearing to not
want her. The recalcitrant absentees had to be reined in before
their quiet escape attempts became a full-blown stampede.
Petula had struggled to think of an occasion to get them all
back, and still had not made her mind up when she gave Regan
the order to wheel them in again. 'Masterly inactivity' was not
her style, action was paramount, even if a plan or point had yet
to be put in place.

'Anyone can admire a view, to live and master a place is the
thing. What about Royce? What did she say, stressing about
her cats and budgerigar again or likely to flatter us with her
company?'

'Actually, she did sound a bit on edge even for her, she was
a bit "what is it this time?". I think she's afraid she's forgotten
something again, another birthday or anniversary. She's getting on.'

'Very charitable of you, hers is not to remember or know why,
hers is just to bloody well turn *up*, you should have just told her
that the pack must not scatter!'

'But that's what you'd say, it wouldn't sound like me if I came
out with something like that... I can't talk like you.'

The snag was that although Petula knew a perpetual state
of crisis was necessary to wield power, the danger of crying
wolf was not lost on her. To maintain credibility she required
a respectable pretext for the gathering. A party for one of her
grandchildren? Hers was not a family that had bought into the

cult of the child, and in any case, there were few on offer. Petula had not been celebrated as one and was careful to not bring too much attention to her own. Other people's youngsters were useful for rallying the troops in a quiet month, but were no substitute for real drama. Besides, quiet months were dangerous for other reasons, people could get too used to them and decide they preferred them to the unquiet kind. For Petula, they also carried personal terrors she dare not share, namely her abhorrence of peace and being left on her own to meet herself. It was no accident that her radio was never switched off and that she was amongst the first of her generation to purchase a mobile telephone, however much it, and faxing, texting and e-mailing, had affected her psychic powers.

'All any of them need to know is that they haven't eaten together for... for far *too* long. And families *should* eat together, I pity people who've been brought up to think otherwise.'

'Two weeks I think, since the last time we met as a family.'

'Nonsense, much longer than that. Why do you feel the need to contradict me all the time, you never used to be like this?'

'I'm sorry, I didn't realise, here...' Regan passed her mother a cup with stars on it.

'That isn't herbal, is it? No, good. Well, I'm not just inviting them round to see their faces, there are things we need to *discuss*.' Petula snorted and took a sip of her tea, the hot liquid scalding the roof of her mouth in a way she found reassuringly agreeable. Why not really upset the applecart and announce an incurable disease? Despite flirting with the idea for years she was sure she had got one... and, if not, what harm would it do to have a very rare affliction she could invent, something exotic with a Latin name that no one knew very much about, *'Don't worry, not a lot of people have heard of it, the great thing is I could still have years left...'*

Petula laughed and put down the cup, her emerald eyes hardening with what might seem to be mischievous resolve.

'The real question is, will the ham be ready in time? Not that any one of them would notice once they get stuck into the booze, the greedy trollops. You know, there are days when I'd sooner eat the people and entertain the ham. Like the pig, often I too feel like a guest at my own meal.'

Control required novelty but could not be gauche. An undeniable lie might set the trap that would finally undo her, far better to tie her deception to facts. Twenty years earlier, if she were to choose an illness, the cutting-edge option would have had to have been Aids, risqué then, passé now; cancer had always been grubby (not to say specific and all too likely), and while there was respect for a heart attack it was beyond her to fake one. Which left the flu, measles and athlete's foot, and who honestly cared about those? Disease would have to wait as it could not possibly live up to its billing. Even if it did, one could not rule out the possibility of her audience embracing shock without remorse, or a mute fatalism that was suspiciously like relief. The obedience a period of mourning would afford could not be manipulated this side of death. Without being able to trust her family's loyalty, it was impossible to play games with it or resort to lesser strategies. Emigration might have once had a similar effect to disease but had been used before, as had threats to sell the house, marry again, and take up the needle and spoon, during a particularly fraught period over last Christmas when they had argued over whether it should be turkey or goose. Petula blew at her tea impatiently, the absurdities even an honest life relied on irritating her greatly.

'Good God, the lengths these people drive you to...'

'You're doing too much Mum, I'm here to help you if you'd let me. Why have anyone over at all? I could just call and say you're ill. Well, you are in a way with all the things wrong with you, and it could just be us then. It'd be way more fun, I'd prefer it anyway.'

Petula rolled her eyes benignly and tried to extinguish the

suspicion that her daughter was no longer entirely in earnest when it came to declarations of this sort, or earnest at all. Was there something she was keeping from her, a heart pricked by jealousy or a mind full of murders she dare not commit? If she could doubt Regan, she could doubt anything. It was disquieting how thoughts slid into unruly pathways, covering ground one's voice would never dare air. Imposing her will on the jetsam and making a decision was the only cure. She would take a stand as she always had.

'Could you boil the kettle again please? This has gone cold.'

Pretexts and excuses were beneath her, she was chasing shadows with both and conceding the moral high ground she required to rule. Asking people to behave properly required no subterfuge, her achievements went beyond personalities. The Heights was an abstract code, a system that would continue without an individual at its head because the system itself was already a person exhibiting a character: her own. She did not want it to work without her, for the dead to be food for the living. She wanted *in*; the world turning by itself an unimaginable proposition. What was would be.

'What are you thinking, Mummy?'

'Ignorance, Regan, is bliss.'

She was spoilt for options, let them all come and she would give them what for. She laughed a little manically, she would simply tell them they were there because she *wanted* them to be. 'I'll rub their noses in my love and give them new faces,' she erupted.

Regan took a tactful bite of her pain au chocolat and affected not to hear.

'Options my dear, they distract and mislead but are the purest measure of success I know, the more you collect, the more memorable the decision.'

In the eternal glory of the present moment, it was easy for Petula to forget a time when she had few if any options at all, a time before the advent of 'the sisters', when she was still a girl and not rage incarnate.

'Roll on four o'clock,' she announced casting her dressing gown onto the kitchen floor, the freckles on her bare shoulders catching the bouncing sunlight. 'When they get here tell them to keep their coats on and join me in the garden. I don't care how bloody cold it is, this is too good a day to waste indoors talking shop over last *year's* ham. What I have to say to them can be said under the sky, under the sky and in *life*.'

Selective glimpses of full nudity were used sparingly but efficiently by Petula to make a point, and as she stood there, proud in her state of undress, her naked flesh a challenge for her daughter to emulate or run from, Regan could not help fearing the performance would be repeated later that day too, and the day after, and the one after that. The future was written, and naked.

'Oh, Mum,' she said and allowed Petula to draw her head firmly up to her breast, neither tender recollection nor hopeful imagining able to suppress what she knew then: that if life could not stop her mother then she would have to.

PART ONE:
Acheron, entry.

CHAPTER ONE:
an ending and an introduction.

How did these things come to pass?

Of Petula's beginnings, those early days in which she was available, fearful and alone, little was known. Her life as a sister began with Regan's birth and Regan knew her as no one else, the frustrated saintliness already in place by the time Regan was old enough to ask her first questions.

'But all that's in the *past*, there's nothing mysterious about it, boring things that happened yesterday instead of today, the only difference is that they happened to me, not you. Really Regan, you don't want to become one of those earnest virgins that squirrel round looking for reasons all the time, a nosy hybrid of Miss Marple and Socrates. Asking people about their memories is opening the floodgates at high tide, darling; you allow a whole clod of sentimentalised excrement to wash through your nostrils. Take my word for it, the second anything enters memory is the turning point in which all this banal *reality*,' she raised her hands to the four corners of John Lewis, York, 'is sprinkled with stardust and a panglossian Cathedral of misty-eyed old balls appears in its stead. They say that time is a great healer but what they don't tell you is that it's time itself that's the big pain. The past is a liar; stick to what you know and bugger the old days. The only old bits worth hanging onto are the parts that create the new.'

From this Regan concluded that the past could not be over quickly enough for her mother and tried to remember as little of her own as she could, which for a time left her very forgetful.

As this sat oddly with the sisters' practical outlook her mother told her not to take her words so literally.

'It's alright to remember where you left your toothbrush and that cherries taste nice, I meant, stop asking Mummy where she *came* from, who Granny was or why Evita's Daddy is different to yours. That's the sort of *boring* past we don't want to talk about. Remembering how to make a cake or to wear an overcoat in the rain is the *interesting* past, whatever a psychiatrist may say to his charges.'

If only this were so. Regan came to feel that of all the hard things to reject the existence of, second only to the present was the past, its vengeful pursuit of her mother impossible to dismiss, the seasonal reminders of its existence afflicting Petula like an allergy.

'And please stop asking me where I came from, I came from my Mummy and you came from me, it isn't *normal* to ask such questions, even at your age my tiny chief inquisitor.'

Not wanting to add to her mother's misery, even if it meant remaining wilfully ignorant, Regan nonetheless formed a view of where Petula had come from, and come from quickly. To be precise, from her first husband with the poor man quite literally still in chase. This may or may not have been her first memory, those prior to it consisting mainly of undifferentiated colour and night, what was beyond dispute was that of all the broken pieces she tried to forget, this was the least fragmented.

It was raining heavily in the late 1970s, Jazzy and Evita were at boarding school and Mr Montague was in the Far East on unstated business that may have been mysterious. Mystery was the mood Regan encountered the world through. Her mother looked like a folk star, her siblings punks, the farmers another species and their children ghosts who shied from her, all mysterious, all unexplained features that came and went like fate. The sisters were the two constants, staring from the panoramic deck that was The Heights into the eye of the advancing storm, wet leaves grabbing and clutching the window like nature's paw prints.

'The noise, it's driving me *maaaad*,' said Petula shivering into her scrappy patchwork shawl, the wind, trapped in the chimney, rattling like a shackled dog against its chain. 'And *rain*, oh for God's sake, tell me it's not true.' Pensively Regan's mother studied the blustery horizon, her beauty brutal, feral and lacking then in all refinement, the gypsy hoops and painted green nails larger versions of the ones Regan displayed on her small wrists and fingers, the sisters already living in tandem, their wild hair a compromise between a mother's nightmare and little girl's dream.

'And to think your mummy could be dancing in a city, dancing from city to city, coast to coast...' Petula's hips began to gyrate under her heavy cloth-work skirt. The fantasy of a dancer's life was later projected onto her first daughter, Evita, though Regan would not find out about that until an argument over money took an unexpected turn, many years later. For now she watched her mother move to and fro with awe.

'You don't talk much do you Chuck? But you have lovely eyes, like mine they are...'

It was true, Regan's eyes were as piercing and watchful as her words were infrequent and flat. At the age of four she was still as silent as she was at three, waiting until she could make sense of the dark and jumbled brilliance of things before opening her mouth. Not until she was seven would Regan grasp that understanding was nothing next to obedience and imitation. And from then on she was fluent in her talk.

'The only argument that ever advances your cause in this life, Chuck, is exceptionalism, being the exception to every rule. This valley is full of dull mothers at home with their dull little children, cowards and jellies; we are the exception, Queen and heir of all we survey. Take it all in Chuck, you never know when you'll need it.'

The heavier weather was moving towards them, thicker clouds forming over the crooked ewes on The Devil's Paw, and with it the figure of a man, or perhaps a tree stump with legs, Regan could not tell, galloping towards them with the storm on his back.

'Look Mummy. There, *that*!'

'Nothing out there but rotting posts and mad crows Chuck. Just because a country landscape changes all the time doesn't mean there's anything new in it.'

'That. Coming quickly.'

'My, we are the talkative one today.'

'There, there Mummy!'

'What are you talking about? I can't see anything.'

'There!'

'Fuck a *duck*. No.'

It was the first time Regan saw Petula show fear, of the kind she experienced when she was lost or woke in the dark on her own. Regan waited for a moment of self-restoration so that reality could resume and her mother return to her imperious self.

Instead Petula froze, the freezing followed by a reduction in colour and stiffening of the jaw, not to attack but to withstand and take ownership of the pain that was about to be encountered.

'Whatever you do, stay in here and don't go outside. And close your eyes. No, come here, we're going upstairs.'

But Regan did not close her eyes and Petula did not take her upstairs; rather, they waited with an appalled and fatalistic tingling, rooted to where they were so destiny could have its way with them and provide Regan with her first memory.

'Not here, not him here. Tell me not,' her mother muttered into her hand, raised like a fist in front of her mouth.

The figure that seemed to move so fast was in fact lumbering up to the house gracelessly, clearing the lower garden fence with much effort, the bobbing head of a broken man fighting to catch his breath slowly becoming visible. Dressed in a shabby tweed overcoat and battered cap, his muddy boots carrying great clods of field on them, the man, seeing light in the house, raised a fist in a gesture of defiance and slipped over backwards. Taking at once to his feet, his short arms disappearing ineffectually under his flapping sleeves, Petula's first husband, Rory Anycock, looked like he might not have chosen the wisest means of delivering his message of hate.

'Petula, I warned you I'd come!'

Anycock's huffing face was a vision of Hogarthian cuckoldry, microscopic bristles wobbling on his top lip, thin legs barely supportive of a pudgy torso, and blubbery cheeks of the deepest purple, indicative of a life of humiliating underachievement. The pretensions of his squire's attire completed the picture of intemperate buffoonery Petula had fled, and as Anycock struggled through the garden gate, she afforded herself a nervous grin.

'What a state! And to think I married that man.'

Regan could not believe how preposterously ugly this gnomic outsider was, far less see any connection between him and her mother, a representative of a higher race as far as she was concerned. In spite of the vulnerability she sensed behind her, Petula had taken care of her thus far: all would be well.

'I told you I would come! Well I'm here!'

'Just close your ears Regan, watch me, like this with your hands. This person is mad. M-a-d.'

Standing before the window, his legs stretched ridiculously akimbo, a hand on each hip as if to draw pistols, Anycock bawled.

'*You* told me to wait and I waited. The mug that waited. So here he is, the waiter.'

A whiskey miniature popped out of his pocket and went to ground with a hollow plop. For a second Anycock stood there, the rain reapplying itself to a face squashed full of rage, his slight moustache trembling with the indignant pomposity of second place. Wiping the sweat and rain off his forehead he snarled inaudibly and raised his fist again. In his anger, skidding from side to side, it hardly occurred to him that in spite of his close proximity to Petula, she was still keeping him waiting.

Petula held Regan closer to her and blew out the pair of candles illuminating the afternoon murk, all the while watching Anycock with barely suppressed fascination. In contravention of her survival instinct, she wanted to know what would happen next, the scene so surreal that she forgot she was its referent.

If Anycock was expecting to be invited in for a cup of tea he was to be disappointed. With thunder creeping up the valley, and the water collecting in puddles at his feet, Anycock drew forward and pressed his face up to the glass and banged hard. '*You* said wait and I waited. Waited and gave you all the time you wanted, time and space and all that. Except that's not what you really wanted, was it? All along you played me, Petula, putting me off and getting further away. You said wait but you didn't wait, did you? Rushing to make your new life here, setting up a nest and getting yourself knocked up by that sharp bastard you always fancied. Give me a year or so you said, so I gave you a damn year, give me another and you got that too. Lord, you must have laughed at me, long and hard, taken me for a mug. I tell you now, I'm on to you, seen through it all, I have. And you should know this my girl. I'm never going to give you that divorce you crave so you can tell that spiv to stick his lawyers' letters. No, I'm not going to let you go, not if we had forever. You'll never be Mrs bloody Montague, you understand me, never... because I love you too much to let you go *Petula*, can't you tell?'

Looking dangerously near tears, Anycock cleared his throat and pointed at the tall figure inside, who was once his to have and hold. 'I'll never meet another like you Petula, no one will, it's why I can't let you go... it's why I've come back for you.' It was a speech rehearsed many times in the cold bed she had left him in and one he was indecently proud of – the words coming out just as he had meant them to, for once.

A peal of laughter, quickly smothered, came from inside, reawakening Anycock's ire.

'Mock me will you? Oh, the things I could tell the world about you Petula...' His voice rose with a righteous anger that came easily to him even in smaller matters. 'For a proud man I wasn't too proud to take, to take, well you know what you are, to take one of those for a wife.'

Regan was to hear a lot about pride in the coming years, often from figures as compromised as Anycock, making her turn against the quality, or at least not take it very seriously from those who insisted upon it the loudest.

'Lying is your calling card Petula. You practise on yourself in your sleep, but I believed, because you were beautiful and you'd have me. And you didn't know how beautiful you were then, did you? It's why I got you, why you took me. See, you always were full of piss and wind, running one racket or another, and I was your jolly farmer until you saw you could do a lot better than jolly! There were bigger game out there, weren't there Petula m'love?'

'Nonsense!' whispered Petula, moving her hands from Regan's ears to cover her eyes, 'I made a second-best bed and refused to lie in it, he's talking piffle. If he doesn't go soon I'll call the police.'

'You going to call the police Petula, or are you going to get one of your lardy-dah friends to get his gamekeeper to thrash me? Or that doctor of yours maybe, oh he liked you too, to commit me eh? Is that it Petula, them men in white coats to take ol' Rory away? I don't think you want them here, them or anyone else! Because you don't want them to know what I know about you, you dirty, well, you know what you are!'

Petula switched her hands from Regan's eyes back to muffling her ears again.

'Jesus. What a bore. Go away, please *go away.*'

'You're a liar Petula! A liar that sells her body for gold!'

'This is too much...' Petula bit her lip yet remained frustratingly short of inspiration. For the first time in their association, the initiative remained squarely with Anycock, but how to get rid of the beast?

'The tales you told me would make a harlot blush! Your parents the aristocrats, or was it royalty? I can't remember! The cock-and-bull family crest you had me hang over the fireplace, the stories of your holidays with Princess Margaret and the Queen! And the truth? You want to hear the truth? A mad old gin dragon with dementia that I had to nurse in our field, who I had to put in *my* caravan and watch and feed! That was Mater! And Pater? Oh this is too good, too good! A card-sharping rake who'd made a run for it on the way to get a cigar from the shops, he had some sense after all. Sisters! Yes, sisters left behind in Singapore you never let me meet! Married millionaires did they? If they existed, if there ever was a Singapore. So much of it Petula, so much of it, one day this, the next one that. Only I remember everything Petula, m'love. And if you won't come back, I won't be the only one who does. Mark these words, I won't go quietly this time. Twice bitten see? Damn you and your lawyers' hush money!'

'Regan, upstairs now, go quickly. Go.'

Regan looked up at her mother and frowned quizzically.

'Please, I know what I'm doing little one. He's mad.'

With sensual exertion Petula rose from her hiding place by the window, ushered Regan away and drew a deep breath, running a shaking hand through her tangled hair.

Anycock squinted, aware of the movement and fearful that he may have gone too far. He had only meant to scare her a little, not scare her away again, but once he started talking he could not stop.

'I can see you Petula, don't you go trying anything. I don't mean you harm, I only want what's fair.'

'Stay where you are,' he heard her call through the glass.

Hearing her voice again reminded Anycock of his pain, hidden for so many days and nights from the one who had caused it, and now free to soar as high as he could cast it.

'I swear Petula, I've come to take you home, before your God and the Law, I'm still your lawfully wedded husband!'

'Hush. You'll wake the dead.'

For many moments he stood there, wondering whether he had been tricked; it would make sense, she was probably escaping out of the front door with her brat. Then one of the many back doors facing the garden opened and Petula walked out unclothed, a northerly wind ploughing into her freckled breasts as hard lines of rain washed through the red thatch which formed a protective triangle round her sex. At once comforting and defiant, helpless but powerful, Petula's propensity to throw herself at the mercy of the elements rarely failed her, cruel nature taking care of its own.

'Sweet Jesus Petula, are you real?'

'Rory, oh Rory.'

With pagan immodesty she strode onto the grass, wet leaves squelching underfoot and hailstones falling all-about, yanked free Anycock's trousers and got down to her knees. Anycock threw his head back, closed his eyes and sighed, 'Have mercy, I'm only a man.'

Soon they were rutting on the front lawn, pools of rain forming a bed of slippery grassy slush under their sodden bodies. A pair of toads hopped cautiously past Petula's crossed fingers, her raised ankles slapping together painfully like clashing rocks on the bone. Pressing her face to one side, to avoid Anycock's whiskey breath, Petula watched a grass-snake curling under a lavender bush for shelter, concentrating on it as if it were a poster, blu-tacked to the dentist's ceiling. Its shiny wet scales reminded her of other more straightforward sexual experiences, its smoothness of past penises she would rather be on the business end of that dark afternoon. Holding on to the hairier part of Anycock's comb-over, Petula controlled the urge to exhale impatiently, the overturned bucket of tripe she married potentially dangerous until neutralised by the panacean solace of ejaculation.

Unbeknown to the actors, Regan saw it all. Whether it was hereditary nosiness or a child's innocent interest she could never decide, a stool by the first-floor window the perfect aerial vantage to observe Anycock consume his fury in a four-minute rut, his buttocks hurrying towards climax like a pair of lobsters scuttling towards the water, sea-eagles circling dangerously overhead.

'Peace Petula, give me peace...'

Later, after they had had tea and a hurriedly intense conversation in lowered voices, Regan spied through a half-open door Petula hushing Anycock again like a baby, his sobbing face buried deep in her lap. 'Shhhh now, you big lump, you'll have to wait and see, I don't even know what I want now, we'll come good again though, one day when we're both ready. Shush. We need forever Rory boy, forever, you think in short lumps, short lumps of time. Time's not one or two sugars, it's a whole mountain of forever. I'll never forget what you've done for me, I promise, never. We'll always be together Rory boy, together in the most *significant* sense. But I need time, more time.'

'I want you now Petula, blazes to later, *now*.'

Petula laughed indulgently at the unsuccessful adult once more resorting to the greed and certainties of childhood, 'Shuuush silly, shush. Later, there'll be more later.'

'You promise, you promise this time?'

'Shuuush...'

Like most problems Petula did not know how to solve, and preferred to bury in a blaze of hectic activity directed elsewhere, this one was tactically set aside, strategically worked around and ultimately, after some weeks, forgotten. Jasper (who later in life would decide his father was a labouring-class hero) and

Evita had their names changed from Anycock to their mother's maiden name, Tanner. Soon after, a stack of Petula's old nighties appeared in a cardboard box at the end of the drive with a collection of letters that remained unopened. Of Anycock, Regan saw no more, his race with the storm never to be repeated.

True to his word Anycock never granted a divorce, choosing unbroken hermitude in his shell of a dilapidated shepherd's cottage instead. The matter of Petula's marriage to Regan's father was settled by her former husband's thoughtful and timely suicide (assisted by gout, alcoholism and tuberculosis) two years later. It was a practical death that any man who had known pain like his would understand. The wedding of the woman he left behind occurred without an announcement in *The Times* or any fanfare, a handful of initiates invited to Glyndebourne one blazing hot weekend in July, the general public never needing to know that they were not invited to an event they thought was already a fact.

In adulthood Regan was to say that it was impossible to know why Petula married her father without knowing why she did not want to be with Anycock. The colossal debts, red nose and farm repossession were obvious factors, but Regan knew that the man who had run with the storm knew too much, knew of the time before the sisters, and that her mother had given herself to him that day for them both. By her teens it became clearer to Regan that it was a sacrifice Petula expected a return on, and that in sisterhood, some acts were more magnanimous than others.

*

The mystery of her parents' attraction would haunt Regan throughout her life. How could it not? If she grasped its nature she would at least see a reason for the pain it begat. Suffering could then be ennobled by logical necessity, it was the only way for it to serve a cause. As long as Petula was that cause Regan held firm; later the need for Petula and logic continued as no more than a nostalgic yearning, whereas suffering remained a perennial fact.

Why Petula and her father made her was the second central question of Regan's existence, following on from her mother's origins, and would always be so as long as their purpose for doing so evaded her. As her psychiatrist would explain, 'the postponement of loving until full knowledge is acquired ends in a substitution of the latter for the former,' and so it proved, questions replacing feelings to no gratifying end. The separateness and distance that characterised her parents' relations were as much a feature of growing up as the school run and successive pets, each parent inhabiting polar tips of passing stars. What light they might cast on their past life they chose to keep to themselves. And still her memory showed her films she could not square with Petula's revisionism or her father's silence on personal matters. There was a day, soon after Anycock's run, when what she subsequently sought in vain was revealed to her, and for once, only once, there was no mystery; her parents were in love and acted like they were. Afterwards she would remember this day more in theory than practice (just as her father had admired her mother's beauty), and later still doubt it altogether. But for one afternoon Petula and Noah Montague made fire in the air, the space between them thrilling, ominous and young.

Hot weather had come very early and unexpectedly, the spring clouds as scattered and varied as a thousand differing destinies. Forecasters warned of tropical temperatures, a hosepipe ban was ignored and the seemingly pointless fashion for outdoor pools in Mockery Gap finally justified. Presiding at the centre of it all were her parents, resplendent in the twilight of their late twenties. Noah Montague sat cross-legged in a lotus position laughing, Petula was half submerged leaning on the pool's edge, and Regan, separated through some accident in priorities, was eating a banana on her own. Others watched the star-crossed couple, athletic and lithe, her father a cross between a Satyr and the star of an adult film, naked save for the black synthetic slip and handlebar moustache, her mother an acid mermaid in a crimson bikini that her nipples stared through. From the darkness of the house overlooking the pool, the curtains drawn as neglected toddlers ranted themselves to distraction, Regan slipped past a stoned au-pair and called out to the adult world. No sound came out of her mouth, only the conviction that she might have been abandoned for good, that the sunny afternoon was infinity and that the moment she was trapped in was a black hole. Now her mother's devotion seemed contingent, contingent on whether there was a man talking to her, since that was what Noah was and would always be to Regan, another man to whom she was supposed to feel closer than the rest.

Brushing past the net curtains Regan made her way down the concrete patio unnoticed, her small steps taken with careful gravity. In spite of all the splashing and chatter, her parents' voices were the most audible without being the loudest, the other speakers timing their silences with the consideration of eavesdroppers.

Petula, though aware of an audience, seemed not to credit it with ears. 'And I just couldn't make him stop crying!' she exclaimed. In the sun, and without makeup, she was lovelier than ever, and Regan waved her banana in the air hoping to catch her attention.

'Really! No stop it. Really?'

Noah laughed baring his teeth, conviviality and ruthlessness taking turns with the sunny disposition he was to maintain into old age. His was the look of a man who had been in extreme situations without drawing absolutist conclusions, and as such, remained slightly untouched by life, so far.

'Mean to tell me he did, eh? Christ, poor fellow must be so far from self-respect that he can't touch the sides anymore. Feel sorry for him, really.'

His voice was lively and deep, words arriving in measured snorts and deliberate abbreviation. 'There's no malice there, a chump, goodish guy who can't move on, world's full of them. Lots of integrity, but integrity can be impractical. Really needs a nursemaid, not a woman. Could be dangerous though, if he's done it once. Nursemaid is what he needs, to look after the poor fellow, give him a bit of mothering.' There was no doubt that Noah wanted the opposite of being looked after, an air of putting others to amusing use inherent in his generosity, the same trope that Petula would eventually adopt to more selfish ends.

'And that nursemaid was me. God, you've no idea Noah, no idea. Seeing him brought it all back of course, I've never been so scared, not of him but of that time. To have a whole time of your life that you can never have back just written off, you've no idea, no idea at all what that's like. All that exposure to another soul and you can't even put it to any use because you don't want to even see them again! Such a waste!' Petula was never scared of decontextualising truth if she thought it would create a favourable impression with her listener, but when she was as aroused as this she stuck to the facts. 'No idea what I was doing,' she repeated. 'All done with now anyway, he got the message this time, he won't be back. It took all he had to try it just this once.'

Noah nodded approvingly, his eyes drawn to her broad shoulders and flatpack back. 'Generally you can take the measure of a man by who he falls in love with, so he couldn't have been a complete wrong un, old Rory, let's give him that, eh?'

Regan dropped her banana skin under a lounger and adjusted her armbands, already too small for her, the plastic tight and constrictive round her little arms.

'Mummy,' she said firmly, 'I think you've been with that man for quite long enough in my opinion.' It was something she had watched someone say on the television earlier that day and she was surprised at how quickly the opportunity to use it had arrived.

Her mother threw her head back and laughed exaggerated-
ly. 'The two of you? Amazing that such different men could
fall for the same lady! I wonder what you both saw in me? Do
tiresome men appreciate beauty? Or is it their miserable little
sagas they love, looking to drag you in so as to dramatise the
misery of their genes?' She laughed again, a high-pitched crack
of the whip that threatened to bring down a passing seagull, the
noise and gesture, for all its unnerving vivacity, perfectly natural and a little frightening. So too were the strong intimations
of sex, sealing the couple into their own world, away from their
daughter and the rest of the party. Regan did not like how this
invisible chemistry made her feel. Indeed, the spoken exchange
between Petula and Noah, lacking physical contact, was more
profoundly sexual than the deed she had observed between her
mother and Anycock weeks before. Ignorant, as Regan still was,
of what sex 'meant', all she could go on was what made her feel
sick, and her mother drinking in Noah's attention, rather than
lying coldly under Anycock, was moving her to retch.

'*Mummy...*'

Noah had filled a plastic glass and, handing it to Petula, picked
up his and toasted her. The lovers had taken self-regard to such
a level that they looked like *they* were the guests they had been
waiting for, everyone else a lesser version of their self-regard.
The moment seemed deliberately staged for them. There was
no rival centre of interest. Regan scanned the crowd with disapproval, blaming it for Noah's chutzpah. Why were they letting
him get away with stealing her mother? It was an audience that
would be pruned, fallen out with and replaced in time, amounting to a 'Mark One' crowd unsure of their value. These men,
more at home in the safer fashions of future decades, straining
in their minimalist trunks, too-tight tops, outlandish sunglasses and clumsily parted bouffants, hardly knew what was expected of them. In awkward clusters they gathered round the pool as
miscast accidents on the set of the wrong film. The women were

the ones in ascendency, buoyed by tupperware and feminism, slowed down by husbands who would provide them with the security that would make the ensuing years so unsatisfyingly survivable. It seemed to Regan when she looked back that this was the juncture her parents were made for, their desire to dazzle and preen the spark that created but could not survive her. Narcissus and Echo, Noah and Petula, the attraction *was* the moment, unrepeatable, fated not to recur the next spring or the one after, however hot it got. Some crucial specific, so seasoned as to remain superficially apparent for years to come, would vanish, the metaphysics of memory slipping towards the materialism of the present, the balance of elements broken for good.

These same elements were broken quickly enough that day by her half-sister Evita, a hefty lump of thirteen, who jumped fully clothed into the pool with a heavy sack of books strapped clumsily to her back. It was the second time she had tried to kill herself in as many days, this attempt more determined than the last. The day before, her mother had rescued her from an open manhole in the road, Evita's chubby face full of terrifying curiosity, an experiment with death dangling in school uniform and sandals. To her mother's happy dismay, Evita's dyed mohican, making her the youngest punk in the county, alerted her to the danger, the bobbing lump of pink hair visible by the upturned manhole cover. Helped by concerned and puzzled onlookers Petula, having yanked her out of harm's way, scolded her daughter theatrically, announcing: 'My children don't always walk in my ways I'm afraid.'

When asked what she thought she was doing Evita had answered that she had 'wondered what it would be like to be dead.' At the swimming pool she went further, shouting 'I want to die' gruffly as she plunged onto the local Member of Parliament, disappearing with him under his grinning inflatable crocodile.

Regan could not recall how her father reacted to this crisis that preempted his last truly tender appearance in public with

Petula. What struck her most about the clamour was that Petula alone overcame her shock and acted, various men waving their towels excitedly, and screaming ladies dropping their sunglasses to no practical effect. Her mother, with singleminded precision, somersaulted like a giant swan in search of a cygnet, her legs all that could be seen of her as she disentangled the flailing schoolgirl from her waterlogged prop. Pulling Evita to the surface with determined impatience, she began to bark orders to the shocked extras, many of whom seemed to be on the verge of spontaneous applause. Quietly Noah towelled himself down, his expression unreadable, the edge of the pool thick now with anxious well-wishers, prepared as one to be led. Petula's eyes searched for Noah and instead saw something that interested her more: power. It was lying there, glancing off the water, waiting for someone to notice it and change everything. The prize was hers to pack up and take home with her. A man she had never noticed before offered her a bathrobe, Evita quite forgotten, and as Petula draped it over her shoulders like a cloak, she reflected on this emerging quality. It was no wilting rose, rather a precious metal, unseasonal, there to wield whenever she chose. Like a millionaire who made money to give it away, Petula had used love to gain the confidence necessary to dispense with it and embrace her true calling. Regan remembered very little else about that day, adults jostling her inconsiderately and a forest of legs smothering her yelps for attention. A particular kind of abandonment was effected as Petula brushed her hand quickly over Regan's hair, while talking to someone else, her interest obviously focused elsewhere.

'She is a little madam, isn't she?'

'So long as she doesn't acrobat off a wall or trapeze into a pool, I'll count my blessings with this one! Listen, do you feel like another drink? Fill me up too, I fancy getting really squiffy!'

Everywhere grownups were shrieking with laughter, Evita's jump effecting a release of nervous energy in the gathering.

Regan felt her guts, small as they were, being controlled by some outside force: she was coming down the hard way. Tears followed. Was it because Petula had forgotten to say goodbye as she entered the next stage, or that Regan actually feared being taken with her? Different days would offer different answers. A taxi ferried the children home that night, a treat, or at least it should have been, as it was Regan's first trip in a hired car.

Superficially life continued as before, which meant existence took on a shallow hue, reality ushered sideways and enacted after bedtime in places a little girl could not go. Under Petula's firm hand, the grand spectacle of the Montagues grabbed the limelight, self-image reinforcing the fantasy and fantasy supplanting truth. This world of appearances with all its garden-party polish would be the childhood Regan looked back on, the music recitals, visits to sculpture parks and banquets at stately homes, all part of her debt to Petula. From this foundation Regan learnt to savour the ecstasy of perfectly executed surfaces, resplendent in their multifarious forms, heedless of all they obscured. Her detective instincts and ontic discomfort underwent benevolent moulding, Petula allowing Jazzy and Evita to go their own way, each a lost cause compared to Regan, her little thoroughbred. By the time Regan entered school she was adept at asking the questions to the answers her mother provided. In omitting to note anything Petula took for granted, Regan gave up memories of her own at the very point she ought to have acquired them.

Noah remained a marginal, if charming presence, his moustache swiftly turning salt-and-pepper. If he chose to see the rise of the house of Montague as an extension of the moment by the swimming pool, he could be excused. Unlike Petula he was innocent of the future. The audience for his family's machinations grew larger than ever, it was just that the society he regarded as unimportant was Petula's true target, and he part of the bait that would draw them in. Regan noticed that her father, never loquacious, and positively pained in the presence of her half-siblings, resorted to a strange kind of silence, one too embarrassed to admit it had lost a winning hand. It came with a wide and mildly gormless smile worn to deflect proper intimacy, reminding her of a louche cartoon dragon that was used to advertise a famous brand of mouthwash at the time. Petula understood her husband's strategic importance and was frustrated that he seemed not to, Noah too much the sensualist to delay gratification for her ambitious schemes, yet remaining an intriguing proposition to others. If his vacillating absence from her dinner table annoyed, or a sinister import was read into the smile that turned sardonic as his fortune was whittled into Warhol prints, renaissance busts and other circus turns, Petula did not allow it to slow her. Family life and 'modest social success' were to continue unabated even with key players only formally present, an arrangement better suited to an idea than people, like many others of that century's innovations.

Full promotion from childhood to sisterhood for Regan would be a matter of time, not choice, and with it the notion that it was better to make it up the mountain than ask what the climb was for. This code would attract success in every aspect of her life with two stubborn exceptions: an uninterrupted night's sleep and romantic love. Sisterhood worked for as long as she was able to convince herself she had no need of these fancies and threatened to crumble if she did not; an eventuality that Petula, with personal experience of the horrors of both, would be prepared for, hand on heart and whip in hand. For time could tell even if Petula could not, that the most bitter threat of all had been there from the start, living in the least celebrated cottage on the farm, The Wart, its youngest inhabitant the sisterhood's last test and first challenge.

CHAPTER TWO:
neighbours and a trip.

It was The Wart's misfortune to sit below The Heights. Had it existed for itself this pretty little cottage may well have been the happiest of homes, but instead it suffered from comparison with its pushy neighbour. The Hardfields had lived there for generations, privately hoping that each owner of The Heights would be the last and that the property would revert to them. Edgar Hardfield had sold the farm to pay off gambling debts a century before, his only condition being that his ancestors be allowed to work the land he lost, with The Heights reverting to them should it ever fall to its original selling price. For decades this long-term strategy did not appear hopeless, or at least not absolutely so. The Heights' middling size told against it, too big to be self-contained or managed easily without help on the one hand, too small to be properly competitive and profitable on the other. Since the original sale stipulated that it could not be amalgamated into a larger property, The Heights tended to attract gentleman farmers and dilettantes, the Hardfields running the place in practice, none of them trying too hard to make it a success or allowing it to be too apparent that lowering the value of the property was their game. Frustratingly, the price for The Heights remained obstinately beyond the Hardfields' reach, there always being some enthusiast seduced by its beauty and ignorant of its trifling potential. As locals knew the holding to be a poisoned chalice, interest came from far and further afield. In just the three years after the war The Heights changed hands four times, the well-intentioned and wilfully blind coming and going in shifts. A stable period in the fifties, during which two old spinsters subsidised it until their trust ran out, was followed by neglect and turbulence. Rich Brazilians bid for it at auction and only visited twice in four years, a couple from London discovered it was too far away for a weekend home and a musician quickly sold it on, having discovered the house was listed and could not be hollowed into a giant studio. In this way hope was kept alive for the Hardfields, the failure of others papering over their own stasis.

It was not until the arrival of the Montagues that the Hardfields conceded that they had met their definitive match. Here were a family of realists who were happy to use The Heights as a front for their property empire on Teesside, collecting at the farm on weekends to polish their new money. Far from being ousted, Benjamin Montague gave the place to his youngest son Noah as a twenty-first birthday present, and the young playboy defied expectations by taking the measure of the Hardfields, renting out the farmland and keeping them on as glorified gardeners for the main house.

By the time Seth Hardfield married Jenny Rowe, The Wart, or Chudleigh as it was known on the electoral roll, had begun to embody the history of which it was the outcome; a battered and beaten air hanging over its untended garden and dilapidated pathway. Unlike his forebears, Seth retained no dream of returning to The Heights or even sabotaging it on the quiet, his resignation shaming him into denying his own property's attractiveness and abandoning projects to improve it. The Wart subsisted in a state of permanent incompletion, a half-finished bathroom and kitchen forcing the Hardfields to clean their teeth at the well, a badly botched annex allowing the snow in, every winter. To an outsider the Hardfields appeared to still believe the long-awaited move up the hill could come any day, why else would they inhabit a building site? Only Jenny's habit of planting tulips every year gave any indication of long-term planning, the front garden a collection of weeds and stones, the back a verifiable jungle of weeds, rotting apples and empty jerrycans.

It was not just the grounds and cottage that stood in painful contrast to the illustrious two towers on the hill. Seth and Jenny, only a few years older than Noah, were a pair tired before their time. An exhausted surliness weighed down their efforts to live a little; the twinkle-toed philandering of the young Montague rubbing salt into the staid youth they had barely emerged from. As Noah partied hard and drove sports cars into hedges, they listened to cricket on the wireless and fixed household appliances. Life was not entirely without its compensations. From the start they were very much in love and instinctively patient with each other's ennui, amusing themselves with their imperfections and failings. Seth, a robust hulk built to wrestle cattle, saggy jowls hanging off his face like papier-mâché sacks, worked energetically in the Montagues' garden in a way he would never have in his own, his wife not minding one bit. His only concession to show was to be bluffly unapologetic in his enthusiasms and honest about what they were. He loved to gaze at sheep (an animal thanks to which his son would one day be hailed as a genius, for putting them into glass cases of formaldehyde) poultry and cattle, maybe feeling an affinity to simple animal life, its ignorance and absence of plans. No one was sure since stating his interests, not explaining them, was his way.

In human affairs Seth was modest and only slightly bitter, the bitterness worked off by sitting alone in unlit rooms and taking long walks under the stars, the walks lasting as long as it took for the twitching in his neck to subside. Never looking forward to anything, or living in hope, meant Seth was free to occupy the present moment in a way few were. If questions of depression ever bothered him he never told, his insistence on being 'normal' meaning that he was too sensible for such things, or his view of normality was; so he ended by rejecting conventional notions of 'depth' out of hand. Such dreams as he had were concerned with rural meditation and not material conquest.

His wife trusted him and never doubted that what he lacked in ambition was made up for in unimaginative goodness.

Jenny Hardfield shared her husband's outlook with an extra level of fearfulness all of her own. For her The Wart was a once-in-a-lifetime gift, a good thing that could easily be taken away unless they bought it, an option her husband dismissed as unrealistic. She hoped, above all, that the Hardfields were needed, occupying a valuable niche between Noah and his new wife Petula, a couple who did not believe in one another, she guessed, and might have need for intermediaries. To make themselves *necessary* was the best way of guaranteeing their future security, as Jenny, originally from Manchester, had never felt settled in Yorkshire. Having children was her greatest wish, and being told she could not, a terrible blow. After a brief period of becoming very religious, which did nothing to increase her egg count, the decision was made to adopt. Helpfully Noah knew a family of Jazz musicians in Scunthorpe who could fix such things, and in the same week as Regan was born, the Hardfields had a baby of their own, a dark little bundle named Mingus. As a three-person unit the Hardfields at last found a stability they had contrived to avoid, the bathroom finished at last, the annex completed and the kitchen installed. If they still did not have much to say for themselves, their silence in no way invalidated a rich appreciation of what they had.

It was sad, then, that Petula should dislike them so much, especially as their newfound contentment coincided with her own grand plans for The Heights, in which she expected them to play a (menial) part. Petula found herself torn between regarding them as useful dullards she respected enough to not mock openly, and fearing them, her husband's kindness and laxity towards the Hardfields striking her as dangerous complacency. What if, she mused, the great nothing between their ears under close inspection revealed itself to be *something*, a subversive something that upset the new order she wished to establish. A firm servant–master relationship was thus enforced, quite at odds with Noah's cavalier slackness, Petula afraid that familiarity could encourage a boldness that would hasten an erosion of her authority. A firm hand with all employees and tradesman, indeed anyone she had no need to impress as being nice, originated from this time, the Hardfields carrying the considerable brunt. They did not mind; like the Test Cricket they faithfully followed, the monotony of suffering that lay before them was welcome because of the remote and hypothetical outbursts of pleasure that might grow from it. The Hardfields were there for the long haul.

For Petula's son, Jazzy, the Hardfields were great trees that reclined under their own shade. Petula and Noah had withdrawn from Jazzy for largely the same reason; they felt that he looked and sounded like a small version of his father, an uncomfortable reminder of a player who had been removed from the board. For Noah there was little more he could do than feed, clothe and stand near the boy in photographs, dutiful indifference tempered by an existential unease meaning the two were destined never to bond. Petula, who had already scolded herself for calling Evita ugly whenever she lost her temper, was even less sure of Evita's older brother, a horrible absence of feeling coming over her in his presence. Jazzy, who was conscientious, imitative and affectionate towards anyone who would let him be, was not yet sharp enough to be aware of this, experiencing her lack of affection as a game of chase. His memory of his earlier life, and the father he was estranged from at only four, left a quizzical vulnerability that Petula could not bear to answer with love, however much she felt he needed it. Her hope was that Jazzy's simple nature was indicative of insensitivity and that what he would never know – a doting mother – would not hurt him too much. The inescapable conundrum, one she disliked herself for entertaining, was that he and his sister held her back, blamelessly spoiling things by their existence and inability to act like children of hers should. In these circumstances it was no surprise that Jazzy should gravitate to the Hardfields.

From them Jazzy developed the notion that the underdog was not always wrong and there was no shame in possessing the face of an Anycock. He had never resembled his father as much as Petula insisted (her obsession planting the thought in Noah's head), Jazzy's pin-point nose and high forehead a boyish tribute to her own aquiline features. As a consequence he grew up with good looks he was not aware of, taking compliments as extravagant praise he thought he did not deserve. From Seth Hardfield he got his two walks, one that he did not know about and one he did. The first natural, head down, his eyes concentrating on his next step, though more likely, on nothing at all. The other deliberate, its manner one of long-suffering patience, the tread of a proud man walking away, his head held high from an argument he did not want, his opponent a lost cause. It was hard to tell which walk was for public consumption, and Jazzy would keep both for the rest of his life, alternating between the two depending on whether he was angry or not.

Without much encouragement Jazzy adopted Mingus as a younger brother and forsook the boys at his private school for village lads, eagerly adopting the locals' accent and manners to unintentionally amusing effect. Jazzy sounded nothing like them, his voice part-Dick Turpin, part-Long John Silver, several miles and centuries south of their Yorkshire vowels, though out of protective kindness they said nothing to make him feel different. In his adoption of a persona, he resembled his mother except a lower-class version seeking to mix rather than stand out, the search not so much for a voice as the rejection of one. Petula saw the advantages in Jazzy borrowing the Hardfields, even if she found his parroting of their country maxims infuriating, with 'No one knows where the shoe pinches except the wearer' always guaranteed to send her into apoplexy. The trick was to send him away to school at the right time; until that bright day the Hardfields could do much as they liked with him so long as he was still there for school and his other 'hobbies'. Besides, their baby Mingus, unencumbered by his parents' genetic inheritance, was adorable, and Petula did not object to Jenny coming up to The Heights to babysit Regan with him strapped to her back. To Jenny these visits were a source of insatiable curiosity, proof that another world existed just kilometres away from hers. Sometimes the women would share a pot of tea together, Petula pleasantly relaxed knowing that nothing she said need be doctored or acted out as the listener was of no consequence.

Instructions from Petula were nearly always conveyed to the Hardfields over the phone (that Petula installed in their kitchen at her own expense), which never stopped ringing. Otherwise there were notes, on endless points of detail scribbled in Petula's demented hand, her sentences virtually indistinguishable from the paragraphs they belonged to. These were usually dropped off at the house as she sped by in her Volvo ferrying her children to music lessons (each was encouraged to play half a dozen instruments), theatre rehearsals, dancing classes and tennis. The usual method of delivery was for them to be tossed out of a moving window, the speeding car veering at the bend, often perilously close to the cottage to avoid a pheasant, badger or hare. Later it was only cars and tractors Petula would swerve to avoid, a few years at The Heights convincing her that the wildlife existed in large enough numbers to withstand the odd slaughter. Occasionally, when she did not have much to do, a state of affairs she avoided like illness, Petula would allow Regan to bring a note in person to their door. This is how Mingus first remembered meeting her, his earlier visits to The Heights blurry memories he confused with a children's program depicting heaven seen at the same time.

The toddlers found each other intriguing, a feeling the mother shared. It was obvious that Mingus, not carrying the

Hardfields' genetic baggage, could be assessed as a little person in his own right. Mingus's large eyes and delicate long lashes reminded Petula of a Pinocchio made flesh, his dreamy slow way of speaking infinitely preferable to Jazzy and Evita's rushed diarrhoeal chatter. By the time they turned four Regan and Mingus were inseparable companions, spending silent afternoons together collecting beetles, ants and woodlice for the micro zoo they curated in Petula's vegetable patch. Slowly the notes, if they were asking something onerous, would come with small presents of food, a stoutly unemotional way of giving those you wished to keep at arm's length tokens of your appreciation. With a large kitchen to play in, Petula discovered cooking and, despite being entirely self-taught, found that she had a knack for it. Jenny Hardfield's appreciation of her cuts of marmite-emblazoned ham showed her there was no outside to her system, anyone could be absorbed by it, even surly philistines like the Hardfields. Without being of a teasing nature, Petula found it satisfying for others to envy her, and food became another means for the herd to sing her praises. As a consequence Jenny Hardfield found the 'necessary' role she sought, that of a sounding board for Petula's more experimental recipes, testing them before they went public. To show it was not all one-way traffic Petula began to buy clothes for Mingus, extravagant outfits of purple corduroy and big floppy Gatsby caps that were as successful at alienating his fellows as Jazzy was at ingratiating himself with them. In one of those selfless bursts of generosity that gave her an undeserved reputation for not being selfish, Petula decided she would take the two toddlers on a trip, albeit one with an ulterior motive, to London. For Regan this would be a fairly run-of-the-mill outing – she had just visited the capital for her eighth birthday – but for Mingus, she guessed, it would be groundbreaking, diminishing anything his parents could have given him. She imagined him looking back at it for the rest of his days as the happiest of his life, like the husbands who remembered their single night of passion with her as the pinnacle of theirs. Unfortunately, Petula was to get her wish, without the fulfilment she thought it entailed.

*

Petula liked to kill several birds with a single stone and the trip to London was no different. Ostensibly it was to buy clothes in preparation for Regan's seventh birthday, lunch somewhere special and catch a children's show at a well-known theatre, but if it had only involved these things Petula would not have left Yorkshire. The trip would serve a more vital matter. By 1979 the problem of how to progress to the next level of societal success had become an obsession for Petula. The Montagues' local standing was second to none, they were welcome in the houses of the aristocracy, highly regarded by the artistic community, such as it was, and an indispensable cog in the county's social machine. Most flatteringly of all, her dinner parties enjoyed unrivalled regional dominance, invitations highly coveted and widely sought after. And that was part of her funk; her renown was all very neighbourly and nearby. Petula's expanding horizons were beginning to keep her awake at night. Getting ahead, once so remote she doubted its existence, was, in practice, one of the most frighteningly easy things she had put her mind to. So why shouldn't she aim higher than bloody Yorkshire?

As a self-avowed enemy of provincialism she had attempted to bring more of the world to The Heights; invitations to Noah's innumerable bohemian friends dotted round the country had pumped fresh blood into the weekends, his money led her to artistic contacts over the Pennines and she was already a patron of any cultural activity within a fifty-mile radius of the farm. It was not enough. The kind of success she desired was 'modest' only because she said so, and local on the condition that she could bring the mountain, wherever she found it, back to Muhammed.

Events or fate, she oscillated over which to thank, rewarded her with a golden egg that surpassed her most extreme fantasies. The hen was the poet Ned Wrath, widely acknowledged as Britain's finest, the wild man of the moors whose work idolised the very place Petula lived. He was to turn forty that year and the regional arts-and-crafts brigade planned to celebrate the event by all means necessary, turning the county into a shrine to Wrath. Although Wrath had actually been born in Croydon, lived in New York for the past ten years, gone to university in Cambridge and married and divorced two black American ladies, his poetry had never moved beyond his native Yorkshire. Volume after volume celebrated hawks, virility, milk-bottle tops and bad weather, the Yorkshire of his memory or mind finding its way from libraries to school texts and from there to the front of mugs and T-shirts. Shatby, an ugly seaside town with several large caravan parks, was the scene of several of his holidays and the place chosen as the centrepiece of that year's celebrations. A selection of the country's leading actors were to gather there and read from Wrath's most famous work, *Raven Did Crow*, a plaque was to be unveiled, and there were rumours that Wrath, who had long planned to 'come home', would do so at last. When his personal appearance was finally confirmed Petula consulted her map: Shatby was only twenty-six miles from Mockery Gap. The game was afoot.

Petula could never be accused of being unrealistic. She knew that she lacked a head start or even a specialist interest in this particular area. Though Petula loved actors, for she was one herself, and theatre, particularly music hall and pantomime, she had little feel for poetry and next to no knowledge of it. Though she readily agreed that Wrath was a rugged hunk, if not an outright dish, she was a spring shower next to the storm of enthusiasts who could recite his interviews backwards. Which left her free to act, coolly, dispassionately and effectively. What she needed to do was work an advantage; The Heights would not be enough in itself and she could be sure that her reputation for preparing a spicy beef stroganoff would mean nothing to Wrath. With the aid of cunning she would 'stumble' upon her opportunity and announce herself by 'mistake'. The answer was the actors, they would be her way in. Four of the Shatby seven were doing a special one-off performance of *Dick Whittington* in London for Great Ormond Street, tickets were exorbitant but attainable. By the end of the day these four would be her lifelong friends by hook or by crook. And through them she would have Wrath to show off to all the world. Several birds, a single stone. It had a wonderful symmetry to it.

*

The train ride down to London was heavenly. The three of them looked majestic, Mingus in turquoise knickerbockers, Regan with a geriatric Bo-Peep bonnet and Petula resplendent in what the tailor had designed for the day, a close-fitting lilac business suit with yellow flared bellbottoms and matching handkerchief, worn as a headband. British Rail had rarely seen their like. The children played a long and quiet game of I-spy with typical and well-behaved understatement as Petula amused herself drawing attention to her painted toenails, laid out on the seat opposite. A clergyman, who clearly wanted to sit there, instead chose to stand blocking the corridor, his gaze held by Petula's wriggling toes, until he was moved on by an impatient ticket inspector who took his place. Idly, Petula closed her eyes and imagined a train full of Tarzans, their modesty protected by loin cloths, all ready to do her bidding in the first-class carriage, Regan spoiling her fantasy with an ill-timed enquiry.

'Does Seagull begun with a "c" Mummy?'

'No, they come from the *sea*, not the letter.'

'I love the sea, I'd like to go there every day,' said Mingus. 'But it would make my parents unhappy as they can't take me and I'm not old enough to go by myself.' Petula smiled warily; the boy's interjections were sudden, unpredictable and often tinged with vaguely adult melancholia. 'And if I did go I might drown.'

She looked into the corridor; a bleached-haired cosmopolit-punk, not unhandsome, shamelessly held her stare, then crossed into the compartment opposite. Attention, especially from unknown and anonymous sources, was glorious. Noah's frequent absences suited Petula, much as it surprised her to admit it. Rory Anycock had been jealously possessive and she reflexively assumed the same stance toward him, the two spending little time apart and forcing one another to account in detail for whenever they did. It wasn't that Petula particularly cared what Rory got up to, or thought he got up to anything at all, beyond the occasional flirtation with his brother's wife. Only that if he was going to grill her ('Who was that you were talking to, you like the dark ones don't you?') then she considered it her duty to be equally quarrelsome in return. What fun she permitted herself was slipped into a shopping errand or long walk, interrogation and suspicion attaching themselves to an ambitious hour of slap and tickle. She lived just two good questions away from getting caught, her lovers men who resented their marriages as much as she did hers, civil enough to get out of her way once she had taken what she wanted. These affairs were Petula's only way of extending herself, her only time on her 'own'. It was in this context that she approached her second cohabitation, her romantic self and practical one by now two separate beings. When Noah had first gone to London for a week she did not know whether she should throw a plate at him and accuse him of a mistress, or insist on going too. Choosing to do neither had been the making of her, for freedom was a two-way street she learnt to make the most of. To think she once feared that love would restrict sexual activity! If anything, Petula felt more comely than she had ten years before when she was still scared of the workings of the heart. What men had lost, she had gained. There were even occasions when she desired herself, closing her eyes during lovemaking and imagining a woman, her reflection, having love made to her.

They hailed a black cab to Biagi's for lunch, so that Regan and Mingus were the first children from North Yorkshire to know the difference between pasta al dente and overcooked spaghetti. The shopping trip passed in a blaze of looks and sideways glances from distracted men and jealous mothers, an irrelevant collection of objects being the only lasting proof it occurred at all. The play itself was terrible, the actors uncomfortable with their dumbed-down roles, the leads trying too hard for the children (who wouldn't have been able to tell the difference if the parts were played by the presenters of *Blue Peter*, Petula later reflected). Getting backstage was easier than she thought, all she had to do was present the children as her outliers; no door remained closed to sweet little autograph hunters and where they went, she followed, her fingers twitching with nervous egotism.

The atmosphere in the changing area was just as she hoped; garish, sincerely insincere and extremely friendly. The space was not so impressive, there was something of the pisspot gloom of the pantry, a line of chairs turned to face a small table of plastic cups and crisp packets, the only concession to show business. Her four main targets were sitting in their makeup, wigs and glad rags, happily rubbishing a well-known contemporary whose profile had recently risen to prominence thanks to an appearance in a Bond film as a charming British villain of questionable sexuality.

'Impotent you say? Well he managed to keep that one quiet for a while.'

'Absolutely, as potent as an empty tube of Colgate. Would have trouble making a budgie come. Always has been that way apparently, even when he was handsome.'

'I'm not old enough to remember *that* far back.'

'Consider yourself lucky, you'd also have had to remember the war and rationing. Anyway, since time immemorial.'

'Wasn't he meant to be some kind of sex symbol back when?'

'Before he married the bull dyke for her money.'

'I thought *she* married *him* for his money? Didn't he come from it?'

'Come off it! No, she married him because he was impotent. Allowed her a free rein with the young ladies.'

'I thought she married him because he was in a Bond film.'

'No, that's the new one, a floozy half his age with her sights set on the pool boy and a generous alimony package I shouldn't guess. *She* certainly can't be with him because of his conversation, he's the most boorish drunk I know.'

'I hate that man starrily, his career arc is as pointless as a rat fucking a grapefruit, must we even mention him again?'

Petula cleared her throat and took a necessary chance. 'I do beg your pardon, but would you mind awfully signing my daughter and her little friend's programmes? You see, you've already made their days and this would just absolutely top it off for them.' She could tell that her hold on their attention was as thin as the skin covering her wrist, and she pushed Mingus forward as firmly as she could.

The actors stopped talking and took notice of their guest. Mingus looked up at them thoughtfully. His sense of what he was doing there was only a little better developed than Regan's, who unlike him had slept through most of the play, but with a bold flourish, he removed his cap and got onto one knee. 'I am Dick and this,' he pointed to Regan, 'is Tom my cat!'

'My god he's a natural! Where did you find the little dear, Alain Delon's purse?'

'Why, on the streets of London of course, with his Tom!' cried Petula curtseying in a way she hoped would make the actors laugh, and did.

She could see an opportunity to show her best side, or at least, the negative better side of her character, and quickly added, 'They both want to be actors when they grow up. So I thought, where would be the best place to take them?'

'Where indeed my good lady, welcome to the Hydra's Head!'

Of the 'Shatby Four', two of the actors were women and two men. The women were the Middleton twins, Esther and Margy, classically trained actresses and proselytising Marxists forever switching sects, specialising in austere heroines and bold spinsters with no need of men. Despite suspecting the sisters of lesbianism, if not actual incest, and balking at their beauty close up, Petula would have found Esther and Margy of great interest if it had not been for the presence of Donald Eager and Max Astley. These slight and delicate thespians were the King and Dauphin in waiting of the Royal Shakespeare Company and British film industry. Eager had been the Clark Gable of his day, albeit a rather small one, clean-cut, bold and officerly with just a hint of the night about him. Despite a good war in the RAF, a pair of very successful Broadway musicals and a second lease of life in kitchen-sink dramas, his flagrant homosexuality had held him back as much as his young rival and lover, Astley, had been abetted by his. They were the meeting point between generations, Astley's rise was swift, brusque and opportunistic as such rises have to be, aided by his shoulder-length blond hair and sensitive frown. Jewish sex comedies, counter-culture love stories and anti-war satire were his chosen stomping grounds, his appeal split between the sexes. A TV remake of a period drama provided the occasion for the two actors to meet and declare their mutual love, followed by frustrated attempts by Eager to leave his wife, which is where they were when Petula said: 'The two of you are just the most remarkable actors I've ever watched,' a compliment that was as honest as it was calculated.

'You can't be referring to *Dick Whittington* my good lady, or else I'd suspect you of insincerity or worse,' drawled Eager, his offhand manner betraying how much he still loved praise of any kind.

'Well you made quite a good Lord Mayor, but I've seen better. No, I mean that otherwise totally awful re-make of *Wuthering Heights* they showed on telly over Christmas, the other actors should have been shot en masse, especially the wet twit they got for Linton, but the way you both played the two different stages of Heathcliff's life, amazing, no one would have thought you weren't one and the same person, yet looking at you now, I don't know how you did it, I don't. It was more than acting, something inside you was the same. Brilliant. Just brilliant.'

'Brilliant? My my, praise indeed.'

'Take it or leave it, only the dim or criminally jealous would think otherwise.'

'I think I'll take it then.'

Straight talking that was not as straight as it seemed was a simple idiom for Petula to slip into, one this audience had sufficient experience of to know they were dealing with no ordinary fraud, allowing Petula to continue. 'But where the dickens did you shoot the thing? I live in Yorkshire but what was going on with the moors? I've never seen them look so... red, red for heaven's sake! Four episodes and not a drop of rain, it was bloody a desert! I half expected to see Clint Eastwood ride over a hill!'

'Independent Week-e-n-d Television,' snorted Eager, killing each word, 'somehow took it into their heads that Malta would be a cheaper place to shoot than Kirkby, hence the farce you refer to. Mind you, back to your first point, given the inauspicious circumstances...'

'We really did shine,' said Astley finishing his sentence, 'yes, for a cut price pile of poo, the worst "Withering Shites" in living memory, we *were* brilliant. I'm just amazed that anyone stayed watching long enough to notice. Still, if it hadn't been for those three weeks in Valletta we would have never met, would we Don?' He brushed a thick lock of hair away from his eyes, 'and life would be very different. This man was my hero, my role model you know.'

'Wasn't he to us all?' exclaimed Margy Middleton, a more homely version of her anorexic sister, Esther, who added slightly less sarcastically: 'Yes, it was almost a national duty to find this man attractive, once upon a time.'

'How I remember,' gushed Petula, leaning forward and showing her bosom in a way that even the gay couple found beguiling, 'they say you should never meet your heroes in the flesh, that they always disappoint; I'm pleased to say that I'm not finding that to be the case, not at all...'

'You dear, dear woman, here, join us, please,' Eager offered his chair. 'Who do we have the pleasure of talking to?'

'Petula, Petula Montague.'

'Donald Eager at your service, Margy, Esther and Max, only the names have been changed to protect the guilty.'

Petula's laugh followed falsity's highest calling, not a note too low or true. She was afraid that at any minute she would be revealed as a piece off a different board, mixed into this set by mistake, and that she must keep trying and not relax for a second.

'Please have my chair.'

'Too kind.'

'Anything for a beautiful lady.'

Petula took her place at the fold-up table, the autograph hunters forgotten for the moment, another bottle of wine quickly opened as she sprinkled flattery far and wide lest anyone feel excluded by her rapid entry into the upper echelons of British acting.

'What I would like to know, love to know in fact, is how you all do it,' she said looking at the Middleton sisters while still addressing Eager and Astley, 'the way you become the characters you play. Is there any hope for the rest of us or do we mere mortals have to rely on make-up and method acting to scale the same heights as you natural players?' Petula frowned for emphasis as she had noticed Astley to do in his promotional posters. Providing her new friends were the object of her effusions they would believe every word, stray off course and praise anyone else in the same terms and they would think she was talking delusional nonsense; the trick was to shut out the rest of the world and its standards of credulity. All that existed was here.

'The short answer is that we are a nest of geniuses and the rest are a shower of jobbing hacks,' laughed Margy Middleton, the two bottles of wine she had drunk before the show combining with the one she had sunk since to induce a certain unsteadiness, 'they can't bleeding act, they just copy, is what they do.'

'So you don't waste time with anything dull like researching characters? Is that all nonsense?'

Margy held onto her mouthful of Muscadet with difficulty and pulled a face suggesting that the answer to the question, were she capable of answering it, would be not if she could help it.

'I find,' said Eager, his sentences inclined to begin as neat summaries, 'that as with life, *moving forward* with what I can best characterise as *vague hope* will offer you far greater freedom than the results of predictive analysis. Specificity and research, as you intimate, are the preserve of the second-rate. No harm in that of course, there's room for us all.'

'I read this theory.'

'Stop there, theory is the revenge of the second-rate against the talented, do not speak to me of it again!'

Petula nodded sagely, it was not hard to see why Eager had earned his moniker, 'the Professor'.

'Absolutely,' said Astley, not to be outdone by the master. 'Overdetermination takes the air out of a role. I please my audience because they please me, and there's something internal to that relationship, a dynamic if you will that provides me with what I'm looking for in a part. Trying to put it together from the outside doesn't work, you need to begin in the middle and from the inside for authentic results.'

'And not overlook the political context,' chipped in Esther.

'Which in itself is no more than saying anything goes,' concluded Eager.

'Ahh yes, a natural selection of accidents, that's what I believe in,' said Petula disingenuously, confident that it did not really matter if she understood what the others were saying as it was a conversation that asked no more of her than she grasp its general drift. 'In fact, I deliberately leave my calendar blank, I hate being hemmed in by plans or detail of any kind,' she lied, glad that the children were still too young to contradict her.

'Plans, God! I think I'm going to miss my train!' exclaimed Esther whitening at the thought, 'I've an early one to catch. I'm meant to be selling the paper in Ilford tonight... I promised Kaspar I would as we've no evening performance. There's a strike on, they're relying on me.'

'Bollocks to Ilford and bollocks to the paper,' said Astley, taking her cup from her and filling it again with cheap rosé. 'I feel like getting properly stewed after that ghastly farce of a play! Who's with me?'

'Oh yes!' said Petula clapping her hands, sure that Mingus and Regan would find plenty to do amidst the props and costumes. 'I could do with getting a bit tight myself!'

'Where did you get that gorgeous outfit made up?' asked Margy, spilling some of her wine over Petula's blouse.

'Shatby, nowhere special. It's in Yorkshire.'

'Shatby, that's funny, we were talking about that place the other day... what for... oh god, what are we doing there again?'

'Come on Margy, the booze is ruining that memory of yours, you'll be fluffing your lines next. Yes, about that other Heathcliff, the intense force of nature that is Ned Wrath,' opined Eager. 'Brilliant man of course, but heavy, heavy-going, not the sort of chap you'd want to get stuck in a lift with. Anyway, he's what we're doing there.'

'Really?'

'Afraid so, we once had to speak at an event together and all he could do was tell me that America was a terrible place for "the black man", which was quite useless information in my case as any fool could see I wasn't black...'

'Oh really!'

'Yes, he's moved from save-the-hedgehog to save-the-world. And he's not even all that young, must be thirty or over, terrible time to get into all that self-righteous crap.'

'I don't trust these single issue politicians,' sniffed Esther. 'Lovely man, heart in the right place and all but the only way we're going to rid the world of injustice is *class*-based politics.' Petula eyed Esther with amused disinterest, she really was no threat to her at all if she carried on like this all the time. 'If we start thinking of ourselves as separate from each other then we're playing the bosses' game, letting them divide and rule, and the revolution can just as well be put off forever.' Esther winced as if the very thought had the power to turn her insides. With her neat and delicately proportioned face, primed with emotion carelessly redirected from one place to another, Petula did not much fancy Esther's chances in any upcoming revolution, decadent late-capitalism seeming just about the right thing for her.

'No I don't see it,' Margy was saying. 'Why can't we be both women *and* Marxists, Red Indians, Hedgehogs or whatever. You know, you have your reality and I have mine, and yours can be whatever you want it to be, so long as you don't tell me what I've got to be in *mine*.'

'You can't be a woman *and* a hedgehog,' said Eager dryly, 'though exploitation is verily egalitarian in its application, I do agree.'

'But there are *female* hedgehogs, Don.'

'But they're not Marxists, dear.'

Petula would not let them stray too far from the hook. 'What *is* your connection with Wrath, do you all know him or something? And why Shatby?'

'Oh, just a curio the agent we all share, the great Tim Tinwood, has got us into, should be quite interesting actually...'

'Of course it'll be "quite" interesting Don, it'll be a bloody honour and a cute gig to be associated with.'

'But he'll be there Max, picking holes in our intonation, diction and God-knows-what-else. He's a bloody fusspot, look at the way he tore apart that documentary Ken Russell made on him, a work of hagiography if ever there was one. He's a perfectionist who considers human life too messy, and us as part of that mess. I'm certainly not looking forward to having to recite him to his face.'

'Still. Have you ever read his *Pig-Man, Dog-Woman*? A masterpiece, it's the volume I'll be reading from, a hugely underrated piece of work.'

'I don't think *under*ration is a problem Wrath's oeuvre suffers from.'

The conversation was pinging along in the direction Petula wanted, this was the way she liked it, speed was the highest value, to move through experience as quickly as possible, attempting to understand *the why* of what she was doing a dreadful brake on momentum. She had brought the horses to water, now they were drinking her bait.

'Don is being picky, I think Wrath is every bit the seer the press portray him to be,' said Astley, 'it's just that we're uncomfortable admitting such a man walks amongst us in this iconoclastic age. I must admit, of course, all the stuff about his plough and penis can be a bit much but one can see what he's trying to do...'

'Oh I don't know,' smiled Petula coyly, 'I wouldn't mind seeing a bit of his plough.'

Astley slapped his thigh and laughed uproariously, 'I'm not above a bit of smut myself, however given Wrath's views on the love that dare not speak its name, I doubt whether he will be up for a plough-share with me any time soon, he's quite old-fashioned like that I hear.'

'Yes, a bloody puritan in some ways,' chuckled Eager, 'I understand that he even thinks playing with yourself is a sin, a waste of good sperm and not at all what the earth goddess thinks we should be doing with our willie winkies.'

'God knows what else there is to do in Shatby! The pictures I've seen of the place look absolutely ghastly!'

'Hold on there...'

'No my good lady, I won't hear a word said in defence of the place, I was in digs, back in '38, playing Iago, my then wife Desdemona and the bloke I was sleeping with Othello, and the landlady would wake us with full nudity, a bucket of oats and a cup of freezing weasel pee, which in Shatby is known as "the full Yorkshire" for breakfast! No, a dreadful place. Let it fall under the same bombs as Slough! I will die defiling its name!'

'I couldn't agree more, you wouldn't catch me even buying petrol there and that's my point, you don't have to stay in bloody Shatby!' Petula protested. 'My farm is a decent distance from town, round the corner but not too close if you know what I mean, so no need for you to be holed up in some miserable seaside B&B... there's plenty of room at mine. Cosy. Nothing spectacular I warn you.'

'Is that so?'

'Of course, it's nothing much to speak of, but you'd be my guests, I insist.'

'What a marvellous suggestion. How generous of you.'

'No, we couldn't put you to the trouble,' interrupted Astley firmly, 'I mean, we hardly know you, though it's very nice of you to offer. You're simply being too generous and you'd regret it later when you found that you didn't like us.'

Petula could not tell whether he was being cautious or polite. Still, it was too late to retreat now, best give it all she had.

'Fiddlesticks, what trouble? I insist you come as my guests. I insist. I'm not much one for entertaining so you'd be left alone, but I think you'll adore what you find. There's nothing so melancholic as an empty space and I have far too many bedrooms in exactly that state. They need filling by bright creative people.'

Reagan watched her mother work the actors from under a large hat she had been playing with, Mingus talking away quietly at his reflection as he posed with a plastic axe, the two children revelling in their invisibility.

'So it's settled? You'll all come.'

'A farm,' hiccuped Margy, her flushed cheeks resembling those on the figurehead of a whaling vessel, 'I don't think I've even been to one since I was a land-girl. Do you have chickens? I like an egg at breakfast. Double yolkers we used to have.'

'As many as you want, chickens and eggs, the whole lot.'

'You old ham Margy, you were never a land-girl.'

'I bloody was, how would you know anyway, you fucked off to America with Mummy before the first bombs fell!'

'I never did! Anyway, Ontario isn't part of America it was part of the Empire then...'

'Oh shut up the pair of you, did I ever tell you about the time I snogged Patton in drag?' guffawed Eager, dropping a turret of ash over Petula's Hermes handbag.

The adults were drinking more and quickly, to slow down just a little tantamount to stopping completely. Petula was being toasted in wild and extravagant terms and appeared to be soaking it all in. Then, at about the second time Regan heard her mother tell Esther she was beautiful, the thin lady burst into tears.

'I'm sorry, have I said the wrong thing?'

Margy took Esther's hand but her sister threw it off and spluttered through her sobs. 'If I am so beautiful why doesn't any man want me, what's wrong with me? Why can't I have children, why can't I find anyone to have children with?'

Petula shot a look at Eager as if to ask, where did that come from, and accepted the swift refill he provided by way of consolation.

'Esther's been through the wars recently, poor girl, lover left her.'

'There there Esther, Petula was only meaning to be nice,' said Margy consolingly; but her sister was not to be consoled.

'Everywhere I go, knowing no man will take me, only the ugly or old ones. Everyone wondering what's the matter with her, why can't she find a man who'll say those sweet, simple words, "I love you Esther and want you"? Why? Why won't they come to me, I have so much of myself to give, why?'

Petula felt her face redden like a hot plate, she needed to cheer this morose cow up and do it quickly or else the wonderful esprit de corps she'd established would vanish as immaterially as it had come. But how to do it? Both men were smiling awkwardly and Margy rolling her eyes in a sympathetic loop of the room, yet Esther showed no sign of giving up her mission of misery. 'Too thin, is anyone too thin to be loved?'

'No.'

Esther stopped crying as suddenly as she had started, amazed at the identity of her interlocutor. Mingus held a handkerchief up to her which she took at once and dried her eyes.

'You are a very pretty woman,' he continued with the utmost seriousness, 'and there is no reason why you should cry, Mrs Montague was saying the truth. You are very pretty.'

Petula could have swallowed the darling boy whole. Even Eager, who was drinking directly from the bottle, looked amazed enough to stop for a moment and express his approval with a: 'My, my. Who taught you to speak like that my boy?'

'Mrs Montague, she talks like me too.'

'Do you really think so?' asked Esther needily, 'I mean, that I'm not too thin?'

'You are just right for a tall lady, just right,' Mingus insisted, his large eyes focused upon Esther's trembling lower lip.

'Just right?' It was the name and catchphrase of a popular brand of cereal though Esther, who usually missed breakfast, was not to know this.

'Just right.'

'Would you like to marry me when you grow up?'

'I don't think I would like to get married until I'm much older, when I am I would like to be with someone nice like you... or Mrs Montague.'

'That's it, now you must really think that I've fed him enough sweeties to start a shop,' said Petula, providing the cue for startled laughter.

Esther was not to be finished with the prodigy and took his hands ceremoniously. 'We're alike you and I, little man, we feel things deeply and say only what we mean. Grownups such as I have much to learn from you my friend.'

'Yes,' said Mingus agreeably. 'Now don't cry anymore please.'

Which actually made Esther cry again but in what everyone could agree was a good way this time.

'What a total, total darling. I love him.'

Uncharitably, because of her good start, Petula felt a strain of annoyance with her small saviour, which she knew to be beneath even her prickly competitive sense.

'He has such an interesting way of speaking. Say something else little man, whatever's on your adorable mind.'

'I would like to come and live here if my Father would let me.'

'What, London?'

'No.'

'This actual room you mean?'

'Yes, it's full of interesting things. And interesting people.'

'Bravo!'

'But don't you want to paint things Mingus?' asked Regan, unconsciously drawn into the act. 'He told me he wanted to paint things.'

'We should have guessed, the boy's an artist.'

'You've never said that before, Mingus. I know quite a few art-ists as it happens...' Petula interrupted, looking to bring them back to the point of their meeting: her.

'I collect things, I put them in boxes and sometimes paint them.'

'Fascinating.'

'Well, that obviously isn't art!' snapped Petula trying to wind the Mingus show down. 'That's just collecting objects and call-ing it art!'

'What things little man, what do you paint?'

Bloody hell, it was as bad as Jesus talking to the elders at the temple! Petula raised her voice a little, she had to, Mingus was actually talking over her and the audience were listening to his conversation, not hers.

'An artist isn't a collector, anyone can do that, to paint Mingus you need *vision*,' she said, gently tugging his arm.

'I collect animal bits, bird wings, skeletons and snail shells and put them in Dad's glass case next to the mantlepiece. And I paint on them sometimes.'

'Oh really Mingus!' She stopped herself, her voice was acquir-ing a tight desperate quality; if she carried on like this she knew she would end up sounding like a nutcase. Her armpits were sodden. This fear wasn't her at all, let the child carry on, remem-ber that the boy was only that, cut him dead at the right time and make a mental post-it to never be caught like this again.

'I like poems as well,' Mingus said, 'listening to them and say-ing them sometimes.'

'You've come to the right place then,' Esther said reasonably, 'we are all poets. Do we know any poems the little man might like?'

Petula felt her heart quicken, the initiative had fallen to her again. Earlier in the week she had worked her way through the poems of Wrath, feeling nothing either way for the most part. A slight stirring of irritation with the longer ones, based on

NEIGHBOURS AND A TRIP

Norse sagas, pleasing indifference towards the sexual parts, the occasional jolt of passion amidst the repetition and gloom and she was done. Afterwards she concluded it to have been a worthwhile experience, even if at the time it was a struggle to keep awake. Her sixth sense told her that it would be well worth rehearsing a poem by heart, one never knew when it could come in handy, especially when one was going to 'bump' into the 'Shatby Four' in a couple of days. The trick was to not be too obvious. Yet the trouble with the trick was that Wrath's masterpieces resisted simple recitation; the interesting poems requiring the reader to discover their genius for themselves.

Unfortunately, there was no shortcut to the understanding of something without making that understanding one's own. What Petula ended up committing to memory was not Wrath at all but a passage that she felt ought to have been him.

Swiftly Petula rose to her feet to greet an imaginary lover, brushing Mingus away as she did so, her eyes closed with concentration, her 'poem' delivered in one long world weary sigh,

> 'Touch me. Soft Eyes
> Soft soft soft hand.
> I am lonely here.
> O, touch me soon, now.
> What is that word known to all men?
> I am quiet here, alone.
> Sad too.
> Touch, touch me.'

Silently she drew back to her chair, a swan closing its wings, picked up her cup, drained it and snatched one of Astley's cigarettes.

He lit it for her. 'Outrageous, wonders never cease, sing that to me again!'

'I couldn't.'

'Where did you get it?'

'Oh, the book just fell open at the right place.' This was exactly what *had* happened, a thumbed copy of *Ulysses* catching her wandering attention when she had all but given up on Wrath.

'Bloody stunning,' said Margy.

'My dear,' Eager took her arm. 'I always thought that Joyce was as a man compiling a dictionary that doesn't need updating, it only need be done once. You've proven it can be done twice. This is news that will stay news. Here's to you and your merry band of players!'

The rest of the evening, for night had already fallen, passed through a tunnel of excitement, running mouths and inadmissible hyperbole, impressions of Kenneth Tynan and Peter Barnes flitting between those of Leonid Brezhnev and Princess Anne. By the end, Mingus and Regan had fallen asleep in a large basket, cradled in each other's arms, Esther photographing them both twenty times before running out of film and starting on the brandy. A burly stagehand carried the sleeping beauties and their shopping to the waiting taxi, Petula staggering up the main isle of the theatre behind them, a shoe in each hand, the breath of the 'Shatby Four' still hot on her freshly kissed lips.

'Darlings,' she shouted at the top of her voice, the sound ricocheting round the red-carpeted vastness of the auditorium, 'till Shatby, you glorious players!'

'Till Shatby, Queen P! And keep the little darlings' programmes handy, we still haven't autographed them!'

She glanced up at the Royal Box, empty yet not without the promise of occupation, a presentiment of the power that would be hers. And then it was over, the lights of Shaftesbury Avenue taking her into their generous and enterprising arms. 'If you have the courage to scale the heights,' they seemed to say, 'then nothing is impossible.' Graciously she blew them a kiss and tumbled into the taxi, crushing most of the shopping as she did so.

'What did you make of that?' Astley turned to Eager.

'A starfucker. She could be the bride at her daughter's wedding, high-voltage, a real pistol... I think she'll do very well by us.'

*

On the train back the euphoria was quickly replaced by disbelief at the unreality of her achievement, as if the right goods had been delivered to the wrong address. Petula was to feel a recurring sense that, grand as it was, success was never quite as tasty as it should be, partly because each success could only happen once and by the time it did, it was already over. Life was at its best when it exceeded itself, and in doing so somehow became more alive, but the lulls that followed directly, though lived, were less than living. Not for the first time Petula had occasion to wonder whether she was an undiagnosed schizophrenic. Which, if true, left her with no one to rage against. No, she preferred to think of this as a rational problem; all would have been perfect if it had not been for a little fly in the ointment, one that prevented her from attaining the complete peace of mind she deserved. That testy scoundrel Mingus upstaging her with his happy-clappy piffle and god knows what else he'd picked up off the television; how could the lad have been so ungrateful? Without wishing to be a Mrs Haversham about it, she would have to lay a frosty egg to prevent future disruptions of a similar kind.

Giving her daughter a quick tug, Petula whispered to the half-asleep girl, 'Regan, wake up, wake up, I'm talking to you. I think the time has come for you to meet more girls of your own age...'

'What Mummy?'

'Girls of you own age and background. You don't know enough of them and you should.'

'Why Mummy?'

'Why not? Now shhh, you'll wake him. Be quiet and go back to sleep. I'm thinking.'

It was unnerving, Petula did not know she was anything like as furious as she was until she spoke. Could it be all the boy's fault? She had to hope that it must be so. Petula turned her head to the window and gazed through her shaking reflection at the black countryside, the rage she could never understand or stem, living over all she saw, the brooding silence of the moon whipping through the passing trees the closest she would come to an answer she had not sought.

CHAPTER THREE,
an aside and an event.

There was danger everywhere. Jazzy and Evita lost their virginity early in life to the same person, the agent Tim Tinwood, then in his pomp and a 'normal' man, the newspaper headlines that would castigate him as a filthy paedophile still thirty years away. Petula would find out about this almost as soon as it happened, choose not to believe it, later claim that it was their stepfather who was responsible, and play politics over the abomination to her death. Both children would go to their graves insisting their mother was devoted to them, a speculative utterance Regan could only repeat in a crowd, usually through clenched teeth. All Petula could do was shake her head with relief. She marvelled at Jazzy and Evita's myth-making from the time they could talk, failing to recognise it as a tribute to her own, their avowed claim to enjoy a special relationship with her belied by the course and content of their lives. That an ideal relationship should exist, at least in theory, remained curiously important to them, however little substance it enjoyed in lived experience. The desire that it ought to amused and touched their mother, who in the lonely moment of the last instance, had very few real illusions of her own.

Whether they were defiantly fouling themselves on the way to the opera at the age of seven, or displaying nasal piercings at fourteen, Petula dubbed her first two children 'attention seekers', lazily characterising their subsequent promiscuity, self-harm and under-achievement in similar terms. It hurt her to see herself in them, the parts she deliberately sought not to recreate, flashes of what she had left behind on the grass with

Anycock returning whenever she glanced at their eager faces. Try as she might, these living embodiments of her former self felt somewhat less than hers, speaking only to her deepest fear: that there was a hidden part of her essence that everyone else saw which would one day be her undoing.

As a consequence of this misconnection, the years of upward mobility were hard on Evita and Jazzy, brother and sister incurring a scorn they could not understand yet were rightly terrified of, their mother capable of anything until her temper, like a fit of demonic possession, receded into glassy formality. Gradually they responded more like the frightened animals Petula was afraid they would become, grunts and hysteria evolving out of dribbling dependence, until she could rightly claim they were 'ready for Borstal', by which time they had other ideas of their lives' eventual destination.

Petula did not think that the public view of her as a doting mother was wrong; there were highly public ways in which she did dote, and the overall welfare of *all* her children was a flag she never tired of unfurling. Sadly for them, Jazzy and Evita had come at a time before the sisterhood when Petula considered herself to be little better than a child. For this untimeliness, over which, she acknowledged, they had no control, the children had her sympathy. To give birth before one was *interesting* enough had certainly been a mistake, whatever unworked-through strangeness in oneself bound to come out in the child. The process of becoming more interesting and self-transparent clashed awkwardly with their growing up, the children needed a mother, not a social gadfly, so inevitably Petula found herself at cross-purposes with their development: it had to be one or the other; them or her. Her selfishness did not go so far as neglecting her protective instincts completely; no one but a freak could think Anycock's damp shack was a better place for children to grow up in than The Heights, and it did her credit to let them know this from an early age. Undoubtedly it served her purpose to keep up a high sense of fearfulness in the children (who were often confused for twins despite being a year apart and looking little alike). Their correspondingly high levels of gratitude to their mother for acting as their saviour meant that whatever else she lost charge of, it would not be their ultimate allegiance. By the time their need grew cumbersome Petula was already trying to live it down, its remnants visible in their hyperactivity and the superficial rejection of the 'lardy-dah' values they associated with her.

Although Evita would reinvent herself as a Seventh-Day Evangelist, later defecting to the Jehovah's Witnesses, and attempt to reconstruct a relationship with the past based on wishful thinking, it was she who showed the first signs of wanting to flee the fanged nest. When not trying to kill herself Evita hatched multiple escape attempts, each more ingenious than the last. Disappearances on school trips, getting 'lost' at airports, catching the wrong trains, and climbing into strangers' cars were all part of her repertoire by the age of eleven. Her success was patchy and she celebrated her twelfth birthday by raising her game, sneaking out of the cinema her mother had left her party in, catching a bus to London and turning up at Vine Street police station claiming to be a prostitute. The desire to enjoy her moment of triumph and show her mother she had got away meant escape and annihilation; absolute and final affairs that brook no looking back evaded her. Suicide proved to be equally inconclusive, Evita always falling a few pills short of a full complement, her poisons turning out to be homeopathic remedies, the leaps to her death occurring from ground-floor windows with no more than a twisted ankle or sprained wrist to show for her efforts.

Stirred into embarrassment, but fundamentally unshaken, Petula took it all in her stride, knowing that her daughter desired to see her broken. The real worry that harm could befall Evita was quickly replaced by social damage limitation as the monotony of dealing with the girl's tantrums acquired a pattern. Every weekend Evita would pack her things into a satchel and set off across the fields 'to Leeds', the drama addiction she had inherited from her mother taking on ever-more-tiresome forms as flight and the suicide solution gave way to immolation. A mixture of half-hearted cigarette burns, scabby cuts and nasty scratches began to appear over her arms and neck, giving Petula hope. Pretending to make a mess of your life was better than pretending to part with it. By the same token, intrusive as bikers, green activists and touring bands were, turning the old piggery into a doss house for ne'er-do-well pot heads, at least Evita was having fun. This curious mixture of tolerance and neglect, abetted by Noah arranging an abortion with Petula's consent over a fling with a 'Southern Death Cult' roadie, meant that Evita knew her mother was there for her in a fashion. Petula, for her part, was torn between completely giving up on the girl, and encouraging signs of life. The most heartening of these was Evita's ballet lessons, the only activity she did not give up as she entered her mid-teens, instead trading them for modern dance. With Petula's voracious support she joined a local troupe led by a former member of 'Pan's People'. The girl's passion for this activity was genuinely disarming, and Petula enjoyed watching Evita's excitement build to the day of her classes. Yet to her disconcertion, Evita demonstrated no talent for choreography, bungling the elegant movements required of her and ending the sessions jiggling round like a plastered chicken, as the other students tactfully left her to it.

Petula knew she was clutching at straws, and rather than risk her daughter's fledgling confidence taking a merited battering, blamed the instructor, beginning by politely questioning her skill and ending by dismissing her as a provincial slut. This was hard on the teacher but good for Evita; ambiguity and mixed feelings were lost on the girl, and in the black-and-white way in which she was raised, the end of the lessons were celebrated as the prelude to a glorious next chapter. With plenty of fanfare and a sharp needle Petula leant on an old girlfriend of Noah's to include Evita in that year's intake at an independent college for dance and the performing arts in Harrow.

The thought that she might have talent proved to be a seductive one for Evita, more intriguing than administering biro tattoos backstage at Crass gigs. Belief in a vocation was a pleasing substitute for withheld love and Evita began to define herself as a dancer. After all, most people who had anything about them tended to be their own inventions, or the successful manifestation of other people's projections.

'Why haven't you finished your pudding, you like trifle?'

'Dancers have to be careful over what they eat you know.'

'Oh, oh good.'

'And I can't do any more lifting, we have to protect our backs.'

'What do you have to lift?'

'That's not the point, lifting is just a no-go area, right?'

Petula saw the abrupt difference this change evinced and began to extravagantly praise the slightest thing Evita might do, be it a headstand or a slight shuffle to a song on the radio, anything to hurry her on her way to the college in Middlesex. Evita's last summer at The Heights passed quickly, and before she had time for second thoughts, she was ready for her new start in 'the Big Smoke', Petula frequently breaking the speed limit to get her there, with the problem of what would eventually become of her first daughter unsolved, yet handily contained.

If Evita's youth was all about leaving home, Jazzy's was largely about staying there, and it took him far longer to decide that he had really loved his mother all along as a consequence. Petula liked this homing impulse no better than his sister's disappearing acts. Jazzy was a ubiquitous presence on the farm, popping up everywhere in a way that might be thought endearing for one who had enjoyed the *Just William* stories as much as Petula had as a girl. Except Petula was no longer a girl and had deliberately set enjoyment aside to become an adult, though she did not yet know it, as she too was still growing up.

Taken at face value, Jazzy's interests were, at least to begin with, healthier than his sister's. Building dens with Mingus, finishing a technically accomplished treehouse with Seth and spending hours in the workshops asking intelligent questions about the use of various tools ought to have won Petula's approval, and that of society at large. Unfortunately, these healthy qualities came with excesses that qualified the good to the point of disqualification. His temper was as wild as Petula's own; the treehouse took four years to complete thanks to his habit of smashing it to pieces whenever he grew impatient with its construction. The dens were actually camps in games of war that frequently ended with other children hospitalised, his partially bent nose, broken twice, dating from this time. Mingus soon grew wary of playing with his older charge, leaving Jazzy in tears when he explained his reasons. Consolation came in tools filched from the farm storeroom, hammers and splints doubling as weapons in his long-running border disputes with sons of local farmers, which were to fester into lifelong hatreds. Jazzy's twelfth birthday was spent in a police cell, events threatening to turn nasty until the French exchange student agreed that the flick knife had been pulled before Jazzy's scythe, the cuts to his shoulder found to be cosmetic once Noah had made out a large cheque to his family. Still, Jazzy's dominant mood was one of needy cheerfulness, which for Petula merely added insult to injury, as the boy had no inkling of how much he infuriated her.

If she found his habit of indulging in all sorts of imaginary weirdness, talking to himself and acting out films he had seen on his own, a tug at her suppressed maternal instincts, his motley appearance guaranteed that the tug remained no more than a faint pull. Clad in Seth's 'hand-me-downs', leaves and branches sticking out of his torn clothes like the distended limbs of a Green Man, Jazzy strutted round Petula's field of vision with the air of a vegetative deity. His ardent desire to be a farmer, expressed through wearing his school uniform with a straw hat and gypsy jewellery discarded by her, was enough to make Petula blush, and she took care to confiscate these items whenever she could. It was no surprise that as he turned into his teens, 'Jasper' was symbolically changed to 'Jazzy' though Petula could not bring herself to call him this, ending up by not calling him anything at all when she could help it.

Just as with Evita, Petula had the sense of watching a tragedy unravel slowly from a great distance, a happy outcome incapable of overcoming the genetic material Anycock had lumbered her with. Bit by bit she observed her son's decline from an eager schoolboy to one whose prospects were no better than that of a menial labourer. She knew his enthusiasm should have been welcomed, but in practice he hindered farm work by his wish to be involved in tractor driving, planting and the other affairs of the bad-tempered professionals the land had been leased to – there being no real farm of his own to 'work'. His fraternisation with local roughs grew increasingly compromising as Jazzy recovered from Mingus's abandonment by terrorising the retired army colonel and wife who lived at the third cottage on the farm, then still called The Jacaranda Tree. Though Petula regarded Colonel Kefford and his wife as crashing bores, it was impossible to ignore the validity of their frequent complaints. Bat excrement through their letter box *was* un-neighbourly, as was a full-scale brick attack on their MG Midget, a firework thrust up their cat's arse and a beheaded bed of roses, the trail of blood leading back to Jazzy every time. Acknowledging the severity of the situation, Noah finally gave up on cheque-book diplomacy and, after the police were called a third time, politely asked Petula for permission to send Jazzy to boarding school a year earlier than agreed. Petula was glad the decision had been made for her. All in all the boy had made rather too much of the place being *his* for Petula's liking, images of him bringing up a family of village bastards on her doorstep and their hanging round *her* farm forever filling her with horror.

The well-meaning interventions of Royce, Noah's childless elder sister, gave Petula her single reservation. Royce was a kindly lady, who seemed elderly even in her late forties; her teenage fiancé having died in Korea arresting any hope that her life would develop significantly from that point on. As with many spinsters of her generation she kept her spirits up with hobbies, *The Mail On Sunday*, gardening and regular interference in the lives of younger relatives. Perceiving no threat in her bumbling advice, usually on how much pocket money to give the children, Petula warmed to her, using Royce as her powerbase for winning influence amongst the rest of the Montagues. Attached to her clapped out Morris Minor, lilac-rinse bouffant and handbag full of melting chocolate mice, Royce was Miss Marple minus the crime-fighting flair. It thus came as a surprise to Petula when her essentially clumsy desire to be something of a godparent to Jazzy and Evita took the form of sticking up for them, however ineffectually.

'*Are they really such bad children, well I don't know, I just don't know about that you yourself say that they didn't turn all that suddenly...*'

As with her neighbours and servants, the Hardfields, Petula felt that there was something about conventionally moral people she should remain on her guard against. It was uncanny how often their innocently helpful remarks morphed into penetrating attacks, before re-submerging again into the harmlessness from which they arose. So it proved with Royce, who bit by bit gave the impression that her everyday homilies were value judgments of the most ominous kind, feeding Petula's hunch that the meek would snatch the earth from the industrious if they were allowed to; all it took was for the industrious to do nothing, for however short a time. Firmly and without fuss, Petula pushed Royce towards Regan, who by now had risen to be such a favourite that Royce had to wait in line as an assortment of well-wishers sought to win favour from the rising sister. It was a tactic that worked, even though Petula could see that Royce still cast a wishful glance at the neglected early-comers, both of whom would have been ready to walk over coals for her, had a grandmotherly relationship been permitted.

Observing Jazzy pack for boarding school the summer before Evita was swallowed by London, Royce, not having seen the boy for months, remarked sadly to his mother, 'you know, they will grow up one day.' Petula felt a distant but implicit threat in her words. For a moment she wondered whether this benign old dear was perpetrating a lifelong con, a game of sabotage motivated by a jealousy for the baby-boomer generation, exemplified by its most shining exemplar. Stopping herself from saying that it wasn't her fault Royce's fiancé had been killed in a war, Petula retorted, 'I think that happens to all of us, don't you Royce? Hopefully once they've grown up they'll appreciate all that's been done for them. If I hadn't said enough was enough to their father, more of a thug than a man, they'd probably be strangling battery hens for a living by now. Instead of having the world at their feet. I know which way I'd like it if I were them.'

'I suppose Noah has helped too.'

'And *I've* helped Noah.'

'Of course you have. Success is a team effort dear.'

'It's certainly felt pretty solo to me. I don't blame him for never really wanting to get involved with them, he hardly knows how to be around Regan so I can't damn the man for not being Santa Claus around those two. Some people are good around children, others aren't. It's the same with animals.'

'Of course. Still, they will grow up one day. I wonder what they'll make of it all.'

'All of *what*? What are you talking about?'

'Oh I don't know, all of this. Forgive me, I'm just doing my thinking aloud I suppose.'

'I've told you what they *should* think; that they've been damn lucky. And if that isn't good enough for them then what do you expect me to do about it? We're all stuck with doing our best. We enjoy every moment for what it was and not for what we'd have liked it to be, and make the most and no more than the most of it. What they will think is anyone's guess. You look at them as babies and you can't believe that they'll one day be creatures that'll swear they were orphans. Newborns tend not to resemble teenage ingrates, but ingrates can one day make remorseful adults.'

'Quite.'

It was not just their futures that scared Petula, it was the future itself, like a villain in leather chaps mincing towards her, the years to come an uncolonised space in which outcomes were the property of no man, or sister either. And the possibility that one day those little harbingers of guilt, Evita and Jazzy, might exact losers' justice for what they would yet become; their future paying the price for her divisive present.

'I've made mistakes Royce, I'll be the first to admit I have, they're both too self-centred and that's my fault. I told them they were right even when they were wrong, and sympathised when what they needed was a kick up the arse. I took their sense for granted and now they're taking me for granted. But I hope to God the world kicks some sense into them,' she said, turning to a row of blue tulips, out early that year. 'I mean, not in a way that would hurt them, only to open their eyes a bit, to build on the work I've already put in for them.'

'Yes,' said Royce, 'that kind of kicking. That was the sort I thought you meant.'

*

Petula's first real test of modest local success, in the severe style, was to turn out to be a no-score draw. 'Shatby's Wrath' was the grandly ominous name given to the day to be held in the great poet's honour, Evita and Jazzy barely teenagers at the time and Regan with her eighth year still to look forward to. Petula's first act, having come back from the *Dick Whittington* outing on what, she decided a day later, was an all-time high, was to agitate against the public officials organising the event and the librarian being appointed master of ceremonies. This unfortunate lady, Ursula Midge, was a devoted and conscientious servant of the community, having lent the young Wrath library books as a boy and followed his career as if he were her own son. She was also forgetful, rather old, smelt of digestives and spoke with a juddering stammer.

'*Thoroughly* unsuitable for the task at hand,' was how Petula surmised her, and with the help of her influential new friends, the actors, displaced the old lady as a prelude to 'tightening up' the order of the day. In practice this meant Geoff Boycott, a famous Yorkshire cricketer, would act as compere (for a generous fee) and the BBC would film the event using a casting agency run by Noah's nephew to provide 'northern extras'. Local participation was restricted to the catering, which Petula had taken charge of. The name 'Shatby's Wrath' was also her doing, the idea coming from the editor of a local paper who had fallen in love with her at the Harvest Festival the year before, and now did her bidding like a reliable mastiff, the dog he most closely resembled. With his help, and that of his equally besotted brother, the former mayor, she ensured that her name would be added to the day's programme just below that of the official sponsors, The Genocider Apple Press.

Once in a position of responsibility, Petula discovered that the old regime had left her a crass leaving present that threatened the day's integrity, namely a 'live' poetry contest that Ursula Midge had arranged with a pensioners' reading group, in the hope that Wrath could judge their efforts after his own reading. This fantasy was quickly scotched and switched to a champagne reception that Petula would do the canapés for, inspiring her coup de grace: instead of everyone hanging on for a gloomy supper at the town hall, a select few, she decided, led by Wrath, were to be invited to The Heights for dinner in the old high way.

With the exception of the actors, who were allowed to overrun, the rest of the day was as closely choreographed as a squadron of Red Arrows, right down to Wrath's entrance in his favourite car, a Humber Super Snipe, thoughtfully lent by Noah's uncle who had a collection of vintage automobiles. Although Petula thanked her lucky stars that her plan was coming together, Wrath's willingness to be feted did take her slightly by surprise as she had prepared herself for some social-ist faux-modesty, especially when the brass band was dropped, but Tim Tinwood, his agent, registered no objections on this or any other alteration. Petula had always worked on the assump-tion that the vanity in even the humblest creative person was the asset that made them most vulnerable to her attentions. Now she felt sure of it.

There remained a single fly in the ointment. Regan had responded to her mother's entreaties to volunteer for every theatrical opportunity open to a child, by being cast repeated-ly as Mary in nativity plays and the 'little girl' in every adult play in need of one. This she took in her usual undemonstrative and stoical style, neither enjoying nor objecting to her duty and earning the nickname 'Still-life' as a result. Petula would have liked her to be more passionate, indeed urged her to be, slightly consoled that at least the girl made up in obedience what she lacked in animation. All this changed when Regan was cast as Tinkerbell in *Peter Pan*, having been chosen, as she always was, on looks alone. Partly through observing Evita's 'dancing', and with the help of the cartoon version watched on her father's Betamax recorder, Regan began to copy the fairy's blithe energy, for she could see that the languid style that had served her so far was of no use in this role. Moreover, the exhibitionism necessary for the part answered a need in her that made her tingle: she wanted to be heard and not just seen.

Rehearsals were a revelation, Tinkerbell easily upstaging Peter Pan, Wendy and even Hook, played by an older boy who would go on to star in a television version fifteen years later. Because Petula was so engrossed in 'Shatby's Wrath', her daughter's evolution from pretty little clotheshorse to bubbling talent was largely lost on her. This was to Regan's relief, as her mother's support had already begun to feel like the control it would eventually end as. Unfortunately, the North Yorkshire sky could not support two blazing stars. Disaster struck, for the opening matinée clashed with the proceedings at Shatby, and as the play could not very well have two Tinkerbells, one for the opening and then another for the following two performances, Regan was asked to choose which she would prefer more, a chance to encounter *real* art in Shatby, or to stick with a childish amusement.

Regan understood her mother was not really offering her a choice. It was only by sacrificing her selfish and juvenile pleasures that she could be sure of equality with her mother, and be spoken to as a grownup and not as the little girl she still was. This was the reward of sisterhood, the egality of two absolute beginners finding their way in the world, the difference in age an irrelevant detail. Over the years, first as a baby and now as a youngster, Regan had acted as a sounding board for her mother's monologues and justifications, her role progressing from that of mute psychiatrist to henchman and enabler. Being addressed as an adult became the gift Regan could not live without; friendships with children of her own age were shallow in comparison. As far as Petula was concerned Regan *was* a person, a lady and not a delightful object to stuff with sweeties. Valuing the respect she was offered, and the responsibility and sacrifice required to keep it, inspired a blind loyalty in the little girl.

Any perceived slight against her mother, from adult or child, was dutifully reported back, as her little eyes and ears patrolled the social frontiers her mother wished to annex. Choices like Shatby were a test, and the greater her self-denial, the closer the bond between the two grew. Centre-stage was Petula's place, not hers. Because this was not formal knowledge, rather a hard-wired instinct, there would be occasions in her life when she forgot it. The decision to turn her back on Tinkerbell was not to be one of them.

'Of course not Mummy, I want to be with you.'

'Of course you do!'

'The play was...'

'Yes?'

'...was really boring anyway.'

'Please not boring, only boring people are bored.'

'Okay, it was a silly play. Babyish.'

'Of *course* it was. Really who ever heard of a great actress debuting as Tinkerbell! Just think of it, they may as well put you on top of a Christmas tree and cover you in tinsel. Fairies with tiny skirts are alright for dizzy shop assistants and factory girls but you have bigger game to hunt my dear. Real actors and real acting is what we are to have for tea; trust me, you jewel, you'll see and hear things tomorrow that you'll remember for the rest of your life...'

And as usual her mother was right. Regan watched Petula hurry off to the car, an important errand in need of her attention, and waited at the door for her mother to call back 'I love you,' as she had seen other mothers do. Instead the Volvo tore off into the mesmerising April sunshine, gravel parting before its fiery tyres, as priorities fell into place and future unhappiness was booked in and all but assured.

*

The big day began badly for Petula, who usually made a deliberate point of not remembering her dreams. She was back in
the past, engulfed in its forgotten essences and boarded-up
importance. Two Red Coats were walking through Butlins holiday camp with a big drum for the nightly 'penny-on-the-drum
parade'. It was the highlight of Petula's stay; every night they
would bang their drum and walk along collecting a large crocodile of campers behind them, singing,

> 'Come and join us
> Come and join us
> Come and join our merry throng.'

The procession began at the Alamein Bar and worked its
way through the main camp into the Jutland Lounge, ending
with everyone rammed in the Ballroom, the adults raising tan-
kards of Beefighter Beer to the new Queen, the children glasses of squash. Everyone laughing and singing at the top of their
voices as the procession wound down and the big band started up, campers of all ages joining in a mad rendering of 'Auld
Lang Syne' and 'In The Mood'. Petula was there of course, at the
head of the procession, resplendent in a big red coat and white
socks and sandals, the other redcoat a little girl she recognised
as Regan. Grappling with her sticks, Petula tried to establish a
rhythm to get the merry throng going, yet her beat was slow, too
slow, nearer a drum-head court-martial than a Butlins conga. No
matter how quickly she pounded the instrument, momentum
was impossible to attain, and as the march began she turned
round to see who was behind her. Her mother and father and
sisters and even Anycock and Jazzy and Evita. After them her
camp pals, the little boys and girls she had made friends with
on the boat from Singapore, every kind face that never refused
her a smile, all looking slightly worried for her but ready to give
their best. Harder and harder Petula thumped, until tension's
release had become preferable to pleasure's accumulation, her

arms and hands sore and tired and to no avail. Instead of growing bigger, the crowd was falling away, some individuals disappearing into bungalows, others hastily turning the wrong way, a hand snatching Regan, and Petula ending up on her own, the ballroom as empty as a boarding school in July.

She woke in tears. The self-induced brainwashing that motored into action as soon as she opened her eyes had broken down. She could remember everything. It all seemed like terrible déjà vu that had only come half-true, the rest of it patiently waiting for her later in the day. With mechanical swiftness she surveyed her past for a prayer, 'Lord, if I forget you today do not forget me...,' repeating it until she was sure it was only words, feeble and human, too small for her predicament. God *was* the situation, not watching it and providing her with lines, it was his immense awfulness she needed rescuing from.

She was saved by a knock on the door from an unlikely ally, her husband, who made a habit of avoiding her until she had washed and dressed.

Gingerly he turned the handle and half-peered at her, the length of his tall body and most of his long face hidden behind the heavy oak door. It had been Petula's idea that they take separate rooms; the house was large enough to cope with it and Noah's snoring, sleep-talking and tendency to need at least his side of the bed annoyed her.

'Everything okay?'

'What do you want?'

Her insolent tone was justified by what she thought of as his shiftiness; Noah's unfailing consideration, however lightly applied, was proof of his guilt.

'I thought I heard you make a noise.'

'I asked you what you *want*. You're perfectly free to chase around the house worrying about noises in your own time. Have you any idea how important today is, how much rides on it?'

'Christ Petula, you're cranking it up a bit early, aren't you?'

'Do you? Do you have any idea how much hinges on today, how much its outcome matters?'

'Well, I know it does to you, I mean, it does, that's actually what I wanted to talk to you about. Something's come up, I'm afraid, no avoiding it, I have to go to London, be there tomorrow morning first thing. Means I have to leave today of course, to get there on time. Damned inconvenient. But no way around it, I'm afraid.'

Petula breathed a sigh of relief, her first of the day. Still, there was no point letting him off the hook too lightly. 'What you mean is, although you know how important today is to me, for your daughter, and probably most of the rest of the county, and how great a part in it I and this house have to play, you're buggering off to London for some "*something*" and leaving me in the lurch, right? In other words doing what you usually do, disappearing when you're needed.'

'Come on Petula, don't lay it on with a trowel.'

'That's you in a nutshell Noah Montague! When the chips are down you always fail to come through!'

'You go too far.'

'How else am I to achieve balance if not by consulting the extremes?'

'I'm sorry? What?'

She shook her head, it was a line she had been beating into shape ever since London, and all to waste on a plank like Noah. No matter, she would have plenty of opportunity to use it again later in the day on appreciative targets.

'Never mind, do as you will, I'm tired. Tired.' And on this point she was in earnest; not only tired but utterly exhausted. To always remain prepared for a battle, one that she would have to start if it failed to rise from natural causes, *was* tiring, especially as the fruits of victory would not be enjoyed by her but by future generations, however much it hurt her to think of them. Like a Communist prepared to lay down her life so the masses could inherit the kingdom of heaven on earth, Petula was ready to sacrifice her peace of mind, such as it was, for her contribution to 'Shatby's Wrath'. In doing so she would become greater than Shatby and its Wrath, so that the hour would come when 'Montague Day' would be how Regan's children would remember the weekend, if only because Petula intended to be around to remind them.

'Well, I wish you every, um, success and hope everything accords to the big plan and all that, Petula. With the thought you've put in, well, I hope it all comes off, eh?'

'Leave me.'

Noah closed the door behind him. Petula lay back down on the bed and looked up at the ceiling, an outbreak of winking the only dent in her immaculate self-possession.

'If I forget you, don't, whoever else asks you to remember them, forget me...'

*

She need not have worried, the day was efficiency personified; like a perfect wedding, it passed quickly and unmemorably, the rigid planning giving every appearance of a spontaneous sequence of events. The actors, audience and Regan did all they were supposed to with barely a glint of improvisation, wayward inspiration holding its counsel in the minor poets' tent where a bar had been set up for marginalised malcontents. Of course, Petula did not enjoy any of it, could not, as it would not have been perfect if she had. The actors would not have soared, the canapés would not have vanished agreeably and people would not have left insisting it was perfect and later on wondered whether it was, concluding that it must have been for someone. It was that type of day, the sort that provides its own meaning so that those that take part in it do not have to, their own pleasures and preferences experienced in enjoyable anonymity elsewhere. Fittingly Petula allowed herself a little time off ordering, scolding and fairly well exploding, to watch the entrance and oratory of Wrath, instinct reminding her that recent acquaintance with a dish was the first step in its consumption.

As usual she had to fight the fear that she had fought too hard for too little. The announcement that Wrath had arrived took her by surprise, and by the time she had successfully cleared the hospitality area, he was halfway to his podium. With the rough assistance of Max Astley, who rather peevishly looked as though introductions could wait, Petula was pushed along a line of other grinning ladies into Wrath's path, Regan lost in the melee. The revelation was that after all the fear and fury, Wrath *was* a revelation, and on first sight to boot. A gaunt man of medium height and build, Wrath's face – almost too serious, wrinkles and creases cutting his forehead into segments and cracked laughter lines bracketing his broad grin – emphasised a care that looked to be punching a way out of the contours of his cruel handsomeness. Under a newly cropped haircut, already grey and dispelling any Byronic glamour, Wrath's black eyes alternated between asking and knowing, a pinched nose and Chaplin moustache throwing any swift first impression Petula wished to form. She could not quite tell whether he was an attractive man who had tried to play it down, or merely a plain one with a very interesting aura. The simplicity of his dress was a study in minimal elegance; an RAF-blue tunic and trousers, both fitted and slightly worn, had been designed by Brooks Brothers to look like they were found on a Ministry of Defence instillation on Ikley Moor, the deception succeeding as ladies swooned, cameras flashed and men thumped him happily on the back, welcoming home one of their own.

'Doesn't he look like himself,' Astley gushed, 'not like that pretentious misanthrope Hughes in his schoolmasterly tweeds and Hushpuppies! He's a good lad!'

'He looks,' said Petula chewing her lip, 'like my father when he was young...'

'A one-off, a complete one-off, here, Ned, Ned! This is Petula Montague, she's taken the reigns and... Ned, just a tick, a second please Ned!'

Petula's disappointment was easy to fathom. Beyond surface politeness and a quick bow of the eyes, Wrath seemed unbothered by her or any of the other stampeding matrons that had gathered for a pound of flesh. Meeting her stare quickly on the way to someone else's, Wrath skipped past Petula, squeezing Astley's ear affectionately, and took his place on the podium. He had certainly been aware of her, she was in a violet frock chosen for its effect on the poetic imagination, but no more than aware. Petula's recovery was instantaneous.

'What a bore for him, having to push past these salivating dregs when what he needs to do is focus. He's actually, probably, quite nervous.'

Astley was impressed. 'I couldn't have put it better myself, Petula. Though if I know Ned he'll be so far in the zone that he won't have noticed a thing.'

'Well of course.'

Wrath's performance was epically and abruptly short, just two poems, neither longer than six verses. The first he roared out, slowly for there was so little of it, the volume of his delivery a device to overcome his fearful and topsy nerves, Petula was right; the rest of the audience confusing it for Viking aggression and loving his colourful directness. Wrath relaxed. He had entered that small segment of omnipotence that public performance occasionally afforded him, one of the happy privileges of talent.

'Thank you,' he said, 'I open my mouth and never know whether the words are going to come out until I hear them.' His voice was unaffectedly northern and there was a ripple of appreciative laughter, for this was his audience, his readership. Having succeeded in providing them with the illusion of unrepeatable significance, they were now ready to follow him anywhere.

'Shatby, what can I say,' he laughed, 'you're a lady. The Atlantic City of the North!'

This provoked a number of 'Hear hear!'s and a group of geology teachers, blind drunk on Buckfast wine consumed on a collective empty stomach, were inspired to begin a rendition of 'For He's A Jolly Good Fellow', the crowd joining in for 'Three cheers for Neddy Wrath!'

Wrath looked ready to strip off and sunbathe in the cloud-broken light; his second poem was quietly and passionately spoken, his face full of reclining intensity and modest assurance. The crowd, sensing that they had been trusted with great art, and flattered by the honour, showed they were worthy of it by applauding madly and heartily. Without consulting the large book resting on the lectern in front of him, Wrath stepped away from it and lifting his hands in a bid to overthrow any remaining self-consciousness said, 'I love you, the ones I've always loved, never loved or never loved until today, all of you. I mean it. I look out at you all and wonder, wonder really what you expect me to say, how I could have got in a position where my words are worth your time, your money, your interest, maybe even your respect. I'll never know, I just keep on with them because there's nothing I know beyond them. I mean it, I don't even know why you're listening, I love you. And I thank you.' Although he was smiling they felt as though he might cry, this unplanned statement, worthy of a Formula One winner, as heartfelt as anything he had ever written.

'Rock on, Shatby!' a fan shouted and Wrath fended off a tear.

'More,' called Petula, 'more!'

No one noticed her, the audience was only looking one way, they were watching a break with planning, here was a free human being and anything could happen next. Petula watched too; Wrath's defiance of the thing that stood before chaos and the void, her belief in a society of fixed mores and meanings, was as compelling and odd as witnessing her house being burnt down in slow motion. To plan what was to happen next was Petula's way of protecting herself against what would happen next if she did not have a plan: Wrath was not like this. Touching his face thoughtfully, Wrath glanced at his shoes and chuckled, 'Here's one you might not have heard before,' adding, 'the good news is I didn't think up the idea. I ripped it off some foreign bloke I thought no one would have heard of. It's all about a naive young idiot hating and loving where he comes from, the first thing I wrote and it's still all up here,' he tapped his head, 'so forgive me if, as the Yanks say, it sucks big ones.'

'An exclusive,' whispered Astley noisily, 'who cares if it's juvenilia, he's giving us a fucking exclusive!'

Wrath shook his head, like one who knew better, cleared his throat and began:

> 'This town of semis, pub, promenade and pier,
> I've seen and walked through year on year:
> good times and great times, sad times and all climes.
> I had you when I were happy, you had me when I were sad,
> with so much incident, feeling, I know,
> it were mad.
> The point of you were heart and feeling
> that I'll seek on sidewalk, chateau and far-off ceiling,
> because Shatby, you were me, and ought to know,
> that I'll carry you, sea salt and vinegar, wherever I fucking go.'

It was enough that he had started and no day for discernment. '"Were"?' muttered Astley to Eager. 'Why all these "were"s?'

'Because he *were* fifteen and from Yorkshire,' groaned Eager, coming up behind him, 'and *were* wanting to be a poet, *like.*'

At the signal from Petula, who had remembered herself and followed the hunch that Wrath may have peaked prior to this unscripted encore, Lady Oswaldo, the famous opera singer who had been born up the road in Swinefield, began singing a libretto commissioned for the day, over the whoops and cheers of the Shatby mob. Perfection was back where it ought to be.

Petula was just wondering whether she was wise to share Wrath with the editor of Faber's new French girlfriend at dinner, and if a tweak to the seating plan may yet be possible, when Astley grabbed her arm.

'Bugger it, the bird has only gone and bloody flown!'

'I beg your pardon?'

'Neddy boy! He's sodded off some place and done it sharpish. Timmy thought he was with me and I thought he was going to the dignitaries for one last round of handshakes, and they thought he was doing that too.'

Petula cast her eye at the group of portly men and women in pinstripe suits and flag-day dresses, staggering about in a drunken dance of backslapping and high-pitched laughter. 'He's certainly not there, not that they'd care now. They're shitfaced.'

'Of course they don't care, he's already worked his magic, and what magic eh? Yes, he's played his part to a T, that's the business end of it sealed up at any rate. We can all afford to go home and relax.'

'But what about dinner?' cried Petula, unable to restrain the desperate tilt to her voice. '*What about my dinner!*'

'Oh,' blanched Astley, rather taken aback by his hostess's need, 'I'd forgotten about that. Forgive me, he'll turn up by then I'm sure, you know what poets are like… Everyone's clearing off anyway, give him a few hours, he'll be back.'

And turn up he did, but with a caveat that a soul less battlehardened than Petula's would have cracked at. Dinner was all good and well, that part could stay as it was, but the location chosen for it was no longer to Wrath's liking. Wrath wanted to stay in Shatby, *his* Shatby, and had made a wonderful new discovery on the walk he took, having vanished at the festival's end. There was a brand new Chinese restaurant on the seafront, Chinkies, that he had never heard of before, and he wanted the party to join him there as soon as they could.

'Chinkies!' Petula gasped and swallowed hard. Now was no time to go to pieces, but the past few hours' wait had been bad enough without that. 'Can we be thinking of the same place? The one opposite the old pier? It's not even a proper restaurant, I mean, they serve prawn crackers and that sweet-and-sour stuff that tastes of goo. All I ever hear is of people going there and coming home *sick*. Really, the place is a hymn to food poisoning.'

'Have you been there then?' asked Royce, who had been following developments anxiously.

'Hardly, I don't need to. Chinkies,' Petula shook her head, 'I mean come *on*! He's supposed to be an intelligent man.'

For the past two hours Tinwood and the other guests, actors and Mayor had hovered round the telephones, complimenting Petula on the artwork, beautiful views and endless succession of cold meats and pâtés that had filled the dreadful waiting. Unsettling as the prospect of crossing this formidable woman was, at least a way out of the stasis had presented itself.

'Yes,' said Tim Tinwood, 'I'm afraid so, Chinkies. I think the idea of a foreign restaurant in Shatby fascinates him, so different from his, er, memories of the place. And he's developed quite a penchant for all that Oriental crap since moving over to the States where they eat it by the bowl-full. Apparently. Or is that Jap food, yeah, it might be, anyway, point being our boy loves it. Still,' he added, resuming his professional face, 'I can't tell you how sorry I am Mrs Montague. So sorry. I know how much trouble you've gone to tonight to make everything succeed and, of course, managed it all in the best possible taste.' Tim Tinwood was scared stiff, though to his credit, did not appear to be. A bent man with a monkish beard, platform shoes and an outfit too flamboyant to be confused for anything other than the attire of a showbiz pimp, which usually disguised Tinwood's furtive nervousness. And his booming stagy voice, borrowed from his clients, dispelled any lingering suspicion that his confidence was a con. 'Give me a luvvie over a bloody poet any day

Mrs Montague, at least I know where I stand with those boys. Actors never let you down. Christ knows what Neddy's thinking of, reminds me of the time he blew me out in Trieste, all because he wanted to rescue some donkey tied up in a field...' Tinwood adjusted his bow-tie and tried to ignore the hunch that he had just addressed a volcano that would erupt as soon as he uttered another word.

'Cheers Timbo,' said Donald Eager through a yawn. The wait had been merely boring for him, hunger, tiredness and aching joints trumping any other consideration. 'Well, now that we know what we're doing, even if we are to feast on muck, can we damn well hurry up and do it. Sorry Lady P, Wrath's a dredge who enjoys ruining everything, what did I tell you? And one other thing, I'm not going to use fucking chopsticks. I hate those fiddly little bastards.'

Tinwood gently removed Petula's wrists from her hips and took them into his moist palms, conscious that this display of affectionate solidarity might occasion a punch on the nose, for Petula, inflamed and shaking, towered over him like an agitated Dominatrix.

'I really don't know what to say, Mrs Montague,' he mumbled through the menacing fire of her silence. 'We can't very well let our prize asset, damn him for being so, dine alone with a lot of rice-wine merchants, can we? I'm afraid he is the star of this particular show,' and correcting himself, 'one of the stars at any rate.' Out of the corner of his eye he could see another succulent joint of lamb being carried into the kitchen, the smell of clam chowder wafting fragrantly through the brightly decorated hallway, bowls of roses and lit candles ready for a night that never was. 'He rang from the restaurant you see, sounding like his mind was very much made up. These stubborn sons of York, reverse snobbery I call it...'

'Leave it Tim,' muttered Astley. 'She's got the message.'

'Yes, I've got the message.'

To Tinwood's surprise, and Petula's own, she did not pull her hair out, stab him in the eye with Astley's new tie-pin, or order her food to be taken to Shatby and rammed down Wrath's throat, all filmed for ten minutes of not-so-commercial air-time.

Instead she gently removed herself from Tinwood's flimsy grip and brushed some imaginary crumbs off her chest. Whistling tartly at Jenny Hardfield, who had been appointed head waiter for the evening, she said, with a carelessness that was meant to be noticed, 'Jenny, we are going to a Chinese restaurant in Shatby tonight and will have no need of the dinner that has been prepared with such great care. Can you pack and freeze what you can, and distribute the rest amongst the help to take home with them. I abhor waste. I know you have Mingus to go back to but would you mind staying on here to keep an eye on Jazzy and Evita... Regan will come with me.'

Both of the older children had been brought downstairs for a cursory and ill-tempered introduction to the guests. Unlike Regan who had stood wide-eyed and silent by her mother's side, Jazzy and Evita had returned to their bedrooms as quickly as they could, scratchy anarcho-punk filtering out from under their closed doors.

'I'd love to Mrs M, but I promised Seth and Mingus I'd be home to make them a late supper. Otherwise I...'

'I'm tired Mummy,' said Regan, 'I want to go to bed.'

'I suppose I should step up,' said Royce, who had been hanging around helpfully all day. 'No one will miss me at supper, even though I did so want to tell Ned Wrath how much I enjoyed that poem he recited last.'

'No, no need for that,' Tinwood raised his hand, the compere demanding silence of a noisy audience, and screwing his small face up painfully he added, 'The fault, or at least the responsibility for this fiasco, is all mine. He's my boy and I should have kept an eye on him. So go, go and enjoy yourselves, I'll hold the fort till you get back. No hurry, no hurry at all. In fact, it won't do me any harm to listen to what tuneless noise these kids consider to be music. Punk's been and gone but it still all sounds awful to me. One eye on the stars of tomorrow, eh?'

'Well, let me put Regan to bed first then.'

Which was all the encouragement the famished party needed as they drained their glasses, crowded into the doorway, and poured hungrily into their cars.

Petula was the first to walk in and coolly stride up to the main table, coming to a majestic halt behind the empty chair next to Wrath. He was alone, drawing a figure of eight on the tablecloth with a damp bottle of beer. A small pyramid of cigarette ends were collected in a saucer; specks of deep-fried seaweed strewn amidst the ash and empty bottles guarding him like sentries asleep in their boxes.

'It looks like you have had quite a party.'

'They say one is fun. Do I have the pleasure?'

'I'm the lady whose house you were meant to be having dinner in,' Petula announced loudly. Anger had settled her nerves most nicely and she was still at a stage of her life where controlled rage made her attractive, its brute aggression diffused in sparkling malice.

Wrath looked up and smiled clumsily. For a second it seemed as though he were about to deliver a clever riposte but instead settled on, 'Dinner?'

'Yes, that thing after lunch but before breakfast.'

'Ahh, that. I think we used to call that tea.'

He was pleasantly tipsy and had, she guessed, embarked on a pub crawl, no doubt conversing with wise fishermen, retired tram-drivers and, by the speed at which a waiter was bringing him another beer, the staff at this strange place. In truth it was not as bad as she had hoped. The walls were decorated with a troop of colourful dragons, all fiery tongues and bulging eyes, that quite appealed to her, as did the hanging carpets and flags, resplendent in matching jade. In fact, she had to concede, once the tanks holding luminous fish, lobsters and pirate treasure were taken into account, Chinkies had made a reasonable aesthetic fist of making up for its unfortunate entry into her life.

Wrath rubbed his eyes and in a relaxed and friendly voice said, 'I'm sorry, I've been carried away. Crazy eh? Who rates Shatby over New York? I never thought I did. So like I say, sorry, I've reverted to being a selfish teenager. I'd forgot there was this infrastructure in place to help me. I told Tim I just wanted to make the day up as I went along, but then the silly prick brings all the rest of this stuff into it...'

'Other stuff? I suppose you mean the bloody hard work other people have put their hearts and souls into for you? I'm sorry, but whilst you sport the pose of a great poet who's above all this pedestrian hassle, others have had their noses to the grindstone. And by the way, hasn't Dylan Thomas already given this "poet-as-a-struggling-alcoholic" a bad name?'

Wrath burst out laughing, 'Christ, I'm not that much of a turd, am I?'

The chairs around them were filling up fast and Petula saw that if she wanted to she could make this man pay for what he had done. She might even get away with telling him that the poem he wrote at fifteen was piss. It would, however, mean ignoring a more enjoyable course open to her. In years to come she would persist in administering a punishment, at whatever cost to her own happiness, because by then keeping accounts was the only way she knew of orientating herself. Tonight in Shatby it was different. She was still younger at heart than she knew, and a glorious impulse to follow the flow surged over the tiresome obligation to be herself.

'Hearts and souls, alcoholism, Dylan Thomas? Sounds like the jig's up,' smiled Wrath, still amused, but only potentially. 'Being found out comes naturally to us all.'

'Sorry,' she corrected herself. Ignoring the interest they were attracting Petula slid into the seat next to Wrath, taking care to straighten her back and thrust her breasts where they could be most easily admired. 'I'm a natural exaggerator, I'm simply unable to prevent myself. I'll have one of those,' she pointed to the beer Wrath was drinking.

Wrath nodded appreciatively, 'Don't worry about exaggeration, all writers are natural exaggerators, it's what makes the important details stand out. Could we have another beer please and some platters, I can't face a full meal,' he said to the waiter. Turning back to Petula, he added, 'I think I'm going to choose liquids over solids tonight. I hate mixing food with gassy lager.'

Normally such a sentiment would have left Petula aghast, as would the taste of beer and the smell of so much of it on a man's breath. She had left Anycock to escape such things, and it had never occurred to her that there could be anything to be said for going backwards.

'I think I may join you on that mission, my appetite isn't what it was,' she said, having looked forward to an extra helping of roast lamb all day.

'I see you've met Petula,' called Astley who had been sat in a nearby booth, the main table overflowing with takers. 'Watch her Ned, she's a woman who isn't scared to bring fire down on her own positions!'

Petula screwed up her eyes to affect annoyance. In truth she could not have coerced Astley into granting her a greater compliment, the act of paying it creating the impression that they had known one another for fifteen years, at least.

'Oh come *on!*'

As in a fairy tale, albeit a Shatby one, two ice-encrusted bottles of beer arrived with a selection of spring rolls and deep-fried lumps that looked suspiciously like scampi; the other diners were already a blur, the restaurant's informality offering unexpected salvation for them all. It was a blur they would not emerge from, in memory or in fact. Not waiting for the entire bottle to be poured, Petula sank the beer in her glass and tapped it impatiently with her knife. Closing one eye, as if taking aim, she necked the second glass as fast as the first and slammed it onto the table harder than she meant to. Her knee was trapped next to Wrath's, both jammed in by the same table leg. In trying to dislodge it she brought her thigh into the equation, the effect thrillingly sexual, their skins as close as cloth would allow.

Wrath smiled gamely. 'Don't misconstrue me for arrogant, we've made a poor start and I don't believe anyone exists for my amusement, but it has to be said, you're a natural comic.'

The ability to make others laugh was one compliment Petula had never been paid, largely, she believed, because nothing could be further from the truth. Trust a poet to get it so arse-about-tit. Still, she wasn't going to disabuse him of so potentially useful an illusion.

'Funny? All the bloody time. That's my trouble, I can't take a single thing seriously.'

'You've seen the funny side of tonight, you're a good sport... I'm sorry, I'm rubbish at remembering names.'

'Petula.'

'Petula. I like that, it's a good name, even if it puts me in mind of screeching child stars with big hair-dos.'

Petula laughed a little at this. 'Success at last. To join yours. I thought your last poem might have been pushing it a bit, but if today wasn't a success for you, don't tell me what is. It'd be too much work to do it again.'

Resisting the temptation to take her compliment seriously, Wrath replied, 'I measure the success of anything by how few of my principles I have to compromise to attain it. Reciting that poem was just something for my conscience, to remind me of how bad I can be even when I thought I was being great. The sad thing is I've written worse.'

Petula pretended not to hear him out; she could not think of what her principles were, offhand, and did not want to go anywhere near the subject of her conscience. 'I thought you recited it so people who like things that rhyme might have something to remember you by. The earlier ones were just too glorious to get a location on.'

'Glorious? You liked them then?'

'Liked them? How could I not, they were brilliant, you stupid man, absolutely so.'

'That's sweet of you, I'm glad you think so.' Modesty had made Wrath's face, thin enough to spread her hand across, appear saintly, and, as if worried that this might be a device to manipulate the unwary, he added, 'I'm good only compared to the competition; compare me to perfection and I'm wanting.'

Petula leant into him and said, 'Balls to that, none of us pass the utopian gold standard, you can only compare yourself to the alternatives, not to what doesn't, and never can, exist outside of your head.'

'Oh?'

'Yes, you can only measure your success by how the others are getting on. That was the Communists' trouble, wasn't it? They live too much in their imaginations and set an ideal standard, and look what they end up with. Something even worse than what we have.'

'How would anyone create anything new then?'

'That's *your* problem, you're the poet!'

Petula emptied the rest of the bottle in her glass, taking care to give Wrath a new one. 'You must think me a terrible lush – a few hours ago I would have driven groceries to your door just to hear you read another of your poems, an hour ago I could have sawn your legs off, now I find I'm back in the fan club. A couple of glasses of beer can change everything; that doesn't say much for me, does it?' She took a sip from his glass. 'Am I being too forward for you?'

'Forward fuck. Go right on, over-familiarity is one of my flaws.'

'And inconsistency mine, friends tell me that enlisting my

support is like quoting the Bible. You'll find the opposite point of view to the one you want support for on the same page... Shit, there it goes again.'

'What?'

Petula tipped back in her chair, scared that she was already falling dangerously under the influence of Bacchus, 'I swear I've said that before, this has happened before.'

'Déjà vu?'

'Yes. That's it, exactly, even my saying this is part of it.'

'It's lucky we didn't start on the fortune cookies.'

Petula pinched his wrist with undisguised merriment; everything from the tablecloth to Wrath's shirt sleeve was imbued with a recurring significance she had felt the flicker of all day. A feeling entirely free of dread had entered the room, a new precursor, the becoming-real of a previously hoped-for possibility: happiness.

'This isn't how mine normally happen, déjà vus I mean. Every time I have one it feels like the thin end of a wedge, another clue that I'm progressing down the wrong road, or maybe that the worst has happened and I'm already at the end of it. This feels like I've picked up a different destiny to the one fate mapped out for me... sorry if that sounds like a line, but there you are. It doesn't sound like a line, does it?'

'Only if you think about it.'

'Whatever you do, not that, none of us are important enough to stand up to that kind of scrutiny.'

Wrath nodded and pushed a plate of cold ribs away. 'All slaw and no ribs, empty vessels.'

'Exactly,' Petula raised her hand to her mouth, a burp uncomfortably close to the offing. 'I just don't think there's that much to any of us,' she went on quickly, 'scrutiny is a process of inventing what isn't there, to hide, basically, nothing at all. That's what I think the substance of most of us is, don't you? A nothing we overcompensate for.' She was going where she felt like going, her first point already forgotten and the next a surprise.

'A cheerless theory Petula, I wouldn't exactly be much of a poet if I went for it.'

'What, you think I'm talking out of my hat? I probably am you know.'

'I'm for inspiration, I can't march about thinking we're banal automatons, each of us powered by our own lack. And I don't believe you really do either, at least not in your own case, or maybe only in your own case...'

Petula, undone and freed by candour, so different to the appearance of it she normally wore, allowed Wrath to refill her glass, enjoying the originality that had only come to her when honesty forbade its opposite. Raising her eyes to his, she saw that he was listening with an intense and fixed concentration. Petula was not used to being appreciated for her confused, uncollected self, her mask too close a fit to risk the unpredictable outcome of such exposure.

'Up to the top please, this is my new favourite drink, what's it called?'

'Carlsberg Export.'

Petula drained another glass. Here she sat, an ideal companion beside her, knowing what it was to be his equal; what should she do about it, stick or twist? A glimpse of heaven may have been enough for most people, but not Petula.

'What is it?' he asked her.

Petula bit her lip coyly. Her bare foot had been pressed against his shoe too long for him to consider it an accident, her toes running up and down the leather like children coursing each other on a staircase.

'What is it?'

'Nothing. Nothing much. I was only thinking how rare it is in life to look forward to meeting a person and find that the anticipation is rewarded. That what I was scared of happening, hasn't.'

'And what was that?'

'Finding out that I didn't like you, or that you didn't like me. That I was a type and that you were too, and that we weren't each other's.'

'What my friends all have in common is that none of them are a type. I write poetry, I don't try and play "the poet" you accused me of back there.' He stopped, his voice not sounding real to him. 'I'm still acting, I can't help it, reading the lines off a script written by identity. But I try and resist doing it on purpose and becoming too preordained. Anyway, you *know* what I do. You strike me as pretty unclassifiable; who are you, Petula?'

'Who am I?'

'Alright, I'll make it easier; what do you do?'

Petula smirked and threw back someone else's glass which was full of a noxious wine that tasted of tomorrow's aspirin. Wrath's leg could have been the table, so firm was its support of her own. 'What do I do? God, how to answer that.' She paused. 'I'm a woman of action, not a perfectly rounded gem or a morsel that a reclusive author knocks out once every fifteen years. I'm a saga to be run ragged with, substantial and episodic. I live in a museum without walls, my life's a wayward story and the way I live it my art. That's what I do... and I hope to die alive.' Petula took Wrath's glass and inhaled deeply, allowing her hand to fall on his lap. She had meant every unrehearsed word of it.

'Is this whisky? What kind? I love the smell.'

'Chinese for all I know. If we were in America, I would tell you that you should run for office. You're a natural politician.'

'Politics? I have none, there's no remedy for this nonsense.' Petula suppressed the desire to move onto Wrath's genitals, balanced inches from her finger tips. She knew if she were not careful she would slip into a version of eternity and leave time and the table altogether. Wrath's careful and wise gaze, possibly an invention of the drink, was having a hypnotic effect. For the first time in her life she was discovering the pleasures of losing control. For nearly the first time she could understand why people drank too much.

'I sense from your answer that you do what you like all day, that you may even be a woman of leisure.'

'Correct. Yet with anarchy comes great responsibility and I'm getting to enjoy the hangovers as much as the parties these days. Have you any idea of how much lamb I'm going to be left with in the morning?'

'I'm sensing you're a complex creation, not a nothing-at-all.'

'Again, correct. I'm one of those things that's better read about on paper than heard aloud. To listen to me is to know I could never work in real life.'

Wrath let Petula stuff a piece of melon into his mouth, confirming her notion that he was as at least as inebriated as she, or did not mind pretending to be.

'Why did you go to America?'

'America, yeah America,' he replied, spilling ash onto his lap as he tried to put out a cigarette he'd forgotten about, 'because too many things were going wrong too many times, that was why, and I was desperate enough to believe in a fresh start.'

'I love it when things go wrong.'

'I bet you do.'

'Why not? Misfortune increases my possibilities, my greatest enemy is also my greatest enabler. That's why I love it when things go wrong... there's nothing like a disaster to bring out the best in me. It's the daily support that people need, my having to be nice to them and say "good morning", that bores me.' Petula hiccupped. She was on the verge of being completely pissed and did not know whether this was the moment to ask Wrath when he would be moving back to England, should she make plans to leave her husband and would he be prepared to move into The Heights. In seconds she would forgo her tactical brain for the evening; she must obtain a concrete advantage before it was too late.

'Excuse me a moment, this beer can make you piss like a horse, don't go anywhere.'

Petula watched Wrath untangle himself from the table and stride purposefully to the lavatory, feeling a simultaneous desire to relieve herself. Best get it out of the way and not waste a moment, she thought, as the jealous eyes of the room followed her to make sure it was not the Gents she was heading to. What happened next Petula could not remember. Perhaps she splashed her face with cold water, took a little too long washing her hands or struggled with the paper towels, for it was a different world she eventually returned to only six minutes later – one in which Ned Wrath had most suddenly ceased to feature.

'Why?' she blurted, for she knew he had gone and only wanted to know the reason.

Astley, who to his immense credit looked genuinely sorry for her, motioned to Donald Eager, who had lit a smelly cigar. Trying to disguise his satisfaction at delivering bad news that he considered just, Eager drawled, 'Well, he was just on his way back to you, back to us I should say, when that waiter,' he pointed at a guilty-looking Chinaman, '*that* waiter called him over to the counter, there was a phone call for him you see.'

'Yep', Astley took over, 'his wife...'

'His second wife,' Eager interrupted.

'Please Donald. I'm sorry Petula, she arrived out of nowhere. The woman must have just got into the country...'

'This country?' Petula felt stripped of her skin, a shock equal to being born had overcome her. If she was not careful she would lose her balance.

'Nonsense Max,' said Eager, 'she's been here for a couple of days at least, holed up in a hotel in Richmond, refusing to leave her room because she thinks our cooking is so awful. She's been ringing round all day and finally caught up with our boy. The bitch told him that if he isn't back before bedtime she'll be on the next plane to JFK without him. And out for a big cut of his goody money after that, if I know the type. Still, all is not lost, he left this for you Lady P.' Eager passed Petula a crumpled napkin and pressed it into her limp hand. Scratched onto it in faint biro was Ned Wrath's New York address, and under it the words, 'I enjoyed bringing down fire on our own positions.'

Petula was to never see Ned Wrath again. As with any famous person, she hoped she would at least bump into him in odd places, before he disappeared completely. At other times she went further and admitted she had spent the most rewarding night of her life with him; in this version she saw them together, the golden couple making the grand entrance, but something stopped her from pursuing this picture in reality. Her correspondence with Wrath, postcards and the odd letter, continued for the next eleven years, one of those false signposts and deliberately misleading clues that kept her going but ultimately led to a dead-end. What it was for him, a fancy not followed or an unconsummated and riveting passion, she never dared ask. Instead she would seek lesser Wraths to spice and season the void left by the first, and with Regan's help hang on to most, the talismanic night at Chinkies marking the last time she would let her guard down with a man. All this was there for her to see on the napkin Wrath left her, the jade cloth his leg rested against, the smell of oyster sauce in her hair and taste of monosodium glutamate under her tongue. Without waiting for her night to end as her day had begun, Petula fled from Astley's sympathetic embrace out onto the pier, her future resigned to a destiny she had not the faith in love to fight.

PART TWO:
Cocytus, Lamentation.

Which way I flie is Hell: my self am Hell;
The mind is its own place, and in it self
Can make a Heav'n of Hell, a Hell of Heaven

– JOHN MILTON, *Paradise Lost*

CHAPTER FOUR,
education and endurance.

The storm was aligning. In the ten years that followed her mother's discreet breakdown on Shatby Pier, which Petula blamed on Chinese food, Regan grew up. To her surprise she was sent away to school soon after the Shatby jolly, and having successfully accepted abandonment as her due, recovered quickly from the shock. The first term away felt longer than life, her boarding-school self the hardened rind of the polite eight year-old she hurriedly distanced herself from. Weeks and months had no meaning, terms and holidays were her new reality and within those she discovered that barbarism allowed no one to rise above it.

Nohallows Hill was an exclusive girls' school for parents who did not wish to share the permissiveness of the 1960s with their children, the former asylum housing over three-hundred daughters of the rich and otherwise preoccupied. Its emphasis on discipline was its selling point though in truth a veneer for a degenerate state of nature, exacerbated by the unnatural absence of boys and young men. It was, in the words of Regan's best friend Diamanda, 'Just like 'Nam!,' an adventure for those girls prepared to ignore their swift dehumanisation, usually a confident majority, and a disaster for the rest. Regan thrived, and developed a detestation for those in her yearly intake who did not. Her unwillingness to occupy subjectivities unlike her own, for however short a time, came from this basic intolerance of outward frailty and with it the habit of holding reflection responsible for every kind of defect of character. Girls who spent too much time analysing the comforts of home, remembering a favourite swing or pony, earned her sullen scorn. 'Get over it!' was all she had to offer flakes, sapping house morale with their finicky digressions and nostalgia for humanity.

Activity was the thing, on the playing fields, in the expensively built sports hall and over the vast school grounds where vicious games of British Bulldogs were enacted until fractured bones or chipped teeth gave the players a chance to hobble away. Admirable as being able to 'take it' and 'take part' was, Regan's indifference to pain robbed her experiences of content, the parlour game of wondering whether she had been happy or not at Nohallows haunting her for years to come. What, after all, was she doing there?

The possibility that her mother no longer desired a constant witness to her life, a little pair of eyes taking everything in, did admittedly occur to Regan when Diamanda, sharing a crushed Battenberg cake sent to celebrate her ninth birthday, told her 'We're here because our parents are assholes, right? But so what? Who cares? Everyone's an asshole, right?' Well, Regan decided, that might be true of Diamanda's kith and kin, Columbian socialist-socialites who furnished second and third homes for the Jaggers, but hers weren't like that at all. She was at Nohallows *because* her parents, or at least Petula, cared for her, Noah having already begun his slow-fade into amiable irrelevance. Making the most of her residency was the least she could do to show her gratitude for the opportunity and, toning it down a little so as to not sound too goody-goody, Regan wasted no time in setting Diamanda straight.

'If only all of you girls could think like that,' her housemistress said after overhearing their conversation and giving Diamanda two weeks' detention. 'I heartily wish there were more like you Regan Montague. You express yourself so beautifully too. Regan Montague, even your name sounds like it should.'

For all her appreciation of her parents' motives, home was not an easy world to return to, however much she missed it at night, when the time came for lights out and she found she could not sleep. To her shame she secretly pined after the gentle inactivity she left behind, naive and basic as it was, next to lacrosse, chemistry and debates on euthanasia. But all that had to be cast to one side, and her new world embraced in all its stimulating cruelty. Staring from her window at galloping cloud formations, fastening animal shapes to her corkboard and dreaming of the day she would accept Mingus's offer of marriage, all now embarrassed Regan deeply, and in a fit of self-disgust she swapped bedrooms on her first exeat home from school.

'Why?' asked Petula, who liked a bit of sentimentality so long as she did not have to have her nose rubbed in it. 'That was the room you grew up in, we chose it for you deliberately, it has a lovely view of the garden, south-facing, and large cupboards we had made at great cost to keep the moths out. Jazzy and Evita would have killed you for it.'

Regan had no answer she was ready to share; things that were important had ceased to be.

'Suit yourself, though I *warn you*, independence for independence sake is as much of a bore as hanging round your mother's apron strings.'

Regan's new choice of abode was an austere guest berth Petula tended to put people she did not like in, and as removed from her lilac den of old as school was from home. Showing a taste for absolutism worthy of her mother, the once-treasured contents of her old life were boxed away and stored in the attic, her other knick-knacks and mementoes trashed or taken to charity. The transition between the two worlds was thus narrowed, reaching its apogee when her mother forced her to change out of school uniform a week into the holidays.

'I will simply not have you going round like that, a dead-end kid, you remind me of an evacuee from the war. They couldn't afford normal clothes so had to walk round in school uniforms until they fell apart. It was very sad.'

'Can't I wear what I want to wear?'

'Not if it makes you look like an underprivileged dredge.'

'What's so wrong with being one of those?'

'Nothing if you really are one. Now go and put something sensible on.'

'She's become a cool customer,' commented her father on her second exeat home.

'You mean an even *cooler* customer,' corrected Royce. Regan's outlook had indeed chilled; like a metaphor that was always changing without revealing its object, adults could not locate a heart behind the glass. Her mother did not need to, she knew she could rely on Regan and required no more than that to enjoy a perfect relationship with her protégée. The further off the others stayed the better; Regan's self-imposed solitude suited her wider purpose. This arrangement was tested only once, and then by mistake.

Unlike school, with its orderly procession of dates and events, The Heights had lost its sense of sequence for Regan; time there did not lead to the future. Perfection had already been attained and it resided in her mother; she could not see past Petula, sitting atop of it all, rendering change a meaningless impossibility. History here did not evolve, there was no such thing as moving up a year, only a stillness that required occasional shoring-up to make it ever more immobile. What hope was there for advancement in this sort of environment? Regan did not put it like this when she asked a very tipsy Royce one December whether she thought her mother would let her pick the jacket she wanted for Christmas, or choose for her, but she came close.

'Read between the lines my dear,' whispered Royce as if danger lurked beneath the very roof they were sat under, 'you'll see what I mean as you get older, as you already can I shouldn't doubt. There's not enough vitality to share round a small place like this. One woman's got a monopoly on the stuff. First she sucked it from your father, his friends and social set, then got to work on the rich and famous. Once she was finished with them she started on you kids; she'll be taking it from the trees and the earth itself next. Why do you think we all feel so tired all the time my dear? She'll disinherit you before she approves of a decision you've come to on your own. Pixie Boots or your choice of husband, you're her little doll, always have been and it's little wonder you should be sick of it.' Royce often said things like this about 'situations', as she liked to call them, speaking obliquely in fits and snatches, assuming her audience understood every word. Tonight she had taken the bull by the horns and Regan marked the moment by trying to deny it.

'You *are* talking about Mummy now, aren't you Royce?'

'Who else?' snorted Royce, quite forgetting she was stirring blood against blood. 'Who else could I mean, the monkey who steals your nuts? A chicken?'

Regan could see that she had annoyed the old woman. 'Are you saying Mummy will never let me buy the clothes I like? Not even when I'm older?'

'Oh come on, you're an intelligent girl, you can't put on that Simple-Simon act with me. Since when has Petula, I'm sorry, your Mummy, since when has she liked people making their minds up for themselves? Look at your Father. Ask him if you don't believe me.'

'But he doesn't mind or care about anything.'

'More like he hasn't had the chance to.'

'Really?'

'It just becomes easier not to argue after a while.'

'That's unfair. Whatever it is that makes Mummy so bossy is also what makes her care so much, you once told me. You must remember? She does too much for everyone, *you* said that. I thought you and her were, well, that you liked each other. You're friends. Aren't you?'

'I've seen a few things that have made me wonder, my dear.'

'What things?'

Royce thrust another lump of cold ham into her mouth and, looking knowingly from side to side, said with the whimsical pomposity that is often the substitute for wisdom or achievement in a person of advanced years, 'Little girls have heard enough for one night, quite enough, and it's time for this one to kiss her Auntie goodnight. Don't you worry my dear,' she tapped her nose, 'remember Royce knows, Roycey knows! And now you know what Roycey knows! I'll take care of you my darling.'

Regan, who seconds earlier had been addressed as an equal, held back from scratching the rouge off the patronising old lady's cheek. Concluding that she would be only a couple of sentences away from wanting to do so again, she avoided Royce for the rest of that holiday.

'Aren't you going to say goodbye to your Auntie?'

'I'm sorry, but I'm about to have a bath, Mummy.'

'Yes. I know what you mean. I'll tell Royce you need to wash your hair.'

Regan lay on her uncomfortably hard bed and brooded over the security offered by eternal stasis, against the risks posed by uninvited change. Though she did not grasp it yet, she was not without her mother's ambition. By the following Easter she had come to the view that it was best to take advantage of her unique relationship with Petula and talk to her directly. It was not beyond the realms of plausibility that her mother already knew how she felt, sympathised with her confusion, and would welcome the opportunity to assist her with inimitable clarity.

Regan was used to manipulating adults in a way that did not count as such if handled with the right amount of roundabout innocence. On her last day at home she took the unusual step of engaging Petula in a rather general conversation on human nature. Not sure whether her daughter wanted something, or was just trying out new hats, Petula tried to humour her as best she could, with one eye on the time. She had an important fitting in Richmond, and did not want to break the speed limit to get there.

'So Mummy, people, greedy people...'

'Hmmm.'

'There's always been greed hasn't there, people have always been greedy, ever since the dinosaurs...'

'Yes, greedy people, living in caves in animal skins, what of them?'

'That's never changed, they were always greedy, but the way they've acted greedy has changed, hasn't it, it's sort of progressed?'

'What are you talking about?'

'Greed.'

'I know that. What are you really talking *about*?'

'People.'

'Hurry up Regan, I haven't bought you up to dilly-dally, it's bad enough having to listen to Royce telling me how she's discovered a new A-road between Spamshingle and Codstock, without having to hear you take the longest distance between two points.'

'What I mean is the way they, they... the way people *express* their greed, that's changed, I think.'

'Could have fooled me.'

'But it has, if you look at history I think it has. Instead of girls and boys being sent into a factory to make money we're sent to school to learn how to make it instead. That's quite a contradiction isn't it, I think. The same quality changes its character over time. Changes for the better too. I mean, it's less bad to learn how to take money from someone legally than to just steal it off a weaker person, I think, like they used to do in the olden days.'

'Jesus Regan, you sound like Plato. Have you some Greek homework to get out of the way? Can't you ask your father about whatever it is you are asking me about, he has to be good for something.'

'No, it's not schoolwork Mummy. I've just been thinking about stuff.'

'I suppose that's what we send you there for – that school you never tell us anything about. Out with it then, whatever it is you're getting at.'

'Do you ever think I might be as important as you?'

'I beg your pardon?'

'Do you think I might count as much as you, matter as much? You might go and live somewhere else and I live here on my own one day, then would I feel as important as you? Live here and be in charge.' Regan went bright red, she did not know what she was saying, only that if she were to express the sentiment she was most afraid of hearing, it would not sound worse than this.

Petula, who had already moved into planning that evening's seating arrangement for Tom Conti's fortieth, brought her full attention to bear on this sudden lapse in her daughter's sanity.

'I know little girls talk and say all sorts of things they don't understand just to watch how grownups react so I'll be kind to you Regan. Have a care.'

'*Sorry, sorry, sorry.* That came out wrong... I didn't mean to...'

'Shut up. Firstly Regan, if you have conversations like this with other people they'll think you're very boring so don't attempt to instigate them or take part in them if someone else starts one, do you understand? Second, silence is golden. You look beautiful with it, use it often, even when you don't need to, it keeps the idiots guessing and saves you from shaving years off your life. Thirdly, I carried you in my stomach, it was that way around alright? I was not born from you, I know you and for the moment, even if that moment is forever, things will remain that way around.'

'I'm sorry Mummy, I'm so sorry.'

'So am I. Don't let yourself down like this again.'

'I really don't know where it came...'

'Should you, despite this warning, find your thoughts running away with you, disturbing that perfect silence I ask you to hold, then consider this. Would you rather have me in control or no one in control? That's the choice. Now go away. You've made me very upset.'

Regan had faced a truth, or at least the possibility of something being true, and was now compelled to forget it, a lesson that was to become a reflex. She would never relate abstractions concerning social progress to the particulars of her life, or share an idea that advanced an interest separate from her mother's again, until life left her with no choice. More positively, delineating a taboo loosened her tongue in public, and Regan became an excellent foil for discussions within agreed paradigms, be they on napkins, theatre programmes, recipes or dogs. With patient gaiety she observed the seasonal ritual of 'modest social success', welcoming its cycles, patterns and deliberate repetitions, as one structurally identical cast after another swapped places round her mother's table. Home did not seem so taxing anymore, and when she passed her fourteenth birthday, and the Eighties became the Nineties, watching Donald Eager perform opposite Julie Christie in *Hamlet*, she considered herself saved from speculative self-indulgence. Choice was a waste of time and freedom a black hole with teeth, the facts were not enough in themselves, to believe in anything she had to *want* to, and it was beyond her to want anything without first receiving Petula's blessing.

Regan's 'personal life' was thus confined to term-time. The holidays, overseen by Petula and quickened by the fear of being outed as boring, which is how Regan now viewed her desire to communicate deeper truths, were an interlude in which she worked on her school persona. At Nohallows she moved through her early conformism to more nuanced positions, retaining only a coy loyalty to the institution through an aloof tolerance of her lot. Regan's carefully contrived air of knowing everything, while saying next to nothing, bordering on world-weariness that would have been absurd anywhere apart from boarding school, won her the respect of her peers; noisy girls who could not sit still or stop talking. Though it was not obvious to her, others acknowledged her as leader of her year, an important, if tacit, position in a system in which hierarchy was ideology.

Few guessed that The Heights was her training camp, albeit a slightly lonely one, with no one to remark on her enigmatic silences or share her long and slightly desperate walks with. To keep her term-time reputation for being interesting and elusive meant seeing very little of her friends in an environment where they may discover that she was not so great after all. For the first few years Regan invited no one to The Heights; her social life, such as it was, continued to be her mother's. Contact with friends her own age was limited to forty-eight-hour stays at their houses, and one-off appearances at parties, always sure to be taxied away first thing in the morning before anyone had enough time to get too used to her dazzling serenity. By imitating the actors, writers and poets her mother collected, Regan exceeded the references of her contemporaries which went little further than *Just Seventeen* and *Dirty Dancing*. Their limited horizons enabled her to pose as a true innovator, even when parroting editorials of *The Economist* and The Smiths' lyrics that she ventured no further than WH Smiths to crib and copy from. Like her mother, success seemed almost too easy, set against such substandard competition, and the resulting confidence was somewhat cheaply acquired.

'Don't you think it's about time you brought some of your friends home with you?' challenged Petula. She had been gazing at her reflection in a mirror she had never looked good in and was feeling peevish. 'I don't want anyone thinking I won't let you have your friends here, least of all them. It's your home too and I thought you'd be proud of it. In fact, I thought this house would be the envy of your year. God knows you're popular enough already. You're invited to things all the time. Think of how much more kudos you'd have if they could all see where you live. You know, I even had a letter from some obscure woman in Brighton thanking you for the influence you've had on her daughter for heaven's sake.'

'Beth's?'

'Whoever; well where are they all, your many followers? Let's be having them.'

Regan went the same colour as she had the day she last crossed Petula's bows, a transgression her mother had forgiven her for by never bringing up. Petula, sensitive to questions of status if to little else, understood the problem at once. Gently she took hold of her daughter's wrist.

'Is there some *reason* you don't want them here, a silly one you can't help having?'

Regan nodded, in plain sight of tears.

'I thought so.' Petula felt her heart undulate protectively; it would not do for the top dog to be unmasked as a puppy in front of her fan club. She would have to think of a way of giving her daughter prime billing for long enough to usher a gaggle of girls in and out of The Heights, their illusions intact. It was an amusing challenge that ought not to prove too tricky.

'Anyway, no rush, there's so much on over the next few weeks that we don't need to find new things to do. Perhaps when you're next home, we could arrange something then. School is such a pressure cooker you need the holidays to vegetate in. It must be a relief not having every old sweat staring at you all the time and knocking on the bog door telling you get a move on. Or changing that channel from your favourite programme in that stinky common room. Quite.'

Regan nodded; her mother always knew the right time to be a naif. Even in her tight-knit group of friends, an elite known as 'The Lasses', Regan was alone, her reticence the invisible curtain that held their worshipful jealousy at bay. The real and sticky mystery of her being was a chimera she did not wish them to probe, her performances and critical notices would only suffer from discovery; far better to trust makeup and lighting.

'I don't know whether they're mature enough to appreciate it here Mummy, it might be a bit over their heads. They act much younger than sixteen, I mean, much younger than you were when you were sixteen.'

'So they might, we should wait until they've grown up a little. I once went to India before I was ready and ended up hating it.'

'And most of their parents are idiots. Or common.'

'Please don't use that word in public. People will think we are snobs.'

In the end, change did not need her or Petula's assent to enter their lives, it only had to wait for nature. The weeks that followed her sixteenth birthday heralded a new stage in her development as adult features emerged from Regan's face like carefully hidden treasure. Dimples fell before sharp angles and her chin and cheeks lost the support of the soft flesh that had kept them company through early pubescence. Regan's height rocketed too, physically turning her into mother's fair double, her tendency to stoop so as to not to stand out corrected by a firm punch Petula did not hesitate from issuing in public. With her beauty increasing by the hour, Regan wondered how best to try it out before it was spoiled or lessened in some way. Reading her thoughts Petula urged restraint, to do nothing on impulse or bland affection, her 'goods' were too valuable for that. In fact Petula need not have worried; Regan's beauty was not the kind that attracted the flies. Regan gleaned for herself that those few boys she came across, especially the hearty ones keen on a girl they could bounce off, could not stand her or stand in her way. Her sleek appearance was fast turning into something frightening, its intimidating unapproachability threatening to become unattractive if deprived of a human airing. With typical adolescent bravura the other Lasses, envious to their awe-enthused cores, decided Regan possessed an aura that could raise the profile of anyone associated with it. Five otherwise pretty girls shed their cheery demeanours and adopted Regan's lost detachment, floating through their parents' dinner parties and the new school year like fragmenting icebergs in an Arctic storm. Soon they were all being ignored by boys, bemusing adults and intimidating their contemporaries, a cast apart in an institution that had no tolerance for factions. The headmistress rang Petula at The Heights, not to necessarily blame Regan for The Lasses, who had by now taken to binding their hair up in handkerchief turbans, only implying that if Regan stopped so might the others. Perhaps Petula might raise the matter with her daughter?

'You want *me* to use my influence over my daughter? Regan is simply being herself, if others wish to imitate her that's a personal matter between them and their aesthetic sense. You say these girls aren't actually *doing* anything wrong, the wrong bit is a sort of attitude you can't put your finger on. So I say wait until there is something you can put your finger on, a rule they've broken; boys, drugs, alcohol, any of that. Then come to me and I'll be the first to lift Regan's feet off the ground and spank her arse. Until then I suppose the best thing for you to do is keep a low profile and try and catch 'em out, because at the moment it seems like they've got the jump on you.'

The headmistress, not used to being told how to do her job, took it because she did not know what else to do, her hand still shaking when she lit a cigarette half an hour after she had put the phone down. The following morning Regan had added blue lipstick to her repertoire, so faint as to look like the rigor mortis found on a corpse, the other Lasses following suit later that day. A line had been transgressed; wearing of 'face-paint' was against the school rules and Regan, though not formally suspended, was sent home a few days before the end of term. Her tribe waved her off defiantly, their remaining time on school grounds consisting of a heady mix of detention, cross-country runs and slave labour.

It was this harsh flowering that increased Petula's estimation of her daughter; her sense of her latent power and future use to her. By the time Regan returned to The Heights, bowed and a little startled at having finally gotten into trouble, Petula was ready to ring the changes.

'Regan,' Petula announced to her daughter, who stood warily by the door expecting a lashing, 'I think it's high time we held you a party, a party for you and your colourful troupe of friends! I expect you could use a lift after all this nonsense you've got mixed up with.'

It was all Regan could do to not moisten herself, with relief or dread she did not know. However, her friends were not here yet and Petula still was – it was too early for a completely spontaneous response.

'You're not *mad* with me then?'

'Of course I'm mad with you, you've acted like a perfect prune. But where did anger ever get anyone? I'm all for moving forward, you know me, my darling, I say it once and never need say it again. On! The road ahead. That's my motto.'

'Mummy, I really don't know what to say, that's so kind of you...'

'Get on the blower and rally the troops, I have something memorable in mind, one to look back on and miss very much when you're older. And darling...'

'Yes?'

'Take that ridiculous blue stuff off your lips, it makes you look like one of Dracula's tarts. No nice man is going to want to get his leg over with you looking like one of the undead. Or thank me for allowing you to remain that way.'

*

Jazzy stared at the hand he had been gesticulating with, and shook his head. His mother's cruelty and kindnesses were unmingled, entire and uneven, which also tended to be reflected in his muddled responses to them.

'I'm *trying*, I'm really *trying* to get my head around it, it's so hard to but I'm trying, give me credit, you've got to give me credit for that at least. Yeah?'

'I *do*, I know how hard you try.'

'You might, but who else does? It's like I'm banging my head against a wall on my own here.'

'No one else cares as much.'

'Is that supposed to make me feel better?'

'I meant no one cares as much as you do, no one's affected as much as you are by all the shit they give you.'

'What, so you think I shouldn't care so much. I should just ignore what's happening?

'*Please* Jazzy.'

'Sure, no, I know what she expects, I ought to just carry on taking it lying down, being pissed on, right here,' Jazzy pointed to his mouth, 'see how much I can take and break a world record for being pissed on, right?'

'You've been through too much, I know it, everyone who really knows what's going on here does.'

'*Pissed* on, I've been, absolutely yellowed.'

'I wish she could see what she's done to you.'

'I've been through more than anyone else could go through. You name one person who could go through what I have. I can't believe what I've been through, sometimes I just sit here and think about it and I can't believe anyone could take all the shit I've had to, from all sides, all the fucking time. Do you even know what I've been through? I've been *pissed* on.'

'I don't know how you've done it.'

'I didn't, they did!'

'I know, that's what I meant. How you've stood it, I mean, the piss and shit, how you've got through it all, and not allowed it to make you, er, bitter.'

'*I* don't know how I've done it, no, I'll tell you why, I've done it because I've had no choice, it was do it or die. I never had any real choice; no, don't say I'm going over the top here...'

'I'm not, you're not.'

'I did it because I care about the place and they couldn't survive a day here without me, not a day, holding this shit together behind the scenes, fixing their lousy window latches and hammering in their nails for them every time they need a hammerer. I've done it, Jill, but it's come at a cost, a price, you know, that price is my fucking *mind*.' Jazzy rapped his head with a bruised knuckle, 'they've done it, done my head in with all their "Heights" bull*shite*. I've had it up to here with it,' Jazzy held a piece of toast up to where he had had it up to, his neck, 'the Heights *shite*, non-fuckin'-stop, never lets up, whenever you think you can have a bit of normality it starts up again, I've had it up to here this time,' the toast was at his neck again, moving in a sawing motion, 'we're off, they can find someone else to waste their fucking lives here, not me, this time I've got to make a stand. My going is the only thing they'll understand, we've got to do it, pack up and start somewhere else. Because this shite, this *shite* right, it'll never finish, never. I can see it going on forever, I mean forever you know. On and on. God, it depresses me so much to think about it. It's so depressing, *so* depressing.'

Jill ran her hand along her lover's dreadlocked hair and rubbed her nose sympathetically against his ear, 'You've been amazing, doing everything for everyone and never getting any credit. I love you Jazzy, I love you so much.'

Fondly, he pushed her away, 'I mean it this time Jilly, there's a limit to how much shite anyone can take and stay sane, right? It's got so I can't even breathe in this place.' He motioned round the table. It was the wrong room in the house to have used as a kitchen, no big windows, gadgets in the way of one another, corners grimy and poorly lit, the perfect setting for Jazzy's despairing digressions. 'What am I supposed to do, I ask you, sit here and take it? I'm trying, but there's only so much you can take before you break. And that's what I think they've done to me Jill, broken me with their bullshit, I can't even enjoy my breakfast any more, going out or even talking to you. It's like there's this horrible, depressing, filthy, shitty thing separating me from all the stuff I used to connect with. Seriously, it's getting in the way of me being able to enjoy life, what's left for me to enjoy. I feel like I've turned into a nutter. I'm a broken man, that's basically it. They've fucking broken me Jilly. That's how shit I feel about it all, it's like none of the good stuff exists for me anymore. She's won, she's got what she wanted, she's taken my minerals. And this, *this* is just too much.'

It was a speech Jazzy made two or three times a week, and every Sunday morning too, groggy and stoned from the night before, if Saturday had been really bad. The loose plaster on the walls and broken appliances stacked by the back door showed the effects of his frustration, as did his sunken knuckles, distorted from punching the oil tank, prematurely greying hair and serrated teeth, the product of too many rants on the whizz. Still only in his mid-twenties, complaint had become a way of life, the news that his sister was to have a large party at the main house, and that his mother expected him to 'buttle' at it inspiring this latest tirade.

'She makes me so angry, I wish I could do something to protect you Jazz. I've a good mind to go up and give her what for, you know. Finally. She can't keep treating you like this. Who does she think she is? It's got to stop.'

Jazzy picked up a bit of loose rolling paper and crushed it in his hand. The song had basically remained the same for as long as he knew the words: how could his mother treat him this way?

'This time she's going to see a different me, she's pushed me too far. I mean, she expects me to wear a bow tie, you know, who's ever looked good in one of those? I'm not Roger shaggin' Moore. We're leaving and that's it. Mark my words and remind me of them, you know me, what I say I *mean*, and what I mean I always do, *always*.'

'It's the unfairness Jazz, it's so *unfair*.'

'She doesn't realise I'm a man of my word.'

'I know it.'

Jazzy nodded, encouraged that his core grievance should have found its way off his chest into the mouth of another, albeit his devoted girlfriend, Jill 'Aries' Cronin.

'I hate the way they've taken all your good energy and given you all their bad. You deserve better karma than this, Jazzy. All you're about is good vibes.'

Which in itself was a matter of opinion. The perceivably unfair treatment between Jazzy and Regan, tacitly justified by the fact that Jazzy was not Noah's son (a biological quirk Jazzy considered tasteless to bring up) steadily defined Jazzy to a point where it whispered to him in his sleep. For all Petula's posturing, Noah held the purse strings, and though he was not averse to financial appeasement, his friendly indifference to his extended family could not survive the tempest of Jazzy and Evita's adolescence. By the time the boy hit twenty-one his stepfather was looking to slash the subsidies that Jazzy considered stingy on account of their failure to keep up with inflation. The moral imperative that this man should pay for stealing his mother from his real father, as Jazzy saw it, cut little ice with Noah who made more of personal responsibility and other fascistic abstractions. Questioning Jazzy's lived experience of inequality, his key to understanding life's many complexities, gave Noah his first black eye and Jazzy his first night in the cells, experiences neither wished to repeat. Wisely their mutual antipathy switched to the cold kind, Noah keeping Jazzy alive and no more, Jazzy doing nothing to make him change his mind or pursue the more generous tack he held out for.

With a care he showed nowhere else in his life, Jazzy refused to openly blame Regan for the way she benefited from his or

Evita's 'neglect'. Instead the simmering jealousy he embraced, albeit hidden within the language of natural justice, grated painfully with his self-image of being a 'laid-back' guy, 'chilling' his way through life. He loved Regan in a brashly sentimental fashion and did not relish either envying her good fortune or others noticing his obsessional resentment. Unfortunately, he was unable to suppress it and would regale anyone from the postman to distant relatives on the subject after the first drink had passed his lips. If only he could be given the means to succeed, he would show them all, and in doing so, prove himself at last. Yet his attachment to the farm either killed him with kindness, he feared, or tied him to a way of life that never raised him further than dependence, he claimed, so in the end he went nowhere.

Petula could never leave a problem unexploited for long and decided that she would eventually have to find a use for her quarrelsome firstborn. Carefully she manipulated him through his many grievances; if he let go of them she knew he would lose his capacity for being played, but, she guessed correctly, bitterness was a path he could not abandon. He was like a dog in search of an owner, his loyalty and fervour wasted on those who did not value it. Times that were merely bad became terrible in relation to what they should have been; poor in comparison to how much his mother appeared to be enjoying life anyway.

Petula had been quick to make the most of her ambiguous relationship to work. The night with Wrath was locked away, the day in Shatby released into the world, the role played by her organisational genius growing at every telling. Events of a similar stature were offered up to her and she was careful to share joint billing with whomever fell under her authoritative spell. Fetes, concerts, outdoor productions of *The Tempest* and Prince Charles's visit to the York Viking Centre all fell under her capable auspices. To Petula's chagrin, though not surprise, her growing renown as an occasion manager did not make enlisting Jazzy to her cause any easier. His childhood rejection of her world had established a fault line neither he nor she could traverse. Even if his fantasy of being a rock-and-roll gypsy had struggled to survive its first encounters with real life, Jazzy had not taken refuge in her dazzling trinity of country life, high society and culture. What Petula needed was a basic change in strategy that could secure the ends she had failed to obtain by more obvious means; to turn what had always upset her most to her ultimate advantage: Jazzy's refusal to move away. True, his farm-bound stasis had known some gentle variations; a few months dossing on floors in Hull, an extended holiday on Australia's Gold Coast, several exchange trips to Corsica and yearly inter-rail adventures, all absentmindedly funded by Noah in the hope that one day the boy would not return. Unlike Evita, who fled the nest having blinded a local lad in one eye after a sexual assault no one could prove, her last-known addresses a series of lesbian squats in Hamburg, Jazzy loved the farm even as he despised its traps and trappings. If it were up to him, his future would lie nowhere else.

'This farm may be your great love but it's a great love that has no room or need for you Jasper. It's what the poets would call love of the unrequited variety, the sort that makes no one happy, capiche? You must realise by now I'm the only thing standing in the way of you and a rocket to someplace else. Noah's been egging me to get you to sling your hook...'

'He doesn't give a shit, it's you who's always hated me.'

'...to get you off the property ever since you landed him that shiner. Your marching orders are on the tip of his tongue, kept only from being spoken of by me, the poor fool whom you profess to hate. But that's another story. The point is you can't carry on loafing round here indefinitely, it *isn't* your home. And your acting like it is sort of makes me feel a bit sick, actually.'

'Let me work here, do that and I'll show you here's where I belong. I'm good for it Mum, I'll show you if you let me.'

'*Show* me? Oh come on, haven't you already been here long enough? I'm sick of waiting for you to wake up and do something manly. You're twenty-one years old for God's sake, in my day that was old enough for you to be sent out to war; in Iran that's old enough for you to be made a bloody General.'

'I love this farm.'

'I wish you'd follow your sister's example and vamoose under a cloud. She daren't come back. Some big brother you were to her anyway, couldn't even keep her out of trouble, and once she shows she has the stones to do what you can't, actually leave, well, even that's beyond you, so you end up writing miserable letters asking her to come back. She's told me! Call yourself a man. Instead of handing out black eyes and pinching the odd arse you should gear up for a full-blown crime. Do something that makes a difference instead of standing in front of me feeling sorry for yourself. Become a mercenary or something.'

'Are you saying I'm not a good brother, that I don't love my sisters...'

'You're not a good brother Jasper, you have never exerted any positive influence over either of your sisters or been a support to them in any way other than rhetorically, and I don't need to tell you where you get that from. Your father was a great one for investing in the bull farm, especially when it came at no cost to himself. But I'm not going to suffer for you like I did for him; you see, this conflict just isn't worth it. The point is, yes, Regan is lucky that Noah is her father, but you, you are lucky that I married her father. Which makes you lucky but just not as lucky as Regan. That's all there is to it. Be thankful you weren't born being barrel-bombed in a ditch in East Pakistan.'

'I can't believe you, where you get off? I don't. I don't get where this comes from... the *evil*, your poison. You, you were never there for either of us, we were practically abandoned when you were out partying with your devils, slags, whoever they were. Do you know what happened to us all the times you

were out, what it was like to be left alone every time? Call yourself a mother? I hate you. You're a fake, an irresponsible monster. *Selfish, selfish, selfish*. You killed my Dad.'

'Oh come on.'

'And you followed the fuckin' money. I reject you with all my
might, right?'

'Which isn't very much is it?'

'You've never believed in us, it was always your shit, we never
had a chance. Your friends fucked us.'

'Never had a chance? Well it's not like the sculpting career
ever got anywhere, is it? How they laughed at me for believing
in you then... You see the trouble is, I have wanted to believe in
you Jasper. Of course I'd prefer to think you're something better
than a deadhead but it's you who's never let me. Never let me
by failing at anything you turn your hand to. Your career as a
sculptor, your chance to be an artist, what happened there, eh?
Oh Christ, I shiver to think of what a prat you made me look;
prat, did I say prat? I meant something far worse that rhymes
with hunt.'

Jazzy had to give his mother that one. It had always been her
knack to find the one aspect of an argument that afforded her a
sliver of validation, and reduce every subsequent disagreement
to it. For a moment, albeit quite a long one, Petula wondered
if Jazzy might have a dispensation for what his teacher called
'three-dimensional art' or what she preferred to think of, until
disabused by the data, as sculpture. On principle she asked
Noah to provide the eleven year-old with the materials, whilst
she offered the moral support, her friends taken aback at the
savage pride she was prepared to take in Jazzy, now that he had
finally shown 'artistic credentials'.

Jazzy did indeed enjoy handicraft, creating and filling small
plastic moulds to manufacture the faces of trolls, orcs and gargoyles, loosely based on swords and sorcery fiends, often producing several dozen at a time. With the tender concentration of one

with little else to do, he stuck these grotesque shapes onto bodies cannibalised from dolls and other family-friendly toys, leaving his mutant creations round the farm to surprise people. Noah lost his aim when he found one leering at him from the top of his lavatory panel early one morning, and his sense of humour when another turned up stuffed in the exhaust of his MG. 'The Creatures', as Royce dubbed the miniature monsters, showed a skill in construction and idiosyncratic touches that could at least deflect questions over whether they amounted to little more than a hobby or not. It was, as Petula made clear to her circle, 'a start'. Ten years later Jazzy was still at it, the creatures having found lebensraum in three sheds, their novelty palling in a way that had yet to affect production. Inspired by the outdoor sculptor, Andy Goldsworthy, Jazzy branched out into transforming burrows, old badger warrens and hollowed-out trees into dens and castles for his charges, attracting a photographer from *Orcwind and Fire* magazine, though sadly not Goldsworthy, whom Petula loyally prepared a herring casserole for in the hope of luring him to The Heights. A showing held outdoors one Halloween, flares lighting the figures' determined silhouettes, and a catalogue describing them as a lost tribe of Yorkshire Pixies, was the last straw for Petula, who, having had the designs rejected by a toy company Noah approached, asked Jazzy to melt the lot down.

'Yes, your sculptural work still turns up in the most interesting places, not private collections I'm afraid. No, the gardener dug up a thing that looked like a dwarf with small pox. Don't think he knew quite what to make of it.'

'I don't want to talk about all that now.'

'No. I bet you don't. What was it you wanted to talk about again, I forget?'

'I want to work here, here on the farm, just let me prove myself, right?'

'Not again.'

'It's where I'm meant to be, please.'

'Well...'

'Please Mum, *please*.'

'There are some things I suppose you could do...'

'Please, I'll do anything, I'm good for it, I can work.'

'By God boy, you'll owe me though.'

'Anything, I'll do anything to work here.'

'Better on the inside pissing out than on the outside pissing in, I suppose.'

'What?'

'You'll see.'

Later Jazzy would claim that he did not know what he was letting himself in for, his dependence on his mother's patronage moving from the conditional to the absolute. As with any farm, there was no shortage of unpleasant tasks that required unskilled labour, and so at his insistence, Jazzy found his adult calling. Not farming but labouring. There was never any question of there being a honeymoon period, his was not the kind of work that allowed for that.

'I assure you that you will learn the true meaning of a thankless task.'

'I've told you, bring it on, it was what I was born to do.'

'Pride before the fall.'

'What is it you don't want to get? It would be so good for you to think I can't take it, but the trouble is I can, I've been *taking it* all my life. I don't care what you throw at me, I can take it.'

But he did care, even if he could take it, at first only a little, soon after a bit more, and eventually very much. Jazzy's attempts to get involved in the more meaningful side of farm work were marginalised and stymied by the tenant farmers who got their kicks watching Petula's boy dig up thistles and nettles for them. Glamorous guests would hurtle up and down the drive wondering who the surly youth potholing the track in all weathers was, or glance across the lawn and marvel how lucky they were not to be digging an irrigation ditch in the middle of a storm. In this way any joy taken in a practical life that Jazzy nursed a passion for merged with a drudgery indistinguishable from a slave rowing his master's galley. Annoyed at his cranky ingratitude, sullen self-absorption, and the thought that she now lived under the same roof as a labourer, Petula prepared her coup de grace. It would come in the form of the 'middle' cottage, The Jacaranda Tree, a gift-wrapped castration she knew Jazzy could not refuse.

Since the military couple had fled, The Jacaranda Tree had come down in the world, ending up in the hands of a family of Sikhs who had violated the terms of their agreement by turning the building into a Temple. With directed needling, Noah evicted the tenants who, displaying a docility unknown in The Heights, left promptly and without argument. The Jacaranda Tree was Jazzy's gift for services rendered, a way of giving him some of what he wanted, whilst withholding the independence he craved. The house was delivered on the condition that his tasks were to continue at a high standard, failure to complete them would mean the introduction of a rent he could not afford; not because Noah cared anymore, his life and interests existed elsewhere, and the arrangement was Petula's baby. But now her son would owe her his adulthood as surely as he blamed her for his past.

'There are just three dwellings on this farm, here's your chance to show what you can do with one of them.'

'I won't let you down.'

'It's not me being let down I'm worried about. Deep feelings are no good without deep thoughts, you'll need to use your loaf on this one boy.'

The opportunity to return the house to its former condition was a project Jazzy embraced, rushing round DIY shops, retail parks, builders' yards and charity shops for trophies and knick-knacks. He made some good beginnings, though, to his frustration, nothing visible enough for the farm at large to remark on. The fiddly details never grew past initial implementation, whereas his weeks in the workshop produced well-made artefacts that had no place in the house he returned to. Meanwhile he drowned under the sheer number of onerous tasks cast his way. By the end of the first year the only concrete change to the building was the name Tianta, which cost sixty pounds he did not have (in conformation with fire-brigade regulations) to register. At home, asbestos boards remained in place, along with leaks, crumbling tiles and lakes of damp; elsewhere leaf clearance, the rodding of drains, unblocking of gutters and gravelling of tracks sapped whatever vigour and vim remained. The cottage, which his mother now dubbed 'The Pimple', remained without electricity until Noah paid for it to be installed properly, the poor plumbing forcing Jazzy to come back to the main house to use the lavatory. Soon, a case could be made for the project having become a burden to the main farm and not the asset Jazzy had promised. His anger, which had been a boy's, now grew to man-sized proportions. Different farm tools bellowed with his rage; the boiler, strimmer, van, tractor and even lawnmower, no season or inanimate object safe from the overflow of his pain.

'I really can't see what the matter is? You've got what you've asked for, how many boys your age can boast their own house and regular work? And what work! You don't even need to get on your bike to find it, no one minds if you're a little late, you can take breaks whenever you like...'

'I... you've tricked me, haven't you?'

'Have I? Have I *really*?'

'This isn't right, no, the way you've made this out isn't right. You gave me guarantees, right?'

'Which you've singularly failed to keep your end of. I don't mind keeping you on, even if you're not up to it, I'll always do everything I can for you, but for heaven's sake please stop this constant whining, it's like listening to an old woman getting her sums muddled up. You've got it in you to be better than this.'

'You've set me up, this isn't fair! How was I supposed to know it would be like this?'

And with his face wet with salt water Petula could see what he meant.

'Nature hates an unlucky man, Jasper. But there's a difference between a man down on his luck and a victim, do you know what I mean by one of those? One who is so unlucky, so often, that it doesn't count as bad luck anymore, the sort of fellow who is an unconscious participant in his own misfortune. You've never missed an opportunity to make it all a little worse for yourself, have you?'

'Christ Mum, can't you just for once make it easy for me and stop the games? It doesn't have to be like this, right, we could all be living in paradise...'

'Well at least you've an honest face Jasper, that will attract sympathy for you if nothing else does.'

Petula was right. The sympathy Jazzy won was heartfelt, his intense experience of victimhood obscuring the respect he forfeited to land it. At times he wondered whether Petula wished to see him humiliated so she could be his only friend; there was never an unpleasant exchange that was not followed by a generous hamper full of goodies. Not that he did not need them; he was not used to living alone. Having rejected his mother's world, Jazzy now found his own not to his liking, the dream of inhabiting his own rural republic failing to tally with the plans of his friendship group. They had fled to exotic imaginings of their own – India, Florida, Tenerife, or London – leaving him very much alone with a local community he remained on the margins of. The Hardfields were always there for love, though their acceptance of their lot made his complaints unintelligible to them, and despite the goodwill shown by most locals, his attempts at farm insurrection were ignored or dismissed. Like the editor of a student newspaper pontificating on world politics, his views were held at too little cost for him to be heard, he was just the boss's son after all, fed, clothed, tolerated, or just about. As his mother said when he expressed his disbelief that she had not been ejected from the house by a mob of downtrodden peasants, 'the labourers on this farm do not live in "The International Working Class", they live in Mockery Gap in a country called England, and if they feel threatened, that is what they will defend. And so long as Noah and I are careful to not take the piss, that's how things will stay.'

Jazzy's self-imposed exclusion bit hard that first winter in Tianta. There was no social overflow from Petula to wet his whistle, so the drug-dealing sons of landless labourers, vagabond crusties and public-school mendicants he had forgone when his sister left, returned. Tianta was the centre of their operations, insulated and filled with sugary cider belches, the stink of hash scones and electric soup. These drop-outs alone had an insight into Jazzy's dilemma, recognising a world that had hurt them too, their stories not so very different from his. Together their defeatism began to reconfigure time and space in its own image, shared dreams giving way to coping strategies, little things to look forward to and unforeseen developments that might be interpreted in a hopeful light. Theirs was an optimistic little community, however much it would break the rules to admit this to the outside world.

For Jazzy life amounted to 'waiting for someone to cark it', an absent step-father or ever-present mother, a waiting game in which time was not on his side. Though the farm was used to living in the atmosphere of untruth, or at least, all of what they could not say to each other, only Jazzy manifested daily symptoms. Occasionally, when he was really upset, he would go so far as launching what he dubbed 'a protective stepping-back', ignoring his mother for as long as he could, which rarely lasted more than a few days, their close proximity and his daily chores making a mockery of any principled stance.

In the midst of his irascible grumpiness it was inevitable that he would find his mother's most lasting gift to him, a prolonged and distracted indifference to real happiness, the most useful mechanism for enduring life at The Heights. With it came his premature stoop and ability to live like he had nothing to lose. Care for the quality of his life would have made him check out years earlier, and maintenance of a cheerful nature would have rendered him more vulnerable to disappointment. In his more speculative moments, stoned to near-incomprehension, Jazzy wondered whether he was not contributing to an epic tale in which someone else had been cast as the lead. In this version his very being was no more than a foil, existing simply to make sense of another man's story, that man's happiness, this other being's eventual fulfilment, as what could he consider himself to be but an onlooker?

Out of his broken social scene came Jill Cronin, who, at four years younger, had taken a fancy to him at the last private school he had been expelled from, she then a diminutive pixie with funny teeth and greasy hair whom he had affected to never notice. Five years and a cumbersome brace later, Cronin could have passed for a great beauty, were it not for a neediness that wrapped her shrunken perfection in a scarf of hyperactive worry. A propensity to read palms, tell fortunes and bring out the tarot deck, her thin limbs buried deep under layers of tie-dye and kaftan, did not blind Jazzy to her elfin sexuality, and the two wound up making love in someone else's sleeping bag to mark their connection. In Jazzy she saw a wounded lion, or rather, the person he still sometimes saw in himself; proud, defiant and fair, his embitterment the result of being robbed of his place in the natural order. As a healer and Jazzy's soul twin, Jill sought to enable him through loving him back to health. In practice this meant moving in to the cottage, asking others to politely move on, listening to his tirades with rapt and undivided attention and massaging his weary limbs once he was done.

If only his potential, or those aspects of his soul she saw, were unlocked, he would emerge into the world as the same irresistible force that squeezed her tits and made her come every night. For Jazzy it was more prosaic: he needed Jill's vote of confidence as much as he was failed to be convinced by it. Unlike her, the weight of history was already bearing down on him, and inside his pronounced defiance was a cynic resigned to the worst.

Nurturing good energy was not enough to make the future a different place from the past, Jill's shock far greater than Jazzy's resigned fatalism, as every watershed proved to be no more than another step towards being absorbed into someone else's life. Their tendency to take each day as it came looked feebler at every turn, Jill's good vibes lost in an endless succession of grey mornings, drizzle and arguments over the benefits of soya milk. Slowly it dawned on Jill, originally the product of a family of middle-class hoteliers, that those who cannot plan a future together probably don't have one, her gentle attempts to chide Jazzy into making decisions grinding to a recriminatory standstill. Gestures and outbursts replaced any semblance of progress, claims that he would drive off and live in a lighthouse undermined in long and oblique letters to his mother asking for ownership of Tianta. Patiently, Jill stood by to watch which way his exhausting combustibility would blow next.

'Do you know how hard it is to know what you actually want in life?'

'I want you, Jazzy.'

'You're lucky you've got it so easy then. I wish I had your bloody certainty,' he smiled and held her hand, 'Jesus I'm lucky to have you, Jill.'

Contradiction followed confusion, the bifurcation of her partner's personality leaving Jill frightened that her love was the only thing keeping him together, his meltdowns as regular as sleep. Tiptoeing around his moods became the safest way of being left alone, countered by her crusading desire to try and save him; which inevitably led to conflict again, the conversations dragging on so that she came to hate the sound of her own voice.

'Please let me help you.'

'What can you do?'

'I can love you.'

'Just leave me, I'm not worth it. You should know that by now.'

Angry as he was, Jazzy never turned directly on Jill, tenderly watching her check his star sign and astrological chart every day, her efforts to suppress her natural anxiety leading to weight loss and short haircuts that gave her the look of a sectioned caterer. Guilt and anger vied with each other as Jazzy wondered whether this was not all part of an attempt to emotionally blackmail him into making more conventional moves to secure their future together. His resistance to Jill's thwarted expectations of him manifested itself in niggling stands; reading a newspaper when Jill's parents came to visit or taking a crap in the middle of a meal, wasting days in which they were meant to do things together by trawling round car-boot sales and hunting pigeons with his catapult. Jazzy's wish was never to hurt her, only to remind her that he was in the constant process of being hurt. The news that he was expected to play butler at a party for his sister's spoilt-brat pack, not even a birthday but a Beano held for the hell of it, renewed hope of breaking the deadlock. Here was an as-yet-unexperienced humiliation that sought to take him beyond what he already knew of the quality.

'I mean it Jill, I'm glad she's done it, really, I'm glad, this time it's different, this time she's really pushed me too far. She'll see, you'll see, too far, way too far this time.'

'I know.'

'Too much, do you have any idea? And idea of how... of how *hard* it is living like this?'

'I know Jazzy, I know, I'm not the one you need to tell.'

'What?'

'I said I know.'

'What the hell do you mean by that?'

'Nothing, please, I didn't mean anything.'

With a firmness as final as one holding onto dear life, Jazzy picked up his knife and drove the handle into his palm. 'Owww!' he cried and threw it at the wall. Leaping to his feet he grabbed his coat and headed for the door.

'Be careful!' cried Jill, strangely heartened that Jazzy had shamed himself into a corner he would have to duke his way out of.

'Jesus!' she heard him shout, 'Jesus!'

There was an involuntary twitch in the corners of her mouth. It took her a moment to realise it was a smirk.

*

Matters were proceeding on a calmer footing further up the hill. Petula woke as she always did in her own good time. Her first thought of the day tended to be a social one and today was very much in keeping with that drill. The room was awash with cards thanking her for the glorious evenings, wonderful nights, beautiful weekends, charming mornings and most memorable few hours that several friends had taken the trouble to reassure her of. The cards had a medicinal effect on Petula, lifting her physically and adding an extra layer of certainty to the many layers she already possessed. Making a mental note to remove the string of cards hanging over the window place that made the room look too much like a hospital ward, Petula cursed another missed opportunity. Ever since Noah had stopped bringing tea and a boiled egg to her in bed, he had threatened to employ a live-in maid, a modest proposal Petula had vehemently objected to, claiming it would be worse than having a spy in the house. She could just imagine the sort of dizzy-looking tart who would come sniffing for that kind of work. Yet her back ached, and knees clicked, and on mornings like this the tart might have been quite useful, spying be damned. Who, after all, would care what a maid saw? As for the interview process, she could always vet it. Old dogs needed work too. Petula's attention turned again to the cards, particularly a large one depicting Monet's lilies taking pride of place on her bedside table. It was from the Countess of Barchester, a woman so desperately agreeable that she would not have been out of place presenting the local news and then changing dresses to announce the weather forecast. In her favour she was still a Countess who wrote a good card, and a valuable addition to Petula's court of admirers. Petula puckered her lips with the satisfaction anyone else would take in a glass of squash on a hot day and reread the card for perhaps the twelfth time:

> *My Dearest Petula, how to do justice to your hospitality; you are a phenomenon! You and lunch were perfection personified, it will be a long, long time before I forget that first bite of quiche! How do you do it? No, I don't want to know, that would be telling after all, and the aspect of you that I find so compelling is your air of mystery, so please never spoil that for me. Anyway, whatever you do, please never ever change,*
>   *Love as always,*
>   *Delicia*
>
> *PS – your son is gorgeous! Please ask him to mow the lawn more often!*

Petula exhaled an appreciative sigh of agreement. There could never be a woman who attracted more flattery that was as nakedly sycophantic, and to her credit, Petula recognised her gift. Once a person paid her a compliment she would fall silent and look at them inquiringly to see if there was any more to come, encouraging them to grope their way further up her flagpole, as if the very act of starting made their eventual destination, complete self-abasement under the shining towers of her brilliance, inevitable. It was instructive to watch how someone wishing to pay her a small tribute would be forced to build on it until she finally acknowledged the compliment, the payer upping their game until they had finally reached Petula's self-estimation. Petula put the card back in its place and wondered how long before its edges would fray and corners turn, it ultimately having to take its place with all the others in one of several files packed in the attic. Without knowing why she was making the leap, Petula suddenly saw herself in the place of the card, packed-away and old, a vision of extinction running through her like a lance. It was an affront that there was an event she knew of that she could not control or be around to *feel*. The cards that had made her so happy just seconds earlier were telling a different story now, representing joys that made her live too fast, too decisively, eating up time in large bites, hastening that moment where there would be none left to enjoy. Or worse, she would run out of life before she had even gotten to the end of her story, perhaps needing someone else to finish for her, to know the end before the grave had even opened.

Petula sat there, leaning against her bedhead for a while, no longer thinking. Outside the early-morning cloud had yet to clear, the subtle gradations between differing hues of white revealing nothing for anyone to look up at in wonder. It took the noisy rattle of a hang-glider engine to bring Petula back to her senses.

What demon had taken possession of her? There was always more to say about life, there were no last words, there was always *something* else, and, as usual, the particular would triumph over the philosophical. She did not have far to look for the diversions that she would later successfully confuse for matters of existential importance. There were, for example, a number of problems she had invented, or made her own, regarding the inauguration of the new bishop, a rather sexy liberal who had come on the scene just as she had found herself gravitating towards Cathedral Christianity. Drinks in the Close fell upon her like a combination of puzzles that could not be solved one at a time, calling for a Eureka moment she would have to put off until after her bath. Her morning was looking agreeably full again, any potential awkwardness raised by that shadowy fog in which she had met herself, forgotten until the next time it happened. After days of unbroken plainness, petrifying stillness and icy showers, the sun was at last breaking through the early spring sky and warming the tip of her nose. Petula ran a firm hand up her long and substantial thigh; she was beautiful and strong, if only she had the imagination to let go of what was, long enough to lie back, close her eyes and touch herself, this would be the time to, but it was too much like self-administering a massage, and she could not get the timings of that evening's dinner service out of her mind.

There was a great clanging from the ground floor, as though the very foundations of the house were under threat from a geological catastrophe, the building vibrating as if it could lose its balance at any moment. Petula snarled and began a slow count to ten. She hoped that it had nothing to do with that business in the attic... of course not, no one knew about that. It could only be Jazzy hammering at the door, no one else would have the impertinence to ignore the bell. What on earth did the silly bastard want of her now?

CHAPTER FIVE,
exile and escape.

The knocking was loud enough to stir Evita, who was lost in an uncomfortable hypnogenic stroll, the attic ceiling the canvas over which she watched her memory advance to the beat of time, without the sequential whimsy that suggested. What she could not see past was the sheer amount she could not account for, the lack of what she could say she had done with it, the misuse of the gift. Time weighs heavily on those of us who waste it, she could remember her mother once telling her.

It had been an hour since she had awoken from a nightmare in which she was pursued by a thing with wet liquorice hair and yellow gums, leaving her with the unfortunate conviction that she had been subjected to an attack by a manifestation of pure evil that dwelt in the house. Since then she had lain as helpless as a baby waiting to be lifted from its cot, old memories struck from one end of her life to the other like a glass on a Ouija board, terror hovering over her attempts to rescue a valued image from the contaminating oblivion of sheer waste.

'Sheesholes on the sheeshore. Sheeshocker: I'm drowning, drowning here...'

Evita was used to waking to unrecognisable situations, or at least ones she could not remember from the night before, always an exile from herself and reassurance, the distance between where she woke and home measured by a sensation that her innards were lain out behind her on a laundry line. It was physically unbearable to be in the presence of thoughts long forgotten and feelings she hoped she had successfully suppressed; the good stuff, if there had actually been any, lost to blue periods on

Turkish smack. But what did she expect, having returned to The Heights with her tail between her legs, late one January night, two months earlier, her homecoming a desperate attempt to cure the habit that had accompanied her round Europe's squats, basements and the occasional loft conversion...

With practised effort Evita turned onto her side, found, lit and drew a nimble toke from the gamey joint she had left unfinished the night before, a dry fissure opening at the back of her throat that no liquid could moisten. A moment or two later she was unburdened of her earlier clarity, that hopelessly arid overview of events that revealed nothing of consequence or importance. In its place lay a richer knowledge, engrossing and fuzzily indistinct. Her soul, the only part of her being she still cared for, remembered with the heart and not the mind. It alone retained ways of relating to those who marked it long after she had forgotten such people existed, their voices making themselves known to her with day-dream vividity. This was much better; Nina, Lottie and the Dutch boy with the kissable dick were all on the mattress with her, stroking, touching and pressing, the air heavy with good spirits. It made her attic nook in The Heights feel part of a wider world and not the miserable corner of Yorkshire she usually experienced it as, her lonely situation slowly conceding its advantages.

For one thing her homecoming had been easier than the months of fearful apprehension that had preceded it. Petula was unflappable, considerate and extremely helpful, her daughter's predicament neither a surprise nor an occasion for triumphant gloating, simply a practical quandary that called for a discrete solution. That first night had been better than she could have ever banked on – countless mugs of Bovril and questions about the differences between heroin and other drugs, no more than an occasional remark on her thinness, and nothing, to Evita's relief, on lesbianism or bi-sexuality.

Her mother's new interests took her by surprise. Petula was

148

due to sit on a 'council' dedicated to eradicating the local drug problem, and had grown close to a rock musician, not the kind Evita had much time for, who had a drug habit of some years standing, so for once there seemed to be the promise of common ground. Evita's presence had to be secret, on that they were agreed, the deception providing a powerful bonding agent. Once again, a discussion as to why her return should remain below radar proved unnecessary. Evita's local reputation would have automatically alerted the police who still wanted her for questioning relating to her act of vigilante justice against the boy she claimed to have been raped by, an accusation neither she nor her mother had ever had much confidence in, the boy having died in a car crash soon after. That kind of attention would only have shone the spotlight on her predicament: penniless, soiled and addicted; a state of affairs she might have found desirable when puncturing Petula's social bubble was a moral imperative, but no longer. Evita shook her head at this reminder of more innocent times and put the joint out in a cup of mouldering tea. It would be honours even on sharing the shame now as her mother well knew. The only other point Petula had insisted on was that if Evita was discovered, they would both make a 'joke' of it yet, unlikely as it might seem, discovery was far from certain in a house as cavernous as The Heights.

The property was an unusual one for its size, its upstairs levels very much existing on a need-to-know basis. Though or because it was often full of visitors only some parts of the house were properly used, primarily those spaces for Petula's public. The corners where guests' eyes did not wander were violently neglected, used occasionally by family or no one at all. It was not unusual for a drunken guest to stumble into a room full of unopened parcels, or venture from one decorated with Whistlers to another full of cobwebs and disorganised memorabilia, the two zones seemingly having no place in the same dwelling. In these circumstances, hiding a young woman in the disused upper tower above Petula's living area, whilst a touch Jane-Eyre, was a conceit her mother would enjoy getting away with.

Having chosen to go 'cold turkey', Evita was ecstatic to meet with her mother's approval for the first time in her life, the all-or-nothing aspect of her daughter's decision appealing to Petula's sense of occasion. With some pride Petula reflected that nowhere could be safer than The Heights, or meet the conditions of isolation, and isolation from a potential supply, as perfectly. The only challenge was to match her daughter's needs as effectively as the Betty Ford Clinic could have, whilst discretion remained premium. Gratefully, Evita talked her mother through what she could expect, thanking and apologising for the inevitable in advance of Petula discovering for herself the hard way.

During those first two weeks of withdrawal, Petula came into her own, the situation playing to all her strengths and asking nothing of her weaknesses. Doing things had always been preferable to forming emotional connections, and Evita was in no state to require more than deeds and actions from her mother, who was delighted to oblige. Petula noticed a rare well-being come over her as she cleared puddles of her daughter's vomit and removed her shitty sheets for burning. In her hours of extreme dependency, Evita groaning and swearing like a geriatric giving birth to twins, Petula saw that what she enjoyed most about her daughter's condition was its need, principally its need of her, the person lost inside that function a distinct second.

Nor was Petula a mere cleaner and wiper. As far as raising, sustaining and keeping Evita alive during that period was concerned, Petula excelled in her nurse duties; a regular supply of vitamins, bananas and scabies cream all part of the traffic to the old attic, still full of Jazzy's creatures and weightlifting equipment. The space, once reserved for all kinds of undesirables Petula would not consent to have anywhere else in the house, had over the years transformed into an overgrown jungle of neglected junk, and thus perfect for their purpose. No one thought of asking Petula what she was doing wandering round the lost parts of her own house with first-aid kits, just as no one would have asked Petula what she was doing in a reindeer outfit and red nose if she had been so attired: she was not the sort of woman to answer personal questions. With Noah away as usual and social commitments generally taking her out of the house rather than bringing callers in, Petula felt a rare freedom, a breezy cheek entering her brazen game. One morning she appeared above her daughter's mattress with a lump of Jazzy's hashish and a wrap of cocaine a guest had absentmindedly forgotten to snort after dinner, the two lesser evils helping her daughter to knock the prime one on the head. Petula finished the remainder over elevenses, and spent several happy hours listening to side one of Fleetwood Mac's *Tango In The Night* again and again, the purposeless repetition as thrilling as gorging on an orchard of forbidden fruit.

By the end of the first month Evita was over the worst, already prepared to think of her addiction as a cry for help and not the source of enlightened pleasure or standard dependency she had previously regarded it as, her gratitude to her mother as intense as her former disdain. And at about this time her thoughts turned, with a heavy helping of guilt, to her brother down the track.

In her time away, Jazzy had faded as a real person, becoming instead a symbolic reminder of warmth and decency. His relationship with her had always been marked by a desire to envelop and protect that she recognised as genuine if only occasionally effective. It was his misfortune to come of age in a family where there was no power vacuum to fill or space for conflicting visions of life. Tenderly she humoured his attempts to stick up for her and understand her suicidal tendencies, recognising that his wish to connect in itself constituted a kindness she would not find elsewhere. Regardless of this, when it came to deciding

151

whom to approach for help of the concrete kind, her dilemma was not long-lived. Evita knew her brother was too like her, fond of gestures and quick of temper, wonderful for a moment and useless over an hour. She did not require a shoulder to cry on, for he had never failed to provide one, rather a powerful hand to pull her out of the excrement she knew he could not provide. Flashes of Tim Tinwood taking her, her screams and Jazzy hammering at the door in tears arose whenever she considered the shortfall between who her brother wanted to be and what he was. She did not blame Jazzy, could not, and loved him more for his frustrated ambition, while at the same time sharing his shame that they could not make it together as a team. Time was casting its judgement. In essence he would remain what he always was: an unsubstantiated intention. Failure, so far, was both their lots in life, the main difference being she had tried to break out and knew it, whereas he had stayed where he was so still feared it. From Petula's remarks she could only guess at what his life had become since her departure, and it was his mother's dismissiveness that provoked their first argument, auguring worse words to come.

'Here's your cocoa and the pills you asked for. I had quite a job explaining to the Doctor why I needed them. He must think I have a recovering addict in my attic!'

'Ta very much, Mum.'

'God I wish you wouldn't.'

'Wouldn't what?'

'Use that awful faux-prole slang your brother does, you know, "ta", "cheers", "yeah", all that bilge. It's like having the stuff they have on the television in the room with you. It's so unnatural.'

'Jesus Mum, I only said "ta".'

'Well *don't*. It makes me *sick*, in fact completely *appalled*, if you must know.'

'You're joking?'

'We ask people whether they're joking because we want them

to be joking. I am perfectly serious. It's bad enough hearing Jazzy chunter on like a cross between Arthur Scargill and Bill Sykes without having to hear you play the same game.'

'You two have fallen out again, is that it?'

'Nothing serious, just the usual nonsense that comes with having him about the place. He's gone and bloody helped himself to a pile of logs cut from one of my trees without asking. The sort of Pikey behaviour he indulges in all the time these days. Trying to get at me without having the courage to come up here and cross cutlasses like a real man. Because he thinks his life has been stolen from him, every little actual theft of his own has a cast-iron moral justification. Trouble is it ruins the atmosphere on the farm and diminishes the quality of life for everyone else; he always tries to involve other people in his little intrigues you see. I've tried to tell him that when two elephants fight it's the ground that suffers.'

'It's natural for every relationship to have its ups and downs Mum.'

'Oh spare me the fortune-cookie mouthwash. You were never that crass. His moods make living in this place intolerable, you should try being his neighbour then you'd know. It accumulates, believe me, watching the same grumpy visage stomp past my window every day, telling me that he's had enough and is leaving here. That's his bloody default position, he'll spend the rest of his life "leaving". I'll be gone before he does. Which doubtless is what he is counting on.'

'At least he loves you, that must count for something, even for you.'

'Even for me... what the hell is that supposed to mean, "*even for me*"?'

'He loves you and I don't think he knows whether you love him. I don't think he's ever known. I think he feels like you abandoned him, and me.'

'Why, because I refused to be one of those huggy-kissy beanbag mothers that never let go of their children? I wish you could see the way love conceals and smothers the things that produce it. Look at the way mothers are with their baby boys, praising and spoiling their every burp and fart, no wonder men grow up to be such self-satisfied bastards. I always tried not to do that, to give Jasper a chance to grow into himself and for you both to be unique and self-contained. What a joke. Look where that's got me.'

'Mum, you're not listening, I said he *loves* you.'

'Anyway, you'll fall out with everyone in your life, you just have to be careful not to do it with them all at the same time. Look at all the friends I have, their variety and differing skills and talents, people of distinction, then consider the hole Jasper has landed himself in, the grim wretches he socialises with, really, it's a point of honour to fall out with a fool like that. And I've held back from saying anything but you always were a lot like each other in the essentials.'

'You haven't changed a bit, you really didn't like us much, did you?'

'Evita, place yourself in my position, you never knew your father, never had to suffer the ape as I did. A horrible, ugly, talentless little man. Once he had finished knocking the stuffing out of me I didn't have much love to give.'

'Hit you?

'Of course.'

'You never told me. And if it had happened, you would have. I know you.'

'There's a lot I never told you. I lived in hell. But that's not the point. To love a child and identify with its fortunes requires you to love the person you have that child with. It's as simple and as unfair as that. And I did not love your father, however much I tried. He was insane actually, there you are. I wish you hadn't asked. Anyway, he was not a person I was likely to produce evolutionary improvements with. He's actually taken my stock back.'

'It just gets worse and worse. Excuses, they're your way of changing the subject, manipulating me into sharing your rage and pain. You've always had a reason to justify nastiness, like you knew you needed one to get off the hook for behaving in a way that comes naturally to you. It's useless talking, you're too well prepared, and the more wrong you are the more dangerous you become, the more you drag others into your craziness. I spent years thinking about it all Mum. I never stopped thinking about it.'

'Believe what you like, talk to whom you like. I could never feel the closeness I desired to either you or Jasper because of that bit of your father in there, taunting me. It was his way of scarring me for life, even after I got away from him physically there was always you two, reminding me of an association no good could ever come from. And it never has. So save your tears, I can see them coming, I don't blame you, it was his fault. You're nearly as much his victim as I am myself.'

'You've no shame! Who could ever beat you in the battle of victimhood?'

'I'm sorry that you should view it that way.'

'As if there's any other way I could! You're meant to be our Mum, you can't dissect us like lab rats!'

'You're missing the point. Fortunately, life improved with the arrival of Regan. In fact, while I can't remember a time when I haven't been forced into tiresome exchanges like this with you and Jasper I can't think of a single one Regan has sprung on me. Not her style. Different stock, different outlook. It runs in the blood.'

'You're unreal. You're trying to tell me the reason you love Regan and not us is because you loved her father, Noah? So she's your *real* child, your favourite. Unreal. Jesus, I mean, what a thing to say to me, even if you think it's true how could you actually come out and say it, knowing how I feel about being no better than shit to you? Fucking hell. I mean, you haven't changed at all. All this time I've been up here thinking you have, I feel such an *idiot!*'

'You've put the words in my mouth and I shan't disagree with them.'

'Fuck you! It's too much, you come on like, like some kind of pantomime dame high on hate. I despise you! Do you know that? The reason you love Regan is because you love yourself, all the rest of this is just... it's just bullshit! More of your lying bullshit!'

'I'm not listening to any more of these choice accusations. If it's a shrink you need you had better find another sap to empty your chamber pot – if you haven't the courage to take the truth squarely on the chin I haven't the energy to coat it in sugar for you. You've clearly learnt very little from your time away Evita.'

Which summed up the next phase of Evita's homecoming with frightening alacrity. With her health on the mend Evita was looking for a different kind of medicine from the sort she required on death's door. She was desperate for a new beginning with her mother; psychic attention and mutual disclosure were the balms that would bring them together, she hoped. All she had to do was break the old cycle of mutual recrimination they had already fallen into. As she said, she had thought about it a lot. Determined to blame herself for as much as she could, and thus encourage similar contrition in Petula, Evita avoided the standard argumentative traps. Instead she embarked on a course of passionate self-criticism which she felt her mother would at least have the courtesy to contradict. Yet even with generous concessions Petula was a hard nut to crack. The very idea of conversational therapy set her teeth on edge and the scale of what needed discussing made a convenient starting point near impossible to locate. Far from interrupting her daughter as she reeled off lists of her past misdemeanours, Petula listened approvingly, nodding to herself and shaking her head with exaggerated gravity, no complimentary admissions of her own forthcoming as it came to 'her turn' to confess. Evita's attempts to induce at least a touch of reciprocity resulted in cross, and increasingly irritable, exchanges that mimicked those she wished to escape the retroactive clutches of. Petula would not play ball and everything was as before.

'You've grown up, I'm glad, it was about time. That is at least what I take your wanting to make a clean breast of things to mean.'

'It's not really that Mum, well, not only that, it's more that I want both of us to open up a bit more and talk properly for once. All my life I can't remember a proper open conversation with you.'

'Personally, it's not the way I'd have gone about apologising, though I credit you for having done so. People can be very protective about their own experience, it's what makes them see the world as they do and they get narky if anyone else has something to say about it. I wouldn't have dared raise the subjects you have. I'd have been scared you'd have ripped my head off. It took you to do it and it's noted. You've grown up.'

'Thanks Mum.'

'No, I mean it, you should learn how to take a compliment. Life isn't all about slings and arrows you know.'

'Great, so is that it then?'

'I beg your pardon?'

'Is that all I get for running myself down, you taking advantage of my honesty to run me down too?

'What are you talking about now? I thought it was all clear between us now?'

'You, Mum, are you so perfect that you don't have any disclosures of your own, any regrets, anything you might actually be sorry for too? Oh, my mistake again, I forgot. You are perfect, aren't you?'

'Good Heavens, drop that tone! Don't be so bloody ridiculous. Or worse, pathetic. I was trying to raise you up a notch. Of course I'm not perfect. And as far as I'm aware I have no recollection of ever pretending that I was. It wouldn't be like me at all.'

'Of course not! Not like you at all! So you're not perfect, can we make a small start and agree on that?'

'Oh don't be so *silly*, I've just said I'm not!'

'Then own up to something, fess up for once! And I mean a particular, not some general imperfection anyone could own up to, like being bad at making tea or finishing someone else's sentences, an actual one please. A real dirty deed that makes you gag when you're reminded of what you are. Come on, I'm waiting. I've been waiting forever and I need to hear words coming out of your mouth that can make me hope you're human Mum, a real human being and not Petula Montague.'

'You're mad, Evita. Schizophrenic.'

'Of course I am, I'm your daughter!'

'Not my daughter in any meaningful way. Really mad, cracked. They were right about you. I'm glad you're finding your tongue again but this kind of insanity won't do either of us any good.'

'Come on Mrs Montague, I'm waiting, I want to know that you have a conscience and feel guilt, that you're not completely beyond good and evil. Speak up Mum, it's only me, you can deny it ever happened as soon as you leave this room.'

'Why should I? Why should I play your tardy little games? I've already told you that you need to see a psychiatrist. And anyway, who in their right mind expects an equal treatment of unequals, a moral equivalence between you and me? I gave you life once when I carried you into the world and I gave it to you again these past few weeks, scraping up your remains and trying to build you back into a person. And now you're making me wonder why I bothered. So you could throw it back in my face? Thank God for Regan is all I can say. Only you could fuck up multiple kindnesses and a clean bill of health.'

'Me, fuck up? Can't you see it's you, that's what we all have in common, you! Of course you can't, how crass of me. This is exactly how you ruined Regan, like you did us, but in a different way all of her own. The thing with you is that you *can* see it, deep down and really, you're not stupid enough to be blind to the obvious. You know you're an insecure fake, don't you? And you know your inconsistencies and madnesses, you're wily enough for that. But when I point them out you run hurriedly along or fight to the death claiming they're anything but. Which is the difference between you and her. Regan's grown up not even noticing hers, a real evolution on you, you were "mark one", you had emotions but hid them, repressed them, but she doesn't have *any*, she's "mark two", an emotional android. The reason you and she have never talked like this is because she doesn't know she can, emotions don't interest her because she doesn't know she has them, and anything that doesn't interest her, simply ceases to exist. You've succeeded in making her what you wanted to be. Not an airhead, an icehead. God help her when one day she suddenly discovers she has feelings. She'll probably die of the shock.'

'Touching, and I thought it was just me you wanted to insult, touching. I think I have somewhere else I have to be. Think about how long you want this arrangement to last; if you're well enough to wound then you're well enough to piss off.'

From this cheerless low Petula took to leaving Evita's food and supplies by the attic door, knocking once, firmly, before abruptly taking her leave. This time there was to be no union of solipsisms, only a burn mark to remind them both that life would have to remain conversationally off limits if they were to speak at all. Tentatively they came back to discussing practicalities again; unfortunately, Evita's improved health soon exhausted this once-promising area and she withdrew into a monosyllabic sulk. Self-flagellation in front of Petula was never likely to occasion anything other than the deepest agreement, a useless gesture and dangerous tactic, for a low self-opinion was the demon that hounded Evita since infancy. Left to brood over her miscalculation, Evita concluded that her universe had shrunk to hold only one person and two concepts: suffering and blame, with the blame poised to tip inwards.

Over the years Evita had clung to the utopian hope that a positive moral could be retrieved from episodic negativity, ennobling her worst experiences with a lesson. This was how she approached being a Montague, a name and a nature that had never suited her un-contrite heart. From the start she struggled with her mother's instruction, or at least applied it unsuccessfully, attempting to copy her approach without sharing her goals. Not for her the audacious tacking between pragmatism and revolutionary romanticism, the close reading of reality and then its creation, a rich husband and nice house. Evita spurned these and longed for a purer kingdom of ends. The boy left blinded in the cloakroom on his eighteenth birthday had been the catalyst, he should have realised she was no one's birthday present. With the help of that abrupt push, Europe lay before her and Evita left with the intention of returning a different person. The first six months were fast-going, friends were easy to make, the conversations ran all night and money was wired to her whenever she ran out. At times she wondered whether her experiences weren't a trifle too *pat*, mugged twice in Amsterdam, an Arab boyfriend in Montpellier who beat her, falling off a moped in Rome and being arrested at a protest in Berlin all reeked of the generic – still she persevered, embracing ever-more-radical manifestations of travelling chic. And for a while she believed she was in possession of her own life, the transformation she sought underway at last.

Her project's undoing was that the qualities and circumstances she craved were too near the privileges and patrician whims she rejected. Like her mother, Evita was liked, when she was liked, for her vim and enthusiasm, eagerly lapping up the nickname 'Passion Machine' from her fellow squatters. Practically she was ready to be useful, tacitly understanding that what she lacked in talent she could make up for in organisational élan. Like the society gadflies her mother collected, the anarchists Evita lived amongst were not averse to having those parts of their lives they were not very good at, run by someone else. Unlike Petula, she could never quite find a way of making her causes serve her. Too often Evita found herself holding the collection box, stuck with a placard or putting up billposters in the middle of night while her savings disappeared into a communal pot. This dug into pricklier aspects of her inheritance; she shared her mother's ungraciousness, a failure to allow the giver to believe she valued the gift as much as they. With the strength of Hercules, Evita could not pretend that chipped mugs, grey bedding and bathrooms without locks meant as much to her as bolted doors, crisp sheets and Branksome China crockery. Her childish fits and involuntary fussiness soon made her an outcast amongst the fugitives whom she had adopted as her new family. Girlfriends, boyfriends, activists and finally fellow users gave her short shrift, the rules governing communal living more ruthless than those of the society she had rejected. All Evita could do was find another city and instigate another cycle, Berlin gave way to Amsterdam, Rotterdam to Bruges, Lille to Cologne, and finally a basement near the amphitheatre in Orange. At every stop Evita met the same fear waiting for her once the smack wore off. Her travels would never yield what she wanted because what she sought resided at home; her mother's approval. Why else had she left? To succeed in the arts, find love and take the same joy in the present as she would looking back on it in a year, were her stated ambitions. Not for what they entailed in themselves but for the point she hoped they would make to Petula.

It was in her last port of call, Orange, that Evita finally gave way to a fit of promiscuity that had been bubbling under the solemn monogamy she had hitherto worked at. The results were mixed, with a marked tendency towards the not-so-good.

PART TWO: COCYTUS, LAMENTATION

As a confused solipsist Evita was incapable of learning from experience. Her kiss said it all; a forward lunge, all mouth and teeth, designed to project power and passion, heedless that its targets often faced severe facial mutilation. Never giving the addressee of her affection a second chance, or way of answering the snog, pinning them under her slavering tongue until it was over, meant she could never learn from another, only repeat the action she hid behind, her energy and self thrown away for little return and no knowledge. At the same time she finally made a go of her 'career', really a euphemism for an ambiguous desire to be regarded as creative in some fashion. The many different disciplines she thought she would be good at meant that Evita did not only live in one imaginary universe but several. Over her last summer she tried her hand at them all, frenetically and in abrupt succession. A bizarre process of self-sabotage bled her confidence of what little lava it still possessed. She developed a stammer when she wanted to train as an actor that disappeared when she gave up, a limp when she returned to dancing, and dyslexia on joining a poetry class. Evita decided she must be losing her mind, her heroin habit, which until then felt optional, calcified into a routine, exacerbating the intense loneliness she now felt at all hours. The old Roman town began to appear in supernaturally shaded hues, certain streets filling her with mortal dread, the amphitheatre wall making her hairs stand up and the tram from Montpellier inducing attacks of the shakes. At nights, in her dank basement room, the devil appeared to her as a pig with a human face, saying nothing, his arrival a wicked witness to her failure. One morning she woke and packed her few belongings into a knapsack, the original suitcase she had left home with too heavy for her track-ridden arms to carry. The mark made by her departure had been etched in vain, her fool's odyssey all but over. With a fortnight's supply of heroin stashed in her knickers, Evita set her course for the attic kingdom that awaited her at The Heights, a sighting of the eighteen year-old boy she had blinded floating past the Ferry back to Dover her last brush with the spectral. At St Pancreas, she stowed away on the Edinburgh train, hitching a lift from Doncaster to Scotch Corner; whatever pride she had left subsumed by the desire that her mother should see her like this, and know that it was all her fault. And perhaps that was what Petula thought as she ushered the emaciated traveller into the kitchen, her heart broken by the vein-punctured scrap that was once her baby girl...

The joint was finished and Evita was having another bummer; how did that happen, happen again? She had been trying to dwell on the positives for Christ's sake, but her thoughts kept coming back to the same juncture... time un-regained.

'Fyuuhuck. Enough.'

She ground out her butt on a Beatrix Potter tea coaster, the frog Jeremy Fisher's face blackening under the crumbling tobacco stub. The deep pink scars she caught sight of on her wrists were a reminder of the times she had hoped maiming herself would awaken her mother's protective instinct. It had not worked, and never would, nothing would change, not her, Petula or the negative current that ran under The Heights. This was always the prelude to how she felt before she considered the only course that felt her own, freely chosen, indebted to no one. Everything is a pain until you accept it, that was her mantra, but she had been given an unacceptably large amount to accept. Suicide, or at least its attempt, was her ownmost possibility, the most authentic deed she imagined herself capable of. To draw a line from nothing, to nothing, cutting out the life between was the dream that drugs had replaced. Without them, it was only the possibility that she could take her own life that gave her the strength to go on, a contradiction that hurt when she laughed.

'Okay.'

From the very first occasion when Evita had asked her mother 'Why will I die?,' she had really meant, 'Why am I here?' The time to halt this question's endlessness had arrived. Getting up from the mattress Evita ran her hand under her chin to inspect a growth she expected to find. There it was, trapped in her fingers, an extra filmy roll of skin. It was amazing how quickly she had put weight on again, foul white-slug-fat collecting round the characterless outlines of her face. That was it.

Decisively Evita felt under the bed to check whether her comfort object was still there. She had been sleeping over the rope for three days now, the knot already tied into a noose. With a vigour that was nearly inspiring, Evita tossed the rope over the main beam and mounted the rickety stool she used to practice the piano on, to fasten the loop. It was at that delicate point in her preparations that Petula, unusually light-of-foot that day, and wishing to share a gripe about Jazzy, unlocked the door with breakfast, which that morning was grapefruit, kippers and scrambled eggs.

Petula had already found her morning an unexpectedly involving one. The crybaby Jasper had all but destroyed her good mood and made serious inroads into her equanimity with a volley of wailing and hollering, as lethal to her mood as a surgical strike on a hospital tent. It was hard enough to remember the amount of salmon needed for the evening's starters, far less that Evita was still skulking in the attic, without his goonshow landing on her doorstep first thing. All that fuss and swearing, in that dreadful accent of his, and just because she had the temerity to ask him to buttle at his own sister's coming-home party! Really, she thought he'd jump at the chance to put something back in for once. It only went to show that one never really knew what would break the camel's back, especially if that camel happened to be a psychopath. It reminded her of those fusspot Cubans rioting in Florida having received the wrong kind of orange juice, concentrate and not freshly squeezed... Come to think of it, an internee camp in Florida might be the best place for Jasper. And not only him but Evita. It was as bad as when they were children, she hadn't known what to do then either.

Unless a problem was effectively eliminated, it would always come back to haunt one; life punished the merciful. If Jasper was a common garden nuisance Evita was a rare weed. Petula paused to collect herself, she was in danger of drifting up her fundamental orifice. Focus. The corridor was thick with the aroma of polish and flowers, the smell of her work. It was delicious. Picking up her tray from the side table Petula resumed her journey and attempted to slow her hurried train of thought.

How long before she could reasonably kick Evita out now that there was no medical need to prolong their mutual misery? That girl, like her brother, could dissemble for England – talk, talk, talk, and none of it the interesting kind, and her silences were even worse. It was time to break the stasis and face her down, present Evita with some practical ultimatum pertaining to the 'next stage' of her recovery, pay her off if need be, the crucial thing was to be rid of her and allow some sort of normality to resume. Having her and Jasper at large was like having to fight America and Russia at the same time, the war on two fronts had done for Hitler and would finish her if she wasn't careful. It was funny how she shared the national obsession for World War Two analogies but identified with the other side, her natural sympathy for the underdog no doubt. Unfortunately, there was no guarantee Evita would go quietly. If she saw she had nothing to lose things could turn nasty; she had always reacted badly to thinking she was no longer wanted, which in this case would be spot on. The alternative was far, far worse though; that she would stay and become another Jazzy. Strong as she was, Petula knew that the lady-in-the-attic days were numbered, it was only a question of a week or so before Mrs Hardfield, or a nosey guest, stumbled upon their secret. That, or Evita might finally develop itchy feet of her own and begin to venture downstairs for nighttime raids of the larder, who knew... Strewth, all this and Regan due home later that morning for the school holidays, it would be a good life if they left her alone for long enough to live it...

'Good morning Evita, I think it's time you and I turned over a new leaf. Don't you... idiot, idiot, IDIOT!'

Evita, her head in the noose, closed her eyes, held her breath and kicked away the stool. Petula was onto her in a flash and for a second the two women struggled, Evita wobbling indecisively as her mother tried to lift her out of danger. Frantically Petula shifted the weight of her daughter's body into her arms and with her foot caught a leg of the stool and dragged it over. Evita's legs and buttocks rested helplessly in her mother's firm embrace. Good, thought Petula, she *wants* me to save her, she's as passive as a mannequin.

'Stay *still*, stay still. *Still* damn it!'

Just as Petula aligned the stool under her daughter Evita lunged again, twisting them both into a clumsy knot of kicking ankles and flailing arms. Before she got any further Petula was on her back with Evita on top, the rope had snapped. Neither of them moved, Petula's head having hit the floorboard with a sullen thunk. Squashed to the floor, hairballs and dust jammed up her nostrils, Petula tried to free her mouth of Evita's sweaty blouse. Her daughter simply lay there, her arms stretched out in a crucifix pose, indifferent to the body fighting for air underneath. With the determination of a survivor Petula wriggled her face free of Evita's shoulder and inhaled. She could see silver stars and strange wispy figurines gliding through the walls like seahorses.

'Thank Christ. For that.'

Evita's sobs, one at a time and then uncontrolled, had a puzzling effect on Petula. The instantaneous relief at having successfully mounted a rescue had vanished. Evita's crying was filling her heart full of the sharpest rage.

'Bitch! *Silly, selfish, little* bitch!'

Evita's eyes were wide open now, red pearls in a sea of salty tears, 'Oh Mum.'

With the agility of a wrestler, Petula swung her leg round

reversing their positions so that it was her sat atop of her daughter, her knees pinning Evita's arms feebly to the floor. 'You may well look scared you little prick. All of life's a suicide mission but only a moron like you could create a mess like this. What the hell do you mean to do trying to kill yourself in my home?'

'Please...'

Straddling her tightly, feeling her floppy body turn to putty between her powerful thighs, Petula snarled, 'Well say something you disgrace!'

She did not expect what came next. With all the fight she had left Evita pulled free her left arm and brought her elbow up into Petula's cheek, making contact with a muffled crack.

Petula felt a door swing shut on her face, hot blood streaming over her mouth and chin, her nose a mix of numb pressure and chilly heat. Tremblingly she touched it and observed a crimson spray volt over her finger onto her daughter's twisted mat of hair.

'You! Why *you!*'

Petula watched her hands go for Evita's neck, her thumbs and fingers and nails forming a second rope over the remains of the existing one, a sweet sensation of total release accompanying a reasonable desire to defend herself against her bestial adversary. She did not know how long this lasted, only that she was no longer angry once Evita ceased struggling, and she lessened her grip. Evita slid onto the floor like a popped balloon, a woozy lifelessness about her that reminded Petula of how people die in fairy tales.

'Evita...

'Evita...

'...*Evita!*'

The body lay there, inert and unmoving, frighteningly still to see.

'Oh my God. *Evita!*'

Downstairs the telephone was ringing. It was a compulsion of Petula's to answer the phone, no matter what she was in the middle of, the device having a totemic importance for her. One never knew who might be on the other end. Swiftly she retraced her steps, having the presence of mind to bolt the attic door from the outside, and made her way down to the second-floor landing. There she cleared her throat and, spotting herself in the mirror, her shirt bloodied and torn, answered the phone with a cheerful nonchalance not normally associated with one who has just strangled her daughter.

'Petula Montague speaking!'

The voice at the other end sounded official and Petula felt the cold hand of destiny play havoc with her insides; it had all gone wrong. She stared glassily at a print of the Cathedral at Reims, long enough for her to preempt defeat and know how badly she would bear up to it.

'What? I'm sorry, I can't hear you, it's a bad line. Could you please repeat that or speak up?'

Yes, it may have all gone wrong but the jig was not up, not until they had her before the beak in leg irons staring at a thirty stretch in the Tower. Fight, fight, fight and never give up!

'Regan! Oh hello darling! What? What! No, I'm fine, of course I am, you've just got me out of the bath. What? What's happened to Regan? You say, a lift from the station, oh, this is Regan! I'm sorry darling, I didn't recognise you, you sound so old! You mean you already *are* at the station, what now? How the devil did you get there so quickly? Yes, no, of course, by train, I know that, you must have caught a very early one. I can't, I'm afraid, my hands are perfectly full here with one thing or another. No. Yes, you'll have to take a taxi. If you don't have the money I can pay when you get here. Yes, see you then sweetie, goodbye... by-e-e-e-e.'

Allowing for rogue tractors and, if she was lucky, an Asian cabbie who did not know his way from Darlington to Mockery Gap, there was about an hour to play with before Regan got home. Long enough to clear up, rebuild the day and start over again. She knew her odds, one disaster at a time, keep each piece separate and throw a bracket round them all. This morning was what the game was all about: establishing her own brand of facts as truth.

Petula strode towards the 'spare' guest bathroom, the least used in the house on account of it not being adjoined to any room, or near one that was in use. It was a long and cold space, not double-glazed, in which the bath had been torn out and a shower installed in its place for variation's sake. Quickly she stripped, soaped herself in a lather and allowed the cold blast of water to do its worst. What had happened? No, that was the wrong question, it could be asked later, would have to be, but for now survival was paramount and she should think of nothing that could imperil it. If she was in shock, and there was little doubt she was, the best thing to do was to use it to her advantage. Stepping into a large brown robe borrowed from the New York Sheridan, Petula stuffed her clothes into an airing cupboard and examined her face in the mirror.

Ignoring the temptation to stare into her eyes, she took a flannel to rub the last of the blood away and see the damage done. Far less than she thought. The nose did not look broken, a little bent, which actually looked sexily distinguished, there was one scratch which she could have done to herself and a small lump on the side of her head no sod would see. Nothing that was not consistent with falling out of bed in the middle of the night after a bottle too many of Chablis. Already she had a picture in her mind of the clothing appropriate to the day, one where glorious normality, restored to its usual place, would revel in unnoticed innocence.

Wisely the offer of paying Jazzy to help at his sister's party had neutralised his latest revolt, at least for the present. Jazzy could be holier than thou about money when it suited his overall purpose, and touchily proud. However, with an MOT coming up on his van, and Bad Brains playing Leeds, his going price was affordably low. It would at least keep him out of the way for the next hour, during which time he might find some consolation in the skinny arms of that emaciated elf of his. Having crossed the landing, Petula took the side staircase to her floor. Outside the sound of the Postman's van coming to a halt on the gravel, letters being pushed through the box and the van's engine starting again sent a chill across her bows. It would be so easy for someone to simply walk in. The front door was never locked. Although she complained about people (and then only some) calling all hours, treating The Heights as an open house, Petula needed them, missed them when they weren't there and wondered what was wrong if a weekend passed without guests. Today, without equivocation, she would be glad to host no one. The trouble was she could not shake the feeling that someone was watching her and could see everything. Usually she would dismiss this as a muddle between what she saw, forgot, and subsequently attributed to another, a confusion consistent with the way her mind was jumping like a stylus in a room of jiving hippopotami, and the erroneous belief that this perspective, or to give it its proper name, God, existed.

This was different, and as she entered her bedroom Petula self-consciously looked behind her, not so much to catch an intruder on her tail, as to show the cosmic force that begat her she knew it was still there. With a stagy flourish she opened the wardrobe and ran her hand over the hangers, the familiar colours and textures comforting to touch. If a grand recording of her life were to be played back to the thousands she had hoodwinked or outmanoeuvred on the Day of Judgement, it was as well to choose something striking to be damned in. Petula found what she was looking for, simple in a wardrobe as ordered as hers, and allowed her robe to drop off her shoulders to the floor. So what if there was a heavenly screening of her breaking a few of the Ten Commandments? Anyone who had been through life would understand, and who was to say the Divinity only gave marks for priggery, there could be points for ingenuity, skill and daring too; the Lord God had created them all. Impartial and disinterested goodness had never made any sense to Petula, a perspective divorced from the person and interest it served was no more than a causeless effect, a meaningless chimera parroted by hypocrites and peasants. True goodness was about energy, how much you produced and the amount you carried into other people's lives, a completely amoral phenomenon and every daughter of Eve's true religion.

Petula pulled on her new, never-worn, cream corduroy jeans, as fitting as tights, and a thin denim shirt. In principle it was a far better thing to be too cold than overheat and the last thing she needed was a red nose. Thankfully, The Heights' many drafts would help her keep cool once the face-to-face stuff started. Leaving her hair down and clicking her tongue, Petula as good as strutted from the room feeling every inch the Yorkshire Cowgirl, a down-home look that could sell cigarettes on advertising hoardings she thought, as she closed the door. Hesitating, she realised what was wrong. Her feet were still bare. Choosing footwear that was suggestive of an immobility at odds with the true speed of events was the touch the occasion required, clogs without socks would do. It was like opening the batting in a game of cricket, a sport she had never had much use for, a mistake was most likely in the first over or so – once she was settled at the crease there was nothing to stop her from going on to score a hundred. Petula paused by the dresser and picked a pair of chunky rings that would have made strangling anyone difficult. In the end it could all come down to details.

All this self-overhearing had left Petula in severe need of a cup of tea. It was a school-girl error she was not going to fall into. For all the philosophers and poets who talked of 'the journey' being the thing, it was final realities that interested her. She had a duty to her daughter to settle before the pleasing consolations of Darjeeling. It was unthinkable that Evita should lie in the open to be found, unlikely though that was. Furthermore, leaving her uncovered would not do out of respect for the dead. Petula coughed into her hand and pulled a face that would have upset her rhythm had she been able to see it. Until now she had not thought of Evita as dead, not really dead, merely as out-of-the-way and no longer a problem. That second part she liked, the first she did not; death was a great destroyer of options, and in this instance, not only for the departed. Wanting someone dead, as she had often desired of Evita, and acknowledging they were (and that one was not entirely blameless in making them that way), made her queasy. Petula had wanted to keep matters on a strictly practical footing yet the inhuman self-discipline this operation required was too much for her. An involuntary eruption of feeling could not be ruled out, better to ask what she felt about the body in the attic now than find out later in public, breaking down over the pudding or somewhere equally incriminating.

Petula had never asked herself a question that had not already been answered in that chamber of justification that passed for her unconscious. That her reaction to the accident upstairs had thus far been a touch un-maternal was obvious. She had spent so much of her life worrying about Evita that it was difficult to remember where love fitted into the relationship. There were flashes, glances that passed between them, especially when Evita was younger, things she had done for her that looked like love, and ways Evita responded that also *looked* that way. They had probably both needed to believe it, suspecting perfectly well that nothing remotely of the kind existed, only sham variations on what the world expected of a mother and daughter. Backdated sentimentality could not sweeten the true and bitter fruit of memory. Evita and Anycock had been too busy tormenting her, creating problems in ways big and small, for her to discover or explore an emotion like care. And what little she had managed saw its potential exhausted in putting out one fire after another. For as far back as she could remember Evita had puzzled and confounded her, an alien being expressing the attitudes, impulses and wants of a complete stranger, albeit a stranger known to and feared by her. Perhaps 'love' in this climate was one of those virtues that could only be preached later, to be discovered in the far-off future like an archaeological relic in the ashes of a volcano. In real time she and Evita had left each other's lives years ago, the incident in the attic that morning a formal seal on a deed already done. All she needed to know about their 'bond' was contained in the last hour, a tragedy to look back on in the complete secrecy of solitude, another cross to bear, all part of the saddest story that could never be told. Petula fought a tear; she could see a friend, an intimate and sensitive one, perhaps even Wrath, looking into her eyes and asking what the matter was and she saying, with the resolve of a stoic, *why, nothing, nothing at all my dear, I was just thinking of how sad life can be at times...* because perhaps, after all, she really did love her.

Petula recrossed the landing, tender misgivings nearly banished to the hinterland of unserious speculation. Of course, there would always be a fifth columnist in her head that would argue that as a mother it should have fallen to her to be the victim, and expired first. If she had known her place, and died not a thousand deaths in Evita's stead, in other words stayed with Anycock, none of this would have happened. True, but this advocate of the Devil would have to insist on her failing the most important test of all, the one owed by her talent to its potential. A heavy hand was pulling her vitality into her southern-most extremities, and out the other end. The idea of her still married to Anycock on that wreck of a farm, frying ham rinds to an audience of idiot children and a husband who'd have been better off perched on the walls of Notre Dame with the other gargoyles, was an offence against life. That's where Nazarene morality would have had her, all the joy she had brought the world wasted on selfish cretins who would not have noticed if she had been swapped for a tent peg, providing it could still poach eggs. Petula shook her head as she watched the four of them (though God knows how many more children Anycock would have had her bear) carrying on like a family in a corn-flakes advert, daily outings to local attractions and holidays in a caravan, one unrecoverable summer after another until they found her on the bathroom floor, frothing from the mouth. If this was the fate Evita's dying had saved her from then who was she to argue? She stopped at the bottom of the wooden staircase that led to the east-wing attic and looked directly up at the door. It appeared as she left it, closed at any rate.

Petula bit her thumb; hide the body under a dust cloth and then what? Was there another way, a stroke of genius that in her haste she had overlooked, a possibility that even now she could hide in the light and pass this off as just one of those things... She took her thumb out of her mouth, of course there was! There was no need for her to resort to subterfuge as though some terrible crime had taken place, this was no conspiracy after all, no, an unforeseen accident that had already claimed one victim and might, if her wits were to desert her, take down one more. In the circumstances, she should proceed guiltlessly and leave the body exactly where it lay. The evidence was entire-ly consistent with a narrative that need not incriminate her in any untoward doings, of course it was! Evita had been ready to die of suffocation when she first walked in on her, was ready to hang herself, for crying out loud! Had she entered the room a second or so later that is exactly what would have happened. All she had done, in a manner of speaking, was allow the girl to have her own way, after having first frustrated her in her enterprise. There was enough truth in *that* version for it to be acceptable in any court of law, if it got that far, which of course it would not; who would think of prosecuting a grieving mother who had already lost her daughter to a hideous tragedy? And again, it was no more than the truth with a small omission or two, pretty well how the greater part of humanity lived their lives from day to day. Yes, Evita had hanged herself and fallen from the ceiling in her death throes. And by the time she had entered the room it was already too late to try to save her life, which she *had* tried to do of course, mouth-to-mouth resuscitation, a dead child in her arms, there was the *real* story.

Petula waited with one foot on the stair for the impact to sink in. Could she do it? Could she repeat it for the rest of her life and never speak the truth in her sleep... No, it would not do, she would get away with it, yes, but her reputation would not, and what use was life without that? The innuendo, suspicion and gossipy malice would follow her around like halitosis... and besides, she did not have the necessary energy to carry on without a breather. If she were to begin this performance it would be one she could never take leave of. She checked her watch, forty minutes had passed since Regan's phone call. Quickly, in-out, hide the body, work out what to do later, then downstairs buttering toast and listening to Radio 4 with the telephone in her hand, awaiting discovery behind the mask of her morning ritual. That was the way ahead. Taking two steps at a time, and losing a clog on the way, Petula bound up to, unbolted and threw open the door as purposefully as any spring cleaner.

She came to a majestic halt; the Titanic had hit an iceberg. As carnivals of bad karma went, this one was proving to be a rare classic. Evita was not there. The chair, the tatty old rope, the mattress and an overturned mug were all present and correct but Evita's body, unless her eyes teased her, was nowhere to be seen!

'Thank God, thank *God* for that,' she said aloud and loudly.

Petula waited for an answer. There was a muffled cry from behind the door and an unintelligible flurry of half-spoken sobs, 'You killed, you would have *killed* me...'

'Nonsense, we had an argument that got out of hand, on both our parts, that's all.'

'You left me for dead!'

'I knew you couldn't have been,' replied Petula thinking quickly, 'your eyes weren't open. Dead people's eyes always are. Anyway, we probably both went a bit crazy back there... though that's no excuse for thinking such a thing. Kill you? Please!'

Evita came out from behind the door. If Petula had undergone a resurrection since they last clashed, Evita was only one step ahead of the worms, her pallor the colour of the sky on a sleety morning and cracked lips a vampiric red. She flinched defensively as she saw her mother, her body undergoing an attack of the shakes. With an exaggerated effort of will she dragged the rack of hair off her eyes and repeated, her voice cracking under a new onslaught of sobs, *'Dead... you left me dead...'*

Her tone was hesitant and if Petula's instincts were right, there was a hint of guilt common to those with memory loss. It was possible that Evita was concussed, confused and, providence be thanked, immanently malleable.

'Cut it *out*! We argued badly, *okay*? Both said things we probably shouldn't have, or didn't mean, and I admit it, I haven't been that cross for a while, right? But that's no reason for you to go off your rocker dramatising everything. It was awful enough without that. Really, you're my flesh and blood! Get a grip of yourself.' Petula could see that she had started to convince her daughter halfway through this but finished anyway. One-hundred-and-eighty-degree about-turns were all about making sure.

'If I hadn't dragged you off me I wouldn't be here now. Come to that, if I hadn't got you down from your hanging tree, nor would you. Insanity. Complete insanity. You could have knocked my teeth down my throat, I had to subdue you, you were like an animal Evita, something wild and dangerous.'

Evita frowned, reality being bent and warped too fast for her to grab the parts she last saw and claim them for what she thought they were. Unsteadily, she lowered her guard and shuffled over to her mother. For a dreadful moment Petula thought she was going to hug her but instead Evita said, 'I'd never have tried to kill myself, never, not any of the times I tried, if I knew that you really wanted me dead, wanted me dead all along... all this time.'

'My God, listen to you, you should be under sedation. There's a world of difference between thinking you have no use for somebody and then wanting them dead, as you'd have it. Give me some credit at least.'

And Evita did; she believed her mother, and in doing so underestimated her. 'Can you blame me, can you? You, your way, it's always been "be my best friend, accept my patronage or I'll kill you." I never obeyed, I was my own person, I...'

'Oh stop it! I have never wanted to kill you, got it? Or for you to kill yourself! I've been saving your life ever since you were a little girl! So don't drag all that mopey gubbins up again, it doesn't suit you, you're too sensible at heart. I'll tell you what happened. You came back home, it began okay, mainly because with all your cramps and flu you weren't fit enough to fight; then we quickly moved from fear and suspicion to irritated contempt with nothing sage or fine inbetween, as it always will with us. I'm sorry Evita, it's who we are and we're far too alike. Make no mistake about it, I'm that rare old bird, one that actually learns from experience. This is what happens every time.'

'Learned, learned what? That you don't want me around you?'

'On the contrary. I've learnt that I don't need you to go away, to die, yes, *die*, for me to miss you. I miss you already Evita, stood here in front of me and not... and not loving me as a daughter should love her mother.' Petula raised her chin, exalted and defiant; it was the kind of inversion of what she really felt that she could produce at a moment's notice, providing that moment was fluid enough, and then believe for as long as was necessary.

Evita had bent her head to one side as if to see some changing object better; the windmill was first a giant, then a windmill again. She was nearly where Petula wanted her, though not entirely there yet. 'You Mum, you may not really want me dead, I'll... I'll give you that then. There, do you feel lily-white now... but there are other ways of killing, you know there are.'

'Metaphorical ones I suppose, this is terribly predictable of you dear.'

'Because you're still a murderer, I mean it, every day you do it and sometimes you even know it. You know all the ways...'

'Spare me.'

'Not listening! By not listening! Ignoring someone's voice, what they want to say with it I mean, that's the same as treating them as if they don't exist. You never hear, you never did believe what I or Jazzy said about Tinwood, one of your precious actors...'

'An agent as it happens, and for God's sake don't bring him into this. It was dealt with at the time. I heard you out then didn't I?'

'That's all you did! We never even told you half of what happened...'

'Well you were both talking complete contradictory mouthwash, how could I be expected to listen to...'

'And worse,' Evita continued waveringly, 'by getting your voice into everyone else's heads so they end up thinking like you. You've never left anyone alone. The swaggering macho woman, my *mother*.'

'Stop it, stop it now.'

'You *hate* me!'

'I'm finishing this Evita. The days of my listening to rants are done. Your performance this morning has settled that for us both. This, none of this, must happen again. So I'll do you the honour of addressing these... concerns of yours one at a time. Macho? I call it grace under pressure, people of my generation are a bit that way, like it or not. Then this stuff about murder without death or whatever, you've got the wrong woman, that's you dear, what were all of your suicide attempts if not self-murders minus the grand exit? All the drama of the real thing without having to pay the true cost, pass that onto some other mug. And you talk to me about not listening. I'm here aren't I? I came back just now to listen; to give you another chance...'

'What Mum, the Devil having a weak moment?'

'Don't be facetious, you don't have the constitution for it. Touch me if you have to, these aren't the scales of a dragon, all this demonisation is pitiful. There is a large and not-often-acknowledged element of self-pity in madness, in giving into and rolling in your worst impulses all the time. I believe it's become something of an addiction with you. I should know. I suffer from my own variation, it's called duty, though I know you regard all that as a waste of time...'

'It *is* all a waste of time Mum, all of this.'

'Far from it. Why should our relationship be a waste of time simply because we don't like each other? I can't think of any-thing more valuable than knowing another person well and intimately, whether you happen to care for them or not. You're the needle I can always pull the thread through. That's how well I know you Evita. I'm sorry you haven't taken the trouble to return the compliment, and instead created this monster ver-sion of me you use to explain each of your unhappinesses. And as for your balderdash about my being a killer, wrong again, the death cult you've joined comes from your father's side of the family. No, I believe in life, there's nothing crazier, you need guts to do it and a decent grasp of the fucking obvious. Once you believe in it you'll believe anything, as nothing, nothing at all, is less remarkable or preposterous than a belief in life. Even a belief in yourself. Try it Evita and pack the rest in. I'm being good to you. When I come back I want this mess cleared and to hear a plan, *your* plan, a plan of what you intend to do next. Right? You look as though you want to say something? Go on.'

Evita was sat on the rolled-up Persian carpet not looking as if she wanted to say anything. Leaning forward in a fug of stunned and gormless incomprehension, she started 'I... sorry, no, you want a plan, I mean, after what happened, what are you on about? I...'

The electronic door bell sounded, changed at Petula's specification to the gong at the beginning of Rank Films, interrupting Evita's reluctant response.

Petula, in a show of great patience, ignored it.

'You were saying?'

The bell went again. Evita looked hopefully round the room, desperate for a hidden witness to step out of a closet and speak on her behalf. A tiredness that felt like the beginning of an acceptance that she had lost again, would always lose at this particular game, was coming over her in agonisingly slow waves. 'I feel sick... I don't know what the fuck is going on. Or what you even... want... from... me.' Evita knew it was smack she needed now, so badly in fact that she could practically feel it working.

'The first honest thing you've said all day. A plan. A plan is what I require from you.'

Evita moaned like a dog tied to a post it wanted to break free from. 'Leave me *alone*, can't you? Isn't it enough that I am broken, that you've made another Jazzy out of me? How can I have a plan when I don't have a way of living yet, or anywhere to go?'

'Ye Gods! Alright, stay put for today. And don't do anything else silly or go anywhere. I'll be back once I can.'

The bell had gone a third time. It was not like Regan to be so impatient. Stoically Petula steeled herself for another unforeseen helping of drama; but not before thanking God that she had not become too old for her victories. If Evita was right and she was a murderer then she was a just one who would only put to death those guiltier than herself. The point, however, was that Evita lacked the guile and strength to convince the world she was right, which, in Petula's book, was no different from being wrong. And at least the girl was alive to know it. A disaster had been averted and the chance that Evita might have been killed in their altercation relegated to the netherworld of unrealised possibilities that never were. Admittedly, there was still the perennial ghost of the low Church moraliser that haunted Petula, the reproach that she might have made a mistake or two of her own, her ultimate triumph notwithstanding. Like a pianist changing styles, it was hard to be completely free of one's old influences. Might it not have been possible to save Evita's life without the unfortunate bit that came after the selfless bit? Some chance! Petula's way of dealing with the problems thrown up by free will and choice was by pretending neither existed; the way she had acted was the *only* way she could have acted and what was done was all that she could do. She was her mistakes and there could be no brilliance or counter-attacks without them.

So it was, that when she finally reached the front door, the bell having just rung for a fourth time, Petula could face the lions with a clear conscience and a smile on her face. The smile disappeared in the time it took her to see her caller was Jazzy. He was scowling and bouncing on the caps of his toes, an arm resting against a pillar and the other balanced officiously on his hip.

Resisting the urge to simply close the door in his face, Petula asked, 'What do you want now?'

'Just one more thing, right?'

'Please God make it quick.'

'I'm not wearing some poxy uniform, if you want me to play the waiter I'm drawing a line in the sand. I won't wear a bow tie, or dinner jacket or any of that penguin shit, alright?'

'What?'

'I can't breathe with anything round my neck, ties make me feel constricted, like there's a snake around my neck or something. And I'm not wearing a uniform that'll make me look like a poof. Not for you, or Regan. I don't do ties of any kind, they're for arse-lickers.'

'So long as you get out of that filthy tee-shirt which makes you look underdressed as well as dirty, dangerous and horrible, and get into something clean with a collar, I really don't care what you bloody wear.'

Jazzy looked hurt; he had not expected a compromise to be so quick or equivocal. It almost put him in the wrong.

'So I don't have to wear a DJ and get done up like a penguin?'

There was a crash upstairs, the sound of a door slamming and legs stampeding down a staircase. Petula quivered. She had not secured her flanks but then she had not thought that Evita would try anything else – her success had felt too secure for that.

'Do I have your word?'

'What? What are you talking about?'

'The bow tie, I ain't wearing one, do you swear?'

'Christ yes, what do you want me to do, sign a court order?'

The feet were on a second staircase now, getting closer by the second, a banging following them, some heavy object being dragged along; a bag, Petula surmised, or perhaps some make-shift club that Evita intended to use for Round Two.

'Is that it?'

'Yeah... hang on, another thing...'

'No, only one other thing; I really do hope you haven't been in your right mind all these years, because if you have, then there's absolutely no bloody excuse for you! We're done here!'

Petula had closed the door on Jazzy's foot, his boot still wedged in the way, and fingers hanging onto the inside handle.

'I ain't through yet! I want to be paid upfront this time, right, not half now, half later... *owww!*'

Petula picked up a bunch of keys and rapped them over Jazzy's fingers, loosening his hold and pushing his wrist back round to his side of the door.

'There's no more time Jasper!'

'You're mad! You could have had them in the door! I'd be left without a livelihood!' he yelled from the other side.

Catching her breath Petula dropped the lock and turned to face the enemy within. The feet had gone some distance away, not towards her as she had anticipated but in the opposite direction, down the back staircase to the door leading to the garden. With Jazzy knocking furiously behind her this was just as well; the two fronts could not be allowed to converge, the centre must hold. Speedily, Petula crossed the narrow depth of the house, through the kitchen to the back door that sat in the middle of the building. Opening it she looked over to the garden entrance at the east wing. It appeared to be rocking against its frame and at the foot of the shrubbery, scurrying through a gap in the hedge, was Evita. Petula watched her disappear, appear again in the back garden, and run on to the outer gate which clanged shut behind her. So the bird had flown. Petula looked from left to right. There was a silence at the front door, the chilly breath of a northerly wind, and a squirrel stealing birdseed from a feeder, otherwise the garden was empty. On her way back into the kitchen Petula noticed a page ripped from an old textbook pinned prominently to the cork-board above the fridge. Written on it, in Evita's ugly scrawl, were the words 'Goodbye Mummy,' signed, 'your greatest disappointment – EVITO.' Well, thought Petula, tearing down the note and throwing it into the compost bin, she was wrong about that – Jazzy was a far greater disappointment, Evita had shown more pluck than she deemed her capable of, even if she couldn't spell her own name at a speed. The phone was going again and the door bell ringing in multiple bursts. She had to maintain focus, there was plenty that still needed doing and she had yet to ring the caterers for the evening's reception at the Cathedral Close, or begin her round up of the yeses, nos or maybes to consolidate a good turnout. Of one thing she was certain, she was unlikely to be seeing Evita again that day or any soon after. Pride was the quality they knocked back and forth over the net. As Evita had been able to reject her again, she was unlikely to forgo her 'advantage' by returning and risking her own rejection in turn. It wasn't, Petula reflected, a bad end to their little war.

'Secrets weary of their tyranny, tyrants willing to be dethroned...'

Rudely and with the single-minded air of a determined zombie, Jazzy's face appeared against the glass of the porthole window over the conserve shelf:

'Half now, half later!'

'Sweet Lord in Heaven! Piss off won't you!'

'I want what's mine, yes or no?'

The front doorbell was still ringing which meant that whoever was there was not Jazzy and, therefore, worthy of her attention. For what felt like the umpteenth time that day, hampered by her remaining clog which had out-served the alibi it was no longer needed for, Petula stumbled back through the house and pulled open the front door, leaning into it to avoid falling over. Some seconds passed as she and Regan stared at one another for what each mistook to be the reasons of the other. Finally, Regan spoke, 'Mum, you look... hot and tried. Are you okay?'

'Me? No, just struck by time's ever-severing wave, that's all my dear! Come in, you must be hungry. I could do with a little tea and toast myself after the morning I've had. I haven't so much as got off the phone yet and have your brother to contend with. It seems as though through some kink in his temperament, he finds my attempts to moderate, to try and make his life better, an affront to his fanatic's code. And do you know something? Your other sister is, I mean was, just the same!'

CHAPTER SIX,
complaints and consolation.

There was something Regan was scared of but she could not see what it was yet. It had not been as sad a first day back as usual, the melancholia of coming home and finding there was nothing special for her to do held at bay until her mother revealed plans for the party she had promised the holiday before. Regan was revolted by her own brattish ingratitude. Gush as she had in front of Petula, the shape of the gift was not to her liking. Having been thrown straight into drinks at the Bishop's inauguration, she had not enjoyed more than thirty minutes alone in her mother's company, and Petula had been uncharacteristically taciturn and distracted over breakfast, certainly in no mood to hear her offer of a party spurned. Instead, having quickly explained the form of the evening, a dinner party quite at odds with Regan's current idea of fun, drinking Cinzano in the woods, Petula handed over a seating plan and changed subjects to Penelope Mortimer's impending trip to Scarborough. Regan listened at a polite distance, her inner weather a squall line of cumulonimbus clouds threatening to break into pellets of sleet.

'So you see, it's *most* important that no one mentions John.'

'Alright.'

'I mean it, it's *crucial* that Penelope sees herself as a writer in her own right and not an appendage to her ex-husband. *Crucial.* It must be dreadful carrying that baggage around. Really, I feel sorry for some women.'

'She *has* written a book Mum. Loads I thought. She can't feel that useless. Or need people to feel sorry for her. Didn't you say someone made a film no one watched about it?'

'Still.'

'Sure. I won't mention him. I mean, I've never really even heard of him so why would I talk about the guy?'

'Really Regan, you don't *half* say some silly things for a clever girl. Who hasn't heard of John Whatshisface?'

To appreciate Petula's kindnesses Regan knew one must separate intention from whatever device, words or gesture her mother chose to express that motive through. A superficial reading of Petula's deeds might traduce a self-aggrandisement that sat at odds with her mother's true animating principle: a desire to assist at all costs.

'The other thing, I can't stress this enough, is for Penelope to feel completely at home here. I want her to be inspired. I want to read about us in her next novel. She has to be able to treat this place as she wishes.'

'That won't be hard, everyone who comes here says they're inspired.'

'She isn't anyone, she's a *writer* Regan, they tend to be more sensitive to atmosphere than your average run of humanity who can find inspiration over sherry in a shed.'

'Mmmm.'

'Mmmm what?'

'Wouldn't a writer like her be more likely to find inspiration somewhere "normal" than a normal person who needs a beautiful house to get them going?'

'*What*? What are you *talking* about, just be nice to her okay?'

Regan could not keep the edge out of her responses; her disappointment was dying to be aired. However she looked at it, her mother's choice of guests for her party was stubbornly eccentric, unless, of course, Petula was looking to assist some persons other than her to have a good time, an option Regan could barely countenance entertaining.

'Don't look so put out, Penelope isn't a monster, I'm sure you'll learn a lot from her. I had even thought of asking her to stay for your party but she's got to be in Edinburgh. Pity. Still, it did give me the opportunity to invite John instead, and he's accepted. He says he's always been very interested in keeping abreast of the young.'

For Regan, this latest kindness was too much like being handed a list of the best novelists under forty and finding the only living entry to be Barbara Cartland, sandwiched between Somerset Maugham and Kipling; these were not the horses she had expected for this particular course. It was not as if she expected to be consulted or allowed to have her way – she was too much a stranger to her own preferences to even know them if called to. Naturally she fully expected her mother's friends to feature heavily in anything Petula had a hand in, it was always so. Several had made a pet of her when she was younger and she played to their patronage. Besides, it was irrefutable that an evening consisting of only The Lasses would border on an uncouth parody of a societal gathering; they were not ready for their own dinner soirées yet, as Petula must have known when she devised the present one. But what Regan had not anticipated were her numbers to have shrunk to only seven (which would be compatible with a day out but not dinner), and that the other *fifty-nine* guests would include people she had never met, or only spied from a distance. She ran over the names again: Landon Trafalgar, Wally Burnbeck, Hayden Fox-Davies. Who were these people? Were they for real? The immaturity of her reaction was pitiful and an obstacle to progress. It was an attitude she could have taken towards Petula's circle at any time in her life and thus missed the social education that marked her as unique in her set. Her failure to embrace this latest challenge was a little girl's conceit. And yet she could not help herself. This was her first real party since childhood and it would be unnatural if her feelings did not veer a little toward self-pity, miserable as it was to paddle in the shallowness of one's vapidity.

'Do you mind reading one of her books before she comes, it would help you know. To get to know her.'

'Um, I have quite a lot of coursework I brought home...'

'Oh, I don't really mean *read* it. Just skim the thing, and maybe the first ten, and last ten, pages properly, you'll get the general idea and the main characters, that's the important thing.'

'Which book?'

'I don't know all their names. Go to the library and ask for the best one, they'll tell you. It's what they're there for.'

Regan tried to remember the other, more encouraging names on the list. Ones she half-knew or remembered from her childhood training: Max Astley, Seymour Barchester, Rex Wade, a lot of men, and one any teenage girl ought, she knew, to positively thrill at the inclusion of: Crispin Fogle, the hunk who had played the 'noble savage' in the last series of *Dr Who*, and was now touted for the main role. How did her mother get hold of that one, she mused; Petula certainly had her finger in a number of pies unknown to Regan.

'I read the first, can't think of its name offhand, had "butternut squash" in the title I think though that doesn't sound right, does it?'

'She doesn't write the cookery books, does she?'

'Oh come on! That's that Delia, plain as parsnips. Penelope was most likely using vegetables as a metaphor for her heroine's genitals or something. She's an author of literary fiction, though don't ask me what that is supposed to be.'

Once Regan could get over the idea that none of this was *her* idea there would be a great deal to enjoy, or if not enjoy, at least the welcome possibility of being enjoyed. To not be found boring by adults was how Regan measured her pleasure; she knew of no other criteria to consult in their company. Her involuntary tics and longings belonged to the world of Nohallows, and as they were no more than a reflection of attitudes absorbed at The Heights, what Regan desired for her own sake remained tantalisingly hidden. Coming top of her class had not given her confidence, simply an understanding of the things she had read, much as leading her year socially had not made her a leader, only the least led of her flock. Her instincts were reliably unsure of themselves. Watching the world through moods she tried to ignore left a robotic residue that her 'real' feelings rarely emerged from. Was this why she knew that whatever pique she felt towards Petula would vanish? Whatever rose from the heart invariably wilted, it was easily the most misleading organ nature had encumbered her with.

'I think there may be a new man in her life, in fact I'm willing to bet on it, Hayden Fox-Davies. He's set to come into a lot of money and is meant to be quite charming though useless in every other way, and he does, poor man, look a bit like Dracula, you know, the Count, Christopher Lee version. He's coming to your party. I think I might sit him next to the Mooncalf.' Mooncalf was the name Petula had taken to calling Royce for an accumulation of offences. As Regan was still going through a sustained and frequently topped-up period of not liking Royce, the moniker met with her approval.

'Yes, I remember his name from the list.'

'His father's second wife has a title. And no children. Fact.'

Just the opposite, thought Regan. The names that interested her most on the list were neither facts nor titles. The names were hopes and her way of becoming the woman who might one day explain all this back to the girl she still was. Metamorphosis was in the night air and she knew she must embrace it. Her last term at Nohallows had felt like a vanishing memory even as it happened, one set of associations falling away in the face of other less certain outcomes. Eras often ended before others realised they had, Regan noticed, and the days of marmite by candlelight, sat in her filthy games kit listening to The Pixies, were fading fast. So too were the purple, green and blue lipstick, her love bites with Diamanda and the freezing Saturday-night ritual of fighting over mastery of the common-room video recorder huddled under blankets and quilts. She was ready to enter another stage; weirdness was a dead end, so far as the world outside school was concerned. In that wider reality all she and her friends represented were smaller versions of Jazzy or Evita, losers, as uncool as they came. Regan had long suspected that she and The Lasses were strange but not particularly interesting, doomed in a context more challenging than one where merely disobeying orders wrought notoriety. She had only to look at their excursions into parties at other schools to see their icy defiance signified little more than an ability to pointlessly baffle, and there was enough of that in normal life to bore the boys without confusing it for a countercultural stance. She would have to raise the subject of change with her merry band as it was out of the question to desert The Lasses. They were her responsibility. How could they not be when she had made them love her by fooling them into believing she was more than they? And somewhere near the un-ignited spark of her undeclared soul, Regan was sure that Petula was proof that this was a ruse that could work forever. The birthday dinner was her chance to traverse universes and begin the second half of her teens. She would take it as confidently as an older girl would a younger one's place in the lunch-line.

'I want to go for a run.'

'What, *now*? It's nearly midnight!'

'I do at school, night-running.'

'They allow you to?'

'Not really, it's just something some of us girls do.'

'How can you know where you're going in the dark? It's bloody dangerous.'

'We carry carrots.'

'Huh. Very clever. So where are you going to run to at this hour?'

'The lake maybe.'

'You must be mad. Well, off you run you unfathomable freak, but make this the last time! I was hoping you'd grow up this holiday. Night-running, I mean, it's not very far off a midnight feast or rounders in a corridor, is it? You're getting too old for all that now.'

'I'm not that old yet.'

'No, but you will be soon. People will stop thinking we're sisters before you know it.'

'No they won't!'

'They won't stop calling us them, but they'll stop thinking it. What they think will be an entirely different matter,' her mother chuckled gloomily. 'Anyway, keep making me proud of you and you'll have nothing to worry about. I will always be there for you.'

Once in her room Regan glanced at her watch. Ten-thirty. The night was cloudless and the full moon blindingly white. Skulking out of school as the rest slept gave Regan the sense that she was in the presence of what no one else was, the loopy dreams of a thousand girls amplified in the intense silence, the only sound for miles the smack of moths flying into the giant electric lights by the main gates. Home was different, running at night here allowed her thoughts to come to her in subtle gradations, vague but sly realisations she would have forgotten over breakfast or needed a week in the sanatorium to recall if she were still at Nohallows. Quickly she stripped off her clothes and changed into the new running outfit she had acquired from a sixth-former for the cost of an old buckskin jacket Evita left behind. The tight leggings and top felt as if she were pulling on someone else's body, a constriction that made her consider her skin, pinch it and wonder what it would be like for someone else to be as close to her as the cold lycra she was embalmed by. Standing in front of the mirror Regan laughed at the alien she saw there, her new Nikes sticking out like Martian hooves, the antithesis of the saggy tracksuit and plimsolls held together by an ugly elastic tongue that had formerly constituted her PE uniform. Though she only half-guessed it, she was in the process of enjoying herself and feeling her age, a frisky effortlessness to her movements like a lamb at play.

Outside it was surpassingly balmy, and Regan began at a reckless canter, the mild air filling her nostrils and lungs when she had expected them to be skinned by the chill. Agile enough to take suppleness for granted, Regan skipped down the gravel drive, the path before her illuminated by the fifth-largest satellite in the solar system, its melancholic beams her floodlit torch. To sustain her pace she often introduced an element of fantasy to her runs, imagining she were leading a marathon with the eyes of the world on her or sprinting towards a drug dealer to kick his evil arse. Tonight her dreams were of a different order, and as the landscape around her appeared to conflate with the orb in the sky, Regan felt as though she were gliding over a lunar surface, past the battered American flag-and-crater-ridden southern highlands of the Moon.

By the time she reached her destination, she was on the verge of hormonal euphoria. The starry constellations of Orion, Gemini and Auriga were emerging over the lake, their reflection quivering like distant eruptions of joy. Below them shone Procyon, the brightest star of all and the one Regan wished on whenever she wanted to extract some small advantage from life that her mother might not be willing to grant her. Feeling like an overfed woman who finds that she cannot breathe because the trousers she habitually wears are a size to small, Regan threw off her woolly hat and let her hair hang down. Kneeling down at the lake's edge she splashed the freezing water over her perspiring face, the effort of sprinting down teasing sweat out of every pore. With a defiant disregard for time and temperature, she lay out and gazed skywards, the tail lights of a passing Boeing flickering high over her pointed nose. It seemed, in the loneliness of her discovery, that this was one of the moments for which the world was made. Happiness was pouring out of her and it did not matter how much she lost for there was no set amount to hold onto; tangled lines of re-creation were carrying her into infinity faster than her doubting laughter could withstand;

'Let me know this always.'

Unlike her mother, Regan stopped before God and knew she always would. There was a thing in life more inhumane and powerful than Petula and she was beginning to suspect she would one day have cause, should she switch horses and bolt, to know more of its oft-spoken-of mercy.

*

Mingus had been out with Jazzy, the skinny art student in drainpipes and raincoat cutting a dour figure next to the blustering wiseacre wrapped in a leather scarf, Stetson hat and yellow wellingtons. That was at least what Jazzy told Mingus over his sixth pint, the ribbing, lectures and bitter confidences all part of their ritual trip to The Condemned Felon. The outing, to mark Mingus's return for the holidays, like so many of their other reunions could be summed up for Mingus by his keenest sensation of the night; one of carrying a bladder full of alcohol that had rested in the same place for too long. Since growing apart in their early teens, Mingus had been round the blocks with Jazzy, the friendship never settling in a form either were comfortable with, yet persisting through habit and Jazzy's devotion to the older Hardfields.

When Mingus first hitched home from art school in Leeds he was greatly excited at the thought of sharing his boundary-expanding discoveries with his old friend, whom he privately worried might be wasting his time in a backwater. Though put off by Jazzy's brash hedge-bandit shtick, Mingus found the continuity he offered comforting and appreciated his friend's loquacious and sentimental airs. A mutually complimentary exchange of perspectives was not, however, to be the order of their reunions. Jazzy had testily spurned Mingus, aghast at being patronised by this self-taught Picasso, making fun of the younger one's pretensions in front of the locals and dismissing him as a wannabe townie and outsider at every turn. Mingus, hurt and bewildered, took his rejection as irrevocable and went back to Leeds at the first opportunity, earning a rare postcard from Jazzy rebuking him for deserting his parents and forgetting his roots.

When it was next time to come home, Mingus made a different kind of effort, on this occasion pretending he had learned nothing in the city, failed to develop in any discernible way, and was still the boy Jazzy had played with in years gone by. He went so far as to help Jazzy with his jobs around the farm, offering his services in as demeaning a way to himself as he could, to cheer and lift his chippy companion. To his bemusement, this made things worse as Jazzy accused him of trying to supplant him, Mingus's insistence that nothing could be further from the truth and that his future lay at the Royal College of Art, not Mockery Gap, falling on overheated ears. Pride stopped Mingus rushing back to his halls of residence this time, the failure of his craven peace offer an embarrassment to him, and so, to Jazzy's intense annoyance, he opted to stay and observe his punishment.

Jazzy decided to flatly ignore Mingus or at least keep an impolite distance, his old friend's 'turn-the-other-cheek' approach striking him as an arrogant conceit, and eagerness to make up proof of his guilt. The trouble was that Jazzy was in and out of Seth Hardfield's workshop too often for indifference to work, enjoying cups of tea with Jenny, and generally treating The Wart as a second home. And in some ways the Hardfields, proud as they were of Mingus's achievements, were also out of their depth in his company, whereas Jazzy conversed with them about a world they knew, the farm, tractor parts, blocked drains and, of course, Petula. The two young men, to spare their elders awkwardness, eventually fell into an occasional and uneasy co-existence, eked out with the help of booze, snooker, marijuana and music. Providing Mingus allowed Jazzy to play the part of elder brother and rural seer on their evenings in The Condemned Felon, and kept the conversation off Freud, art history and the wilder shores of the universe, he was cheerily tolerated. As Mingus was used to surprising people, his anticipation of reactions that were surprising and often hostile had become a way of life for him. He did not expect to be treated as he treated others because he expected his treatment of others to be misunderstood, and their treatment of him to be based on misunderstanding. His optimistic attachment to life and tacit belief in destiny were his protecting angels; this and the abiding certainty that he was always going to be alright. Petula had once said to him, 'You and I are survivors and survivors usually do a little bit better than just survive.' Even when he did not know whether he was doing well or not, or questioned whether he ever had been happy, he'd answer yes in an instant if he were asked to live it all over again. He wore the attitude quietly; people who liked him noticed it in his unthinking confidence and swift, lightly critical eyes. People who did not, drew away uneasily, scared that if he were to look at them for too long he would find something out. Jazzy, though he did not know it, shared his mother's innate distrust of Mingus, who was no more his creature than he had been hers years before.

The two young men staggered out into the car park, Mingus relieved that another session was finally drawing to an end. Their last conversation had hovered close to unintelligibility, Jazzy not caring to explain himself and Mingus too drunk to mind very much, conscious that last orders had already been called.

'You going to drive back? Jazzy?'

Jazzy was staring ahead and saying nothing, usually a bad sign when his final drink had been whiskey. It tended to mean that the subject was going to be changed towards a matter his companion was not going to like, possibly to do with the companion himself.

'You alright?'

'What?'

'Alright, are you?'

'You know what?'

'Eh?'

'Let me tell you *something*. You know your trouble Ming? Your trouble is that you've never really known what it is to suffer, right?' Jazzy began, his eyes focusing once more. 'Really suffer, you know what I mean Ming? Everything's just come to you on a plate because of that talent of yours, you're an arty fucker, right? People who have talent that isn't so obvious, ones like me that have to work for everything they get, you won't ever know what it's like to be one of them, to be the bloke who mows the lawn with his teeth, one of that mass of, mass of stinking half-talented ones. I mean, I'm not saying I'm one of those, but nor are you, you know what I mean, like? That's why my Mam used to spoil you and not me. She knew you were artistic, always, you know, making things and drawing attention to yourself. That was what you did. You got more attention than I did. Period. Period. Not that I give a flying fuck about it now.'

'So what are you talking about it for then?' Mingus replied, laughing disingenuously.

'Fuck you man. My Mam gave far more of a shit about you than me, right? Did everything for you, nothing for me and my sister, my real one. You'd talk about it too if it were the other way. You would, of course you would. It was all about you and Regan, like fuckin' Barbie and Ken. It made me want to puke, truth be told.'

'Thanks for telling the truth.'

'I'm telling you that's the way it was.'

'It's the way you remember it.'

'You're too young to remember, too busy lapping it up.'

'My Mum and Dad, they listened to you, they still listen to you. More than they do me, you know, and I don't mind. Everyone finds the audience they deserve.'

'Don't be snark.'

'I'm not, I'd like them to listen to me but they don't know what I am really on about most of the time.'

'Because you don't talk to them on their level, fuckin' chuntering on about Andy Arsehole and the Noowah Yaawk scene, you can't expect them to be interested in all that shit. It's different anyway. They're hicks like me. Country people, normal people. That's what I'm saying, right? I have some normal people in my life now. Have you any idea what it was like growing up with someone like Lady P for a Mam, have you man? A nutter who keeps it coming from every orifice? *S-h-i-t*, of course you haven't, you had it easy with your parents, they're salt-of-the-earth normal. I never knew a normal day with *Petulaaah*.'

'She's strong, not as a person, but a strong character.'

'Naah. Bollocks. Ahhh, she's not strong, that's just what people say, she's crazy, not heavy, a ding. I've got evidence on her. Know how she operates, oppressing your mum and dad, oppressing me, what's the matter, you don't think so? Don't you care? She's an oppressor. You've seen how I live, the fix she got me into. Anger, man, I feel anger about it all. You should too. You would too, if you weren't so soft.'

To be angry with someone in retrospect for something you signed up for struck Mingus as revisionist flakery, yet it was difficult to remember a time when Jazzy had not been angry, the sour phase having lasted far longer now than the sunnier warmth that preceded it. Of course people could be expected to be sensitive over what they chose to make of themselves, so with a tact so well learned as to have become intuition, Mingus replied, 'I see it. That side, nicer to the people she invites to dinner than the ones cutting the hedges yeah, I see, that's her.'

'Shit yeah, always losing it with some poor cunt. She's a

conductor of, you know, of anger, wipes her pain over you and makes it yours. That's the trick, I mean, that is just the trick. And she doesn't work, never has, never met a deadline in her life, just gets others to work for her. All those poxy events, I mean, what's that all about? And what does she know about real life, what it feels like to be us, what goes on in our... in our brains, right?'

'Nothing.'

'*Nothing*, exactly, so we're in agreement, she knows *nothing*. I was watching this thing the other night, it was like all about, all these talking heads were talking about, talking right, about how this certain kind of person is completely mad. And I can't remember the name they had for being this off-your-head, in this particular way, right, but anyway, that was Petula, this name they had, that was her in a nutshell.'

Mingus nodded. He thought of Petula, and then only rarely, as an aloof fantasist who existed very much as a winter blizzard; a natural phenomenon that could be beautiful providing you were wrapped up well, watching it from afar. From the time she had banished him from Regan's life as a small boy he had felt a fatalism regarding any attempt to renew contact with her. In truth he suspected he would be regarded as a contamination and crushed underfoot like a beetle that could not find its way outdoors, if remembered at all. It was a potentially upsetting experience he would rather avoid.

'I don't think she liked me as much as you say Jazz. I mean, I'm flattered you think so, only I didn't feel the love you're talking about so much. I do remember falling off Regan's birthday party list before I was out of shorts, and that was a time ago, years. And she's hardly said a word since, Regan or your mum, we're talking longer than when I went away, way before then. She just stopped coming to my house and I didn't get invited to yours. It was hard enough to still play with you, and that's only because you've never cared what your mum thinks, so you went ahead and were friends with whom you wanted. I'm not first name on the team sheet anymore with Petula. If ever I was. I was just some weird kid for her daughter to hang around with when she was small.'

'Of course, I'm sorry man, yeah. It makes my shit itch, being played off like this, played by my own flesh and blood, and us turning on each other, you and me, it's not right. I didn't mean any offence, right?'

'That's okay.'

'No, that's what it isn't. Not okay no, not right, no. I haven't even said about the worst of the shite yet, you're not going to believe this. A fucking party for Regan, for Regan, and she, Mum, I mean Mam, she expects me to sing and dance and God knows what other shit at it, I shit you not padrone. Your father's right about her, about the... he's *wise*, imagine the shit you have to be acquainted with to be so wise, that's him, you know, Seth...' For a moment Jazzy looked lost, the moonlight casting its spectral hand over his guileless face.

'Yeah, I know, my Dad. Seth, what did he say about her?'

'That's none of your business to know! What happens between, said right, between me and Seth, stays between me and Seth!'

'Sure! Only, I, well, I didn't know he had an opinion on her.'

'How can you say that? How can you stand there and say that?'

'You what?'

'Your trouble, you know Ming, the trouble right, and this is wrong, so wrong of you man, is you don't *respect* that man enough, you don't know what you've got in him, that man, that man is a *genius*, a real one, not some arty twat, a real salt-of-the-earth legend, right? So you can keep your Salvador shitheads because I don't need 'em. Your father, he is *the* fucking man, right...'

Mingus was smiling now, guiding Jazzy towards his van. 'And

you talking about him like that makes me see red Ming, really, because he deserves better than you. He deserves me and you know it. Talking to him like you're some kind of professor of... of shite basically, right. Where do you get off?' Jazzy snorted charitably, 'You don't see it, that's the trouble, don't see what's really important in life, had your fucking head turned, haven't you? All that art-school bull*shite*, you've forgotten what really matters in life, family...'

Jazzy had reached the van and was fiddling with the key.

'Shit. G-o-o-o on, *get in!*'

Mingus yawned. Years later he would hear people lecture on the dangers of drink-driving and wonder how his erstwhile friend had ever survived so many nights like this.

'I feel like walking.'

'What, upset you have I?'

'No, no, just want the air.'

'You mad? It's freezing. Actually, it's not that cold, might walk myself. Nah, fuck it. What do you want to walk for?'

'I like walking at night.' And it was true, Mockery Gap at night was the only way Mingus could stomach the place and free himself of the associations he had thought he would have outgrown and replaced by now, but probably never would.

'To yourself be true, to yourself be enough, that's what I say. See you the other side, there's some shit I need to talk to you about before you go back, to Leeds, seriously, serious stuff, so don't go getting dragged and mounted in the bushes by anything *naaaasty*, walking at night, arty twat!'

'The dark is scared of me.'

'Of course it is. We need to talk. Okay. You take it easy now. I love you man, you know it, don't you? Wouldn't talk to you like I do if I didn't, I'd do anything for you. Love, it makes my world go round. Would yours too, birds like you, I've seen 'em. Look that there's no one in the road, yeh; my bloody rear-view's buggered. Love, think about that man, *think about it.*'

Love. Had Mingus been where he wanted to be, romping with Regan in a loft in Greenwich Village, he would have told Jazzy to shut his impertinent mouth when the subject of the younger Miss Montague came up. But as he was nowhere near this desired end he could, to his shame, share some of the sourness of Jazzy's critique, particularly the sense of becoming a person of less importance on the farm. The matter was not as clear as it was for Jazzy, as Mingus guessed his fate rested as much on future wars of appropriation as it had the meagre pickings of past campaigns. Furthermore, he was confident that love would have its say when it came to the matter of endings, at least in his case.

Like a young Yuri Zhivago, Mingus had abandoned himself to a life of tragedy, so far as love was concerned, the day he found out that Regan had left for Nohallows. True, he was young, extremely so, not sexually active and incapable of understanding abstractions cognitively. However, his eight year-old self could grasp the basics of a broken heart and reel from the sudden disappearance of a loved one, the true helplessness of childhood revealed as one paradigm hastily gave way to another. There had never been anything filial in his regard for Regan, quite the reverse, his feelings were as romantic as befitted an imaginative boy who regretted being at least a decade too young for marriage. The suddenness of Regan's removal was a crime against induction, and like a faithful canine pining for the return of its owner, Mingus drove his parents to desperation asking when Regan would come back, incapable of telling, in spite of his preternatural canniness, that they grasped what he could not.

After the first two summers, Mingus gave up on vocal expressions of his grief and brooded inwardly, wandering along the tall hedges that separated the Montague world from what he was fast understanding was his, in the hope of hearing a rustle from the other side and being reunited with his amour. It did not happen; Regan had other things to do – in London, York, Shatby or indoors, always elsewhere and never at a loss, which was where Mingus usually found himself. Slowly he came to understand that he had loved Regan as a beautiful aspect of his own early existence, later as a symbol and, once she was about to evade his orbit, as a girl. In her absence, the risk of deifying her was overwhelming and it was to girls, flesh-and-blood ones who he could actually come into contact with, that Mingus knew he must turn.

There had been a number of them, first at the local school and then at college, who were taken with his quiet elegance, unashamed oddity and dark good looks, their attention obstinate enough to wake him from his internal dwelling places. Suffering had grown tiresome, as had wondering whether he was a latent homosexual or idealistic fusspot, which in Mockery Gap amounted to near the same malady. Embarking on his own sexual revolution, he discovered, despite a false start with a girl who spent an hour looking for a condom, that he was not impotent, the female form was his preferred erotic outlet, and that if he thought of Regan, his climaxes could be quite satisfying. A number of girls fell in love with him, and though he felt some responsibility for that, his eyes were too focused on escape to go through the pretence of teenage relationships, based on adult equivalents copied from Australian soap operas and tiresome situation comedies. Art school offered an opening at a slightly more elevated level. A humourless affair with one of his tutors, a bitter crone who had said it was impossible for her to make friends with other women under capitalism, had not answered any questions, and nor had a Greek beauty who had pretended to carry his child in a bid to get him to marry her. As with his studies, matters of the heart were hard work (he would enjoy the artlessness of being young much later in his thirties), with one fling after the next mimicking the exact inconsequence of the last. Girls who were tired before their time were drawn to him, mistaking his surface seriousness for nullifying maturity.

This was enough to keep his hands full, but not to forget Regan, or more precisely, her continued existence, doing things at the same time as he was, in different places and with other people. The thought tormented him to a point where it ceased to make sense and he began to wonder whether a thing he cared about so much could even exist outside of his mind. Unfortunately it could, and he saw just the right amount of Regan in the holidays to appreciate the objective fact of her being, glimpses of her fair hair pirouetting past The Wart on her runs his ideal of overflowing beauty.

Waving to her from the kitchen window, a shy hello at Christmas and answering a few questions on the Easter Monday walk comprised the larger part of his annual points of contact, though he noticed she often looked sad, which he took to be, he did not know why, a good sign. Animated by a shrewd self-deprecation that came close to insincerity in his attempts to protect himself, Mingus was always going to annoy the sisters; Regan wondering whether he was making fun of her, Petula detecting chippy impudence in the way Mingus made so much and little of 'what he had been up to'. Nevertheless, she found him watchable and amusing, a face pressed against the glass, refused admittance yet cheerfully game. Doubtless he was a kind of enigma, but not one Petula could take credit for and, therefore, a potential problem to be isolated and perhaps preserved.

For his part Mingus tried to resist the essential deceptions of nostalgia, reminding himself that being cut or rejected by someone could make one think one liked them a lot more than one did, and that Regan may very well be no more than the pretty little rich girl the songs had warned him of. Might her stellar incandescence be a product of his own longing for perfection, or at the very least, a gross overestimation of what was after all only a human being? His insides told him otherwise and reluctantly he accepted that he would never be able to banish Regan Montague from the totemic position she held over his affections.

'Mingus,' his mother said tenderly, not quite able to believe that she had summoned the courage to raise the subject, 'it's no good mooning so. She'll be bound to marry some other bloke and make you unhappy for wanting it to not be that way. You'd be better off larkin' about with one who cares for you, this village is full of girls who'd give you the time of day.'

'What are you talking about Mam?'

'You know what.'

'Mooning? You what! Not me, you're going mad!'

'I don't want you to be hurt. I mean, what do you two have in common? Who's to say if you'll ever even talk to her again! Not properly anyway. It's no basis for love, Mingus.'

'Love? Come on... I don't know what you're on about love for. I've never said anything about love.'

'You don't need to.'

'Agh, you've got this so wrong.'

'Please listen to me Mingus, I never lecture you or tell you what to do with your life. Please, it'll bring you no good, caring for one who never even stops to inquire how you are. You're not in her reckoning pet, I'm sorry, you're not.'

Mingus knew she had a point. The holidays were long and interminable, Regan had every opportunity, should she have wished, to drop in for a cup of tea, ask whether he wanted to go to the cinema or join him on a trek in the woods. With so little to do with one another's present lives, it was not difficult to imagine receding into one another's past. What was their token communication, stacked with significance his end, if not a memory in the process of fading until there would be nothing of substance left to animate it all? So, once again he decided to stop thinking about her and had then gone on thinking about her without much interruption until his latest trip to The Condemned Felon, for if there was one thing that marked this obsession, time spent thinking about Regan passed quickly.

The quaintly dilapidated pub was tucked into a bend at the

bottom of the steep hill that The Heights sat atop. By cutting directly up, past the giant lake that the Montagues had put in to announce their arrival, Mingus could be up at The Heights in half an hour if he did not spare his legs. He had made a link between his thinness and sex appeal and decided walking was the best way to naturally maintain whatever advantages his real parents had given him. With the exception of his first few seconds of being awake, where he experienced Edenic bliss, Mingus found the countryside annoying, mainly due to the absence of city dwellers. Natural beauty was a distracting backdrop; faces were the thing. So much so that he did not notice much about the walk up, the strange glow of the moon, the wood full of noises or the abruptly still spaces flanked by circles of bent old trees, the dead air that surrounded them causing him not the slightest disquiet.

It was not until he came to the clearing that led to the lake that his heart began to beat to the rhythm of human interest. He could see a shape lying in the grass, a mermaid or siren, certainly not a run-of-the-mill night prowler, and he knew at once, knew because it had to be so, that it was Regan. As casually as a man emerging from the woods in the early hours of the morning could, Mingus came off the slope and walked towards the water's edge, from where he hoped to make himself visible without scaring her.

Regan knew she had company. The figure smashing its way out of the undergrowth, silhouetted in the moonlight, was not difficult to notice in an otherwise deathly tranquil clearing. Her first thought was that she was completely safe. This was not a poacher or a rapist. From here her process of elimination was as fast, though more unexpected than Mingus's, since unlike him she had not spent the last few years musing over her neighbour. The boy she used to play with was as boxed away as the rest of her childhood mementoes in the attic. Consequently, there was no reason she knew of as to why she was sure it was Mingus, or why she should have been glad, past natural relief, that it should be so. Mingus had certainly meant far more to her than any of her other companions prior to the age of eight, but having decided to write off everything she had felt before the age of twelve, it was hard to know how she should rank the affections of her earlier self. Mingus was unquestionably, from the little she saw of him, appealing and possessed an arresting face, though Regan's relative sexlessness and absence of romantic élan meant that such observations counted for little. The greatest sensual pleasure she had been able to tease out was a pleasant tingling round the chest whenever Sebastian Coe raced on television, and then only a half-hearted simulacrum of passion that ended before the finishing line. There was also a bicycle saddle she had enjoyed sitting on for vague and disconcerting reasons and a somewhat forced crush on a friend's older brother, diminished by the discovery that he was 'a gay'. It was high time for something *real* to happen, now or never, and it could not be never but nor could it be now; oh what to do! With studied absent-mindedness, as if to say 'what else could a girl think of in the circumstances', Regan peeled off her top and lay there, her small breasts stiffening in the misty chill. There was no time to take herself by surprise, it was already done. Immediately she thought better of it, scared by whatever madness had taken possession of her, and rolled onto her front assuming the position of a nocturnal sunbather. Resting on her stomach, her chin propped on her fists, Regan wondered whether there was enough time to get her vest back on again before Mingus reached her. The figure had stopped but was not far away, and could almost certainly make out the details of her movements. She would have to brave it out.

Mingus had noticed this feverish activity without knowing quite what it denoted. He hesitated, conscious that he had never had to start a conversation in these circumstances before, aware too that caring too much could be his undoing. Success often fell to those who had learnt to not place any value on it. He had waited for Regan for a very long time, things could fall into place but people rarely did, yet here she was. With haste, he strode up to her and asked the stupidest question to ever have taken leave of his mouth: 'Hi, you're Regan, aren't you?'

Regan looked up, as stunned by the inquiry's assumed ignorance as the asker, grateful still to have been given a line to pull on. 'It can't be that dark Mingus.'

'No.'

'But this is a bit random so I don't blame you.'

They both laughed. Mingus stared down by Regan's bare back, 'Were you, were you thinking of going for a swim, now?'

'Um, sure.'

Mingus turned to the water. Despite the warm evening, it looked very cold. He had not swum in the muddy brown lake since he was child and was fairly sure Regan had not either, but here she was, poised to take a midnight dip, alone with him and on the verge of removing the rest of her clothes. Keeping his feet dry was outrageous: he would hold his manhood cheaply if he did not do as fate bid. Anyway, with the amount he had drunk there was more chance that he would drown than freeze. Better that than a marathon dance of nerves and intensities brought on by recollecting an opportunity squandered ever after.

'I'll come too, if that's alright?'

'Sure, why not?'

Regan could think of several reasons why not, and was determined that whatever else happened, her knickers were going to stay on in the water. Getting up, her arms covering her breasts awkwardly, she grimaced, 'This is just so random.'

'It is, yeah…'

'Random.'

Random summed up more than Regan's evening (why had she taken her top off, and having taken it off agreed to swim? To save embarrassment? She was not embarrassed, no more than being by the lake in the first place had embarrassed her, which was not one bit). Her misgivings were those of agency rather than shame. At heart she felt she was an arbitrary person who never knew why she was anywhere, randomness was welcome for the variety it could bring, and with it the hope that something would turn up worthy of being imbued with value and transform her into a woman of destiny. With Petula in charge of the significant decisions, it was sensible to leave the rest of her life to chance. That she was on the verge of making a choice that might count as important, awed her. It was slowing her joints and binding her limbs, a weird density pushing her back from the deed she was set to embrace.

'I can't believe we're doing this,' she murmured, the first of her trainers kicked away, the second resting obstinately on her ankle.

To pretend the present was past, that anything she was about to do had already happened and that this swim was old business to be finished off and not the instigation of the new, was how to proceed.

'It looks chilly, doesn't it?'

'We should just go for it. I only need to get these off,' Regan undid the shoe and tugged at her lycra leggings, 'they're kind of like painted on...'

'Do you want a hand with them?'

'No, um, no I'm okay.'

Neither her legs nor her breasts, voice or words seemed to belong to or want to have anything to do with her. This radical disassociation of feeling was of a piece with Regan's acceptance of the arbitrary and fed into what little she'd had to do with boys. Romance, or more explicitly, kissing, on those rare occasions it occurred, had been as good as forced on her. Floppy mouths that tasted of Dutch courage trying to prise apart her firm lips, were how her dates concluded, courtesy of lads who, having asked her out, did not know what else to do. Like her mother, her way of giving into temptation was to pretend that she did not have a choice, yet unlike Petula she did not feel temptation's call. 'Just be yourself,' she remembered Diamanda saying, absurd advice, as what could be less relaxed and more harrowing than being that? Would going with the flow be any different this time, she wondered? Her gut, a rarely-listened-to part of her anatomy, told her that it might.

'I'm nearly there.'

Mingus was stood with his back to her. He had stripped to his underpants, obviously mindful of the same sanction against total nudity as she, his arse not much bigger than hers, and was eyeing the water as something to be conquered. Without facing Regan, and taking a lot on trust she thought, Mingus bounded into the water and roared with shock as his legs, tangled in weeds, gave way and propelled his body forwards. Bathing in icy water was a great leveller and Mingus was overjoyed to find Regan plunging in by his side, aborting an attempt at breaststroke and instead clinging limpet-like to his boney hips, her legs hanging through the gaps in his elbows as he drew her close. Even in the cold water his erection was hard enough to support a building, and as he bent to face her face, she pressed her blue lips into his neck with an urgency neither of them were prepared for, and bit him.

'Regan!' It was an uncontrollable exclamation of hope revived; the idol Mingus had prayed to, on faith alone, was real. Quickly her mouth found his and her tongue, licking away hopefully, slipped between his chattering lips like a spilt oyster and completed a brief circle before losing all feeling in the warmth of his response. For a moment they held the kiss, Mingus splashing from foot to foot to keep their balance, Regan revelling in the absence of that quality.

Both felt an urge to begin a disorganised conversation in which they said everything on their minds, no matter how unrelated or potentially compromising of former attitudes, but each was salient enough to know they had to get out of the water first or die of hypothermia. On shore huddled under Mingus's trench coat, matters felt different. Now Regan was sure that not knowing what to say was, for once, a sign that she understood the situation better than she would were she talking. Fortunately, Mingus felt no pressure to say anything at all. Reeling from the number of potential scenarios with Regan he had run through and prepared for, he was happy to now have no need of them. Reality was a far better place than the dress rehearsals of yearning had prepared him for.

'Strange,' Regan said at last. Their shivering bodies were so closely entwined that they were practically wearing one another, and though it did not matter what she said, it was time to confirm their closeness in words.

'Strange,' she repeated, '*mad*.'

'Yeah.'

They agreed without really believing it; for very different reasons each thought their presence by the lake to be one of the saner acts of their lives.

'Do you still like to upstage little girls at their parties?' Regan asked.

'I do? I mean I did?'

'It's what my mum said once.'

'She didn't tell me.'

'Perhaps she was afraid she might upset you.'

Mingus smiled broadly; the prospect that Regan might have a sense of humour was one he had never considered.

'That's good of her. I have a thin skin. Very sensitive.'

'So what else have you been up to when you're not doing things like this?'

'I don't think I've time to tell you.'

'You've had a busy few years then?'

'It's a long story.'

'I like quick versions the best. '

'I've been preparing to be good at what I want to do when I leave here. Be an artist.'

'That's cool. I'm not good at anything really.'

Mingus adjusted her head on his shoulder so as to look at her eyes, which had lost their far-off veneer and were inquiring and desirous. His first thought was to tell her he loved her though he feared that could ruin everything, and more importantly, give something of his away that may never be returned, so he said instead, 'Do you remember the party where we were all done up as animals? Had our faces painted by the famous artist friend of your mum's who fell out of that balloon on telly. What was her name? Anyway, I was a fox, all covered in stripes so I looked more like a yellow zebra, and you were a...'

'A rabbit, she made me a sad rabbit! Why couldn't I have been something else? It's not fair, it was my party!'

'She was a painter, a famous artist, she must have seen deep-lying, sad-rabbit tendencies in you.'

'Are they still there?'

Mingus could not honestly say they were: the sad rabbit had become an antelope. They kissed again and it was, when they looked back on it later in their lives, as good as they thought possible.

'You're still a fox.'

'You...' Mingus had to say something that was true of how he felt, whether it would run the risk of making a fool of him or not. Some sincere expression of care was, in its way, as important as getting into the water, for if he were silent, that first act of courage would remain incomplete.

'You've one of the most beautiful souls I've seen in my life.'

Regan laughed, though to his relief not cruelly. 'I've come across quite a few people with mixed motives recently...' She knew it was her wont to see through emotion and thus miss the point of it, a cheap cleverness that passed exams but forgot sunsets. Without the mediation of any mental softener, she thought about Mingus liking her, the reality of it, and stopped breathing. It was a simple thing but even a simple thing was composed of smaller things that could not always be summed up simply, and by the time she began to breathe again, she found she was too scared to speak. 'I don't know what to say, I... I like your soul too.'

And there she lay, wondering whether she would be expelled from instinct forever, until Mingus pulled down her wet pants and made careful love to her. Afterwards she ran her hands over his body so as to remember it when he was gone, for she had no intention of seeing him again and thus risk what had already passed.

CHAPTER SEVEN,
malevolence and misunderstanding.

It was close now, Jazzy could feel it move over the fields and up the hill. He was not following the news that morning, the broadcaster's voice dispassionately moving from the funeral of Terry Thomas to the funeral of the Ayatollah Khomeini without indicating a preference for either, and the main feature of the breakfast programme the wholesale massacre of a small town in Angola he had never heard of. It had once been suggested to Jazzy that if he were to focus on current affairs his own problems would not seem so onerous, an absurdity he dismissed with a sad shake of the head. The only way a massacre in Angola could be worse than being asked to waiter at his sister's party was if he were forced to undergo one after the other; and in all fairness, those who perished in Angolan massacres were pretty used to doing so, whereas Petula was always thinking up novel ways to torment him, the kind that would not take second stage to goings-on in Africa. Jazzy stubbed out the joint. It was risky to be toking this early in the day, but as he had hardly slept, the demarcation point between the night before and morning had faded into an indecipherable formality. He looked at his watch; six forty-five, Jill would be up in fifteen minutes for her job at Pug and Sons, a local solicitor's where she was a typist, much to Jazzy's disgust. They did not, in his opinion, need the money, and even if they did Jazzy never noticed it being spent on anything worthwhile, only bills and repairs that should have been Noah's responsibility. By choosing to work at Pug's Jill was as good as using her salary to normalise their oppression, especially as she ring-fenced it from him in an account they did not share, ostensibly 'in case they had children'. It was yet another example of her failure to live in the present. He wished he had thought of putting it like that the night before instead of knocking the bedroom door off its hinges in a fit of frustration, sending splinters flying into every corner as he stomped his foot through its plywood frame. He could not remember precisely what had sparked the argument, only that one occurred on his return from the pub and after a muddled start settled on a few well-worn themes, continuing until Jill was too tired to speak and nodded off. The first time this happened Jazzy had shaken her awake again, furious that she was not ready to take his pain seriously enough to stay up and keep him company with it. But Jill had looked so angry the second time he had done this, spitting at him in point of fact, that Jazzy was taken uncharacteristically aback. No matter what the provocation Jill did not normally react in this way, all the more startling since after snarling at him she had promptly fallen asleep again without so much as an apology.

With a bong in hand and a rug slung over his shoulder Jazzy decamped to the kitchen to recover from his shock. Getting wasted was no longer a simple way of passing the time; it really worked. At least this way the first thing Jill would feel on rising was guilt for having as good as banished him there, stoned and alone. He could not countenance, however cold, uncomfortable or paranoid he grew, slinking back into bed and giving her the solace of hoping she had not hurt him. Jazzy also enjoyed the feeling of losing control, or more control than he was normally used to losing, staring out into the vastness of a world he was but a tiny (but very angry) part of. Rather than diminishing the size of his problems when confronted by the universe, agonising by the window expanded Jazzy's angst into something as large as the sky itself, propelling him to dizzying and sublime fits of pique. Problems and regrets attained new heights of clarity and catharsis, as his conversation with himself rose to dazzling peaks of eloquence, the only pity being there was no device to record and play back the results of his adventures in solipsism. Having reached enlightened self-knowledge, Jazzy's voices evaporated into puffs of smoke enabling him to drop into a peaceless slumber, coming to once his face rubbed against the sticky linoleum table. This cycle had gone on for hours, broken by a vision at five in the morning of a cluster of clouds that formed a giant Peace symbol in the sky; Jazzy taking this as a sign that all would be well, then deciding an hour later that all wasn't, which was where he remained until Jill quietly entered the kitchen. Her hair was lank and wet from her rushed shower, a cheap over-sized blazer and grey skirt giving her the air, as Jazzy so often said, of a cut-price Member of Parliament.

There were signs of irritation round Jill's twitching lip that made Jazzy feel as though last night's argument was in danger of being carried into breakfast more seamlessly than he would have liked. He had prepared for this eventuality, working out several versions of what he wanted to say, though by the time the cocks had started to crow, his preparations had distilled into just two words, 'Fuck you'. This morning some instinct, possibly tact, held him back, for there was a new element in the mix, one he had seen signs of but never apprehended before in her dewy eyes. The best way he could characterise it was rebellion, which was absurd, as Jill had no cause to throw over any authority he was aware of other than the one that ground them both down, The Heights *shite*; yet it was evident that it was nothing so general as their overall situation that caused her to pout angrily as he cleared his throat.

'Well, another night where no one's the winner,' Jazzy offered diplomatically, drawing heavily from his joint, 'same as it always is. No winners, only losers.'

It was a tacit understanding between them that though their arguments usually originated with Jazzy, the reason they did so was because of Jill's lack of understanding, so that officially the blame lay with them both. It kept their relationship on an even keel without one feeling more put out than the other, whoever may have been more at fault for their most recent spat. Jazzy did not mind taking his share of the knout and would have eventually made it known that he regretted any harsh words he could no longer remember, so long as Jill acknowledged the aggressive passivity that had provoked them. Quid pro quo. What he was not used to was being looked through like he was not there. Must he bear the guilt of confusing himself for someone else lost in his own life? No, he would not allow the tables to be turned. He put out the joint and pushed away the ashtray calmly.

'Jill? Jill, I'm talking to you, *right*?'

Jazzy looked down at the joint he had just crushed. If he straightened out the stub it was probably good for another couple of tokes, and to be honest, he could use the help. He drew the ashtray over again and lit the stub, the flame from the zippo catching his lips and blackening the end of his already-sooty nose.

Coughing, he tried again: 'The thing with fighting, right, is that there are no winners, period; you'd may as well dig two graves. That's where it leads, seriously. This can't keep happening to us, turning on ourselves, fighting amongst ourselves, you see what I'm saying? It's madness. As above so below, you know?'

If she did know she was not telling. Jill was not only ignoring him, but curling her lip as she stepped over the broken shards of door in a way that made it look like she thought him at fault for the damage, shaking her head and laughing sardonically to herself. Jazzy sat upright in his chair, all pretence at being relaxed dispelled. What he was detecting was a frightening lack of respect. He was not used to it. Jill loved him and her high regard, though he often brought it into question, was a factor he could always take for granted once the drama ended, as he now decided it should have.

'Are you listening to me? Am I talking to myself here?' He could hear the panic in his voice, trying to control it as he went on, 'We're trying to have a conversation, yeah? So why am I hearing only one of us talking? It's time to cut this shit out! Come on Jilly, grow up. I'm talking to you!'

Jazzy was no stranger to not getting what he wanted from life. What he had no experience of was to lose what he previously had; it was unacceptable, if not impossible, that it could be happening, he and Jill were spiritually conjoined and her respect for him was an essential part of that covenant. She must really be going mad.

'Jilly, sit down, I'm trying to talk to you for fuck's sake, you've got to listen. Are you alright, you don't look it... is everything alright?'

With her back turned to him Jill filled the kettle and pulled out a mug, only one, pointedly ignoring her usual custom of filling a pot for both their uses. If this was a glimpse of a new order, one where the most basic customs common to their shared life were not observed, the future was a desolate and unnatural place he had no wish to appease.

'Jesus, I'm asking you how you are! What the fuck do you think you're *doing*? For fuck's sake sit down and look at me.' Jazzy's teeth were clenched together; if she did not listen to him he knew he would end up throwing something. No, that was no good, the broken door was proof of that, and God knows how many other objects had been martyred to his temper; he had to try another way.

'We've got to talk about this, if we stop talking we're dead, you've got to keep communicating Jill, it's what makes us humans, right? We're humans, *right*? Come on, talk to me. For fuck's sake talk to me or I'll break something!'

Jill said nothing, nothing to that or any of the other conversational openers Jazzy tossed her way over the following five minutes. With her back still turned to him, she drank her tea, at what must have been a scalding temperature, and, with a single-ness of purpose that did not come naturally, moved to pick up her bag and leave the house.

Jazzy was not going to let her get away so easily, and though it would have been simple to trip her – she was walking past him like a robot with limited programming – he did not want to give her any excuse to be angry. The moment called for subtlety; he knew he must effect a thaw without turning up the heat.

Grabbing her arm as she bent down to pick up her handbag, rather harder than he meant to, Jazzy pressed his face to hers and whispered hoarsely, 'I love you, why are you doing this to *us*?'

At the angle at which he held her it was impossible for her to not look into his eyes and balk at the proximity of one she believed was stronger than her. She had nowhere to go but to return his stare and, from there, crack.

'What do you mean, why am *I* doing this,' she broke, 'why are *you* doing it, always doing it, every time you come back pissed?'

It wasn't the reply Jazzy was hoping for but if she was talking to him then he had won her back; Jill did not have the nerve to resist the most powerful emotion she knew, the need for a bit of passion in life. 'Good, we're getting somewhere. At last. You've been looking at the symptoms and not the disease. So what if I come back here wrecked, why do you think I do it? Yeah? You think I'm destroying myself for *fun*? For *fun*? Come on, you're cleverer than that. What sends me that way? Exactly. Dig deep-er. This isn't about me coming back pissed, right?'

'What? What are you talking about?'

'I'm talking about you, I'm talking about us. You need to work out what you want Jilly, seriously, because this is crazy, the way you're carrying on, you're in a crisis. What do you want? I can't keep pretending everything is alright when you're going round the bend all the time. Why do you think I step up and try and get a rise from you? You've got to work out what you're all *about*, what you want from life. And it's not just you, right. You need to work out what *we're* all about, you know? *Us.* I mean all you're going to do acting like a pissy secretary is leak away this thing we have, that we've worked so hard to keep when everything's been against us, wanting us to fail, my mum, Noah, your parents, everyone, they want us broken up, destroyed, finished, right? Yeah, you know it... and I know you don't want that. To give them the satisfaction of having broken something beautiful.' This was his trump card. The siege mentality of love against the odds, engendered and strengthened for having been attacked from all sides. It was Jazzy's usual way of effecting reconciliation, tried and tested in the history of relationships since time immemorial and a tribute to the unconscious way he had picked up elements of his mother's statecraft.

'I don't know...'

'I *do* Jilly, I *do* know. I know what's wrong and I know what's right. Now come on and get real, right. I'd give anything for us to be happy, why do you think I keep on here if it isn't for us both? You think I like it? You know better than that. Don't let them win, don't let them beat us, don't give them the pleasure. It's what they want, have done all along. I love you Jill, can't you see that? It's the most obvious thing in my life, the rest of it's shit compared to that. Why else would I fuck myself up if I didn't care?'

Jazzy raised his arm, a prominent cut from a smashed vase dispatched a week earlier trailing down his arm like a malevolent centipede, 'Why else?'

This was too much for Jill and she burst into tears. Tears, Jazzy calculated, she needed to shed to be herself again. To be herself and to be his. Tenderly he comforted her, holding her in his relieved grip until she was finished and ready to leave for work.

*

Breakfast at the Hardfield's was never the most talkative of meetings, Jenny's banal and often surreal ramblings constituting the spoken part of the ritual, Mingus's head buried deep in *Melody Maker* and his father's in the *Daily Mirror* the rest. One of them would occasionally chip in to ask Jenny to repeat a detail out of courtesy for having prepared the meal, or chuckle contentedly if there was an anecdote she seemed particularly pleased with. Father and son took care to not be too funny themselves as Jenny was not a woman who was at ease with the comical, restricting themselves to a little gentle teasing if the moment required it.

Jenny had been talking for over half an hour, deliberately taking her tea as slowly as possible in anticipation of what she hoped would be Mingus's eventual arrival. By the time he joined them, grinning imbecilely, she had nearly run out of things to say, yet seeing him look so handsome and happy, she tacked back to a story she had finished earlier, and resumed it with gusto.

'So I said to her, "What did *you* just say?" and she said, "Well what do they do? That's what I want to know, just what is it exactly that they do, tell me that?"'

Seth, busily buttering another slice of bread, grunted loudly. He had, for once, been listening and appreciated the story, or at least appreciated that it had only been told once before.

'And I said, "How can I tell you? Who's to tell you because it's not a thing to tell, not this, not really, so who's to say?" It isn't is it? A thing you can just be one way or the other about, at least I don't think so, do you?'

Emitting a consenting humph, Seth piled the bread into his mouth, making more communication between them temporarily impossible. Mingus was sat with his head resting on his fist, looking like an engraving of the young Keats, his love-lorn look suggesting that he could easily put up with a thousand such stories today.

'And she went, "Well *I* say. Nature. It's just sat there, what does it do?" and I really can't believe I'm hearing this so I crack and say "It's nature Marg, it doesn't have to *do* anything," and she just sits there and says, "Well who says it doesn't? Flowers, I mean what do they *do*?"as if I'm the one missing some really important part of what she's trying to tell me. I mean *really*! And on she goes, I don't know whether she's on the Mogadon again or what, and now she's telling me that if nature were to disappear tomorrow, and I ask her what part, and she says flowers, then she says she wouldn't even notice it gone, can you believe. Because the only part she's interested in are the whales, *whales*, I mean for heaven's sake, so I knew what to say to that, "Well whales are just sat there Marg, they don't do a lot either, maybe swim a bit to stop themselves from drowning but what do they *do*? Not much but it's no reason for their not being allowed to exist is it?" and she said, "Alright, stuff the whales too, give me something useful any day," and I go, "What's useful?" and she says, can you believe, she says, *"Michael Douglas's bum!"* Well I say, what do you say to that!'

Seth scratched the back of his head and refilled his cup. Mingus stared dreamily into the hazy morning light filling the room with its wondrous aura; life was too good. He barely noticed the plate of food his mother put down in front of him, breaking off her story to do so.

'Anyway, I wasn't letting her get away with that kind of smut, not at the expense of whales and flowers so I said, "Well it's very pretty, nature, prettier than your Michael Douglas, the chubby womanising so and so, and if it wasn't for nature, he wouldn't even have a bum and nor would you!" He makes me want to wretch really whenever I see him, he's so awful, carrying on as he does at his age, he must be at least forty now...'

'Oh he's not so bad' said Seth.

'Oh he is.'

'I liked him in, what do you call it, *Easy Rider*, with the motorcycles.'

'That was Dennis Douglas pet, Henry Fonda's son, the Douglas we're talking about is Burt Lancaster's boy, and I didn't have very much time for him either, truth be told, divorcing all his wives.'

'You're thinking of Kurt Lancaster love. And it was someone else that did the divorcing. A woman, not a bloke.'

'Lancaster Douglas, that's it, well he was no better. Anyway, what I told her is so far as nature is concerned anything that makes life easier on the eye is alright by me, eh Mingus, that's what an artist would say isn't it? Even a chocolate orange.'

Mingus, full of the glorious anaesthetic of the night before, his miraculous accomplishment teetering on that point where sensation is lost to memory, and memory to a glorious future, merely smiled.

'Eh Mingus? That's what an artist would say, isn't it?'

'Sure Mam.'

Jenny basked in the comforting glow of approval and, not appreciating that she had been delivered a feint, moved onto other matters at the very point her son had hoped she would shut up shop for the day.

'How was Jazzy last night? That pub does good business out of the both of you. You two do enjoy your evenings there, don't you, up all hours nattering away, I wonder what you find to talk about, I'm not sure there isn't a girl or two you keep down there, in The Felon. Is there? Jazzy was always turning up with someone new before he got mixed up with that little thing. How's he doing with her I wonder? It feels like ages since we last saw him.'

This would have normally annoyed Mingus. It was bad enough spending an evening with Jazzy without being asked by someone who had seen him only the morning before, and every other morning for countless years, how he was, as though he might have undergone a sudden change that afternoon and become a butterfly. It upset him to see his family absorb Montague gossip and absurdities with their own, depressing him even more when his mother thought this trivia might act as a bridge to reach him.

'There are no lasses in The Felon Jenny, it's a drinkers' pub.'

Jenny chose not to hear the note of caution in her husband's voice, and continued with her well-meaning interrogation, 'So what did you talk about love? I bet Jazzy was still raging about the party eh? You should have seen his face when he came in yesterday, ooh it was a picture, I don't think we've ever seen him so angry, have we Seth? Oh I do love his moods! And when he holds court. Telling us what she could do with her filthy uniform and all sorts. The way he was carrying on I thought that boy, that boy will have a heart attack before he's thirty, honestly, he was fuming!'

'I can't remember what we talked about. But it sounds like you already know how he is without me having to tell you Mam.'

'Oh he must have said something, didn't he say anything about the uniform? He must have, she really knows how to push his buttons, she does. A uniform, you have to laugh. You'd think she'd know him by now. '

Mingus took a bite of egg and drew the sports section of his father's paper towards him with no thought of reading it, merely to establish a barrier between his ears and his mother's chatter. He hated himself for it, but loathed what he perceived to be his mother's brute ignorance, his father's, so much plainer, always much easier for him to bear.

'A blazer I think,' said Seth, hoping to draw attention away from his son, 'she wants him to wear a blazer. Like one of those stewards on the QE2.'

'He'll look *ever* so nice in one of those. If she gets him into one that is! I should have a word with him, there'll be some nice girls there I'll bet, she's bound to have some of her friends there, pretty friends at that girls' school, Regan I mean, he'll want to look his best in front of them, *they* won't mind him in a uniform I'll bet, he'll look very presentable once his hair's swept off his face. It really doesn't suit him so long. I'm surprised they don't get his nose when he goes in for a haircut.'

Dimly Mingus became aware that he was listening. His mother had used a name he did not want to hear uttered by anyone else, not yet anyway and not in connection with Jazzy.

'That might turn Jazzy's head, a lot of pretty girls for him to run round after, "bring us this, bring us that", he'll end up loving it I'm sure.'

'He's got a girl Jen, stop making trouble,' interrupted Seth, 'he's as good as married to Jill and she's good to him, nice and sensible. He needs that. He's not the most grounded lad. Very up-and-down.'

'At his age he should be footloose and fancy-free, eh Mingus? He'll have a crop to choose from at the party however much he might not want to be there. Every grey cloud eh?'

'What party Mam?'

'He's finally awoken! The great sea beast! I thought you'd never stir, and what time did his lordship get in last night I wonder?' Having achieved her objective Jenny switched the onus of her conversation to things that really interested her. 'Were you wearing enough clothes last night, it was freezing, you don't want to go back to your college with a cold, you'll be ill all term, you're thin enough as it is and that coat you always wear is useless...'

'What party? What girls are you talking about?'

'When?'

'Just now, you were saying that there was going to be a party somewhere here. *What* party?'

'Oh! Haven't you heard? I would have thought Jazzy would have talked about nothing else. He was so worked up, I mean, really, it's only a *party* I told him!'

'No, I don't remember. He didn't say anything. *What* party? No, hang on, he did say he had to be butler at something... but *what* party?'

'Don't worry love, it's not going anywhere!' Jenny was beside herself, she at last had something to say that might interest her son, a golden nugget that would ensure that for however short a time, he would actually listen to her.

'Come on Mam. What were you on about?'

'The party of course, your old friend, *Regan*, it's her one, she's having it.'

'What? She's *having* it or she's *had* it?'

'Oh, it's still to come, but not long to go.'

'Soon then?'

'Yes, she's having a great big bash put on for her, a coming-out kind of thing I think they're called. Petula's arranging everything of course, so you can guess what kind of party it'll be from that. Frocks and dinner jackets and all sorts. Honestly, I think she'd be just as happy if she were left to it in a barn with her friends. All that sort of razzmatazz is wasted on the young, even her sort.'

'When... when's all this meant to be happening?'

'In a week!'

'It isn't.'

'It is!'

'No.'

'Well why not? As far as I know the Montagues don't run their social plans past you first do they dear?'

'I'd have known if it was happening. She'd have said something.'

Jenny laughed outright, 'Are you having a laugh love? When's the last time Petula Montague sought your consultation, really!'

Seth folded his paper in two, the passion in his son's voice waking a protective instinct that he felt helpless before.

'I know her better than you do, she'd have said something to me.'

'You must be out of your mind Mingus, I've known Petula before you were even born. Of the two of us it's me that knows her better, really it is. She invites me into her house, has done for years. We were quite, quite close once...'

'I don't mean bloody Petula, I mean *Regan*!'

'Oh I see! You mean her, do you. Regan, well. I don't know what to say. Poor boy, you thought you'd hear from her... well, I don't know what to say to that, I mean, it's been a while since you and she were going to each other's parties isn't it? Not exactly last week that you went off to London together is it? And really, there is no need to swear at me, really there isn't.'

'She'd have told *me*, of course she would.'

Jenny laughed again, a little startled, 'Is there something you're not telling me Mingus? Because from where I'm sat this is a little puzzling, love. Is there any reason why she should be telling you about her parties other than politeness?'

'It doesn't matter, it's nothing.'

'Don't clam up pet. It looks like it does matter. If there's a story I want to know, I'm your mother.'

Mingus had pushed away his tea and was looking slightly manic, a rare trace of colour emerging from under his olive skin. Jenny felt something she had hooked withdrawing to a place where it would never take her bait again, as if a once-in-a-life-time opportunity to break the riddle of who this stranger was, and gain an understanding of her son, was on the verge of being lost forever.

'Come on Mingus, you can talk to us. Have you been... in touch with Regan?'

'I said it's nothing Mum. Just forget all about it, alright? Why do you keep going on?'

'Now Mingus, you don't need to be like that; if there's something you know that I don't...' Jenny paused. It struck her that she had enjoyed delivering news of the party precisely because of the effect she was sure it would have on Mingus. Her responsible motive for doing so was to drive any fanciful ideas about Regan out of his head, and if the most direct way was also likely to be the most painful, then he would thank her once the pain wore off and good sense prevailed. But she had an irresponsible reason too, motivation so unmotherly that she wondered in the brief moment it took to acknowledge it whether it were hers at all or some miasmic confusion brought on by a badly boiled egg.

'My, what are we all so het up for dear? We were only talking. And it is only a *party*. Let's just calm down a bit. I can't see why we can't have a conversation about our neighbours without your going all wild. There's going to be a party in the house, they've had lots of them, the only difference is that now it's the daughter's turn, and if you ask me, she'll turn out just like her mother because that's what her mother wants and her mother is a woman who always gets what she wants. Not like me or your Dad. Or you even.'

Mingus stuck his fork into the end of a sausage and watched the fat ooze out onto the plate, the dead pig undergoing a second death as unwanted food he would play with.

'Forget about it, just think of me as mad, alright? I don't want to know any more so just shut up!'

'There's no call for that! I mean, be sensible, you've had parties you haven't invited her to, haven't you Mingus, plenty, and I doubt she's made a fuss over them... scowling at her mother for no good reason; of course she hasn't.' Jenny was angry with her son; his belief, unarticulated it was true, that he could waltz into a world that would not have her or Seth, and belong in it, was alarming enough on its own. What made her sick to her heart was that he might be right. She wanted to protect him from becoming the plaything of his betters, a grownup version of what she had seen him turned into as a little boy. It was to her great shame, and would be whenever she had cause to remember it, that she relished what she said next: 'Perhaps you could go love, they need another waiter...'

Seth glared at her and put down his paper.

'For God's sake, Jen!'

Mingus sprang from the table and headed straight for the door. Once outside he thought there must be some mistake, he knew Regan inside out, their souls had met, she had practically worn his penis and made love to him with it, how could she have neglected to tell him about a party? It was inconceivable that there could be anything about Regan's life his mother knew that he did not, how could there be after what had passed between them? And how ridiculous it would seem if his very next communication to her was a question, or worse, a tiresome request.

There he stood like a carpet that was about to have the dust beaten out of it, looking towards The Heights in the hope that it was not too late to hear an invitation being issued from Regan's open window. Nothing came. Mingus tried to catch his breath, even though he was not in the process of moving anywhere. Perhaps it was because it was only a party, a thing of shallow insignificance that Regan did not wish to waste her own time with far less his... but if the party meant nothing to her it was even more reason for her to have told him, passingly and lightly, of its existence. Could she be ashamed of him, a boy suited to the dead of night but unfit for daylight consumption? It was too awful to contemplate, which of course did not mean it was not true. The weather was crisp with what Mingus now took to be dark potential. His heart was broken, too easily he knew, its course not his to command but frighteningly not Regan's either. He felt for it with his hand, its survival no more assured than a blister which the most indifferent remark, however slight, could rip and empty. Life, at least his, was destined to be tragic after all.

Taking off across the fields Mingus began the journey down to the lake. He knew he would not find Regan there but he did not know what else to do and could not bear remaining with himself, not in motion.

The walk already felt like an exercise in nostalgia and by the end of the holiday would, to Mingus's unconsolable disappointment, prove to be that, the real object of his journey having undergone the mental taxidermy common to those things that are no longer one's own.

*

Regan did not consider eavesdropping a noxious habit. Usually she lacked the relevant context to understand what she overheard. An absence of success in gaining any advantage from her nosiness made up for the frequency with which she sped round corners she had been lurking behind, a moral balance struck between failure and pointless deception. Despite being as affected by their lakeside encounter as Mingus, the practical side of Regan's nature had triumphed and she woke in the knowledge that she should seek medical advice. To that end she needed access to the telephone as she had only a vague notion of her gynaecological position or what clinical steps she should take to avoid having a baby or catching Aids. Needing the telephone badly on any given morning in The Heights was an exasperating condition, and it was best to simply dismiss the idea or walk down the track to the The Wart or The Pimple to use theirs, as guests frequently had to. The Petula Communications Cooperation was in full swing by eight o'clock and did not subside until ten-thirty at the earliest, particularly in the run up to 'an occasion', which was how Petula divided up her life, Regan's party having become the latest such event.

Dressed in one of Petula's robes, her bare feet covered in dry mud and bits of grass, Regan tiptoed down the corridor, her mother's voice booming under the floorboards a minefield in the process of detonation. There were phones on every floor, each wing and most of the main rooms, added to which was Petula's new acquisition, the cordless phone plus the mobile brick she travelled in the car with, but only one incoming line to the house. The temptation to simply pick up a receiver and listen to who was on the other end was great, Petula's half of the conversation plainly audible to all but the hard of hearing. Usually boredom prevented Regan from this subterfuge, that and the number of times she had listened listlessly to calls before, the conversations all part of an interchangeable assemblage of chatter that seemed to have replaced the role of silence in her life. However Petula's telephonic activity had been so relentless that morning, a menagerie of shrieks, growls, inducements and hushed whispers, that Regan, who had hardly had time to drop off to sleep before this onslaught began, wondered whether this could possibly be business as usual, or the prelude to an blow-out which superseded what even The Heights had born witness to.

'Tell her *it is* top bloody priority, okay?'

It took Regan a few moments to work out what this latest squall was about, and even then she was surprised when she discovered.

'I don't see why she shouldn't, I mean it's simply not on to cherry-pick what one does or does not turn up to. Friendship doesn't work like that, the shame is that she seems to need to be told. I need to know by today, at the latest. Got it?'

It was the party Petula had promised for her which she had completely forgotten about. Judging by the racket, it was still very much on her mother's mind. Regan's incredulity centred largely on how Petula could have become so animated about it, having held, attended and turned down a flock of similar occasions as a matter of course on a weekly basis. In any case, her party was likely to be a second- or third-division affair compared to the cream of Petula's calendar, hardly worth testing the strength of her popularity over.

'In that case tell her it is an emergency, I want my daughter and her friends to be stimulated, not bored to bloody death. Stratford can bloody wait. Tell her I said that, yes, tell her from me, she's been bloody useless the last couple of years, she'd doggy-paddle across the Atlantic to watch Jeremy Irons take a shit on Broadway, the least she could do is repay some loyalty and make a young girl happy. Yes, very virtuous, I know, that's me all over, very good, good job, *byeeee*.' Petula hung up with a flourish and congratulated herself quietly.

Stopping by the phone on the upstairs landing, Regan waited for it to go again; a lapse of about thirty seconds had passed since Petula put it down. Her mother usually liked to savour her chats before embarking on more. She did not have to be proactive this time as an incoming call rang impatiently, Petula allowing it three rings for the sake of decency before picking up.

'Petula Montague. Good God, do you know I was just thinking of you!'

Regan rather absently lifted the receiver a fraction after Petula's noisy declaration. The call must have been part of an ongoing conversation as her mother leapt into the middle of the matter at hand, her tone appeasing and compliant and therefore quite unlike her.

'Yes, of course there'll be *girls* Tim, loads of the wretched little things, it is a girl's party after all. Are you worried about the ratio, don't be, I mean there'll be plenty of older women there too; no, not geriatrics, but mainly it'll be girls, quite a few of them at any rate. How many? Well Regan's invited eight or nine I think. You don't think that's enough? No, it isn't really is it? I can get her to invite more, no I'm sure it'll be enough notice, these are teenagers, I'm sure their diaries aren't full to bursting, they are a bit scattered but their parents could always pull their weight. Yes, yes, I'll make sure we only ask the pretty ones! I don't want Crispin Fogle sat next to some virgin with spots and braces either. Of course, I know most of your clients are used to models at Cannes, well, I can't promise them that but some of these girls, once they've got a bit of makeup on them, well, you'd never know how old they are. Yes, real stunners. Oh, you are pressing me a bit, did he really say that, that he wanted to know what the filly situation was? Cor, what a way of putting it!

Well assure him as his agent that he has nothing to worry about
on that score. You are insistent Tim, incorrigible... Regan, well
of course she's beautiful, she's my daughter, yes, we'll sit her
between Crispin and Dex. Yes I quite agree we don't want to
waste her on homos! You really are too much Tim! That's my
flesh and blood you're talking about! Please! Stop it!'

Tim Tinwood was sure he was too much, but having gone all
the way before with this woman's family why not do so again?
He had yet to meet anyone who was as crazy for stardust as
Petula Montague, or one as likely to give in to audacity as use
it. Tinwood had sailed too close to the wind in his time, and
been burnt often enough to develop an astute sense of whom
he could afford to be 'himself' with. Petula had first struck him
as a terrifying Gorgon who had strayed into the wrong epic, her
interest in showbusiness verging on the arbitrary, but halfway
through that first day in Shatby she fell into place, and by the
time he saw her return to the farm in tears after the debacle at
the restaurant, he knew she was a woman he could work with.
Far from being a formidable matriarch, or a randy rack of mut-
ton that wanted to hump a poet, Petula was going for something more complicated, the ultimate ineffability of her search
its great weakness. What she wanted from her actors, scribes
and artists was an immaterial reward she did not believe she
deserved, a return she was afraid she was not good enough for,
worrying her to a point where she must have it at any cost all
the time. The desire for this kind of invisible distinction, a social
substitute for religious grace, was the mistake many a merito-
rious person who believed they were not 'good' at anything fell
into, except in Petula's case it was a raging, warring complex
she was barely conscious of the consuming force of. If Tinwood
was right, and the years had not disabused him, he knew he had
her down for what she was and, having got her, was careful to
instigate close observation with a view to never letting her go,
his client list the perennial bait she could not resist the lure of.

MALEVOLENCE AND MISUNDERSTANDING

For a visibly sweaty man, who overcompensated for his nerves with colourful and aggressive verbiage, it paid for Tinwood to know his way around the sewage system of human insecurity, as it paid him to know the canals, estuaries and lakes of high aspiration. The rule of thumb that rarely let him down was that a person's natural state was the opposite of their self-image, all one had to do was hold one's nose and try not to laugh at the mess created by the conceptual confusion. In this respect Petula had been a stickler, and with a carelessness he really ought to have checked, it was impossible to not have a little fun with her when the occasion demanded.

'Oh do, do come off it Timmy. I mean come on! He should be here anyway, do we really have to promise him that? No, I'm not saying that that *might* not happen, only that saying it definitely will is a bit much really, isn't it better to just let nature take its course? Oh you're only joking? Well of course, ha ha!'

Surprisingly, making a conquest of two of her kids while the others fled to Chinkies had given Tinwood sleepless nights for over a decade. With a past like his the security of the present moment was never more than a denunciation away. That sibling sandwich was a risk he would never repeat, certainly not with upper-middle-class children who had access to materials, and in deference to that fear he had been careful to avoid physical pen-etration below the waist, though both Jazzy and Evita had had to clean their teeth and wash their legs once he'd finished with them. Still, they hadn't been hurt, violence was a line he would not cross. How the English hated a fuss, anything to avoid one and its sequel, social embarrassment – only violence could rouse them to anger, and then only sometimes. That's why no one had come after him. It owed a great deal to the culture he chose to operate in, never leaving any marks and picking his victims well. Kids who did not wish to get into trouble and parents who would rather the family suffered in secret than gain a reputa-tion for scandal or unclubbability, and failing that, little brutes who knew they would never be believed. Without a cassock or schoolmaster's robe to hide behind, allies like these were a necessary part of his success, for unlike some contemporaries, he did not waste time giving promises of television appearances or trips to Chessington Zoo to silence his victims. Whatever else they might say about him behind his back, he had the integrity to get his share of candy without recourse to any soft-soap bullshit, a point of principle of which Tinwood was proud.

'But he can't sleep *in there* Tim. Diamanda, yes, Diamanda, Regan's best friend, Diamanda, she's already in there with two other girls. I'm having to get a bunk bed in or sleep them on the floor in bags. He won't mind that? You *are* impossible Tim! I've half a mind to let you organise this thing on your own! Really, you are, no don't, stop it, that's just being wicked!'

Tinwood reckoned on at *least* fourteen years' grace before most children started talking, allowing for a handful that never would and a brave few who had never stopped. As far as Petula's two were concerned that time was up and who knew what buried tales might be finding their way up to a bosom buddy, social worker, or worse, a journalist. Of course, his fear depended on the youngsters wanting revenge, their not enjoying his 'breaking-in' ceremony and growing up with a view to avenging their lost innocence. Yet it did not have to play out that way, however bad it might have seemed from their end at the time. The brats might even move to a more nuanced position as they matured. Perhaps even a grudging gratitude, or kinky acknowledgement that had it not been for him they would never have been set on their way as sexual beings, free of the ridiculous hang-ups he grew up with.

'I know it's a party and I should loosen up, that's easy for you to say Tim. But I'm the one that has to bloody live here after you've all gone! You should try living in the country, absolutely everybody remembers everything!'

He was a gambling man and there was no sense in exchanging

pleasant memories for panic, that was doing the prudes' work for them. Life was nothing without a little sugar and spice and if the price for a wild night was ten sleepless years then so be it. Anyway, the key was their mother's reliability. Petula either knew and did not care, knew and did not believe her children or did not know but would not have cared if she had. And now the same woman was helping him arrange a ball for a roster of the randiest young actors in the country. Ludicrous! Even if he had wanted to proceed along other lines how could he resist steering the evening into an orgy? The cast and location were just too perfect.

'Be sensible Tim, this is North Yorkshire, not Monte Carlo, Greenwich Village or, I don't know, *Soho*. Yah I know all that but *come on*. That kind of entertainment would not do. It would be like putting Audrey Hepburn in a triple XXX, you're getting carried away. No, I mean it, I'm going to have to put my foot down this time. The youngest person there will be no more than *fourteen*. Be sensible for heaven's sake! No I've already said I *mean it*, do you want me to get arrested?'

Tinwood had not the subtlety or patience to consider a fourth position that his hostess might hold regarding the defilement of her children. Petula did not want to know because she knew she would have cared if she had. Like a student of history offered proof of her country's past crimes, Petula chose to embrace the myth of imperial glory, paternalism and a rose-tinted past over the painful reckoning of famine, war and disease ushered forth by revision. Pretending that Jazzy and Evita's outbursts regarding their rough use at the hands of her most useful contact, a man they had never liked, were 'true' did no one any good, casting doubts over the mental health of both children if anyone else were to find out. Recognising the accusations as backdated inventions calculated to hurt her, the crimes they fragmentarily accused Tinwood of copied off an American network drama, spared her the humiliation of having to destroy a network of friendships she had worked hard to sustain. And in fairness, there had never been an occasion when either her son or daughter had come to her in a calm and considered fashion with a report of what actually happened, only snippets worked into shouted arguments and denunciations that amounted to little more than garbled innuendo, making it quite impossible to know what they were talking about. A court of law would have dismissed the whole fuss in a finger flick, though thankfully, neither child had the confidence in their lies to take matters that far.

'Does he really? I'm... I suppose I am a bit, why? He doesn't seem that sort of person in his films. You know, looking at his roles you wouldn't automatically think that of him! Christ Tim, you don't 'alf represent some fruitcakes...'

Later Petula would wonder whether there wasn't *something* to these frenzied outbursts, even allowing for their inconsistencies and contradictions, lapses of cohesion and confused chronology. The thought that her children were far too like her, given to the odd infelicity or lapse into unspecified exaggeration, and therefore not to be trusted, was weighed against other emerging concerns. Their behaviour, always curious, was simply too deranged, once they entered adolescence, to not be laid at the door of a trauma. The last place she wanted the finger of suspicion to fall was at her door; after all, what had she done wrong? And it was no use blaming Anycock, useful as he was for that purpose, as the exhibitionism her children excelled in owed nothing to his brand of self-harming, but essentially private, madness.

Petula suspected that an 'incident' at school, cubs or brownies, that Jazzy and Evita had conferred over and decided to 'share', pooling both their experiences into a single fabricated narrative, may have actually taken place. This 'incident', however coloured by fantasy, might even have contained aspects of the hysterical excreta aired during their recriminatory fits. Crucially, in the light of her theory, Petula's genes could not be held to account for Jazzy's lousy taste in girls or for why Evita blinded a lad who tried to peck her cheek. Satisfied that this mysterious 'incident' offered the explanatory potential to the riddle posed by their socio-sexual absurdity, Petula made the mistake of ground-testing her speculative discovery on Jazzy one evening. His response, a descent into tears and a sobbed request for her to leave Tianta immediately by the nearest exit was not what she had expected. Later still, in the years after Noah had delivered his killing blow, Petula decided that the true identity of the 'abuser' was her enigmatic former husband, claiming to have known all along, her only crime blind loyalty to a secretive predator. By then those who would have benefitted from this belated admission had moved on to new torments, as indeed had she, Tinwood having tired of her for reasons she struggled to come to terms with or understand.

'I still haven't decided which table I'll sit at or who I'll be next to... What? No, I mean me of course, who *I'll* be sat next to, yes of course I need to sit next to someone, what do you think I'm going to be doing, dancing on the tables?'

Petula's pride recoiled slightly as she wondered what exactly she was trying to sell here; not herself, that much was becoming clear, but an aspect of herself, or to be cruelly specific, what she was capable of delivering. Never in her years of social haggling, playing off one circle against another, a person's pride off another's vanity, had it been made as clear to her that the guests in question would come because of what she could offer, not for who she was, an illusion she would have liked to cling to for at least a little while longer. She was not *that* old yet.

'Yes, well I'm afraid he will have to sit next to me; yes, I know, of course I can't speak French but nor can bloody she! No I *don't* want to sit next to Margy, I'll sit next to whoever I should so bloody please to sit next to. And I don't give a toss if he's never heard of me, the pleasure will *not* be all mine, that I assure you.

What do you *mean* you want something in return? What, you're back to that bedroom again; for God's sake, I've already told you, there's at least room for three in there and we've problems enough with space as it is; have you any idea how many people we're going to be trying sleep in this house? Honestly! The whole thing is turning into a perfect nightmare.'

This conversation was the beginning, Petula would reflect, of the slow erosion of hope, followed by her confidence, that would end with her strafing the county with repeat invites and endless summons. Yet the mania to be at the centre of things did not allow her to pause as she breathlessly promised Tinwood the ground-floor bedroom she intended to put the girls in, adding that yes, he could jolly well share it with them if he was that desperate for company! All so she could be at the right hand of a promising young television actor who would never, to everyone else's surprise, rise further than Mr Darcy in a forgettable adaption of *Pride and Prejudice* that was eclipsed by the one posterity remembered, shot a couple of months later. It would take another fifteen years, and a handful of men and women to come forward with stories of how Tim Tinwood stole their childhoods, followed by a lengthening queue that extended into the hundreds, for Petula to say she had honestly never cared for the man, and despite general scepticism, mean it.

'What, you really think they might use *this* house to film? No, I mean that would be wonderful, of course it would. How could I have any objections? I'd be thrilled, but, no, it's just that I could imagine, and I know this is obvious, I could imagine this place working better for the Brontës than Austen. No, of course I'm not going shopping but weren't her books set in Hampshire? I mean, would that matter? Splendid. Oh, you'll never guess who else might be coming...'

Regan heard all this in a mood of puzzled incomprehension. Did her mother love this man? Why did she think he would like her any more by mentioning that Diamanda's parents knew the Jaggers and by putting on a silly pleading voice that made her sound like Widow Twanky in pantomime? The multitude of people her mother was capable of becoming, often within a moment of one another, while remaining resolutely herself when called to, was a way of being in the world that struck her as daringly pointless. Regan did not ponder the puzzle for long, the ways of Petula often eluded her, and her own concerns were a circle she must square. Mingus was still inside her, her mother had to get off the phone fast so she could ring Diamanda and find out about morning-after-potions and the other ways of holding off pregnancy.

'Perfect, perfecto, absolutely, ring in an hour, I'll have had a chance to have talked to them by then. This is going to be a good one isn't it? Yes, I feel it in my bones too! And about time, there have been too many damp squibs and half-chances, time for an event with some real welly, I couldn't agree more. *Excellent*, speak in a bit.'

Petula could hear the tell-tale creaking on the landing, her daughter had risen. The sisters swapped places, passing each other on the staircase in an affected hurry, with a cursory 'good morning' disguising Petula's interest as much as it faithfully conveyed Regan's lack of.

'I just need to use the phone for a bit Mum,' Regan called once she was a safe distance away, 'I'm getting Diamanda to bring some clothes over and need to discuss sizes,' she added, hurrying into ground-floor study.

'Feel free, it's your house too. Your telephone too, come to that.'

Petula waited to hear the heavy oak door slam; her daughter had yet to learn the art of closing anything quietly, be it a car boot or biscuit lid. Not wasting any time, she proceeded as quickly as she could to Regan's bedroom and allowed herself in for a brief snoop. There had never been a point in her life where she considered her daughter's property or affairs separate from her own (though hers were certainly separate from her daughter's), or that covert access to them constituted an invasion of privacy. The principle reason she waited until Regan was out of the room before prying, aside from paying lip service to another societal norm, the cult of the teenager and their tiresome insistence on needing their own 'space', was that to ask permission would be too much like taking an inventory. The truth was, rooting round in other people's things without their knowing gave Petula a thrill she was too generous to herself to deny; especially when those things could nearly be her own, the differences between her and Regan's taste intriguing and, where too great, troubling.

Petula knew she was holding Regan to a severe standard, and wanted very much to be kind in her judgements. Sadly such reservations went out of the window when confronted with the full horror of Regan's bedroom floor. At her feet were a pair of knickers stuffed into one cup of a bra, a trainer lodged artlessly in the other. The craze for wearing 'training shoes' outside of a school sports day, or marathon, dismayed her, but that could at least be put down to the madness that lay behind generational shifts; it was Regan's underwear that was the deeper worry. Regan's panties were altogether too plain, minimal and utilitarian to qualify as instruments of seduction or even of use. Petula understood comparisons were lazy yet felt compelled to draw them anyway; what she wore next to her skin was lacy, expensive and intricately detailed, the product of a different kind of civilisation, one dedicated to seduction and not brute function. Regan's choice was alright if you expected to be experimented on by space creatures or mounted by the Russian Army but there was nothing in the thin black strips of elastic to attract a repeat booking from an English male with an ounce of discernment.

Stepping over a pile of what-she-knew-not, Petula pulled open a drawer. As she feared, the panties on the floor were not a one-off, there were handfuls of the tiny terrors stuffed orderlessly amidst socks, chewing gum and wristbands. It seemed conceivable that Regan was developing what was usually known as an interior life, or at least one Petula could not see, with its own reasons and motivations that weren't hers; what did these tiny panties mean: lesbianism or a desire to pursue a career in gymnastics? In the past Petula could read Regan easily, she was a girl for whom whatever happened occurred on the surface, visibly and without the need for interpretation. Petula had hollowed out that inner space that constituted Regan's centre so nothing in there should surprise her. How could it when she also provided the filling, creating a more compact, predictable and passionless version of herself in her daughter's deepest recesses? But the lycra monstrosity Regan jogged in, punky yoga tubes, and miscellany of books (if Regan read there was never any sign of it in her conversation), told an alternative story. How did all this stuff get here and when, Petula wondered, did the psychic growth spurt that mothered it occur?

Diaries or letters might have provided a clue. Petula had searched in vain for these on previous occasions, Regan's one holiday journal of their trip to Austria a summer ago an embarrassing synthesis of guidebook wisdom and adult malapropisms, though not so worrying as finding evidence of an independent mind. Such written correspondence as there was pertained to the utterly trivial, postcards and thank-you letters, no doubt replying to equally innocuous examples of the same genre. If Regan was taking herself seriously she lacked the confidence to leave an account of her achievement, the dissimilarities Petula feared real, yet petty, expressions of outward differences she could easily tolerate.

As she was about to leave Petula noticed the stack of novels on Regan's bedside table. Lying on top was the new Wrath, *If I Should Fall from Grace with God*, sent to Petula earlier that year with a barely eligible scrawl in the cover hoping that she would find time to read it 'in her museum without walls'. In sending her each of his new titles Wrath had sought to keep a memory alive, rather than offer the spectre of romance, much to Petula's dismay. She dearly wished the package the book had come in had contained something else, a note on headed paper detailing his flight times into Heathrow, a hotel address or a postcard of a Scottish Loch he intended to meet her at. Having pulled the jiffy-bag apart and checked each page hoping a letter would fall out, Petula was left with another volume of poetry that did not rhyme and a canonical memory she had returned to far too often. Angrily she vowed to not play the game of trying to read between the lines of the poems or hope they were addressed to her. Anyone could buy and read these words, deluding themselves into pretending they were the latest muse – what she wanted was handwritten confirmation that she was the one he saw when he closed his eyes and thought of England. Petula was worn out by the detective work required to live on scraps of comfort already in the public domain. It had ruined her enjoyment of his last four volumes and she vowed to leave the next unread. Unfortunately, having Wrath's words so close to hand was more than she could manage. With the desperation of a student who has just a night to revise for an exam, Petula tore into the volume in search of northern sirens, Shatby beauties, mythological earth mothers and even brief encounters in Chinese restaurants, anything for evidence that she had scraped along the sides of an artist's consciousness. Instead she saw page after page of ungainly and incomprehensible prose, essays of a kind, masquerading as poems, scaling the heights of neither. Though she would not have swapped Wrath's remembering her for the world, Petula was too much alive to hope pleasant recollections of what did not happen were a reasonable substitute for what she hoped still could. Casting the book deep into a pile of unread litter, Petula resolved once more to steer clear of Wrath's poetic offerings, until such a time as her name appeared in print as the dedicatee, at which point the quality of the work could go hang; she'd defend each turgid word to the death. But until then...

Credit to Regan though! Back for a day and a night the little reprobate had already been through her study and pilfered a book. Regan was a chip off the old block all right, her sneaky ingenuity nearly making up for the theft. Petula delighted in her own inconsistency. There was something rather sweet in picturing the scene, Regan's determined little frown as she checked to see if the coast was clear before making off with her trophy. Still, it was puzzling that she should actually have tried to make a fist of reading the thing. Petula opened it on the page Regan had marked, and to her disconcertion, found a long passage underlined faintly in pencil. Had Wrath done that or was it Regan's work? Petula had grown so disenchanted with the rolling, aimless, drone of words, that she could not remember noticing any annotations in the text Wrath might have left for her. Nonetheless that had to be the more likely explanation for the highlighting than Regan making a connection of her own. Briefly Petula considered taking a rest from herself and simply putting the book down; all this over-stimulation would result in exhaustion before luncheon...

'The unhappy few who want order in their lives and a sense of growing and progression suffer terribly,' Petula whispered, hoping that the sound of her voice would tease out whatever sanity slept in the text, 'there is always the shape of the individual day to remind you. It is a microcosm of man's life as it gently wanes, its long morning shadows getting shorter with the approach of noon, the high point of the day, which could be likened to that sudden tremendous moment of intuition that comes only once in a lifetime, and then the fuller, more rounded shapes of early afternoon as the sun imperceptibly sinks in the sky and the shadows start to lengthen, until all are blotted in the stealthy coming of twilight, merciful in one sense that it hides the differences, blemishes as well as beauty marks, that gave the day its character and in doing so caused it to be another day in our limited span of days, the reminder that time is moving on and we're getting older, not older enough to make any difference on this particular occasion, but older all the same.' Petula blinked to ward off a hovering migraine; she was already struggling. She considered tackling the sentence again, before deciding that it was better to plough on to the end lest she give up altogether. 'Even now the sun is dropping below the horizon; a few moments ago it was still light enough to read but now it is no more, the printed characters swarm across the page to create an impressionistic blur. Soon the page itself will be invisible.' I wish, thought Petula. 'Yet no one has the urge to get up and put on a light; it is enough to be sitting here, grateful for the reminder that yet another day has come and gone and you have done nothing about it. What about the morning resolutions to convert all the confused details in the air about you into a column of intelligible figures? To draw up a balance sheet? This naturally went undone, and you are also perhaps grateful for your laziness, glad that it has brought you to this pass where you must now face up to the day's inexorable end as indeed we must all face up to death someday, and put our faith in some superior power which will carry us beyond into a region of light and timelessness. Even if we had done the things we ought to have done, it probably wouldn't have mattered anyway, as everyone always leaves something undone, and this can be just as ruinous as a whole life of crime or dissipation. Yes, in the long run there is something to be said for these shiftless days, each distilling its drop of poison until the cup is full; there is something to be said for them because there is no escaping them. Our belief in them is what will not go away, even after what we believe in, ceases.'

Fuck a flock of ducks, what pish! It was all Petula could manage to not shout 'Off with his head!' at the top of her lungs. Wrath had really gone off the boil, off the boil and mad and dull all at once, like a hideous cocktail with the wrong ingredients drunk lukewarm from a test-tube. Talk about trading on your reputation; clearly the world of poetry was as manipulable as a seating plan at Ascot. Congratulations of a kind were grudgingly due. Wrath must have succeeded in making a lot of intelligent people feel very scared to pull off publishing this kind of discursive flannel. Petula put the book back as she found it, feeling slightly queasy.

The negative reaction was consoling, easing Regan's defection to the world of words and the very slight possibility that her daughter saw something in the long-winded dross that she did not. It would also soothe, for the rest of the day, the sting of not having Wrath in her life and the absurdity that she had any grounds for thinking she ever would. Delicacy forbade her making any mention of her curious, yet hopefully meaningless discovery to Regan, interesting as it would be to probe. Better to think of the theft as a harmless gesture of independence, a cheap way of acquiring depth no more serious than pinching pennies from her purse. Regan's intellectual development would, when it finally ceased to evade Petula, come as a shock, for in all her years of foment, Petula assumed her daughter was simply reading to pass the time. And so did Regan, who understood her own interests through her mother's perceptions of what they were. Rarely had so much text moved from page to person without that individual noticing its accumulation. Regan's reading had metamorphosed from a weak pose struck for reasons her mother more or less suspected, to expressing an unspoken, and unthought, tendency towards local truths and universal freedom, a private consolation that would eventually announce itself in public ways no one had associated with Petula's pliable doppelgänger.

The study door slammed to a close. Petula had lost sense of time; how long had Regan been on the phone, that was the real question! She was never normally one for nattering away; well, at least there was no mystery why – who wouldn't be experiencing that beautiful combination of anticipation and dread that presaged one's first major social engagement?

Passing her on the stairs, Petula, again affecting a great hurry, gave Regan a wink that had the disconcerting effect she hoped it would, leaving Regan with the fear that there were no secrets in sisterhood and her conversation with Diamanda had been overheard.

'Will you be needing the phone again? I've a number of important calls pending,' Petula called breezily from the study door, determined to show her daughter that she liked privacy too, 'all for your benefit, you know. The party, I mean.'

'No thanks, I need a lift into town though, when you're finished, if that's okay.'

'Why, is it urgent?'

'No, it's alright, I'll ask Jazzy.'

'Oh, I wouldn't do that if I were you.'

'Why not?'

'Because he's completely mad and would probably end up driving you to Hastings.'

'Don't worry, it'll be nice to catch up with him...'

It was not nice to catch up with him at all, but still preferable to having Petula drop her outside the Doctor's, as at least Jazzy would not think of asking her what she was doing there. Regan had never experienced a silence that the instigator found so difficult to self-enforce, Jazzy straining and grimacing his way through their journey, shifting in his seat and muttering cryptically into his arm. Evidently the way was being left open for her to ask Jazzy what the problem was, or to simply offer an apology to be on the safe side. Regan felt too nervous to try, an intervention likely to provoke the avalanche he was desperate to release and she, at least for the moment, to avoid. Their parting and her decision to take the bus back was a relief, Regan resolving to not ask Jazzy for anything that might be construed as a favour until she had given him a chance to air his latest malady.

The nurse at the surgery, having established the circumstances of the seduction the night before, gave Regan what she needed with only the briefest joshing, suggesting that it might be a good idea to take a condom out on her next night run, given that one never knew who one might meet. Regan considered this well-meaning advice unnecessary. On the journey back she permitted herself to finally remember Mingus, and to establish why, despite an oceanic longing to step from the lake into the sea with him, she could have no more to do with the boy.

It was surprising, having waited to be guided by feelings in the past only to find that none came, to discover two powerful and contradictory emotions, side by side. Her desire for Mingus was wild, uncharacteristic and most likely a manifestation, if it existed, of love. Regan could not tell whether this was a predictable response to having sex for the first time or whether it predated the loss of her virginity and that she had always loved Mingus. Fun as it might have been to wrack her history and un-plunged subconscious to find out, the distinction was largely academic as nothing rested on it.

The second conviction was the one she knew she must obey the logic of. Erroneously Regan accepted the bogus divide between heart and head, the binary opposition making more sense to her than a world of supposedly nuanced shading. Whatever stood in opposition to her happiness arrested spontaneity, which was as it should be, as caution had always greater weight in her eyes than joy, and other dangerously irresponsible concepts. Of this Regan was sure, with a certainty more powerful than faith. To disobey the imperative of denial would mean she was lost as a person and to the future her mother was preparing her for. Behind it lay a prejudice against love she had accepted unquestioningly from Petula. Fear played its part too; Regan was scared of finding out that love was not true and that to sustain it required delusional levels of stupidity she might not have. The night with Mingus by the lake had been perfect, and perfection needed defending against life's degenerative tendencies. Regan knew Mingus loved her back, and by quitting at the top she could save them both from disappointment; Mingus would never have to grow bored of the 'real' her, allowing Regan to remain interesting, moonlit and immaculate forever.

Blind to the romantic element inherent in her analysis, Regan drew on what she took to be her superior maturity. If she could show she was stronger than love, harder than feeling, and superior to sentiment, who knew what she could go on to achieve as an adult? Fortunately for her, she was beginning at a more evolved stage of social development than an ordinary teenager. Unlike Mingus she already understood that independence was a more advanced state than dependence and that love, for all its promise, was the handmaiden of need. It was also uncool. Regan felt that her sacrifice would set an example that a woman of greater experience would approve of, however much it hurt the girl she still was.

Regan could still not leave a decision this big entirely to emotion without some practical research to justify her conclusion. Subsequent enquiries into Mingus's character yielded a girlfriend in Leeds, and more than one in York, an older woman in London, and a number of 'possibles' in the village. He also lied a lot, was pretentious and fake, would never make it as an artist, could not even paint, and put objects he found in glass cases and called them art. These blandishments coexisted with a tendency to copy his ideas off other people, drink and smoke too much, and borrow money and sponge with no thought of ever honouring his numerous debts. All this from two short conversations with her brother and mother! Admittedly none of it fitted with the other more generous accounts she heard about the place, but by taking Petula and Jazzy at their word, she at least hoped to take the sting out of any future doubts.

They were to meet again once that holiday, along the track on the morning of Regan's party. Mingus looked ill when their eyes met, the weight of all he wished to ask leaving him grossly over-qualified for the confident and easy greeting the encounter required. He felt touched by the unreality of things, the confusion and sheer embarrassment at having been cut by the love of his life rendering him no more capable of speech than a terrified mute. He had, to assuage his own incomprehension, decided that Regan's gross indifference to him was his own fault, and in this way, had given her a motive he could at least understand. She was a rare and precious thing who had been humiliated by his desire to physically possess her. His raging itch must have destroyed her impression of him as a celestial being, reducing their intimacy to the level of debased lust. No wonder she wanted nothing more to do with him; he was no better than an animal in her eyes. It was better to take possession of the tragedy in this way, and blame himself so as to get over it sooner, if ever he could. The alternative, that Regan did things like this all the time, and so for her, it constituted no big deal, was unacceptable.

Stuck for what to say, Mingus foolishly, for it could be no other way, asked Regan for the only thing it was in his power to offer at that moment. Would she like to go for a walk with him? Regan replied, airily, that she needed to 'chill' as she was busy later, which was the type of balanced answer Mingus dreaded. Shaken by this humiliation, and left with no reply, Mingus carried on his walk alone.

Regan felt like a bitch immediately afterward, before experiencing an exalted sense of power. Had she not shown she was an adult at last, wiser and more accomplished than Mingus and his pointless walks? It was an impure high and could not last. The space still to come, the future, a concept she was in thrall to without the least idea of how its subclauses, time and regret, worked, had other plans. Those few weeks of holiday had represented radical freedom; rare avenues of choice where her causal chain had come loose, leaving Regan undetermined by the patterns of the past. Her tragedy was she could see, even then, how simple it was to act freely, and pick a juncture where she might emerge recast as herself. Instead, like a wistful flirt tied to old codes of courtship, Regan substituted volition for a parasitic notion of what she thought Petula would do in the same situation, and missed her chance.

The cost was enormous. By turning her back on freedom Regan had to accept the moral responsibility for what followed as surely as if she cast the winning vote for a madman who brought the world to wrack and ruin. To her horror she discovered that her decision to reject Mingus trapped her in a new cycle of predestination, without choices or options, binding her to an irreversible logic that would take years to play out. However hard she struggled there was no way out, only a single course to follow determined by the act before it, narrowing her life to a predictable series of mistakes she was helpless to prevent. Free will grew to be so much a stranger to her that when, hidden in a tiny corner of her future, the opportunity to choose rose again, Regan remembered her last taste of freedom and put her hand through a window in disgust. Time and regret had had the last word.

But before that she had a party to attend. Regan walked back to the house cautiously, sensing something come and then go; the sky a royal blue, a trickle of condescending pity coming over her as she imagined Mingus's lonely life on the farm in years to come. She had guessed that if she saw him again it would be awkward and it had been, though at least it was out of the way, and there had not been any embarrassing scenes. Things were often not as bad as one thought they might be, and, sensing the worst was over before the worst had even begun, Regan congratulated herself on a situation well handled. It was just a shame that she could not tell her mother about it.

PART THREE:
Styx, hate.

But from inward motion to deliver
sweet, sweet, sweet poison for the ages tooth:
Which, though I will not practise to deceive,
Yet, to avoid deceit, I mean to learn.

– WILLIAM SHAKESPEARE, *King John*

CHAPTER EIGHT,
a party and a punishment.

It was only meant to be a bit of fun. The day of the party was overcast and treacly, crystals of salt sticking to Petula's body like handfuls of sand, putting her in mind of a Tennessee Williams play, the absence of a breeze most unlike Yorkshire and the opposite of what was forecast. With slow imprecision the rain clouds finally assembled, releasing only a few soggy flecks, the weather neither breaking nor clearing but congealing colourlessly with god-like indifference. Petula found that she had very little appetite for breakfast and none at all for lunch. With Noah away as usual and Regan shaking like an intoxicated foal, she felt an unwelcome ring of isolation form round her as the hours slid away and the desire to retch grew. It was unpleasant to observe that she did not have her usual grasp of what was stippling across her mind, mad and wild thoughts that seemed to come from the very heart of the house itself. With great determination she acted her way through the labyrinth of preparations and duties, harnessing her fears to commands that somehow managed to overlay them, the surfaces holding out against her simmering depths until it was time for the first guests to arrive, and all hell to break loose.

*

The party was out of control from the very start. Petula had made it clear to Tim Tinwood that she did not want B-listers telling anecdotes about people they did not know, only the crème de la crème of his client list, with a contemporary twist if possible. She had got her wish – with a twist. The crème de la crème had arrived drunk and drugged out of their contemporary minds. It had been typical of Petula's life that no sooner had a fear manifested itself than reality would do its best to outflank it on a platter. And so it proved. Petula turned to Tinwood, first out of the minibus, and said,

'*My God!* What have you done to me? They're all absolutely wrecked! I was expecting something to go wrong, but this...'

'Oh come on Petula! Live a little, it's a party! Party time! Eh?'

'It bloody will be but shouldn't be yet. This lot look like they've been on it since *breakfast*. They're bloody sozzled Tim!'

'Come come!'

'Jesus, you can barely stand yourself! And what about him still in the taxi? He's fast asleep!'

'Don't worry... I'll get the driver to give him a poke. Got stuck in a bit, earlier on. He's Bobby.'

'What?'

'Bobby, a good lad, normally.'

'I am frightened, I am. What the *hell* were you thinking?'

'Relax, okay, relax, it's not as bad as it looks. "Forget your fears babe," we're all just here to have a good time!'

In fact Tinwood was not so immune to fear as his phoney protestation was intended to suggest. Getting the actors Petula wanted had been quite a sell, harder than the same proposition would have been a couple of years earlier. His efforts had forced him to cast a wary eye over his association with Petula and reappraise her market worth. Doubtless, she had delivered good times in the past. But to a spunky young actor asked to attend a dinner party, not even a rave, for a teenager they had never met held by a pushy mum they had also never met, in Yorkshire, verged on the otiose. The days of stating that there was this incredible force of nature they just *had* to meet seemed innocently passé when fed to a generation gorged on cable, air travel and Sunday shopping. Tinwood was left with no choice but to sell the evening as an outrageous orgy in the making, which of course he had no objection to should that promise come true, presenting Petula as a high-class brothel madam, happy to line up a troupe of schoolgirls for their delectation. Though exaggeration and unthinking misrepresentation were his stock and trade, Tinwood couldn't now nullify the fear that he might have gone too far on this occasion, allowing his loyalty to Petula to run amok. But how else could he have got them there? The five young actors, single, pandered and gullible, appeared to have taken him at his word, referring to the party as a 'jailbait fuck fest' in a conference call the day before. Fearing his own hyperbole, Tinwood had made a belated attempt to play matters down to no good effect, and had no choice but to encourage the actors, travelling up together on the train, to loosen up with a few sharpeners in the hope that the booze might take the edge off their predatory instincts, a ruse that was over-successful in its application.

Which was only the first reason for his odyssey of anxiety. Tinwood had, when confronted with the reality of another trip to The Heights, reacted with delayed dread to returning to the scene of his earlier crime. Every time he put the debate to bed, another aspect, usually the one he hoped to have resolved, returned in a marginally altered guise to take him, once again, through the gauntlet of doubt. True, his principle of acting as though nothing had happened had served him well on the myriad of occasions he had gone back before, neither of the two molested children anywhere to be seen, nor even so much as mentioned by their mother. But was he pushing his luck in persisting and hanging on, when the world was not exactly short of parties and hostesses he could defect to? The unease would not go away and so, like his clients, Tinwood had started on the booze and pills, the result being that as his party approached York there was not one of them who was not stage drunk or speaking amphetamine logic. By the time the train finally pulled into Darlington, Tinwood had started to imagine he was a General in the Spanish Civil War every time he went to the lavatory – his tried-and-tested way of knowing it was time to switch to something less toxic. Out came the brandy miniatures and, with the counterproductive inconsistency of a novice, the new 'sedative' he had scored the night before: 'E'.

Petula watched the mob enter The Heights, so elegiac in the dusk now the sun was finally visible as it set, with intense dismay. It would have to fall to her loyal nucleus of Eager, Astley, Marg and Esther to save the evening, that or the few local celebrities she could count on to stem the Dionysian outbreak. Unfortunately, she knew in the instant it took to consider it that this strategy would fall short of solving the problem. The small number of invites and gaggle of inexperienced girls were a regrettable combination; there was simply not enough fondant in her cake to disguise the taste of the inebriated thespians, who would stand out in a Viking raid let alone a sit-down dinner. She would have to scrap it out head on, ask them to pull themselves together and compel the fools to behave like the professionals they professedly were. Actors were like most pansies; they liked a good scolding.

'Fuck a *duck*!'

To her horror she had spotted one, an actor, the cover star of the current *Radio Times*, urinating over the side of the house as the Bentley bearing Landon Trafalgar pulled up, the gap between the roses allowing the deed to be perfectly visible from the drive.

Trafalgar, the septuagenarian owner of Trafalgars, the north's largest department store, looked on with astonishment as the new Doctor Who, Crispin Fogle, wiry and impudently handsome, attempted to tuck himself in, the most important part of the operation remaining stubbornly beyond the reach of his flies.

'You're hanging out lad,' Trafalgar shouted gruffly, showing remarkable powers of adaption, Petula felt, in the circumstances.

Ignoring him and tittering like a small child, Fogle skipped up to Petula and offering up his moist hand, which she did not take, said, 'I'm so happy I could shit in a Tardis! Tee heeee! Sorry! I'm still in character, it's the sort of thing *The Doctor* says you know.'

'Not in any of the episodes I've watched.'

Laughing feverishly Tinwood pretended to slap Fogle, before not pretending to grasp him in a headlock and bundle him through the front door; a manoeuvre he accomplished without resistance as Fogle had decided to pretend to be a dog, and was woofing happily at the new arrivals.

'Think we need to splash some water on this one's face!'

'Exterminate! Exterminate! Woof woof! Arf Arf!'

Watching them barge their way towards the hall bathroom, a bushy eyebrow raised, Trafalgar grunted peevishly, 'I know I'm just a simple rags-to-riches cloth merchant Petula...'

'Oh Landon, please, you're so much more than that... and always have been...'

'...But you do have some funny friends. The kind of funny that doesn't make me laugh my dear. I'm most sorry to say.'

Petula blushed – must she have been mad to think she could invite a blimpish clothing mogul and the new Timelord to the same event? Diversity had always worked in the past – the greater the range of faces the more intense the reflected glory in knowing them all. Creative people enjoyed the company of money as much as money enjoyed the company of genuine talent. And as for the generation gap, wasn't that meant to be shrinking again with everyone becoming more alike and wearing the same clothes? That last part, at least, was borne out, as Fogle and Trafalgar were both in jet-black smoking jackets, but as for the rest of it, Petula was not hopeful. Whatever force it was that usually allowed her to proceed with assurance in a forwardly direction evidently wanted nothing to do with her today.

'Not my friends Landon, friends of friends as it happens.'

The old man looked at her pityingly.

'I've sat you in between Cordelia and Daisy, Regan's class mates... one girl to every bachelor,' she added unnecessarily, trying to laugh and squinting instead. Trafalgar's wife of fifty years had died only a few months before and Petula, a close family friend, had been asked to read at the funeral. The silence was tense and heartfelt. Her mouth was stuffed with corpses, could she get nothing right?

'Boy to girl is what I mean... my seating plan.'

'It's hot tonight, too damn hot,' Trafalgar said loosening his cravat and walking in.

Behind him were Astley and Eager. The years had been honest to both, Eager resembling an archbishop with a twinkle in his eye, Astley a robust parish priest, his hair shaved in a grade-one now, both dressed in black robes and white silk scarves.

'Ye Gods am I glad to see you now,' Petula blurted, grabbing Eager's wrinkled and heavily tanned hand, 'it's been a sodding nightmare I tell you, no help, lugging round big tables by myself, a nightmare with this Japanese caterer Regan absolutely insisted on, sushi's it with these girls at the moment, goldfish food as far as I can tell. Anyway, everything a recipe for total confusion, and then some, and with this seating plan, Regan trying to bloody change everything, why I don't know, just so these girls can all sit together, I mean, what's the point, don't they see enough of each other at school? Chaos. Absolute *chaos*. And then to cap it all this lot, my God, did you see the state of them?' Petula beckoned towards the noisy shouts echoing along the long corridor which was now doubling as a dining hall, 'I don't know how Tim got them into that condition, all five and Tim too. He had to practically wrestle one to the ground just now. I thought he'd knock my eye out. I'm scared, I admit it! No, okay, not scared, but you know, it's just not right, this is my *home!*'

Petula's choice of a thin black dress was wise, as the effort of the last speech had released enough sweat to glue it to her body, damp patches glistening all over her powerful equipment. Affectionately Eager released her hand, glancing at her nipples with thinly disguised beguilement.

'Upstarts,' he muttered with friendly annoyance, 'cheeky upstarts.'

'And look at *that*.' Petula pointed to Rex Wade, an ex-*Blue Peter* presenter cast as Will Scarlett in the new series of *Robin of Sherwood* who, having been carried into the house by the taxi driver, now reappeared with a rose thrust between his teeth, the bush he had plucked it from a rare 'Alchymist' imported from North Carolina.

'You're going the wrong way,' she called, 'it's inside, the party is inside, okay?'

Wade grinned, losing the rose as he did so, the flower scuffed underfoot as he careered into the wall. From his place on the floor he blew a kiss at a nearby daisy and then, in an apparent change of heart, burst into tears.

'Well go on, help him,' Petula barked at Tinwood, who had reappeared from the bathroom, a hastily received scratch scrawled along his cheek and neck.

'Okay,' panted Tinwood, 'okay. Christ. I'm knackered already!'

'Phew, it's a bad crowd Tim's been knocking about with, bad news all round Petula, I told you that when you first asked "who's new?",' said Astley. 'You ought to have taken heed. Sorry to say I told you so, it's such a bore to be right about such things. I take absolutely no such pleasure in being so.'

'But they all look so *nice* on the telly,' Petula protested, 'how was I to know they'd be such bastards in real life? I mean that bloke laid flat out looked after the garden in that kids' programme, *Blue Peter*, that must count for something character-wise, right?'

'Crap,' drawled Eager, 'he did whatever Tim dug up for him, they're a bunch of cocky young pricks, dancers and rent boys, not serious. Malleable and disposable automatons. All pulled off those dreadful soap operas or kids' TV for their fifteen minutes. Not actors at all.'

'Well they took me in, just as well that I adjust quickly to shocks,' gurgled Petula, 'I had half a mind to call the police, really, when I saw them roll up.'

'Shocks is all it is, Tim's way of showing us all how young and with-it he still is. Give them ten minutes of the cold shoulder and they'll be eating out of your hand. Ahhh, here she is, the girl herself. Regan, what does it feel like to be the centre of all this attention?' smiled Astley, and gave Petula's daughter an affectionate hug.

Regan, following the black theme that had been suggested without being insisted upon by herself for the want of any other idea, was dressed in a cat suit a couple of sizes too large for her. Rather than show off her slim physique, it hung off her like an astronauts overalls draped over an ironing board, offering little hint of what lay underneath.

'Am I?'

'Of course you are! So how does it feel?'

'Terrifying, I'm not sure I like it. I can't believe how nervous I was earlier. Silly, because it's only a party, I mean I know I shouldn't be so scared. Am I supposed to be so unrelaxed that it's impossible to enjoy myself?'

'Nonsense' said Astley kindly, 'to be the object of any gathering induces nerves, whatever the occasion. It's as close as most people get to going on stage. Just so long as the nerves are kept under control. Once it starts everything is usually okay, and anyway, worrying should be your mother's job, you just revel in it all.'

Regan smiled as warmly as was sensible in the heat and turned to Petula with something like impatience. 'Mum, I think you'd better come inside for a minute, I can say hello to people out here, one of the actors, the one who used to be on *Grange Hill* that's meant to be sat next to me, he's just been sick *every-*

where. No one really knows what to do about it, I've asked Mrs Hardfield to clear it but I mean him. No one knows what to do with him, he's just sat down in it and refuses to move. So I thought that perhaps Diamanda could sit next to me instead because he looks like he could do it again...'

Petula was already on her way, she had noticed Regan's tendency, inherited from her, to shout loudest at what she desired the most, puking actors were probably her cup of tea, she just wouldn't bring herself to admit it yet. As for the vomiting thespian himself, a jug or two of water and a cup of coffee ought to sort him out. If it didn't she would take it upon herself to personally batter him to death in the pantry with her new chrome saucepan stand.

Entering the landing area Petula barged straight in to Chips Hall. At one point she had designs on Chips for herself, then as a possible suitor for Regan, but like a lone centre-forward unfortunate enough to come of age between two brilliant striking partnerships, he had never enjoyed his run in the team and had to be content to fill in wherever he could. Now in his late thirties, still single, a successful property developer but explicably bitter, his face lewd and eel-thin, Hall had resorted to ever-more-sycophantic ruses to hook his hostess's attention, which on this particular evening could not have been further away from her priorities.

'Petula, this is really, really lovely. I love, I really *love*, the black drapes. Really, really, gothic and, I dunno, creepy, but in a good way, yah?' Hall's features were mildly intriguing until he came to use them whereupon his narrow head and slick-back hair resembled a sculpture that had lost too much clay, less a matinee idol than shifty police informer. 'I just *wonder* where you got all these drapes from, India or a local market? Really, really plush, you know, profound and plush.'

'Not now Chips!'

'Oh, is something the matter?'

'For God's sake, in case you've been on another planet; the Vandals are sacking Rome...'

'Oh what? Those noisy plonkers who came barging in? Who the deuce are they, I don't recognise any of them, I thought they had something to do with Regan to be honest with you. Snotty arrivistes, one of them's just thrown up actually. Can I do anything to help?'

'Save yourself Chips, I'm equal to it.'

'Just say if there is...'

The scene that greeted Petula as she strove along the corridor was about as bad as it could be while remaining within the bounds of possibility. The actors were assembled in a rugby huddle, mid-song, the puking one of their party still on all fours and attempting to scale Diamanda's leg, mercifully out of his own vomit, but showing every sign that his repertoire was on its way to encompassing sexual assault. Petula issued her warning shot, 'Mr Wade, there's an important phone call for you, could you not come into the kitchen and take it?'

The other guests were milling round the tables doing their best to regard the disruption as normal and even entertaining, with the exception of Landon Trafalgar, who with his hands behind his back and head down, was patrolling the room like a police Alsatian. Though the tables were all laid for dinner, a directionless ennui had infected those who would normally take a lead, bringing home to Petula her pivotal importance on that most misleadingly simple of operations; making things happen.

'Mr Wade, I must insist... you're holding everything and everyone up...'

Jenny Hardfield, having stood to attention with a mop and bucket, quietly went to work with the professionalism of a council worker falling on bubblegum stuck to a park bench. Wiping her hands on her apron she looked at Petula and confided in a hoarse stage-whisper, 'I don't think he can hear you, they're singing too loudly. And such a horrible song, don't you know.'

'Of course I don't *know*, I'm not a bloody rugby-playing medical student, how would I know about their beastly songs!'

'Well nor are they, medical students, they're *actors* Petula.'

'Oh for crying out loud! When Jazzy gets here ask him to report to me, I think I really may need him for once. Thanks for your help with the sick. I would be able to do nothing without you.'

'We love blowing our own trumpets, they make such a beautiful sound...'

Petula tightened her fist and felt a volley of battle-hardened indignation proceed up her spine. Just as she was about to pull Wade off an admittedly unresisting Diamanda, thus crossing all lines of civility and as good as confessing the evening had got off to a disaster, she felt a spongy poke on the shoulder; the soft finger that she had been sure of on impact seemingly dissolving into her skin like a warm icicle as she turned to face its owner.

It was a young man, or at least she thought so, of delicate composition, considerably shorter than herself, and deeply pink of face. Glaring up at her triumphantly with an expression of flustered expectancy on his rouged lips, he poked her again, this time in the chest, and raised a mascara-smothered eyebrow theatrically. Despite the many conflicting dramas vying for her attention, none of which were remotely comedic, the youth's appearance was such an affront to the laws of geometry and proportion, that Petula smothered a giggle under a gasp. Her first thought was how could he have possibly reached her shoulder, his arms were stubby and starchy, the sleeveless silver lame vest he had chosen for the occasion a poor advert for his flappy biceps and potbelly.

'I suppose I'm to be sat next to *you*,' he announced pompously, 'they always call for Tackleberry you know! Tackleberry! Wherever I am, they ask for me, by name. *Tackleberry* they say! Where are you, where is *Tackleberry*? I'm the one they always ask for. You see I don't just act! I play and sing on records too, that's

why I'm in such demand. For parties and social gatherings, like,'
he made a circle in the air with his fat index finger, 'this one,
whatever it's supposed to be. Tackleberry, you see! Even you
asked for me, so I must be right.'

'What?'

'Tackleberry, I'm the one they always want.'

'Who are you?'

'*Tackleberry* you nincompoop! The name on everybody's lips,
the one they all want to be.'

'My God, you're the actor, aren't you, who's going to play
Darcy... you *can't* be. No...'

'Just played. We finished shooting on the first of last month.
Near a dour little market town in Hampshire if you must know,
the weather, oh the weather!'

'Shooting? No, that's impossible. Tim said that... told me
you'd be shooting in Yorkshire later in the year. You can't even
have started yet, I mean, you've got to choose a location for the
house first, and you haven't even done that yet... have you?'

'I assure you we have, if you don't believe me then consider this: I wouldn't come to Yorkshire more than once a year at
most, no matter who asked for Tackleberry!'

Petula tried to flatten the shock – it was one thing to be lied
to and used by Tinwood; however the revelation that *this* was
Maurice Tackleberry, the next Mr Darcy (what kind of adaption
could he have been cast in, a *Muppet Show* special?) was as cruel
as reading the tag upside-down and grabbing a present meant
for someone else; the memory of confusing her elder sister's
golden slippers with her own plain pair one Christmas was still
an outstanding piece of childhood debris she had failed to dis-
pose of. Tackleberry reminded her of those slippers.

'I must say, since we wrapped, I have rather let myself go,' said
Tackleberry squeezing the fold of his belly, 'you don't know what
a pain it is to be put on horses and stuck in corsets. They forced
me to eat nothing but greens and lentils for a month before pro-

duction. Forced *Tackleberry*! It completely did my bonce in. I had terrible headaches, there was a day when I couldn't even get up. Never again! From now on Tackleberry chooses his parts, never again will a part choose Tackleberry!'

Tackleberry, his bleached triangular quiff extenuating the broad dome that supported it, untucked his skin-tight vest, which helped disguise the stomach he no longer bothered to hold in, and drained his glass of champagne. Stamping his heavy motorcycle boot onto the floor suddenly to muffle the unmistakable thud of a fart that had caught the seat of his leather trousers, Tackleberry helped himself to a handful of passing venison cocktail sausages, and repeated, as if to mollify any lingering doubt, '*Tackleberry!* That's who they always ask for!'

'I'm surprised they get the chance to, or even a word in edgeways, you talk too quickly.'

'I find my own voice and manner reassuring, it reminds me of who you all think I am.'

'Yes, the great Tackleberry, I'm surprised you don't remember.'

'When you act it's easy to forget who you're meant to be. Here, give me your glass, I want you to have mine.'

'What on earth for?'

'You'll see. What on earth are those morsels, going there on their sweet little way?'

'Crepes Jambon Fromage: posh pancakes with ham and cheese.'

'Meaty cheese! I want to make them mine, the sloppiness and crumbliness appeals.'

Petula now remembered Tinwood's cautionary remark about Tackleberry, another of 'his boys', discovered at a roller disco in a suburb of Coventry or Solihull (Tim was never fussy about where he had to dig for the muckiest of his human putty), waiting, no doubt, like the others for opportunity to knock. Despite being, in Tinwood's words, a genius and the next Jason Connery, Tackleberry was 'prone to sudden fluctuations in weight' which meant, in plain English, that he would have been handsome had he been three stone lighter, or at least, might then have borne some resemblance to the beefcake in tights Petula saw on the resume she was sent. The other actors, horribly loaded as they were, at least had the virtue of resembling small aspects of their photographed selves. How Tackleberry had become Darcy without life-endangering surgery, involving entire strips of his body being sliced away in time for shooting, flummoxed her. Though not as much as how this pastry-shaped blob had been offered the part in the first place. Petula had noticed him loafing about earlier in the day, making a nuisance of himself round the food, and hoped he had something to do with the lighting or catering, a disc jockey at the very worst, but this? No one deserved Tackleberry on the same day as Wade, Fogle and Tinwood's other thespian discoveries.

'Is there any reason why I should be sat next to you, why you asked for me, why I might not be put to better usage elsewhere?' Tackleberry inquired, pulling a bit of skin as lustrous as sun-dried dog excreta off his crusty forehead. He was close up to Petula's face now and looked like he had blown his nose over a container of talcum powder, fine specks of cocaine dotted about his nostrils and chin, his pupils pulsating dangerously. 'I'm half-Belgian by the way, it's why my voice is so high, and my diction so damned good. No one would know where I'm from, not even the Belgians. Are there any others here? I hope not. I hate them. But why am I sat next to you? I thought I might be placed next to one of those pretty little foxes. I thought that was why you might have sent for Tackleberry.'

He pointed at Diamanda who was leading Wade by the tie in the direction of the hall lavatory, Landon Trafalgar a few steps behind apparently unsure of whether to intervene or not. Elsewhere, to Petula's surprise, if not alarm, several guests appeared to be following an 'if-you-can't-beat-them-join-them' policy, empty wine and champagne bottles being changed for fresh

PART THREE: STYX, HATE

ones at a worrying rate of exchange. Even Astley and Eager, standing protectively at Regan's side, seemed to have managed their objections to the next generation and were hurling the fizz down as fast as Fogle and company.

'You know, I don't think too much of these crepes,' said Tackleberry, melted cheese oozing from the corners of his overfull mouth as though he were a sandwich toaster, 'I *far* prefer the ones in my local cafe in Bruges, they make them with a type of honey you can't get in this country, made by very rare Belgium bees. They have a special jar there in the cafe just for Tackleberry. And jam too, made from very exclusive dates you can't buy in England. I like to dip my finger in and just suck. Ha! Do I shock you? Yes, that's Tackleberry, absolutely outrageous, you just ask Tim! Now, are you going to introduce me to any of those pretty little foxy foxes, eh?'

Petula shook her head, scanning her fury for a convenient and representative place to take hold of, and do justice to it. Not only was this idiot, one who would probably refer to himself in the third person even if he was not high on drugs, not to her liking, but it seemed as though he had the audacity to consider her beneath his! Should she blame herself, and thus pretend she was still in control, or strike him in the face and find someone less militantly ignorant to be infuriated by? It was dreadful to move so suddenly from being socially accomplished enough to not take anyone in her circle's explanations for their own behaviour seriously, simply assigning them their real motives, to actually having no idea what was going on, nor means of stemming this tide of destruction.

'The danger,' Tackleberry was saying, 'with my style of acting is to end up hemmed in my own little universe and occupy it too perfectly. That kills my range, leads to typecasting, leads to stasis, yes, you're following me? Which is most tedious, the typecasting, verily, verily, verily. At the moment all anyone thinks of when they want Tackleberry is of a big gorgeous boy in tight riding pants and that's just so boring from Tackleberry's point of view! Because Tackleberry is so much more than *just* that. Don't fence me in. I am a creator, not a copycat. I've told Tim to send them my scripts, I write too you know, it's all my own work. I want real roles, the grittiest I mean, but all they want, the clowns! All they want is a pretty arse on a horse! They all want Tackleberry, a piece of Tackleberry. But the wrong piece, because Tackleberry is not just a pretty arse, no, no, no, he is so much more than that. So much more, *yes*, I must *insist* on that point. Anyway, what about those foxies? I'm ready for some fox fur. Foxy, *frisky* foxies! Frrrrrr!'

Tackleberry scrunched his face up and squinted like a mole confronted by sunlight, his hands raised to his chin in homage to that creature or another, Petula wasn't to know; 'Find me foxies or I will hurt you! You do not want to feel the bite of Tackleberry!'

'What? I've absolutely no idea what you're talking about... Get your hands down from your face, you look... ridiculous.'

'Foxy time!'

'Stop talking. I don't understand a single thing you're saying... I don't, so stop it... *please*.'

Petula was telling the truth. She was experiencing an attack of violent incomprehension she could barely bat back. Its cause, though vague, was nastier than any foul energy that could be attributed to Tackleberry alone. The will to resist his spiel, far less answer, was undergoing a reverse metamorphosis; the swift current of her anger slowed then reversed by a dam of paralysing disbelief. What was going on?

'The foxies, the foxies!'

'Stop that, just shut up!'

'Girlies, foxy ladies, you know the kind, paw lickers!'

'My head... I can't bear this, I feel weird... bloody weird... I think I might be sick...'

In what seemed like slow motion Petula watched her hand

open and the glass Tackleberry had given her tumble to the floor, roll to a halt and be crushed by a passing boot. The boot looked like Jazzy's: heavy, clumsy and angry. The sort of boot that liked to stamp and thump, trampling down any more delicate object that crossed its path. Petula hated boots like that; she was on the side of the glass. She smiled sympathetically at the broken vessel, admiring the little shards ground into smithereens, their many splintered parts glistening like precious stones. Her fascination was mingled with a keen appreciation of danger; the room bristled with threats of every kind. It would do well to remember that the accident had occurred a long way away and therefore had nothing to do with her; she was safe, only an observer. All she had to fear was the voice she could no longer hear, her own, a pointless little secret best kept from the outside world that knew another voice, still hers, only less so; one that could be heard every time she opened her mouth. Let them connect her to that! Still, she was damned if she was going to make it easy for them by speaking: there was too much to enjoy in the glorious and over-directed silence that had discovered her. The rest of the room was flowering into a cartoon jungle last seen on children's wallpaper, as wondrous to Petula as it was familiar to the macaws and toucans that populated its branches. As remarkably, there were trees she had never noticed before, growing alongside the chairs and other wooden objects in the room. Whatever was made of a natural substance, be it cotton, metal or flora, appeared to be accompanied by the place that produced it – looms, steel-mills and flower beds hovering round the guests like old cine reels, while the head of a cow, twisting from side to side, struggled to get its front and hind legs out of a leather armchair, oblivious to Chips Hall who sat slumped in its path. By way of contrast, plastics and other man-made fabrics fizzled and spat under her gaze, tupperware containers burning like oil-wells and polyester shirts shrivelling off men's backs as if struck by napalm, her own silk dress dissolving sometime earlier into gooey scales. What the hell was happening? Of course Petula knew she must be seeing things, while remaining equally sure she was not. Was that how going potty worked? Hallucinations affected the eyes: this was the whole book of Genesis. Both views must be correct. It was a little shattering that she had never noticed this before; if two things could be true of the same state of affairs no wonder everyone always thought that *they* were in the right. Might every great mind simply be a doubt away from its opposite position?

Petula's neck stiffened as she stood there aghast at the implications of this latest discovery, Tackleberry still jabbering away like a sermonising whisky priest, her own expression as inflexible as one lifted off a medal. She was quite lost, her former thoughts characters in a story that had gone wrong. Memories rushed to greet her by the thousand, the assigned masks they had previously worn cast off as new and frightening faces took their place; a past that no longer agreed with her, the voice she wished to suppress leading the charge, yelling at the top of its jeering range: '*What overpriced counterfeit reality do you live in?*'

Everyone's first reaction to the truth shaped as an attack was mortification, she knew that, it was what one's second response was that counted, and Petula was not to be caught short in quick succession. She had to snap out of it. With a determination that verged on the demented, Petula tried to move her face away from Tackleberry's diarrheal flow, at the same time as silencing the voice of her conscience, if that was what she could hear yelling behind her ears, along with all the other debris erupting under her unconscious. The mental part of this operation, or the resolve to attempt it, was easier than its physical execution, for her head would no more bend than the Queen's leave a ten pound note, the effort of trying to move leaving her wobbling with a crooked neck. Could anyone, she panicked, notice this? After all, she hadn't said or really done anything yet; perhaps she was still safe!

'I like fox hunting you see, in chaps, tight you understand, because Tackleberry likes to feel a bit of Tackleberry.' Tackleberry had seized his genitals and was mimicking the movement of a rider, edging closer and closer to Petula's leg as if riding a rocking horse. Behind her she sensed Tinwood peering over her shoulder, a boxer hoping his trainer would give him the wink to throw the fight, glad that she was bearing the brunt of the punches. He was an awful man yet even this fact did not matter as much as it had a moment ago. Restoring order was pointless, the temptation to let go for the first time in her life utterly compelling; the room and the party were past saving, she had may as well take her place in the madness. But first she had to clear her way out of the undergrowth. Chandeliers, tablecloths and candles were covered in the wild jungle habitation that had always, she now guessed, been there, hidden behind the force of habit that stopped her from noticing this and so much else. Her guests, for example, were squawking birds and she a lion, a lion queen, lazy and tired after all her kills. The parrots, the cream of local society, were taking their cue from Regan, a subdued canary, and had each picked an actor, vultures all, to accompany them to their various bird-tables. With intense and forced jollity these minions were looking to engage the birds of prey in conversation, riding roughshod over their fear with the help of even more drink. The thought that she was paying for this fiasco, indeed, that it was her daughter's coming-out party, was a tempting offer from reality to get a grip again, yet the call of the wild was too strong. Besides everyone was enjoying themselves, it was feeding time! The exception was Trafalgar, a felled elephant, who was disconsolately heading back along the corridor to take his leave in whatever giants' graveyard his kind returned to. There was no time to stop him as Crispin Fogle, the young Doctor Who, who had been sat on the other side of the hall watching Tackleberry, stood on his chair, and pointing accusatorially at his fellow actor, leered at the top of his voice:

'Who's that ugly *cunt*?'

Tackleberry yelped as though stung by a ferocious wasp and ducked behind Petula, knocking Tinwood into the path of Jenny Hardfield and a platter full of braised partridges.

'You see,' he howled, 'I told you, they're all jealous of Tackleberry!'

'Go away, leave me be,' hissed Petula frantically, pulling free of his wet grip, her words vibrating like chords on a strange musical instrument.

'A cunt with feelings!' cried Fogle. 'True poetry,' he went on, 'is absolutely indifferent to the form it is required to take, and so is the true poet. Hear me, for time is short and happiness, wanton whore that she is, is a very tight pussy called, I forget her name...' At that he fell of his chair. Having landed he made no effort to get up, awaiting rescuers. Regan bent down and with the help of Astley hauled Fogle to his feet. Although he was grinning stubbornly, there was a dark thicket of blood oozing down the side of his head and his arms were flopping back and forth like a broken ventriloquist's dummy.

'Fogle, you're a *disgrace* to the profession,' hissed Astley into his ear, crossly lowering him onto a chair, 'snap out of this and try behaving like a human being for God's sake.'

'Oh naff off bumboy,' snapped Fogle, his goodwill having deserted him. 'He must die!' he shouted, pointing again to Tackleberry who was cowering on the floor, 'exterminate! exterminate! *exterminate!*'

'Help me!' screamed Tackleberry, scrabbling up to Petula's waist, 'I'm marked for death, tripping my nuts off too! This has all gone wrong, so wrong for Tackleberry! Help!'

'What? What are you marked for? No. Stop. No. Stop. This. It isn't right, whatever's happening to me... is wrong too,' gasped Petula, this time sure that a device had abseiled into her brain and was talking on her behalf, 'make this stop, stop! No! Tripping what nuts? *What?* Oh God, I've been drugged haven't I?'

'I thought it would be fun, I thought it would stop the night from being so bloody boring! I've never even tried it before?'

'Tried what? Please, I'm scared!'

'What do you think, acid! And I've had two!'

'Two *what*?'

'We're on LSD you silly bitch!'

'How? How could *I* be?'

'I gave you my drink; it was spiked. In case I didn't meet any foxies and had to sit next to you.'

'What?'

'To loosen you up and make you more interesting; I was bored!'

'Bastard! I'll fucking kill you, I'll report you to the police...'

'Those birds, keep them away from me,' Tackleberry pointed to the partridges, scattered over the floor like discarded toys, 'the gravy they're in, it's *speaking*. Saying the most horrible things! Make it stop!'

Petula looked down and to her horror saw that Tackleberry was right, the oily backs of the birds appeared to be moving in concert and in doing so disclosing secrets about the marinade, for though it was the gravy that spoke it was the marinade it derived from that possessed the knowledge, had always possessed the knowledge for it was a *sage* and *wise* substance... Petula cupped her ear and listened to its song of strange and wonderful sufferance, an aromatic melody that would put her off rich sauces for the rest of her life.

'*Strewth*, this is strong,' Petula exhaled. She repeated herself as firmly as she was able, mindful that it fell light years short of what she wished to express, which was that she was in the very mouth of madness. Her breathing was heavy and ponderously slow; it was an achievement to have been able been able to breathe so well in the past, taking oxygen really was very hard work. Gradually she noticed that her feet, formerly the most reliable part of her body, were losing their footing and that she was stooping at rather an unsustainable angle. Next she was at ground level taking her place with her new friends, the birds, where there might be safety in numbers. She was a lion queen no longer. With no clear idea of where or who she was anymore, and no memory of who she had been ludicrous enough to believe she could be when the occasion last arose, Petula saw what it all boiled down to: control or its absence, the light and dark of her life. Why was she so scared of being abandoned by her great comforter? The answer was obvious. There were no fellow pilgrims in this valley. Without the protective veneer of control she was completely alone with the earliest fact she had ever grasped; that she was an irredeemable and friendless failure.

'It's a disaster,' she muttered. It was expected yet still a complete shock. The iron law of life, win or lose, and she on the wrong side of it for once, cast amongst the beaten and hated. She had arrived at her eternal destination; the roasted skins of the cooked birds far too like that of charred human flesh for Petula to believe she was not in hell.

'It *is* a disaster,' said one of the partridges, closest to her hand, with an empathy no human was capable of.

'I *know*,' Petula replied, wiping away a tear.

The tenses had switched, her modest successes a feature of the past, the future the property of her critics. If she were only stupid enough to enjoy second best, to lounge safely through existence like the hedonistic zombies who were careering through her wine reserves, then she too might discover the joys of waking up and remembering nothing. Like children who would rely on the memories of adults, destined never to discover that recollection was the proper completion of experience, this carnival of stupidity possessed a lightness that would always elude her. It was not fair. There was nothing about pain she did not already know and no God, even one she did not care to be observed by, could inflict a trial as pointless as this without even the consolation of a lesson learnt.

For the second time that evening Petula felt the nauseous after-burn of a notion she had never hitherto entertained. She *had* been taught a lesson, a lesson in being made to feel awful, a condition she took pride in foisting on other eminently deserving souls when their behaviour compelled it. Without it control would have amounted to no more than self-control, the part of that activity that interested her the least. Her mood of lingering devastation must be what it felt like to be on the receiving end of her ire, to be someone else that *she* hated! For a hopeful sanctimonious second Petula tried to convince herself that she hated no one, but it was no good, she hated plenty. What, then, to do? Wake up tomorrow and resolve to never make anyone feel as bad as this again? Or slowly weave another version of events that she, or at least the others, might believe? One where she had simply twisted her ankle when that noisy Belgian barged into her: there had been no singing marinade, self-doubt or road-to-Damascus experience to report of. The backstage area that had witnessed it all was no more than her own mind, which for political purposes did not exist. On.

She had been sat on the floor for less than a minute, a broken aqueduct in a ruined city, arousing the concern, if not the suspicions, of Astley, who tapped her on the shoulder and asked gently: 'Are you alright old girl? Donald tells me that wanker Tackleberry has been poisoning people's drinks.'

'I think I might have succumbed to a dose,' said Petula, standing slowly to attention, 'nothing I can't manage or rise above.'

'Then you're one of the lucky ones. Those two,' Astley pointed to the Winkles, Petula's solicitor and his wife, 'I think they've got psychosis or the like. Tackleberry gave them a tray of fizz when they got here. And the rest, as they say, is mental history.'

From behind a long green curtain that mercifully appeared to have lost its jungle trappings, Petula could see two sets of feet, a man and a woman's, meekly peeking out from under the cloth.

'They've been there for the last ten minutes and the couple they arrived with are hiding under their coats upstairs refusing to come out, or take questions.'

'Jesus, I don't know how I'm ever going to make it up to them. What should I do?'

'Best make a joke of it when, and if, they are restored to their senses. They'll be too embarrassed, hopefully, to press charges.'

'Nothing like this has ever happened here before.'

'I can well believe it. I'd have to go back to a food-fight with The Who and Olly Reed since I last got caught up in this kind of carnage!'

'Where the hell is Jazzy?' asked Petula with some of her old authority. The whereabouts of her son suddenly seemed by far the safest thing to worry about. 'He's meant to be conducting the main course, not that anyone would have noticed the starters anyway,' she added guiltily, trying to avoid eye-contact with her old friends the partridges. 'If we can get everyone sitting down then at least there's a chance of reinstalling order. Let's knock some heads together...'

'Listen Petula, don't take it to heart, I can see you're not feeling yourself, this party can take care of itself. Why don't you lie down...'

'No. No need.'

'No I mean really Petula, you look a bit peaky to tell the absolute truth.'

'Nonsense.'

'I'm just thinking of your best interests.'

'I'm *fine*, alright!'

'I'm sorry... I didn't mean to offend.'

Stunned at her own anger Petula wavered and in a fit of inspiration raised her voice even further in the hope of making a joke of her outburst. 'No offence taken. Fact is, I've rarely felt perkier, perky okay, not peaky! Don't worry about me. I've plenty of perk. I'm perky alright...'

Finding that Astley was looking at her as though she were mad, Petula quietened her voice in stages, pretending it had never been raised in the first place. 'Forget rest Max, I'm *alright*, I don't need that or wise words, I'm relying on your presence alone to sustain me, together we can... make things a little better. I'll just need a little help from my friends. Oh look, here are two now...'

'We were looking all over for you Petula!'

Margy and Esther Middleton, retaining the slight and slightly larger relationship in relation to one another's size as they had when Petula first came across them years before, grinned together and asked, 'Where were you?'

Rather than admit that she had been far below eye level communing with the first course, Petula replied, in an attempt to replicate her overpowering best, 'I am this house which is why it's no good looking for me in it, I am everywhere,' laughing she gestured at the ceiling and doors to give them the general idea.

The sisters smiled too politely: they had either heard this kind of thing before or else there was another aspect of Petula's countenance that disturbed them.

'Like God,' said Astley helpfully, 'everywhere and nowhere at the same time.'

'Don't mention him,' said Petula, glad to get a bit of sympathetic banter going, 'avoiding him is why I can treat life as my special place of worship; it's the one place he's guaranteed never to be.'

The Middletons chuckled deferentially at this and Petula felt a rush of self-restoration pass through her. Perversely she knew this must be another attribute of the drug, but it was so welcome that she forbade herself to quibble about the source.

'Could someone get that fire down,' ordered Petula, a command helping to further settle her nerves, 'it's like having the bloody devil in the room watching you all the time.'

'I won't put any more logs on,' said Astley, and whispering in her ear, 'sorry if I misjudged you Petula, didn't mean to send you to bed.' Loudly, he turned to the others and added, 'It looks like it might be a bit too late to do anything with the seating plan, so you might like to join us Petula. A few of our table have already dropped out by the looks of it.'

Petula glanced the length of the long hall, the tables arranged in a broken line, their occupants manifesting some of the more extreme aspects of the human condition. Despite the sound and fury there were absences and gaps, with the room no more than two-thirds full. A number of the older guests had followed Trafalgar's example and filed off towards the exit, others sat in stunned and comatose shock as the actors picked them off, one by one, couple by couple; the fervour of the few failing to disguise the passivity of the confused remainder. More disappointing for Petula was the behaviour of those pillars of the community who, taking advantage of the mayhem, had simply copied the actors' thirst for annihilation: Tom Scone, the ex-Mayor of Shatby, pinching Jenny Hardfield's bottom and guffawing uproariously as his son, the current Mayor, tipsily followed his lead.

'Are you all meant to be sat together, I'm sure I didn't mean to put you all on the same table,' said Petula, doing her best to ignore the evidence of her senses. Picking up the card next to Eager's she frowned and shook her head thoughtfully, 'Donald, case in point, you were supposed to be next to a lovely old friend of the family, Chips, Chips Hall. Why don't you help me find him?'

'I'd rather *not.*'

'You spoil sport. I'm giving you an opportunity to meet new people!'

'But what if I don't want the opportunity? I'd rather be a spoil sport than take my chances on a table with any of that lot.' Eager thrust his thumb up at the next table along. Two of the actors were arm wrestling as a third put out a cigarette on a chewed partridge wing. The Corbetts, cousins of Noah, were looking longingly at the trickle of departing guests, and Mathilda, a friend of Regan's, was biting into her hand to stem a flow of tears.

'You see Petula, I've got to this place in life where I prefer people I know. Boring of me, but there it is.'

'Don't you think dispersing our numbers will be a better way of quelling the rioters, Don?'

'No, I don't,' said Eager, 'and even if I did I wouldn't want to, if you see what I mean. Really Petula, I'd rather just enjoy myself if that's alright. I've already fought in one war. That was enough.'

'But we can't just ignore them as they tear the place apart...'

'Why not?' said Astley carefully lowering Petula on to the chair next to him, 'I don't think they're capable of much more monkey business anyhow. Let's not give them the satisfaction of giving them any more attention. Don's right. Let's just try to enjoy ourselves.'

Petula could feel her position undermined by her allies' complacency. She did not know whose behalf she could pretend to be indignant on. Her anger was at its most effective when hidden behind the guise of defending those who could not defend themselves. But there were no takers for her kind of wrathful protection. This time she would have to come clean and express it on behalf of herself.

'It's just not good enough, we can't let them get away with it,' she protested, 'they've tried to ruin the evening, created a horrible ordure and God knows, probably trashed my reputation into the bargain. I'm finished in Yorkshire!'

'Not at all,' said Esther taking Petula's hand into her own and caressing it. 'This is exactly the kind of mayhem the country bourgeois thrives on. They'll be talking about it for the next twenty years alright, but not for the reasons you're afraid of. It's the perfect antidote to their stuffy, frightened little lives. You've opened their eyes to another way of being, a new reality.'

'Me? I haven't done anything of the sort, have I?' protested

Petula, squeezing the actresses talon-like finger needily, 'do you really think they'll forgive me?'

'Oh more than forgive you, they'll thank you!'

'Even though I didn't want any of this to happen?'

'Don't be so naive Petula, of course you did! Why else would you have brought, and not by chance, a lot of stuffed shirts into contact with a different world? Tonight was what you meant it to be, whether you know it or not!'

'God, not more negative solidarity Esther,' spluttered Eager, 'you don't mean to pretend the bozo army here are some kind of freedom-fighting anarchist collective?'

'Well why not? If their targets are the same as ours.'

'*Ours?* Piss Esther, unadulterated, leaking, yellowy piss. Don't include me in any of this Maoist balls. You're moving towards even greater stupidity than when you hung about with those Trot poseurs of yours. I sometimes think your only public ambition is to remain left of left of centre until your dying day, despite every provocation to switch. The irony is, looking at these wasters,' Eager allowed his large hands to take in the room, 'the man I'd like to hand them over to would be your Chairman Mao. He'd know what to do. And he wouldn't waste time with any flowery eulogising; they'd be sent off to a labour camp without so much as a by-your-leave. I agree that there is something fundamentally *uncivilised* about right-wing politics, but for this rabble there is no excuse.'

'Donald, there are parts of you that are absolutely uninhabitable. Mao would support their protest.'

'Protest?' asked Petula shakily. 'Who are they protesting against, me? What have I done?'

'Why, not you silly, you've given them the *stage* to make their protest.'

'I suppose that is what it is in a way,' said Petula, 'tonight, their way of showing they don't enjoy the same things as us... that we're irrelevant old farts.'

'Don't you start Petula or else there will be no one left to hold the line,' counselled Eager, 'getting pissed on somebody else's booze and dropping your trousers is bad manners, no ifs or buts. Protest, balls!'

'Look at those two square up, delusion versus illusion,' interrupted Astley diplomatically, 'anyone fancy taking bets?' Petula's solicitor, Jerry Winkle, having mustered the courage to leave the safety of the curtain with his wife, a paper crown sat clownishly upon her head, was cast in a struggle to retrieve a fur coat from Tackleberry, who having surfaced with it from under a table, now refused to let go of it.

'It's *mine!*' screamed Tackleberry, 'it's my *foxy!* No one can take my foxy away!'

'Blast you,' groaned Winkle, the sleeve of his black-and-white check suit a victim of this frantic tug of war, 'blast you!'

'Foxy!'

'But I'm its rightful owner! Give it back or we'll, we'll sue you!' screeched Rowena Winkle, holding on to her husband's wrist. 'It cost a thousand pounds!'

'To wear that suit and marry her, he just doesn't care does he, your solicitor, you've got to admire a man for that, even if he is a limb of the law,' laughed Eager cruelly, 'I'd help him if it wasn't for our table's neutrality. You know, I do have to agree with Esther on one thing. I have always thought some of your local associates were a little on the stiff side Petula, but really, they never deserved anything like this. Bleeding Tinwood. Go on Max, give him a hand and get the coat back. And poke that piss-weasel Tackleberry in the eye from me.'

Astley got up custodially and then sat back down again. 'Actually, I think it best to honour first impressions and stay out of this one.' Tackleberry had abandoned the coat and was lying, like a beached seal, on his front and beating the floor with his fists, one eye still following the relieved Winkles who were embracing to mark the end of their ordeal. Taking advantage of his adversaries' hubris, he reached for Rowena Winkle's ankle without warning, and bit at it testily.

'Rabies! He's given me rabies!'

'Should we invite Regan over or do you think she's alright where she is?' asked Margy, ignoring the clamour. She had collected a respectable stack of partridge parts on her plate, and as the others had chatted, finished the best part of a bottle of champagne, her hands, the food, the drink and her plump mouth forming a conveyer belt of efficacy and speed.

'Where is she?' asked Petula, afraid that in her paranoiac preoccupations she had left her daughter behind in the world, untended and without a guardian.

'Over there and taking it all in her stride,' said Eager, 'you must be very proud of her. She is splendidly unruffled.'

Petula felt got at; an unflattering comparison had been left out for her to wear. It was hardly her fault if Regan shone simply by virtue of having no responsibility or stake in either the evening or life in general. She was sat on the table furthest from theirs, at the end of the line, listening to a group headed by Royce, and nodding with the airy indulgence she often showed towards bullshit in public places. Petula suspected that Regan's view of people was hesitant and uncertain, likely to fall into place when they were nice to her, certain to turn sour once they were not, contravening her own preferred way of dealing with the mob. It was doubtful whether Regan yet had the guts to cut an undesirable ex-shag at two paces or turn the other way from a lovesick fool who could ruin her life. Until she did, she was no threat to the world, or, for that matter, to her. Theirs was a love that must always recognise rank; the only people Petula loved that still interested her were the ones who left her wanting more, and she would induct Regan into this knowledge, if she could first get out of this night alive. As it was, of the two, Regan was having the easier time of it: Royce was making her excuses and saying her goodbyes, a casualty Petula was glad the party had claimed. There was still no sign of Jazzy however, and acting on the assumption that a traffic jam of food must be building in the wings, Petula shouted to Hardfield who was hovering by the table, 'Tell that Japanese bloke to bring forth the sushi. We can't wait all night.'

'What about Jazzy, Petula, don't you want him to conduct service? You were ever so insistent about that, you know you were, you said Jazzy had to do it.'

'Oh for Christ's sake forget all that! People are starving here, get the fishy stuff out quick, alright? They'll think it's only another starter anyway. Don't worry,' she added quickly to Margy, 'the sushi's just a trendy decoy for the girls, there's real food to come too. Meatloaf and lots of it.'

Margy wiped her mouth of partridge debris, and to conceal her embarrassment at being singled out as a proponent of the benefits of meatloaf said, 'I actually quite like sushi Petula.'

'So,' said Tinwood, 'do *I*.' The agent had reappeared with a goofy grin, his shirt stuck unflatteringly to his chest and a powdery stack of mucus hanging dangerously from his left nostril, poised to fall like a globular icicle, 'this is a hell of party Petula, I've just been talking to the most interesting young woman who I believe is a mate of your daughter's, Belinda or Melinda? I think she'd be a good fit for the next Radio One road show...'

'You mean you've plied a minor full of cocaine you slimy swine. Honestly Tim, talk about two worlds colliding, you've turned the evening into a complete circus! Half these people are in fear of their lives, and the rest have left, and you haven't even the manners to bloody apologise,' said Astley, his hand resting protectively on Petula's shoulder. 'We've told Petula to not mind, but can you blame her?

'*Whooah*, steady there Max. Hold those horses! It wasn't *my* idea to bring the boys along, it was Petula who asked me to, as it happens.' He pointed a finger accusingly at his hostess. 'She insisted. And I obliged. That was all I did, obliged. Okay?'

'Oh, you're very obliging, only following orders,' said Eager, 'so much so that I think I may be looking for a new agent on Monday. This, along with you allowing Larry to get ahead of me in the queue for the part of the old boy in Brideshead, which I tried to forgive you for but can't, takes the biscuit. It's closing time at the last-chance saloon for you Timmy boy.'

'I got you the part as the family doctor, didn't I?'

'Piss to that; I wanted to play Lord Marchmain and you were bloody well instructed to fulfil that aim!'

'You know, you're getting kind of irascible in your old age Donald, you always were a bit, but it's beginning to get very noticeable.' Tinwood wiped the cocaine-strewn snot off his nose and raised his eyebrows at the others. 'What's got into him?'

'I'll tell you what's got into me, you flaky fraud, years of accumulated disappointment, try that for starters. Followed by the shameful way you've repaid Petula's hospitality this evening, how's that for a bolt on?'

'Please gentlemen, this isn't the place,' intervened Margy. Turning to Petula she said, 'I agree with Esther, I don't think the evening is ruined at all. Weddings are simply pantomime, and funerals so depressing; only a good dinner party like this without speeches offers any hope of sincerity. And isn't that what we have here? Look, hardly anyone has touched the wine, here,' Margy filled up her glass and did the same with Petula's, 'cheers, here's to many more wonderful evenings!'

With a practised flick of the wrist Margy consumed the contents of the glass in one and mechanically filled it again. Her eyes popped, then glazed quickly over. Repeating the process, she threw back her glass a second time, and reaching for the bottle, proposed a toast 'to those nice men, Donald Eager and Tim Tinwood,' sliding down her chair as she did so, her breasts resting on the table beside her empty plate.

'Does she look okay to you?' asked Petula despairingly, another sliver of acidic dread worming its way through her gut and stoking the fear that her psychedelic turn would never end.

'She's pissed,' muttered Eager, 'not that anyone would regard that as an exceptional state to be in, given the current melee.'

'Yes, to the great Donald,' agreed Tinwood mischievously, his chemical balance poised most nicely after that last line. 'Who's that girl by the way, the short little thing in the tights, she's a pocket rocket. I'd crawl over broken glass to empty my 'nads in that!'

Petula – who to her disconcertion had watched Margy morph into a wasabi-glazed salmon, further proof that the LSD was not through with her – had only just thanked her stars that everything else was normal, when she noticed Tinwood unravel his tongue and mutate into a lizard with red stools on its face. 'What did you *say*?' she asked, her voice tilting towards panic.

'I asked who she was,' replied the lizard, the fork in its tongue darting about lasciviously as it spoke, 'that chick has an air of the castanets about her.'

Tinwood was inquiring after Diamanda, Regan's best friend, dressed in a black boob-tube with 'minuscule but perfect' emblazoned across it in silver, her appeal attributable to her entropic green eyes which patrolled a pert, lively face. Having come alone out of the lavatory she had retired to with Rex Wade ten minutes earlier, she was on her way back to Regan's table, the actor showing no sign of surfacing from the same commode.

'She's got the right stuff alright,' slithered the lizard, 'Carmen incarnate for sure, but oh-so-forgivable.' Petula tried to ignore the hissing abomination, and instead watched Diamanda, who had at least retained a human shape if not her modesty. Her assured manner was more conqueror than conquest, and with a crude wink, Diamanda gave Regan a high-five and whispered something into her ear. Almost simultaneously Mathilda, another of Regan's friends, left the table she was on in tears and sobbingly rushed up to Regan to recount what seemed to be a tale of great importance. Pressing enough for Regan to look down the room and catch her mother's eye, the drug exaggerating Regan's precise beauty to a point where Petula was afraid wings were about to grow out of her back and she would fly to the heavens. The vision, far from disturbing her, successfully changed her mood. Her daughter was beautiful and she had made her daughter.

'There looks to be quite a little drama brewing,' commented Eager.

'It's… it's so *compelling*,' said Petula, the pace of the drug shifting gears once more. She had become the lead camera in a film, and was eager to see where the script would take her next. The action looked ready to absorb its audience, as Regan strode past the tables that separated them with an expression of controlled concern, perhaps worried by the way her mother was busy chewing a fork without any food on it.

'Mummy, are you alright?' Regan asked, gently taking the item of cutlery out of Petula's hand.

'What! What?'

'Calm down Mummy, are you alright?'

'In a manner. Why is everyone asking everyone, I mean me, whether they're alright, I mean whether I am?'

'Are they?'

'Could you get out of the way please, I'm trying to watch what happens next.'

Obligingly, though not without some reservation, Regan did as she was bidden, adding quietly, 'You looked like you were having a bit of a bad time.'

'What *is* going on over there I wonder…?'

Mathilda had returned to the table whence she had come and slapped the actor who had been asleep in the taxi earlier, Bobby Stack, sharply across the face. This caused him to laugh shrilly and for her to weep even harder than before. The scene was abject and in poor taste; Petula really would have to have words with the director if things did not improve.

'It looks like a lovers' tiff, the same the whole world over, they could pull their fingers out a bit more and *entertain*,' she mused aloud. Petula was conscious that others could hear her criticisms, especially as she was speaking them aloud, but this felt of no consequence. Keeping secrets from the outside world was unnecessary. The film was everything, her own narrative put temporarily on hold until she could get to the bottom of who had decided to stage this drama in her house. Unless, of course, the answer was that she had... that she was, as Esther had said, responsible for all this... this whatever-it-was.

Feeling queasy, Petula vaulted over the thought and returned to the movie. 'So who started it, what's behind the fight?'

'That's what I was I was going to tell you Mum, there's been some unpleasantness and an accident. Involving one of those actors, the *really* drunk one. It's quite serious actually.'

'I can see that! Your friend's belted the poor blighter in the face. Fascinating. But it's fine now, he's making a joke of it. Look he's laughing.' Which was true, though there was nothing funny, or fine, about Stack's laughter, its piercing ripples closer to the caverns of Mordor than Blackpool Pleasure Beach.

'That's not the accident I mean Mummy. Diamanda and that guy Rex, well, they sort of went to the toilet together.'

'The toilet...?'

'Yes, together, well, he basically led her there, followed her I mean.'

'Oh yes...' Petula was out of the story again, the weird voyeurism of the preceding few minutes draining the prurient curiosity out of her like the itch from a bite. It was startling: how could she have ever been so taken by this sordid exchange? The effort to retain a static sense of self, or point of interest, was a challenge she had persistently failed to meet. The drug had beaten her hands down, she must establish supremacy over it or drown the next time she met its current unawares.

'I think he said that he wanted to show her something. Anyway, something happened and he ended up banging his head, quite hard, against the lavatory seat. I think he's still unconscious now, actually. Don't worry, Mrs Hardfield is going to look after him and has already called an ambulance, I think.'

'Fine, fine, fine,' said Petula impatiently, 'bully for him. Hospital is probably the best place for the man. And what about those two? What's all that about?'

'Right, well that guy has really upset Mathilda.'

'Where, I can't see a scratch on her? She's quick to tears, isn't she?'

'I didn't say hurt, I said upset. Not like that, he's hurt her feelings, he's been really out of order.'

'How?'

'I don't really want to say Mum.'

'Oh come on.'

'Really.'

'I'll ask her myself.'

'No, don't do that, please. The guy, Rob his name is, he said, he asked her if he could fuck her in the mouth.'

'Right, and then what?'

'That's it. And now she's going home, she's asked if you can call her mother so she can collect her. They don't live so far away, near Wetherby.'

'I won't be ringing anyone. I can't leave the party. Tell Mathilda where the phone is and ask her to do it herself. Or else leave it for bit, wait until she gets over it. And don't worry, none of this is your fault. It's more the kind of thing that happens when you get a lot of interesting people together in one place. Stuff can get a bit unpredictable, which is part of the fun of course, but also the risk you run.'

'Sure. Are you positive you're okay Mummy?'

'Of course I am, can't everyone just shut up about that for a bit? I simply had a funny patch, well, a couple, thanks to that idiot I was talking to earlier overdoing my drinks. Listen darling, I know the evening has been slightly uphill until now, but it isn't too late to enjoy the last ten yards, so go and relax and let your hair down before you wake up tomorrow morning with any regrets.'

Regan nodded hesitantly, thinking that she could have offered her mother much the same advice.

'I mean it Regan, stop observing and go and enjoy.'

Feeling the futility of arguing the point, she turned to look for Mathilda, who had vanished into the bathroom Wade had yet to emerge from. Rather than follow her, and pre-empt another unfortunate incident, Regan stopped Jenny Hardfield, who was carrying a large tray of faux medieval cocktails specially prepared for the girls, and took a sip from one. It tasted flat and furry, an alcoholic mousse for minors.

'Yuk!'

'Careful with those,' warned Hardfield, 'truth be told I tried one myself earlier and I'm feeling a bit tiddley still.'

Regan laughed impishly, sticking her finger into the lumpy brown mess and licking it, 'You'll be okay then, this is the night of the living tiddlers.'

'Isn't it just? On my life, I've never seen anything like it!'

For a wayward second Hardfield, her smile flickering wonkily like a fading image on a malfunctioning television, reminded Regan of Mingus. This struck painfully at a part of her being that was not prepared for it. Regan had already briefed her friends on Mingus, moving swiftly through tenderness and sticking to a formula she had rehearsed earlier, that 'He and I no longer fit into each other's lives,' worked from a line in *Dynasty* that had impressed her. If her friends had looked puzzled as to why she should wish to airbrush her first real boyfriend from her life Regan affected not to notice, Diamanda's question, 'But what does *he* think?' a surprise. It had not occurred to Regan that Mingus would think anything; his thoughts were not a part of the equation that concerned her. The belief that there were living beings at the business end of her actions enjoyed a formal reality that was still highly disembodied, a notion brought uncomfortably to boil by Hardfield's smile. What had she really done to Mingus? Left him behind, that was for sure, and in doing so caught her first glimpse of a karmic return; hurt done to others was the hurt one would be left with when they were gone.

Seizing a fresh goblet Regan sucked up the froth and smothered her self-reproach, wheeling it to the rear view of her mind with a determination her mother would have envied. Needless torture was the last activity the hour called for. Of pressing relevance was her mother's insistence that she should take advantage of the occasion and party. To decode: if she wanted to get wildly drunk in front of Petula, this was the evening to do so, a smokescreen for any sin she may commit or have committed in her name.

Having approached the evening nervously, expecting Petula to make a great show of her as she had at previous parties, abandoned to boring or overbearing men, possibly even forced to make an impromptu speech in fancy dress, it was a cheerful surprise to witness the pantomime anarchy of the past hour. Undeniably, her mother's best-laid plans had been thrown into disarray, yet Regan could not help feeling secretly proud of the mess, and enjoying her association with it. If The Heights had burned to the ground there could not have been any more to talk about than there was, and it had all gone down at *her* party. The other girls would look back on it and discuss this night until they were old women, and, of equal importance, all of Nohallows would know of it too.

It did not really matter to Regan that the actors lacked star quality; this was no loss: she had never believed celebrities were mysterious or inspiring figures and had only ever looked up to Petula. Possibly they were not so pitiful underneath it all, even though Regan could not see that far down; either way, their personalities would gain in even the most cursory retelling. For their misdemeanours it was likely Petula would be blamed, which probably explained her jarred and awkward manner, for her mother was certainly suffering for their art while Regan, in the cold recesses of her un-fully-formed heart, had not felt a thing, her mother's pain provoking only slight curiosity. Petula's bullishness, which Regan knew to be a transparent deception, freed her from any formal obligation to worry, it was true, but if she loved Petula should she not feel more of her distress? Or was she really such an ice queen that it did not matter who it was, mother or lover, they could all fade away and radiate so far as she cared? The thought and its chilly undertow, similar to her snubbing of Mingus, was monstrous, but its promise of increased power as mechanically seductive as oil reaching an engine. There was nothing ennobling or wholesome about its path. A blackly erotic and refined cruelty underlay it, Regan could sense it in the seat of her pants, an intimation that she had been working up to this for years: a persona of her own to get behind and cultivate at last, 'The Ice Queen', perfect because it was perfectly true. All she had to do was pick up the crown of identity and put it on.

She was interrupted by Chips Hall, who had been thinking of some pretext to approach a girl, any girl, and act as her White Knight.

'Yah, I thought so, I recognise you from somewhere, are you one of the actresses from that show?'

'No, I don't act.'

'Really? You do in a way though, don't you?'

'No, really, I don't.'

Hall squinted and clicked his fingers in an attempt to pretend to guess who Regan was. 'But I've seen you before, I thought it must have been on television, either that or you look really, really, like some girl I've seen on telly.'

'I've never been on telly.'

'Then why do I know your face? Who do you remind me of? You're just not what you seem, are you?'

Regan could see that he really did not know who she was, also that it was too late to dismiss Hall. She would listen to a minute more for the sake of politeness at the end of which she could disclose her identity and icily excuse herself; he would be the Ice Queen's first victim.

'I suppose you must be connected with Petula in some way, most of us are, she invited a few of her daughter's chums, enough to try and palm this event off on her anyway.'

'Did she? In what way?'

'Don't be naif, when is the gig not about Petula? She barely gave me the time of day earlier, busy charging after what's-his-name, you know, sucking up to those degenerate pups shipped in from central casting like they were, I don't know, like they were Burt Reynolds or someone. She's getting too old for it…'

'She's not old, she invited them for a bit of fun, for everyone to enjoy.'

'Really? She invited them for herself; it's all about her, trust me. I hear she regards her daughter as a less satisfactory version of herself,' Hall added knowingly rubbing his nose, 'I mean, what's all that about?'

Regan twitched her lips so as to speak but found she was speechless, desiring instead for Hall to spontaneously combust and to do so while remaining alive, so as to better feel the pain.

Hall nodded and with a confidential smirk went on, 'Yah, they call them "the sisters", funny eh? A cut-throat partnership if ever there was, that's her over there isn't it, the daughter?' Hall asked, pointing to Mathilda, who having briskly walked back from the toilet with a horrified expression, had stopped at Petula's table. 'I haven't seen the little one since she was sent away to school. They do look a little alike don't they,' he added, 'filthy tarts the pair of them…'

'Excuse me?'

'Ha, I... I hope I haven't put my foot in it, you know, one hears things that'd make your afro curl about those two. Well, not so much things, more opinions, you know, about some stuff, yah?'

'What is it you're trying to tell me?'

'Oh, nothing really. They've just got that thing really, that way, you know, of looking I mean, in common, yah? A bit of the cathouse, a bit dirty,' Hall smiled feebly, 'you could imagine the same bloke going for them both and them obliging, heh heh, hope I haven't overstepped the mark?'

'Not at all; we, my mother and I, have exactly the same way of smiling falsely,' Regan replied, 'when people are boring or rude to us. Goodbye, whoever you are.'

Petula watched Regan march away from Chips Hall with a tinge of disappointment. Having lied to Mathilda about her mother being called, successfully negotiated the release of the meatloaf from the kitchen, held off the ambulance man who had allowed Hardfield and Eager to drag the still unconscious Wade to the front door, thus keeping the emergency services at arm's length and avoiding an unnecessary scandal to add to the others, Petula was quietly coping. Even the LSD had settled into a contained pattern, leaving her fellow diners only partially transformed, so that their mouths and teeth retained animal features, leaving the rest of their faces largely human, and with most other perceptions under surveillance, and taking every second as it came, Petula felt capable of an accurate third-person value judgement. The arrival of the meatloaf was to change all that, though for the moment, she was sorry that Regan appeared to have given Chips short shrift, however correctly she had assessed his oily smarm. This was one occasion where standards were an impediment to growth. Chips might have been yesterday's man, and a bit of a creep, but at least he was a known quantity to lose one's virginity to, and a far better inductor than the acting troop, who did not look capable of a single sustained sexual act between them.

'Goody,' said Margy, who had opened an eye, and then another, her nostrils succumbing to the overdone stench of burning meatloaf, 'here come the mains!'

Leading the procession out of the kitchen was Fogle, the lord of misrule, who had appropriated the chef hat Hardfield had been wearing and, dressed in an apron and brandishing a torn oven glove, held a pair of tongs in the air, shouting, 'Make way for the meat! Black, burnt and beat! Make way for the meat!'

Behind him a line of hired help were carrying trays on which generous cuts of loaf, far from its best thanks to delays, sustained reheating and Fogle's kitchen invasion that resulted in it being trodden over the floor and inexpertly reassembled, then hidden under handfuls of parsley to better conceal the damage, finally made its way to the diners.

'I expect it's all ruined,' Petula commented realistically, 'held up by all that pointless sushi and my son's vanishing act.'

'I don't know,' replied Margy, 'food is food, and meatloaf is pretty good at retaining its flavour.'

'For the first few hours anyway,' qualified Eager.

Laughing as though he possessed some secret, Fogle passed their table and lowered a plate of cuttings towards Petula, for her inspection. 'Meaty treaty. Have a sniff matey. Slam in the Lamb!'

'Push off,' Petula growled, an element of Fogle's plate nonetheless catching her attention. 'Here,' she said, standing and taking the plate out of his hands, 'what's all this?'

Petula's fingers tingled most unpleasantly. What was before her eyes could not be what she thought it was. It could *not* be. No. Not that. Not even Fogle would have done that. He couldn't; it was simply too barbaric to credit.

'What is it Petula?' asked Astley, returning to the table, Fogle brushing past him in paroxysms of laughter.

'He *can't* have...'

'Can't of what Petula?'

'Shat! Shat in the meatloaf!'

'You what? You're not serious?'

'Not me, that bastard over there, taken a shit on the meatloaf and put a piece of parsley on top. To try and get away with it!'

Astley looked aghast and took a step back, as Margy narrowed her eyes with the intense curiosity of the very hungry. 'Looks alright to me...'

Petula raised the plate to her nose, the smell was foul yet resided in a corridor of ambiguity. Yes, the meatloaf was indistinguishable enough from shit to look like it, the steam flying off rancid enough to smell of it... Petula acted on a wild instinct and, grabbing at a chunk, bit deep, flakes and juice running over her lips, a portion diving down her front, and all to no avail – was it shit or was it meat? She was eating it and she still couldn't tell!

With her mouth full, and spitting lumps over her dress, Petula gasped, 'It must be food otherwise I'd be sick by now...'

Tinwood was sat opposite, slapping his thigh, doubled up in laughter. 'Oh Petula, you're too *much,* too *much*...'

'Easy Petula,' said Astley offering her napkin, 'I think you might be seeing things there. There's no shame in admitting it. You've been drugged for God's sake. The Army used to use that stuff for experiments. Here, let me take that.'

Petula handed the plate over to Astley and wiped her face and hands, the relief that she had not eaten a mouthful of thespian poo offset by the horror that she had been prepared to.

'Credit to you for taking the big bite! No one gets out of here alive!' guffawed Tinwood, quite carried away by her display. 'It reminds me of a time I tried to eat an ashtray thinking it was birthday cake at Freddie Mercury's! Too much!'

Petula was speechless. Tinwood was right, this was too much, she did not deserve her life. She didn't deserve life full stop. There really was no excuse for her at all.

'Oh don't be such a dirty ape Tim,' objected Esther, 'anyone can see that Petula isn't feeling herself.'

'I...' Petula was about to protest that she felt fine, but what was the use? She had been struck by the lowest blow of them all; it was official, they had started to make allowances for her. The sympathy that was to be swiftly followed by pity, a redrawal of respect and, finally, blistering irrelevance, had begun. Unfortunately Petula had no choice but to take it: it was the best deal on offer and her only way out. Time to admit she could no longer take any responsibility for herself, having long-lost any claim to be in control of the evening.

'Yes,' she muttered, 'it is all rather a shame, still if it hadn't been for that bore Tackleberry...'

Even this, Petula knew, was at best another ineffectual face-saver. She had recently taken to describing people that made her feel uncomfortable as bores, at the same time as finding relief in people she had previously regarded as boring. Tonight she had found and been found out; the set she wanted to play with was not the deck she belonged to.

Picking up the glass that she noticed in front of her, half in the hope it was laced with hemlock, Petula took a despondent sip and watched Tinwood hatefully.

'What are you laughing at?' she hissed, suddenly very angry. 'Don't you know you've ruined my life?'

'Trust me Petula, I'm not laughing at you, these sniggers are driven by nerves alone.'

'Because you know you've ruined my life.'

'No Petula, you're wrong about that,' said Astley, 'no one's ruined your life, you've had a rough time, that's all.'

'Not bad,' murmured Margy, helping herself to another portion of meatloaf, 'it's actually not bad.'

'What do you bloody care, you'll be back to London tomorrow and it'll be like none of this ever happened. And that'll be good old Petula used up and tossed out...'

'I only said the meatloaf...' countered Margy.

'Not you, *him*,' said Petula, pointing to Tinwood, who was try-ing to keep a straight face.

'Look, cool it okay, I wasn't meaning to laugh at you personal-ly... more the situation, okay? I mean, am I the only person here who can take a joke?'

A figure not dressed for the party was coming up behind Tin-wood, part Guy Fawkes, part, as far as Petula could ascertain, avenging angel of doom. She blinked, convinced she must be hallucinating again, the figure seemed to differ in colour and composition from everyone else in the room, marching forth in a reality of its own.

'The important thing is that no one's been killed, so some proportion here please,' ventured Tinwood. 'Granted things have got a little out of hand, but there's no need to exaggerate our difficulties, we're all friends, let's not get so uptight.'

'I know, I know,' said Petula, Astley's hand leant reassuring-ly on her trembling fist, 'just that you don't know how much work, no, not only work, how much *hope* goes into something like this... It's, it's... sometimes I think it's all that I *have*.' Petula felt like crying again, not a solitary emission, like the one she released earlier, but a full-blown thunderstorm of tears; it was a wonder she hadn't thought of doing so earlier. Glancing over Tinwood's shoulder she saw the figure she had noticed come closer, checking her tears and shaming her admission, its frankly sinister comportment sobering her enough to ask, 'Who's that?'

'There, there Petula, don't go upsetting yourself anymore,' consoled Eager, 'we'll look after you now. Friendship's good like that, you can't remain the gift that keeps on giving all your days, you should allow us to help you more. Do you not know the meaning of remorse?' he tutted, glaring at Tinwood.

'Can everyone lay off demonising me for a sec and stop tak-ing themselves so seriously? You're all way too po-faced, what's wrong with our having a little bit of fun, eh?'

'Hang about,' said Astley, 'looks like um, some wurzel wants a word with you, Tim.'

The figure that Petula had noticed appear from nowhere, had actually been in a corner of the room for a considerable part of the evening, nursing its pain and biding its time, wondering how best to express the rage of decades past. Dressed in his flat-brimmed cowboy hat and poncho, Jazzy did indeed resemble the man with no name, the uniform he was to have worn buried beneath his protective outwear, any thought of fulfilling his official functions as head waiter abandoned the moment he had laid eyes on Tinwood, recognising at once the man who had, as he had so often said, ruined his and his sister's lives.

'I say, Tim, do you know that fellow, he seems to know you?' said Eager. 'He seems most certain of it.'

'Who?'

'Behind you.'

'That's your son, isn't it Petula?' asked Esther, amused at the handsome lunk dressed like a tramp glaring over Tinwood's shoulder. 'My, he's grown if it is...'

Petula decided that she might cry those tears after all. If things could get worse they surely would. Of course it was Jazzy, why, on an evening such as this, would it not be? His motivation was as clear as diamonds; Petula could curse herself for her oversight later, for now she would have to take another punch where it landed, or more aptly, Tinwood might have to.

'Hello there,' said Esther. 'Have you come to join us? You're a bit overdressed if you have, it's boiling in here.'

Tinwood, sensing a weak wind up, stayed as he was and bent forward to help himself to the meatloaf. 'Tell whoever it is that I want some chilli sauce with mine! I'm not tackling any of this stodge without it.'

Jazzy, dispensing with introductions, grabbed Tinwood by the curly sides of his hair and, with cultivated and well-rehearsed malice, thrashed the agent's head down against the corner of the table twice, before anyone thought of restraining him – his mission brought to an inchoate end by Esther, who took to her feet and got between his hands and Tinwood's limp head. 'Are you *mad*?' she shrieked above the noise.

Drawing away, Jazzy kicked Tinwood's chair from under him, and watched him go to ground in shock. Tinwood's fear was greater than the physical damage, which consisted of a small cut above the eye, as he feared a vocal denouement would now follow the assault, listing his former crimes to all those present.

Bringing his boot in, Jazzy kicked Tinwood in the thigh, hard, forcing him to retreat under the table, then, without letting his eyes leave Petula who had been his target all along, shouted, 'There! You made me do it, you never believed me. You believe me now?'

'Oh grow up!' was all Petula could think of to say.

'What's all this about?' asked Esther.

'Ask her!' yelled Jazzy pointing an accusing finger at Petula. 'She knows!'

And at that moment Petula did know, and in fact, could not see how she ever had not. Tonight she had perceived Tinwood for what he was, had in all probability always been, his essence seeded to the core, only her desire to mix with the famous and credible blinding her to his very obvious limitations as a friend and person. Which, and in this lay an even greater source of discomfort, meant that Jazzy, absurd as he was, had been telling the truth, or expressing a part of it, all along.

'Ask her!' Jazzy repeated, foam bubbling at the corners of his mouth like an overflowing mountain brook. 'You're the only ones she's ever cared for, fallen over doing everything for, no one's ever done anything for me! No one's ever helped me. I can go to hell and die for all she cared!'

'Really, this boy is most manic,' said Eager. 'Petula, I must apologise, I think I ought to take my leave now, this is all getting to be a little too much for me. I admit I like talking about violence but I draw the line at having to see it – however blame-worthy the victim might be in this case.'

'No, stay!' commanded Petula, scowling at Jazzy who was reciting his litany of injustices past. 'He's harmless, all he's good for is talking through his jockstrap.'

'You all think she's a saint, she's taken you in, like you wouldn't believe. We get the crud, you get the good stuff, she's false, a fake! Can't you see that? Open your eyes! You knobs! She's made mugs of you, right? Taken you all in. Every one of you is a puppet in her scheme, right? But not me, not me any-more!'

Petula mentally crossed herself. Of course Jazzy had not been right; he was too much of a fool to ever be correct about anything, least of all the contents of his personal experience. So what if Tinwood was a louse? That proved nothing and took nothing away from Jazzy's mania. God how easy it was to hate the boy, the worst night of her life and he had gone and found a way of making it worse. The chippy, verbose, gangling, little, but not anymore, *bastard*...

'I don't see what that has to do with you coming in here and bashing Tim,' said Esther, a remonstrative hand on his shoulder.

'He stole my innocence!'

Petula sneered scornfully, 'Well, couldn't you have come in and made that point instead of half-beating him to death like a one of those football supporters.'

'I believe in direct action!' shouted Jazzy defensively.

'So do I!' intervened Esther.

'Don't encourage the oaf,' hissed Eager, and with an air of impatient irony, 'can't you see he's dangerous and completely deranged, probably on the same drugs as Fogle's crew.'

'I'm not on drugs! This is direct action!'

'I beg your pardon; what I meant to say is that you're a very *serious* young man.'

'Direct action? Don't make me laugh!' taunted Petula. 'This

is what I get for feeding delusion. What great examples of your direct action I've witnessed down the years, very direct all right, just not very much action. Big talk and no movement.'

'I *act*, I act all the time.'

'Exactly, it's all an act, all for show. You haven't the patience, the tenacity, the application, to go beyond that. You're too emotional to ever make a sensible plan and stick to it, so where are you? Standing here buggering up everyone's night with the sort of whinging piffle I have to endure every time you open your flap!'

Jazzy reddened and waved his arms in an angry, though not entirely synchronised, gesture of rebuttal. His characteristically passionate outburst had, he noticed, taken some of the sheen and most of the terror out of his impressive assault; even Tinwood had recovered sufficiently to smirk at Petula's put-down, and find his way back to his place at the table.

'I don't have to prove myself to you, you or anyone, right, especially not you.'

'Oh but you do! Go on, show us some more of your direct action!'

Jazzy's eyes reddened: it was not at all clear whether he would pick up a fork to stab Petula or use it on himself. 'You don't believe me?' he practically choked, 'Watch me!' Making an about-turn worthy of the parade ground, Jazzy quick-stepped past the bemused tables of guests straight through the hall and out into Petula's study, a byway whose glass doors led into the conservatory.

Petula greeted the sound of smashing glass with a shrug, and the second messier break that followed a few seconds later, with stoic forbearance. 'Bound to be worse, he has to smash a whole plate to get out of the conservatory, any fool could walk right through the study doors. They're flimsy wicker things with a thin sheet of glass in the middle. It'd be bloody draughty if the worst of winter wasn't behind us.'

Behind him Esther followed in keen pursuit, sympathy for the underdog in conflict with her courtly appearance. Under her cropped blonde hair majestically coiffured and ankle-length dress weighted down by a heavy belt of red pearls, Esther was a minor Scandinavian royal engaged in a game of hide and seek, only a small badge of the Chairman betraying her firebrand inclinations. The man-boy she wished to parley with had left a number of calling cards on his way out of the building, his trail hopelessly easy to follow. The study doors had been kicked clean off their hinges, the conservatory window, as Petula guessed, smashed completely; shattered glass filled an assortment of pot-plants and cacti, and beyond the detritus, Jazzy plodded into the night like Frankenstein's monster, heedless to her calls to stop. Tripping over the end of her dress, removing her shoes, and catching up with him only with the greatest difficulty, Esther threw her body before Jazzy's, blocking his way with her skinny fists.

'Stop,' she gasped, beating at his chest, 'you mustn't think everyone is against you. I want to help, if I can. If you'll let me.'

Jazzy brushed her aside and through gritted teeth, his head shaking from side to side like a dinghy in distress, muttered, 'Out of the fucking way, what do you know about it? Leave it be.'

'Nothing,' Esther fired back, 'I know *nothing* about it, I admit that, but I'm willing to learn if you'd give me the chance. It's a start isn't it? I want to help you.'

'I'm warning you, don't mess with me.'

'*Please...*'

'You're playing with fire!'

'Do your worst! I'm here for you!'

'Why, what am I,' Jazzy spat, 'to you? You come here, feel sorry for me, and then leave, right? A holiday in someone else's misery, right? I know how it is with you people, your kind.'

'Please, don't do that. Don't lump me in with the others. I'll tell you what I think...'

'Save it, I've heard it all before.'

'I think you're a man in pain, a man in a lot of pain, most of it coming from a place he doesn't even understand. And I care about that, whatever you might think of me. Help me learn from below!'

'Stop, stop it.'

'It's the truth. You're in so much pain that I don't even know how you've been able to go on for this long. How have you?'

This was too much for Jazzy who, to Esther's relief if not satisfaction, threw himself onto the grass, flinging off his hat and plunging his head between his knees, the tears that followed an artless mix of grunts and breathless snorts, moving her to exclaim, 'Good grief, it's been that bad, hasn't it? You poor boy, what have they done to you?'

When he had collected himself she was at his side, an arm wrapped round his neck, her tender hand stroking back his hair softly. 'There, there, you need to get it out of you system, that's all, I bet a big man like you doesn't get to cry very often. Or let his feelings go. It's good to from time to time, even for a big man like you. See, doesn't it feel better now? It's nothing to be ashamed of, getting it all out of your system, to show emotion for once...'

Not wishing to disabuse his comforter of her assumption, there hardly being a day when Jazzy did not grant his feelings an outing most men would envy over a lifetime, he lifted his head to hers in assent and blinked. The muggy block of cloud had lifted, leaving grey cirrus filaments trailing across the night sky; the faintest breeze leaning into them both.

'How does a person come to have as much pain as you I wonder,' Esther asked, brushing the corner of his eye lightly, 'to be so exhausted, so tired, so misunderstood?'

'It's because I'm working-class,' Jazzy replied, inspired either by a far-off Soviet satellite that had mastered psychic control over Yorkshire, with a view to fermenting class war, or by a half-buried hypothesis he had overheard in another context, 'and so was my old man, a farmer, dirt-poor, all his life. Chewed up and spat out. She never forgave either of us for it. It's the bottom line for her, always was, always will be. She hates me because of my roots, right? Because I never betrayed them. No matter what bribe she dangled in front of me. Never. I am who I am. Jazzy.'

Nothing could have delighted Esther more than this class-based analysis, and as she ran her tongue firmly over Jazzy's stubbly upper lip, teasing the corners of his mouth, it occurred to him that he really had stumbled upon something here. Petula's hatred of him was that of the imperial colonist for the native; his response redolent of the slave who struck back and cast off his master's yoke. In this account Tinwood's guilt was greatly obscured, and as Esther's tongue worked its restorative magic, Petula, past injustices, and his new-found guerrilla identity, were all forgotten too. At the unbuckling of a belt, the back lawn of The Heights resumed its traditional function as a mating ground, Jazzy swiftly climaxing not inches from where his father entered his mother, all those moons before on the night Anycock ran with the storm.

'You beautiful boy, you just needed someone to listen to you, you don't have anyone who does that for you, do you? To simply listen, it's the hardest thing... but not for us women. You need a good woman in your life.'

'I have one,' he blurted in reflex and watched Esther instinctively recoil, 'well, a girl, anyway. But she doesn't understand, she's no woman,' he added hastily.

'Oh. How remiss of her...'

There was a palpable change of mood, though not so great as to entirely diminish what had gone before, not for Jazzy at any rate. His hurried copulation with an actress he could not really claim to have found very attractive, nor had any thought of at all until the urge was upon him, was not what he was expecting from the party, and despite later deciding he had been used, Jazzy knew that he felt a lot less angry once the deed was done. Esther kissed him awkwardly on the nose, and quickly returned to the party, leaving Jazzy lying on the lawn, gazing at Altair, Deneb and Vega, the triangle of stars that lay above Delphinus, or 'Job's Coffin', the cluster he hoped would bring him luck ever since he first spotted it as a small boy.

Observing Esther's return, Petula, who had offered a brief interpretation of what had occurred to a small group, including Regan, stressing Jazzy's resentment of the humiliation of wait-ering, the part of his motivation that she guessed would attract least sympathy in those he was due to wait on, called, 'Bloody hell, did he wallop you?'

Esther had lost her belt of pearls and the seam of her grass-stained dress was torn, exposing a tusk-white leg and grazed knee.

'God no, nothing like that, I fell trying to catch up.'

'What for? Couldn't you work out he's bog-brush mad?'

'I thought it best to calm him down. I hate leaving anyone like that, in the state he was in.'

'I prefer people who quietly give in to their tears, obviously taking no pleasure in them, than those who theatrically pro-claim their arrival with a shift in their being,' proclaimed Eager grandly. 'What an indulged boy he is.'

'Don't be so stuck-up and inhuman, he's just a child!'

'Did you stop to see the state he left me in?' Tinwood protest-ed, applying a napkin with unnecessary vigour to the tiny cut on his head, to force a bit more blood out, and biting into a little pill he held under his thumb. 'Did the poor lad say why he decided to pick on me as the sacrificial lamb? Or was I just sat in the wrong place, at the wrong time?'

'You must have reminded him of someone he doesn't like,' said Eager.

'No, I wasn't playing the role of policeman, that's the last thing he needed,' replied Esther, 'he wanted to let it all out, cry I mean, he's at a difficult age I think, the whole world against him, you know. He feels out-of-place and out-of-sorts.'

'You're telling me!' sighed Tinwood, secretly delighted at how well his luck had held out, his secrets safe. 'Tell that to my poor bloody head!'

'Oh you've survived worse Tim.'

'Easy for you to say, you're not the one who nearly had their brains dashed in! You honestly seem to think I'm bulletproof, you say anything you like to me, and I'm not meant to feel a thing, but a yobbo can assault me before all and sundry and all anyone cares about is what society has done to alienate the delinquent prick!'

Despairing of the postmortem, which sounded like the amplified buzzing of a telephone left off the hook, but might have been a pair of flies making love, she was undecided – the LSD having skewered her hearing – Petula clutched her daughter by the arm and said with what authority the night had left her, 'Everything in this life seems so definite, except why we're here, or how we got here, I don't know what to do about it anymore...' She stopped herself mid-sentence, rinsed and exhausted. 'Please at least tell me you're happy, that there's some point to this debacle of an evening.'

'I beg your pardon Mummy?'

'Happy?'

'Yes, yes I am.'

'Good... in that case, the music, what about that?'

'He's here.'

'Just get it started. You'd may as well. There's bugger-all else to fall back on.'

'Now? It's a bit early still.'

'Is it? Why, what's the time?'

'Only just gone nine-thirty.'

'*Jesus!* Is that all... I feel that tonight has lasted all my life. No,

I mean I've been alive for all my life... Balls, help me, what was I saying?'

'Music.'

'Right, okay. Tell the band to start. Dinner's a complete washout. Apparently the cake has already been attacked by those hounds, nothing left of it. And no other pudding. Best get this over with, throw everything that's left at the wall and see what sticks. Bring the band on, wherever they are, if they know any old numbers they might even raise a smile from our poor, poor friends. Our true ones, the only ones I should have ever thought of... Sorry, I'm rambling. What is it? Why are you looking at me like that? What have I said now?'

'Um.'

'Um what?'

'I don't know where you got this band idea from Mum.'

'*What* are you talking about? Didn't I give you several hundred pounds to sort out a band, wasn't that the *only* thing you had to do? You asked to do it yourself for God's sake, this can't be my fault too!'

'You didn't say band Mummy, you said *music*.'

'What are you playing games for? Music? Band? Same bloody difference. Don't split hairs. Where are they?'

'No Mummy, remember, I told you I hired a DJ, there is no band, we're having a DJ, that's him setting up his decks now.'

'A *disc*jockey?'

'A DJ, Mum.'

'Is that what I paid an arm and leg for to come all the way over from Majorca or wherever it was, a disc jockey? Some joker putting on records? You know in total it cost me more than booking David Essex for your father's fortieth! Tell me you're joking, please! There is a limit you know Regan.'

'Not Majorca, Mummy, Zer0 has flown over from Ibiza and...'

'Zero? As in naught, nothing, oh, for God's sake, don't you do this to me too. I thought you had brains. The sushi was bad enough, but you're either being taken or taking me for a proper mug. Tell him to clear off, it'd be better to have an absence than a con man laugh at us.'

'Mummy, please.'

'I mean, couldn't you find someone a little closer to home, Ripon or Darlington, it's not like he has anything to do except stand there all night. You don't have to be Roger Daltrey for that. It would have been cheaper to get a jukebox in.'

'Mummy, please *don't*. Look, I really want this to work. And I explained everything before, don't you remember? Zer0 is a different type of DJ, not one that stands around at weddings taking requests, we're really lucky to get him, he's part of this new style, a different type of music, he doesn't just put on records, he mixes them up, it's as hard as being a proper musician... *more* difficult actually.'

'Come on. Spare me the hype.'

'No, I mean it, he expresses his feelings and makes up his own sounds using old records, but they don't sound old, it's harder than being in a band because he's on his own and doing something completely new and original without help. He's an innovator.'

'My, aren't you the little convert, where was I looking when all this was going on? Obviously not in the same discos as you.'

'I've liked this kind of music for ages Mummy, well, since I first heard it, really, you'll be surprised. It's *really* good.'

'Surprised? Don't worry about that. I already *am*. And at you most of all!' Petula surveyed the slightly emaciated hunchback in baggy jeans, a hooded top and ludicrously greasy ponytail, struggling with a heavy case of records, who for all his surface anonymity still exuded the lazy authority of one who knew what he was doing.

'So that's your Zer0. You know we had all this in the Seventies with *Saturday Night Fever* and Studio 54. There's nothing new under the sun. He reminds me of a ticket tout. Perhaps I should applaud him for his career change. At least the Bee Gees and Nile Rogers looked the part. I suppose he hasn't made a nuisance out of himself, though for the life of me, I don't know what you could possibly see in him, he's... most unprepossessing.'

'The actors are prepossessing Mummy, and look how they turned out.'

'There's no need to be sarcastic, for God's sake, I only invited them for you and that's how you thank me...' Petula checked herself. Anger was clearing her head but there would be time for that later; there would be time for everything later, she must simply get to the end of the evening first, and defer her comeback to a better day. Tactical delegation was what this wobbly juncture called for. 'We've paid for him so he may as well do his thing, whatever that thing is. Those tables, they'll need moving too. That's all there is left for it. From here on I bow out, I did my best, whatever you may think...'

'I know you have Mummy, you know I do. I'm sorry everything has been so...'

'Yes, yes. I did everything I could with what I had, it's up to you now. So go, and good luck, it's thankless out there, absolutely thankless.'

'Mummy, I...'

It was too late, like a fading chanteuse who had been coaxed out of retirement one last time only to find she could not face it anymore, Petula turned her back on her daughter and retreated to her table falteringly.

'It's in your hands now darling, your hands now...'

'Game over Petula?' asked Tinwood, happily puffing on a cigar, 'surely too early to turn in?'

'I don't see why not,' she replied, 'I've tried everything else. Except I'm not in the slightest bit sleepy, even though I'm too tired to walk and have almost no control over what's coming out of my mouth. Or going on in my head, although that has a got a little bit better in the last few minutes. That said, I really think

I can put my finger on it and say that I have never felt worse than I have tonight. So thank you for all your help, you were most invaluable in dragging the world as I've known it down around me.'

'Not again Petula, I thought you were perking up!'

'Really? When was that exactly?'

'Please, don't be like that, it hasn't been all that bad, listen, you know what you could use, I've got just the thing, a little friend that could give you a lift.'

'Not on your life! I've had it with your suggestions thank you very much! You and I are through after tonight Tim, I mean it. This has been too awful. I want no more of you. No more.'

'What did I do? Seriously, I've got just the thing for you, I swear, without a few of these I'd be as low as you are...'

'I'm not low!'

'Alright, alright, I didn't mean low, I just meant down, I mean tired, but these pills' – Tinwood reached into his pocket and pulled out a cellophane bag that contained what looked like small aspirin tablets – 'they've kept me *up*. And I don't only mean up, I mean up, up and away, *high* as you like and no complications, just on it.'

'That's your secret is it? I thought it was that you were just a selfish shit who didn't care whose life he turned up in to fart all over.'

Tinwood threw his head back and laughed, 'No one grows up wanting to be Satan! My problem is the things that make me happy seem to be the same things that make others miserable. I've feelings too you know, have you any idea how much money I raised for charity last year? There's more to me than stage villainy!'

'Really?'

'Sure, sure, I'm always the bad guy, but look at it this way, at least I'm having a good time! You want to stop being all paranoid, that's the fault of that shit Tackleberry spiked you with, no one needs that, but these Es, they're a totally different bag. Seriously, they just make you want to chill and be mellow, you know, dance a little, go for a little boogie and kick back... I've taken another after I got belted and I'm already, well, judge for yourself. I feel good.'

'I suppose you do look pleased with yourself, but when don't you? You were grinning like a moron and stoned on those things when you arrived. You've one of those faces.'

Tinwood winked lopsidedly to acknowledge the closest thing to a compliment he was likely to receive, and waved the bag playfully under Petula's nose.

'Oh put it away, the last thing I need is any more drugs. Period.'

'I swear! Take it from the doctor, one of these is exactly what you need right now, you'll be back on your feet and in the control seat of the universe before you know it. It'll completely cancel out that trippy crap you had before, you'll be reborn, not in a heavy way, trust me, let me make it up to you, you've got to get on one, here. I'm taking another, we can have half each.'

'Half? And what would that do?'

'Try one and see!'

'No, no. It's the last thing I need. I mean, it might mix with this dreadful thing I'm already on and I might die.'

'Impossible! You don't understand drugs Petula, that's not how they work, this one would actually work as a literal corrective to the LSD. Please, it would be so good for you, and you'd make me feel a lot better. I really want to make this up to you. I want you to see I'm not the snake I let myself be made out to be. These drugs, they really help people, help them to feel beautiful and sexy and free. Seriously.'

'Hmmm, well, the wound may as well be healed by the spear that caused it...'

'Exactly!'

'I suppose I don't have anything to lose; here, give me a whole one, in for a penny in for a pound.'

'That's more like it!'

Petula took the pill and swallowed it with a mouthful of flat champagne. Nothing happened though she was not expecting the heavens to open, merely the consolations of a dull sedative. She looked down at Tinwood's knee. He was tapping it repeatedly and clicking his fingers, nearly in time, even though there was no music playing, or was there? It took her a few minutes to decide. Sound was coming from the speakers, only it did not conform to any musical notion Petula had encountered before, closer to a long whistle punctuated by drum claps and crashing cymbals – a woman moaning over the top and a piano crashing down the stairs, all that at a suffocating pace, but not *music*. Evidently DJ Zer0 had started his set, much to the delight of the remaining actors, who formed a circle round the small podium he had erected, and were wiggling and writhing to his strange clatterings, filling the hall with whoops of encouragement, helping the din to grow progressively harsher. For a while, how long she did not know, they sat there, ignored by the dancers who all seemed happy being left on their own to jump about badly.

'Have you ever heard of this stuff before?' Petula asked Tinwood at last. Her desire to accrue novelty had somehow been reawakened and trumped her instinctive disapproval at her house being used as a church of electronic voodoo. 'It... it *burns*. It's not like music at all, is it? There's quite a lot to it. It's... quite... clever... really... don't... you... think?'

'Of course, who hasn't heard of it, it's been playing in clubs for the last couple of summers. It's why the kids are all wearing those smiley t-shirts.'

'Right, of course...'

'To be honest, it's crap if you're not on drugs, but we don't need to worry on that score, I've another bag in my travel case.'

'I'm... I'm alright with what I've got I think.'

A tune buried within the main track, which could have been part of the US military's *Star Wars* programme, so closely did it suggest laser attacks and interplanetary chaos, struck at Petula's pressure points, her lower body responding positively without bothering to consult her brain or existing notions of taste. Low ripples of bass were rattling tables and chairs as if a small landslide was in progress, a plinky-plonk organ starting simultaneously with a choir of sampled orgasms, and a lone bleep holding the whole flow together, DJ Zer0 working faster than any jukebox Petula had slipped twenty pence into. In point of fact, she had never listened to anything that could change so quickly, every decision she made about what she thought of a track lagging behind its latest turn, her knees and ankles keeping abreast of where she guessed the beats might appear next, the noise entering her as might an infection.

'It's speeded-up elevator muzak, basically, isn't it?'

'Yeah, yeah.'

'I like it! Really! It feels like I am standing on an earthquake...'

Tinwood had closed his eyes and was twitching his head up and down in short jerky movements, his face a reflection of the deepest bliss. To her surprise, Petula felt like she might like to experiment with the same response, her decision delayed by a familiar voice. 'Petula, I had to come back, there was something I wanted to say to you, it was no good slinking off like that, not my style.'

'Oh not now...' Petula muttered.

Mishearing her, Landon Trafalgar took an empty seat next to hers and, surveying the scene, which admittedly, could not be said to offer much to the uninitiated, remarked, 'Yes, I thought you'd feel the same way, this is going from bad to worse. It wasn't my place to tell you what to do at your own show but I should have stood to and presented my services earlier, aye, to have offered to clear out the trash while there was still time. Instead it's gone from bad to worse, aye, bad to bloody worse... Kick over a rock and look what crawls out: *Gecarcinus quadratus* – Halloween crabs.'

Petula found herself nodding without really agreeing; it seemed easier than giving an account of her changing feelings towards these rock dwellers, especially as they were so recent and liable to further adaptation.

'Can you pass a glass of water, I'm feeling thirsty.'

Not acknowledging her request, Trafalgar continued, 'I've often wondered how you've coped, with no man round the place, no one to take care of you as a man ought. It's not right for a woman of your age, of your calibre. Forgive me if it's not my place to say it, but I've thought it many a time, you out here on your own, that husband of yours never here. Away again is he? Yes, he's always away, even for his own daughter's coming-out ball. Well, it's alright when things are working out, but what about when they're not? You take my point, I hope? In the spirit in which I make it? Yes? Yes, there's a sensible lass. I came back because I wanted you to know that the help you need is here, I am that help, all you have to do is give the word. Just the word, you hear? Even now.'

Petula would have been only too ready to agree with this sombre analysis at any number of points that evening, accepting Trafalgar's courtly offer of protection, were it not for her welcome slide into anarchic bliss, occasioned by DJ Zer0's mix-mastering skills and, since there was no point in ruling it out, the little white pill from Tinwood's pocket. Taken from the perspectival shifts of the last hour, Trafalgar's return was a most unwelcome intrusion on what promised to be an interesting new experience. Petula attempted to smile meekly but her attention had moved to the music, which she now wished to get up and *react* to, instead of being trapped in some grim overview of her life with a man who could sober up a carnival of drunks.

'Aye, you look like you've been having to squeeze the laughter out tonight my dear, that's the thing about so-called good times, there's always something bogus about them, especially when we have to try too hard for too little, if you take my mean-

ing. So tell me to shut up if you want to. I don't mean to pry into
what isn't my business, not my style, which is why I say stop
me if you feel so inclined. Aye, tell me to shut my big lid; but
you know sticking my nose in is not my way, never has been. In
normal circumstances there would be nothing to say. But look
at this lot for crying out aloud Petula, just look at them. They're
not your sort of people, they're not my sort of people, I don't
know whose sort of people they are because, and I'm going to be
perfectly frank with you here, they're *not* people. They're rats,
furry-tailed rodent scum to a man jack, every one of 'em without
exception, look at them for shame, call that dancing? Call that
music? They look like they've spent their lives cavorting round
the sewers of Scunthorpe. Not a decent lad amongst them. Say
what you like about me, people do, but in my line of work, and in
all my years in that work, real work mind you, not the prancing
and posing this filth call graft, the one thing in all those years
I've learnt, beyond any doubt, and if you'll pardon my French
because there's no delicate way of putting it...'

Please, please, get to the point and then shut up, thought Petula,
squeezing her knees together to resist the urge to get up and
dance. Dance, dance and dance, it was all she yearned to do, her
limbs contracting in mighty explosions of energy, as if a great
wind were blowing her forward, her body seeming to have made
the decision to fly for her...

'...So if you'll forgive my bluntness and excuse my calling a
spade a spade, I'll put it to you in terms any layman, fitter or
joiner would understand: I know cunts well, every kind of cunt
mind you, not just the ones that normally hang round with you
or were brought here tonight, every kind of one. Now that is
something I've wanted to say to you for a long time, never knew
how, never felt like it was the right time to, but the despicable,
yes despicable' – Trafalgar crinkled his nose as if he were trying to avoid inhaling a decomposing object that pervaded the
air – 'display of bad manners that I saw, and still witness, here,

tonight, forced my hand. You can't go on like this Petula! Letting weak and evil people decide your priorities for you, you need a firm hand. No stop, let me finish, I know you're an iron lady, one of the flintiest, but that's not my point. Even the strongest need guidance and help, that's what I had my Bessie for, and now she's gone I need someone else and so, well so do you. That man's no good for you, if he was he'd be here, at your side, making a stand. What I'm saying is you need help to drive the cunts out of your life, and then to fasten the hatches and not let them in again. Oh I know this isn't the language you'd normally hear me use, but why keep lying to ourselves? Help me Petula, help me help you! Help drive them *out*, my dear, and together we'll drown them like the vermin they are! There, I've said it, and be sure of it, once we've achieved their drowning, and by God we will, well then – no, let me finish – then you'll be ready to be led into the sunny uplands of common sense and, if I might so bold, good companionship with one worthy of you.'

Trafalgar cleared his throat, his face quite violet after the exertion of delivering this speech, and, leaning forward in his chair, waited for a response, the heavy force of his breath spreading cheesy moisture over Petula's already soaked arm. Not knowing how to reply, Petula sat on her hands, all the better to trap them and stifle the overflowing desire to wave them in the air. She had always known Trafalgar was a stentorian bore, but never realised he was quite this nutty.

'Well my dear? What say you?'

'I really could use a glass of water.'

'Water be damned! About my offer girl, what say you to that?'

'I...'

'Aye?'

'I...'

All Petula could think of, absurdly she knew, was asking Trafalgar if he wanted to dance. Irrelevant as her unmade offer to take the floor might be, it was still the reaction least likely to offend the man. The music had grown so loud that she could hardly hear the bulk of his speech, and what she had heard annoyed her, not on account of Trafalgar's words or intentions, simply because it was talk, and talk was one activity she wanted no more of at present. She was wasting time, Petula needed to dance and recognise the authority of the virtual remote control planted on her back. This device, installed by whatever laboratory Tinwood's ecstatic pill had been devised in, enjoyed complete control over her future movements; the thought of potentially gyrating against a speaker making Petula tremble all at once. She was not herself, but this time it was a blessed release. Tinwood had, against all odds, come good!

Licking her lips in anticipatory pleasure, not caring whether the technological intensity of the latest track excused her rudeness or not, Petula edged her chair away from Trafalgar's and prepared to get up.

Trafalgar appeared not to notice this tactical displacement. 'What say you Petula? A man can hardly reveal all that I have and not expect a word or two back, can he? That would hardly be in the spirit of the game. The game, you hear? Make no mistake, a game is what we're playing here, the life game, aye, high-stakes poker my dear, the roulette wheel, the card table, I make my move and then you, my prickly pear, pull out your little finger and make yours? Hmmm? Now I know you may have found me shocking. You wouldn't be the first, you might even have thought that I didn't have it in me to be such a coarse old badger, eh? I don't say it was easy for you to hear, but what's the use in forcing the back door when the front one will do very well for the same purpose? Eh? You don't, when all's said and done, make friends with a pirate like me for reassurance but for the challenge, aren't I right? Come. We're friends. Speak openly, I won't bite!'

'I...'

By now Petula did not have any memory of why she was friends with Trafalgar. Far away in the distance, she recognised a lifelong tendency to befriend the powerful, rich and established. Whether this was the best way of ensuring her security or a means of joining their number Petula could not decide; only that her pursuit had forced her to overlook their glaring character deficiencies, namely that most of them were as dull as Trafalgar. Like that other great imperative she followed at all costs, fawning obsequiousness to the glamorous, creative and exciting, her desire to know every wealthy person who crossed her path was unquestioning and long subsumed into instinct. As such it did not really count as a decision, far less a conscious choice, inspiring Petula to exclaim, 'Friends? Us, Landon? I never had any choice. I sought you because of the way I am!'

'*Exactly*, you put your finger on it my girl! We were made for each other! Neither of us had a choice. Oh, I grant you, we're not everyone's idea of star-crossed lovers in their first flush of youth but chaff to that! I always knew you saw me as another father, yes, a father figure, to replace the one you never had. And soon you'll learn I can be much more than that!'

Petula nearly choked on her tongue. This put things into clearer focus. The impatience she had always blocked, towards this man and every other local worthy she toadied to, along with the years of being subjected to their judgments, small-mindedness and irritating unawareness of other minds, spilled out into a curtly-put, 'No! No! You're wrong, all of you!'

'Yes, yes! We understand each other only too well; don't be too clever and not good enough, our connection is an exceptional one lass, exceptional! We understand each other, you can't take a thing as important as that for granted, I'm old enough to know. Be sure of it. Being right is one of the few things I've been able to enjoy in exactly the same way through the years, a pleasure that's never changed. And by all the angels in heaven, I'm right this time too! Love has no time limits.'

Trafalgar was right about his base assumption, Petula could grant him that. She *did* understand him, understood him well and despised what she understood; she had had enough of taking her place in a game of societal musical chairs that dignified one aspect of her being and neglected every other. To look at what it had incubated and ultimately led to, namely a septuagenarian shopkeeper in a smoking jacket slobbering sweet nothings to her, was indictment enough of her former policy. What could be more ridiculous than cultivating a father figure when she hated her father? In fact, hated all fathers; no man had sired her, she was the product of pure alchemy. Tinwood's television trash were rodents, on that Trafalgar was correct, but in controlled circumstances they were devourable, whereas this old man was food for the moths, and more importantly, they were *dancing* and he wasn't. Petula stood up.

'Where are you going? Not out there, with them, surely?'

'I'm sorry Landon, there are other guests I have to see.'

Panic seized Trafalgar, and he lunged for Petula's wrist.

'I've made a fearful ass out of myself, haven't I?'

'No more than I have. Would you please take your hand away.'

'Listen to me Petula, you must listen to me, I don't usually announce my goals until I've achieved them. I took a chance with you and...' It was a weak countermove, Trafalgar could see that Petula was gazing longingly at the dancefloor. The actors had been joined by a surprising number of guests, the party, against all odds, finding its collective pulse thanks to the enigmatic nonentity behind the decks.

'It's no use pretending to enjoy yourself, no one will believe you, you don't fool me like that!'

'Please stop squeezing, you're hurting me.'

Trafalgar let go of Petula's hand and surveyed her with compassionate distaste. Deciding to give her one final piece of wisdom, but catching her impatient eye, Trafalgar abbreviated it at the point of delivery. 'You know Petula, you do very well, but you can't abolish time. You're larger than life now but only because you're scared of it. Mark my words and mark them well...'

Petula was already away, throwing first one shape with her hand, then another, coyly circling the cluster of ravers without knowing if she could shake off every last semblance of restraint and respond to the music in the sole way it demanded. To her immense satisfaction she found she could, the rhythm disarmingly easy to follow so long as she did not mind moving in a way that had little to do with her existing ideas of dance. Petula had lived through the Sixties, not the swinging version, yet close enough to copy the manic deliberation of the girls she watched jive on television on the few occasions when the opportunity to do so herself arose. Tonight the music asked for no such accompaniment, simply for her to mirror its chaotic assemblages and sometimes clear circuitry, which in practice meant that Petula began to jog sideways on the spot, her arms flying about either side of her like an excitable lollipop lady.

'Yo, yo, yo!' hollered Fogle, taking a break from blowing the referee's whistle round his neck, 'Look who's got the bloody spear out of her arse and's going for it!'

'I'm loving it,' shrieked Petula, 'really, really, really!'

'You *what*? You *what*, you *what*, you *what*?'

'Loving it I said! *Loving it!*'

Petula had moved to a new country and had no use for old customs. Let somebody else pick up the pieces and worry. Qualifications be damned, when had she last experienced her body as an instrument of wonder, been lifted so high and taken so far? To feel this attractive normally would be an effort contrived entirely from the subtle and patient application of makeup; tonight the love was bubbling forth from within. Christ she felt sexy! And not just her, they all were, every shambolic set of limbs and feet, entwined together and communing in a huddle of love.

'I love it!' Petula repeated, 'Louder! Louder!' A wistful falling-away was easing down her sphincter like the airiest and most erotically satisfying fart ever slow-released. 'Total heaven,' she gasped, 'to be alive. Whooh!'

'Whooah, Petula! I didn't know you liked to dance!' croaked Tinwood hoarsely, suddenly aware of her at the centre of the melee. Touching her face, with near-animal curiosity, he added, 'You're feeling good, right? All that other shit just a bad memory?'

'Good? Too good, I love it!' Petula laughed, this simple affirmation nearer to the truth than any other spoken alternative she could think of. 'Really I do!'

'Cool,' Tinwood intoned, a clumsy slowness to his movements which meant that he was lagging behind the accelerating beat. Wiping back his sweaty combover he gave Petula a cheeky thumbs-up; she winked back, the two of them children in thrall to their new toy.

'Nice one!' he sniggered.

'You too!' she found herself saying, 'Alright! *Let's fucking dance!*'

Petula felt an intense connection with the agent, and realised that it was shared with all her fellow dancers, the room, and life, divided between the movers and the statically bemused. Those on their feet were enjoying an identification stronger than politics or religion; it was enough that an individual should choose to join the dance, no matter how grievous their prior shortcomings, to belong.

'Shake a leg girls!' she called over to Regan's table, her voice drowned in the squelching bass, 'This... this stuff's tremendous!' Manically, and not a little unhingedly, she pointed to the decks and gave a knowing thumbs-up.

'I can't hear you Mum,' Regan shouted back, the relative darkness sparing her blushes.

'Forget about it, just get your arse over!'

For Petula, judgement was an annoying memory that no longer worked, this abolition of standards arriving in time for Tackleberry who, having reemerged playing an imaginary flute, was hopping about blowing raspberries dangerously close to her toes.

'Who are you, the cunty Jester?' Petula yelled.

Tackleberry performed a little twirl, and caressed the air, his stubby shoulders bopping back and forth as he held his hands round a virtual neck that he seemed intent on clumsily strangling.

'Come on, come on, everyone come on!' beckoned Petula to all-comers, '*Come on in!*'

Nestling up to her backside was Fogle, rubbing against her sticky dress with the crude audacity of a one-man conga line, and beside him Chips Hall, bending awkwardly and clutching his sides, in an attempt to get down with it, for it now seemed the thing to do.

'Connect woman, connect,' Fogle breathed heavily into Petula's ear, his face balanced on her neck, 'you got to *connect* with yourself, I demand it.'

'Oooah...'

It was like gorging on a dirty chicken kiev she had just got out of the freezer and could not stop eating, she knew she should desist but Petula couldn't, the garlic as good as dribbling down her chin. 'Connect me,' she replied, 'go on. *Do it...*'

Fogle's hands were all over her, their bodies moving in an electronic tango, the partners dissolving into a shapeless libidinal movement, Petula so far from shame that Fogle could have entered her there and then for all she cared. As in the height of her lovemaking, Petula was giving into an injurious and sweet pain she could at last express, a feeling of absolute relief that was not secret anymore... their dance was like that but without the beauty, without the point, and without the impediment of personality and character; they were inhuman shadows, no more real than the DJ's flickering strobes and half whacked-out smoke machine, puffing away doughtily behind a curtain.

'Yes, yes, yes...'

There were no indications of reality, Petula did not have to make the abstractions concrete, only take another beating from the ever-present drumroll and scream as loud as she could, 'I could do this forever!'

'You know you could baby, you know it.'

Petula closed her eyes, and reached out for the ghost in the machine. In the past her love of landscapes and skies had not so much disguised as announced her longing for immortality, the hills and stars as permanent and unending as she wished her future incarnations to be. She was where she wished to be; pure soul. And the music kept playing on...

'Yes! Yes! Yes!'

Regan watched her mother, half-absorbed, half-disturbed, mindful that this was the moment she most feared the arrival of, the part when Petula enjoyed herself more than she did, but for it to happen like this, with her music *and* her friends dancing round her mother like bees buzzing round the queen... It was too much, and quietly, in a way she hoped would attract no attention, she broke a breadstick in half and stabbed both ends into the table.

'That smoke eh? It's like bloody tear gas,' said Eager, offering Regan his handkerchief, 'reminds me of the bloody war. Can't say what this music reminds me of, one of those Earl's Court light shows I think, before they show you all those new cars no bugger can afford to buy.'

Regan felt grateful for the old actor's presence, and thanked him by accepting his handkerchief and blowing her nose into it. There were tears in her eyes but they were not falling, simply staying where they were, and doing nothing.

'Sorry.'

'Think nothing of it.'

'Some skins are thinner than others, some skins are thinner than other skin's mothers,' growled Trafalgar barging into them, a bottle of brandy in hand. 'Watch that one,' he went on, pointing at Petula, 'she's a great dame for hiding in the light.' Taking a hefty swig he collapsed into an armchair and surveyed the scene with an exaggerated scowl. 'We could have almost had it all lass,' he grunted. 'There, right there for the taking,' he added, clenching and unclenching his hand.

'Hmmm,' chuckled Astley, joining them both and handing Regan a beaker of champagne, 'so... tonight... I think it's gone quite well, don't you?'

All three of them burst out laughing.

'You don't feel like dancing my dear?' asked Eager.

'She makes me feel like the family's grey sheep,' said Regan without thinking, 'you'd guess she'd spent her whole life just waiting to jack her booty!'

'Sometimes the simplest possible answer is not always the most obvious one. I think she's tired and unhappy. Those aren't high spirits Regan; they're your mum's way of trying to forget about it all.'

'What's she got to forget about? I mean, she has the perfect life, hasn't she?'

'Has she? Did she tell you that?'

Regan opened her mouth to reply only to find she possessed no answer. Inquiringly she peered over the dancefloor, and at her mother's latest manic display of energy. Petula, sensing she was being stared at, looked back. It was the first check on her rush. Regan was casting a critical eye on her, and indeed, would seem different to her from that night on. A moment earlier Petula had briefly felt something snap and give way in her ankle, but quickly danced over the abrasion. The pain may have affected her acumen; why else was she wasting time mooning at a party pooper who lacked the wit to seize the moment as she had? If Regan did not know how to enjoy herself she jolly well did, and there was not a moment more to lose. The night was getting away from them. Petula was in agony and yet euphoric. Life was sweet. Record decks were her new favourite instrument, verses and choruses could go hang – she had seen the future and could dance to it. Grabbing the whistle off Fogle's neck she blasted it for all she was worth. The music was just as beautiful as it had been before, Fogle scooping her off the floor and rubbing her in toxic perspiration, the swelling ankle forcing her to dance on one foot now, anything to keep up with the changing frequencies, anything to keep up with the others, anything to keep up with all this marvellous... ecstasy.

*

Jazzy stabbed his knife into the ball, left by the son of one of Petula's guests from the summer before, and watched it deflate under his hand with no obvious satisfaction. He was used to carrying on with a conversation long after it was finished. Music was thumping over the lawn, shrieks of laughter carrying across the garden and down the hill, to where he was slumped on the drive, weighed down by a jagged melancholy that had struck his legs dead. Embracing his pain, Jazzy stretched out on the track in a star shape, the heavens too far away to be the coded shapes and messages which would normally have vied for his interpretation.

The gravel beneath him kept him bound to earth, it was prickly and rough, like cut hair stuck in his collar, the irregular incisions probing through his clothing a reminder of nature at her most closely inhuman. Jazzy wondered whether an untimely accident might qualify as a suicide attempt; it was not impossible, a car quickly speeding up the drive unlikely to know what it had hit until it was too late, his sorry flesh mulched into the potholes he so loathed to fill in life as his soul ascended to a far kinder place...

Thinking better of his personal dissolution, Jazzy crawled into the bank and wiped the lingering taste of Esther's lip gloss off his mouth. Revenge had not tasted as sweet as it should, his vindication at taking the war back to Tinwood ebbing before he even finished his correctional beating, with the effects of his redemptive fuck nearly as fleeting. He sighed. For this he had waited so many years; there was no such thing as victory, all roads led back to life.

Before him, crouched in the incline, sat his bungalow, squashed by the unkempt bushes and overgrown hedge that ringed it off from the rest of the farm like a wall, shabbily anonymous and unloved, easily confused for another of the estate's condemned relics. The hedges had grown so high that his little garden had developed its own weather system, frost covering the mossy grass as no light could get in, the building utterly overwhelmed by the bocage that hid it from view, lending it the look of an underground bunker.

He had no wish to go in and resume his life, the one he so often complained he 'wanted to be left alone to get on with'. Jazzy's longing lay in the opposite direction, to rejoin the party he had all but debarred himself from; the lights, laughter and noise that tauntingly continued without him at The Heights. Was he the rejector or the rejected, banisher or banished? In all the to-ing and fro-ing Jazzy had forgotten the order of sequence. Nor did he have any great wish to remember, suspecting that to do so might lead him back up into the path of advancing traffic, with Esther's thoughtful kindness lending a gratuitous helping of self-reproach to his usual diet of thunder and woe.

'For fuck's sake,' he mumbled, his rolling papers stuck together and tearing at the first ruffle of his impatient touch. Crossly he fumbled in his pockets for another pack, finding only a twisted bit of fruit-gum foil and an unpaid parking ticket. It was too much. Could not, for once, the lies be the truth and he, and not his sister, be the heir anointed? He would be a good and kind and generous ruler, no one would have anything to fear from his reign, there would be no reprisals, no recriminations, no hangings or shootings, only justice and peace. The tatty grey shawl of internal exile, dragged by a king never-to-be would be cast off for good, replaced by the dignity and fellowship of a Camelot in which he wielded Excalibur. This fantasy was at once so pathetically base, yet nakedly true to his unacknowledged intentions, that Jazzy winced, glad that no one could peer into his mind and listen. What burnt his conscience most deeply was that the sensible, and still very good compromises once open to him, were all but impossible in the stew he had helped to prepare, simmer and bring to boil. It was hardly conceivable that in his short life he could have gone from living in a rural palace to dwelling on a frog's bottom just yards away from his former splendour, the juxtaposition all the more torrid for his trying to convince himself that his lowly hovel represented progress. It was not that he really cared about the trappings of wealth or status (though he had to confess to a soft spot for comfort), just that in the absence of any other trappings they were preferable to his meta and physical stasis.

Jazzy stepped over the broken gate and approached the side door, the front one long-obscured by rotting piles of wood that waited there, year after year, for cutting. The bungalow walls, originally granite-grey lumps of concrete, were buried under thick smears of brown algae and creeping ivy, the small windows practically eyeless, hidden under the detritus of a prolonged winter and delayed spring. Loose slates hung menacingly from the roof, blocked and broken guttering patrolling the building's fringes, the chimney that had twice caught fire the Christmas before reduced to a crumbling red stump. Broken glass, fragments of brick, rusty beer cans, dog bones, soggy newspapers and torn bin-bags populated the garden, choking the snowdrops and daffodils, with what grass remained thin and irregular thanks to the all-seasonal shadow cast by the vegetative fortifications. Some of this, Jazzy had to concede, was his fault, and some of it not, a life wasted apportioning the blame all he had to show for his years as master of this mess. Having never wished to acknowledge the entirety of his character, his feelings, no matter how repetitive, came as a reliable surprise to him. The geographical upshot of this failure to progress was marked by Jazzy's attachment to the same spot, however much he had grown to hate it, and the expectation that it would, without his lifting a finger, one day change for the better.

Jazzy nudged open the door, which was warped and stuck against its frame, its shaded location affording it no exposure to the sunlight that could have shrunk it back to its former shape. He was, he knew, all too ready to embark on an argument, as what he required now was complete understanding, in whatever form he decided it should take; and what human could give that? The thought of Jill, sat all night watching television, sipping cider and doing nothing to help him or housekeep, suddenly enraged him; he needed a partner, not a passenger, though just as quickly his anger palled. She was as much a victim of their exclusion as he, and to that end, he must show her more compassion and thoughtfulness, however hard it was to stick to this resolution in practice; her simpering agreeability too often stoking the rage it sought to placate. But for all her talk, what had she ever done to concretely help him? He needed a doer, not a dippy chatterbox...

The dim hall, packed with obstacles of every kind; broken video recorders, stacks of mouldy photo albums, an iron mangle and second-hand fridge, awaiting use or sale, always insured a collision or two, doing nothing for Jazzy's mood as he approached their living quarters at the other end of the dank building. Despite the exhausting vexations of the past few hours, Jazzy was alert to a subtle difference in his hearth. The bedroom door was closed, thin shafts of darkness pouring through the cracks in its rickety frame. On a normal evening Jill would have been curled in front of their small black-and-white television that was enthroned on the chest of drawers at the foot of their bed, until she fell asleep to the dulcet burrs of closedown. Instead the kitchen light was still on and a familiar noise, not immediately identifiable but one he had heard her

make many times before, was being emitted uncommonly loudly. Without having made his mind up as to why, Jazzy felt a volt
of apprehension puncture his gloomy irritation, followed by
fearful disbelief. Quickly he stumbled towards the kitchen and
snatched open the cloth partition that acted as a door, tearing it
down as he did. Once in, he could not quite believe what he saw.

His partner, or at least, the soles of her feet, were waving to
him, like hands raised during the terrifying descent of a roller-
coaster ride. Between them were the olive oven-bun buttocks of
his neighbour, never before observed in this position, pinning
the rest of Jill to the sideboard that had been all but broken
asunder in his last climactic strokes of lust. How, thought Jazzy,
had Mingus got his arse that colour living in Yorkshire? Fighting
the urge to be sick, he realised it was of no accord. His partner was being fucked by another man. Squeaking like a spring
relieved of a great weight, Jill started to jabber a torrent of loving nonsense into Mingus's ear, his slight body leaning into
hers, as he slowly fought to recover his breath.

Time, a lot of time, appeared to elapse before Jazzy heard
himself shout, 'Right, *right*! That's enough, I've seen everything,
what the fuck is this? What the fuck are you two doing? Don't
deny it, *I saw you!*'

Mingus bolted back, losing his balance on account of the
jeans still rolled round his legs, and fell as heavy as a plank
onto the floor. Panicking like a writhing fish out of water, he
accomplished the buttoning up of his trousers from where he
lay, so that as he struggled to his feet and faced Jazzy head-on,
he could at least parry any incoming blows with his modesty
covered.

'Get out of the fucking way, I don't want to see you. *Cunt.*'

Lamely, Mingus hung at Jazzy's side, as Petula's son glared
at Jill aghast. Unlike her lover she had been slow to remorse,
and whatever shock registered by Jazzy's entrance had gone by
the time he laid eyes on the face he thought he knew. There was

a twinge of regret on her lips, but not the kind Jazzy sought, rather a feline crossness at not having been afforded the time to enjoy a post-coital cuddle, having sampled the rest of the goods.

'You could at least *pretend*,' yelled Jazzy, 'do you know what you've just done to me? Christ, I can see the come dripping down your fucking leg!'

'Don't make it worse,' she said quietly, 'I know it looks bad.'

'*Looks!* Bad? Bad! What are you talking about? You haven't seen *bad!*'

'Jazzy, please.' Mingus had unwisely put his hand on Jazzy's arm in an attempt to recover the situation. 'I'd just come to say hi before I went back... and then...' Pausing, Mingus followed the line of Jazzy's look down to Jill's naked thigh, a trail of what he left further up on its way down, his qualifications nefariously inadequate in the face of such physical proofs, 'I didn't think anything would happen... and I'm so sorry you know...'

'Nothing happened! You're trying to tell me *nothing happened*? What kind of mug do you think I am?'

'No, I said I didn't think *anything* would happen...'

'Christ! Are you going to get it out and fuck her all over again? Get your hand off me you cunt!'

'I'm sorry. I... it's not as bad as it looks! I mean, it's not happened before.'

'Too right it hasn't boy, I'd have known, what? You think I'm a fucking mug now?'

'Jazzy... we were just talking, and then...'

'You can't deny it, I saw you! Right, I *saw* you!'

'I'm not trying to deny anything.'

'Just stop talking, okay? Shut up, I want you to shut up now. I'm going to tell you what's going to happen; you're going to shut up. Or I am going to punch you, right?'

Jill had adjusted her skirt and, having reached down to pick up her panties and stuff them behind the radiator, was watching the two boys with a dissociative interest, as if she were waiting for a quarrel that had begun long ago to finally resolve itself.

'I swear this has never happened before Jazzy.'

'I know it's never happened before; you snake, you think I could live with someone you'd been stuffing and not know, right? I know it's never happened before. But everyone knows what you are, you know that?'

'Okay, you can call me anything you like. You can hit me if you like.'

'Just shut up, I don't want to talk to you, you fuck off, fuck off right, you just fuck off, stop speaking, I don't want to hear you, okay? Just fuck off out of it. Now, fuck off!'

'Please Jazzy...'

'Go on, get out, get out before I hit you. Fuck off cunt.'

'Fine, if you want to hit me hit me, if it makes you feel better. I want you to hit me, go on.'

'I said get out, get out of it, cunt.'

'What are you going to do to her?' Mingus pointed at Jill who, having lit a cigarette and reached into the fridge for a can of cider, had admittedly never looked so capable of looking after herself.

'It's none of your business. Friendship over, right? That's it. I want you out of my life. That's us finished, for good, right? *Over*. Hang on!' called Jazzy, 'Where the fuck do you think you're going?'

'You told me to go.'

'You think you can just walk out of here after this? That I'm just going to let you get out of here scot-free after what you've done? This is my home, my house, my table, my chairs, my food and drink and my girl, right? No way, no way are you going to just waltz out of here after what you've done to me, no way! You lay one in her, take a piece and not pay for it.'

'What do you want from me? I said you could hit me.'

'How about you begging forgiveness for starters, on your stomach like the snake you are, and you, you slut,' Jazzy glared at Jill who was nonchalantly sipping from her can, 'I haven't even got started on you yet!'

'Why don't you sit down and stop working yourself up. You know Jazzy, this is probably for the best,' said Jill, the perverse beginnings of a smile tickling the ends of her mouth, 'I mean, we haven't been getting on for a while, have we?'

'I don't believe this! Are you mad! I can't believe what I'm hearing, right? You should be on your knees begging me for forgiveness! What have you been telling her?' Jazzy asked, ramming his fist against Mingus's shoulder, 'Turning her against me because of some bloody book you read at your college. Yeah?'

'Grow up.'

'No,' said Jazzy, pushing Mingus again, 'you need to hear this and listen for once' – Jazzy tapped his ear vigorously – 'you've made her think you understand her, right? That you're so weird and cool and intelligent, completely down with women and understand their feelings yeah? That's not you man, that's *me*, so stop pretending to be me and find some tail of your own, you poof!'

'Oh fuck off. She's lovely, too good for you, I never did it before but it isn't that no one else would have in my place, anybody would have given the chance! You're the joker Jazz. No one will tell you, but so what? Somewhere in yourself you know you are.'

'You mind your manners or you die motherfucker!'

'Go on then, kill me you prat!'

Jazzy lunged forward but Mingus had already taken the precaution of driving his fist straight into his erstwhile friend's ribs. Something cracked. By the time Jazzy had recovered his pose Mingus was gone and Jill had opened another can of cider, a provocation too far for Jazzy who pulled it out of her hand and smashed it against his head. The physical pain was neat shorthand for what he was feeling inside, the second self-inflicted blow from the can releasing a catalytic torrent of invective that

Jazzy was soon lost inside, his injuries hanging out in all their betrayed and humiliated agony as the cider streamed down his snarling face.

'How could you? In *our* home? The place where *we* live? No! No! *No!* I won't have it, I won't have it! You owe me an answer, right? Are you listening, can you hear me, are you bloody deaf, dumb and blind all of sudden? Speak for Jesus's sake, I'm not having this again, it's answers you owe me, answers, a reason, *get it*? A reason why you had to destroy our life here, kill our lives, why did you do it Jill, why?'

Jazzy had earned the right to ask, their shared past acting as a deposit before a future he never once doubted they'd still share, the shock that Jill might have wanted to do what she did more appalling than the actual crime. The deed could be palmed off as mistake, the heinous spell of an outside influence, but her motive could not. He needed her to admit that she was as sickened by her reasons as he, and then the healing could begin, albeit it within the frame of perpetual and unconditional contrition.

'Listen Jilly, all that you love is all that you'll ever own, you leave love and you're homeless, right? What you've done, right, is *disgusting*, no one could argue that, but that doesn't mean I don't love you. No, because I can't help that part, so don't piss on me by using that against me, okay? Don't piss on my face... you're a bitch but I love you!'

Before this storm Jill said nothing, no words at all, not to Jazzy's exhortations for an explanation, apology or answer, his hands coming close to but never actually touching her; not with so many other things to break first.

'Jill, are you fucking *listening to me*?'

In the morning there was a fist-sized hole in the oil tank and an empty place beside him in bed; Jazzy would tell anyone who listened that Jill had not wanted children, the explanation more consoling than the letter she sent a week after her disappearance, the contents of which he could never bring himself to accept, his remaining contact with her limited to the dreams she haunted, inconstantly and in different forms, for several years after.

*

Petula could hear the phone ringing and opened her eyes with no idea of where she was. The throbbing pain at the bottom of her leg was so extreme that any movement, past, present or future, seemed beyond her. The ceiling was certainly consistent with her bedroom, and the smell too; the incongruity therefore, must lie in her. Panicking, Petula reached down to her waist and to her relief found that she was at least partially clothed and that her underwear, though ridden hard, was firmly on. That she was lying the wrong way up and in a wretched tangle with some other sleeping thing constituted a problem of a lesser order, until confronted, at which point it would doubtless seem just as bad as the thought of finding herself naked had seconds earlier. All she could be sure of was her shame at having let herself down irrevocably in public. The back beside her bore this out; it belonged to Chips Hall, thankfully also clothed, his appearance more frightening for only appearing to be sudden, the truth being that they must have both lain there for several hours. And not only him: lying sideways at the head of the bed was Eugene Tackleberry, snoring grossly into her favourite lavender-scented pillowcase.

Instinct warned her that she must move quickly, but movement was impossible; her ankle had swollen up to the size of a small football. It was excruciating enough simply lying there, would she ever be able to use her foot again? It felt doubtful. The dawn of a brand new day and she had already reached the end of the line. She was a prisoner in her own house and a hostage to her memory loss, horrible forgotten spaces opening up all around her, talons real and imagined poised to claw her into the worst of all places: current reality.

The phone had started to ring again; hearing it was pure torture on account of her natural urge to answer, and her new one to hide forever from its awful reach. Petula felt it was time to try and say something but her throat was bark-dry and tongue too thick for her to dare risk inhaling her own breath. What had it all been about, and what had it all been for? The night was a myth. Life was a myth. She was a myth, oh no, no! Images were returning to her, followed by trickles of remembered sensation, the party was much worse than mythology, it had been a tragi-comedy-tragedy... Fogle, the partridges, Trafalgar... she was finished, finished as a serious force for modest social success, all thrown away for a wonder drug and an appalling rake with nice bone structure who may or may not have chewed her face off in full view of her daughter, *her daughter*, Regan, that was the worst of it! What respect could she have for her now?

'My God, *Regan!*' Petula choked, her voice sounding like something being flushed down the lavatory, 'Regan!' – what must she think of it all?

There was an abrupt knock on the door, bringing Hall to with a grunt, 'God, what a party. *My* oh *my*. Monster-mash blowout...'

Petula was lost for ideas, in too much pain to physically prevent more embarrassment but incapable of issuing the vocal command that could at least keep whoever was knocking on the other side of the door.

'Tell them to shut up!' snapped Tackleberry, burying his head under the pillow, 'I need rest. Tackleberry is not very well.'

'Nor am I,' called a voice from the floor, probably Tinwood's judging from its subterranean rasp, 'has anyone seen my watch? It was an Omega...'

'Petula, Petula,' the voice from the other side was Hardfield's. 'Can I come in please Petula? It's ever so important.'

'No, don't,' croaked Petula feebly, her voice hardly rising

above a hoarse impersonation of a whisper, 'please don't. I'll be up soon.'

'Speak for yourself,' sniggered Tinwood from the foot of the bed, 'I need a bloody drink, a G&T, and make it a strong 'un. Aspirin ain't going to cover this mother.'

'Tackleberry is going to die.'

'I'm sorry Petula but I really have to speak to you at once, it's urgent.'

'Get on your broomstick and fuck off, whoever you are,' Tinwood growled, inspecting his bent glasses.

The door pushed open and Hardfield meekly cleared her throat, what awkwardness she may have registered in the scene more than tempered by the news she had to share.

'I'm sorry Petula,' persisted Hardfield, 'but it really is most distressingly pressing, don't you know. Otherwise I really wouldn't have bothered you.'

'I know, but not now, please, not now.'

'It's the Police.'

'What?'

'It's the Police, Petula, on the phone you see. They want to speak to you if they can, I said you were still asleep.'

'The Police? Why? A drugs bust? *Shit!*'

'No Petula.'

'But you said the Police...'

'Yes, the Police Petula, I said you were still asleep, and they said fine, so I said what does that mean, and they said that's alright, they'd come straight over.'

'Why? What the hell do they want? Why do they need to see me? What have I done? The drugs weren't mine!'

'That actor Petula, the one that hit his head funny on the lavatory, you know, the ambulance came for him, well, he didn't get better you see, he didn't get better at all...'

'No... this isn't happening.' Repelling a force heavier than herself, and with great effort, Petula sat up. Once upright she was struck by a dizzy blow to the head, seemingly inflicted by no more than gravity, 'I think I'm going to be sick, please, someone bring me something to be sick in...'

'Oh oh, chunder city, call the life guards!' laughed Hall, who in contrast to Petula was very much enjoying himself.

'What happened to the idiot, they found drugs on him did they? What did he tell them, that I was selling them?' Petula coughed, fighting back the bile that was swirling round her throat. 'He was on the bloody drugs and bloody bought them himself, it was his own fault that girl belted him, self-defence, he must be mad to press charges.'

'He can't Petula, he died on the way to the hospital.'

'Sheesh,' mumbled Hall, 'what a bummer.'

'Petula, Petula, are you alright? Can I fetch you anything...'

Hardfield's words were in vain; Petula could not hear them anymore, her nervous system having made the decision to faint for her, her body swooning over the sheets before flying head-first, hitting the floor with an conclusive thunk. For her the party was finally over.

CHAPTER NINE,
reputations and reversals.

The wind changed direction, again. The next three years saw Petula rise from a celebrity to a legend. Notoriety was the open prison she operated from, protected by a healthy reputation for madness, a short fuse and the ghoulish rumours surrounding the house on the hill: wild orgies, black magic and psychedelic experimentation constructing a dark halo over The Heights, Mockery Gap's own Castle Dracula. This myth-making was supported by the voyeurism of the village itself, proud of its newly acquired reputation for the dark arts, and pleased to have come out of the twee shadow of Richmond and Shatby. Scandal added to Petula's lustre, there being no firmer stamp of exceptionalism than having one's guests leaving one's party dead in an ambulance. The judge who decided that the verdict of death by misadventure for Rex Wade would be punishment enough for Petula, supposing the damage done to her reputation should render further prosecution unnecessary, did public opinion a disservice. Society, contrary to the formulations of reason, was to prove a far more perverse referee than either the Law or Petula could have guessed, her glamour now enhanced by a macabre and dangerous mystique.

Death (though, crucially, not her own) opened doors for Petula. Aiming higher than fate would allow her to go ceased to be a problem. People whom she would have once sought to cultivate were frightened of her in a way they had not been prepared for, allowing her to ruthlessly press her advantage. Choosing to come out on the front foot, exactly at that point when conventional wisdom said a defensive feint was called for, was a move so audacious that her critics were left with nowhere to go. Instead, the malcontents who whispered that Petula had tried a little too hard in the past found they were prepared to make the extra effort themselves when faced with social irrelevancy. Besides, they knew Petula's weaknesses and how many sugars she took in her tea; she had played coy with them before. Put up with her for a bit, safe as they were behind their electric gate codes, then watch her choke on her own hyperactivity, the same way she always had; all they had to do was to sit tight and allow the storm to pass.

These relics of the old order underestimated her. Petula no longer cared for their patronage, oblivious to the blandishments and bribes dangled enticingly within reach. Whereas she had never known how to say no to society before, living under the shadow of eventual rejection, she now discovered that it was good for her soul to do a bit of rejecting of her own; the more indiscriminate, partial and obscure, the thinner the explanation and more oblique the motive, the better.

Sensing that this reprieve called for a stylistic overhaul, Petula cut her cloth accordingly, ditching the Eighties and their superannuated notions of demi-monde chic by her back door in shiny black bags for the council to collect and recycle. Adopting an ivory cane (her ankle had never properly recovered from the party), and alternating between a voodoo cockerel handle and a shrunken celtic chieftain's skull, her hair straightened and dyed a witchy black, the ample curves of her hips slimmed into prepossessing onyx frocks and androgynous business suits, lipstick a light grey, Petula was reborn as a more curious and less corporeal being. From tasteful overstatement, Petula's appearance grew seductively quiet, her transparent smocks verging on the bland until her public noticed who was wearing them and how little she had on underneath. Accordingly she approached fewer people and fewer felt inclined to approach her; the summer garden parties, soirees for favoured neighbours, and use of

the house by the local great and good, phased out in sniffy dos-
es. Each purge fed a dynamic of further trimming, and by the
second anniversary of Wade's death, the annual invitation to
The Hunt to have breakfast on the front lawn was dramatically
rescinded, joining tactical entreaties to minor royalty and charity galas on the scrapheap of recent social aspiration. Petula's
former constituency did their best to hide their shock; should
it not be they, after all, who were doing the banishing? But by
then it was too late: they were already experiencing the shame
of exclusion, victims of the temporal trap that believed the
future owed them the same reassurances as that time of greater
success: the past.

All this clearing of space did not mean that Petula became
a hermit. Into the void rushed Danish directors, one of whom
mooched hopelessly round her for a whole summer, the nou-
veau riche who repaid her suppers with holidays in Sardinian
villas, nightclub owners (these men fascinated Petula, their
knack of making punters pay handsomely for the privilege of
inclusion running parallel to her own modus operandi), nervy
music producers and, of course, the new breed of DJ, hot out
of Detroit and Chicago, Ibiza and Goa, the exorbitant cost of
white-label vinyl meaning that Petula's record collection quickly
outgrew her children's. The effect of this social spring-cleaning
was positively rejuvenating; deep house and rare groove blowing over the lawn on Sundays where once the sound of church
bells, string quartets and The Eurythmics would have had to
suffice. Among her new associates Petula began to refer to herself as a businesswoman, and though taking no greater control
of the day-to-day running of Noah's various concerns, amused
herself with the purchase of shares and various other invest-
ments, noisily bringing attention to her activities, careful then
to make fun of her prowess in a very 'Nineties' parody of showing off. Her financial portfolio was more than an interesting
diversion; it led to personal consultations, and with embarrass-

ing ease she found that she had become a local expert on commerce, taking care to not allow herself to be put in a situation where she might really be put to the test. Confidence and common sense, the perennial substitutes for knowledge and learning, were all she needed. No longer did Petula lie awake with the usual fear of having become old news. And not for nothing did Royce say, by way of an admonishment that delighted its target, 'My, look who's changed with the times... or have the times changed with you?'

Amongst her old set who survived the cull Petula made a greater fetish of 'quality' than before, eventually divorcing it from any real-life examples so that it became an inhuman standard of acceptance, keeping the survivors on their toes and sparing them from the liberties they might have taken had they been at their ease. Between exactingly high criteria and misanthropy Petula patrolled the line, mindful never to cross it, her brand of energy too canny to deprive her tribe of the hope that she would one day forgive them for Regan's party, the moment her old world let her down.

Naturally the psychic tax that had to be paid for not coming clean about what she truly thought, feared or loved, was not cheap – Petula did not expect it to be. She willingly paid up, and would have sold her soul many times over rather than face a reality she was not the master of again, or be reminded of what enforced admissions to the self had cost her, on the night she heard the partridges speak. Those scars were the vengeful phantoms that drove her forward and spared her the humiliating agony of looking back. Why should she, when she knew what was there? Ample proof that a world that had not succumbed to her principles of invention was not a habitat that could support one such as her. Petula's aims were thus constant with her founding principles: power, control, proof that she was alive and that others knew it, realistic substitutes for the self-knowledge she had no use for, her credo to win and never to know. It was the same hemlock that had always been her tipple of choice, drunk in the belief that though it passed her lips, it would be someone else who would take her place and die.

*

Whether her mother's latest round of social roulette evinced the last sighs of her exhausted genius or the beginnings of another metamorphic cycle, was a worry Regan pretended to regard as a blessing. Though she had not yet come to the conclusion that Petula might be in it for herself, Regan had only just stopped short of it the night of her party, and wondered how she could have got so close to so demonstratively slanderous a belief. Pique had to have lain at the heart of her misjudgement, the discreditable envy towards one whom she still fell short of the mark of twisting her logic and robbing it of its informative potential. As such, Regan's satisfaction at watching Petula topple dangerously was a discomforting shock she could no longer pass off as a priggish anomaly. The shame of her mother drunkenly letting off steam at her party paled in comparison to her response to it – coldly looking down at the one she owed her every thought to. Witnessing others, particularly the old, enjoy life too much (the thought of anyone younger than she being happy was merely weird), triggered a reflex to criticise in Regan, her judgements delivered from a chilly and secluded perch that bore no resemblance to anywhere she wished to nest. This was the flaw in her project of existential self-creation; her ice-queen persona had flopped because it was no persona at all, simply a sop to her natural failings.

There was little point in saving herself from what must have already been evident to others. Regan knew she was the selfish one, the pain of the admission easier to bear if she was brave enough to acknowledge it was her fault, and not that of the value system she inherited. But this charitable concession did little to put out the fire that Petula's second and third coming had lit in her daughter's troubled heart. Regan continued to feel one thing, while trying to think another, ensuring that her conscious and unconscious minds settled on opposite sides of the room where they remained eternally unreconciled.

For her mother matters were simpler. Regan's relative failure as social bait had led her to drastically reassess her daughter's going worth. This she conveyed by loosening the reins and lessening the interest she took in the unremarkable doings of Regan's life. Accordingly Regan plainly grasped that spending her free time at The Heights in Petula's company was beginning to get on her mother's nerves. Much as her siblings, she saw that life on the farm necessarily meant taking second position; in her case, becoming a paler version of Petula. Frightened at the insidious feelings that were likely to overwhelm her if she stayed to embrace this fate, Regan decided to leave at the first opportunity, and embrace the same fate elsewhere, having already unconsciously substituted Petula's goals for her own. With tender self-deception, Regan flattered herself that she had affected a genuinely original synthesis, using the mistakes of others to avoid more of her own. Inculcated in the dogma that Evita and Jazzy were failures for having gone against their mother, leading their lives as pathetic replies to the overweening glory of Petula's, their independence a pathetic sham, Regan sought to maintain the old code in new territories and export her mother's gospel. Embracing the concept of necessary distance, Regan split their world into complimentary zones of influence, separated by age and a little geography. Henceforth she could enjoy her own life, enhanced by the best advice a girl could leave home with, far enough away to neither antagonise nor irritate the free spirit she sought to emulate. Petula, recognising that her hold over Regan was still secure, yet annoyed by the way her daughter dithered over her destination, swiftly prepared her charge for a gap year temping at Chase Manhat-

tan, followed by a place on the newly instigated Business Management degree at Cambridge; Regan's first preference for Art
History loftily pooh-poohed as so much old hat.

Cambridge in the mid-1990s was where Regan now awoke,
at first confusing the ringing of her mobile phone for a crying
baby, then, on identifying it for what it was, cursing the fact that
it must have also woken the boy beside her, an undistinguished
Argentinian hockey player she had picked up the night before
at the South American Society Barbecue. The grizzly highlight
of this hearty cross-cultural gathering, concerned for the most
part with exchanging ideas on how best to roast meat, was an
ex-shag of hers throwing himself into the charcoal pit to stop
her flirting with her current bedmate. Fortunately on-the-spot
first aid had reduced the jilted attention-seeker's injuries to a
small patch of burns along his hands and neck, but not before
he had noisily and publicly accused Regan of being responsible
for his poor exam results and emergent suicidal tendencies.

It seemed to Regan as though every third boy or fourth boy
she slept with fell in love with her or manifested the signs of
some perplexingly intense obsession. It was puzzling, as Regan
knew she had given no more of herself to these lovelorn lads
than she had to their less insistent counterparts, both kinds of
couplings unilaterally tepid and perfunctory. Out of her incomprehension grew an intolerance with what appeared to be no
more than immature play-acting, a sham that men that could
not accept that there was not *that* much to anybody, herself
included, played out in the vain hope that it would prove they
were different. Their only distinction was their hopeful idiocy,
fed by power ballads and teen flicks; self-deluding Romeos all
haunted by their own most human *lack*. It was no accident that
Regan sought out tepid conformists, irrespective of what it was
they had chosen to conform to, be it rugby-club ethics or their
father's dentistry practice. The more indifferent and vague
these boys were over who they were, the easier Regan found it

to pass the time she required them for – passion and fireworks the domain of charlatans and romantic losers.

A narrow, thinly tanned ankle caught against hers and the Argentinian, with the lazy entitlement particular to the other South Americans Regan had known intimately, opened an eye, glanced at her vaguely, and turned over to make up for the sleep lost during their divertingly brief union, which, Regan remembered, had ended in tears. The tears were of course his – in all probability prompted by the memory of a distant and betrayed girlfriend lighting a candle for him in Buenos Aires. As Regan had fallen asleep to his lopsided sobs she had wondered, briefly, what it was he had found attractive about her, and while attempting to focus on that thought, nodded away on the back of dark galloping horses. This morning he appeared to be exacting his revenge; short bursts of phlegmy snore breaking through his irregular breathing, and the faintest aroma of burnt carcinogenic gas rising from the sheets on his side of the bed. She reached down; there was dry come on her thigh, *again*, proof that an event could register as itself, without her having to notice. The ringing had stopped, and though she felt the groggy privations of having shared her bed with another, Regan knew she would not go back to sleep.

The fresh start in Cambridge was not the great panacea Regan had initially hoped for, the city and its life too close to her previous existence to signal the rupture she would later decide she needed. Her flat, taken at the start of her third year in a new block of studios far from the university and its trappings, reflected an isolated state of mind, one that was grimly made up, and owed little to local colour or conditions. Regan's decision to lodge alone was an act that dismayed those friends who wanted to be proven wrong about her, her determination to find a place too expensive and small to share an unqualified success. Pegasus Court had yet to meet with Petula's approval, since after the first year she had stopped visiting Cambridge, driving

REPUTATIONS AND REVERSALS

straight to London instead, which did not prevent Regan from hoping that her mother would give its sparse interior the grunt which granted her qualified assent. The flat's eggshell-white walls, nuclear-bright window fittings, cream ceiling and carpets were difficult to keep clean, so beyond those guests necessary to prove its existence, Regan discouraged visitors. To those who made it up, the space sat as an odd fit for a young student, the cheekier comparing it to a Martian escape capsule, an after-death experience or, once they were a safe distance away, the final word in consummate zen blandness. Regan heard it all, and would have preferred to live on a stack of shelves than return to her college and its traditions, which like talk of 'community' or 'seasonal spirit' carried, for her, the suggestion of showering in someone else's sweat.

Living in a glorified hotel that denied the very question of taste conversely answered a need close to rebellion in Regan, buried below the comforting explanations and other diversions invented to deny the basic tensions in her life. Having wasted a year in New York, put on weight watching Jerry Springer, and suffered the loneliness of a lowly bank teller, all to provide her with 'real-world' experience, Cambridge felt like it could be public school mark-two. Quickly perceiving what was required of her if she was to achieve conventional popularity, Regan braced herself for a repetition of the cycles she had undergone and overgrown at Nohallows. But to her dismay she found that she could not comfortably tread the same water twice. Often Regan found her thoughts turning to the recent past: the toasty junior common room in winter, her legs entwined with Diamanda's; nighttime by the lake at The Heights and Mingus's serious and forlorn face, fresh humiliation still burning in his cheeks; a reddening squall forming over Shatby harbour, her snug in her mother's Volvo, the hail pelting the bodywork. It was an effort to move forward.

The habit of self-discipline insured that her body did its best to ignore these distractions, and get on with what was expected of it. Regan began to lose weight again and fraternise with her neighbours in the medieval quad she was housed in: a mix of sporting enthusiasts, brainiacs and self-hating revolutionaries well below the level of Petula's most average fare. Very little about these 'new' characters took Regan by surprise, their identities fitting them like worn laundry that nothing could rescue the faded novelty of. Everywhere she looked it was the same old story as school; the gowns worn to college dinners where grace was still observed, hockey and rowing, lectures in an English heritage site and the services of an agreeable porter who reminded her of a male, whiskered Jenny Hardfield. It was as if, barely out of her second decade, she was already doomed to live her life again in the same musty rags as before. Even her subject, a supposedly innovative borrowing from the Harvard Business School, turned out to be no more than a depressing extension of common sense; a less conscionable sociology for the Nineties that killed conversation dead at a succession of tacky freshers' balls, her dates more interested in the fact that she had once danced with Crispin Fogle, in any case a lie, than in her 'funky' new course.

During her second year Regan withdrew from college life and moved to a terraced semi-detached student residence in a slightly seedy area near the train station. It was by far the murkiest property she had inhabited, her warring housemates a clumsy parody of whatever family life had previously been played out between its French-mustard-coloured walls. Lost afternoons sipping tea, gobbling up Hobnobs and arguing over which episode of *The Fast Show* to watch might have shown Regan how the other half of college lived, had she still cared: an irredeemable ordinariness, lightened by marijuana and hiding one another's socks, filling the vacant columns of her dwindling ambition. House politics – who had eaten whose Ryvita or left pubes in the bath – were a world away from the camaraderie of

Nohallows, revealing a tenacious and childlike resolve in Regan to get her own way. Hurtfully her fellow lodgers began to refer to her as 'Brat', and in doing so, provided the pretext for the occasional cold fury in which Regan would castigate them all as second-raters, tearfully returning to her room to make pointless conversation with her latest fuck-buddy, picked up at some woeful college event.

Having broken the taboo of sleeping with someone she cared nothing for the second time she slept with somebody, the former head boy of a Catholic school whom her circle insisted was good-looking, Regan slipped into promiscuity quietly but completely. Convinced she had no sex drive or people skills and thus needed plenty of sex with lots of people to remedy the defect, Regan cantered into horizontal affirmation with the assured nonchalance of a seasoned rider. The overriding flaw in her worldly veneer was her not being able to consult her own judgement; every time she tried to work out whether she was attracted to a boy, fuzzy and indefinite images would emerge of Mingus. Sex quickly became a way of switching these pictures off, Regan consoling herself that her proclivities had at least saved her from falling in love, and thus ruining her young life in the way her mother had frequently warned of. Regan thus remained the same inscrutable force in her relationships as she did outside them, growing no nearer herself in the privacy and privileged attention of her partners, than she had on her own.

By the time Regan moved to Pegasus Court, her father's generous allowance topping up that of her local-authority maintenance grant, minimalism had taken root in all branches of her life, an overriding desire for simplicity, no matter how her reductions twisted or diluted reality, an unwavering constant. The gang of wits that had dubbed her 'Brat' adjusted the nickname to accommodate 'fuck-happy robotic', Regan's appearance with knee-length felt boots, leggings and a silver roll-neck if going out, and Nikes, leggings and a bronze turtle neck when staying in, doing little to deflect their snipes, and her hatred of bright but shapeless leisure-wear positively confirming them.

Even her most loyal confederates had to concede that Regan's superficial otherness might not amount to anything deeper than borderline autism: a young woman who lived as she danced, exactly and precisely, free of the waft of hyacinths her partners sought to detect in vain, her spirit a grounded betrayal of the ethereality promised by her Waterhousian beauty. Mercifully Regan was modest; lacking the passion to do anything else she did the best she could, her real goals and motives occasionally coming to her in dreams she forgot on waking, the early promise of sophistication having by now faded into an atomised cleanliness similar to that of any other chilly weirdo.

The sting in the tail of her inverted osmosis was that Regan could feel Petula slipping away, like a crane gliding into the setting sun, without her. For as long as Regan was consciously able to perform the operation, her life had ceased to be a succession of 'nows' and consisted of a stream of 'thens' whose value consisted in her being able to tell her mother about them later. Her mother's ever-decreasing interest in her tales hurt – Petula only reaching animation when she detected the seeds of a challenge in Regan's anecdotal recollections, otherwise content to give every sign that listening to her daughter posed something of a struggle. During Regan's last trip to The Heights, this trend had crescendoed to insultingly absurd proportions. Regan had only to embark on her narrative stride for Petula to leave and answer the door, reach for the telephone, or rise suddenly to retrieve a boiling kettle, the act of having to hear to the end of a sentence sure to send her mother into fluctuations of unrelated activity. Regan was left with the hurtful intimation that there had been an argument neither could remember having that had nonetheless changed everything.

'...it made it really nice to spend reading week somewhere different this time.'

'Sorry, what was it you were saying?'

'Me and Jeremy, you know, Jeremy and I, we decided to spend reading week in Bath, you remember, where his sister lives, the one you liked, she was wearing some bit of clothing you liked, remember? I went there before when you had to go to that jazz thing in Switzerland; it's a bit like Cambridge but I actually I prefer it because Bath...'

'Hold on, just a second, I'm going to have to take this, I think it's from Cory; he'll be calling from Vancouver, so I simply must. Anyway, I think you've told me that story about Roy and his baths before...'

Regan was practised in distilling complicated emotions into simple expressions of hope, a thick skin the requisite counterpart to putting her clothes on in the morning. Even so she could not resist the impulse to feel sorry for herself, however hard she tried to not allow it to show; she had followed the rules, obeyed the instructions, ignored her heart and distanced herself from unsuitable friends. What more could she do to take her place at Petula's right hand? Warily she toyed with opening up in such a way as to benefit from advice, a tested way of securing her mother's attention.

'I do sometimes get a bit lonely at uni, Mum. Like you must living out here I suppose.'

'Eh?'

'Lonely. Living on your own can get lonely can't it?'

'You must be *joking*. I don't get a moment's peace.'

'But don't you get tired of being around people all the time?'

'Why should I? We're meant to be social animals, aren't we? You're the one complaining about being lonely, I'm not surprised with that long face darling, I told you moving to that housing estate on the outskirts of town was a peculiar idea. Who'd want to go there when you have all that history on your doorstep? Town's the place to be at your age, where the action is.'

'It's not a housing estate, Mum, and anyway, that isn't the problem, I meant more that...'

'That you don't have enough friends? That's the fault of your Nohallows girls, it's stopped you seeking fresh blood. So long as you know you have them to fall back on, you can't be bothered to make the effort.'

'Not that. But I do find it hard to really get to know new people, I suppose.'

'Put yourself about a bit love, make them need you more, become invaluable, you know, so that whenever so-and-so needs such-and-such done they call you, otherwise it'll flop. You get out what you put in, all that nonsense, your gym teachers should really have told you about that long ago. It's a chore, but the only way you can be sure of grabbing the audience you want is by not giving them any say in the matter, get in their faces, don't leave them with any choice. That's the thing. Otherwise you're wasting your time, and life is all effort and no bloody reward.'

And for the last term Regan had done precisely that, returning to social functions she had recently thrown over, dating boys in a pedantically old-fashioned way that involved seeing them more than once after she slept with them, eating in pizzerias, shopping in Waitrose, dressing up in Rag week and using her Fiat Uno at the drop of a hat to convey friends to lectures, debates and jamborees; not quite hating every minute of it, but close enough to wonder whether Petula realised one woman's Daiquiri might be another's prune juice. It was not as if Regan was blind to her mother's point – she might have to do all the driving, but the punters were in her car and would have to suffer her presence at the controls whether they liked it or not. Rather, such a service, in one who revealed little, risked relegating her to the status of a trusty appendage. Lacking all will to force her personality on those who came to rely on her, Regan found that her wheels were never really in motion, simply spinning in mid-air as the remaining term of her last year passed her by.

Regan was not sure when the phone had started ringing again, only that it had been doing so without interruption in the time it had taken her to rise, clean her teeth, and slug back the better part of a bottle of half-frozen Perrier, gagging as the fizzy current of water tore down her throat and percolated noisily in her taut chest. Still it rang, the Argentinian muttering something in Spanish and pulling the duvet over his ears pathetically. It could only be her mother, the ringing itself reminding Regan of her voice. Only Petula could hold on for so long, despite her calls drying to a weekly overture usually delivered last thing on a Sunday night, for the want of anyone else to relate the weekend's events to. But if it was Petula it might be important, certainly out of the ordinary, enough for a daughter ravenous for a helping of validation to grab the receiver and intone emotionlessly, 'Regan Montague here.'

'At last,' said Petula, 'what the hell kept you? I thought something had happened. Don't make me wait like that, I beg you, not *that*. Oh forgive me darling, I don't mean to sound mad, I've been trying to get hold of you all morning; really, oh it's so, so awful. No, I mean it, simply awful. And terrible too, frankly. Just... just terrible. I never thought I'd see this day, I mean actually be alive if something like this happened to me, to *us*. Don't even ask, I can't believe it's even really happened. I don't mean that it hasn't, only that I can't believe it. It's like it's happening to someone else. Someone I hate. God knows how long it must have been going on for. And it's my own fault. Always insisting on seeing the good in people. Or being too busy trying to do good to notice the bad under my own nose. Sorry. I know I must sound absurd to you. Oh forgive me!'

'What, Mummy? What is it you're talking about? What's happened to you, are you alright?'

'Of course I'm not!'

'Then...'

'No, I can't. Just horrible, I'm sorry, no, no, it's too much. Frankly I'm disgusted, to tell you the truth. Yes, to be frank, disgusted. Sickened. Completely. It's *disgusting*.'

'I'm sorry Mum, but what's disgusting?'

'Have you opened your mail yet?'

'No, I just got up, I've been at a...'

'Then go, go *now*, at once, you'll see then.'

'See what? What am I supposed to be looking for Mum?'

'A letter of course, he's sent one to you too, read it and then call me back. At *once*. Please darling, I need you now. We're like sisters.'

And forgetting anything that she may have ever harboured against her mother, Regan bolted out of the door, tumbling down the narrow steps to look for a letter that would explain it all. There, sitting atop a scattering of leaflets offering deep-pan pizzas and fried battery hen at discount prices, was a crisp envelope with a foreign stamp on it. There was a desolate air about the scratchy handwriting, the black ink and white paper ominous in the way that only news which considered itself bad could be. Should she open and read it or phone her mother right away? Regan could not remember what order she had been asked to perform her duty in, her gut telling her that even though the letter was addressed to her she was prying in the affairs of others if she pulled it open. Natural curiosity was too great, and ripping apart the edge, Regan sat by the door and experienced, though she was too preoccupied to know it, an unpleasant turning point in her reading life. From that morning on she would be scared of letters, the brush of mail being pushed through the letter-flap, postboxes and red vans innocently going about their business, all of these would make her shudder. Her preferred mode of communication would, like Petula's, become the telephone, or failing that, yelling out of the window into the street. When she had finished reading she sat where she was for a while, staring up at the milky morning light pouring through the frosted-glass window above the door, and celestial beings, their thin traceable lines moving like ghosts across into the walls separating her flat from the next.

Slowly she followed her path back up the stairs, the letter dangling dangerously from her twitching fingers, and on opening her door, glanced round the flat. Its essential similarity to the one she left some time before filled her with frightened disappointment. She checked herself in the mirror, as if to see where the enormous changes she had been told of had taken place. Had they registered on her face yet? Did she look any older? The letter seemed too small a place for them all; the information it alluded to clearly in the world, but not in a world she belonged to, at least, not yet.

'What took you so long? I've been standing here for an age, waiting,' her mother snapped.

'I'm sorry, I was really quick I thought.'

'Did you get *it*?'

'Yes. I've got it with me now.'

'Then read it for God's sake, read it to me.'

Regan did as she was told, slowly. When she had finished there was silence the other end. It struck her that the time it took to read the letter was probably the longest she had spoken to her mother without interruption for years, an irrelevant yet teasingly satisfying accomplishment.

'Mummy, are you still there?'

There was coughing and what sounded like a wet hiccup.

'Please, please, again, slowly if you could, I need to sit down and hear it again, I'll tell you when I'm ready. Okay, just a minute. There. I'm ready, go on. Louder this time please.'

Regan, growing used to operating in shock, began to read again, the experience of being carried on the back of her nerves slightly exhilarating.

My Dear Regan,

*Please forgive the gap between my letters, I have never been
very good with words, or found a voice I am comfortable with
to address you, either now or when you were a small girl.
Cambridge must be a thrilling place to be at your time of life.
I wish I could have followed your progress more closely. I remember going to Cambridge once, years ago, to buy a cap, the kind
that people once wore to drive. It's funny how all men used to
wear hats but don't anymore, the same thing happened with
beards I suppose and god knows how many other trends and
peccadilloes down the ages. I used to have a moustache when
you were growing up, I wonder whether you remember it? I don't
know when I shaved it off but when I did people said I looked
younger or older; I can't remember which. So much for small talk.*

*I am leaving your mother and nothing anyone can do will make
me change my mind about this, so please don't try – in essence I
have always been a waverer but on this I am adamant. I will also
be leaving England, for good I hope. For some years I have had
another family, here in the Philippines, by a woman who has been
as good as a wife to me. I have accepted her children as my own,
even though they are of another race and colour, for a simple reason. I have never lived in the presence of so much love and simple
understanding. I wish you could know it for yourself. But now my
partner here is pregnant, with twins, and naturally she is asking
me for a commitment which after all these years of devotion it
would be dishonourable not to make. Please be clear; I have no
plans to divorce your mother or change your lives in any way.
Everything will go on as before and none of you ever need want
for anything; I mean your step sister and brother too. But I shall
no longer be with you, if ever I really was. You've seen so little of
me these past few years that this may make absolutely no difference to you in practice. For me it will make all the difference; for*

years now my soul has felt like something dragged along in a sack, and my life in England a lie that serves no one apart from your mother. Am I not, as much as you, her own work?

If you can forgive me, or wish to know who I am, I will provide you with a return ticket to Manilla any time you like, but you will not see me at the farm again.

Love

Your Father

Ps: Be assured that money will never be a problem, I have written to your mother on the subject and will oblige her in any way she asks, as I always have.

'Ha!' laughed Petula scornfully, '*ha!*'
'I'm sorry Mummy, but that's what it says.'
'*Ha!*'
'Do you want me to read it again?'
'*Where* did that little weasel find such fine and flowery words… he certainly never spoke them to my face. No, I got the weasel and you get Sir Walter Scott. In all our years he never strung a sensible sentence together or uttered a single thing of sense. I don't, I just don't understand where all this piety has come from. It wasn't there before. Look, can't you tell him that you love him and need him?' Petula added, almost absentmindedly.
'*Sorry?*'
'In a letter back or something, tell him how much he means to you, you know, make him realise that he should come back?'
'Seriously Mum? You can't want anything more to do with Dad after this, right?'
'What?'
'You can't want him back, already?'

'No... no, no, no. Of course not, no, just thinking aloud. No not thinking. Losing my mind. It's been terrible, too *terrible*, I'm not myself. He's succeeded in driving me crazy, that's it, he's finally done it. Sweet heaven, what did either of us do to deserve this treatment? I mean, you, his daughter, what have you done to deserve it? Apart from to trust and depend on him. It's *disgusting* and *vile*. No, no it's more, it's more *evil*, the man's *evil*. You can't treat people like this without being evil. If the definition of evil is doing something like this then yes, he's evil. How could I have never seen it?'

'I'm... I'm amazed too. It's so... so weird! You aren't the only one, I didn't think he could be so determined about anything. Like, he never has been before. It's like he's suddenly just taken a bravery pill or something!'

'Yes, determined! Where did he learn to be so determined is what I'd like to know! But that's the thing with ditherers, they're all opportunists, no matter how long they dither their decisions always seem to come out of the blue. That reminds me, did he ever *touch* you?'

'What?'

'You know, touch you, sexually?'

'No! Of course not, no, why?'

'Oh nothing, just another possible angle. But how could he have done it, that's what I want to bloody know! How could he have actually gathered his wits enough to ship out and not give himself away first!

'Did you only find out about it today?'

'This morning! Like you, at the same bloody time as you! I had no idea, simply no idea. About this bloody double life of his. All men are perverts and liars, nature's fault, but this kind of caper, he should have been a bloody spy! He'd have made the perfect assassin. I gave my whole life to that plum, everything, tied myself to the bloody post and stood before the judgement of my peers, everything, I sacrificed everything I had! A husband, children, my good name, everything! And now he repays me with a letter... I'll be honest darling – when the facts catch up with "love" you need something pretty powerful to keep your relationship going and maybe I *did* take my eye off the ball, a bit, but what did he have to offer to keep me interested? All that man did was lollop, lollop, lollop. Lollop around doing nothing and expect to be taken care of. Is it any wonder that I should have found other things to do with my time than wilt in his shadow! It's not my fault, I didn't do anything wrong, do you understand me, I did nothing *wrong*!'

'I know! But perhaps it's for the best Mum, do you see what I mean, you may not think so now but it could turn out to be. I've no respect at all for the way he's treating us, we don't need him, and if this is what he's really like, aren't you better off with him gone? This is hell now but... but don't you think that it could all be part of our destiny?'

'*Destiny?* You're saying that this is destined?'

'Haven't you thought of it too? That it's our destiny that Daddy should do this and for us to be rid of him. Things happen for a reason, right?'

'Stop it, stop it! Justifications are just an excuse! Is destiny any more than what simply happens by mistake? Things don't always happen for a reason darling, they only look like they do to idiots!'

'But...'

'No! No, no more. I can't bear it, please, I can't.'

'Shall I call later?'

'No! Don't leave me now! I need you!'

'I'm here Mummy, I'm here for you. I was just thinking, this is strange, I've the letter in my hand and the stamp on my letter, it's, well I think it's from the Philippines. But the postmark says York even though the stamp is foreign... that's kind of fishy, yeah?'

'So?'

'Is he in the country do you think?'

'No! Of course not, he's a born coward! You should know that, you get your courage from me. I got the letter treatment too, like you, a shabby shower of obfuscation, the same as yours. Full of foul cant and lies. I'm surprised he didn't just send a fax.'

'What did it say in your letter?'

'What is there to say? Accusations, waffle. No answers. There was nothing in it... Like him in that respect. Nothing to the man, absolutely nothing, he'd rehearse his quips a whole day early if he thought he was going to meet you; a most unnatural man. God knows what went on in his... in his demonic mind. He gave away sod all, so vague, what woman and what kids? I mean, what the bloody hell is all that stuff about a family in the Philippines! It's the first I've heard of it! I thought he was working his arse off out there getting ideas about fertilisers. That was what he was supposed to be doing, what he kept telling me. Months he was away, which at least fits with what we've learnt now. And do you know the worst part about it? There's nothing more manipulative than making someone think they know you when they don't, and God, what scope I gave him to do that! I was his collaborator, his accomplice...'

'He was practically always there, abroad, wasn't he? Away and travelling. He always said it was really boring, that there was nothing worth talking about when I asked him what it was like to be travelling all the time.'

'Ha! I wonder what that bitch looks like, how big her tits are, tiny I expect...'

'Mum...'

'Oh for God's sake do you always have to be so bloody *cold*? Really, dealing with you and your brother is like the difference between being burned or frozen to death. What's wrong with you? My husband has just left *me*! Aren't I entitled to wonder for what *minger* I've been dumped?'

'You haven't been dumped Mum, he's just decided he doesn't

want to be with you and I guess there's never a not cruel way of that happening...'

'Alright then, I've been swapped for someone else and it's all perfectly normal and I'm overacting like a child. Happy?'

'I'm sorry, you know that isn't what I mean Mum. He hasn't told you anything else then? I mean, you don't know what comes next...'

'Nothing, absolutely no clues, nothing. He's left us high and dry, nothing about her, and nothing about us. A practical and emotional vacuum. How are we to go on? I've no idea how we'll keep the wolves out. Rally, we must rally. When you're struck by lightning that's all you can do.'

Regan would, when prying about in her mother's study the following day, find a letter from her father that ran into ten sides of foolscap paper, a verifiable diary of her parents' life together, ending with a list of figures regarding continuing payments for the private clinic Evita was kept at, Jazzy's ongoing subsidies, Petula's many ventures and an allowance for them both that made her gasp. Regan had always believed her mother's fiction that they were poor, or relatively so. For now she replied, 'Do you still want me to come home at the weekend or...'

'No, now, come now. The weekend's too late. We've got to be together at this time. There's so much we need to discuss, to be sure of again. Foundations that need to be rebuilt, yes, we have to build again, from the bottom up. And not on sandalwood or clay, we need bricks. We can't let this be it for us; stronger, stronger, we have to come back...'

'Stronger.'

'Exactly. And trust, it needs to be rebuilt too. Between you and me, I am afraid I have let us become strangers...'

'No!'

'Please Regan, that's very good of you but it's true. We need to get to know one another again. It's socially necessary for us to. Together we *are* something.'

'Oh Mum. I know.'

'Of course you do, you're my daughter.'

'But I was going to bring Jeremy...'

'Who?'

'Jeremy, remember, I told you about...'

'Yes, yes, if he can leave at once bring him, we'll need help to break up the misery, if not he can bugger off. Passengers are the last thing we need. I'll expect you today then, come what may, and darling...'

'Yes?'

'I care about you more than anything else in the world. So be careful not to drive into the hard shoulder.'

Regan glided onto the sofa, lightly like a petal evaporating in a storm. She was weightless, the shock of her father's abandonment less affecting than the tremulous vibration issued by her mother's offer of a sisterhood reborn. Reaching over to her stereo Regan thrust the graphic equaliser up and, turning it on, adjusted the dial to Radio Three. It felt like what Petula would do, or at least might have done had she not 'got into' dance music, to celebrate a moment like this. Wistfully she closed her eyes, less a person than an instrument of a higher purpose. The room shook to the glorious force of Wagner's 'Das Rheingold', chains rattling and dragging this way and that, as the Argentinian, now fully clothed, shook his head sympathetically and made his way out unnoticed.

*

An hour later and Petula was ready to make her next move. For much of that time she had been sitting down. Her habit of skipping meals, currently last night's supper and that morning's breakfast, had led to the desired loss of weight (her bad leg meant that the pounds could only be controlled by denial), but also to physical unreliableness. Standing during a crisis was no longer an option. Never one to learn nothing from adversity, Petula had decided that sitting made her less evasive and more accepting of feelings that in the past she would have strode round the room to avoid. This was a time for sitting; she had been hit hard and wished to let the blow rest where it fell.

In obedience to a suggestion she was rapidly tiring of, Petula took a sip of green tea and curled her lip, her expression suggestive of a young Elvis trapped in the body of Diane Keaton – if the young playwright who had recommended the drink were to be believed. His days as her court favourite looked as numbered as those of his preferred beverage, the idle sycophancy of her set indicative of the complacency and aimlessness she had confused for 'a cutting edge'. Despite its bitter flavour, there was a dignity in soothing her woes with a stinking cup of boiled water, especially as the consolations of alcohol were the rational drug of choice for an unwanted wife. Petula glanced at the bottle of Johnny Walker sat by her wastepaper basket, resigned to facing the next few hours without its help.

The old playroom, now her study, having undergone a patient and orderly phase that ran against her preferred way of using it, was a mess. Her immediate response to Noah's news was to look for the files sent by a private detective commissioned to follow him years before, the findings salty though considerably less seasoned than what she presently took to be the case. Sensibly she saw that old facts, however useful if she were looking to retain a wavering Noah, were useless now he had moved beyond her 'protection'. He was not the only attachment she was waving goodbye to, with him would go a world view that underestimated the separateness of other people's existences, their version of their own realities and disregard for her formal dominance over them. Carrying on as she had could only mean applying a botched analysis of the future and misunderstanding her past. Petula knew that if she did not pit herself against the questionable character of anything that seemed obvious, she would sink into the tired and loudly voiced delusions of victimhood she had spent her life denouncing. There was ground to make up and she would have to hit it running.

She snorted; if only it were that easy. With one eye back on the bottle of scotch, Petula drank the murky green tea to the dregs, its promise of preventing cancer forcing her to keep it down, and the telephone erupting into song again, though for once she wisely ignored its summons. It was time to admit, if only to herself, that just as she built Regan up too high, and buried Jazzy and Evita too low, the glaring failure with Noah was to make him think he was not necessary, when what he represented – a successful if highly relaxed marriage – was a cornerstone of her success. Noah's affairs were known to her, a simple way of extending himself beyond the confines of his prescribed role, but to fall in *love*, for she was sure he had, with an Asiatic floozy, ground glass into her assumptions. Had he not given up on love by now? It was not fair that he should be in thrall to the emotion, and causing her pain into the bargain, while she had sought romance without success ever since her marriage deprived her of her greatest asset: her unrealised potential.

'For you have mistook me all this while...' she muttered, wiping a clod of green sludge off her gums. The belief that it was possible to actually know someone else had been based on the strongest of intuitions and the flimsiest of evidence. Softly Petula touched her stomach; she could feel several types of burning there, the most pointed of which was humiliation. The thought that someone else, a Polynesian beauty plucked out of a Gaugin, was enjoying what she could not, namely Noah's finer points, whatever they still were, made her miss him with an intensity she would have thought impossible a day earlier. Worse, it forced her to remember the man she had fallen in love with: Noah as he was before his great withdrawal, spilling champagne into goblets as their open-top car sped through the villages of the lower Loire, hair tumbling into her freshly kissed eyes. Petula reached for a tissue in anticipation of the expected tears. None came, despite her desiring the release afforded by their arrival. There would be no redemptive flood to wash away the memories, she was stuck with them. It was her own fault: she had started with so many. Even as the years became more alike, Petula had privately mourned the driver of that car as he shrank and faded, her love dying in stages, this final blow actually softened by countless smaller passings, yet a stubborn remnant of that initial glut still flickering at the periphery of her vision.

'Shagging tarts in Shatby, that's all I thought you'd dare to do... oh Noah!'

How had she allowed it to happen? Noah had been scared of her and outwardly conformed to the minimum required of him; he followed orders and never downed his tools in protest, Petula could count the number of arguments they had had on her fingers and toes. But he achieved all of this without ever losing the relaxed and inattentive air of one who was getting his sex elsewhere, she grasped that much. Fear of taking her on deprived him of the means to impose his wishes against her far stronger ones, he could not push it or else he'd lose her; that was their relationship in a strap-line, disappearance was his only way out. Petula just wished he had the style to fake his own suicide. She must face it; their marriage had ended before she realised it and she had probably been single for the best part of the last two decades. Her delusion had been total. Petula tried to laugh out loud but the wheeze she heard was a bitter relative of what she wished to be buoyed by.

'I wonder if you still care about me?' Petula asked, addressing the empty chair Noah had last sat in four months before. She had grown far too used to letting him out of her sight; they had probably spent no more than four nights together for the entire year, and then exchanged only cursory greetings. What was mad was that she could have convinced herself that this was an unremarkable way to carry on, and that many 'happy' people lived this way!

Petula could sense her contrasts close in on her, nothing stranger to her than the distance between normality and abnormality in the same person; she wanted to follow Noah's lead and seek liberation elsewhere; she wanted to walk out of the door and find him repentant; she wanted to hunt him down, tear off his goolies and wear them round her neck as a message to his new lovers. She was going to pieces and had to reassemble, so with that heightened sense of evolutionary knowhow, which never failed her, this was exactly what Petula did. She rose, ran her feelings under a cold tap of instant forgetting and squared up to the mirror. Her face was ever so sexily ravaged, but otherwise similar to the one she had been so pleased with the night before. No one would tell the difference. Yes, it was time to make her next move.

Ignoring what an hour ago she could not believe, Petula leafed through the stack of sheets that comprised Noah's letter, arriving at the page that contained the bottom line. These were the facts most resistant to emotion, the ones that the rest of their lives would hinge upon. Skimming over the columns of figures, financial enticements, and other sops designed to assuage her disappointment at being ditched, Petula homed in on the greatest surprise of all; Noah's willingness to meet her face-to-face and grant her a divorce:

...if, in spite of all that I have written to persuade you that it is in neither of our interests, you still want a divorce, that is, absolutely insist upon one, which I most assuredly do not want for the many good reasons I have already given, then you shall have your way Petula.

Allow me to surprise you again. I am currently staying in Gales with Royce and will be there for two more days before going to

*London, and from London back home, which as you now know, is
the Philippine islands. All you have to do is call me before then
and ask for what you desire and I'll contact Jacksons and get
them onto it; I give you this chance Petula. I owe you that much, I
grant you. I will also be in Shatby concluding some business this
afternoon, the 9th.*

*I knew from the moment I realised I had to do this, that I could
never have told you all I have face-to-face, and I'm sure you know
why. You know me. But if you wish to see me in the flesh, if just
to vent your spleen, I will be at our table at The Elephant's Nest
Hotel where I proposed to you, between the hours of 3pm and
4pm today. If you do decide to come please bear in mind, hard as
I know it must be for you, that I have tried to be as kind and
reasonable as the situation permits me to be, and that making
myself do this, and lay myself open to your hate, has taken all the
courage I have, and more. Perhaps, if you do come, after we have
discussed the terms of the divorce, we could take a short drive
together to some of our old spots? Just a thought. However,
Petula, I must make myself clear on this one point; if I neither
see or hear from you in these next two days I shall resist a divorce
with all my might. I may not be the lion you are but you know
that I have my resources and have no wish to see my property
needlessly split and devalued to satisfy antiquated and vengeful
notions of separation...*

And nor, if Petula were to be honest, did she. Being bumped
off The Heights, her headquarters and the foundation of her
self-belief, held absolutely no appeal at all, with the very unpre-
dictability of divorce and separation, and the potential loss of
assets and lawyers' fees, a game of Russian Roulette she had
no wish to enter. However, an arrangement like the one Noah
suggested, so like her existing life that it would make no odds
to anyone who did not know the truth, was a tasty consolation

that need not make any observable difference to life's surfaces. Indeed, now that she entertained the thought, why should the world discover anything at all? She had hidden far greater secrets than this in her time.

Petula reddened. It did not do to have the law laid down to her by Noah in such maddeningly arrogant and inconsiderate terms, and more importantly, *she* knew the truth; what he had done and sought to get away with, and so would everyone else in the time it took to tell the first caller. What respect could she hope to attract once the community learnt that despite being cast aside, she was willing to stay on at The Heights, like a wedding dress that had been stored simply because of the bother it had taken to make? A life left shielding her ears and closing her eyes forever; a sight and noise that would never go away? No, to carry on 'as normal' was an outrageous suggestion made by a criminal who would escape the shame of living with his crime by having no honour. Stuck as she was, she could not do that.

Petula shook her head at her own perfidy. She must stem this suicidal recourse to pride before something came of it. Of course life ought and had to continue as it was, the outrage committed against her demanded no less. The danger to her reputation could best be met directly by an outrageous lie, or two, or three, or however many it took, so long as no one heard the truth. Yes, people *would* find something out, but the *what* of what they would find out was the only thing that counted. And it certainly wouldn't be a précis of Noah's letter, whose fate belonged deep in the archives. The account people would be drip fed, incrementally, was a different kind of beast, truer to her feelings, and less faithful to Noah's actual movements. He had never been any good at getting his version of events out to the general public, a stuttering, faltering fumbler who had meekly accepted her right to speak on his behalf. Which is what she would continue to do, with an added passion. Noah's self-exile could not have played into her hands any better. With him out of the way there was nothing to stop her from saying that their separation, yes, their separation, had been instigated by her on account of his philandering; in fact, she had banished him, throwing him out and telling him never to darken her door again. Humiliation management of this sort, in which the disaster could be carefully phrased and presented to the world, might alter the meaning of her misfortune completely. What she would lose in absolute pity she could retain in measured sympathy; she was still the wronged woman, though crucially one whose face was saved through bold and forthright decisiveness. Not for her the messy compromises of standing by a proven adulterer, nor the ridicule of the cuckold's horns; there would be no second chances for Noah, there was only one way to stand up to infidelity and that was to send it back to the Philippines with no return ticket – she could stand for Parliament on that kind of platform!

As ruthlessly neat as her solution was, Petula could still make out the flapping strap of a loose end. A divorce may have been out of the question yet she wanted to punish Noah by making him *think* one was on the cards; she owed him and her self-respect that much, even if she had no intention of countenancing one. But to her horror, the idea of actually seeing him rendered her physically weak, her stomach rinsed by dread. It made no sense: being able to boil Noah in a barrel was just what she thought she would have yearned to do. Instead, and entirely out of character, she was fearful of what a meeting might entail. It was too soon somehow. Petula tapped her finger lightly against her forehead, imagining that it was a woodpecker and her skull a tree.

There, it was there. She could not face Noah because she needed time to disguise her sadness as anger, vulnerability as fury, hurt as scorn. It could not be done at once. The firestorm burning through her was too unpredictable, it could change direction at any turn, leading to a scene that may compromise her; a tearful break down or sobbing pleas to come home; anything was possible. Noah had her at his mercy, and acknowledging how was terrible: Petula could understand why he had done it and gone and left her – would she not leave herself if she could? By tomorrow she would have forgotten and replaced this insight with recriminatory self-justification, but at that moment, and maybe for the rest of the day, she saw things as Noah did. This admission, tied to the practical difficulty of raising the prospect of a divorce, when Noah was in a position to call her bluff and actually make one happen, rendered any meeting a strategic nightmare. To run from him, though, was unthinkable; she would never be able to take herself seriously again, and crucially, she would lose the only hold she still had over Noah; his fear of her. But to gaze back into his grey eyes? No. There had to be a solution... some way, or one she could turn to create the confusion needed to halt the flow and claw back the initiative.

There was a quick volley of forceful knocks at the door, followed by a long unbroken hammering characteristic of Petula's closest neighbour, her son.

'Jazzy!'

The noise accelerated and stopped, a scraped about-turn and gravel crunching under the sound of heavy work boots, the force of their tread purposefully ground down to emphasise the agony of every step.

Petula chuckled giddily, her relief deliciously sweet to taste. 'Oh *Jazzy*, your time has come at last, Pegasus, my winged messenger!'

What better way of looking like she could not accept reality than sending Jazzy out as her special envoy, charged with telling Noah that she was too angry to see him? Jazzy was guaranteed to make a mess of his errand which was exactly what she wanted. In ignoring Noah's terms, and announcing that his mother demanded a divorce and expected him at The Heights with his lawyers by the end of that week, Jazzy was as good as helping Noah onto the next plane. Cast as an unlikely saviour, his presence at The Elephant's Nest in her place was the best way of saving her self-respect, frustrating Noah's attempt to impose his terms with her consent, and leaving her free to pull herself together and counterattack. If this meant she was 'stuck' with an arrangement identical to the one outlined in his letter, so much the better, though Noah would never know that, leaving her proudly above the fray! This was more like it!

Petula navigated her way round the strewn files and scattered photographs to the window, and pulled it open. Briskly, she stuck her head out and closed her eyes, sensitive to nature at its most supportive. Spring was speaking the urgent language of regeneration, birds she did not know the names of working in cooperation with one another to feather their nests, their circular calls doing much to reassure her. Even if she were living through a period she would look back on as hell, somewhere a pair of lovers were waking up to an era they would remember as the best of their lives. Petula wished them luck, whoever they were, liking herself much more than normal for doing so.

Drawing back into the room, she glanced at her watch; no time to prepare. This would be a performance in the finest traditions of heartfelt improvisation, the one marker to never lose sight of being that her intended target was human too, however far ahead his start was. Flinging on a wispy grey cardigan and grabbing her cane, Petula bounced stiffly down the passageway to the front door, lifted the latch, and progressed over the sunlit threshold of her empire. The brightness was obliteratingly pure.

'Even on your best day your shit is just as weak as mine my love,' she huffed, her agony still inches behind the grim and somewhat sad smile she had forced across her face, her squinting eyes dribbling a watery saltiness she quickly thumbed away.

Jazzy had been in a tolerably good mood until he noticed his mother following him down the track, gaining ground in a way that suggested she had something to tell him. His own reasonable spirits were based on his latest piece of news; he had been accepted on an upholstery course by the local sixth-form college, a desire that had become a somnambulant obsession for him these past eighteen months. It was the third evening class that had accepted him in that time. Inheriting his mother's panache for transference, albeit on a humbler scale, he sought to pretend that he was responding to her nagging, slugging up to The Heights to grumpily announce another activity he had enrolled on, while privately revelling in the thrill of accomplishment. However, the sight of his mother advancing at an eager pace awoke old fears, and like a police car passing a reformed criminal, Jazzy reflexively feared the worst from her approach.

Petula noticed her son's brow darken and waved her cane gamely. She did not want to frighten him off. At times like this she knew she had drawn her children too deeply into her warring ideology, siring a pack of Frankenstein's monsters who had swallowed, inverted and intensified their maker's mark to an imbalanced extent. All their hatreds and prejudices were her own, but too defining of their being and inattentive to that pragmatic moderation required in a war where not every attack could be frontal assault. Fear and anger, which for her were the telescopic sights she saw the world through, in themselves constituted the world itself, threatening to bubble and boil out of control in Jazzy and Evita; Regan choosing to shudder to death in the cold on terms equally as extreme. Admittedly the minute they abandoned their genetic inheritance and toned things down, Petula suffered a different kind of apprehension – they were no use to her if they became wholly individual entities, no longer bound by the matriarchal traditions they shared in common. Her task was to maintain their aggressive posture while being careful to not release them for the kill. When in years to come Petula read of how Pakistani Inter-Service Intelligence played the Taliban off the United States she recognised kindred spirits, sad to acknowledge that they had managed their game far better than she.

'Hullo there, Jazz! Hold up, stop. Something serious has come up, extremely so. For all of us. You have to hear this.'

Jazzy scratched his mottled chin sceptically, halting his legs though still moving quickly away with his eyes. 'I told you I'd replace that lawnmower, didn't I? Don't know what happens with that catch, every time, but it doesn't click properly, right? There's no spark... but it wasn't me that broke it.'

'This is *serious*,' insisted Petula, badly out of breath, 'red alert okay? You must listen to me.'

Looking worried, Jazzy offered, 'You know that course in Richmond, right, remember me telling you, to fix the old sofas? I'm on it, they accepted me.'

Petula grimaced sympathetically, seeing that Jazzy was trying to fend off what he believed would be an attack. His conscientious effort to find a craft he excelled in had won her pity; she knew he could not succeed, but watching him reminded her of when he was a little boy trying to walk. There was a living, vital sweetness in his making an effort that was, nearly though not quite, as attractive as attainment, and she admired the quality all the more from knowing that one more failure would probably kill it for good.

'That's great, really, but we have to talk properly about this other thing, you have to hear me out...'

'Yeah, but with the bookbinding and fieldcraft courses I'm on, which together makes three, right? With all of them I could go back and do A-levels if I wanted...'

Petula nodded impatiently, her pain recent enough for her to control the desire to cut Jazzy short, a sensitivity to all suffering the moral outcome of her own.

'See, with more qualifications, right, the whole bottom line for me changes, aye, I enter the rat race at a whole new different level, for sure, that's a given,' he tilted his head for emphasis, 'but like it or not, you got to play the game, right? And I can take the extra, no worries, grafting's no problem, you know what I'm like, I graft and graft...'

At least he would have some help, Petula thought, now that Jill had flaked into the night without so much as a 'Dear John' note to thank the family for five years of rent-free living. Her replacement, Spider, who in actual fact resembled a grazing bison, was an improvement in several respects, even though Jazzy wrongly feared she would be a slither too far down the social slope for his mother, her turquoise tattoos and chunky forearms anything but demi-monde. Jazzy would have been correct if Petula still judged her son by her own standards, but she had long ceased to, using Jazzy's own stunted yardstick to measure matters. With its help, she discerned that Spider was a loyal, stubborn log, who would sooner shave her armpits than welch on the man who had given her and her children a home. All three of her rotund freckly tykes, the fruit of some earlier tryst, amused Petula greatly; they were cheery, observant boys who would wag their tails if they could grow them, following her Range Rover up and down the drive like young Masai on safari. This new family had curtailed Jazzy's drinking and self-pity, if not his marijuana use, and their kitchen still reeked of wacky flapjacks and cookies, in much the same way as his years of bitter self-righteousness had mellowed into a not-quite-convincing stoicism. And despite the presence of children, no one could call Petula 'Grandma' yet, a prospect Jazzy had disqualified her from when he had demanded a vasectomy as 'the world's too dangerous to bring any more little ones into'. As far as Petula was concerned, so long as his brood's population had peaked, and kept its distance, they, their house, and her increasingly infrequent contact with her son, were part of a history that had moved through harm to harmlessness, distinguished largely by its lack of prominence in her life. But Noah's flight had changed these comforting assumptions, upsetting years of stability, and necessitated the creation of an on-the-spot deputy.

'So what I'm saying, right,' Jazzy droned on, 'is that my prospects are moving all the time, right, I can see things happening

I couldn't before, and that's all to the good, right, my handle on work is firm, my skills base is sound, right, I'm broadening out and upping my game...'

'Please Jazzy, I know this is all very important but it can wait, really it can wait. I'm in the *shit* and so will you be if we don't act in concert at once.'

'You're what?'

'The *shit* okay? We're in it, deeply, us both. I know, sadly I'm not joking. This is *serious*.'

Jazzy's mouth fell open, astonished to be included in the same brown waters as his mother.

'It's bad, okay? Very. And we need to keep our heads and help each other, so I require you to listen to me, and to do so carefully. Your *full* attention. Let whatever differences we've had be put to one side; it's *that* important. There may even be some way out if we can both keep our heads. I'm not asking you to do everything, just turn up, okay?'

'What's happened?' he blurted hoarsely, his voice tightening. Jazzy was far from used to being his mother's confidante and could only imagine what horrors they were faced with if she had resorted to such a desperate step.

'I've discovered that your father, sorry, Noah I mean, he's been having... having an *affair* behind our backs; well obviously, but I've only just found out about it this morning... and, well, as I am sure you can imagine, the consequences for our lives are going to be serious.'

'Fuck me!'

'I know it's hard to take.'

'Fuck me!'

'Quite.'

'Fuck me! Fucking hell! Fuck me!' Jazzy had reddened dangerously and seemed to be at risk of losing control of his bowels, straining his face and hopping from foot to foot most curiously, Petula thought, as the corners of his mouth whitened with spit.

'Please, let me finish,' said Petula raising a hand calmingly, 'and please slow down. I know this is hard...'

'Fuck *me!*'

'Right, but I'm not going to let him get away with it, and I won't put up with it, okay?' Petula took a step back; her son was performing a sort of Rumpelstiltskin dance around her, reminding her of the little victory jigs he would perform after smashing up his treehouse or stoned round a fire at the outdoor parties that speckled his teens and early twenties. It was not the sort of response she was look for.

'Jazzy, please, like I say, we're not going to take this lying down...'

'*Bastard!*'

'I know, I know. He's not going to get away with this but...'

'I should fucking coco! *Bastard!*'

'Right.'

'The dirty, dirty, d-i-r-t-y *rat!*'

'Right, agreed, but let's try and keep emotion out of it, for the moment anyway. He's been having this affair right under our noses, I mean behind our backs, oh bother... I'm finding it difficult to speak, sorry.' And she was. Petula felt like she was about to cry, and sensing the hopelessness of holding back, let the tears, which in fact were sequel to the exasperated trickle she had rubbed away earlier, come forth.

'I'll fucking do the bastard!' cried Jazzy, jumping on the spot now, his face contorted into an approximation of neolithic outrage, 'I'll take him, I'll take his teeth! Jesus, he's been asking for it, well now I'm delivering, I don't like *snakes* that go behind people's backs, I'm going to tell you what I'm going to do...'

'No Jazzy, please, stop it, it's hard enough as it is.'

'I'm going to take the *snake* and I'm going to cut him right up, cut him and scrawl our initials on his belly, right, and play noughts and crosses with a blade between his *snakey* eyes, fuck him up real bad, that'll teach Mr *Snake* a thing or two, right...'

'Oh God.'

'If *snakey* wants to play games he better learn to play mine...'

'Jazzy, Christ, listen to me and be sensible for God's sake *please!*'

'No Mr *Snake*, two can play at that game, you're not the only one that can bite!' cried Jazzy, swirling like a Dervish in his sea-shanty of outrage.

'Jazzy, snap out of it, please, you're scaring me,' yelled Petula grabbing her son's arms, as his glazed eyes beamed with religious conviction, 'situate yourself and get it together, I'm going to need you, *please!*'

Jazzy blinked, his strange visions of reptilian death suddenly passing. '*Fuck*, how could he?' he muttered, 'You're the best woman on earth any man could hope to be with.'

Petula noticed a lump form in her throat. It was the same size as one that had appeared in her son's as he spoke these words.

'You're such a wonderful lady, Mum...'

'Stop it, stop it or you'll get us both going!'

'He can't, he can't be allowed to do this...'

'I know, I know, but it won't do any good crying or getting any more angry, please Jazzy, listen to me,' said Petula, squeezing her son's clenched hand. Grasping it and firmly holding on, she continued, 'You're going to have to exercise grip, this is going to be one of the trickiest situations we've faced down in our lives. I asked him to come here and be some kind of man about it, to face me and...' She stopped herself; in this version she was going to say she had asked him to the house, which made no sense if she was going to then say that she had thrown him out, but Jazzy spared her the difficulty of embellishing further.

'And he's bottled it, right? He has, hasn't he? Hasn't even the decency to look us in the eye and fess up...'

'Exactly, exactly that. In fact, he's says he won't come any closer than Shatby, and he'll be there today... and that if I want to go and talk to him I have to go there and do it, on his terms, you see. He wants it all on his terms.'

'Outrageous! Completely out of order.'

'It is, he is. It's obvious he doesn't love us anymore, maybe he never has, anyway, without love you can end up doing anything to anyone, they don't exist for you as people. That's why he can treat us like this, the only thing he's ever loved is his own comfort, having me slave for him all these years...'

'Tell me about it!' cried Jazzy, not to be denied his turn, 'He never loved me either, never, he just tried to control me, and use me to get you. He needed me to pretend we were a normal family! Children and all, we were a smokescreen, so he could do what he wanted... behind the scenes. He practically killed my real father! Oh yeah, there was a lot that went on behind the scenes I could tell you about,' Jazzy foamed, warming to his theme, 'there's stuff he's done that means I can never look at him in the same way again. Things I know right? Shit that happened...'

Petula covered her mouth to disguise the smile she did not want her son to see. His face was lit again with that crooked evangelical sheen that was visited upon him whenever he talked bollocks, warning her that if she did not calm him down again he would soon be of no use to her.

'I don't doubt that, don't doubt it at all. That's why he's staying away, he'll do anything to avoid coming here. Well, I won't see him there. I have my dignity...'

'Of course you have, he can never take that away from us, why the hell should you go? You're the one who's been shat on, he should be at your beck and call. Not you his, he should be crawling and grovelling, that's what, and even then, that wouldn't be enough. Grovel, he should be made to grovel.'

Petula nodded; Jazzy was working his end ingenuously. 'And I want a divorce Jazzy, honour requires it and I'll accept no less. That's what he's scared of you see, no question of that, and I'll take him for every penny he's worth. If I don't, then, well then you work out what will happen. It doesn't bear thinking about. We'll all be at his mercy.'

'Jesus. I hadn't thought of that. He can do whatever he wants to us, he could throw us out, right? Force us to move on?'

'Of course, the place is his, but if I do get him where I want him, in the courts, then things might look up for us if you see what I mean. For all of us. He wouldn't be so powerful then.'

Seeing that Jazzy didn't see what she meant, Petula pointed down to towards Tianta, his cottage, and then back up to The Heights. 'All this would legally be *ours*, don't you see? We could have security for the first time in our lives, be real masters of all we see and survey! And if it doesn't work out like that, we'd still have a very good chunk of it. We could set ourselves up somewhere else, not have to watch our backs all the time, or sleep with one eye open wondering what the hell is going to happen all the time. You understand? We'd be *safe* for the first time in our lives.'

Jazzy had stopped jerking round, and looked to be carefully processing this line of reasoning which seemed to explain much that had previously been inexplicable to him.

'You'd be entitled to half, right? And me, your blood, would have half of that, right? Half of your half I mean? Would it work out like that? Not that I'm out for anything mind...'

'Of course!'

'I mean I don't want more than I deserve, I'm no operator; just a fair recompense for all the years I've kept this place together, worked its fields, tended it, made sure everything was going properly, you know? Only what's right, what's rightly mine from graft, that's all. Only what's fair; only what's right.'

'Yes, of course! But we can talk about all of that later. That's all just detail. Now's the time for us to try and reclaim our family, Jazz,' exhorted Petula, twisting her face into an expression she knew Jazzy would employ if he were giving her this speech, 'to say no to this injustice, no, once and for all, *no*! And to step up to the plate together, it is the plate isn't it? Yes, to step up to it and be counted, to be a family again, are you with me dear?'

At that moment Jazzy choked, and for a wavering instant Petula was scared she had gone too far and caused him to swallow his tongue. Prolonged inspection showed how wrong she was. He was gurgling with tears, thick flowing streams, babbling brooks and overflowing eddies, so unlike her feeble emissions that she waited and watched in quiet awe. Petula had always been taken aback by the willingness of people to reveal the pain they were in, envying them their naivety.

'I'll do whatever it takes Mum, but... but I just don't understand,' Jazzy grumbled through his sobs, 'why everything has to be so hard all the time. Why can't we all just get on for once? I mean, you and I, we're getting on, but then this comes along and...'

Taking Jazzy by the neck, Petula administered a hug that was not quite sure of itself, Jazzy returning her effort with interest, and simpering into her hair. 'We were so happy, so happy here before all this started...'

Petula could not bring herself to admit that it was disasters such as this that provided the very glue that held them together; instead she sighed bravely, 'I know dear, our family motto ought to be that we succeeded in making a hell out of heaven. Much to all our shame. But don't let that blind you to what he's done; whatever you and I are, he's worse. That's why we have to stand up to him, why it's so important, stand up or be crushed. That's it, our only choice. And this is our chance. We have to look upon it as an opportunity.'

'I know, I know. It's the only way you can make sense of it.'

'Not make sense of it, that's the way it is, the way things are! We can't sit around blaming ourselves. We're just as much victims as we would have been if he'd mown us down on the pavement in one of his old sports cars. That's why we have to act; to protect our lives here!'

'But there's something about this place, you have to admit it, that breeds it, trouble, breeds trouble...'

'What? What are you talking about?'

'You know, this place, The Heights, right? It's like a curse, yeah? It's cursed, like there's some kind of crazy jinx on it that fucks with anyone who lives here, right, what else could it be, for shit to keep happening like this? And all of us, we're all feeding the curse, giving it the bad energy it needs as its food, keeping it going like, and totally screwing ourselves, aye! And even now, right, even now, I'm helping it by fighting Noah. And the worst thing is I've no choice and nor have you. You see what I'm saying? That's how it works. I know you're right, we've got to do what we've got to do, but I'm doing wrong somehow by doing it, you see what I mean, obeying the curse's commands...'

Petula gently let go of him. She had forgotten that listening to Jazzy was like staying on the lavatory for too long; once the essential business was over there was a temptation to remain that had to be resisted. His facts were all over the shop but she sensed his heart would go in the direction she pointed it: he was equal to the task she had in store for him.

'Jazzy, forget about curses, just stop all that okay? They're not what fuck up life: people are. Noah is. We need to focus and you need to pull yourself together, okay?'

'But I still can't get my head round how can someone do evil to those who have never done him wrong...'

'Forget all of that, okay? All that background stuff, it's by the by, you have to learn to seal your own wounds, and do it without the help of those who inflicted them on you. Believe me, acceptance and adaptability are the way to go, deniers are broken by life. Listen, for me Noah was just someone who I allowed to borrow me for a while, that's all. Do you understand what I'm saying, all this philosophising and looking into the matter deeply can wait. There's a job to do and you have to be in the right mindset to do it – I'm relying on you now. You're the *man* of the house now.'

Jazzy coughed, and stared gravely at his feet.

'It's just that when I think about stuff...'

'Poppycock! Thinking gives you too many options, action narrows them down. The closer you are to action, the fewer options you have. That's the way it's meant to be, men are supposed to be simple doers, and leave the thinking and handwringing to gays and geriatrics. You're a man Jazzy, a soldier, and I need you to be one for me!'

'What do you need me to do?'

'Excellent, that's the ticket. Now I'm going to have to get you to go to Shatby in my place, as my representative okay? You go there and you tell Noah that a divorce is what we want, got that? Jazzy, are you listening, can you hear me. Look at me.'

Steadying his lachrymose lower lip, Jazzy raised his eyes and nodded, wiping his nose on his sleeve, 'I hear you.'

'You've got to say yes Jazzy, I need to hear you say it. That way I know I can rely on you but I can't until I hear you say it. Please be balanced, not too angry and not too sad, you have to say you can do it...'

'Yeah, yes. I'll do it.'

'Bravo! That's my boy. Now there's not much else for you to do except go there and repeat what I've just said, okay? That a divorce is what we want and we won't accept anything less. But you need to be in control, nice and calm, everything has to be just so, no scenes, no threats, no stamping up and down or breaking things, okay? We don't want him calling the police and painting us to be the villains. It's about getting something done and not merely trying to prove a point. You're a man now and I want to be proud of you, no palaver; simply deliver the message and leave, understood?

'Yeah, yeah. Completely, you can rely on me to do this.'

380

'Yes. I know I can.'

Judging this to be the right moment, Petula gently elevated herself so she was level with Jazzy's forehead and kissed him there.

'You have my blessing, you know I care very much about you.'

'Me too, me too, you're everything Mum, everything...'

Liquid was once again freely flowing from Jazzy's eyes and Petula was on the verge of wrapping up and giving him her car keys when she noticed Spider plodding up the hill gingerly, her wild stacks of black hair collected in an irregular bun. Despite her uncertain gait, there was a protective determination in her large bog-brown eyes that suggested a desire to circle the wagons if necessary, her loyal heart alert to the possibility that her partner may be suffering cruelly. Petula did not mind that Spider, wrapped in a goose-shit green shawl, should be wary of her – one never knew when that might become useful; the alliances of dusk had a way of transforming into twilight's encumbrances. Mildly entertained, Petula watched Spider grope her way up to where they were, an abominable snow-woman coming to terms with a new landscape, her posture hopelessly compromised by her upper body weight, which consisted largely of her medicine-ball breasts. These burly twinned cities were in danger of scraping along behind her like soup cans, Petula thought, the strain of her panting and puffing painful to behold, yet behold it Petula did. Her actual face, the same dark gypsy tan as Mingus, was very pretty, and strongly sexual. It required little effort to imagine Spider's bent body operating on all fours, and with an awful slip of focus, Petula saw this enchanting troglodyte pounce upon Jazzy, their mating ritual witnessed by the forest under a killing moon, Spider burying her son's knobbly carriage under the seat of her worshipful flesh as she triumphantly rode him, on and on, towards a truly Homeric climax.

'What is it Mum?' Jazzy had noticed his mother's attention wander away from the path of greater intimacy, and was already beginning to miss the most powerful ten minutes he would ever share with her.

'Oh nothing... those, over there,' Petula pointed at a cluster of peonies, their stalks not entirely solid enough to carry the weight of the flowers bursting at their heads, 'they're the bright shoots of everlastingness, aren't they? So beautiful, so reassuring, all will be well, yes, all will be well...'

'It will be Mum, it will be, be sure of it. From now on.'

'Of course it will... In fact, if you feel up to it, you might mention to our runaway when you see him that the Philippines is no longer a land of lawless opportunity, they have extradition laws now, I've read about them, and he'd be better off trying his luck somewhere else, New Guinea I think. More his line.'

'Philippines?'

'Oh, I'll explain later!'

Jazzy smiled wisely, it was an expression Petula could imagine taking people in, should he have recourse to do so in future, along with an earthy charm he might like to cultivate.

'The world will be too small a place for the runaway by the time we're through with him. This is only the start Jasper.'

'Jazz,' called Spider, 'babe, are you good, everything okay?'

'Yes babe,' bellowed back Jazzy with a great sense of occasion, 'today everything is good. We're a family again.'

Petula winced, for as much as the sentiment touched her, the blustering finality with which it had been conveyed did not. All this was stalling, she was standing at the start of a new act, and needed to be alone again in peace to prepare for the next step, and then for all the ones after that.

'Go Jazz, here are my keys, keep your mind on the job, and God bless you. Now go.'

coupling and coming.

Petula's problems were about to take another unexpected turn.

Jeremy gazed across the narrow gap that separated his knees, thighs and compressed genitals from Regan's, and marvelled again at how he could not find this girl more enticing, her physical existence meeting many if not most of his requirements for formal earthly perfection. To observe her at this distance was to run his eyes over a menu of sexually enticing positives: narrow and viciously pruned eyebrows, toothpick-thin lips, blonde thickets of hair piled upon her head like dainty pineapples and a sculpturally finished carriage that looked to have been lifted from the Galleria Borghese; all bound in skin-tight velour tracksuit, completed by her maker's crowning achievement – thin, probing fingers that Jeremy really ought to have built into his morning masturbatory tussle, squeezing the fleshy circumference of his jutting cock, instead of politely observing them on the steering wheel of her Punto, tapping away in time to the inoffensive chart-hop dilution Regan preferred to the gangsta-rap compilations he had assembled for their journey. Then again, Regan might have actually considered finding him a bit more attractive herself; could he be any less so than the acned toads, hedge-creatures and greasy nonentities she wasted herself on? Jeremy knew that this was to miss the point of their relationship, yet it was a point his vanity enjoyed flying over, allowing his ego an airing before being caged within the sulky-superior silences he usually expressed it through. Besides, he knew he *was* attractive, not simply because when he asked people they usually replied in the affirmative, though that was certainly a relevant part of his conviction, but from the deepest sort of lusting after oneself.

From an aesthetic point of view, Regan had picked her 'special friend' with a similar care to that she took with her clothes, her human attire combining the same qualities of comfort and decor as the inanimate kind, Jeremy a mute Sancho Panza to her stunned Quixote, their deficiencies of character the pull and limit to how well they worked together. Taken on their visual impact alone, they were a success, looking as though they ought to be a couple who would come to a happy end several years hence. Jeremy was tall, and though conscious of it to the point of stooping slightly, offered an instantly recognisable silhouette, his giant elemental shoulders and trunk sending plenty of undergraduate hearts aflutter. He was easy to spot, lunkishly barging to the front of a queue or appearing from under a bridge on the towpath where he took his solitary and sullen walks. His features were solidly assembled and brick-like, built to an exact if rather universal specification for balanced male handsomeness that Regan deluded herself into thinking was an acquired taste of her own. Though spurning athletics and team games of every kind, his figure was equal to tossing a caber, a bunch of muscles seemingly constructed without the help of any exercise, other than the hours he spent at the obscure gym he and Regan frequented, popping out of his vests with careless virility. This near-caricature of complete masculinity was accentuated by his unusual fetish for clothes that were at least a size too small for him. A visible brief line, and a penis he could not stop fiddling about with, its outline crushed in his spray-on jeans like a broken bar of chocolate, were too absurdly sure a way of announcing he was gay to be confused for it. Regan loved the vulgarity but was not turned on, conscious as she was of the sheer number of vulgar townies who would approach them on a night out, her companion a beacon to the basest forms of lechery, fielding off multiple inquiries about whether he was a personal trainer, Chippendale or adult-film industry worker, every time they visited a club. This fanfaric sideshow detracted from the relationship they were not having, the juncture between it being too early for them to embark on one, and then too late, traversed suddenly.

Jeremy had heard there was no such thing as an impossible sexual combination but he and Regan were, he had to admit, looking an increasingly unlikely one. He reproached himself for not having made his move on the first occasion they shared a bed together after a night on the town. The two drunken clubbers had collapsed onto Regan's polar-white eiderdown, just inches away from an exploratory kiss. Then for some reason Jeremy could not remember, he had started to tell a story about a relatively dull acquaintance of theirs, perhaps to add some credit to his own role in a largely pointless anecdote about swapping coats. Regan fell asleep as he was talking, and he had lain there, watching her, scared that to wake her and try now would only be tragic or disappointing. The following evening it was Jeremy's turn to pass out, following a round of tequila shots on an empty stomach, the alcohol working too well to offer the Dutch courage it was downed for. Botched misses and squandered chances piled up, other lovers coming and going to ease the disappointment, as instead of the revelatory intimacy their initial attraction had gleefully anticipated, their chemistry remained stubbornly tepid, if occasionally furtive. In six months the closest they got to doing 'it' had been talking about it in the hope of birthing an act that would not come of itself. Regan, developing a tall tale she had eavesdropped over her mother's table, told Jeremy, stoned, that her fantasy was to have rough love made to her on a beach as a line of men, Magnificent Seven style, took turns to stand on a rock and masturbate over her and her lover's rutting bodies. It was a heartwarming lie, Regan expecting a layer of the filth she had heard so much about to rub off on her, and having done so, finally inspire Jeremy to pin her against a wall and fulfil his biological duty. Jeremy, not to be outdone, though missing the point entirely, slowly reeled off an exaggerated director's cut of his sexual history, tongues and fingers counting as lays in his telling, played out in places boys who did not have anywhere to go back to would use: the floor of a secondary school at four in the morning, the empty garage of a relative, a Church altar, a suburban footpath. These drearily episodic tales did little to raise the temperature between the potential lovers, and nor did a pornographic film they sat awkwardly through, the actors ugly beyond words. In the meantime they became friends, the first of the opposite sex either had properly made, for Mingus, whatever he was, had never counted as anything so straightforward as a chum in Regan's reckoning. Tenderness gradually clouded the erotic component of their relationship, bringing about the filial bond Jeremy had dreaded in its place; coziness a damning admonishment to his thwarted testosterone.

Despite choosing a Business Ethics course with the ambition of one day managing a nature reserve, Cambridge, or at least the university and its environs, was an intimidating proposition for Jeremy, however much he tried to conceal it with diffident and sometimes pouting bravado. Regan quickly grasped this fundamental insecurity, perceiving how the college and its communal rituals challenged her friend's natural shyness and desire for a privacy he had never known. Both Jeremy's parents had met at their local bank where they had been tellers from enrolment to retirement, his brothers resentful planks who saw women as their enemy, his sisters older and always pregnant, their home a cramped nettle-green bungalow on the outskirts of Swindon. Jeremy freely confessed to her that the sum of his family's collective existence was to live quietly, understand absolutely nothing, and die quietly. It was a fateful path he lived in half-hearted terror of, lapping up Regan's tales of The Heights and of Petula's experiments in public taste with relish. Being in Regan's company was as good as renouncing the maudlin genealogy of his forbears; his father's grey hush puppies, his mother's hair nets and shower caps, his bunk bed and yellowing Formula One duvet, all flushed away; a world so thin that it would take a Montague or two to thicken it to a width he could be proud of.

Jeremy did not require Regan to issue her invitation to The Heights again, not even when he was told that their plans had been brought forward and they were to leave in an hour, all on account of her mother having been unexpectedly heartbroken. As he had often pretended his parents had divorced simply to make them sound more interesting, Jeremy was stimulated at the thought of encountering a real-life tragedy in progress. What did it matter that he had failed to obtain his oats with Regan? He knew from experience that finally getting to sleep with the object of one's dreams was a hollower victory than the wait prepared one for, enticing potential so often lost in the crudity of its obtainment. To be held at arm's length with Regan was still preferable to the alternative – a relationship with another slapper he would have to apologise to his mates for. And who knew, perhaps on her own turf Regan might grow into a friskier proposition, luring him onto a four-poster bed like some latter-day Anne Boleyn, with the promise of an orgasm that would last three quarters of an hour and a peerage at the end of it.

Embarrassed at the extent of his imaginative impertinence, Jeremy tried to strike a deliberate note of wonder. 'I don't think I've ever been this far north before,' he said, 'the funny thing is, near where I come from, they do these adverts for bread, and basically pretend that our town is in the north, you know, the whole lie is set a hundred years ago, and they pretend that's where the bread is made.'

'Where's that?'

'Shaftesbury, it's called "Gold Hill", an old cobbled street that the advert says is in Yorkshire, because it looks like it should be. The voiceover is shit too, some old paedo telling you how they baked it in the old days.'

'But you're from Wiltshire aren't you?'

'Yeah, but the two places are practically next to each other.

Wiltshire, Dorset. You can catch a bus in five minutes.'

'Right.'

'Alright, so maybe they're not that close, but you told me you were from London when I met you!'

'You wouldn't have believed me if I said I came from where I do.'

'Correct. I figured you for somewhere like Cheltenham or Henley.'

'People don't get the Yorkshire connection because they're always looking for the wrong thing. Not me basically.'

'Like what?'

'Leeds United, Nora Batty, Alan Bennett, Little and Large. I don't have the accent, the attitude or look, nor does Mum or many of the people we know, not the ones we know really well anyway. Maybe my brother does, sort of... actually I wouldn't know how to describe him, anyway, don't worry, we probably won't even see him.' Regan felt a nauseous rustling in her chest, like an intruder forcing open a door she wished to keep shut. The thought of Jazzy always seemed the first step in a journey she would rather not embark on, her lack of compassion for his 'predicament' a source of embarrassment to them both.

Jeremy helped himself to another fruit gum, shards of the sticky sweet entwined in his teeth. 'Posh people are the same all over, they're like their own country,' he mused in the slightly childlike, even feminine voice he sometimes adopted with Regan, and never used round anyone else. 'You've all got more in common with each other than you have with any of the ordinary people you live near.' It bothered him that he had never found a natural way of talking, silence always feeling the most natural state for him to remain in.

'We're not that posh,' Regan replied, 'trust me, compared to some of the people we know we're like, like the worst most lowly peasants, you know? Nothing special. Common even.'

'That,' said Jeremy professorially, 'remains to be seen!'

He reclined in his seat with the assurance of a judge at a private members' club, and bringing his knees up to the dashboard with an insolence he did not really feel, attempted to whistle along clumsily to the music. In truth he was really on-edge. The ticklish prospect of finally meeting Petula was daunting. Would she consider him a groaningly dull upstart from a far-off place no one had heard of? There was not much use in opening with the Hovis gambit, that was for sure, which put into sharp focus how little he had to say for himself – nothing amusing, intelligent or intriguing at any rate. What if she saw him as a potential son–in–law and delivered the full treatment: 'So, you think you can marry my daughter, do you?' Did he really know how to fend off the unfriendly attentions of a woman who ranked the great, fashionable and creative in her address book? Would she even deign to notice him at all? He could only go down in Regan's estimations once Petula had shown him up as a mediocrity, yet he had to try, even if his chances were no better than a tulip surviving a nuclear winter, he still *had* to try.

It was safest to put off any more second guessing until it was too late to worry, which he calculated would be some minutes before they finally arrived for high-tea, supper, dinner or whatever it was the Montagues called their late-afternoon meal. Out on the road the landscape and weather were growing ever more alien. He was right; they were definitely in the north now, and Jeremy imagined how the air, inaccessible in a car travelling at nearly ninety with the windows up, must feel: clear, cleansing and sharp, like a ghost stroking his face. Maybe that was what entering Regan on a lonely moor would be like, surrounded by a flock of goats and the skull of a kite, the oceanic purge his body owed to itself reaching its final consummation, Regan lying under him, her haunted eyes staring into his, knowing she would never be so satisfied again. His penis began to harden, and tactfully, he drew his hand over his crotch. The motorway appeared to be the dividing line. To his right Teesside; all pillars of smoke, defiant chimneys and winking lights, sullen in the browning cloud, the industrial working class challenging the flâneurs of Mockery Gap to neither forget nor write them off; and then the other side, where they were headed, a maze of crooked black lanes and craggy slate walls that led into the mountainous expanses of North Yorkshire and The Heights. Destiny, Jeremy thought, that was the most effective way of controlling his nerves, to accept that he was doing no more than being driven towards his fate, already too late to plead nerves or insanity.

'Let me get my tape on,' he said reaching back and rifling in his bag, 'Yorkshire needs to hear it.'

'Needn't worry,' said Regan, 'my Mum has probably already got it.'

She watched Jeremy pinken and curve away catlike in his seat.

'But I haven't,' she added, 'please, let's put it on.'

*

Jazzy was no fan of towns in general, nor Shatby in particular. Indulging in his weakness for misrepresentative generalisations, he regarded mid-size dwellings as a poor substitute for the extremes of the city or countryside, their existence a challenge to his view that life was an all-or-nothing affair, rather than the confused patchwork of compromises that kept a roof over his head. Because of his prejudice against places of average population, Jazzy had tried to give Shatby a wide berth, its continual presence at his operational frontiers an unwelcome reminder of a parallel route he might at any time be forced to take, should Petula give him his marching orders. It was typical that Noah had chosen a location that he would have had no desire to visit of itself, or even on account of his present mission, for which he felt ill-exposed and unprepared.

And what was Shatby anyway? It was not distinguished by narrow cobbled streets, a beautiful ruin or two, an abbey whose bells provided order through windy October nights, a world-class oyster restaurant and a tidy marina, nor a resurgent new-age community selling crystals, gems and spells from nicely smelling boutiques; none of that was Shatby yet this was where Noah had decided the next era of Montague history should be made! Crippled by an ugly working harbour, resembling a Soviet era port, and large connecting A-roads that split its sea-side tack and low-rise bungalows from the newer tower blocks that could have been lifted from Sheffield or Leeds, Shatby was low on magic and high on loss, the moors just far enough away to make the walk there along the duel carriageway lethal, and as Jazzy indicated to turn into the old town, he made the resolution to never come here again. He had met his match: Shatby had out-depressed him.

For Jazzy the weedy bank of shabby granite council houses foretold humiliating failure, a grey army looking down upon a soon-to-be-vanquished foe, compelling him to move his van to the opposite side of the road and park outside a boarded-up semi, its overgrown and untended garden comfortingly like his own. The grubby particulars of seaside life – a seagull tearing apart a turquoise crust of bread, the news emporium selling peanut brittle instead of papers and the drizzly Februaries that could never be told apart – were all harder for Jazzy to bear than the rural grime he felt safely camouflaged in. With an air of minding his own business, he thundered awkwardly across the top of the old town to the war memorial that overlooked the central thoroughfare which led to the seafront, the two sections of Shatby immortalised by Wrath as 'a dead body held up by a broken leg', a copper bust of the poet parked at the centre of the prominent traffic island. Down below, amongst the fading Edwardian hotels, sat The Elephant's Nest, once a fashionable place to take tea and gobble 'little rascals', gnarly current cakes that could blind a gull if launched with enough malicious force. Naturally Jazzy had never entered the place, though he knew the twee Brontë Museum next door with its collection of spooked dolls, a dozen for each sister, staring out to sea with their eyes of blackened plastic, and the pier where an upmarket shop that prepared North Sea skate in breadcrumbs and lemon, instead of batter and vinegar, had opened next to Chinkies, now renamed The Oriental Rose. Jazzy had no use for any of these seafront consolations, heading straight for Saint Elmo's Fire, a garish American theme bar announced in shocking pink and yellow lettering, partly hidden by the broken Fifties slot machines and jukeboxes stuck outside as ornaments. It commanded a partial, though disguised, view of the entrance to The Elephant's Nest, and it was here that Jazzy ordered his first pint of the day, a flat American pilsner that smelt as if it had come from a vat the brewers had burped in. Jazzy quickly ordered another and, ignoring the other drinkers, a cross-section of the elderly, unemployed and soon-to-be-institutionalised, took a stool along the thin bar that ran next to and along the window.

What the *fuck* was he doing here when all was said and done? That was the insurmountable horizon under which all other questions had to be asked. How nice it would be, he pondered, wiping the thin trickle of syrupy froth from the first sprouts of grey on his upper lip, to deal with happiness for a change, however short-lasting, instead of steeling himself for more carnage. Could it not be someone else's turn to be stoical about pain, and his to be stoical about pleasure? A wise man, he knew, ought to be able to see beyond both, but it always seemed to be his role to bear up nobly to misery, which felt real enough to him, and never to 'see through' the so-called illusions of happiness, which he would gladly risk being fooled by for once. Even so, Jazzy could see why Petula thought he was the perfect patsy for this job, his honour at having been chosen short-lived. Knowing him uncomfortably well meant that his mother saw enough self-destructiveness in his character to finish the process others had started, or to put it bluntly, the ideal cannon fodder for any suicide mission going. The dubious privilege of telling the man that effectively bankrolled their lives to go to hell would normally have fallen very much within his remit, though not, it seemed to him, on the one occasion it might actually count. Far from feeling like an avenging angel about to mete out justice to a cowardly want-away, Jazzy was frightened from the moment he had been left on his own in the van. His mother had got it badly wrong, or at least failed to examine her options carefully, certainly so far as his personal position was concerned. It was alright for her, she was Noah's lawfully wedded wife and therefore safe, but who was he to this stranger now? If Noah no longer loved or needed to mollify his mother, what cards did her son by another man have left to play? What if Noah simply told him to sling his hook, would Petula be in a position to protect him or might he emerge as a makeweight in a larger game he would be excluded from? The possibilities, combinations and likely outcomes all stank.

Jazzy felt his skin slide slowly off his face, the alcohol working to the detriment of his confidence. As though catching up with the decisions of an amnesiac, he noticed that he had ordered two rum chasers with his Budweisers; all four glasses now stood empty. It was inexplicable. To hold inebriation up, he ordered a packet of pork scratchings with his next pint and checked his watch; quarter of an hour to go, enough time for a quick crap and swift change of scene.

Returning from the urinals, the stink of disinfectant furring his nostrils, Jazzy tried to dredge up memories of past resolution as a way of steadying the shaking hand that had made a mess of wiping his bottom seconds earlier. It was only Noah, who even at his most threatening was a thousand times less formidable than a legion of gnats. He had been more than equal to him before, even going so far as to refine and make an art out of giving the man shit. On coming home from the pub and finding his stepfather awake, Jazzy would stride into the kitchen and sit head-to-head with his enigmatic benefactor calling him every name he could think of. Eventually this had turned into a Friday-night ritual, Noah never uttering a word back, only smiling broadly at the clock and stirring his tea. But the last time Jazzy had put him to rights in this way was six or seven years earlier, and on that occasion Noah had actually risen, taken the kettle off the Aga, and left to drink something stronger elsewhere.

Beyond cursory farm-work discussions, awkward appeals to borrow more money, a tedious Christmas lunch Jazzy was too stoned to take an active part in, and the occasional grunted greeting, no meaningful contact had passed between them since. In the intervening years Jazzy had crossed the crucial threshold from adolescence into adulthood; would the old rules, and allowances, still apply, now he was nearly a man? He could think of no reason why they should. His features had begun to fidget without moving, and his arse itch with unridden shit. Jazzy glanced at a care-in-the-community candidate who appeared to be watching him, muttering intently into his fingers. Tuning in to the diversion, Jazzy tried to untangle the babble. It sounded as though the old man was asking him for help, and leaning forward Jazzy caught what sounded like: 'Can you help me die?'

Recoiling, Jazzy ducked protectively behind his pint, and pretended to ignore the elderly retard. He was ready to put his foot down with all the stubbornness of the truly weak, if only his preemptive moves hadn't felt like reactions to a hand he had already been dealt. He could not get past the sacrificial quality in his errand, the recurring fear that he would have to be mad to trust his mother any more than he did Noah. There were times, many times, when he honestly thought she loathed and reviled him, or was it rather a case of his hating her? No, that was unacceptable, he could never formally admit to hating anyone, that was what bastards did... even though hate had always helped his thoughts cohere, his memory establish patterns, and identity converge round a single governing idea: kill or be killed. But that was ludicrous too – he was a lover, not a fighter, only entering battle to protect his integrity and those who sought his help. This was his story; he knew what he thought, or what he had told himself to think, for so long that he had stopped thinking about it, rendering his mind as unreflectively predictable as it was prickly. Jazzy's true motivation came to him unbidden. In the lively moment of the last instance, his hate laid the red mist he needed to face his persecutors. Without it, and the necessary loss of control it afforded, he was alone and without armour. And that was the crux: the more in control he was the more frightened he felt; he needed destabilisation, craziness and bile to act, even on the smallest of things, be it arguing the toss with a traffic warden, yelling at slow drivers, or giving Noah Petula's ultimatum. Hate was the magic potion out of which his strength derived.

It was not, Jazzy decided as he gulped his lager down, a bottleneck of swilly liquid stuck above his Adam's apple, normal to feel this way – mad and torn up one minute, terrified and lost the next, the blind panic of how he was to live and make ends meet chasing a bundle of rage round in endless circles. There had to have been a reason why he was like this, an external cause or, more relevantly, some state of affairs or person he could blame for making him this way?

It was the moment his unconscious had been waiting for, the practised manoeuvre that worked every time, and on cue, his reasons came running towards him, every embittered ranting promising a return to the old certainties with extra lashings of customised self-justification.

Of course he was entitled to be exactly as he was. There were watertight causes for the fear that had driven him to the toilet, irresistible arguments he could genuinely respect himself for entertaining. He was a tool to be swapped or discarded, the expendable spoke on the farm wheel, charged with doing The Heights' dirty work. With nothing to lose it was inevitable he had become an attack dog. Family had changed all that though, real 'family', whether they were his natural 'blood' relatives or not. The needs of Spider and her children had drawn him into life and rendered him unique and irreplaceable, freeing him from the burden of independence that caused so much misery in the past. With lives he was now responsible for, he could not afford to take chances; his missus and the kids depended on him. It wasn't for him to go charging in rashly, fighting Petula's battles and issuing her deranged ultimatums, especially when she had lost the plot so badly. The game had moved on. Unless he reigned her in, she'd land them both on the council-house waiting list before they were within sniffing distance of a pay-out. For all her experience of war, his mother had never realised that there was a time for anger and a time to be smart. Jazzy shook his head and smiled benignly; she was at her most wrong precisely when she thought she was right. Not that he was perfect; he had made the odd mistake of his own, trying too hard when the answer was to take a chill trip and trust karma. Sometimes it was best to simply leave well alone and watch the river flow by. Forcing the issue had always been Petula's problem; he would not make it his.

Jazzy returned his attention to the pensioner, and watched him repeat his obscure request for death. The poor bastard was pathetic, the threat he posed laughable, and ensuring that the man could see his compassionate smile, Jazzy put a pound down in front of him.

It would be irresponsible in the extreme to follow Petula's orders to the letter and arguably criminal to obey her at all. This was a matter all parties would have to take their time over, there would have to be discussions, lengthy ones, perhaps chaired by a neutral, perhaps overseen by himself, everyone having their say and listening to everybody else, especially those most affected – him, Spider and the kids – in a calm and just atmosphere, a properly grown-up context for an adult solution. Jazzy brought down his pint, firmly, his chest filling with exalted self-righteousness. He could even foresee his spiritual health benefitting from this kind of steady and negotiated vision of the future, one where round-table family conferences replaced shouting matches in the rain; his soul was a thing he could grow into, and in growing into, build. There was absolutely no point whatsoever in getting het up and making irreversible decisions before there was a plan in place. Jazzy straightened up and ambled to the bar, ordering another pint and chaser, changing his mind and asking if they served mild, before accepting a glass of the same piss as before, and, nonchalantly, started to roll a fag. Smacking his lips, he looked round for a light. What he really fancied was striking up a conversation; this change in outlook deserved celebrating. Sure, the situation was still catastrophic, but no longer serious; shit like this had happened before and shit like this would happen again, nothing fundamental would change, it never did. He was the man again; sole possessor of insight and the guardian of all knowledge.

Wandering toward the lavatory Jazzy felt an enjoyable kind of urination coming on, the complete reverse of the urgent sort that bothered him earlier, or the stubborn constipated crap that would not quite come before doing so most unpleasantly. This was a royal toilet trip he did not really need to take, a deliciously decadent relieving of oneself that kings who had nothing to do all day must indulge in. The alcohol was certainly kicking in. Stopping by the door of the gents, Jazzy made a sympathetic motion of the head to an ugly youth at the jukebox, half his size, struggling with his selection, and called, 'She Sells Sanctuary', one of the half-dozen tracks he felt could compare to the lively piss he was about to take. By the time he jigged back through the plywood door, guided by an almost mystical jouissance, the driving guitar on the track he had asked for had filled the room in a way that was embarrassing the other drinkers, the mismatch between the music's attack and the desire of the patrons to remain hidden too great. The boy had followed his orders, tickling Jazzy's notion that he was a natural leader, and punching the air raucously, he wandered up to his new friend. The boy's slitty eyes stood to attention, leaving Jazzy in no doubt that he had enlisted a loyal rookie into his tribe of pacifist outlaws, an obliging boy buried under the stringy beard he was too young to grow.

'I've put it on all five goes,' he said breathlessly, 'all *five*.'

Jazzy acknowledged the offer graciously with a tilt of his thumb, the howling vocal enabling him to feel like a holy chief riding into chaos, armed only with a peace-pipe and the wisdom of old, ready to teach the squabbling white man how to live in harmony with his dead ancestors – and given his pivotal position between Petula and Noah, how far was this really from the truth?

'I used to sing it with my band,' lied Jazzy, 'we covered all kinds of shit.'

'Were you a singer then?'

'Not to start with, but I was better than the singer we had, so I sort of took over, right. Little prick called Mingus, used to live round here, he was the original. I found him fucking my girlfriend when I was on tour, you know, beat his fucking head in. No choice, know what I mean.'

'Where's he now?'

Jazzy looked at the floor. 'Six feet under mate. It was the only way it could go.'

Everything was getting mixed up in a rather wonderful way. Putting his hand, almost fatherly, on the boy's sunken shoulder, Jazzy noticed that his thoughts had turned to drugs, and so asked, loudly enough to be heard over the music and therefore all through the pub, 'You got any blow?'

The boy chortled eagerly, 'Yeah man, yeah. Loads.'

Jazzy, close to his face now, peered at his new friend; here was a youth who did not look like he had any drugs that he had not already taken.

'I just need enough for a joint.'

'Right, right. But it's all at home.'

Jazzy looked about cautiously, 'I can't really leave here. I've got something I have to do. You know, an important job, I can't leave to just fuck off some place, you get me? But maybe you...?'

'That's okay, I'll go and get it, yeah?'

'Good lad.'

Jazzy watched the boy walk round and past the other drinkers, timidly annoyed at having their afternoon disturbed this early, and raised his fingers in a peace sign to him, as he left the bar. The barman, a permed lummox in a Hawaiian shirt who had replaced the girl Jazzy had been ordering off, beckoned Jazzy over. 'Be careful with that kid, he's hit his head a few times if you know what I mean. He's not 100%.'

'Who is?' Jazzy shot loyally back. He raised his eyes at the clock: zero hour; Noah should be arriving at any minute. He chuckled, remembering that Noah was not meeting him here, and that in fact, Petula's husband did not know he was meeting him at all. He had never thought of Shatby as being a town fit for secret assignations, but perhaps Petula was right and there really was no such thing as a boring place. St Elmo's Fire certainly had more going on than he would have previously given it credit for. His judgements ought to be more generous in future.

As he returned to his seat he found another pint he could not remember ordering.

'From me,' gargled the disturbed old man who had asked Jazzy to kill him earlier. Without questioning this kind gesture, Jazzy slurped at it thirstily, its tastelessness facilitating its windy passage, and resumed his vigil at the window, a little confused at what he was meant to be looking out for. Of course, *Noah*.

And then he saw him. What first struck Jazzy was he was much taller than he remembered, or at least, not shorter. His memories of him must all have been of Noah sat down, as he could not picture him with legs, which was crazy as he knew he had never had to get about on a wheelchair... God, it was happening. Jazzy clasped his forehead despairingly, he was pissed, incontrovertibly under the influence to a point where the distance between fact and frog-shit could be measured in finger flicks. Blinking hard, he attempted to focus on the rangy, pole-thin figure, taking the steps two at a time. Dressed in a dazzling linen suit and straw boater, Noah was exuding the confidence of a buyer walking through groves of soon-to-be-condensed fruit juice, and not the retiring matrimonial fugitive he had banked on bullying. Noticing another rum chaser arrive by his side, and attempting to ignore its entreaties to be drunk immediately, Jazzy pressed his face to the glass to better inspect his target.

As he was about to enter the rickety doors of The Elephant's Nest, Noah peered behind him with the sixth sense of a practiced adulterer, and appeared to hold his gaze at the window Jazzy was perched at. His evenly tanned face, sporting his trademark moustache, clipped militarily, was in fact doing no more than taking in the North Sea, staring beyond the pier into the scummy ocean froth. Jazzy did not wait to find out. Obeying his schoolboy instinct to hit the deck, he threw himself to the floor like a whipped dog, much to the amusement of his new friend, the suicidal drunk, who, having cheered up, rasped: 'You hiding from a woman or the law lad? Haw haw!'

Gathering his dignity, Jazzy quickly sprang up and rushed through the bar to the fire escape. Once on the pier, he pulled his woolly hat low over his eyes, and marched with his head down to the entrance of The Elephant's Nest, but instead of following Noah up the steps, he took a right and walked round the block onto the main road leading away from the sea. Not stopping, he retraced his steps back up to the war memorial, and only there did he rest for a moment and rub his overwrought heart, which was beating sickeningly fast. He was a great one for seeing complexity wherever he looked yet when it came down to it was all very simple – he was running away because it was the smart thing to do. And weirdly, propped up and panting by the obelisk, Jazzy discerned why Noah had come clean, damn the consequences. Secrets inhibited their keepers more than the deceived, and comforting retellings of reality were a crime to oneself. Fighting the urge to throw up, Jazzy grappled with his tin of tobacco, papers and filters flying over his feet. On his hands and knees, his eyes tight with rage, he cursed an existence that was all lessons and no learning. The first spits of rain had begun to land insultingly close, leaving him little option but to stalk back to town in search of shelter and another drink, his message to Noah temporarily waylaid in his hurry to forget it.

*

Regan pulled their bags out of the boot, finding at once that Jeremy's was too heavy for her to take any further. Making her mind up to call him she watched his progress, over the gravel she had taken her first steps on as a toddler, passing the point of no return, as Petula came out of the front door to greet them. He was on his own now. Jeremy had proceeded ahead of Regan unwillingly and only at her insistence, since, knowing that her mother liked men who showed initiative, Regan had forced him to lead from the front. She was as desperate as he was that Petula should admire him; he was her find.

Regan watched them approach each other, Jeremy bombing up like a fell walker eager to complete a disagreeably jagged peak, her mother betraying no body language she could recognise. All she saw at this stage was that it was mercifully unhateful; Petula was not above redirecting her ire at whoever she happened to land on. Her near-androgynous twiggyness, clad in flimsy Gucci rags suggesting a humility she intended to be obvious in a subtle way, did nothing to disguise the risk she posed to the too-eager-to-please. Regan left her holdall where it was and, straining painfully, hauled Jeremy's sack over her shoulder, determined to play second fiddle to a fault. It crossed her mind that her friend was either planning on several changes of clothing a day, or looking to stay longer than the couple of nights planned upon. His bag was as heavy as meteorites.

'Hey, Jeremy...' she called protectively.

To her slight annoyance, though understandably, Jeremy appeared to have forgotten her, and hobbling awkwardly over the crude indentation that was supposed to be a speed ramp, Regan wondered why her mother had not come to greet her first. The thought was selfish and frighteningly base. It was as if a reflex churlishness was there on the drive, waiting for her to come home, step on, and carry in on her shoe.

'To be contemporary you must be predictive,' she heard Petula say, responding to what was most likely a compliment. From the expression on their faces it looked like they had both noticed something neither could remark on, and seeing them absorbed in one another's company, Regan dropped the bag, which was on the verge of breaking her back, and walked over to the neat line of cars parked in the yard.

Petula had never taken any interest in vehicles, there were no other guests expected, yet here stood an Audi estate, two Golfs, one of them brand new, a Range Rover and a Porsche; what did her mother want with them all? There was no denying the show-room flashiness of their shining bonnets and gleaming tyres, especially considered in the light of her childhood transports, a mud-splattered Volvo and her father's old MG, impossible to sit in and forever breaking down. Of the few conversations they had actually had in the past decade, Regan recalled her father gently steering matters round to her mother's spending, this miniature tribute to Beaulieu Motor Museum indicating that he may have had some cause. Regan would never have described Noah as flinty or selfish, but as Petula had so often said, he tended to think of things in individual units, himself fore-mostly, rather than in abstractions like family, herself and Petula, to distil it to its essence.

And so what if Petula used a different car every day to plunder Waitrose? Regan noticed she was doing it again, inexplicable droplets of negativity infiltrating her thoughts like bearded fireworms, banishing the generous sanity they brushed against. The desire to act as a censor, brimming over with petty moralising, was little better than coming out straight and telling Petula she was jealous of her, for what else could lie behind it? Unfortunately Regan could not entirely help herself, weakened by the effort of having to pretend she was feeling other than she was, in her mother's company.

Regan glared at Petula, who still had not said hello, hoping to attract her attention, and at Jeremy, who had not bothered to even thank her for the lift. It was a kind of mania that she could not keep down. Neither of them had done anything wrong. Regan tried smiling, found that she could not, so clearing her throat, called: 'So now you've met Jeremy...'

For some hidden reason she hoped never to discover, her mother was actually listening to Jeremy, who was holding forth buoyantly, coming in stronger than she would have thought possible, though judging by what she could hear, courting disaster. 'I can only imagine. You know, what you are going through, being lied to by someone you trusted, whom you probably thought you knew inside-out, I mean, it must be one of the worst things to wake up to, being jilted by a bloke you were married to, so confusing, it must be doing your head in...'

Regan practically choked. Talk about diving straight in at the deep end; now she feared for him! Jeremy's lack of tact was a lack of breeding, it always showed; *they* never guessed that the confidence they believed was expected of them came across as

PART THREE: STYX, HATE

simple vulgarity. Regan stopped herself again, loath to divide people in this way, and quickly amending her prejudice, decided Jeremy was a victim of nerves. She would have to come to his aid.

Her concern was misplaced. To her amazement, her mother did not cut him short, choosing instead to pick up where he left off. 'Yes, confusing is it in a nutshell. We confuse who we want people to be with who they are, allowing them to live up to a lie. It reminds me of that saying, I only consulted it this morning when the bomb dropped, "an atheist who values his life will let himself be burned alive rather than give lie to the view that is generally held of his bravery". Which says it all really. At least, for me. We're actors who read our lines off the identities others give us. Basically, that is it. It's little wonder that we hardly know who one another are, despite sleeping in the same beds with them for years.'

'For sure, it's impossible. And great that you're able to be so philosophical and cool about it Mrs Montague.'

'Regan hadn't told me that you read philosophy? The subject fascinates me to tell you the truth, without it I don't know how I'd have lasted this morning out. It's been hell from start to finish.'

Without *it*? Regan reserved the right to feel some confusion of her own. Had her mother not rung her that morning for comfort; was that before or after burying herself deep in Heidegger and Heraclitus? Petula was a rock alright, but Regan could not remember her mother being *this* stoical on the phone, nor very much about her previously-existing love of philosophy either. What she had observed was that, like many an improvisational actress, Petula was handy with quotation.

'It's good of you to come anyway, new people always lift me up. No man has killed me yet.'

Petula's spirited patience with Jeremy became her, but Regan also found her forbearance annoying; what would become of their new intimacy if the suffering that announced it was already over?

'The important thing is that you look great Mrs Montague, I mean it, really fresh, given what's just happened. Not many people could bounce back this quickly. You know, I wouldn't have believed you've been through what you have, if Regan hadn't given me all the details.'

Regan cringed; she had provided Jeremy with no more than a few guiding lines; it could only be seconds before Petula exploded.

'That's an observation that loses nothing from repetition, please make it again.'

'You look great! Your husband must be a madman to up sticks.'

Petula laughed, and casually held her arm out to Regan, touching her shoulder familiarly, while keeping her eyes firmly on Jeremy. Regan could not understand what was happening; had it been anyone but her mother she would have thought her manner unbecomingly flirty, which was of course impossible.

'Don't be too hard on him, he was Regan's father you know, whatever his other shortcomings. It's no one's fault really. We simply became so much ourselves that we stopped being aware of each other except as characters bound up in our own fantasies.'

'What a lovely way of speaking, do you always talk like this?'

'I don't know, I would have thought you'd already have had some experience of me knowing Regan as you do, perhaps she's inherited some of my habits of speech.'

For the first time since arriving Jeremy turned to address Regan. 'If you insist, but if you don't mind my saying so, it's no puzzle where she gets her looks from. And her brains. It would be an act of philanthropy if you went out and had more daughters! Mind you,' he added, lowering his gaze to Petula's bosom, 'Regan hasn't got... no, nothing! Forget it!'

Petula scooped back her freshly trimmed wedge of hair, to indicate that though she had heard compliments along these lines many times before, she was still willing to accept them. 'Ha! No, don't underestimate Noah, there were brains on his side of the family too, I couldn't have stayed married to a complete plank.'

'But he couldn't have thought deeply about leaving you, or else he wouldn't have done it!'

'Thinking, as such, wasn't really his forte, but he was a useful manager.'

'Who wants to be a manager?'

'That's not quite what I mean. Look, I judge a man's competence and stature by how many different worlds he can *manage*, and there have to be at least two on the go for me to rate his achievement,' Petula pouted, showing her game face. 'As for Noah, judging by his dingy affairs, he must have been managing at least six or seven, whereas my son, you've yet to have that pleasure, he exists in one and can't even manage that. He was supposed to phone me earlier, I charged him with a little task. He and I fight at different weights, I *heavy*, he *light*. Anyway, forget that, what I'm trying to say is that I can't be too hypocritical. Noah and I were alike in more ways than people think. And I might have enjoyed the odd dalliance or infatuation in my time too. I'm no innocent myself you know, so you see, we're all hypocrites. We just hope that knowledge of that hypocrisy makes us nicer people. Which is why you won't find me bitter about any of it.'

'That's magnificently big of you Mrs Montague. I'm kind of startled by your attitude to tell you the truth.'

'Petula, please, call me Petula. Or else I might go off you!'

'Sorry, Petula! So, was there, if you don't mind my asking, someone else involved in this? A third party?'

'Jeremy, sorry to interrupt, but you sound like you work for the *News of the World*!' Regan interrupted, 'You can't ask that.'

Petula waved Regan's objection away. 'You could say so. But a love won at the cost of another enters the world in a diminished state.' Petula's voice hardened, a sudden knotted quality making the words atonal. 'Noah's killed his chances of future happiness on that score,' she coughed angrily, 'I actually feel sorry for the little table dancer he's ended up with, I think that's what he said she was. God alone knows what she expects from him or what he's promised her. That's their business. But one thing is for sure Jeremy, they're not going to get it from me.'

'Why should they?'

Petula threw her arm back at The Heights, as though unveiling a portrait. 'All I asked for was this, a beautiful home where the world would leave me in peace to live my life. No one needs more, or to live anywhere larger than the average home of the British middle class. Millionaire ranches and helicopter launch pads are not my thing, I leave that to others. Yes, this is about right for me so far as privilege and luxury are concerned, the rest is just conspicuous consumption. But what I love I will not give up. Still, that's just my personal opinion. Others,' she looked at Regan, 'might differ.'

'You're right,' said Jeremy eyeing a forecourt the size of a small park, the building behind it larger than any private dwelling he had ever been invited to, 'this is about right. You can't ask for more.'

'Thank you, yah, that's it, exactly, this *is* about right, and I have always found that I can trust people who like it here, who *feel* the energy of this place. And can't stand people who don't. They're not for me at all.'

'I feel it alright. The energy.'

Regan listened open-mouthed, her disbelief incapable of finding a toehold that would allow her to disrupt the performance. Had they any idea of how stupid, false and venal they sounded? She could not believe a word of what she was hearing. What was all this about her mother's 'infatuations' and 'dalliances'? She had overheard scurrilous slander, so typical of village life, whispered by poisonous gossips, yet never credited it as fact, nor seen anything that made her suspect it could be, apart from that one night with Fogle. Yet if Petula was gaily admitting as much, the truth must have been under her nose all the while. Which was crazier still; why would her mother confess to being a hussy in front of someone she had never even met before? Who exactly was the idiot here? And why stop at that revelation? All her fanciful poppycock about a 'table dancer', and 'being left in peace to live her life', the stuff about consumption and hypocrisy, it was a sham, all of it, as was Petula's entire countenance with Jeremy. What was she playing at – had grief sent her mother mad? For the first time in their association, Regan thought she might be blind to something that everyone else thought obvious, and that loving Petula most did not mean knowing her the best. She looked at them, grinning, immersed in their bottomless, nauseous nonsense, and said, 'Mum, what are you on about? Are you feeling... alright?'

'Do you think you'll remain, after this, on good terms with Regan's dad?' asked Jeremy, Regan's question having as little effect on his hearing as the sharp squalling of gulls over the freshly ploughed fields. 'Will it be a good break-up, do you think?'

'That all depends on what you mean by *good*, Jeremy.'

'I'm not sure. No, you know, I'm sorry. Regan's right, I'm beginning to feel like a snoop sent over here to doorstep you! I've already bothered you with enough questions, probably. I don't want to overstep the mark on our first meeting!'

'Don't be so silly, my life is an open book, anyone who knows me could tell you that. I'm not interesting enough for secrets... though I have a few.'

Regan clenched her fist so the blood showed, not that anyone was likely to be looking. She could have killed them both, couldn't they just shut up and be quiet and resist the urge to say another stupid word? Why was her mother leading this idiot on? It was desperate, she absolutely had to stop them from talking and proceeding as they were, but short of telling them to hold their tongues, which she knew she was incapable of, what else was there apart from storming off in a sulk? And that, she guessed, they would not mind at all. It was all too like the mistake she committed when she made 'Never talk to me like that again' her catchphrase when she started Nohallows; raising negative capital had never been her forte.

'Would you take him back? I guess that's what I'm getting at, do you give people second chances?'

'Are you mad? If he sets foot in this place again, I'll have his bloody guts for garters!'

'*Touché!*'

'Oh how crass!' said Regan.

'The good terms I want to be on are his knowing his place,' continued her mother, ignoring her. 'Crossing me by coming back here, for whatever reason, is out of the question. From now on he lives in the shadow world he has chosen to inhabit. I've no place for him. I don't blame him for being what he is, and I don't want to waste the rest of my life hating him, but that doesn't mean I actually want anything further to actually do with the man.'

'Boy, I wouldn't want to be in his shoes if ever you get hold of him!'

'No, you wouldn't. His problems, those that will flow from this decision, are just beginning. But he never was any good at seeing that there would always be consequences. There is a saying...' Regan groaned loudly, but Petula was unstoppable now, 'an old saying from these parts that says that you had better trust your mistress more than your wife. I dread to think what dirt that little squaw must have on him by now, probably enough to get him to invest in a line of those clubs he met her through. And I'm sure she has got a troop of brothers and sisters, all dancing on little tables of their own, who all require paying too, regularly on the bloody hour. He'll have a whole caravan of dependents before he knows it, and not one of them, mark me, that will be prepared to look after him in his dotage, as I would have!'

'Mum! I don't think it's right for us to call this... person, names. Or make assumptions about her and her, her culture and family.'

'Sorry darling, I thought that would be kinder than referring to her as a *whore* or whatever you'd call an individual you'd find on a card in a taxi office in Manilla.'

Regan quelled her agitation with a diplomatic 'Please Mum, let's change the conversation.'

'Don't take me so seriously darling, you know how I like to lash out for sport!'

At least Petula was talking to her. Regan noticed her mother's hands were shaking and that beneath her bonhomie, her pallor was as pale as Alaska. Instead of understanding her curious behaviour as a symptom of grief, Regan saw she had rushed to judgment once again. What she ought to have done was take her mother to one side and tell her it was all going to be okay. As it was, the pressures of the day were in danger of spoiling their reunion.

'I know this is hard for you Mum, but mightn't it be a good idea to take a bit of time out and a rest? Lie down a little before tea? You don't want to wear yourself out. Today has been absolutely mental for you.'

'Lie down, why?'

'Because, because you've had a really hard day of course.'

'Hard? On the contrary dear, as I was about to say to Jeremy, I'm entering one of the most fascinating challenges of my life. The only hard bit about it is the point of the axe I'd like to bury into that little trouser snake's head, should your father ever bring her anywhere near here!'

I can't listen anymore, thought Regan. Jeremy was guffawing and slapping his bottom as if his hand belonged to someone he wanted to stop. Loudly, he blustered, 'Regan said you were a woman of steel but nothing could have prepared me for the real thing, I mean nothing! And please don't take that the wrong way, I'm beginning to think that there are more sides to you than a... than a crystal!'

'A crystal? Oh come on, can't you do better than that?'

'No, I can't actually! Regan will tell you. I'm no good with words.'

'That I can hear for myself!'

'So be it, but that's still my analysis. You're about the most many-sided person I've met! So deep, there's just so much to you.'

Petula clicked her tongue saucily. 'Is that right? Your *analysis* eh? Well, if you have one of those in you, perhaps you are a two-dimensional man after all Jeremy. And I bet it's that second dimension that takes most people by surprise!'

In spite of this being the most cutting thing he could remember anyone saying to him, Jeremy intuited at once it was anything but a put-down – he was being enjoyed. 'I don't know how many dimensions there are to me. I've never stopped to ask who or what I am,' he said, the truth being that he had never stopped looking and so far found nothing, 'but go ahead and have a pop, I deserve it, for being so nosy and presumptuous... Still, we were talking about your dimensions weren't we? How many of those are there I wonder?'

'Can we go in Mum?'

'Just a minute dear, let me answer, it isn't such a stupid question,' Petula winked, but at Jeremy, who was grinning lewdly. 'I don't deal in dimensions, so you'll get nowhere asking about those. I'm the same all over, all the way from the bottom to the top,' Petula ran her hands up her haunches to her sides, stroked her chest, and practically purred: 'So you see, I reside on the surface.'

'You mean you only show people what you want, right? I find it hard to keep up with you!'

'You're not meant to. The only time I stop is if I'm looking forward. I've not much use for pausing in the present. And none for the past.'

Jeremy was beside himself with glee. Petula was validating him and, he suspected, opening up in a way that was rare for her. He was conscious of Regan's surprise too, and fully expected her to later congratulate him on the feat of drawing her mother out, as his success must have been as pleasing a shock for her as it was him.

To cap his euphoria, Petula thumped him on the shoulder. Without taking her hand away, she squeezed his powerfully developed bicep, and practically grunted into his ear, 'That's some meat on you there. You're a regular bit of eye candy, aren't you? I bet you could push back peak-time traffic, if you wanted.'

'Come on!' Regan interjected, 'Time to go in.' Her mother was leering over Jeremy, reminding her of a twelve year-old stalking the captain of the school football team who, alert to her intentions, was contracting with pleasure. Whether it was mental damage, as Regan hoped, or the pathetic obliviousness of one caught in the hypnosis of mutual attraction, as she could hardly credit, the conversation was about to become physical.

Tugging Jeremy by his free arm, Regan pulled him away, dragging him up towards the house. Petula stood rocking, her balance momentarily upset, a bemused expression concealing a rush of irritation at her daughter's possessive insensitivity; young people always got the hump when one of their number broke generational ranks and gave age its due. 'Has all that student ragging and boozing gradually changed your existential landscape my dear, you weren't like this when you were last home. You seem a bit hungover today, a bit tetchy...'

Regan, trying not to snarl, replied, 'I don't drink that much, nothing like your friends. But I'll admit I'm tired, you woke me up really early this morning with your call, remember?'

'Who doesn't imbue occasionally? But there are ways of handling it Regan, I prefer to let others inspire me out of my dark corners. You seem a bit out of sorts. Why don't *you* have a lie down before tea?'

Misunderstanding the stand-off that, in reality, neither side thought they were having, believing the antagonism lay completely with the other, Jeremy got between the warring protagonists and laughed, 'Ladies, a contest to see who cares more about who! Crazy, you don't know how lucky you are. In my family we're always fighting to see which of us is the sickest and in need of a bit of sympathy; the way you two put each other first is awesome, I mean it, totally awesome.'

Petula raised her eyebrows at Jeremy, as if to say, this one is your problem now. 'I'll see you both for dinner, it's late already, forget tea, an event for old ladies, Regan will look after you Jeremy. A truly unexpected pleasure. Regan only seems to know other girls, it's good to have a man about the place again.' And smiling coyly, she about-turned and walked back to the front porch, her cane left on the gravel behind her.

Regan let go of Jeremy's arm which she was on the verge of twisting, the momentum to share the pain she was in was growing irresistible: she had forgotten she was a girl and become rage incarnate. Was this how it was for Petula, she wondered, every time she witnessed her mother's eyes flare up and heard her scream?

'She's fearless, like nothing could scare her, not even a nuclear war!'

Jeremy's voice was awestruck, thought Regan, as she replied impatiently, 'Why should it? I'm sure she thinks "our side" would win.'

She wanted to add that if he thought he was making a friend in Petula he was very much mistaken, and even put it in that nasty way, following through with a jab about how she would make him one of her creatures, but these unspoken slights horrified her more than the events that provoked them, and Regan consoled herself by kicking at the gravel.

Little did it matter, as Jeremy was looking at the house with his tongue sliding about his chin. Without knowing whether she meant to offend, knowing only that she had to be by herself for her own protection, Regan turned back and headed to her bag, still beside her car.

'I wish I had a mother who talked like her.'

Regan snapped over her shoulder, 'Be glad you don't. Anyway, I hope you don't mind, I'm going on a run.'

'Cool, I'll come with you, just let me get rid of my things.'

'No, no, I don't want to trouble you.'

'You won't be, I want to come,' Jeremy was alongside her smiling cooperatively, 'I'll bring in your bag.'

'I need to be on my own, okay? I just need to be.'

'Why?'

'Because I do, alright? All your questions are really pissing me off, if I'm honest.'

'Shit, I'm sorry; what did I say? I'm sorry.'

'Yeah, me too.'

'But what about my room Regan? I don't know where I'm meant to go!'

'Mum will help, you two look to have hit it off.'

'Are you alright?' Jeremy looked at her carefully now, and Regan saw the old fear slowly reappear over his questioning face.

'What do you think? Yeah, of course I am. I've just got a lot of stuff of my own to think about. I don't need you there, with me, when I do it.'

'I promise I won't talk. You can think.'

'I'm sorry, that's just the way it is. I don't think it ever worked, us exercising together, anyway.'

'You what? I thought you loved it when we did. I know you did, I was there, we worked out well together! I don't get what I'm meant to have done wrong. Why are you so pissed off with me all of a sudden?'

'Please Jeremy...' It was then that Regan saw what she had toyed with all along, the dirt under the fingernail of an other-

wise-clean hand. An intentionally vague idea, within which lay
a specific one: an excursion down to the lake that would lead to
a re-run of her seminal night with Mingus, clarifying her relationship with Jeremy, and by proxy, with all men, once and forever. If Regan had the courage to read her thoughts exactly as
they were, this symbolic encounter was what Jeremy had always
been groomed for. And as a true, but generous narcissist, her
task was to use her beauty to give Jeremy back to himself, making him more aware than ever of the body he loved, his own,
leaving her with an idea of herself that might also give meaning
to her lovemaking. Not very romantic, she had to admit, but
theirs had always been a practical arrangement, and there was
no reason to think that their kissing, scratching and pawing,
however passionate, would traverse that fact.

The very thought of physical contact seemed utterly gross to
her now, and as she watched Jeremy's stupid expression turn
into one of hurt, it was all Regan could do not to spit in his face.
She had gone from thinking he was one of her closest friends
and a possible lover to considering his existence disgusting and
hating him completely in a little under ten minutes. And for
that she had herself to blame, and her mother to thank.

*

Jeremy did not know what he was doing, sitting on his bag
as though he were waiting for the intervention of a National
Express Coach to bus him out of trouble. There were no shortage of other more suitable objects for him to sit on in the room,
which, in his dejection, he had failed to acknowledge. Comfort
was insignificant next to his fearful disappointment at having
ruined months of work and preparation, all through his refusal
to continue in the role Regan had assigned him. Could he really be blamed for finally breaking cover, having been presented
with the opportunity to engage with a beautiful and intelligent

woman, instead of standing there like a sullen lump who needed Regan to translate for him all the time? What else could explain Regan's sudden coldness when he had played his part to selfless perfection, if it were not for his playing it too perfectly? Regan had not wanted her supply of new blood to exceed room temperature. In showing his hand, and raising his status above its expected place, he had ceased to be her cuddly-toy bodybuilder, and paid for it on the spot.

With bathetic self-pity, Jeremy considered the works of art that appeared to have pinned him to the lowly corner of the floor he could not wriggle off; circular spot paintings evoking windscreen fly splats, ringworm traces and police fingerprints, a horror show that bore witness to his shame at having allowed Regan to dismiss him like a dog without producing so much as a bark in his defence. Like a good canine, he had done as he was told, and trooped through the house to the bedroom he had been allocated, brushing off the atmosphere and smells longingly imagined during those expectant months in which he had patiently waited to be invited. And all for this; to be plonked on a sports bag wishing it could all be over, and that he would wake at home in Swindon eating macaroni cheese in front of *Match of the Day*.

With Regan strutting off to change into her running gear in the car, of all places, having insisted that he follow her directions to the chamber her mother always reserved for 'single men', and not accompany her, Jeremy had finally got *it*. Regan was not angry with him for teasing her mother out of herself at all: she was mad with Petula for bringing out the best in him! Jeremy sighed at his courtly naivety: he had not seen this one coming, he, the piece of meat in a generational hag-fight between incumbent and pretender! Flattering as their attention was, there was little point in succumbing to the compliment – men like him were the first to be tossed under the wheels of the carriage when the search for a scapegoat began, the fate of the gigolo in history a notably ignominious one.

Was it better to simply call for a cab and leave straight away? The nearest train station was not all that far away. No, the nagging persistence of self-love held him back. Though Jeremy understood that he had flown close to the sun, revealing a bright and witty aspect of his character in front of Petula, Regan's subsequent disgust had delivered an unexpected gift. Yes, it had plunged him into despair, but just as significantly, her irrational rage proved his ultimate innocence. Without self-condemnation, there was a stubborn part of Jeremy that was not ready to go anywhere, however awkward it was to remain with his pitch so thoroughly queered. Or was it?

Quietly the first stirrings of indignation were taking shape: it was highly unfair being shaken from a joyful trance in which everything appeared to be going brilliantly, to then be cast into a situation where it was not. Jeremy's crude grasp of what he supposed was Regan's rivalry with her mother was no stronger than a sinning drunkard's attempt to piece together his walk home, yet he was sure that having been caught in the cross-fire, he was at least owed an apology from her. An explanation, however, was unnecessary – his vanity saw to that. Regan and Petula were loaded and sexy, meaning that neither had any real reason to be unhappy, and, as he had never heard Regan speak ill of Petula, only the instant spell he cast over women could account for their sudden animus. It followed, then, through no contrivance of his own, that his position in the house was still a useful one, and it was too early to give up. Providence had sent him on a mission to smooth out the differences he had ignited, possibly showing both that he could be a friend to each in his way. Who knew, were he able to affect a reconciliation, he may end up with one on each arm, or at least the pick of the two! Wasn't there meant to be a jacuzzi in the basement?

Put out as he was, Jeremy was beginning to notice the positive aspects to his surroundings, which he no longer feared he might be thrown out of at any minute. The 'paintings' excepted, which were the worst kind of weird toss, the room appealed to his sensibility to such an extent that he could hardly credit that it had not been curated with him in mind. A spanking new mauve armchair, scuffed to appear antique, emblazoned with heart-shaped Union Jack cushion, sat beside a thin table displaying Esquires that looked to never have been opened. Their aesthetic juxtaposition struck him as not being far off perfection. Resting above both on a thin metallic shelf were a pair of Warhol prints of Muhammad Ali and a black-and-white photograph of Charlotte Rampling in a string-bikini, the rest of the room a similar compliment to high-flying alpha masculinity – dark-grey towels of all sizes and a silk gown laid out neatly at the foot of a king-size bed, presided over by a Giacometti style pole on top of which was a thick candle that resembled a chopped-in-half dildo, its end unlit. Jeremy stood up and popped his head forward to give it a good sniff: at first it was like inhaling the musky crotch of an ancient sex-god, before fumes of burning leather evoking a fire in a Porsche 9-11 ashtray brought his nasal hairs to attention. The seductive aroma, every bit as effective as Viagra, tilted him heavenwards, circumnavigating his social pain, and drove straight through to his animal senses. Layer after layer of the nasty apprehensions he could name, or at least reductively misrepresent, fell away, allowing him to get in sync with the warmth in his balls again. It almost did not matter that he had no plan of how to survive the next few days, or hours, if he was spared so long, because when life was this pure, he *knew* everything would come up roses. And what was more, he felt up to fucking for England if called to, the operational readiness of his genitals the bellwether and yardstick of his cerebral health.

'Am I a disturbance?'

Spinning back, Jeremy lost his footing and smashed straight into the shelf he had been admiring, his considerable weight knocking it off the wall, the glass on one picture cracking and another smashing underfoot as he tried to restore his balance, the noise worse than the damage, he prayed.

'Oh I *am*, aren't I? I thought your hunter-gatherer antenna might have forewarned you of my arrival.'

With cowardly reflexivity, Jeremy found that he had assumed the defensive posture of an old codger fending off a nest of hornets, his arms raised protectively over his head to parry away the hovering swarm. Overcoming his clumsy response, with startled difficulty, he grimaced and wiggling a bit, tried to look as though he had been shadow boxing, this being the least embarrassing alibi he could improvise.

Petula stood there in the doorway laughing, dressed in nothing but a loose white t-shirt that reached the top of her knees and a pair of pink sparkly flip flops. In her hand was a plate of rare-beef sandwiches which she had already put down on the bedside table, a finger raised to her lips inquiringly.

Jeremy watched, or so he thought, his previously established kudos dribble away. 'God, I must be living on the edge, edge of my bloody nerves!' he choked, blasts of crimson erupting and spreading through his cheeks, his face a cheap jam sandwich. 'I'm a world away. Sorry, you must think me a, um, total jerk. It's all been happening a bit quickly today. I'm having trouble keeping up, I'm not used to all, well, getting my head round being in a place like this one, you know...'

Petula did not say anything to this, only stood in the doorway, and, laughing a little at him, bit her thumb cruelly.

'I'm sorry, it all got a bit weird back there didn't it? With Regan I mean, I think I pissed her off,' Jeremy could hear the words redact in his mouth, stupid meaningless noises missing their mark, anything to appease his shame at being caught fantasising aloud. 'Anyway, she's got the raging arsehole with me, you know what I mean, I mean, sorry to put it like that, just that I've never seen her react like she did... I didn't really know what I had done wrong, to be perfectly truthful with you. Oh bollocks, you probably don't even know what I'm on about. You know, back there outside the house? When we arrived, she went a bit funny on us, with me, didn't she, didn't you think? And now she's gone on a run by herself. Which sort of makes it a bit pointless my being here.'

Petula shook her head, whether positively or negatively Jeremy could not guess, and stepped decisively closer.

'And I've just got to thinking about it, really deeply,' Jeremy blabbered, 'and then you surprised me, because Regan cut me up pretty bad, you know, to take me so far into myself like I was just now, you know, lost in thought, more than I should have maybe, but her attitude I mean, though I guess you might think I'm reading too much into it all. Bollocks, I'm talking shit aren't I? Sorry. I was so looking forward to coming here. So much you know. Seeing your place, meeting you at last, but I ended up being too nosey, too familiar, nerves I guess, upsetting everything, and kicking up a lot of awkwardness. I did, didn't I? I bet you two don't often go cold with each other like that? I'm not saying you did, you know, it may have just seemed that way. And to mix all this into the pot with everything else you've got going on anyway, I feel totally shit about it. Adding to your problems when that's the last thing you need. I just don't know how it happened, I mean I do, oh, you know what I mean. It's just, I don't know, you know how you want things to be and then how they are?'

'Do shut up!'

'You what? I've put my foot in it again haven't I?'

'Stop talking. You know, you're far prettier when you just say nothing. And go red.'

'When I do what?'

'Red. Like a girl. A stupid little girl. A tart. Which I think you are in part.'

'I don't get you.'

'No, you don't do you, *getting it* isn't your forte. You're more of a thing to be got.'

'I'm a what?'

'Very slow on the uptake; all Regan wants is what any female who could stand being honest with herself for two seconds wants. But self-honesty isn't her. She trusts myths, resides on surfaces and holds to the stories we tell about life. I know myself, I should have encouraged her to know herself too, but I couldn't without spoiling her.'

'I thought you two were meant to be alike? Regan said they call you "sisters".'

'That's for idiots who think they're being clever. How could we be? I was forced to understand what I am from an early age. I know my wants, she has no idea what hers even are. Even an ox like you must know what I *want*.' Petula drew up to him.

Jeremy practically squeaked, positive that he must have misheard Petula's words, if he were not so excited by the intention they laid bare. 'I don't think I follow, are you saying Regan is actually a bit *thick*?'

Petula was now so close that she knew he would be able to sniff the alcohol on her breath. She avoided touching Jeremy, though her smell and aura were as good as inside his, and lowering her eye over his crotch, noticed that his penis was hardening into the thing she could trust to close the conversation. 'Can't you find anything more interesting to talk about, or is it that I scare you?'

'I don't know what you mean.'

'Do you even know what is under here?' Petula asked, raising her vest and pointing her breasts, far larger than her daughter's, into Jeremy's unbelieving face, 'would you like to twist these as you fill my jacksy?'

'Jacksy! That's your arse, isn't it?' muttered Jeremy, his hands dropping to undo his belt buckle.

'Arse, fanny, you put it where you like.'

'Now? You're having me on. Right?'

Petula paused, her damp hand on Jeremy's waxed chest stuck

like melted marshmallow to plastic; 'I'm asking you to be so kind as to put the fire out in my nerves and fuck me, you stud.'

Jeremy already knew that, it was his experience that physical contact was always more assured if he kept himself waiting, however artificially, a moment longer than he had to. Any more than that and he might succumb to the kind of shock that did not favour the spontaneous maintenance of the male member.

'Well then?'

He grunted; when reality exceeded his wildest fantasies it was best to just go with it. And go he did. To his unconcealed satisfaction, Petula was as good as her word and over the next forty minutes did not try and stop Jeremy doing what he wanted how he liked, drawing him deep into his bovine nature by whispering, during the finale, 'I can smell the lion reek of the other brutes that have possessed me,' her finger dug deep into his anus. That was enough and Jeremy noisily relieved himself in her for a second time, almost putting her back out, his previous climax having wreaked havoc with her bad leg.

'I told you I wasn't going to come in you,' he said, just after he had, hoping she would not mind.

Petula trembled; God it had been ages since anyone had got sounds out of her like that!

'I'm too old to have children, silly.'

'Uh, I didn't want to assume.'

'Okay, now shhh.'

It reminded her of those orgasms of long ago, which rose out of nature and physical activity, rather than a conscious decision to move things along a bit so that one could get up and put the kettle on. She reached over and patted Jeremy's arse, admiring his pornographic tan line, bubbling with a lusty goodwill that she had difficulty recognising as her own. Sex like this belonged in its own space, whatever reassuring stories one made up later about it being like the other times. Erotic pleasure had once been tremendously important to her, the very point of her social preening, before the dance itself became the object and the thing to be looked forward to. For a tottering moment Petula wondered whether she got her priorities confused: were not social snakes and ladders meaningless if they did not end in the recuperative and immersive wholeness that only a good shagging could afford?

She was thinking about this when she heard Jeremy mumble from his pillow, 'Is it normally like this for you?', his neck hissing sweat.

'Always. Because I'm just *so* good,' Petula replied immodestly, glad that chutzpah was not reducible to morality.

Jeremy gazed up at her reverentially, his chin propping up his head, trying, though not too hard, to take in what had happened. Generally he was scared of discovery; insight interfered with his enjoyment of things. This coupling was different and unlike any other; there was more here than there had been with anyone else, and his body had become a source of new information that he did not dread the burden of. Complex and exciting configurations were suggesting themselves to him, their approach cerebral, though softly so. Quickly he tried to remember the key metaphor or picture that would make his thoughts as necessary to others as they always seemed to him; he knew his vision was still within reach but he would have to be bold to see it. Yes, it was there alright. Petula's vagina was a cave without a roof, and, high in its vast expanses, was her true self and all that had been hidden by her formidability; there a different person awaited him, wet, playful and unassuming. He was not sure if he could ever get round to saying that, but it was wonderful to watch it be from his place in the shallows below. Jeremy could imagine not wanting to masturbate the following day, as even his onanistic tussles would have the consequence of reminding him that they could never top this. His muscles were turning to fluid, he was adrift in deep waters and there was no land in sight, and he did not mind in the slightest, for what use was terra firma when he was at once useless and utterly justified before the goddess?

'What are you thinking, you beautiful interruption?' Petula asked, stroking his thick sticky neck.

'I wasn't,' he lied, only just stopping himself from saying to her that her pussy was the sea and her anus the earth, 'I just don't want us to ever have to leave here. This room. It's like its own world in here. No one can disturb it. It's perfect.'

For once, Petula had to agree with such isolatory sentiments, her thoughts moving away into a most pleasing waltz of their own; lost impressions and once-cherished memories, fleeting and profound, bobbed about the etheric surf with newer sensual creations, a merry-go-round of the past and present that washed away the hurt of the morning, relinquishing it as barely there. She tried to picture Noah naked with his new lover and found she could not. It was a waste of time to attempt to concentrate on any one idea. If she tried to ground her perceptual arsenal, all she found waiting for her was sex, the flux and not the fact. Closing her eyes, she succumbed.

Perhaps she had been asleep, but before Petula was properly aware of it, she was nimbly hurrying through the subject in a more cut-and-dried way, airy mediations superseded by the dates and times of all of the fucking she had ever had. It was incontestable: there was a lot of it, and remembering herself as the one who did it all was not nearly so nice as the way she had been feeling earlier. For one thing she did not know why she had never admitted to herself that she had failed to properly re-sexualise after having Regan. That birth had left her as awkward in her body as one who had never had sex, a disjointed maladjustment lingering for years after. Putting her beauty into the service of societal advancement helped conceal the obsession that things were over for her as an erotic player. Not that she had stopped having sex; indeed, Petula had embraced an industrial policy towards fucking that sought to obliterate the fear that inspired it. In her defence, it had not seemed so desperate or sordid at the time, simply the *only* thing to do.

Petula could no longer feel Jeremy's body against her own, the room was as motionless as before but something had come over her, best characterised as an indigestible clump of regret. As a believer in 'natural' law, over the humane or moral kind, sex with whichever of her friends' husbands she liked was as pure a reflection of nature's pecking order as could be found outside a wildlife documentary. Over the years she had re-written the Ten Commandments as she had gone along, her circle of acquaintances large enough to support a vigorous approach to infidelity, and there being no point searching further afar, with heaps of pliable flesh within driving distance. Formally successful as she was, the experience seemed to damage the men she chose as well as their wives, and on her second or third romp round the circuit the difference was noticeable; her lovers had either given up or wanted to run away from her. And what, in a man, was natural about that? She had robbed these beta-boys of their natures as well as their wives' trust, forgotten or blanked those whose appetite for abuse was not endless, and kicked her heels at home when there was no one left to fuck, complaining that Shatby was not Ashbury. Had she really enjoyed any of it? No, she had put up with the mechanical ritual of undressing, humping and dressing which, save for a second of sharp relief before the end, was all it amounted to. And she had continued in the hope that one day she would get better and enjoy it again, and, even more hopefully, not be afraid anymore. But fear of what? Of so many things, not least that an honest appeal for help would result in her extinction.

Petula noticed that her hand had left Jeremy's neck and was trembling in mid-air, the configuration of snow-clouds produced by the dust floating through the light had darkened into hailstones and the room was slowly beginning to re-situate itself in the world. It was time to interrupt herself and exercise grip; she needed to get out of there, fast.

Jeremy knew nothing of this, his mood lighter than a troop of helium fairground bunnies. Nakedness had always carried the stigma of exposure, and in his nightmares he was often chased in his birthday suit through public buildings, his clothes disappearing as quickly as he found them, the jeers of his pursuers getting closer as he struggled for breath. For Jeremy, concealing his nakedness in suggestive clothing meant remaining in control of it; total nudity was as bad as a leaked secret. As much as he enjoyed showing his body off before sex, he would rather have made love with his clothes on, and could not wait to cover up and withdraw as soon as it was over. But not today. The room could have been packed with the Aberystwyth male-voice choir and his cock would not have crinkled an inch: bare-arsed nudity was the perfect condition to reside in, proof of his triumph. Unfortunately for his newly-earned serenity, this conclusion drew him towards a crude summary of events that somehow sold them short, quite unfaithful to the sleepy wisdom he had only seconds earlier been afloat in. This was a lecherous version that begged for an audience to delight in a vulgar overview of his achievement. Put simply, and once thought of in its most basic form, there was no other way of putting it; it had taken months of ground work with Regan to get on the wrong side of a rigid scolding, yet here he was having splayed the hips that bore her wide open! What need did he have of her daughter's approval when he had rammed Petula senseless – the view of her on all-fours asking for the door to be slammed again likely to provoke erections well into his old age! This was, he knew, deliberately getting it wrong, even though it was strictly what had happened, but the facts minus beauty and mystery did not amount to the *truth*. Even so, the tabloid editor in him was simply too stubborn to revert to ethereal delicacy now that his horn had taken over. If he got Petula to take it a step further, which would not on this evidence be difficult, and ply Regan with one too many glasses of wine over dinner to loosen the pole from her hole, they'd probably end up in a threesome by the fireplace! The erotic possibilities were multiplying quickly, and Jeremy could see a future 'arrangement' developing where they could meet for an orgy every month, maybe not always at The Heights, that might get boring, but in posh hotels and maybe other countries, and even film themselves doing it. Why the hell not, lying still and being fucked on camera would tick both of Regan's boxes – passivity and making an exhibition of herself – and 'the sisters' could easily afford the equipment, so what was to stop them? Had not the last hour shown all things were possible? The momentum was unstoppable, Jeremy could not help it, and though he knew he was losing something precious for good, he moved his hands roughly up Petula's thighs, and lifted his forefinger to commence proceedings.

'Ouch! Careful.'

There had been a marked change in her, of that there was no doubt; Petula was as dry as a Saharan drought, and her hand, dead and cold, slapped his away angrily. Jeremy sniggered, and tried again, this time even more forcefully, ready to instigate a new game for them to play.

'No, it's too much, Regan could be back any minute, there's nothing to stop her just walking in,' she snapped, unable to disguise the tremor in her voice. What had she done?

'*Relax*, come on.'

'No, I can't!'

'Don't worry about Regan.'

'One of us has to!'

'No really. About Regan, she might not mind as much as all that... she might even think, think it's funny...' But Jeremy could already feel that particular hope evaporating; he must not get too far ahead of himself, Petula was obviously toying with him again. 'Stranger things have happened, eh?'

To show she was not on the verge of becoming a different person, Petula brushed her hand over the battered end of his throbbing phallus and forced the corners of her mouth up. If the spell had broken for her there was no point ending things as quickly for him, he had done nothing worse than be himself in the face of unspeakable temptation. 'I've got to hurry away, we can't be found like this. I'm sorry, but we can't.'

Jeremy had a stupid look on his face, the possessor of a secret that could enhance his standing if only the world knew, its arrogant simplicity amusing Petula as she exited, and annoying her madly when she entered the kitchen four hours later to find it still there.

CHAPTER ELEVEN,
missing and misunderstanding.

Was it too late? In the showery mist it was hard to tell whether the day had already turned dark or not, and Jazzy found that he was no longer sure of where he was. That he was still in Shatby, and outdoors, was not open to question, though from there his narrative tailed off into conjecture, notions of sequence and temporality suspended until such a time as they made sense again. When that would be, Jazzy did not know, though tomorrow morning might not be a bad bet, if ever it came, and without any attempt to conceal what he was doing, he released a bilious swell of streaky hops over his trousers. Swearing at what he thought was an unfortunate gust of wind, but no more than his stumbling backwards into a public bench, not a speck of puke having missed his person, Jazzy pulled off his woollen hat and fumbled about wiping himself down, before giving up and throwing the soggy item over a wall.

'Shit!' he yelled at the elements, 'Motherfucker! Mother made you mother *fuck* you!'

He had stopped at two or three pubs he had not noticed the names of, since dodging his date with Noah at The Elephant's Nest, and, frowning so as to remember them better, Jazzy tried to focus on what had occurred in their interiors. That he had been poisoned, he was in no doubt. The landlord at the last boozer was a notorious pervert, famed for drugging customers so as to have his way with them over a keg in the cellar. It was the dodgy pint that tasted of eggs that could be blamed for the digestive purge he stank of, and thank God he had run and retched without paying, or else he'd be in a coma by now, chained to a radiator and made filthy sport of.

The other two pubs, or one, he was not sure, they looked alike and may have been different bars in the same building, had refused service. Remembering that spooked Jazzy, as he had been many times drunker in the past and still been obliged by friendly publicans who could see he was a good lad only letting off steam. Which implied that the management's decision to first ignore him – he had waited at the bar for an eternity – followed by telling him he should go home, portended to something worse than a comment on his sobriety. Could it be a pronouncement on his mental health? Whichever authority decided these things had judged him not right in the head, all because of something he could not help; his essence, soul, or whatever it was he gave off when standing there waiting for a pint. It was horrid to be picked out and reviled, to arrive at the same fate as Evita, his sister, sanctioned off in a clinic refusing all contact with her family: is this what awaited him? Stumbling a few paces forward, Jazzy deliberately sat down with the intention of registering a protest against his condition, just as a braking lorry spotlit him and a voice called: 'Get out of it, you're on the fucking road, cunt!'

A little later Jazzy discovered his legs again and checked his pockets to see if he still had his wallet and keys. On finding both miraculously there, he gazed slowly from port to starboard in time to see the mist lift from the sign of The Saint Elmo's Fire. He had accidentally contrived to walk all the way back down to the pier without realising. Bringing his finger up to his temple he tried to unpick how this could have happened, and finding, after a while, that he had forgotten what he was standing there for, Jazzy decided he needed the reassurance of familiar surroundings.

Once at the bar with a pint in hand he looked round for signs of friendly life, and to his manifest relief, there were plenty. Walking towards him, excitedly, was the ugly waster he had adopted as a disciple when, in another frame of mind altogether, a celebratory joint was what the moment had called for. For quite different reasons, the same drug would still be most welcome, and rising to his full height, Jazzy did his best to look master of his movements, smiling to himself as if having remembered something wildly amusing.

'This is the top lad I was talking about,' gushed the boy to a companion who had followed him over to Jazzy, somewhat too readily. The man was Jazzy's age, wore a heavy centre-parting that was on its way to becoming long hair, and a stretched smile at odds with his gnarled, pocked face.

'How do you do, I'm Adrian,' he offered, his voice plummy for the location, 'but you can call me Ade, everyone else does. I heard you play in a band, sing, is that right? That's exactly what I came north to form you see, a band. I was at Leeds, at the uni, and it was all a bit gothic if you know what I mean. I want something more Seventies, natural, a bit more "All Right Now", like in the Levis ad, you know the one I mean?'

'Ade plays keyboards,' offered the boy, 'he's fuckin' ace, like that Jean Michel whatsit! The French bloke with the shades, you know.'

'This is a bit of a classic way for a group to meet for the first time, isn't it?' continued Ade, reaching ahead of himself, 'I can imagine us all looking back on this evening, in the future, when we're asked questions about how we first came to together to do such great things as a band, you know, a retrospective on our career...'

'Save that for later,' Jazzy interjected, worried that he would lose his train of thought if he heard any more chunter. 'What's your name again?' he asked the younger one.

'Nigel.'

'Well Nige, did you fetch the weed? You know, you went home for it, remember? You got any on you now?'

'Yeah, it's all in here!' the boy patted a knapsack that Jazzy had not noticed. 'With *loads* of other stuff. I got the works here, hash, pills, whizz.'

'No, just weed, let's go back to your seats,' continued Jazzy. 'Me hands are freezing, no good for rolling, you think you can skin one up? There's a good lad.'

'What, in here?'

'Yeah, why not, it's a shithole, no one will mind. Under the table, nice and shifty like.'

The boy looked to Ade for a second opinion. Ade nodded with some urgency, either impressed with Jazzy's gumption or having decided that it was a small enough initiation to undergo for a prospective lead vocalist.

'So are you still with your group, or are things on a bit of a freeze at the moment, I didn't get the name of the band either, but Nigel tells me you were big in the States and that you used to play with Billy Duffy of the Cult. Is that a fact? I used to really dig them.'

'Duffy? That *dick*?' sneered Jazzy, not really interested in pursuing this line, but stuck with having to make the best of it. 'He's a poodle, we chucked him out and his curlers; I fucking hate all that hair metal, you know what I mean? Fucking posers.'

'What, you chucked him out of The Cult? So you're still with them? But isn't he?'

'No, not the fucking Cult! Hell Sanctuary, the band he was in before them, he played guitar for us but I told him to knock off all that rock-star crap or piss off. Had to chuck him out in the end, didn't I?' Jazzy could hear his words slur, not that it mattered with company that at better times he could have done without. 'And The Cult, Astbury and that lot, they were the only ones who would take the dick, once I was through with him.'

'Hate Sanctuary, yes, I think I heard of them, it definitely rings a bell. What the hell happened to you guys anyway, one minute you were big and the next...?'

Jazzy examined his new companion, a posh plonker he could

basically say anything to, none of it would make any difference, they would both talk shit at each other and then never see
one other again. 'We became Hate Bastard, and Hate Bastard
became Hell Bastard, and that became Sperm Sanctuary, and
Sperm Sanctuary, they became Sperm Yard, who became Fuck
Claw, that became Fuck Hammer, and the Hammer are who I'm
with now. Got it, or do I have to write it down for you?' Jazzy
winked at Nigel who appeared to be transferring his allegiance
back to him, Ade's questions slowing down a fast time.

'Wow, yeah, that's quite an evolution for you guys. And what
about the rest of the band, you didn't say, where are they now?'

'In the States, touring, coast to coast, with a bit of the mid-
west, and some of that deep south thrown in too. You know, a
proper national tour.'

'Right. Why, if you don't mind me asking, aren't you with
them? They can't be much cop without their lead vocalist!'

'I had to stay here, didn't I?' responded Jazzy, a touch of
aggression in his reply, 'To look after me sick mam, right? Me
dad shipped out, the wanker. Why are you asking so many questions anyway, eh? Who gave you the right to be Columbo, eh?
We've got a way of doing things round here, it's called minding
your own business, right?'

'My apologies, I'm sorry, I only wanted to know what your
situation currently was because I want to form a band. And like I
said, I've been finding it a bit difficult to get all the parts together.'

'I'm not surprised.'

'Oh?'

'Yeah, and I could tell you why too,' said Jazzy poking his finger into Ade's pigeon chest, 'because folk round here are going
to think you're a southern wannabe who doesn't know a Leo
Fender from a Les Paul, got me? Coming up here and asking all
these stupid questions. What do you expect? You're lucky you
haven't had your head kicked in.'

If it was Jazzy's intention to give offence it was obvious he had failed, even in this modest goal. 'That's it! That's exactly it!' cried Ade with the fervour of one saved. 'That's the exact reason why I need someone like you to help inspire me and get things going in the right direction, why I'm in here tonight! Really, I can't believe it, I've been waiting for someone to say what you've just said all my life, really, this is just too serendipitous...'

'Is that joint ready yet?' Jazzy asked Nigel, the three of them having managed to retire to a corner table, despite Jazzy dragging his leg behind him like a smashed post.

'Yeah, it's in front of you boss.'

'Champion.'

Jazzy looked down and made eyes at the joint, thick as a cigar, lying procumbent on his beer mat, an uncomplicated joy to behold. Trying to stylishly flick it up to his mouth, the doobie fell through his fingers, causing him to scramble about on the floor, and in so doing, reveal the full desperateness of his condition. Eventually, after having nearly lifted the table up with his head, and lost the company a round of drinks, Jazzy allowed his prospective band mate to rescue it for him.

'That's it, now spark up the bastard.'

'What, in here? Shouldn't we go outside? It's a lovely evening,' replied Ade, striking a slightly flirtatious note that Jazzy was not too far gone to notice.

'No one will fucking care, this is Elmo's, right? Folk come in here to die. Get on with it yah poof. No offence to your kind meant, like.'

'Oh, okay. Here I go, there, you have first bang.'

For the next few minutes Jazzy was only conscious of the hashish he was able to suck safely and hold in his system without choking, the talking continuing at a lively pace with only his occasional interjection mildly affirming that he was still there. Slowly Jazzy grew aware of a shifting onus away from band talk to more abstract planes, Nigel laughing automatically at anything Ade uttered, the beauty of it being that if Jazzy had not been much interested in them before, he really did not give a fuck now. Filtering them both out he closed his eyes and was drifting into Jill's arms when he was bought up with a jolt, an unbearably life-like vision of his mother sat next to him shaking her head had materialised without warning. Resisting her gaze, for Jazzy feared he would hear her voice next, he began to hum, which acted as a cue for the conversation to grow ever louder, though not loud enough to silence Petula's summery of his prospects, stated in a crystal-clear staccato. 'Not all our lives are equally important because we don't all treat life equally importantly.' These words, still horribly relevant, were first uttered in her Volvo as she collected him from Smeekdales, the last school he had been expelled from, twenty years earlier. Jazzy balked: he had to get out of that car!

'NO MUM!' he blurted, knocking another pint away and reaching for Ade's face.

'I'm sorry?' Ade laughed nervously, pushing away Jazzy's trembling grip. 'Not when I last looked mate. I think you'll need to go home to find her, she's not here,' he smirked, and took the joint gently out of Jazzy's hand. 'You just need to slow down a bit, you seem a bit wound up about something.'

Jazzy peered into the shark-blue eyes of his maternal predator to discover Ade's instead, their patient accommodation light years away from Petula's inquisitorial pointedness.

'I wasn't talking to you lot,' Jazzy replied, reminding himself that they could see nothing of what was in his mind, and that it was as well not to let them know they were bedded in with a lunatic, plagued by visions of his mater. 'Just getting shit mixed up, is all. Been on it all day, haven't I? Anyway, sorry.'

Apparently satisfied with this, Ade continued, 'No seriously, artists, writers, musicians, basically people like us, we're the kings of existence, I mean, there are money men out there who long to be us, but not many of us that long to be them, right?

Well okay, we could use their money but we don't want to be them in any other way do we? I mean listen to this' – Ade pointed up to the speaker above the table – 'who wouldn't swap a million quid of a yuppie's earnings to play the axe like *that!*'

Jazzy knew it was pointless to answer, he had said similar things himself, in a mood identical to his companion. The music sounded like a fair attempt to live heroically; it was the same song he'd heard earlier, striding out of the lavatory that afternoon, before his relationship to hope had suffered its latest cognitive setback. Now the forceful riffing was a diminished thing, of less interest than the hat he'd thrown away, which begged the question whether his disenchantment lay in his auditory cortex or with the hackneyed playing itself. Dope always did this to him, and for a moment Jazzy felt exhausted by it all: the insights that were not really insights, the answers that were questions, and the questions that were always the same ones as before.

They were interrupted by the hollowed-out pensioner who had bought him a pint earlier barging into their table, a concerned look on his face. 'The landlord is calling the Police, you can't smoke that waccy baccy in here lads, best make a run for it! I heard him only just now say he'd call them.'

'Whooah there! Do you know how many fewer people this kills than the booze you imbibe so freely?' retaliated Ade, pointing to the smoked-out stub. 'I can tell you the statistics if you like. You'd be shocked by what they prove.'

'That's not the point you silly *bastard*, they've called the Police,' cried Nigel, panicking, 'Me mam will disown me if I'm sent to Borstal! We've got to get out of here. *Now!*'

'Bollocks has anyone called the police,' growled Jazzy with Pretorian calm, pleased by the intrusion, 'he said he *would* call the police, didn't he, the landlord? I heard him only just now too, heard him say what he has millions of times before, that he *would* call the police, but he hasn't and won't, just like he never has all the other times. And I'll tell you why. Because once they start poking round in here they'll find a lot of other stuff he doesn't want them to. Like his whole money-laundering operation right? That's correct friend, this place, this entire town, is run on the black, you got me? The black economy right, you ever hear of that? He's full of shit that landlord, and the only people who believe him are those that want to. Like you mate. You want to join our conversation? Ask nicely, and don't come talking shit that could get you smacked if the wrong man heard you; aye, it could happen. If you want us to say thank you, or owe you a favour, forget it. There are smarter ways of doing things, you know what I mean? Acting all weak and pissing yourself is just fake, see?'

The old man, even in the dark, looked hurt, inspiring Jazzy's Churchillian flourish, '"I lied on behalf of truth, and acted falsely because of sincerity," you know who said that? Me old mam. Bet you didn't think I could say things like that. You know what it means? It means that even if you come across as phoney, your heart might still be in the right place. So take that look off your face, no offence meant, right? Here, pull up a pew. All friends again.'

The old man's cheeks seemed to stiffen, and bending down with creaky dignity, so his bristles rested against Jazzy's own, he gasped, 'Living is a frail thing; each of us has to live with his own version, lad. You mind how you go, you got the same problems as me, I can see them written large; you need help.' Defiantly he hobbled back across the room without giving Jazzy time to put his arm round his shoulder and make friends, as he was now disposed to do.

'Arrogant dick,' Jazzy said to himself. 'Any of that joint left?'

'Fuck, that were weird, well *freaky*,' muttered Nigel, and started laughing, nervously with relief, at first, and then succumbing to a tide of titters that found everything funny, Ade joining in once he saw things the same way, and Jazzy so reluctantly that it could hardly count as mirth. The old man's rejection was

nothing next to the recognition that he was obsessed, absolutely and without salvation, by his mother, and to what end? To sit
here knowing he had failed her again without the strength to
rectify his latest mistake, one that could still be faced down by
simply walking across the road and facing Noah.

'*Freaky*, man, well *freaky*!'

'Who was that guy?'

'I dunno. But he were *mad*! Can't believe I took it seriously;
the filth, like they'd care what goes on here!'

'Yeah!' chortled Ade, 'Absolutely spot on, oh my days! It's
all mad when you look at it! My absolute favourite expression,
sums it all up for me, "it only hurts when I laugh!"'

Jazzy was finding the opposite to be the case; for him it
hurt nearly all the time. Like the others he was unable to take
anything seriously, without seeing anything in the least funny
about not doing so. Listening, speaking and believing were all
equally ridiculous in principle. There was a pin-prick of satisfaction to be found in knowing this, though nowhere near enough
to compensate for its truth. As long as he was afraid, he would
never be free. Communal canned laughter would not change
that.

'Cheer up chicken, it may never happen!'

Jazzy scraped his chair away from the others and the table,
Ade quickly rising and steadying its back so as to stop him from
rocking over.

'Let me go will you? Who asked you to be my fucking mate?'

'Hang on, there's no need for that...'

'Just leave me alone, will you! The pair of you, leave me be!
What are you, *gay*?'

For a second Ade and Nigel struck a worried note, glancing
at each other carefully, before doubling up helplessly with yet
more giggling.

'Bloody hell mate, no offence, but you've got to admit, you're
bloody hilarious!' cried Ade, banging the table, the snot stream-

ing down his face, 'I thought you were really upset there, for a second!'

The greatest deflation of all was that Jazzy knew he would return to his normal everydayness again and all this vividity and self-honesty would count for nothing. Sat there, pissed, stoned, detached and furious, a brooding testament to the inevitability of Petula's predictions.

'Yeah, whatever, I like to give folk a good time,' he murmured, half covering his face. It was all he could do to hold back the tears, and he was glad that Spider was not there to comfort him, again, as even her kindnesses were coloured by his mother's rank disapproval of their union. Petula had made much of warning him that the worst thing he could do in life was make a poor relationship, which would ruin him forever, and by his own count he had made at least two: with little Jill to show he could have a girl that attractive and with Spider to prove that beauty was only skin-deep. In both instances, the first mistake and then the reaction to it, the person had not been as important as the point he wanted to make; but to whom? Petula, of course, first, last and always, Petula.

Ignoring the cackles of his companions Jazzy drew up to the table again and drained the remainder of Ade's pint. He still missed Jill with a disorientating savagery. To begin with he hoped her departure would follow the pattern of their previous quarrels, where each would find they were as unhappy alone as they were together, and that if their togetherness was no more than the sum of their combined individual unhappiness, at least they did not have to endure it alone. That was not to be. After her letter, Jill vanished as completely as one who had never been. Dawn calls to her parents' house, painstaking surveillance of nearby haunts, and messages on local radio, all failed to winkle her out of whatever parallel universe she had melted into, forcing him to acknowledge that she *really* did not want to be found this time. His failure gave him an incentive to try and hate her a bit more, dwelling on all she had inflicted on him, loudly protesting that her replacement was thrice the woman she was, none of which addressed his need for her sharp little tits, so much tastier than Spider's loyal and supportive cumulus sacks. Jazzy clutched his chest; absence made the heart lose weight, and he genuinely doubted whether he had it in him to get up, leave the pub, find his way to the van, and return home without stopping at a lay-by for a Jill-related wank.

Blind as a fist he rose, then quickly sat down again, waiting until the room had at least become shadows and shapes, rather than fateful blackness, before embarking on his flight. Moving his lips silently he mouthed, 'Please God let me see.'

'I think he's lost it,' said Nigel to Ade, tapping his head, '*well-gone.*'

'Always the way with chippy ones, they can't handle their ale.'

'You better not be talking about me,' Jazzy grunted from the side of his mouth, and with one last effort, propelled himself off the chair and onto the floor with a crash.

No one helped him to his feet. Instead he lay there and heard Ade reply to the leader of a group of noisy students, standing on his stool and shouting at them, 'Death-machine-infest-my-corpse-to-be! Justin! Thought I recognised you, how the devil are you, you old bastard! And more importantly, how did you get on with band recruitment?'

'Crap! Couldn't find anyone here who could play drums or bass! Just some old sod with a mouth organ! How about you?'

'Well, I thought I had a vocalist, but look at the state of *this*!'

Jazzy heard a squall of merciless laughter that had everything do with him circle overhead, and, taking care not to be drawn in, which was not hard, since as far as the pack was concerned he was over, he groped slowly along the floor, until in one giant roll, he was picking himself up off the pier, bent over the rails, and vomiting over the bubbling surf below.

Rising from beneath it all, as alone in her infinite condemnation of him as if she were the only person God created, was Petula. Outside her he was nothing, and alone also nothing. The breaking waves were provocative, a taunt that suicide was an option he had never examined closely enough, Evita having robbed even that of its seriousness. Like his sister, who made an attempt on her expensively maintained life every few months at The Priory, Jazzy could not recall a time when it was worth getting off the slippery slope because he could not remember a day when he was not already sliding. What could be more useless than a single achievement he could be proud of in the face of so much slippage?

Through the moth holes in his trench-coat, and the creaky armour of inebriation, Jazzy shivered. Rolling barrages of wind had drilled through both, each gust carrying handfuls of cloudy vapour that splattered across his numb face like so many slaps. Thoughtfully he turned his back to the sea and lifted his collar up, as if there was someone within him he still desired to protect, and with his head down and homing impulse locked in, Jazzy made his way back towards his parking place without further delay. The police found him on the hard shoulder some hours later, the remains of a baby fawn splattered over the front of his van, the driver slumped in the back under some wet newspapers asleep, his trousers pulled down to his knees.

*

Back at his place at the bar in Saint Elmo's Fire, Noah had watched Jazzy crawl out with hesitant interest. He never had understood that boy, any more than he grasped why some people wished to make easy things difficult, or how some could suffer so much while others glided through life untouched. Acceptance and adaption were two qualities Jazzy had recoiled before; to deny what was, and to fail to embrace destiny's flow so that he was forever facing the wrong way and blocking the flow, was all Noah could remember about watching this strange lad 'grow up'. How could people be so dim? Noah disliked ungenerous judgements and quickly amended this one, hoping that Jazzy would find the same understanding in life as he would one day in heaven, should he ever get to grips with either.

'You know him?' asked the old man pointing in the direction of Jazzy's flight. 'A head case that boy. A friend of yours, maybe?'

'No,' replied Noah, 'I've never quite attained the virtue of friendship.'

'That, that's shrewd that is!' the old man seemed pleased with his answer. Outside the police had arrived and the bartender was pointing them in Nigel and Ade's direction.

Noah had savoured his tea at the Nest, confident that Petula would not show her face, correctly guessing that they both had far too much to lose by anything as juvenile as taking anger seriously. He had waited there far longer than he intended, taking in the surprisingly fruity sights of an averagely prosperous tearoom, and having tipped the waitress heavily, was ready to celebrate with something stronger than Earl Grey. He was reasonably sure that Petula would believe his Philippines yarn, at least for as long as it mattered; the invention of an alibi far easier than having to spell matters out in a way that was guaranteed to inspire everlasting conflict.

Noah finished the gin and tonic and adjusted his cravat, noting that in spite of being dressed for a regatta he had attracted very little attention in a place where his fellow drinkers looked to be one change of clothes short of penury. Not attracting attention was what he liked; or at least only the discriminating kind, as he sought no life beyond his own for insight, and was unable to imagine any cares past those that came automatically to him, safe in the scepticism that if life had not already existed, he would not have believed it possible. It was time to turn to the petite waitress who had followed him over from the Nest, and leaning into her to let her know he knew she had been there all along, he asked what she planned to do for dinner, as he knew a very nice place round the corner that served oysters.

*

The wheel had come full circle, the arrow turned target, thought Petula, trying to avoid looking at Jeremy who was not trying to avoid looking at her and, in fact, was doing his best to not look anywhere else. Matters were barely improved by their being the only two people in the kitchen, Regan banging about noisily upstairs, slamming drawers, flushing lavatories and stamping on loose floorboards, in what sounded like a tribute to the sonic-effects division of the Radiophonic Workshop.

God, it was a mistake to want anything too much! Petula scolded herself for her impetuousness, pulling out the salmon from the fridge, and stalling for a way of prolonging the simple operation of turning about and placing it on the table. Elaborately she paused to sniff its pink midriff, wasting a second or two before scowling at its clipped tail. It was hard to credit the time when she would have cherished the memory of a man's member over the real thing, or stimulating gossip before actual stimulation. That was how she had got into this mess, by neglecting her elemental impulses and paying the price when they had taken her by surprise, all in the form of the grinning messenger camped before her. The evidence was all about the place. Parts of The Heights had grown to resemble a North London recording studio; minimal slats and blinds preferred to roaring fires, salad replacing blood-red roasts, and a treadmill in the hall where a long walk, interrupted by a hump over a fallen tree trunk, would have sufficed in the past. Arid sexlessness did not suit her; there had been too much dark and tasteful inertia and not enough life. No wonder Noah had wanted out. Putting down the salmon, Petula allowed her eyes to meet Jeremy's, and fighting back a fear that rose through her entrails like fire, she watched him lick a finger and wink cheekily. With a bit of rational panache, Petula puckered her lips and nodded back, acknowledging him without, she calculated, encouraging him to say or do anything stupid. Jeremy looked appeased, and possibly a little disappointed by only this quasi-affirmation of their earlier intimacy, sinking back in his chair and giving Petula a glimpse of the sombre self-pity she would have to prevent him falling into, if their secret was to be spared an airing. Steadily she leant forward and asked, as dispassionately as being a few inches away from his face would allow, if he would like some wine with his meal. Jeremy shot a glance at her as if to suggest that this was not good enough, the tone falling far short of what he expected, and without answering, pushed his glass forward. Petula poured, affecting not to notice any brewing hostility. Her guest looked like he was waiting for someone who was never coming back, though fortunately he himself did not know this yet, still banking on an eventual return.

Abruptly kicking the kitchen door to one side Regan marched in, asking with loud and strained disinterest, 'Didn't you say that you bought a pair of new kittens? Where are they then?'

'I gave them away, they were too wild. I should never have got them, I've never been any good with animals.'

'Yes, you prefer *things*, don't you?'

'Some things.'

Petula could tell at once Regan suspected nothing, reality too outrageously complicated and unimaginable for her to keep up with by means of ordinary calculation, her daughter's battle the same one she had been fighting that afternoon, prior to their competing armies' realignment. Normally she would have found Regan's tone intolerable, though normally Regan would never have adopted it, and in light of the tone she would have used had she known the truth about Petula and Jeremy, it seemed a small and temporary price to pay for the maintenance of a deeper kind of order. There was also, not that Petula would have consciously credited it, the outside possibility of a lingering guilt slopping over the sides of the lid held firmly over her conscience. She could not tell whether she had actually done anything wrong or not, her moral code weighed towards her never being wrong, simply because she was who she was and winning was the thing, her survival requiring no less. Nonetheless, her instincts were mildly reproachful in this instance. Even if she had not sinned, she had committed a handful of acts that might upset someone she loved, were they to learn about them. That was as near to self-admonition as Petula dared, and cared, to go.

'I've actually gone off the idea of cats. They're more like foxes and bats than real pets. Ever since Goblino died I've never really taken to another.'

'If you couldn't deal with them Mummy, you really shouldn't have got them, the kittens.'

'I didn't know they'd claw everything in sight.'

'Why not? Didn't our old kittens always do that?'

'Do you know, I can't really remember. I never took much notice of them before, but now that I'll be alone in this place again... I might actually want some furry company.'

'That might not be the case for much longer.'

'What do you mean?'

'Nothing, only, I'm sure people will still visit like they always do. That you won't be alone for long. Definitely not long enough for pets.'

Jeremy coughed loudly and pushed his glass forward towards Petula, who immediately filled it to the brim. It was an old rule of thumb of hers that careful and selectively applied wickedness often went undetected and unpunished, but the strain that gave into its own appetites was always destined to end up in court condemned. Which made it all the more important that if she were cunning, she should be diabolically so, treachery accepting no half measures. It all hinged on whether she could get through dinner without allowing Jeremy to open his mouth or give the game up in some other way, before finding a means of persuading him to leave without arousing suspicion. With that accomplished she was safe and could deny everything if ever he later decided to tell-tale – distance and the lapse of time having long rendered his story unbelievable. But how to get through the next couple of hours, which already promised to be excruciating beyond belief, without giving herself away? Hell would be something like this, an eternity in which to explain one's perversions to those one most wanted to keep them from. The conversation would have to move off cats and onto matters more interesting sharpish, or else the sheer pain of having to listen to more mealy mouthwash might force him to squeal.

'Fish?' queried Regan with forced tartness, rolling her eyes at the salmon, 'I doubt that will be enough to fill Jeremy up. He eats like a horse at college. Didn't I warn you? I thought you knew?'

Jeremy grunted in a way that appeared to neither agree nor disagree with the statement, the imbecilic smile that had so irritated Petula when she first entered having re-emerged in the hope that Regan's bitchy solicitations would rouse her mother's jealousy. Observing him from behind the bowl of lemons she was toying with removing from the table, Petula decided that her tête-à-tête with Jeremy carried most of the hallmarks of a masturbatory experience, rather than the meeting of souls she was scared it might have been. In its essentials it had almost been the perfect pornographic transaction; a virtual fuck that left nothing changed in her life, its tax a purely psychic one. And as with pornography, she had approached Jeremy in a hurry and with single-minded determination and left him in boredom, distraction and shame. Who knew, perhaps his ardour had also vanished with his climax, though if it had he was not showing it. On the contrary, it appeared as though it had grown scarily into ardour-*plus*, his eyes pressing against her like a row of bodies in a rush-hour train carriage. Which, of course, was the crucial way their union differed from the consumption of pornography: here the pictures and images could talk back and tell all.

Not looking at Jeremy meant having to pretend to find the plate, the fish, or Regan interesting, and judging that the last of these might enable conversation to move on the most quickly, for Petula could not stand another second of silence, she said to her daughter, 'I like your top, it's quite, you know, *punky*. Not very you, actually.'

'I'm sorry, how not me?'

Petula could have stamped on her own toe. Had she reached an impasse where she was incapable of offering even a tactical compliment to her daughter without opening the gates of hell? The flimsy article in question was a cheap cheetah print of Evita's that Regan had rediscovered and contrived to render faintly glamorous.

'I just recall seeing it somewhere else before.'

'I got it out of a box of Evita's things.'

'I thought I recognised it from someplace, near but far, if you know what I mean. We haven't heard from her for a while, anyway.'

'Yes Evita,' Regan turned to Jeremy and added, faux-helpfully, 'she's a sister of mine we never talk about, mainly because she's completely mad, though that's not the only reason, she's also, or was, I'm not sure, who can keep up, a drug addict, and a bisexual. Then she became a Christian Adventist or a Krishna or something like that for a while, and then got committed to a snooty loony bin full of rock stars who want a week out of their lives. Except she's been there for ages, and despite loads of doctors listening to her problems she's never actually got any *better*. Which makes you wonder if whatever they're making my father pay for actually works. Anyway, the point is she won't see any of us because she thinks we're all evil; well me, Mum and my father, anyway. I don't know what she thinks of my brother, though she believes the world has let her down so she can't think too much of him either, as they at least used to be a *proper* brother and sister. Unlike me.'

Jeremy, taking this history in his stride, pulled his fish apart, and with heavy and deliberate movements began to eat with his fingers. His general character was getting more determinable, and Petula was going from disliking it a bit, to hating it quite intensely. As if looking to complete the effect, Jeremy belched loudly, and wiped his hands on the tablecloth with feral relish. A vapour trail of swiftly digested fish oozed across the table and Petula held her hand over her nose. What on earth, she wondered, could she say to this boy on this, or any other subject? The only natural way she could be in his company was as a lover, anything else jarred, offering either too little or too much. As for Regan, she appeared to be enjoying Jeremy's table manners, incorrectly intuiting that they were directed, in the main, against her mother's snobbery, and not at them both as living entities of all he had suddenly decided he most loathed.

'Yes, a good man, a nice boyfriend, might have helped sort her out. She never had one of those,' Petula offered uneasily, not sure which port of greater safety she could steer the conversation towards, 'reality could never support some of the wilder assertions she made about it, boys tended to find her a bit too intense...' Petula faded out and abandoned ship, staring at her raised index finger as a last resort.

'Why was that, do you think? What was her problem? She was good-looking, guys liked her, they were round here all the time when I was growing up. Why was she always so angry with them?' Regan asked, with an insistence her mother knew no good could come of.

Looking to make light of the inquiry, Petula replied, a little too violently, 'What's got into you darling? You know we don't like to rake over the sordid and silly affairs of Laurel and Hardy!

There's nothing interesting to say about either of your siblings that they haven't already said, far too many times, about themselves.'

'You say so, but I hardly know the first thing about them, and I never really got what all their ranting was about. It was just stuff between you and them. But they're my family too after all, aren't they? My brother lives just halfway down that track and I hardly know who he is now, never see him, and can't remember when we last spoke or about what. And as far as I know, we haven't even fallen out. It's just kind of naturally-unnaturally happened!'

'*Half*-brother, he's your half-brother.'

'I wish you'd stop saying that, I'm tired of that distinction. It isn't natural, it's like you deliberately want to keep us apart.'

'You'd have every reason to be grateful for "that distinction" if you knew half as much as I do.'

'But I don't, do I? That's the point, why else would I be asking you questions?'

Petula twisted in her seat, the first clods of lava that forewarned an eruption bubbling up. 'You can't really mean to tell me that you care about a woman who hasn't the good grace to send us so much as a postcard, after all this family's done for her, that you actually *care* about what this ingrate's "love life" was as a *teenager*? Is that what you're really asking me? I was making conversation, I didn't seriously expect to be hauled over the coals with this nonsense.'

'It's time I knew something about her. We grew up in the same house but could have been on different planets for all we had to do with each other. I don't know whether you didn't want us to mix in case she influenced me or what, but it would have been nice to have been given the *choice*.'

'Phooey! You saw all there was to see! A highly strung spoilt brat who, in the absence of any direction in life, sought to embarrass the only person ready to show her any kindness.

Myself! Who but a psychiatrist could be interested in someone like that? And as far as keeping you apart is concerned, I didn't have to. Evita has only ever been interested in herself. The reason I may have shielded you from her influence was because she was so jealous that she'd be liable to harm you. Do you know, I once stopped her from pouring a cup of tea over your head as a baby! I had to keep you apart for your own bloody safety! She'd have killed you!'

'Then I'm sure that I *do* want to know more about her, actually! Yes! How could you have got my sister to hate me without even knowing me?'

'Regan, you're having a moment of madness. It will pass. You need to calm down, we have a guest here. Don't lay yourself so open in public. Her hating you had *nothing* to do with me.'

'Drop the double standard, you've been laying yourself open in front of Jeremy all day! You don't mind telling him things I've never heard before, stuff about yourself, so why hold back with me when I ask about Evita?'

'Christ! Well since you beg me to speak of it,' Petula had raised her voice and could not stop herself, 'your *sister* moved from seduction to hostile contempt too quickly, that's why no boy stuck around. All one had to do was leave his calling card to became the object of the most curious hatred. She was so terrified of rejection, so eager to preempt it, that she chased them off before they had the chance to properly pull out! The possibility that it might not happen never occurred to her. She was in too much of a hurry to show she didn't care. There were a couple of alright ones who tried to persevere, I can't remember the names, but they were broken reeds by the time she was through. She couldn't trust anybody who'd give her the time of day. There it is, happy now, glad that we've had this adult conversation? Strewth, it's like having to swim in the *gutter*, speaking of this stuff. I don't know what's come over you.'

Petula knew all too well that she could have practically been speaking of herself. At least it was one way of getting it all out, she supposed, emptying the bottle of white into a half-pint glass normally used for water. In quite a different register, she continued, 'I know he's your father, but he was my husband, and his disappearance shouldn't be a green light for us all to go mad. I can't think why else you'd speak in so... in so *unfriendly* a fashion. It's important we don't all lose our minds at once. We can come back from this if we just all pull together.'

Jeremy clucked harshly and, getting up, brushed into Regan, who was still balanced against the fridge, and ran his hand over her bottom. Then, his other hand on her hip, he shoved her away, and, adjusting his jeans, began to scrutinise the wine rack above the sink. Scratching his chin, in a grotesque imitation of a connoisseur, he pulled out a bottle of red, and swung it down onto the table with a thud.

'The bottle opener is just beside the tap,' said Petula, 'I assume you know how to use one. Please savour it, that is a rather expensive vintage you've chosen.' She was finding that as she did not trust herself, her tendency to try and persuade others only increased, and that the world, especially this small part of it, must live with her version or pretend to. It really was that simple. She smiled sadly at a crease in her trousers, and tried to ignore her anger. Despite their tightness the line was obstinate and would not go away, and running her finger along it, she brushed an imaginary crumb off her lap. Would Regan stick or twist, for it felt, at that moment, that their relationship depended on a contrite and submissive response that Petula did not think her daughter had it in her to give.

'I was just taking some interest in a part of our lives you never let me talk about.'

'Oh, was that it? Jeremy, could you stop looking so pleased with yourself for a moment and help me out. I don't like switching colours, but I'll join you in a glass, if I may,' she said, holding hers up to him for a refill. 'So are there any more tedious lines of enquiry, or will you sit down and eat something now dear? You look too thin you know, I was thinking that when you got out of the car this afternoon, but didn't want to say anything knowing how sensitive you are. There's soup here, Jeremy hasn't looked at his. Have some, Royce brought it round yesterday, it's probably quite good. Broccoli, or some other green thing you'd approve of.'

'It can wait,' Regan hedged, making the most of her rare anger, 'everything you've just said, I mean, all that stuff about Evita, how can you *know* all that, what was going on in her head, her motivation? You always speak like this but how can you know?'

Petula snarled superiorly. 'Please darling, you're beginning to sound like a second-rate mind. I'm her *mother* for God's sake!'

'No, just listen for once! Why do we have to stop talking about this just because *you've* had enough? I haven't! And you being her mother doesn't answer anything...'

'No, no, of course, it doesn't, do continue, let's give Jeremy a real show eh?'

'Were *you* actually there all that time to see what was going on in her mind, and watch all the neurones or whatever they're called click in her brain...? I mean, only God is supposed to be able to do that, right? But you do it all the time...' Regan's voice was shaking and her teeth were chattering. She was not at all pleased with her effort so far but she was too angry to stop. Compared to Petula's speech, which in truth had deeply impressed her, her rebuttal was little better than face-saving qualification. Once more she saw herself playing the part of herself unconvincingly, the daughter faking the standard adolescent line in the face of the slow and sudden accumulation of wisdom that was Petula. What did her mother see when she looked at her: a feeble pretender thrashing at what could not be kicked away, whose self-discovery was that it was no self, only an echo? Or did Petula secretly fear what she could become; an agent of rebellious pandemonium, the first crack in the ice? It was an emission of confidence worth riding into battle on, and she pressed, 'Maybe she rejected others because she felt rejected, by *you*?'

Petula snorted, 'Hurrah, which book did you throw that up out of? Please Regan, I've already warned you, you're speaking like some common redbrick militant and I can't have it, I *won't*, you're too good for that.'

Breaking wind sharply, the chair sounding as if it had been cracked in half by a bull-whip, Jeremy tipped the rest of his glass into the bowl of soup that had sat there untouched, and drawing it to his mouth like a chalice, drained the lot, a mixture of caramelised broccoli and red wine sloshing over his cheeks, chin and neck.

Ascertaining that the evening was going bad in ways she had not even allowed for, her gut instinct and pessimism having grown pretty much interchangeable, Petula moved her foot up to Jeremy's, with the intention of re-establishing contact. If sleeping dogs were to stay asleep she needed to throw them the odd bone, and bringing her boot forward, to kick him playfully, she instead launched an angry blow to his shin, causing him to grimace like a removal man lifting a bed. Glowering, Jeremy grabbed a piece of bread and stuffed it into his mouth to confuse the pain, Petula's attempt at under-the-counter flirtation coming off as a warning shot, her crackling adrenaline too intense to smother her true feelings towards her guest.

'Instead of telling me I'm unworthy of a reply...'

Petula tried to block out the words. It was enough to know that she would rather accept death than admit to having made a mistake, without having to hear it from Regan in politically correct jargon. However much she wanted to explain that there were no villains and no victims, that everyone was both and took turns at being each, introducing this level of ambivalence into their dynamic carried dangers worse than those already unleashed. She would have to embrace sainthood for the moment, while praying Jeremy did not become too insufferable in the time it took to work out how to expel him.

'...because it isn't a reply, is it? It's basically just more *manipulation*.'

The word brought Petula to her senses. 'Manipulation? Ha! Stop it! Any person who knows their own mind, or can make their case clearly and would like others to agree with them, could be accused of that! Can't you see that you're doing exactly the same thing, only inexpertly, trying to get me to accept your underlying reasons for thinking what you do – but with less success?'

Regan opened her mouth into a beautiful oval shape that no sound passed through, reminding her mother of an exotic fish swimming from one side of a tank to the other to find, once again, that the context of its journey forbade it to go any further. Petula turned to Jeremy. 'The stupid thing is that she doesn't even know if she likes this sister of hers, so instead, we get to hear all this dreck about manipulation!'

Jeremy scratched the table and issued a screeching meow, the inference that Petula was most herself when she made no effort to be nice, mirroring Regan's own solid grasp of the fact that her honesty was often synonymous with unpleasantness.

'Manipulation, *please*! You'll be talking about star signs and crop circles next. And whatever you say, none of that slush about how a desire to defend oneself mutates into the exploitation of others, I've heard it all from your sister, and she nicked it all off Channel Four. You can actually read, so you've no excuse.'

Regan had no adequate reply. A disabling inertia, too heavy to be panic, had come between her and her anger. Was this all she was conditioned for: to only agree or disagree and not understand anything in between? Thinking for herself sounded so simple in theory; if only she were able to find a subject her mother was not already right about, then she might be able to start. When she thought of family, all that really meant was Pet-

ula, the others never amounting to more than bodies encountered in familiar spaces, the question of whether she 'liked'
them or not as remote as whether she 'loved' them, and equally
as irrelevant. Who had Evita been to her? An intimidating prospect more complicated and enthralling than herself whom she
would have liked to have been noticed by. Instead she received
mistrustful acceptance from her half-sister, punctuated by outbursts of unnerving friendliness that struck as suddenly as ill-
nesses, Evita's smiles too nervous to settle or reassure, however much the cessation of prickly sensitivity was greeted by the
family as a holiday. Growing up expecting her relationships to be
stampeded on by the more determined ones Evita was ready to
have, her cares and interests like those anonymous Argonauts
written into a film for the Minotaur to pick off, explained why
she secretly pined for Petula's patronage; Evita being too much
like their mother for her to stand a chance in an equal contest.
Regan had never confided in her sister, or supported her and
Jazzy's rebellions against Petula, shattering any hope of an alli-
ance between them, because it would be as pointless as going
to war with herself. There was one thing she remembered Evita bringing up in arguments that had always put Petula on the
defensive, however, and she tried it for herself now. 'Evita told
me you could only love people who didn't scare you. She said
she scared you, but if you had the courage to be a feminist, and
brought her up as one, instead of relying on men all the time,
you'd have been able to bond properly. That's what she said.'

Petula, who looked run-through by a lance at the mention of
fear, and raised to heaven at the reference to feminism, spluttered: 'So that's her take is it? *Feminism* would have saved us
from ourselves. All us *wimmin* together, loved up on polytechni-
cal lesbianism, standing up to nasty old patriarchy?'

'Yes, well, no, only part of it, her perspective I mean.'

'Is that what you call it? Patriarchy, you do realise, is just
another phrase for trans-historical permanent reality?'

'Look, this isn't an argument about politics, it's about our family and...'

'Isn't it? Trust me, so far as perspectives go, you'll find that it's my one that tallies with all that reality stuff out there that you seem so unbothered by, not Evita's pissy little intersectional self-justifications. And whilst we're at it, could you, or anyone, explain to me the difference between a feminist and an ordinary woman these days? What does one do that the other doesn't? I mean, really, what does a woman think she's doing calling herself a feminist at all, it's such a miserable little alibi! And there are so many braver ways of making an impression. Evita once told me that her sleeping with so many boys was an act of feminist defiance; I told her that the real surprise isn't the number of people we've slept with but the number that we *haven't*! Think of it, the billions and trillions of men we haven't fucked! Haven't fucked yet and never will! *They'd* like to do it, *we'd* like to do it, if certain conditions were met, and yet somehow we can't get our act together! We ought to be telling strangers that it's their turn next! There should be copulation in the streets! Feminist my bony arse! I wouldn't cock a leg on one!'

Jeremy watched Petula light up and egg herself on – it was like listening to a poem while watching a contest – her eyes alive to how much fun she was having, even if her code of conduct would not admit it, and Regan, shivering behind her sanity, sincere in her thwarted desire to leave the world having learnt something, while hating every step of the dance. These were the sisters he had resolutely failed to live in the moment for, projecting his way through the last two terms in the shabby hope that he would one day be admitted to this famous kitch-en, where whatever-it-was was supposed to happen. And so it had, though not in a way that had any need for witnesses or survivors. Jeremy couldn't deny it any longer. He was the guest of people to whom he would never mean any more than noth-ing, no matter how many times he met them or years he spent attending their parties, get-togethers or weekends away. It was a play that nothing outside of the two sisters could explain, his birth, experiences and continued existence utterly superfluous to the outcome. Lying naked with Petula had meant nothing to her, no more than his earlier attempts to clown around and generally try to make a charming nuisance of himself had. Even offensive and calculated vulgarity was a waste of time; between him and them was an electric fence powered by eternity that would never be breached, and he had been a detestable fool to think otherwise.

'Come on Regan, why so shy, isn't this the kind of conversation you thought you wanted? To play grownups with your shallow half-wit of a mother?'

Jeremy stood up, not yet knowing what he was going to do or say, only that he could not remain silent any longer and still command the self-belief needed to live out the rest of his life. Petula barely noticed him rise, though Regan did, potentially grateful for a sacrificial distraction.

Before Jeremy knew it, he was talking, and could hear his voice speak as if listening to a pre-recorded broadcast, with the sensation that what he was saying had already occurred, and that he was merely laying rightful ownership to it, overwhelming. 'What I want to know is why do I have less right to *exist* than you two? No one's ever given me, my mum, dad or anyone I know, as much talk or attention as you two do each other. Quacking away like the world doesn't exist, it's not *right*! There are babies that die without anyone knowing who they are. You think you're the best people in the world but you're dregs, you're just where you are because of luck, that's all, because *you*' – he pointed to Petula – 'married who you did and *you*' – he turned to Regan – 'had her as your mother, and that's it. None of what you take for granted has anything to do with you, but you act like it was created off your own backs and you have a right to it all, and talk about yourselves like you're something important. You *aren't*. The person who does the paper round is more important than you. You don't deserve any of this and you're spunking it away and too busy doing it to realise you won't get the chance to have any of it back. Luck doesn't repeat itself till it's blue in the face and you lot have had more than's fair. It's not right! You're really *bad* people!'

'At last he speaks!' laughed Petula dryly. 'Perhaps if you'd tried engaging in a more human way earlier we'd have taken more notice of you. And not just you, but your mother, father, the dead children, the paperboy and anyone else in the world you cared to entertain us with the existence of!'

'Just *fuck off* will you?'

'Please Jeremy! Don't speak to my mum like that!'

'And you can too!'

'It's alright darling, Jeremy is on his way to becoming a nicer person. It'll just take a little more time and practice than he thought. We all need to be patient for him.'

Jeremy had turned his back to them and was grabbing coats off chairs, lighting on one of Petula's Barbour jackets that lay over his Puffa. 'Nicer *person*?' he yelled at the garment, 'you can talk about nice people! Perhaps that's what we should have discussed after I stuck my cock in you, yeah? How *one* goes about becoming a *nicer* person? What about that, eh?'

'Since you ask Jeremy, I'll put the answer in an idiom that won't confuse you: you enter a room, like this one, look around for the biggest cunt in it, and if you can't find one you leave, because that cunt is you. Nice-person conversation over.'

'Don't try me, I could take you out just like that! You can't get away with treating people like this, not me anyway. I'm going, off!'

'Then you'd better go,' said Petula quietly, folding her arms and haughtily staring past him at a painting of an octopus on an operating table, that she had kept meaning to move, but was now belatedly grateful to have hung in her line of vision.

Regan had gone white. She watched Jeremy, his eyes nearly crossed with fury, struggle to get his arms into the sleeves of the coat, pulling it on the wrong way like a madman strapped into a straightjacket he was trying to escape. Without stalling to correct his mistake, Jeremy stumbled away from the table, arms outstretched before him, tripping through the kitchen door face-downwards into the corridor. His obvious distress and the leery clumsiness of his flight excited a pity in Regan that her mother did not share.

'Never mind, in life you don't always have the conversation you were preparing for,' Petula called after him loudly, to establish before them both that Jeremy had already left their lives, if not the actual building yet.

'You can't treat people like this!' he yelled back, 'you *can't!*'

'Drunk out of his mind, the poor fool,' Petula added, the hint that Jeremy's mental state had been the real subject of their conversation all along, implicit. 'No helping him now; the bottle has broken and the red mist released, he's his own worst enemy. I could see that as soon as look at him.'

Regan was already following Jeremy out; she could think of nothing else to do. Gaining on him, taking at first his sleeve as he shook off the jacket, then hanging onto his bare arm childishly, she pleaded, 'What are you doing! This is crazy. Let's talk about this!'

'THERE - IS - NOTHING - TO - TALK - ABOUT!'

'But there is!'

'No, it's too *late*, I won't be treated like some joke. I'm not some piece of shit off the street that'll stand for it, I'm not! I'm going! I'm not a worm, I'm *not* a worm!'

'I know that! I'm not saying you are!'

'Take a look at yourself, you don't even know you're doing it, the way you've treated me, it's disgusting!'

'What have I done? I honestly don't know what I'm meant to have *done*!' cried Regan, her earlier aloofness forgotten completely, as she tried to drag Jeremy back down the corridor, and then onto the floor with her. Jeremy, making no effort to protect her against his superior strength, swung her ungallantly against a case of glass starlings. There was an ugly crack, the front of the cabinet fracturing like so many tentacles against Regan's protectively raised arm. Broken bits of glass confetti fell everywhere, covering Regan's hair and clothes, shards crunching beneath Jeremy's feet as he pounded on.

'It's too late, everything's too *late*, alright?'

Regan knew then that if she were to let him leave in this state, it would end a stage of her life she had no wish to pass through or ever have over, and because of this it was imperative that he should stay, allowing her to return to a largely imaginary normality. She also feared that she was to blame for his outburst, having had it drilled into her that passion vouched for the correctness of one's cause, while cold restraint equalled guilt.

On her feet, she sprinted past him, blocking his way towards the front door. 'No, I won't let you do this! You're being absolutely crazy. I don't even know why you've flipped. So I had an argument with my mum, so everyone argues, and maybe it was boring for you to listen to it and I acted like a bit of a brat but...'

'Just leave it! Please leave it! I cared about you, you know that, really cared about you! But I never want to see you again, I'm through with you all, you can take your hospitality and stick it up your arses for all I care. I'm through. I don't ever want to experience Montague hospitality again! You saw what's been going on all day. What's there not to get?'

'Jeremy, *please*! You don't mean it, you're drunk and crazy. It's been a crazy day for us all. Don't do something you'll regret. Please. Stay and sleep on it!'

'Do you know something? I was actually dreading coming here, you know, dreading all of this ever-so-fucking-superior bullshit, dreading it for months and months, and you know what? It was even worse than I thought! I'm through with you, that's it, don't you understand, I don't ever want to see you again! Now get out of my way.'

'Don't be mad, what about your bags, they're still upstairs, and where will you stay, you're lost out here in the middle of nowhere! You don't even know where you are Jeremy, for Christ's sake, at least stay for the night and we'll call a taxi for you in the morning. You don't even have to talk to us or see us if you don't want, but don't just leave like this. You're being completely *mad*.'

'I like the way you care about me now! I'm through. I've told you to get out of my way, I won't tell you again. You better get the message.'

'But Jeremy, you're being absurd, you sound just like my brother...' Regan could see it was no use, the more she returned to her solicitous self the more of her there was for him to throw back in her face, her kindness and his savagery feeding off each other inversely.

Without her actually getting out of his way, and without Jeremy exactly looking to avoid her, they found themselves having much the same exchange beyond the door; the full moon spotlighting two shapes grappling against one another, as Jeremy pushed Regan forward like a car charging through a crash barrier, shouting, 'Get out of my way! Just get out of my way!'

'I'm not in your *way*, you're in my way!'

'Move will you!'

'That's what I'm trying to do!'

'No wonder you two love actors,' he yelled, 'you're unnatural like they are, you don't get the "real" in real life. You're denying reality, I want to go and you won't let me!'

'I'm not going to let you be such an idiot, I'm not going to let you make this our last word!'

Continuing in this manner they progressed, surprisingly easily for two bodies thrusting in different directions, to the bend on the gravel path Jeremy had so charily proceeded along earlier that day, Regan's pumps muddied by a mole hill they detoured through, her jeans splattered in loose earth. She groaned, and finally admitting defeat, uttered: 'Slow down, please, you're hurting me. I'll let go if you let go of *me*.'

'Let go of *me* first then.'

'You're hurting me! Let go!'

'No, you let go! You're the one still hanging on to me!'

'You stupid dick, I can't, you've got me by the wrists!'

Fired on by an anger he could not, even after Regan's earlier attempts to soothe it, believe was not justified, and furious that she had finally shown signs of kicking back – he the fond abuser she must take for granted – Jeremy lifted his arm to let go of her wrist, bringing his hand back down far harder than he intended. There was a rip, and he saw that he had torn a strip off the front of her paper-thin blouse.

Aghast, Regan pulled away. The flimsy garment flopped down below her waist, and drifted off onto a bush. For a hesitant instant Jeremy froze, scared that some line had been crossed, which it had, though neither of them knew what it meant yet. Finding it less embarrassing to continue on his insane course, or else force a situation where he was asking to stay and she telling him to leave, Jeremy tore down the track, running quickly now he was free of her. Regan watched him go, deciding that if he got to the gate without stopping she could just as well commit herself to following him all the way to Richmond in an unsatisfactory game of chase. The gate was the cut-off point; once he reached that she would give him up as lost and return to Petula empty-handed. The gate would show he really was serious.

'We love each other, we're friends,' she bellowed as she watched him vault over the gate and continue down the hill. In the distance she heard a car blow its horn twice, the local custom for a vehicle approaching a blind corner.

'Jeremy,' she whispered, 'don't be such a dick...' A vision of her life in Cambridge without him flashed up and vanished. She would have to arrange things differently now that they hated each other; the holiday to Thailand she had been looking forward to was certainly out, shared lifts to hockey, and George's party would be a bit awkward now too... perhaps he wouldn't go.

As she walked back to the house, Regan really felt that she had lost something bigger than a friend, and for reasons impossible to pinpoint, had been shown what a hateful person she was at heart. Entering the kitchen, she was about to share as much with Petula, when her life was saved from this judgment by her mother's speedy intervention. 'Whatever you do, *don't* blame yourself! I know you Regan, and you need to know that it is not, that it is *never,* your fault. And don't think so for a minute. Blaming oneself is just the position a bully wants to put you in. It's how they work.'

'But he was so... *angry*,' Regan said doubtfully.

'Not angry, *mad*! Obviously. There's an important difference.'

'I've never seen him like that.'

'You wouldn't have, they're good at disguising it, that's the way with abusers, and then slowly, slowly, *suddenly*, until it all comes out.'

'I guess.'

'I *know*.'

'But what was that horrible thing about his sticking his, did you hear? His you-know-what, in you? Why would he say such a thing?'

'Mad! That's what I'm trying to tell you. As I say, it's the only explanation. Put it out of your mind. Forget him and everything he's said. None of it matters, none of it is true. He's not worth another second of our attention.'

'I guess he'd have to be crazy, I mean really medically mad, to come out with something like that... that, you know, *twisted*.'

'Well of course, that's how some men are. In his case I'd say he didn't even realise how far gone he was, and probably thought he was just yearning for a little unqualified joy when he left the house this morning. But there was a nasty, nasty side to him, I saw it at once with all his toadying and flattery, and to then go from that to being... Darling, what's happened to your blouse? You're in your bra! Did he try and molest you? The filthy animal!'

'No, no, it was a mistake. He tore it by accident. I think he thought he'd gone far enough at that point. He just ran off and I let him go. There was no point after that. He didn't even seem angry, you know, at the very last. It was like he was coming to his senses but knew he couldn't stay after all that.'

'Oh I bet he did, all wars are popular to start with and I've never seen anyone try and start one as hard as he did, but isn't it funny how belligerents always expect the war to end when they want it to? The bloody *bastard*, I'd like to tear his shirt off and see how he feels!'

From Regan's shaken and quizzical expression Petula feared her daughter was attempting to hang onto a hard-won thought that she was not ready to give up so easily; she would have to make more reassuring noises to capitalise on and make fast her extraordinary luck. 'Here, put this over you at once' – Petula handed Regan Jeremy's fleece and, seeing what it was, quickly replaced it with her shawl. 'You're probably in shock, it's hideous to be spoken to like that, no one feels themselves afterwards, your heart burning and beating and your back up and worst of all, your mind playing all those horrible words over and over. It's just too awful. I've faced it on and off all my life. I'm sorry your turn has come, but you'll be better prepared for it the next time it happens. Come on. Come here and give me a Montague hug. We both deserve one. With the day we've had.'

Hesitantly Regan shuffled toward her mother and stopped, paralysed by a sluggish reluctance to accept that the chapter was closed, Petula having to lean over and actually pull her into her embrace.

'Let's just chalk this down to another man we've seen off,

dear! Another silly-willy full of wounded pride, just like the others...'

On that final point Petula was not wrong. Jeremy was so full of what she ascribed to him, but also shame and remorse, that he was hardly aware of the Land Rover until he smashed into it at full tilt, Jenny Hardfield only able to apply the brakes after her front wheels had travelled over his trunk, the back two pasting his guts over the road. The mystery of what a young man, drunk or on drugs, there was not enough of him in one place for the coroner to discover which, was doing charging down the road from The Heights at the dead of night, marked a turning point in how indulgently such losses were viewed by the local community and in Regan too, who, wishing to avoid more fatalities, never brought a boy back home to meet her mother again.

PART FOUR:
Phlegethon, fire.

If you gave me a fresh carnation
I would only crush its tender petals,
With me you'll have no escape
And at the same time there'll be nowhere to settle.
And if you're wondering by now who I am
Look no further than the mirror –
Because I am the Greed and Fear
And every ounce of Hate in you.

– THE JAM, *Carnation*

CHAPTER TWELVE,
fighting and finality.

At last it had happened. The decision to kill Petula was one Regan and Jazzy came to on their own, without conference or the faintest notion that the other sibling was being edged towards the same desperate solution to what neither guessed was a shared problem. Nor did they hold the thought in its raw and reductive form, instead discovering, like a tadpole in a petri dish, that it had been growing unwatched all along – Regan believing she loved her mother right up to the night she saw she hated her, and Jazzy long entertaining the notion that nothing would change until his mother passed, without recognising he willed that day on with all his heart, until it was forced from him. Theirs were separate journeys, taking very different routes, made at contrasting velocities, the slower reaching its goal faster, and the quicker drawing the same conclusion later; speed for once being of no account in this race to a conclusion neither had forewarning of.

Like a voter who puts a cross beside the same colour at every election, Regan was too party-orientated to question the self-evident truth that her mother was wonderful, the pace at which she attacked life preventing her from focusing on the passenger left on the platform, in this case herself, mouthing back the opposite of what she thought was the truth. Jazzy, on the other hand, had less distance to travel, nursing so many conscious grievances against his mother that it was an effort for him to think of anything else, from the time he brushed his teeth, to passing out; the shock for him not that he hated Petula – he believed that all along – but that he loved her, and it was because he did that the only course left open was to stop her from hurting him any more. Their decisions, however, were identical in the relief they brought.

These decisions once accepted, neither brother nor sister had cause to consult the past again, question the righteousness of their motivation, or blame coincidence or bad luck for the parlous desperation that drove them to leave the world they knew, and enter a secretive hell in which their most intimate imaginings and longings lay beyond the law. Both had heard it said often enough that if this or that had not happened, a certain conversation not overheard, the wrong bit of gossip not shared, the rain having fallen on that day rather than on this, then destiny would have happily resolved its tensions in a way compatible with everlasting satisfaction. This they no longer believed. The tale that life had fallen foul of malevolent chance, altogether too rosy and itself worthy of a Hardy novel, was pushed by their aunt Royce in an attempt to build bridges, without straying anywhere near the sore core of their purulence, her optimistic characterisation of their dissatisfaction as accidental, too hopeful by far. Royce would have been better served consulting the Russian novelists of the nineteenth century. Here she would have found a pushy and inexorable fatefulness, born of an eternally present horror, capable of being challenged at any time and therefore tragically stoppable; had there actually been a possibility of the challenge succeeding and tragedy avoided. Regan and Jazzy lived through slights, slings, tedious lunches and spontaneous gatherings, where all it should have taken was to ask Petula what the hell was she doing and could she please stop, to prevent the fall into criminality. Simple as this sounded, Jazzy and Regan had danced to variations of this tune for years, forever slipping up on the oily blatancy that underwrote their mother's rule. All Petula had to do was simply deny that she knew what they were talking about and that there was any problem at all, only a mania the siblings had built up in their own minds, which is exactly how it would look to others once she had knocked their paranoiac querulousness into touch, and followed through with a speech that would shut them up for another two years. Regan and Jazzy would *still* be stuck with a version of themselves they despaired of, to be endured until its cause had gone, or, more likely, by their dying first (having never really lived), their mother scolding the undertaker for being late and reciting the funeral addresses over their coffins to a Cathedral packed full of her chums.

The step from conceding that only death, the black attendant, terrible and unconditional, would stop Petula from enjoying the last word, having exhausted the civilised problem-solving consensus, was a stroke from admitting that beneath this thought breathed another, with a crucial prefix: nature could not be expected to act on her own – if they were to enjoy the carefree mornings of a Petula-less future, it would need help. They would have, sooner or later, to pick up the slack reigns of their personal agency, otherwise Petula was going nowhere and nor, more as to the point, were they. Doing *something* in this context did not yet mean murder, and might even have entailed being able to persuade Petula to up sticks and leave the country, or convince her to simply leave them alone to live undistinguished existences away from her orbit and interference – these un-fatal remedies quietly suppressing the one true solution over a decade of wishful prevarication and second thoughts, matricide still too preposterous for them to contemplate.

Outwardly none of this was obvious, the slide towards barbarity concealed behind the dignity-sapping patronage that suggested a misleadingly cyclical picture of life at The Heights continuing without interruption. For his well-wishers – Jazzy had retained his gift of cultivating enduring pockets of sympathy – there was enough to celebrate in the solid and joyless progress he displayed on the farm, tackling chore after task, supported by Spider and their cottage full of her children. With a dogged persistence luckier people showered in cheap praise, and a firm handle on the irruptions that had previously played havoc with his nervous system, Jazzy applied himself to a life nearly free of hope, ambition or direction, and in this way was closer than ever to the peasants of the past he imagined a kinship to. With muted satisfaction, he observed how well he could manage his days without being inspired, stimulated or particularly happy, a competent and fierce worker; loyal too, as there was no question of his ever labouring for anyone anywhere else, the slow pace of his achievements – a bodged door that saved Petula the cost of a replacement, hedges trimmed like crew-cuts and drains as leaf-free as the trees they fell from – marks of a hair-splitting thoroughness that not even his mother could dismiss the solidity of.

Occasionally Jazzy would disappear without a word for an afternoon, adding to his portfolio of tree sculptures dotted round the grounds. An old oak suffered creatures like those he moulded as an adolescent carved into its trunk, while a totem pole of related freaks appeared at the base of a red beech by the lake. An outbreak of experiments with the branches of ash trees, sharpened like spears, followed, and a quintet of small conifers were turned upside-down and stuck back in the earth to mark his fortieth birthday. These playful forays in to wood-art led to Jazzy's eventual pièce de résistance, the result of several months' covert labour and one weekend's noisy construction work. With stubborn meticulousness Jazzy had set about a cluster of birches and stripped them of their bark, uprooting and replanting them over forty-eight hours by a remote south-facing border of the property, the straight line of trees pointing like cruise missiles to a world beyond The Heights in what may have been a homage to either war or peace, attack or defence. His feat took those few walkers who saw it by surprise, whilst causing no one any offence, and very little comment, Petula slyly not giving her son the pleasure of raising even the slightest objection to his relocation of natural resources. Soon after that Jazzy sulkily switched back to the creation of small moulds, this time mostly in the form of elves and fairies that he sold at local markets with Spider's jams and cordials, the resemblance between these figurines and his old girlfriend, Jill, obvious to those few who still remembered her.

There were other more prosaic changes. Jazzy was no longer considered a 'colourful' character, at least as far as his clothes and physical appearance were concerned. Turning his back on the harlequin garments and loud togs of a medieval troubadour, Jazzy submitted to overalls and construction boots like any other mid-life labourer, his earrings, nose ringlets, Celtic bangles and love beads vanishing, the best of the trinkets going to Spider's children, their original owner content to blend into the ordinary and unremarked-upon world of the average man. The relaxed drift towards an assimilation with his surroundings was roundly welcomed by his neighbours, Jazzy finding that middle age was not the cruel trick he had been warned of, rather a condition unusually suited to his staggered acceptance of ennui. Naturally he would have preferred life without the patch of scarlet veins that shot up in rivulets under his cheeks, the shying of hair, which fell in twisted clumps once the dreadlocks were untangled, and disabling pain that broke out in places he had taken the obedience of for granted. All that was as miserable as it would have been for anyone else, his fierce work ethic alone disguising the full extent of the maladies that functioned as a tag team, one ailment passing the baton to the next in an uninterrupted slow roll of illness and aches. Indoors, Jazzy would lie on the saggy, battered old couch, salvaged from one of Petula's spring cleans, and groan, but outside, the general levelling particular to survival into his fourth decade heralded doors, albeit it narrow ones, he welcomed the opening of.

It was gratifying to reach a point in life where he could call people 'son', 'young man', or 'kid', and not have them laugh behind their hands, and say of young women, 'Well she's only a lass', and have their mothers chuckle in agreement. Nearly as pleasing to him was huffing and puffing as he raised himself from his stool to buy another pint, and have the barman nod with stony empathy, enjoying the doleful respect of one who had seen it all before, even though as a forty year-old there was not quite so much need to make all that noise. His crowning triumph, however, was his assumption of a wise and patient smile as someone else tried to explain themselves to him for once. Then he could mutter and tut and shake his head with the best of them, as he explained to the sufferer that there was nothing new under the sun, that life was a bastard, and that his would be another pint of mild with a Bell's chaser, before winking at whoever else happened to know he was right. The older farmers and cash-strapped labourers would make a place for him at the bar, linger in conversation, ask after his health and exchange jokes, the purpose of which was to signal acceptance and not mirth, often at their own instigation. Jazzy could easily slip into the ebb and measured silences of a conversation on nothing much, always generous with his time even when busy, his past intensity and rowdiness a bit of a joke to be laughed off like a plaster cast on a broken leg at a farm show.

Not so far below the innocent consolations of mediocrity, Jazzy did wonder if his improved standing might not be attributable to a less-than-noble perception, in short, that his fellow sufferers now liked him because they saw his life was just as fucked as theirs. To them he was no longer a silly little rich boy in a paisley waistcoat, showing off in the cider tent, or a highborn playing at being poor, but a man whose prospects they could honestly believe in the irreversible shittiness of. Jazzy did not dwell on the porous base of his popularity for long; tolerable inclusion was not so bad, and nobody could question the one solid achievement he had devoted his life to – to stay in a place where he was not wanted for a very long time. Jazzy had always been as committed to The Heights as the firmest advocate of Volk to their Fatherland, its soil as valuable to his survival as his own blood. Now the rest of the community had caught up with his passion and returned the compliment; even Petula no longer asked him how many more years he intended to linger under her feet for, his existence on the farm having slowly transmogrified into a process as natural as cutting the grass.

Under the veneer of good-natured placidity, Jazzy drilled himself to ignore those questions that still filled his sleepless hours, fearful ones like where had all the (good) time(s) gone? Would he ever get to sleep with anyone else before he died? Should he and Spider have had children or were hers enough to kill him on their own? Was it too late and financially prohibitive to hire a private detective to find Jill? And most potently of all, nice as it was that Petula was no longer horrible to him, what would it take to make her finally love him? This last question was usually presented in a milder form, just before he lost consciousness, so that when he woke, he could dimly remember the terrain it was posed on, without actually remembering asking it, which prevented him from making fateful progress towards the drastic answer his salvation required.

In truth, reaching forty had freed Jazzy only of his least noticeable eccentricities, his neuroses burrowing underground into subtler and more remarkable forms of disturbed oddity. Without registering what was happening, Jazzy redirected his anxieties into curious obsessions related to finitude and erosion, as an experiment to see if any substance could really change in life, having already decided that his own life could not. As the seasons passed, he grew into the overseer of the erosion of minutiae, dedicated to the use and wearing out of records, jackets, boots and old vans, until they rusted, their grooves wore through, their linings were torn, or they were otherwise rendered unusable by smelling so awful that public opinion forced him to cast them aside. Spider would catch him holding filthy trainers up to his nose and examining old jumpers for new holes, tugging at the loose elastic of underpants and picking paint off battered tractors, all part of a daily ritual devoted to the total consumption and finishing off of things, especially hand-me-downs that he was always on the lookout for; his violent elation at the point of their falling apart, or being thrown away, practically orgasmic. This quest to watch items that no one else wanted die or expire, joined the host of other habitual secrets – talking to himself, pulling his ear-hairs, taking a pornographic magazine into the farm toilet – that he considered at once too boring and too shameful to share, while at the same time very much looked forward to and indulged in daily.

Practised as his attempts to smooth out, re-describe or blot out the existential wrinkles were, there were white stonewashed walls, blank malignant days, that he could not help hitting with the force of a power-saw. Twice a week Jazzy would suffer a 'crisis morning', usually Monday and Tuesday, often Sunday and Monday, and sometimes all three, where he felt too miserable to fall out of bed and subject himself to the whirring blades of ongoing reality. At these troughs he saw himself as a horny lead on the set of a pornographic film who finds that he cannot perform, and despite being exactly where he wanted to be, lacking the one thing he could always take for granted: an erect member to make all those naked bodies work for him. Like the impotent actor, Jazzy was on the spot he loved more than anywhere else in the world, the farm, surrounded by nature in every beautiful variant and guise, but to his recurring disappointment, somehow unable to take advantage of it all. The world was massive in theory, he only had to look at a map or drive into Middlesborough to see that, but the only part of it he could ever see himself in remained minuscule and resistant to his stewardship. The conundrum, shaped in what amounted to Biblical time, was finding its formulation: he could not survive anywhere else, but when would 'home' actually be his?

Jazzy's response to responsibility without power was that of the Stakhanovite packhorse, renewing his efforts to visibly be seen to be working even harder, and thus earning the right, in the eyes of the public if not his mother, as their opinions may sway hers, to be thought of as at least the second-most-important person on the farm. Although Seth Hardfield had been appointed farm manager after Noah's flight, regularly reporting back to the absent master much as he had always done, he had, ever since Jenny's accident in the Landrover, lacked initiative, allowing Jazzy to make himself truly essential to The Heights' upkeep, doing the jobs that Noah knew needed doing, and Seth was too long in the tooth for. Under Jazzy's watch the fields were sublet, the shepherd's nook turned into a new barn, his mother's flower business planted, primed and packaged, essential maintenance turned into a fine art, and most tellingly, Petula was forced to lean on him in a multitude of personal ways that compromised her claim that she could rule alone, or survive without his help.

He was faithfully on-call as her driver, the old injury and the onset of arthritis making the manipulation of the clutch and brakes painful for Petula, when not playing the part of her foreman, relaying and enforcing messages and commands she found too tiring to look into or deliver herself, and eventually, a kind of confidante; Jazzy's need to share his thoughts with his mother largely ossified after so many years of finding them unchanged, but hers, however, growing more urgent and in need of sharing with age. Without exactly finding themselves on the same side, or sharing an identical interest, circumstance was creating a bond between them that compromised Petula as much as it encouraged Jazzy.

This move towards generous accommodation seemed no more than 'doing his duty' to Jazzy, who would never have attributed an ulterior motive to his becoming his mother's reliable working limb. Contradiction, however, lay under the blankets of his sweaty selflessness. On some days he tried to spend as little time with his mother as possible, on others as much; watching Petula disgusted him, her selfishness and pretences repellent, but it also inspired;

her unwavering self-belief and almost total mastery of him a feat he could not help but remain in awe of. To be the fly on the wall or the mole tunnelling under the foundations into the throne room, both a trusted insider and a loathed outsider who would never fit in all at once, kept Jazzy confused as to his own reasoning, the tacit direction his life had taken fundamentally mysterious to him, as its honest slyness did not fit with the person he had long ago decided he was.

Petula watched his savage devotion and never for a moment assumed that it could be as entirely disinterested as her son wanted her to believe. Petula understood that she would have to pep him up from time to time, and leave a brace of low-hanging carrots in his path to prevent rebellion at whatever point Jazzy saw he was not going to get what he could not, until then, admit he wanted. In the short term simply taking him into her confidences over matters of mingling and indeterminate value worked wonders, though over time she would have to promise more, as even a faithful retriever had to hope that one day it would be fetched from the kennel and allowed to lie by the great roaring fire.

Her chosen means was to appeal to what she thought lay behind many a selfless life; an unacknowledged desire for property and wealth. In doing this Petula gambled recklessly, needlessly leading Jazzy into temptation. 'Accidentally' letting slip one night that a third of everything would be his when she died, she handed Jazzy a practical motive for the darkness that would follow, though neither had any inkling then that the seeds of transgression were scattered. Her lie was transparent to anyone but a wishful thinker, as she had no intention of divorcing and risking the loss of anything valuable to her in her own lifetime, while the very idea of a world others would inhabit after she had gone lay beyond her imaginative powers; if Anycock's children wanted a legal right to Noah's estate let them marry him themselves! Yet in the absence of any other goal to work towards, her empty promise, so easily disproven had Jazzy thought to probe, repeated whenever she was tipsy or simply wanted to play with him, became the emergent focus and stimulus for his existence, providing a vision of generational succession he could not rest till he had. Tragically, especially as it was never in her power to divest what was not hers, Jazzy would have been happy with so much less – credit, respect, an acknowledged role on the farm with securities – his innocence contaminated simply because his mother was not in the habit of playing for stakes any less dangerous.

Petula gave the matter of murderous incentives very little thought; she was enjoying her new wardrobe, her games with Jazzy a pivot to enable her to get on with the more important developments in life. She had graciously settled in to the role, while working furiously hard to create it, of a national treasure with countywide renown, fusing her past selves into a grand synthesis of her previous styles, pretensions and modes of being. It had always been a knack of Petula's to know, like the rock star shedding skins or opportunist switching sides, which role best suited the stage of life she had just reached, and so it continued to prove. Years in the public eye had trained her in the discipline of ruptural adaptability, picking the loose clothes that disguised a thickening body, and those identities most likely to keep her at the centre of attention and power; wisely, for there could be no question of allowing standards to slip when even her most fanatical followers were at least forty-nine percent sick of her.

Correctly adducing that to chase society nakedly would be unseemly and unbefitting a woman of dignity, secure in her own worth and indifferent to the dictates of fashion, but that to not do so would be a fate worse than being forgotten, Petula was incentivised to find ever-more-ingenious ways of drawing the crowds in. The device she settled on was beautifully appropriate to a grand lady nearing sixty in a new millennium: family.

Loudly she declared that her main obsession in life was family, indeed always had been, that she was a woman who had sacrificed her life for this tribal concept, and now longed for nothing more than to be surrounded by those she had lifted out of nothingness, her two children with Anycock excepted. With her cover story established, and received wisdom dumbly echoing her platitudes, Petula had the alibi she needed to justify the continuing string of parties, dinners and lunches that people who were not related to her were still expected to attend. What family that did come was not necessarily her own – in fact, rarely so – but obscure cousins, uncles, aunties, step-brothers, sisters and even ex-partners of Noah's. These joined the other 'motley randoms', as Regan dubbed them, who belonged to friends Petula had come to regard as 'family', her personal bloodline represented only in her own, and Regan's, selves. The press-ganged collection of wealthy, bemused and easily bullied relatives would arrive quietly and sit about in the corners of Noah's house and wonder what they were doing there now he was gone, until the first string of real guests arrived. Then pride and the belated recognition that they were somehow related to this shrill iron-age queen so keen to claim possession of them took over, enabling them to play their parts to clumsy perfection, the other guests wondering why these clownish losers had been invited in the first place until they remembered that Petula, bless her, loved her family.

These back-to-basics feudal meals, held on the elongated rectangle table that Petula insisted on calling round, in homage to Arthurian legend, occurred at least once a month, Regan still called on to attend, irrespective of where she was in the world or her life. The food was always more lavish than the occasion required, Noah's retainer covering multi-option courses that would have had their proper home in Michelin-starred restaurants, chefs being hired for a weekend, entire meals driven up from London, and on occasion, prepared by Petula herself, aided by a reliable army of caterers and housewives, eager to see the inside of The Heights by whatever means necessary.

However, not all the food was eaten and not all the people who were invited came, the banquets becoming an altogether more confused gathering of odds and sods than Petula would have liked to present them as. The 'main attraction' was a decidedly anti-systematic collection of whichever distinguished persons Petula could get hold of from month to month. What constituted a desired guest was no longer an absolute value so much as a slippery slope, the slightest perception of stardust of any colour or kind being enough to have her throw herself, gracefully and with restraint, at the intended target, wielding them into her orbit. Property developers, archbishops, television anchormen, the head of Chris De Burgh's road crew, antique dealers, the Master of Hounds, a recently divorced head teacher of the local choir school, a handful of colonels, wing commanders and brigadiers and their wives, sat next to what remained of her old faithfuls; Astley, the Middletons, Chips Hall and whichever unfortunate happened to be the local Member of Parliament at the time. Through sheer weight of numbers, and a constant rotation of faces, Petula was able to shore up her power-base in quasi-conventional ways at the very point that the conventional, once again, wondered whether the time had not come to finally wash their hands of her. Sadly for her haters, Petula could manipulate their social rituals to political effect so much more effectively than they, sharing no more confidence in their judgement than they had in their own, thus forcing them to abandon plans of ushering her into purgatory for a life of crimes she had probably got away with.

It was impossible for anyone but a fairy to keep casting spells without running the risk of being thought something of a fraud, even by her friends, and it was this criticism Petula most often heard made of her, usually in the form of a bogus compliment pertaining to her longevity. Never failing to project her fear outwards, her critics as scared of her intentions as they were her actions, Petula would home in on the slight and wait patiently for a confession. This torture could continue until the confessor had owned up to the absolute opposite of what they had actually said, no context or occasion too public or embarrassing for Petula to renege on her full pound of flesh, as when it came to shame, she had none to lose. Even talk of entering local politics, on a vaguely green-national-Thatcherite platform, was enough to force councillors to grant her planning permission for a giant solar-panelled bantam-coop, and turn down the Council's bid to build ten new social houses over a grubby acre of field she insisted was the home of some shrewish vole, or stoat.

Privately she suffered as never before, or at least believed she did, not remembering all of the past, and knowing nothing of what still lay ahead. Trips to the hairdresser were like watching a natural-history documentary; her overgrown hair sprouting like grass from a neglected pavement, its pruning a reversal of the natural order and way of stopping nature from reclaiming its own, for she felt more dead than alive. Years of failing to enjoy things for their own sake, but for what they could yield, led to a strange philistinism at odds with her patronage of the arts, and a boredom with herself almost as great as her fear of being left in her own company. At times Petula's eyes would go cult-blank as she repeated her dogmas to others, the impression that she had ceased to listen to herself even as she expected others to, difficult to shake. With no clear direction or idea in dominance, it sometimes seemed to her that her paths had thematically criss-crossed into a dizzying headache of 'anything-goes', both in her own sphere and the world at large: kaftan dresses mixing with Barbour jackets, invitations to Crufts with the Q Awards, and rugby at Twickenham with London Fashion Week. Returning to never saying no to anything, and requiring everyone else to say yes, was debilitating, and she fought down colds and a flagging immune system with a cocktail of organic remedies, and when they failed, an arsenal of chemical ones; her war-chest of pills and potions packed into the boot of the Volvo, and splayed over the floor of her bathroom. If she was not hosting 'home-games' at The Heights, she did not like to spend any longer there than she could help, its role degenerating into a pit stop on a never-ending nationwide tour. During these pauses for breath, Petula observed the signs of her unravelling with a semi-detached horror akin to floating over an operating table. On hot days, to find something to do, she would produce fuming stews and sweating hams that went straight into one of her vast freezers, as she nervously nibbled cheese and biscuits and chain-smoked, a habit that she had come late to, having picked her fingernails to death. On freezing days culinary logic was turned the other way, and Petula would prepare chickpea tuna salads and sorbets that would be thrown away untouched, her staple in all weathers marshmallows and donuts, gorged on until the sink was clogged full of sick.

Sleep, an activity she had never had much interest in, could no longer be taken for granted simply because she was tired. In the finest traditions of the uncanny, three o'clock in the morning was her witching hour. Whether Petula had gone to bed one or six hours before made no difference, for three was where her day always started, and barring a possible eclipse between the hours of seven and eight, consciousness was her lot from there on in. What she was conscious of was primarily a vision of the world without eyes, its goodness all dug out, that lay beside her like an unanswerable question; her experiences, friends and lovers all sucked into the abyssal throat of the phantom she shared her bed with. If she tried to define a memory, scent or song, it would totter and blur, vanishing beyond her grasp, its disappearance a punishment for daring to set herself against life by absorbing its rewards and ignoring its price: that all counterfeit purchases will be returned in the end with interest.

She was, of course, getting older; that was all, she sometimes hoped, it was or could be. Petula would repeat this homily as daylight reassuringly brightened the deathly gloom of her bedroom, nature's circuitry kicking into life with the loud hawking of crows and Jazzy's hacking cough. With characteristic tenacity Petula kept plying the common-sense solution to her wobbling secret life of night-doubts and day-dread, throwing half an hour with the Two Ronnies and a packet of custard creams at the problem; the novels of Dan Brown and Ben Elton providing backup, the lower the artistic merit of her comfort aides, the greater the safety on offer. Towering above all of these was the level-headed constancy of Broadcasting House, its audio blanket covering every room, Petula's mind protected from the accusatory emptiness of silence so long as she could hear the received pronunciation of Radio Four blaring from all six of her radios.

For days she would survive in this way until it was time to go again – to host another function or attend another party, to keep going as only she could, as this was no less than what her sanity required of her. There was no other dynamic that could force Petula to accept and compromise with situations and concepts not of her own making, or rescue her from her bleak imaginings, than the social whirl that was gradually killing her. Only public life, played out to the painful utmost, limited and restricted her to the real, keeping the hour of three o'clock hidden in that gloaming corner of the psyche it belonged to, while to the world she continued as tiringly and (nearly as) triumphantly as before.

Encouragement was not hard to come by, and there were still enough devotees cheering her on, who saw her as their leader, enabling Petula to make minding their business her job. With the omnipresence of a writer of the future who only gave interviews and didn't write books, her flower-arranging 'firm' a pretext to enter and organise anything from corporate events to weddings, Petula spread her advice like fertiliser, nowhere safe from its energy and spite. And for those few who dared escape her there were always her famous rages to look forward to; over the phone to local tradesmen, at the openings of gastro-pubs she had not been invited to, and down the long thin corridors of The Heights on her own and drunk out of her mind, raging at still not having *got* anywhere in life, her achievements as mystifying as the questions asked by the silence she wished to drown in valedictory shouts.

Meanwhile Regan continued to make as little of her life as her mother seemed to have made as much, or at least so she believed, as Petula truly confided in nobody and laughed away her daughter's suggestions that she might be overdoing it, or resemble anything less than ecstatic good cheer. When asked how she was doing, Regan never made any comment more revealing than 'Alright,' sometimes going so far as to offer 'I'm okay, pretty good,' which she wasn't, yet the alternative, to tell the truth, would have left her tongue-tied in search of where to start.

The decade after Jeremy's death passed too quickly in her own company, only slowed by her interminable pilgrimages home to fulfil her role as Petula's loyal dauphine, the weaker their actual intimacy grew the tighter her mother tied their formal knot. With the exception of six weeks in Swaziland teaching Aids orphans how to count, Regan was never away from The Heights for longer than three weeks at a time. Even this separation was reduced by Petula ringing every other day and reading aloud from her engagement diary, Regan's patience rivalling a nodding dog that could no longer take the benefits of mutual masturbation for granted, their phone calls an exercise in testy submission.

Regan's home was an old property of the Montague family in Kensington, the top floor of a dinky mews house decorated with a set of Howard Hodgkins an obsessive gallery owner left her in his will, having overdosed in the ladies' toilets at Stringfellows after she had refused his rash offer of marriage (Petula had unwisely offered the man some hope on her daughter's behalf, rectifying her mistake by not making a second and mentioning it to Regan). There was little else in the flat to show who was living there: one of Jazzy's creatures, a bow-legged faun with its maker's sad smile, balanced on its hind legs, tactfully hidden behind a photograph of Regan and Petula taken at Astley and Eager's civil union on an otherwise bare white mantelpiece. Below it sat a cream hi-fi, surrounded by stacks of intelligent-house CDs, Regan's living quarters a tidy duplicate of her student dwellings in Cambridge; her personality blended into a pale invisibility, the only objects to fall outside its pallid character the floating particles of dust missed by the cleaner and a pair of carefully tended window boxes that offered a tender reminder that Regan might wish to exceed the terms she had set for herself.

As Head of Entertainment Law at the William Morris Talent Agency, Regan was in a job she sometimes thought she must have been in training for since the age of six. Here she observed other people's more interesting affairs, there to draw the line when they could not, amend errors they had not noticed, and facilitate the more exciting progress of those better suited to the limelight, lessons well learnt through her life as Petula's understudy. Her sweat-less aptitude to cut very quickly through what other people regarded as complicated problems, and the pace at which she could attack administration others found too dense to decode, combined with a cybernetic memory for tedious detail that could outperform any computer, meant her boss's job was hers in less than three months of enrolling as her assistant; Regan's lack of a law degree was no impediment to making the niche hers for life, should she wish to travel no further than the top.

Professional success was not deliriously satisfying, as she would sometimes imply, to excuse not having a husband or children yet, nor a total disappointment, as her friends tended to conclude when they saw her leave a party early looking listless, withdrawn and flat. Regan's embrace of neutrality was deliberate, at times seeming like the grownup version of her school-girl ice-queen persona. But these efforts to dull her sensibilities and exist in unconsidered blankness were fated to fail, despite appearances. Like her mother she could not help but consult her extremes, bobbing about in a state of sometimes painful happiness, or, more often, unhappy pain, her occasional jouissance never vivid enough to count as complete, while her inattentive self-neglect was too refined by habit for her to notice the agony she was in – clues like sleeplessness and inexplicable crying fits easily dismissed as natural phenomena connected to being a woman in a city in the early twenty-first century.

To remain in attendance to Petula meant maintaining an element of eager infantility – a need to fake interest in her mother's doings, feign childlike delight at trifles and wide-eyed innocence at reheated gossip – that Regan found increasingly unnatural as her twenties wore on into her thirties. It was only possible to continue with the deception by making a studious effort to pretend to be simpler and less intelligent than she was, in a way her mother could still find charming and becoming, if not entirely believable. As the years began to impersonate eternity, computational responses and disingenuous enthusiasm replaced strained but genuine points of contact and conversation; Petula not minding a bit so long as Regan remained obedient in her outward comportment. For Regan, doubt had become an article of faith, and for all her talk of how wonderful her weekends at The Heights were, it was always a deliverance to leap into her Punto and hit the motorway back to London; solitude as welcome to her as it was repulsive to Petula. Regan could no longer ignore, at these times, how the entire routine was wearing her down, her smile pepped up by Botox treatments so that it could hold even as the rest of her drooped, the world never seeming so large and unexplored, nor her future such a prison of predictability, than when making the journey back up the M1 to Yorkshire.

Her cry for help came while fighting off a Maltese shipping-magnate friend of her mother's in the library one evening. Hoping that he could enjoy a post-dessert squeeze with this skinny tease, he discovered Regan staring emptily at a volume of Boswell's letters to Johnson, his lusty advances tipping her over into a gruesome sobbing mess. Having scratched the hand he lay amorously on her thigh, and fractured the finger he ventured up her skirt, she warned him that she was in the process of having a nervous breakdown and that it would be best if he returned to the dining room for coffee and brandy. This had the effect of assuaging his vanity, and taking pity on Regan he arranged, and paid for, an expensive course of psychiatric help; she rewarding his kindness by showing up for dinner at The Caprice, but withholding the businesslike hand job he'd hoped might be thrown in as an encore.

The Harley Street sessions themselves produced no break-throughs, Regan sticking to the public script of her life, much to the psychiatrist's frustration. The opportunity to talk and think about herself divorced from her life's strict narrative struck her as a perverse trick she could not see the purpose of, the neat sterile rooms too like her flat for her to feel that she had entered a disinterested atmosphere. After the five weeks and ten sessions had run their course, she refused the advice and option to book any more, diplomatically claiming that she did not have the money for this kind of indulgence as she had some outstanding dental work to pay for.

But that was not quite that. The not-too-delayed consequence of failing to open up was behaviour altering. Regan suddenly stopped acting altogether and simply accepted her mother as a sullen ox would the branding iron. Gone were her gushing questions, thoughtful appraisals of non-problems, and the mechanical shaking of her head whenever Petula made another insightful contribution to conversation. Meals passed without Regan paying attention to anything much, never giving the impression she would prefer to be somewhere else; rather that she would be happiest if she could be nowhere at all.

Though Petula noticed this decrease in attentiveness, amounting almost to a polite sulk, if not entry into a post-self, she could not pretend it displeased her. Regan was unaware of it, but her shocking beauty, enhanced by looking extremely pissed-off, was still as big a draw amongst Petula's male guests as her cheesecakes were to their greedy children. So what if she was not having the time of her life? Regan's mute petulance amused Petula, while frightening her just enough for her to hold her even more closely in her maternal armlock.

Intimidatingly remote behaviour, however frostily gorgeous, saw to it that Regan was appreciated at a distance more than enjoyed up close by men of her own age, and by the time she reached thirty, she still had not enjoyed a relationship that had lasted longer than three months. Eligible men would go off her after short and passionate courtships, for the same reasons she would go off them if she beat them to the chase, her brief dalliances a race to see which party could terminate the affair first. It was chilling how the reactions of her suitors mirrored her own, irrespective of the difference in their personalities; their rejection of Regan utterly practical and without spite or passion, her being dumped no more than an expression of rational taste – an exact reflection of how little they meant to her in reverse.

Regan could not decide whether she was as dull as she found them to be, or as she once overhead an 'ex' say, 'It's never like you're in the same room with her, even when she's sat on your lap.' Had she contrived to become a missing person in the company of her lovers? As ever, it seemed to her that she was paying for an earlier mistake that had become a first-order tragedy, the kind that neither she nor mankind could do anything about (her mother and the continuing violence in the Middle East were examples of two others), lest she identify its source. In this case she accepted a notion that had haunted her for years: that her rejection of Mingus had permanently undone her so far as becoming a spontaneous and natural sexual actor was concerned. Mingus was so persistent a feature of her emotional memory that she no longer cared whether she was paying undue emphasis to him or not, as even if she was mistaken, the frequency with which she dredged him up from the past, and her excitement at remembering their brief union, bestowed a creation myth on what might otherwise be a causeless penny-dreadful. At its most basic, nothing else had felt as right as the idea of them together; a teenage construct that had survived unchallenged into her thirties, her swift glimpse of transcendence defining that time of her life in honeyed sepia – her leggings, the laces of her trainers, the emerging breasts that never grew any bigger, Vanilla Ice, the first Gulf War and Twin Peaks – all signifiers hanging above the trap door she wished to plunge through, waking naked by the lake and impaled on his shivering thinness.

It was on a morning when she had been considering memory's buried treasure more than normal, inspired by a dream the night before in which she was a nurse in an institution and Mingus a needy patient, that Bronwyn Robinson, a high-maintenance Australian popstar with highly contrived reputation for being low-maintenance, her bubbly candour and saucy sincerity the work of her publicists, rang the office and brought Regan's inertia to an end. Robinson wanted to pull out of the Welsh and Northern Irish legs of her tour and fly straight to New York the following week, missing the tedious (for her) party William Morris had arranged for their staff that she was due to sing at, in order to attend a hot and much-talked-about show at The Gagosian by a rising star of the art world, a young Englishman known simply as 'The Magus'. Regan had been busying herself suppressing a book by Robinson's embittered ex-manager, Timothy Tinwood, who was himself facing charges related to child-sex scandals dating back to the Seventies, in which he claimed that his protégé was a plastic surgeons' pin cushion, show-room air-head and selfish martinet, who had stolen his ideas and other people's songs. Regan's work in keeping this libellous tract away from the shops had endeared her to the star as a woman of some use, and to show that she was not completely without gratitude for their work on her behalf, Robinson had insisted William Morris be represented on this trip by Regan, who practically alone in the office had never knowingly heard one of Robinson's songs all the way through, and cared nothing for her renown.

Robinson's esoteric reason for picking Regan above all others was that she found her absent air unthreatening, complementing the saccharine violence of her own finely-strung personality. And as an added bonus, Robinson had noticed from the invite that The Magus, like Regan, was from Yorkshire (Robinson had turned down a number of invitations issued by Regan on her mother's behalf to stay at The Heights), offering an opportunity to try out her northern accent on the plane, with a possible seduction of the wunderkind in mind; the commercial potential of this union easily worth letting down her Caledonian fanbase for.

Regan knew enough of The Magus's ascendancy to know that this camera-shy, limelight-avoiding recluse was her very own Mingus, his stage name a silly magician's contrivance that appealed to his sense of the stupid. News of the show did not then come as a mind-altering shock, though to hear him coyly alluded to by Robinson still made her want to rush to the office kitchen and puke, her cheeks abruptly changing colour once she had dropped the receiver. Until that morning Regan had watched Mingus's rise from afar and nervously, avoiding his Hoxton Gallery and White Cube opening, the early Saatchi shows and public commissions, and even the giant wooden etchings of a lake, an anomaly in his work, that decorated the headquarters of the Halifax Building Society. To her enormous relief he courted an air of inscrutable elusiveness, avoiding having his picture taken or appearing in public, which was all to the good, as double-page interviews in the Sunday supplements would have scared her from entering a newsagent's. By keeping her distance Regan could pretend that it was not really Mingus all this was happening to, and that it was perfectly bearable that she was not at his side to enjoy her portion of his glory. Interestingly Regan also noticed that his rise was as profound a source of discomfort to her mother, who never mentioned it, as it was to her. Rather than take credit for a man she knew as a little boy, an open goal for Petula if ever there was one, the subject was ignored to a point where Jenny Hardfield – justifiably proud that her son's glass installations of dead cattle, empty pint glasses and torn condoms were on their way to making him a millionaire – dared not share her joy when the two women bumped into each other. Whether Petula could not stand the success of one who had not relied on her to achieve it, or was in some obscure way envious of the attention he had garnered, Regan could not make out – the closest they came to broaching the subject were her mother's numerous broadsides against 'the curse of crappy conceptual installations that you find everywhere like fox turds, I mean, where the hell is the *joy* in that?' Regan had to admit that she did not like this development in modern art any more than she enjoyed dwelling on the garbage it was based on. Mingus's work may have been more sincerely felt than the tacky rubbish his context-switching contemporaries lifted off the skip and stuck in galleries, though it was not, in Regan's mind, any less dull or ugly for that distinction. Even if she was mistaken, and Mingus's masterwork, a room in the Tate Modern that replicated what she knew very well to be the original interior of the St Elmo's Fire, long since pulled down on Shatby pier, was as the critics proclaimed a multi-functional advance on Duchamp's *Fountain*, she would not have missed an episode of *Friends* to visit it again. She prized Mingus for the soul that brushed past hers, its trace lying dormant over her own ever since she had seen daylight, blinked and scuttled back into the dark. The external expressions or trappings of that life-force, like the applause of the art mob that claimed to have discovered him, were a matter for a world that did not know what she did: that the broken air-conditioning units or painted ping-pong balls in chrome cages could shatter and rust; it was the boy she loved.

Robinson's phone call punctured an embryonic wall separating her secret existence from a real person she now had no excuse not to interact with; to remain passive as good as running away from a chance, at last, to direct her life towards the object of her reverence. In rejecting Mingus, Regan had tried one route: to become someone her mother would approve of; why? Because in doing so she would remain someone her mother was not jealous of, a price she was willing to pay to court her approval. It was time to accept, not having sought one herself, that life was offering her a second chance; the intensity of this knowledge convincing Regan that she would risk everything that sustained her, but could never bring ultimate happiness, and fly out with Robinson that Monday, come what may.

In the event, simply by not contradicting Robinson, a car, tickets and reservations at the newly opened Soho House New York were arranged, and their seats on Concorde, only months from being decommissioned, booked. The office in London did not like it; a black mark Regan could live with, never having done anything to court outright dislike before, beyond exhibiting more conscientious, thorough and punctual behaviour than the average cultural-industry worker felt comfortable with. The decision made, Regan teemed with hesitancy. To follow through or not to? Within the hour she was on the phone again, her weekly conference call with the old Nohallows girls, who, in true contrary form, she hoped would tell her to pull out and come to her senses once she had announced her news.

These four young women, outside of her memory of Mingus, and the reality of Petula, were the only constant in Regan's life, their lasting friendship a rare source of enduring pride and reassurance. Regular 'reunions' were a shared joke, as there was no need to reunite a group who had never stopped seeing one another; a blizzard of postcards, phone calls and group holidays steeling them through their individual life-trials far past an age where school ties fray; newer replacements never threatening the primary bond forged on the hockey fields of Nohallows. Less kindly, Regan had gone from being the gang's beacon and intimidating figurehead to the girl they all secretly worried about and felt slightly sorry for. She sensed this, though hoped it was her paranoia working overtime, as to be an object of pity was only one step up from the revulsion Jazzy and Evita inspired in her mother. Nevertheless Regan's leadership of the gang had dissolved into an honorary role, and the thought that the others were ahead of her on life's way, and she left behind, a constant self-reproach, culminating in her suggestion that they should meet for a weekend at The Heights for the first time since the unfortunate death of Rex Wade. Regan had designed this break as a way of showing her friends how content she was with her freewheeling independence, beholden to no man and glad to be single, putting any ideas that she was on her way to bitter spinsterhood out of their minds. The weekend had also been carefully picked and arranged to *not* include Petula, who was due to be away shooting grouse with Tim Rice near Oban, leaving Regan in a position she had rarely been able to take advantage of before; enjoying the freedom of The Heights without Petula. Fortunately, her impending trip to New York would not interfere with their jolly, and might even have endowed her with genuine happiness to share with her friends, were it not for the perverse desire to sabotage her adventure, before it had begun.

The dynamic of the girls' friendship had altered only a little over the years, Regan's silences quietly interpreted over time as awkward rather than above it all; otherwise the girls bantered as before, taking only the slightest notice of their individual fortunes and circumstances. Each shared enough in common with all to prevent formal sub-alliances or factions from developing within their set. Diamanda was cynical, brash and single; the lead singer in an all-girl Clash-covers act who had toyed with lesbianism, her main income coming from her modelling career. Men, she liked to say, were nothing more than sluts and cunt-teases, good only for starting wars and carrying her into cabs when wasted. Daisy had married a much older man, a successful architect and sincere Methodist whom they all teased her mercilessly about, but liked well enough; her five children and converted barn in Surrey were the closest any of them had come to achieving conventional bliss. Mathilda and Eloise were more fragile and less set on their courses: the former having been left with triplets by a serially unfaithful husband, a racing car driver, whom she was in the process of divorcing; the latter a successful television comedienne who had used her excessive girth for her act to an unfortunate degree, and whose primetime show would in all likelihood be axed if she ever now lost weight.

Despite their differences, Regan still feared that she was the odd-woman-out, the others comfortable in, or at least honest about, whatever unhappinesses they encountered, displaying a refreshing levity she could not ape. Privately she apprehended that Daisy and Diamanda's opposition secretly united them; Elouise shared Diamanda's performing background and Mathilda related to Daisy's domesticity. Added to that, Daisy's love for her children ran through and was intimately connected to her love for her husband; she loved them from the start because she already loved him – meanwhile Mathilda had circumnavigated her husband and become quite separate from him to the point where her feelings towards her children could not save their union, but as a mother was still closer to Daisy than Regan ever could be. And most unfairly, Diamanda, ostensibly Regan's best and oldest friend, was too amused by life to share her anxieties, busy making a joke of everything like Elouise, whose self-disgust had always been her route to popularity. True, just as at school, they all enjoyed setting themselves apart from the scaly rump of humanity, yet alone amongst them, aloof withdrawal for Regan was not an act, but an alienated fact. Thankfully her depressing digressions on isolation, usually framed in an anecdote indirectly alluding to her having no other real friends, could always be cut short by one of them making her laugh, dissolving distance and stroking the hairs of her doubt back into an orderly gradient.

Biding her time while peering into the soupy muck of her hot chocolate, the powdered milk collecting round the sides of the cup like elderly spit, Regan dug her plastic spoon into her palm and waited for an opening, her heavy and irregular breathing a hint that she had more to say than usual, though not a strong enough sign for her friends to stop talking.

'You're at a personal best aren't you? I watched you last night and thought I'd never seen you so big. How do you keep putting it on?'

'Posh ice cream.'

'And you can still have *sex*? Neil, the sleazy div, what happened, did he succumb or stick with someone smaller in the end?' Diamanda asked Elouise.

'He came to me, of course he came to me, he's my skinny counterpart, he thinks I'm a niche and we help complete each other.'

Talk had so far been dominated by Diamanda and Elouise; the latter having proudly announced that she was sleeping with a television anchor-man known to them all, and married to a more famous television anchor-lady they all despised.

'So what happened?'

'Funnily enough he was completely pissed and it was my turn to be totally sober. I had to take his trousers off for him, he was a mess, blabbing that he didn't know what he was doing and that he'd never cheated on her before. Which must be bollocks. He's too practised.'

'Rather you than me, it sounds horrible.'

'No, he pulled it together after a bit. The disappointing part for me is not being able to see what's going on anymore. I just can't get that bird's-eye perspective since I put on the extra pounds.'

'Who can without mirrors?'

'Don't either of you just want to forget about yourselves for a moment and simply enjoy what's *happening* to you, directly I mean?' interrupted Daisy, determined to remain part of the conversation. 'The last thing I want to see if I'm horny is me naked. I just don't see what's so kinky about watching what you're doing when you're making love.'

'*Making love?* Please, please stop making me sick; thinking of you getting horny, and that could only mean with your husband, which means I have to think of him too, is too sicky for pictures.'

'So it's alright for you to yak about it all the time and not me? Just because you think seedy and gross is cool?'

'Only if it was with someone interesting. I still remember when you used to pick up Korean students in nightclubs Mrs Tinder!' said Elouise, her voice a thin squeak packed in thick casing, 'You were *filth*, I don't care what you tell the world or you husband these days, preaching your gospel of parsimonious mating to people who don't know your dark heart. Once filth always *filth*.'

'You're *vile*.'

'There, go easy on Mrs Tinder,' said Diamanda, 'if she's made a life decision to pretend she enjoys having intercourse with her children's father then that's up to her. Even if it means lying to old friends shamelessly.'

'Life decisions, Diamanda? *Please?* You haven't even made any to regret!'

'I've made two, only *two*,' Mathilda cut in, her lisp complimenting the slur that was the result of prematurely middle-aged drinking habits, 'who I married and where I work. Those were the only two. And they took turns at being shit, and were even sometimes shit at the same time. And you've no idea how much thought went into those decisions either...'

'Those are the two, the only two, most people make, and most people regret,' Daisy said kindly, in a way that suggested she did not go in for such errors, adding with pained languor, 'You know, you did do the right thing telling him to leave, Mathilda. Duncan was never any good. We all hated him from the off, especially Diamanda. He was a proper bastard, a cliché.'

'That's why I like small decisions,' Diamanda cut in quickly, 'so I can change course before a good thing deteriorates into a shit one; you know, when the same parts you loved to start with begin to assemble in a different way that looks decidedly shitty? And I like the beginnings, what's so important about going on forever and ever until the end? Two or three good times early on, move on, meet someone else, fail again, There's no shortage of takers, we've hardly met anybody yet!'

'Some of us *like* permanence Diamanda, and don't want to keep chopping and changing all the time. I want what makes me happy to survive as long as I do and to even outlast me,' said Daisy, impatiently, but with faked annoyance. She knew what her friend thought, knew that she did not agree, and that this unbridgeable chasm would make absolutely no difference to either of their lives or friendship.

Diamanda snorted, 'Try writing a novel then. You can't be talking about people when you say things like that. What's permanent?'

'Maybe she means a novel? It'd be as difficult as making a dream interesting; I don't know how anyone can read one let alone write one. I haven't finished a book since the twins were born,' groaned Mathilda.

'Oh, you know, there's always when they're are asleep,' Daisy laughed, 'I'm halfway through Proust now.'

'I'm too pissed to even understand what's on the telly by the time the kids have gone to sleep.'

'What the hell are we talking about anyway?' asked Diamanda, 'I've only got half an hour until my shoot, someone say something interesting please, or else I'll have to accept that you're all just a bad habit I can't kick.'

Regan took the plunge, 'I'm going to New York on Monday.'

'So what? We can all go on airplanes now sweetie, now that we're big girls. And you're not the only one who's been to America now, the rest of us have caught up too!'

'I know why you're going,' Elouise interrupted in a shrill accent that she took to personify the New York art world, 'because there's some really interesting *white* building they just put up that you have to go and stand in and look at the ceiling of?'

'Has someone been lying to you about the constancy of the coke out there?'

'I bet you they've promised you something, haven't they Regan?' carried on Elouise, 'Fly over there for free, be fucking bored out of your mind, come back, but at least you didn't have to pay for the flight out or the canapés, am I right? Corporate cack in excess? Trust me, you'd have a better night out at the Clapham Grand.'

Regan was used to their overflowing spirits washing through her usual evasions, and rather than follow her opening remark with what she had intended to say – 'I am not sure I should, I think I'm making a mistake' – she felt a surge of boastful pride replace her hesitancy. Whether it was because she found her own thinking wonderful when she reached the subject of Mingus, or because a decision was tantalisingly close to being aired – the actualisation of self-invention simply a few words away – would be a question she would save for the plane ride over. She blurted: 'I've been invited to an opening at The Gagosian for your *information*, by the artist whose show it is. And I am taking Charlene Robinson.'

'An artist? What, you mean one of your mum's mates? And why's Robinson in the picture, I thought you said she was a bloody harpy?'

Regan beamed inwardly, 'No, one of *my* mates actually, Mingus, you remember him, he's called The Magus now but it's the same guy. And Robinson's just along for the ride, she thinks I am great for some reason. There are people who do you know!'

'Hang on, you're not going out to *fuck* someone, are you?'

'What? No! What are you on?'

'Mmmmm, sounds very much like a transatlantic booty call to me!'

'Fuck off! I can't believe you sometimes!'

'But then what? Something similar, to test the water right? Mingus... Magus, oh *that* guy! Jesus Regan, you're so fucking transparent! I honestly don't know why you bother!'

'You're thinking what I'm thinking Diamanda?' laughed Eloise.

'Pure serendipity! Of course she means him! The one she fell in love with when she was about four!'

'What are you talking about? I never did!'

'Oh come on, it's *obvious*, you've practically said as much when you're pissed, thousands of times!'

'I don't ever remember saying anything of the kind to you, any of you! When have I ever talked about him?'

'Elouise is right,' cackled Mathilda, 'you always bring him up if you're off your face, and don't even realise you're doing it, hoping we'll ask you a few probing questions. It's *so* obvious that he's the love of your life. I can't even believe you'd bother denying it! You're insulting all of our intelligences. Collectively! Hef hef! Bad girl!'

'I don't know where you've got this idea I'm in love from,' Regan stammered, 'I mean, I haven't seen him in years, years and years...'

'We know!' they all chimed. 'And that makes no differences whatsoever,' added Diamanda, 'everyone has a love of their life, and if it's someone you never even see then it's even easier to believe that they're the one that got away, and that everything would be oh-so-different if you only took them up when you had the chance. There's no time limit to this stuff, it's unlike anything else.'

'Look, you've got this all the wrong way, it's not that big a *deal*, I just thought it would be interesting to see what his work is like, having known him before.'

'Bullshit! That is just such *bullshit*. I remember one time when we were off our tits you told us all he was your first shag, that time when we were camping outside Guildford, on that hill when those guys stole our beer stash, remember? You know what, you should go over there and fuck him good,' said Diamanda, 'give him something to remember you by and then never return his calls; think of the power you'd feel!'

'You're mad! I wish I hadn't said anything now...'

'Spare us, you're gloating! You want the whole world to know you're alive and capable of love!'

'Don't worry Regan,' said Daisy, rushing to her aid, 'there's nothing wrong with obsessing about someone all your life, Proust is full of it, even if we *are* too close to the stories we tell to know whether they are true or not. But good luck to you, it's about time you got hitched.'

'But I only want to see him to catch up!'

'Whatever! No one believes you, and even if we did, catching up is always the first stage of long-distance seduction. *He'll* know what you're there for, trust us. Transatlantic *booty* call!'

Regan broke the plastic spoon she had been bending; Mingus's reaction had not been a factor she had seriously considered until now. 'Do you think he might freak out with me turning up out of the blue?'

'Why the hell should he, you said he'd invited you didn't you? He's obviously just as obsessed as you are, or else he wouldn't bother chasing you after the zillion years or so since you last got jiggy. It's weird enough that he got in touch with you.'

'I suppose. But I'm not obsessed, please get that out of your heads! I'm only... interested, that's all.'

'Oh save it, just do it, get over there and do it – tell him you love him, get married, have babies, and stop playing games. You'll put yourself and us out of your misery,' Diamanda said impatiently, 'and it'll be about time, we were all getting sick of your Lady of Shallot routine. Stumbling around and looking for someone to save you and pull you out of the water.'

'You don't think I'm mad then, or a bit sad and going backwards?'

'Of course you're mad but who cares about that?'

'But I don't even know if we'll get on or have anything in common anymore, I could be murdering a good memory for no reason at all. And making, you know, a fool of myself.'

'You don't *need* to have anything in common if you're in love!'

'But I don't even know that I am!'

'I think if you do love him you'd know about it,' said Daisy. 'Would you be in pain if you didn't go? Think of it like that. Pain doesn't need to be put to the test, it's not like love like that, when you're in pain you *know* it. Would you feel shit if you didn't go?'

'I'd regret not going, yes. I mean, it would be something I would look back on and... not feel good about.'

'Do it then, for God's sake do it! I used to think you never lose people you love, you meet them in other people, and you always have the memory, but life doesn't work like that; each time you fall in love is a one off, and memories are just pictures. Send him our regards, we're lovely girls really.'

'Diamanda's on the money,' said Mathilda, 'if I had anyone who wanted to shag me in New York or Newfoundland, I'd be on the next plane over, no questions asked.'

'It's the three stages of love,' concluded Diamanda, 'the religious, the romantic and the practical. You believe in it, you believe in him, and you could probably get on together in the practical sense, so get on the plane. It's now or never, pilgrim. You've waited too long.'

Regan felt a bleak exhalation in herself. She was about to step into complete freedom; empty, dreadful and empowering, if obeyed – remembered in impotent agony otherwise.

'I'll go. Thanks. You know I love you all too, don't you? I do.'

'Oh fuck off with that. Just don't come back and start telling us about how wonderful your sex life is, we've all done it and there's nothing new under the sun, even if the boys do keep on coming...'

*

The solstice always came too early; the sense that decline had begun and darkness would slowly filter back into the sky scared Jazzy into using every available hour of light for noisy and demonstrative tasks to prepare for winter's approaches. That, at least, was his alibi. Cynics doubted whether it was really necessary to install another gate in a fence that already had one, erect a deer-watch to replace the contraption that had only gone up the year before, or build another shed for logs that hardly needed to be cut as they would never burn, now that the farm was centrally heated, and so on; the questions pursuing the tasks like hounds after a hyperactive hare.

It unsettled Jazzy if folk thought he was simply doing nothing; an overgrown man-child clinging to the hair of his nanny-goat's beard. When hard at work he was beyond the judgement of others, an essential human service protected from criticism as long as the graft was in plain view. Onerous exertion, Jazzy was sure, was the simplest defence against anyone who might ask what he was still doing in a place he first proclaimed his desire to leave twenty years before, his unfulfilled proclamation drowned under the activity of the fret-saw and clawhammer. Whatever one thought of the necessity of such work, it was undeniable that the fruits of his endeavour littered the farm like beer cans after a party, a range of objects as disparate as shoe trees and tree houses, plywood boiler covers and oak compost holders, all bearing their maker's mark: exact and technical finishing worthy of a spin bowler on a sticky wicket.

Having ended his daily flagellation when the last of the hired help left, a Sisyphean re-creosoting of posts, Jazzy had spent the last hour of this particular evening on his own pretending, successfully, that the rest of the world did not exist. By seven o'clock the farm was a shimmering finery of nature's many tiny parts, or depending on how he squinnied, a vast collage in flux; the late-evening sun burning away until the sky became a pale-blue furnace, layers of nocturnal light that would dazzle until the sun rose again illuminating all below in eerie greys and whites. Jazzy loved it; it was why he was here and nowhere else. In the still-fading streams of yellow and red, the clouds drifting through slow explosions of colour, their shapes and shades migrating into ever-gentler combinations until they blurred into what passed all understanding, Jazzy knew he stood at the helm of the ship, the complaints of the day no more than an unreliable friend who had let him down, again. An elemental breeze, faintly frosty, broached his nostrils, filling them full of hope and banishing lesser concerns into languid inconsequence. He lapped the freshness off his prickly moustache; above all else, out here the world *forgave*. Alone, Jazzy recognised a miraculous vastness that might even have been the work of God; the smell of bonfires and lavender bushes a fragrance worthy of a deity, the crushed thyme he carried in his pockets serving the same function as a wedding ring would to any other man. Death as a form of cosmic reintegration had never made better sense; here he was a believer, and would remain one until the time came to speak again.

The Heights, which Jazzy's eye would always end up wandering down to, infused him with ticklish excitement, its wood and white-stone walls suggesting a shifting mirage of permanence, no more stable than the slashes of sunlight – tiger stripes of scarlet and orange – that bubbled between the shadows of creeping ivy, wisteria and honeysuckle. He could not quite put his finger on what he felt when he saw the house, nearly daring to admit to a thought that was not his, but that he knew himself capable of entertaining, on the condition that he would never have to spell it out, even to himself. His reluctance to cerebrally verify this desire did not stop him from experiencing it as a vague and heartfelt aspiration: that by luck, justice or natural disaster, all this would one day be his, and if it weren't, he would at least be here, the trusted and acknowledged power about the place.

The hope was too mean, silly and selfish, spiritual in inspiration and materialist in application, not to say optimistic, for Jazzy to own up to. He could not believe anything he wanted that badly could turn out in the end not to be true. That did not stop his loud hints to Petula that the farm would collapse without him and his boastful acceptance of the title 'foreman', which had officially been Seth Hardfield's position, until Jazzy encouraged him to take early retirement on a full salary, helpfully provided by Noah's preference for a quiet life. Hardfield may have still reported to Noah from the armchair next to his fireplace, but it was Jazzy's work he was reporting on now, and no longer his own. From here it was only a tiny step to complete control, yet not one Jazzy was ready to take, yet. It seemed clemently disgusting to think that this was all that his brief acquaintance with consciousness came down to. Possession and ownership were not how he would like to see the world, and equally importantly, not how he wanted others to know he saw it. But the facts, he hedged, might very well force possessive ownership upon him. For when Petula finally got round to divorcing Noah, a course of action Jazzy had been advocating for some years (and why had she *not* done it yet?), and retired to London (another move Jazzy had been the advocate of), with Evita in rehab and Regan signing contracts in Soho, who else would there be to fly the flag for the family? And who else knew where all the keys to the tool shed were kept?

When Jazzy looked at it like that, accompanied by the chants of cuckoos and the flowering of roses in reds so precise as to venture on the unnatural, he grew overwrought. What was to stop this process of evolutionary elimination but the continued intransigence of a single stubborn and embittered old lady, who could not even cut her own lawn or deadhead a flower without his help? And that was the point; Petula had become a windy glove-puppet, incapable of sustaining the conditions upon which her life relied. That was why his speculative project was worth persevering with, even if he would not admit to having one, as in the end, patience, forbearance and loyalty, resentfully given or not, would receive their karmic due. How could they not? He was *so* close to what he wanted.

The marvel was that these disembodied calculations could inform Jazzy's entire existence, while not even consciously registering as thoughts; a script he had written down to the last hyphen and full stop, but never dared read back, aware of itself as directional reassurance rather than as the cold-blooded plan it was. This failure of honesty was where Jazzy's ultimate undoing lay. Expecting a higher power to extract his dreams from where they slept and execute them for him, leaving him to pick up the crown from whichever branch destiny had thoughtfully left it to hang upon, was too passive a strategy to succeed in a world Petula still ran. He would have to try harder.

Jazzy's unreflecting reflections were interrupted by Petula's ageing Volvo Estate, the car she always chose to drink-drive in, holding to the maxim that no one could die in them, however pissed they might be. The dented V.240, looking as though it had been rolled in a drag car rally, veered carelessly from bank to bank, the driver in a rush to get to the house before she was missed. Wedging it at an awkward angle under a pear tree, Petula hobbled away from the vehicle like a guilty vandal before a broken window. Jazzy smiled indulgently; there were no other witnesses. He knew the keys would be left in the ignition for him to park the vehicle in its proper place in the forecourt in good time for normality's resumption the following morning. His mother was indulging in an uncharacteristic guilty pleasure: several rounds of gin with the 'Wild Geese', a handful of divorcees, or as good as, whose husbands had either quit or eschewed all resistance. These late-fifty-something ladies gathered in one another's living rooms in a combative huddle of inventive gossip and injured self-righteousness, offering balm for each other's wounds and salt for everybody else's. Petula's quiet adoption of the set, whom she had cheerfully looked down on in the past, was now as established as a goose's hold of an intruder's leg, evolving from her just happening to 'drop in', to becoming a central mainstay at these loathe-ins. Naturally she would never deign to hold a meeting at The Heights, nor would her new friends expect it of her, their social thirst easily quenched by the great Petula Montague entering their world again, for she had been friends with them many decades before, as an honorary complainant.

For Jazzy it showed overdue human fallibility in Petula: a woman who could waste her time in wasteful pursuits like anyone else who had problems they could not face. Flatteringly he knew he was a cult figure amongst the Wild Geese, a dependably handsome face who was often called in for a beer and motherly chat when Petula had forgotten her way to the car, or fallen asleep on a settee. And the manner in which the tipsy ladies fussed over and infantilised him, with musty undertones of repressed longing, reminded him of what it was like to be wanted, his undisguised enjoyment at having his long arms fiddled about with and pinched all part of the fun.

However Jazzy did not like the order of things, or their look, when he entered The Heights' kitchen; his mother had emptied her handbag over the table and was comparing bottles of pills under torchlight, a spirited means to ward off the inevitable need for glasses. Like him she also feared winter, and turning on an overhead light would be a way of acknowledging its onward progression.

'Everything okay, Mum? You look stressed. Anything you need help with? Just say.'

Petula yawned like a creaking door; it was all too much like reading a book she could not remember. She was sure the mood of the text had entered her sensibility, but as to the detail, she had no idea; what was it she was meant to take before bed to help her sleep? Her last gin, a fifty-fifty mix of flat tonic water and Gordon's, had seemed so necessary at the moment of its suggestion, but she remembered nothing of drinking it, or whatever else she had consumed to make her completely forget her journey back home. She had recognised nothing; where did any of those lanes lead to? She hoped she had not killed anyone; she never had before, if she did not count her daughter Evita. No, that was wrong, she had only nearly killed her that time in the attic. Yet people had died on the way out of the house through no fault of her own. No one could blame her for that. At least she was home. What was she doing again? Petula dropped the torch and shuffled over to the fridge where an emergency supply of her favourite nightcap awaited her: a large jug of elderflower cordial diluted with Blue Nun wine.

Still unnoticed, Jazzy pulled open the door of the fridge for her and watched Petula tip the mixture into a tupperware beaker left on the worktop for such occasions. His mother appeared to have given in to a series of mechanical reflexes, and was safe until the moment came when she was forced to decide again. Although he had grown used to seeing Petula in ever-more-vulnerable states of intoxication, there was an exaggerated stateliness to her movement that he found he could not take seriously.

Still she did not register his presence. Standing right behind her, Jazzy whistled the melody to 'Maggie's Farm' note-perfectly, and still not able to attract Petula's attention, sung the opening of the old Bob Dylan classic, 'I ain't gonna work on Maggie's Farm no more...' The song, played loudly out of his bedroom, and later from his van and cottage, had always been employed to annoy Petula, successfully doing so ever since he went through a phase of referring to her as 'Maggie', an unflattering comparison to the then-Prime Minister, twenty years before.

Tonight it did not. Instead Petula stared emptily in the direction of a mauve orchid on the windowsill, her lifeless gaze seemingly borrowed from some less expressive person. Panicking slightly, Jazzy sang a whole verse, and had got to raising his voice at the chorus and banging the side of the fridge in time, when Petula turned, barged past him and vomited into the sink.

Ten minutes later they were both sat at the table drinking tea, accompanied by tumblers of whisky and stilton and gherkin sandwiches. The mood was affectionately strained, like old friends willing a parting, so they could remember one another happily unencumbered by reality.

'That was very, very, nice of you, thank you,' said Petula with her mouth full, beckoning for a re-fill, 'carrying on until the bitter end, it's what I always seem to do. I honestly had no idea where I had got to. It's a bit frightening actually, it must have only been minutes ago but I can't remember *anything*. I mean, I remember Mina pouring me a drink and thinking it was time to go home, but how I got here... and then this. Have we been talking long?'

'Nah, I just got here and found you. Forget about it.'

Jazzy had yet to utter anything of consequence, unable to measure how drunk his mother still was, and unwilling to have to repeat himself all over again in the morning, as he often did after having wrongly calculated she was sober enough to remember their conversations the next day.

Testing the temperature, he offered, 'Still, what a lovely night, what a sky. Beautiful. I could never live down in a valley, always a hill for me. I'm not a valley dweller.'

'Eh?'

'And the weather, glorious, absolutely glorious.'

'*What?*'

'The weather, it's been good, aye.'

Petula's expression changed as if she had discovered something nasty in her food, her eyebrows forming an arch of sudden annoyance. 'Good weather? *Good weather?* What on earth has that got to do with me?'

'I was just saying...'

'Good weather is one of the great deceptions performed on the nervous system! A way of pretending life has really changed when in actual fact it has just slapped on the makeup. Don't talk to me about it, please... One day the sky will go black and everything will simply stop. Good weather? Whatever next! We'd may as well talk about what will be on television this Christmas!'

Jazzy laughed uncomfortably, 'I know what you mean,' which was a lie as he didn't, 'but until that day cometh, life goes on eh?'

'Exactly, it cares too much about bloody going on to care very much about whether we're still in it or not, so please no more mention of the Hardfields and their bloody untalented son. It was all anyone could talk about tonight, all I could hear, the silly old gin dragons. Nothing else to do except tout and dissect other people's business. That boy hasn't a drop of talent anyway.'

'You what? I thought we were talking about the weather! I don't give a damn about that talentless little git Mingus, if that's who you mean. Don't pin any interest in him on me, he's a sneaky piss-weasel.'

'Exactly! Love thy neighbour bollocks! What a thing to do to us, abuse our hospitality by attempting to make out that that bloody son of theirs is some sort of media star. A big name! Do you know, I think he once had it in his mind to seduce Regan? The cheek! Storming the art world! It's all his mother can go on about apparently, some bloody show in New York she's been invited to. I mean *her*, that woman who can't even spell Matisse, in New York, really! It would be like finding out that the Queen's got a todger. She doesn't even know where America is. And *Mingus*, that's another one we can chalk up to Noah and thank him for, bringing him here as a baby. That boy hasn't a single thing going for him more than you, except a talent for self-advancement. Look at the way he tried to use me! And he was only three at the time! Artwork balls. I'd take your bloody creatures any day, foul as they are!'

Jazzy, whose quiet hatred of Mingus was another of his life-sustaining obsessions, would usually have joined Petula in her mood of vituperative spite, yet tonight he checked himself from going any further, or encouraging her to continue. There was a flowing quality to her invective that worried him; it was rolling out too quickly and haphazardly. Without careful steering, it might easily be his turn to be run over next.

Smiling with considerable effort, he stated: 'Still, Mrs Hardfield's alright isn't she? She's not her son, and Seth – what can you say. Forty-five years' loyal service. What a bloke, salt of the earth. What you see is what you get with him. We should all try and love our neighbour eh? That's what the good book says.'

Petula, who though used to Jazzy's middle-aged conviviality found its commonness more offensive than the purposefully inflammatory persona it had superseded, exclaimed: '*Love?* Now you're really waking me up! Love what? What are you gabbling about?'

'Your neighbour, you know, me and the Hardfields, your neighbours. The Bible says you should love us Mum!'

Petula looked at her son as if her were mad, implying perhaps that if she did not love him she was not exactly ecstatic about herself either.

'I don't know what you are talking about,' she said at last.

'Anyway, forget about it, it's not important.'

'Quite. My God, what's wrong with them...?'

Petula was staring at her fingers with alarm; her wobbling

digits were threatening to escape from her shaking hands and crawl across the floor in search of a new body to attach themselves to. Whatever she had gained in clarity from heaving into the dishes, was lost in the last throat-full of Scotch. She felt chased and harried by a vengeful abstraction. There was a thought that had occurred to her earlier, strong enough for her to pull into the side of the road, only to forget what it was; its terrifying force falling away as abruptly as a half-realised déjà vu. But it was back again now, no longer an immaterial terror but a common enough problem for people her age.

'God,' she groaned, 'this is it, isn't it?' Her life would never get any better than this and she did not have the heart to rally and stop it from getting any worse. 'And to think I used to believe I was *different*! Instead of just a silly old bat like the rest, redeemed only by hard work, never having had any talent, but now too pissed and lazy to even slog. How *profound*! Even my problems are a milkmaid's. In what way am I still different? In absolutely *no* bloody way at all.'

'How much have you had tonight Mum? You're a bit of a mess if you don't mind me saying. There's nothing wrong with you that a bit of sobering up and sleep won't fix. Do you want me to help you up to bed? Here, put that down and let's get shifty, eh?'

Petula sniggered, tickled by the suggestion that she might be making too much of her difficulties. Was it simply that she was still very drunk, and nothing, certainly not anything that might occur to her before she fell asleep, would mean a thing by the time she came to remember it all tomorrow? To sleep and wake and not feel the slightest difference from the day before, oh God, she was going in a circle again, this had all happened to her in the car, before she had pulled over into that lay-by, full of crushed cans of Tango and shredded pornographic magazines. She had stopped the car because she wanted to give up, and then forgotten why she had. What was so important about whatever she was trying to recollect anyway? And what would it change if she could still remember? Of *course*, there was no *point*! That was it!

'God, it's all so pointless,' she tutted into her tumbler, eying the orange-gold content with an absence of the cynical optimism that had got her through every single day of her life.

Jazzy fiddled with his glass and laughed weakly. 'Alright. Don't go to bed, suit yourself. It's funny though. Do you remember the days when it used to be me who would come in here all tiddly like, and you and Noah that would have to sit and hear my story? And you'd be the ones telling me to go to bed! It's like we've switched roles now, eh?'

'I don't see how, you still seem pretty tiddly to me.'

'Oh come on Mum, be nice.'

Petula burped noiselessly, and pulling the jug of elderflower wine towards her, muttered: 'You'll never, ever, have the satisfaction of hearing me agree with you...'

Jazzy dug into his pocket for tobacco, and considered his next move. Earlier he had intended to make a short speech on how it would be more expedient for money that was going to be spent on the farm to be paid into his account directly in a single lump, than his having to justify every expense on a case-by-case basis over the telephone to Noah, who was ignorant of local conditions. The hope that a cosy nightcap or two might get his mother to agree to this progressive step seemed reasonable, given that anything which loosened Noah's hold over their life was generally welcome. But seeing how much the worse for wear she was, as confused and clumsy as he had ever witnessed, led him towards thinking she would be better served being escorted directly to bed by force.

'This tastes awful, have you put thinners in it? Or Lucozade? It's meant to be equal part cordial and wine you know. Drink speaks for all my wants and my wants are all a bunch of *cunts*,' Petula slurred. 'What is this awful stuff? What have you put in it? Are you playing games with me too?'

'I haven't touched it.'

'Oh haven't you? So I suppose it gets drunk all by itself does it? Don't think I don't know about your little raids, you and those children. Nicking the Green & Blacks out of the larder and as many cases of the Blue Nun as you can carry. For your parties.'

'I've too much taste to touch that stuff, don't put it on me.'

'There's nothing about you I don't know *boy*.'

Jazzy was about to say that his mother should go to bed by herself or risk a strong-arm escort. A reservation, not edifying or pretty, held him to his seat, and left the words unspoken. Seeing Petula totter in this state presented a ghastly opportunity to break with the preassigned moves and countermoves that regulated and filled their exchanges with content of the utmost predictability. He did not want to play with Petula, as he sometimes did with a lack of charity he could not help, her furious seriousness making her drunken condition a thing of mockery. That was a game he was ashamed of enjoying, suitable for rebellious children, but if a man of his age wished to get on then it would require learning things she would never be ready to disclose or discuss in her right mind. Slumped over her tumbler, wittering on in frowsty semi-consciousness, meant that she could not be better primed for interrogation or being led; it was an opportunity to snatch the power from her side of the table, and turn the screws, for in a fair fight he would have no chance.

'Do you ever think of my Dad?' he started.

'Yes,' Petula answered immediately, 'of course I do. Though I thought you'd finished about all that stuff, you know, how I as good as killed him, a while ago.'

'I have,' said Jazzy taken aback, already frightened that he had underestimated the speed at which Petula could re-discover her cognitive bearings. 'What I wanted to ask was what you think about when you remember him. He was a big part of your life once. But we act like he never was. And you know, when you think about it, what's yours was his, right, and I guess what would have been his is as good as mine, which makes what's yours sort of mine too. And it all started with him and, well, it'll all end with me I guess.'

'*What?*'

'You know, basically what I just said, right?'

'I've no idea what any of that gobbledygook is supposed to mean, and I am amazed you do. But as for your father, well, I think nothing of that unfortunate man that you will want to hear, nothing that you're capable of understanding, I am afraid.'

'Try me. I know you think I'm a bloody idiot but I get things well enough.'

'You have wise-man airs but you understand zilch Jaz, always was, always is.'

Jazzy ground his teeth and feigned an ironic countenance. It was too soon to bring the subject over to the question of dynastic succession, especially as he had no idea of how to steer her towards this enormous subject without sounding grasping. He decided to stick to curiosity, for the present.

'What do you think about when you think of him, then?'

'Try this. I think about *me* Jazzy, and not really of him at all, I think of knowing him for all that time without his knowing he was going to die. And I think of the door that suddenly slammed shut for him, and hasn't for me yet, and what he might still think of me if our places were switched. And I think of how much of a nicer person he would have become if he had lived for as long as I have.'

'But...'

'*Shut up*, I haven't finished! I think of him dying angry and ignorant and simple, and of all this life stuff being completely wasted on him, because the further into the future you go, the more you learn about the past, and he died too early to learn anything. He'd never even been abroad, not once. Or been further south than Burton, poor man.' Petula stopped and sneezed into her cup. She could remember Jazzy's father turning down the chance to share a holiday in Brittany with friends, telling her that she would not go either, since with her imagination, she did not need to travel to a far-off land to know what it was like. She had agreed, not realising that the future would be just such a place. She looked back at Jazzy, who was mopping his scrunched-up eyes with a tea-towel.

'Anyway,' she continued, 'he said he would die *happy* if he expired within walking distance of where he was born, and he could walk a long way, so who can say he lived in vain? I don't know whether he really meant it though. Not that, or any of his other oaths and loud predictions. Because it's usually not the stuff you really want to happen that comes true, rather more the rubbish you spout when you're not thinking about what you're saying. That's the stuff fate will call you out on. Every time I say I hate this place or my life, which I know is quite a lot these days, the chances of my reaching happy old age here lessen. Whether I mean it or not. We exaggerate the difficulties we face because it's wrong that we should face any difficulties at all. Just look at a baby when it starts crying...' Petula allowed her sentence to putter out, the plane she had been flying slowly dematerialising until she was left with just her feet for pedals. There was something wrong with her insides, a sour aftertaste, like a marmalade in which the oranges had been substituted for carrots; she may have looked the same but did not taste so, her essence had been substituted.

'Hell, I'm *burning*, burning up. Well, do you know what I am talking about? Are these the answers you wanted? God, I sometimes hate the sound of my own voice, of *me*.'

Jazzy said nothing; he knew what his mother meant all too well. Memories of being teased for his privileged existence as a boy with a rich stepfather, a big house and a bathroom the size of his friends' cottages, all used to undermine his son-of-the-earth credentials, shadowed his every protestation of poverty.

And his response to his underprivileged tormentors so blunt that it became as big a part of the ribbing as Noah's wealth itself: that he would be perfectly happy if he grew up to live in a draughty old shed and grow wormy cabbages. And now look at me, he thought, trying to avoid his mother's remonstrative gaze.

Petula flinched as she observed her son's downturned mouth, doing its best to not give up its shape altogether and open up into the dark hole that preceded a howl; this boy-man whom she could never rid herself of, residing beyond, but still in sight of, her love. How alike they were, dependents both, confusing selfishness for doing what it took to 'survive', all so they could sit in a tiny corner of England that they had confused for existence itself, and blame others for their unhappiness. 'We just haven't come *far* enough have we?' she offered, brushing a tiny blob of hardening mustard off her nose. It fell into her drink and started to dissolve. She considered taking his hand in hers but dismissed it immediately as ridiculous. It would only embarrass them both later.

'No, I mean yeah,' replied Jazzy. He had no exact idea of what he was negatively assenting to, only that this kind of mood made him intellectually agreeable.

'We haven't changed, worse luck, but the times have,' continued Petula, nearly sentimental now. 'You'll realise it for yourself one day, how lucky you are to not know what will happen next. As you get on. And get old, you either pretend to be a saint, or degenerate into a pest. What you won't do is stay the same, that's the same as degeneration. And if *that* happens no one will care what you are anyway. It happened to me and it will happen to you. We're not that different, worse luck. We're denying progress by simply turning up in our bodies every day.'

'I feel finished at times, if that's what you mean,' said Jazzy, doubting very much whether his bright mood earlier that evening had ever really existed.

'What *are* we still doing *here*? Alive I mean. This isn't our time

Jasper. What have we left to discover, or offer?' Petula snatched her drink and gulped at it. Wiping her mouth she continued: 'Most people who really count and knew me twenty years ago probably think I'm already dead.'

'Maybe we're being spared for a purpose? Do you know what I mean?'

'If so we're hardly going out of our way to discover what it is. How long have you been here, how long have *I* been here? And what have we done with our good luck? With all this good fortune we've been drip-fed? Composed symphonies? Written novels? Found a cure for the common cold? No! Simply plotted different ways of fucking one another up!'

'Oh come on Mum, it's not that bad, is it?'

'Seriously, isn't *it*?'

'Give over. We're a... we're a family! There's both good, right, and bad in us. We've got to stay positive.'

'Why should I? What's the point of us?'

'Steady, right? You're losing perspective.' Jazzy moved Petula's tumbler, and the by-now empty jug, onto his side of the table with authoritative ceremony. It had been hazardous of him to test the power of the snake by prodding it when coiled; Petula's venom had never travelled an orderly path.

'Oh that sounds clever Jasper, perhaps I am being a perspective-less ninny?'

'Don't be like that, please Mum. Be nice. We're not plotting against each other, just the opposite, we're supporting each other. And what you've got to remember about this world Mum is that none of it is serious, you've got to remember it's all just a game, right? A game played to certain rules that stop you from taking it too seriously, from forgetting it's a game, right?' Jazzy was attempting to rally; he tapped his head woodenly. 'A game, yeah? And if you forget that, then you can go a little bit gaga, yeah, that's the rub.' Describing life as a game was still the profoundest card in his deck; a PE teacher had once made a great impression on him by making the same point, and having found his mother's musings more upsetting than revelatory, Jazzy had no choice but to lay it flat. 'People who can't see that, well, they can't see the wood from the trees or the fish from the fowl. And they can end up a bit twisted. I don't want you to end up like that. There's no need.'

Petula looked ready to laugh. 'A *game*? I suppose I would rather play a game than go to war. But that doesn't let you off the hook, because you still have to win both. Plots or no plots.'

'Life isn't like that Mum. It's not all about winning and losing all the time, and you can win a war by not playing if you see what I mean, just by living in truth and sticking to your principles, like Gandhi and, you know, flower power and the hippies. All of that lot.'

'I'm sorry, but you said life is a game, and war is part of life, so how is not playing it any answer at all?'

'Well, war's a game too, isn't it? Like I said, and,' Jazzy scratched his head, his thread was out there somewhere, '...and you win a game by, well, by *playing* it, and... sometimes *not* playing it can be kind of like winning too.'

'No, you're going nowhere. An endless succession of soldiers have to be killed to win a war. There's nothing playful about that. And winning and losing are different things, and it matters which is which. And we aren't winning, I tell you that, because winning feels very different to this, however you wish to muddy the waters. You're a muddle. You were *always* a muddle.'

'Just *cool* it, right,' said Jazzy, losing his cool, 'I'm not looking to have an argument with you tonight. Winning, right, it isn't everything, not like how you say it is. If you've really *tried* your hardest, really given something all you have, isn't that the only thing that counts? How hard we've tried? That's all I'm saying. Effort's the thing.'

Petula bared her teeth; how this line of excusing failure reminded her of all that had irritated her about her son as a teenager, a state that had seemed to last until he turned forty; the clumsy stupidity masquerading as wisdom, the self-important ignorance behind his sententious questioning, and the tantrums which followed any attempt to set him straight.

'Please Jazzy, anything but that, tell me for God's sake, who's interested in how much effort you put in? If trying your hardest isn't good enough, all that shows is that you *aren't* good enough. It's not complicated. The rest is just stuff we invent to make children feel better when their test results come in, all scribbled over in red ink.'

'But not everyone can finish first, can they? The whole thing about places is that there's a first, second, third and last too. Someone has to come bottom and don't *they* deserve to be loved for themselves?'

'But by whom? Only other losers who don't matter to anyone of distinction and character. No one else counts, the detritus you talk of is just here to make up the numbers, so there's less chance that decent people die in car crashes!'

'And I suppose that's me, isn't it? The "detra"-whatever-you-call-it. Jesus you never *change*! Never. Do you know that? And I mean, haven't you ever wanted to, haven't you ever thought how much better you'd feel in yourself if you had? If you just tried, right, to not be you for once?'

'Change? Why should I change...' Petula reached out for her beaker and Jazzy moved it further away, forcing her to grin at his cheek. How badly had she ever wanted to change? Not all that much, it had always been a dangerous notion. Certainly never enough to make a decision that would be as large as her life, exchanging the existence she had for one she did not know she could yet attain. 'There isn't time to change, not enough time in one's life to do something that *big*.'

Jazzy struck his chest martially. 'That's a cop-out if ever I heard one, I'd have expected more from you Mum, there's bags of time, how does that song go, "we have all the time in the world...."'

'There you go again, misunderstanding everything all the time! All we have is the present moment which we can enjoy *as if* we had all the time in the world. The line means embracing a cherished illusion. Christ, I may be a senile old lush, but you make me feel like a raging genius Jazzy. Really.'

'Maybe you are one?'

'Oh stop it, you've never been good at sarcasm.'

'I wasn't being sarcastic. Sometimes I think you are a genius, not the good kind, just the type that wants to make the world into a hell for every other poor sod who has the bad luck to live at the same time as you.'

'Behind every piece of bad luck is a bad decision.'

'*Shit!* This is why I can't even talk to you. Why it's easier just to walk away.'

'Oh? And is that why you thought you could take advantage of my reduced capacity to cast me over the coals?'

'What's that?'

'You know, you're trying to take advantage of me being a silly sot. So you can ask me what you might think are tough questions in the hope I tell you this or that, forgetting it all by the morning, yes?'

Blushing and at high speed, either to cover his embarrassment or because fate had cast the words out of their hiding place, Jazzy asked: 'So will you marry again?'

'I've already done that twice, isn't it time you tried?'

Jazzy snorted derisively. 'I'd have to be in love first. We don't all marry for money and a big pile.'

'In the past, self-interest was nothing to be ashamed of. It was what constituted a sensible person's character, and everyone expected to encounter it in anyone sane. If you read novels you'd know that,' Petula replied defiantly.

'Yeah, that's as may be, I wasn't alive then, and I don't have time to read. But I'd still need to be in love to marry.'

'Well, don't you love that person you've been living with for however long, I lose count now; don't you love her, your Spider?'

'We're not like that, it's more of a practical thing, we care about each other but… you know, it's not so romantic, we're more partners than, you know, lovers. She's my companion in life. There isn't that passionate part anymore, and there wasn't ever really that much of that to begin with either.'

'You could have fooled me, walking round holding hands all the time and writing each other poems, you said.'

'Yeah, we've had special moments for sure…'

'And you're always banging on about how much she means to you, how I'm looking down at her and her little termites all the time, and how she deserves my respect. Don't tell me that's all another load of your blah-blah?'

'You stop that or…'

'Ha!'

Jazzy threw his beaker against the wall, and watched it bounce off and loyally roll back across the stone floor to his boot. Squeezing his fist, he wanted to yell 'Aren't I the one who's meant to be asking the questions?' but knew that a pat line from a police drama was the admission that she was waiting for: that he would never overtake Petula. Instead he cried, 'Christ, it's not that *simple*! Not everyone is like you, clear-cut and cut-and-dried!'

'What complicated feelings you harbour Jasper. How hard it must be to grope about in the shadows. I've seen the two of you walk around the place holding hands, you said she was very dear to you, that she was your whole life; your words, not mine. Who would be blamed for thinking you were in love? I merely remark upon what you offer up for my consumption. Wasn't that the impression you were trying to convey? The point you were trying to make?'

Jazzy raised his hands in exasperation. 'Blimey, you sober up quickly in the race to become a bitch again! We *do*, you know, care about each other, a hell of lot. Of course we do. But it's not like, like it was with *Jill*. We've a different kind of understanding from what happened with me and her. It's not the same for me and Spider.'

'And does the Tarantula know that?'

'No, of course she doesn't, and don't go telling her anything either! It's none of your business anyway. This is one thing I don't want you fucking up for me. I was in love once before and you showed no respect, don't ruin this too.'

'I don't know what you're talking about, I always liked Kitty or whatever her name was, it was just difficult to get a word out of the girl, that's all. She seemed perfectly pleasant to me. In an unassuming way.'

'No, stop right there. I don't want to hear it, that ever-so-fucking-nice bullshit, save it, I know that's not you. You, you treated Jill like a second-class citizen, an underling. I was there, remember, I saw how it was.'

'Well she seemed terrified of everything! Still, I grant you, she was... clean and pretty well turned out. I've nothing *against* her.'

'That's big of you. So very good of you Mum now that you've done your worst and driven her away. What relationship could survive in the atmosphere you create here? And think about it if you care at all – where round here am I ever going to find another girl like that eh? At my age. I'm getting old too, I feel it every day when the bones pop as I get out of bed. Jill was a one-off, a complete babe, right? Someone I could really fall headlong and head over heels with. Oh aye, you only love like that once in your life. That was my chance, and you robbed me of it!'

'Now who's getting maudlin? I don't know what I'm supposed to have done or not done. You may well be right about Kitty, but you're wrong about the one part that actually matters, that isn't what love is, what you say, a *once-in-a-life* chance. You're worrying over nothing if you think it is.'

'Oh no? Like you'd know would you? Spare me that act!'

'I don't want to spare you, I want to *help* you. You ramble on about love, like you ramble on about everything else, but it's not the unique event you think it is. Love makes use of us, replaces us, reassembles and finds different combinations; it's the most active force in the world,' Petula sneezed again and slapped the table for emphasis, 'because it's not about *us*, we're at *its* service.'

'What the hell is that supposed to mean?'

'I'm saying that it chooses and discards individuals, and is only *sometimes* about them. Your turn may come up again. Who knows?'

'And that's meant to make me feel better?'

'Oh grow up! Can't you see I'm trying to get you to a place in life when you can finally become a man, a real one and not some popinjay who struts around like some extra from *The Archers* spouting homilies! All this stuff about Jill is just more retro-active nonsense, and it's typical of you. I never heard anything like it when you were actually together. You're just making it up now so you have an excuse to hate me!'

'Your trouble is that you don't know me, you never have. If you had you'd know that you're the hater and I'm the lover!'

'This is turning into something it shouldn't. You're provoking me now.'

'So what? I'm telling you the truth: I loved Jill and still do! If you knew me you'd know that. And the past, up here in my head, is the only place I can still see her, thanks to your treating her, and everyone before her, like *shit*. And then you go and blame me for living in the past.'

'Stop this obsession with the past, stop thinking of it as a paradise, really, I implore you. It'll only break your heart! Like dwelling on the death of an old friend. You've got absolutely no idea of the problems you're creating for yourself. You never look ahead.'

'What's the point in lying to yourself? You were saying the same thing not a moment ago, about how we're all washed up and have only our past to keep us going. I'm not going to bullshit you, you're right, you had your day, it lasted for a while, a whole lot of people came here and did some crazy stuff and then buggered off to leave you sitting in the kitchen on your own with me. And I had a past *too*. Don't deny me that, and it was Jill. Everything about her and that time is better than what this is, right. The sky was different, breathing was different, the colour of everything, more special, purer. Sometimes when I'm falling off to sleep I remember it, feel it just as it was. It's silent, there's no separation. Life is all one thing again. Fuck it, what do you know about it eh?'

'Everything in fact.'

'*Bullshit.*'

Petula put her glass down. She could see and hear nothing, sense only a glowing red dot in the far distance, slowly advancing until all beneath it would become an entropic desert; the black-tempered need to injure her son absolutely beyond her power to control. There it was, it was time to release the heat; rising she shouted, 'Damn you, you gangling idiot! Don't be so bloody, bloody... *wet*! You're wet on the insides, you're so wet you'll turn to muck! I can't even hear you without seeing rivers of liquid silage bubble before my eyes! How I bore you I will *never* know!'

Jazzy had also stood up, Mark Antony to her Brutus, and was pointing at his mother's face so closely that an inch further would have resulted in him jabbing out an eye. 'Not even you can take the happiness I've had from *me*,' he proclaimed grandly, 'it's sad to see you reduced to this, a pissed-up old witch. You always were black all the way through, but never so evil as the booze has made you. So what if we're both outcasts in our own time? I have less to lose than you, because I've never been anything anyway. But at least I know what it is to really be loved by a person, and to love them back. That's the only difference I need between us to walk out of here with my head held up high. Held *high*!'

Petula shimmied Jazzy's tumbler over to her side of the table and drunk most of it to buy herself a sliver's respite from her bilious choler. She wished she was not doing this, still doing it at her age, but was powerless to stop what was coming.

'My head held up high, do you hear me, held up *high!*' Jazzy repeated, smashing his fist down on the table.

'*Idiot!*'

Petula shook her head rancorously. Self-restraint; ought she to experiment with this alien notion or continue as she always had, towards ever-harsher forms of indiscretion? To hold back was too like acknowledging her drift towards death, that final threshold which, once accepted, towered over every other trifle; each smaller self-imposed limit a way of reconciling her to a temporal nature she had always wished to exceed. Far better to speak up and allow the scalding fire of her temper to burn all before her; 'I know about the letters!' she shouted, 'You didn't know that, did you?'

'What?'

'The *letters*, I bet you don't know anything about them, do you?'

'You what? What bloody *letters*?'

'You never had to read her letters did you? Horrible drippy things that came for, oh I don't know, maybe six months or a year. Dreary second-rate rubbish they were too!'

'What are you talking about? Whose letters?'

'Don't be thick! Letters that that girl wrote you, the one before the Spider that you can't shut up about. She got your name right, but for some reason they were all addressed to the main farm house; there must have been about five or six of the things. I read them and threw them all straight into the bin. Nauseous little missives, really *awful.*' Petula curled her nose up and drew her shoulders in as if to protect herself from a nasty draft. 'Let me see, first I think she wanted you to take her back, and she was sorry for humping whoever it was you caught her with, next she was upset you hadn't replied, and then the rest were all rather pointless ways of making those same points, but without any useful upshot. And finally she wrote to say that she had gone to live in Australia with another woman; yes, she became a lesbian. Or it might have been America; anyway, quite absurd.'

'You're lying! Lying! I don't believe you, you'd never have kept them from me. You can't keep secrets. You can't keep your mouth shut. I know you!'

'Why should I have told you? They were boring, *petty*, silly little notes from a mousey mediocrity. A silly little bitch who would have ruined your life if you ever got back together, though granted, at that stage I hadn't realised you had it in you to do so much worse! And don't get me going on secrets,' cackled Petula in full flow, 'whether they fiddle their expense claims or fiddle with kids, there isn't a secret in this county I haven't encountered. Yes, that's right, I know everything! Who fucked whom when they were married to whomever, the whole tawdry history of this place written and kept in my archive!' Petula slapped her forehead, her rings breaking the thin skin into tiny bruised cuts; 'I know everything! Did you get that? *Everything!*'

'If you're telling the truth, if for one moment, right, for *one moment* I really believed you, I could...'

'Yes?'

'I could *kill* you!'

'Go on, what's stopping you?'

Jazzy beat his chest with his fists. 'For crying out aloud! What kind of thing are you? I could kill you! I could really kill you! Do you know that?'

'You can't! It's already too late! You could have just now but you didn't! You told me instead! And you'll never find it in you again! You've never had the courage to act on what you really want. And you know how I can say that? Because I *do* know you! I do know you, you idiot!'

'You're talking about what *I* want? All I want, all I ever wanted is to be left alone and given a chance to run this place!'

Petula screamed with laughter. 'Is that all! Then you really will have to wait until I die! But beware! The spider and the fly usually die together because the spectacle of their squabble offends whatever higher power happens to be having its lunch! You won't outlast me by a single day! Not a single sodding day...'

'Damn you to hell, I *hate* you, Mum, and I mean *hate* you! Some bad thing deserves to happen, some very bad thing *needs* to happen to you. I'll never forgive you. Never, forgive you for... for... *for this!*'

Petula carried on guffawing like a fairground ass, her body rocking unsteadily with mechanical merriment. As she correctly guessed, Jazzy had given up thoughts of dashing her head against the wall, though not for the reasons she thought. A new spirit of calculation had entered him as swiftly as instinct; he knew he could kill, the question was how and when to do so, and get away with it.

'You've got to avoid holding things against people for the rest of their lives and yours, their lives *are* how they pay for their mistakes! Save yourself a chore and forget about never forgiving me. Oh bless you, look at your face, do you have an idea of how ugly you are when you're this angry? It's amazing how much you resemble your father! Really. I've spent some time with some rough customers, long service in hard stations, but in a mood, you take the whole tin!'

Petula started to sneeze with diabolical mirth, the snot streaming out of her nose and collecting on her chin. She closed her eyes and carried on shaking her head, the situation, all situations, too funny by far.

'Bless me, you've given me a much-needed laugh!'

Without a word Jazzy turned his back to her and tore out along the corridor, wondering how the world could have changed so much in an hour. When he had got back to the cottage, he coldly relayed the events of that evening to Spider, omitting those parts that would embarrass him or compromise their domestic arrangements, and finished by swearing that this latest outrage would be the last. Spider, having already commented that he seemed like a different man, assented gladly to his proposed way of ensuring that Petula's days were numbered, and having made love to confirm the unity of their intent, fell asleep in his arms. Jazzy awoke with pins and needles some ten minutes later, and waited until morning before the feeling returned to his right side, thoughts of murder most final sustaining him through the hours of darkness.

Petula did not notice him go; the drink had turned another corner with her, allowing her to mistake a fruit bowl she was laughing at for Jazzy's ongoing presence for twenty more minutes, by which time she had forgotten the content of what had passed between them, losses of temper and memory occurring simultaneously, and remembered only that he had upset her in some way, provoking another of her flying furies of which he would doubtless consider himself the victim. The kitchen had grown dismal and all of a sudden Petula had no idea what time it was, the suspicion that it might be late afternoon in winter fuelled by the cold clicking of her joints. Taking her plimsolls off and putting them on her hands like glove puppets, having them 'argue' in the voices of Jazzy and Anycock, amused her for a time without wholly extinguishing the fearful appeals of moral reproach; had she gone too *far* this time?

Crossly ticking herself off for listening to the conversation of phantoms, she clambered up and walked the length of the house, stopping in rooms and spots she normally had no use for, as if to say hello, not quite knowing where she was for periods; her confusion strongest whenever she glanced out of the window, the view full of a colour she did not recognise. Occasionally a sense of emergency would creep into these wanderings; the need to find the lavatory a periodic interruption; the usefulness of switching a light on another. Robotically she would miss both cues, walking into tables and sicking up on her leg. The smell round her began to grow rancid, nature's call repeatedly absorbed by her slacks, but not knowing what the stench was or where it had come from, only the faint memory that something awful had occurred kept her going, before sleep overtook all, and the horrors of the night joined those others in the overhead locker of accumulated regret.

Waking on a rug at the bottom of the steps, shivering, Petula struggled to free her hair of the scarf she had confused for a nest of nocturnal vampiric crows. The desire to protect oneself, and its mutation into the exploitation of others, was what she had thought of every time she passed the Hockney portrait of Evita in the hall before passing out, and she could still hear the thought repeated as though a tannoy had been set up in her skull. Were there other people in the building who had wired her to it in her sleep? And whose voice was it she could hear, Wrath's or some old hag's, about to announce the results of the sack race at her school sports day? The house was alive with strange utterances.

Quickly she wrapped her shawl bedouin-like round her head and, scared stiff, crawled back to the kitchen, encamping under the table where she resolved to count down the minutes until daybreak. From every corner of The Heights disharmonious and weird entreaties threatened to materialise into a concrete manifestation she could at least identify, without being so kind as to actually do so. There was nowhere to hide, but she was not sure who was watching her or why she was desperate to be hidden; she could be seen and heard everywhere, that much she knew. Struggling to her feet and banging her head against the table, Petula stumbled into the hall again and grabbed a large Ming vase out of which she discerned painful groaning, lifting it toward her ear like a giant shell. To her horror, a fearful version of 'All Things Bright And Beautiful' was being sung backwards by a satanic choir, the racket booming deafeningly if she held the vase to her right ear, but changing into a creepy murmur if she switched to the left. Nervously she moved the vase to her eye and peered in; what the hell was in there? Like Alice, but not in Wonderland, Petula saw a frightened woman peer back out into her mouth, deep down into the darkness where her secrets were hidden. It was not her nerves this time, the Devil had come to collect. The house terrified her. She wondered how she had never noticed before. Petula started to scream and cry and jabber and mewl, until she could no longer hear herself, running about in the early-morning light locking doors and closing windows, without the presence of mind to know why or stop.

Rising later that afternoon, Petula was relieved to find that reality was nearly the same as always, at least as far as the weather was concerned, and taking the precaution of avoiding Jazzy for the next few days, she returned cautiously to her established routine.

*

Nothing had been as Regan had foreseen. To start with she and Robinson were not seated together on the plane – she in Economy, Robinson at the front – her one trip up to see if she could share some First Class sushi a short one: Robinson was unconscious in a silk eye mask with 'Fuck' and 'Off' stitched into the eyes in glittering emerald beads. Regan did not sleep, read or gaze at accompanying clouds, only blink and brood about what she was doing, having never given in to a comparable impulse since that fateful night by the lake. However she sought to justify her journey, she was going a long way on very little, and would not have been doing so, she saw, if she were not a very unhappy individual. The plane was full of omens she tried to ignore; the laboratorial hum of the air conditioning morphing into the guitars on The Rolling Stones' 'Gimme Shelter' for the

duration of the flight, the man next to her resembling an over-
weight Jeremy exhumed from the grave, and a flat Coca Cola
that kept repeating on her comprising the third prong of Satan's
trident. She had been asleep for perhaps a second when the
plane landed so abruptly that she thought it had crashed.

New York was not bright, interesting and loud, but overcast,
indifferent and noisy. Robinson's insistence that she lie spread
out in the backseat of the car in a sleeping-pill hymn to oblivion,
forced Regan into the front like an anxious domestic, ruling out
any residue of camaraderie that might have survived the flight.
The driver, a balding man with halitosis, or possibly a lively
hencoop at the rear of his mouth, leant over every few minutes
to tell her how Robert Morley had asked him to slow down in
the red-light district, noting conscientiously that nothing had
come of it. The atmosphere in the car was lonely and detached
from the city outside, suggestive of unfulfilled hopes and wasted trips, Regan thought, as she scowled at the aggrieved face she
caught sight of in the wing mirror.

An ugly kerfuffle at the hotel was caused, without his knowing, by David Bowie, who was also going to the Mingus show. His
being housed at the last minute in the suite Robinson had originally been booked into prior to the Thin White Duke's gazump-
ing, forced a hasty retreat to rival premises that would provide
a room of similar specifications, on the basis that she be down-
graded to a building where her neighbours were senior execu-
tives and lawyers, and not Elizabeth Taylor and Prince Nelson
Rogers. In a catty and lingering rant that ran from the reception
to the dining room, back to reception via the bar, and out into
the foyer, Regan began to experience the first inklings of the
'what-am-I-doing-here' feeling she was so scared of encountering, recognising it as the harbinger of more misery to follow.
Sure enough, on the way into the lift, still screeching at all and
sundry, Robinson's foot was caught momentarily in its closing
doors; how hard no one knew, but she threw herself onto the

floor howling, clutching the injured limb like a Premier League footballer looking for a free-kick. The next hour was a whirligig of activity, and before Regan had time to find her room, she was taught another lesson in how some lives are more important than others, as the hotel doctor, a surgeon who was staying on the same floor, another doctor from the general hospital, and a private podiatrist all announced that although they could find nothing *technically* wrong with the foot, Robinson would need it bandaged and rested for several days; the suite immediately transformed into a state-of-the-art medical facility. To Regan's alarm, Robinson assumed that the best thing for her to do now was to stay in the suite with her as a companion in pain, feeding her Häagen-Dazs and taking phone calls, thus causing another altercation in which Regan left the room almost in tears, but at least left the room, a portfolio of obscene antipodean slang following her out into the corridor.

Splashing her face, and dressing in clothes that did not reflect her in the sassiest light, for in her current mood she did not know what could, Regan fled for a cab, only to feel conspicuously alone with razor-wire butterflies, robbed of her cover in Robinson. The taxi abandoned her a block away from the venue with an hour to spare, leaving her a sixty-minute window to pace round the warehouse district in heels wondering again, as she hoped she would cease to do once things got going, what the hell she was doing in New York.

With the hour over she found out that if she was there to view *art*, such an innocent alibi, she was still the very first person at the gallery, for who else but the mad woman of Mockery Gap would turn up to a society event bang on time? Detecting an unhealthy lack of respect for herself that she hoped wouldn't show, Regan stumbled down the velour steps, past a podium where anyone worth having a camera pointed at them would pose, a line of burning torches, and a pair of giant 'Matey' Bubblebath Sailors she presumed Mingus was responsible for, into a narrow tunnel that led to another world. Waiters dressed in overalls and boiler suits approached her, carrying trays of champagne and absinthe cocktails, as behind them, in what resembled a stonewashed sports hall, glass cases full of refuse and obscure tat mutely kept their council. Hung above her from the ceiling in giant parody of a pub sign was an illuminated plaque, with the title of the show, *IN THE ABSENCE OF A SOLUTION TO THE WORLD'S PROBLEMS I GIVE YOU A WORK OF GREAT ART'*, squashed on in bubbly pink neon lettering.

The room was vast and utterly without atmosphere, less a gallery than a post-modern marketplace in which deals were done; the sense that she had wandered into a commercial hub nauseously omnipresent in the sound of the Stock Exchange, streaming into the hall through hidden speakers. Snatching a drink and taking it to a far-off corner, where a line of squirrel skulls had been arranged along a strip of asphalt next to a packet of tapioca pudding entitled *'MORE SIGNIFIER-LADEN BRILLIANCE'*, Regan feigned absorption in the hope that anyone who saw her would not know at once she was friendless and, were she not so anxious, already quite bored. After several painful moments, impossible to measure other than in intense rivets of fear, the room filled up. Regan was easily absorbed; there were many people, it turned out, who had come on their own, and they were all grateful for a floating companion, however disengaged, to disguise the fact. Managing to avoid looking at any more of the artwork, as very few others had even seemed to notice it, Regan spent the next forty minutes being passed about like a relay baton, in brief conversation with an underwear manufacturer, a moaning rapper from Bristol, a Columbian artist whose parents had been kidnapped by the FARC, and a well-meaning banker who insisted on showing her how she could hear New Order's 'Blue Monday' on his mobile telephone, thanks to evolving technology. Pleasant as they all were, Regan would not have travelled from The Heights to Darlington to see them, far less undertake the actual journey she had just suffered. Taking a long time over a trip to the lavatory, she was thinking that it seemed as though the least painful course open to her was to taxi back to the hotel to be alone with her shame, and fly out the following morning, when all at once she was standing face-to-face with him. It was a close-run thing to work out who was more shocked, and in her astonishment, Regan tried to barge past in the pretence that she had not seen, or did not recognise, her oldest friend.

'Regan... *Regan*! Hey Regan, stop, it *is* you! What are you doing here?'

'What?'

'Regan, it's *me*! It's me of course, this is my show! What, I mean, what brings you here?'

'Oh Christ, *Mingus*!'

'Yes, Mingus! How come you're here?'

'I was, erm, invited.'

'Well that's, that's amazing! I had no idea, no idea you'd be here. This is just amazing! How long has it been? No, forget it, it's just *amazing* to see you here, to see you again, it's been so long! Who invited you? No, forget that, it's just amazing. Amazing that you're here full stop. Do you live in New York now?'

'No, London; do you?'

'Most of the time yeah, I've got a barge in London too, that I sometimes use.'

'Wow. Two residences!'

'Yeah, two, three really if you count the place near Palma. And four if you count my parents'!'

'Palma? Wow! Things have really come on for you!'

'Yeah, they have, I mean, everything's changed a lot since we last... saw each other.'

'So I see...'

Regan was stuck. Mingus was not quite as she remembered him. He was no longer skinny and gave the impression, in his tailored-to-fit clothes, of cool coordinated strength. Wearing tinted glasses and with an at-home-in-the-world gait, he conveyed something that she had not expected; the air of one who had no real need of her. The entire room was here because of him, no one else cared who she was, and she understood she had only seconds to say something to hold his interest or draw him in, before the crowd took hold of him again. It was startling that she had even had him to herself this long and the bridge she had to cross was already drawing up; she had no idea what to say and nor, now, by the look of things, did he. He was still smiling, sincerely; at least she had that.

'I'm sorry, it's so crazy seeing you here Mingus! You know, I know you've more right to be here than me,' Regan began again, 'and this is a really daft thing to say, but I don't pay much attention to the art world and I didn't know you were this Magus character I'd heard the name of; I probably should have *guessed* but I didn't make the connection,' she lied, though only in service of her point, 'and it's surreal just to see you in this context and know all this is your life now. Unbelievable really, I should just stop going on about it I know! But it's so different from how I was used to seeing you before.'

Mingus frowned. 'In Mockery Gap you mean?'

'Yes, I don't think we ever saw each other anywhere else, did we?' she said, hoping to deliberately miss the point, if there was one.

'You don't remember that time in London then, when we were small? I often think of it.'

'Oh!' Regan was more elated than embarrassed; if he could remember that after all that had happened to him, then there was hope. 'Of course! I wasn't counting that, I meant as grownups!'

'Grownups?'

A tall black woman in a painted-on pinstripe business suit walked through Regan and took Mingus's arm with calculated authority; 'Darling, what a lot of wankers there are in here tonight. I can't wait for us to get away; fucking Americans; I told you an artist doesn't turn up to his own shows.'

Mingus smiled apologetically, and touching Regan's shoulder as he was dragged away, managed to say, 'It was really nice to meet you again after all this time...'

As Regan rushed to the entrance a few moments later, tripping over stray feet and barging into swinging elbows, she was collared by a grinning man she recognised as the pompous bassist of a seminal three-piece rock group that she could never remember the name of, their tunes synonymous with building-society adverts, property development and bleach.

'You're Petula's daughter aren't you? Do you remember me? I was at a party of your mother's years ago, you couldn't have been more than a girl. How old are you now?' He was already too drunk to consider such peace-time breaches of etiquette as rude, and pressed against her so his arm was resting round her neck. Without waiting for Regan to answer he continued, 'And how is *she*? You know, I once did quite a lot to try and help her. It's been years since I last saw old blood and guts; I suppose she's still going strong?'

'Yes,' Regan somehow managed to say; how she did not know. His breath stank of canopies and cigarettes and riddles of the lower gut. She might yet be sick if she breathed in another word of his, but his hand was on her wrist and he was not letting go.

'Hmmm, but she's never been any good at understanding other people's terms of reference has she? Oh my, I am sorry,' he placed a hand on her chest flirtatiously as he belched, 'but perhaps you and she are just the same? Weren't you called, even then, something like "the sisters"?'

So this, Regan thought, is what it is like to be brought back to life only to be killed all over again. Holding a hand to her mouth, she wriggled the other one free, and turning, ran into the tunnel towards the muggy aquamarine light.

*

Regan lay fully clothed on her bed, and gazed toward the open blind, too upset to make any other concession to the world of being and doing. It may have been a moment when, were she the type to end her own life, she would have. But Regan took consciousness and public opinion too seriously to consider suicide, understanding that in her case it would make her look a fool and spoil whatever fleeting satisfaction she may yet obtain from eating chocolate and buying a newspaper. Balance, as always, oversaw her torment with smug dispassion.

There were several angry messages from Robinson awaiting her, not so much pouring salt in the wound as mocking her notion that she mattered enough to even be wounded. Lacking the passionate conviction to call her back and tell her to fuck off, Regan resolved to say very much the same thing to Robinson over breakfast, by which time some sense of worldly care may have drifted back to her. For the moment she was a nothing, fit only for the purest melancholic and unfiltered wonder, lying there listening to the passing traffic, wondering where all the different cars were going. This was not what she had expected to be doing on this particular night, but why should she have anticipated any other outcome? Of all the nights of her life, what tiny proportion had been spent in the company of anyone who cared about her? She was lonely, of course she was and had always been so; Petula may have kept her physical company but even then she was alone, cast as her own witness, her actions remembered only by the unnoticed subjectivity whose proper name was Regan Montague.

Gradually Regan began to replay and rehearse what had happened at the gallery, the worst bits first, next the dull parts, and then finally all of them together. As she did so she found herself searching for an explanation that would not incriminate her as a sad loser, or a desperate old maid. More than that, she had to embrace the painful observation that Mingus had not taken an oath of celibacy until she re-entered his life, far less waited to sail away with her in a pea-green boat and be married under the light of a full moon, so like the one they had made their unofficial vows under. Instead, she reached for what would play kindly to her feelings, and help facilitate the dignity she knew she would need to clean her teeth and wash her face in the morning. Her preferred version went something like this: she and Mingus were a modern-day tragedy, star-crossed lovers who had the misfortune to have met on different stages in life's way, when neither of their realities were the other's truth, hopelessly ill-served by timing and their own chronologies... It would all fit nicely into a song, but was not enough to stop her tears, which knew another version. Regan allowed the water to come, if anything overjoyed to have the company, the effort of having to prepare a successful account of the night for the girls too reminiscent of the 'back-shadowing' her mother had practised down the decades. She had sat as a girl, out of consideration and politeness to the feelings Petula would not own up to having, and listened to her mother alter the significance of the same events with endless invention, adjusting them to her current goals or audience to save her from having her humanity remarked on, or the ordinariness of her existence judged. By remaining stronger than anyone else, empathy would always be an impossibility, yet this was what Regan sought, even as her friends took care to not show too much of it, lest they shatter her self-image as a tower of ice. Let the world laugh then; it would be worth every humiliating second, if scorn were the prequel to empathy, and inclusion into the human condition. Mingus had simply repaid her treatment of him in kind, with the merciful qualification that at least he had not done so deliberately, whereas she had spurned him because she had allowed herself to think that she could do better, and that his love was the first of many. In doing so she wished to remain true to her mother's example, and the selfless warning that men who loved were the most deluded of all; Regan not able to see that Petula could be selfish even in her kindnesses.

Regan lay there for an eternity trying not to think of these things, thinking of them, then trying not to, failing to, and thinking of them again, before catching herself and starting the process from scratch. And then the phone by the bed went. Her first reaction was to leave it, assuming that it was Robinson looking for a little bit of afters, or worse, wanting to make up now she had hit the minibar. But a more powerful instinct, indistinguishable from hope, threw her arm over, and reaching as far as she could, she pulled the receiver to her ear. Blankly she said, 'Hello.'

At first all she could hear was a lot of noise, a spaceship of macaws being eaten by jungle parasites, before realising that the loudest of them was actually shouting her name, 'Regan, *Regan*, it's me! Shit, I'm so glad I've got you! This is about the *millionth* hotel I tried and I was about to give up! Seriously, I'd called everywhere, so this must be, I don't know, *destiny*! Sorry, I'm wasted, I know, but I couldn't stop myself, I needed to speak to you. Jesus! I've spent years just thinking of you! Do you know that? I think you're great and I can't believe you came all this way for nothing! I've got to give you something... I've got to let you know you're great, *great*!'

'I think you're *great* too!' she shrieked, 'Thank *God*, oh I'm so glad it's you, you don't even know!'

'Not as much as me! I didn't think I'd find you, I tried looking for you again round the gallery, then different hotels I thought you might be at, but you went for the Cinderella moment, you hated the show I guess, yeah? That's why you left?'

'Yes, no, well partly! But it doesn't matter, I don't hate you! I just don't understand the work.'

'Bollocks! That's a cop out, just say you hated it! I don't mind, I think it's fine, loads of people do! There's nothing to understand, anyway, every universalisation is a dilution as well as a reaching-out, I'm not surprised I alienate people. Who cares if I do?'

'That sounds very theoretical.'

Mingus laughed. 'It's not meant to be, I'm trying to be stoical, theory is how untalented people get their revenge on the talented someone once said. I don't know what I'm doing. There's no plan, people are free to think what they like, especially *you*.'

'That's why you're so successful, everyone does think what they like, you've given birth to an entire industry!'

'Bullshitters all of them... I... do you want that... think?'

'I'm sorry, I can't hear you! It's getting too loud where you are... you're breaking up,' shouted Regan panicking, 'can you say that again?'

'You're... my...'

'I can't hear you! Please, you've got to be *louder*.'

'You're my destiny, which is why I only know one half of it. My half!' she heard Mingus yell over the music. 'When can I see you again?'

Without missing a beat Regan said, 'The Brooklyn Bridge, this side, tomorrow morning?'

'God, I'd love to, but I might still be fucked! I've just taken a hundred mushrooms!'

'Fuck! Then the next day, same place, dinner?'

'Sure... sure... yes! Time?'

'Nine, I love you, see you then!'

'Me too...' The line had gone dead. Regan felt lifted off the bed, tossed into the air, caught again, and embraced by the cheers of an adoring crowd. She wanted to sing, take her clothes off and run up and down the corridor pleasuring herself; life was as much, and more, than the dreams she had always regarded as beautifully constructed placebos. In her happiness she turned on the television, stuck as how else to celebrate the moment, Rod Stewart on MTV in tight pink trousers only just coming on when the phone by the bed rang again.

She felt sick; this time she knew it was not Mingus. Cold sweat had replaced tears as her excrescence, and she waited for the phone to ring off, which after its thirtieth ring it did. Almost instantaneously her mobile began to bleep, and finding it quickly she shoved it under the sheets to smother its vibrating call. After a very protracted period of time it stopped, and the landline started again, Regan holding out until the thirty-first ring before picking up.

'What the *hell* took you so long?' screamed her mother.

'I'm sorry, I was, I was asleep.'

'It must have been a very deep one.'

'I was completely out on sleeping pills. Zonked. Sorry.'

'You should watch those, they'll drive you bloody barmy if you're not careful. Anyway, at least I've got you.'

'How did you find me?'

'Why does that matter?'

'I'm just surprised.'

'Your office told me you got caught up in some dreadful business involving that circus clown Mackpiece or whatever stupid thing he's calling himself these days. I thought you could use some moral support.'

'You're not coming over are you?'

'No, don't be ridiculous, what would I want to get involved in that idiotic caper for? No, but I need you back here pronto.'

'What? *Why?* I've only just *arrived...*'

'I know you've just woken up, but you're not sounding very clever; are you alright? You don't sound... altogether sane. Or right in the head.'

'I'm tired Mum. I was asleep. It's the pills. But *why* do I have to come back?'

'Did that little bastard blank you? He'd better not have! He'd be nothing without us, *nothing!*'

'You mean Mingus?'

'Who else do you think I bloody mean! I'm worried about you!'

'No, no! Of course not, no one has blanked me. There's nothing, absolutely nothing to worry about. I promise. But I don't understand, what's so important that you need me back right away? Are you alright? Is everything okay at home?'

'Forget about *me*. What's so important about where you are that you *can't* come back? New York is a bloody terrible place, muggings, crack cocaine, subway rapists! I want you out of there now, before it's too late and something happens. You've got to come home.'

'Mum, don't be crazy! I'm perfectly safe here. Nothing is going to happen to me.'

'Please Regan, I credit you with intelligence, you're not involved in something stupid are you? There are many ways of making a fool out of yourself, and you don't need to get on a plane to New York to find out about all of them.'

'I have things I need to *do* here. Work stuff too. Why do you need me back so badly? I'm meant to be in the office here in New York for work, it's important. I have to stay. Really, I have to.'

'Nonsense, just shift a gear and get on that plane tomorrow. Stop *arguing* with me and just do it! I've checked times, there are at least three leaving before nine o'clock. I have plans for us this weekend and also have something to tell you, something very, *very* important that I can't simply say down the blower.'

'What is it? Why not?'

'Are you even listening to *me*? I've already told you what you've got to do. You are being a bit thick aren't you; I've just said in plain English that there's a matter that would require us to meet face-to-face, it's far too important to blurt out now, you never know who is listening on these lines, and still you disobey me, still you ask *why*...'

'But Mum, I'm meant to...'

'Regan! *Regan!* Are you not listening to a single *word* I am saying? What's the matter with you girl? I require you to be here in two days' time, which gives you more than enough time to travel and rest, all of tomorrow in fact, and most of the following morning, which is a timeline I don't think unreasonable in the circumstances. Most reasonable in fact. And what are you doing in New York anyway? I'm told the woman you're with is certifiable and that Magnum is already yesterday's news. A charlatan and imposter. A madman and a drug addict. And besides, I can't stand physical attraction, it's so... so *obvious*.'

Regan could say nothing. She and Mingus were primed for a future they would not inherit, like vines wrapped round each other's stems so neither of them would ever meet the light. What a lot of time she had spent thinking about something that was never going to happen.

'Regan!' Petula barked, 'Are you still there? Can you hear me, are you still there?'

'What?' Regan practically snarled back, unable to stem her mother's will, more powerful than fate. 'What is it you want me to do? Travel all the way back to bloody Yorkshire like I do all the time to meet you at home? That's fucking crazy Mum! I've only just got here! Are *you* drunk?'

Ignoring her question Petula sighed and replied matter-of-factly: 'You're to meet me in Bath, I agree Yorkshire is a bit much, I've booked us in for treatments, spas, facials, manicures, that sort of thing. *Bath*. Everyone needs to be fussed over now and then. And we need to keep our defences up against illness or worse. I'll be outside the station in the Audi, nine pm sharp, Friday evening. We can have dinner together. You'll need something decent after all that airplane and American food.'

'I have to stay here...' said Regan, no longer believing it was possible to, but owing it to the future she would never have, to protest to the bitter end and die fighting.

'Don't be so *ridiculous*, we've already finished with that conversation. I need you here. With me. I won't have it any other way. Do you understand? Of course you do. You damn well know you *do*. Nine pm. Bath. I'll see you there. And don't worry if you're a little late. We'll have *plenty* of time. Goodnight, and don't forget to set your alarm.'

Throwing the phone across the room Regan flopped down to the floor and wept, beating at the carpet ineffectually with her small fists. After a while, wanting to make more of her despair, she moved to smash a window, the glass eventually shattering on her third attempt with the table.

The doctor who helped with the stitches, fortunately on her upper arm and conveniently out of sight, came straight from Robinson's suite, and along with the management was most understanding of the accident, believing Regan had been driven to her act by the pressures of toiling for an employer they could all agree was a nightmare. Regan thus saved herself the embarrassment of having to explain her predicament, or invent one. The following morning after just two hours' sleep, Regan took a taxi, which stopped at Mingus's gallery where she left a letter she hoped would explain everything, and from there to the airport, and to Petula.

PART FIVE:
Lethe, forgetfulness.

*Isn't it queer how we go through life, always thinking
that the things we want to do
are the things that can't be done?*

– GEORGE ORWELL, *Coming up for Air*

CHAPTER THIRTEEN,
kindness and killing.

It turned out that the very important 'matter' her mother had asked Regan to leave New York and journey to Bath for was too delicate to mention right away. Contrary to her insistence over the telephone, Petula preferred to overlook Regan's impatiently careworn expression, and to warm up on less distasteful topics, including the colour of the Hardfields' new Saab and Royce's litter of Springer puppies. She shushed Regan when she brought the 'matter' up in the steam room, asked her not to mention it during their facial, played deaf on the treadmill, ignored her reference to the subject over dinner on their last night, and exploded when Regan raised it again as they parted at the train station.

In a stormy and perplexing dressing-down, attracting the attention of the entire concourse, Petula screamed at her still jet-lagged and by now thoroughly exhausted and farouche daughter, 'Have you *never* had anything so terrible on your mind that words fail *you*? Experience that simply defies expression?'

'But I thought you couldn't wait to tell me!'

'What are you talking *about*? Of course I could *wait* to tell you. Otherwise I would have told you over the telephone!'

'So I don't understand why you can't now? I'm here, aren't I?'

'My, I've bought you up sheltered and protected, you really have no idea what I'm talking about, have you? No, no idea!'

'But...'

'Have you not the slightest shred of empathy for my suffering? I who washed your baby feet in the bath?'

'How can I when I don't know what it *is*? All we've had this weekend is the usual trivial pursuits, with a load of activities chucked in. Any excuse to be too busy to talk seriously. But here I am, and I still don't know what I was meant to travel halfway round the world for!'

'Stop bullying me! On, on, on you go! You never let me speak or leave me alone, following me everywhere like my shadow! It's like being chased, ravaged and roasted by a bossy Pekinese! I'll tell you in my own good time! Until then, leave me *alone*!'

'But Mum...'

That time turned out to be the following weekend, when to Regan's horror, Petula decided to remain at The Heights after all, having cancelled her shooting trip in order to catch up with Regan's gang whom she claimed not to have seen 'since they were little girls'; factually untrue, though in the spirit of a greater truth, as Petula had never taken any interest in them on those occasions they had met, from little-girlhood onward. Had her vexation not been so transparent, Regan would have found an excuse to cancel the expedition, instead of driving up to The Heights as a condemned woman would, expecting the farce of a show trial, followed by the inevitable denouement, a short trip in an open cart, and death.

This time things were exactly as she had foreseen. The weekend was a disaster; the most miserable she could remember. If her flight from New York had crushed her will to live, a ghostly and confused message from Mingus on her answerphone at William Morris the only evidence that she had ever wanted to, the reunion with the girls squeezed out what endured of her instinct to exist. Petula did not leave them alone for a moment, stage-managing every molecule of the trip with an attention to the molar architecture of their movements that made her previous efforts to show guests a good, if closely managed, time seem laissez-faire in comparison. There was not a single conversation that was not led, overheard, interrupted or redirected by Petula, into the kind of inane, irrelevant and intense small talk that Regan would have gladly gone deaf not to have to hear again. Meals were formal and punctual, name cards at set places, Petula dragging her arthritic and increasingly unbendable legs behind them on short walks, forcing them out of politeness to plod at a snail's pace, and listen to her complaints and intermittent put-downs. A desperate last-minute trip into Leeds was called off because Petula wanted them to watch *Antiques Roadshow* with her, which was in Shatby that week, with Regan delegated to fetching mugs of tea and snacks for her friends, their virtual servant, as Petula feigned outrage that the guests should have to do anything for themselves.

Saddest, for all of them, was the decision to curtail their rambling soirees before bed on Petula's insistence: she wanted the young women up fresh and early for her three-course breakfasts, consisting of prunes, porridge and Aga-baked eggs and bacon, which she suggested they prepare together. Her friends, collectively alarmed but too sensitive to convention to refuse to comply, increased the number of cigarettes they had to leave the house to smoke, gathering in the garden furtively and whispering that they could never remember the woman being *this* bad and how the *hell* could Regan take it? Understanding that Regan's trip to New York had been a trophy-less hunt, and that her failure was in some way connected to the mournful figure she cut under her mother's dictatorial gaze, meant that ongoing and pained glances were the only real communication they had with her all weekend, the anticipated 'catch-up' never to happen. And as the girls headed away in taxis to the station, to breathe the air of freedom and lambast the prison they had so recently escaped, Regan, guessing that the moment when it might have meant anything had already passed, asked once again: what was Petula's urgent secret? With monumental unconcern her mother replied, 'What? Oh *that*, nothing really, I can't remember now. I'll let you know if it comes back to me. I wouldn't worry about it if I were you. There's so many things on at the moment that it's easy to confuse their importance.'

Regan could not recall how she got to her car, remembering only that she hoped her legs would carry her that far, and
that if she fell, she did not end up eating gravel and being sectioned. The weeks that followed were no better. What intellectual life that survived her inferno of inward recrimination was
spent checking the internet for varying definitions of madness,
schizophrenia, bipolar personality disorders, dementia, Alzhei-
mer's and mixtures of all five – a medical explanation for her
mother's behaviour occasionally bringing her a crumb of comfort; the hope that a hidden illness may have begun a degenerative disease of the brain easy to reconcile with the facts, if not
with the way they made her suffer. Daily, Regan resisted turning the television on and sitting in front of it doing nothing, or
simply lying in bed and not moving; a lethargic demotivation
replacing the prosaic dependability of her being. Bizarrely, once
having forced herself into the office, her work was the one constant she could still rely upon herself to engage with normally,
performing her tasks no better or worse than before, the terror
that Mingus would call again forcing her to explain her terrible
life to him, or of her ringing him to volunteer the same, keeping
her awake and wired till five. However there was little disguising
the shell-shock of one who had been through too much to ever
talk of it, which preceded and overshadowed her every utterance – whatever words she managed being empty replacements
for more important ones that would not come.

Twice in a month Petula called her back to The Heights on the
pretext of discussing an important matter again, once in a flood
of tears, which continued throughout her stay precluding any
confession, the wasted journey creating the need for a second
trip where her mother finally promised to tell all. Nothing came
of number two either except stilted and mechanical meals with
people Regan may or may not have barely known, registering
no impression on her as she was not there, or anywhere. Where
Regan went to, she could not remember, becoming aware of her-

self again only as she floated back to her food, imagining her knife and fork stuck in her mother's back, neck, or wedged into her lower abdomen: a human carvery with nothing left on the plate. And then she would shudder all over, and pass the salt, as someone was always bound to want it. Her belief in her wretched destiny was now so singular, and her mother's place in it so secure, that nothing else appeared to be required of her. She knew an event would occur to set her free, but as it was beyond her power to instigate it, there was nothing else to do but passively accelerate towards inevitability with open, if somewhat floppy, arms.

Jazzy was having no better time of it than his sister. He was all over the place, lacking the singleness of purpose that required one who wanted to kill to graduate to the status of murderer. This was especially evident on those mornings when he would have quite happily called out 'good morning' to his mother, even if by the afternoon he wanted to bury a hatchet in her head, the ever-changing tenor of his temperament never so obvious as when he had to rely on himself to alter a situation. This inconsistency was more than a stumbling block; it meant that he had to be in the *mood* to kill to actually be able to do it, as well as believe in the need to, which was by far the easier part, as the theoretical case was watertight. Finality, though, had never sat well with him. What if, after he'd done the deed, he wanted it undone? How would he know how he would feel in a week, and who knew if how he felt then was any more representative of his true feelings than what he felt now? Or perhaps neither of those were the final truth and for that he'd have to wait another month? Never having gone anywhere in his life, Jazzy had never had to consider reversibility before, let alone an absolute and irreversible plan that he had not talked about for years first.

There was much, though, in his favour; almost too much. Unlike most killers, his problem was not one of trying to lull the victim to a quiet spot to do away with her, or arranging an obscure pretext for a rendezvous out of the blue, but being positively spoilt for choice and context. Not a day passed that did not brim over with opportunities to dispatch Petula into the next life, and not just any opportunities but nigh-on perfect ones where she would not know it had happened, far less who delivered the blow.

These opportunities brought the inevitable day closer, which only increased Jazzy's anxiety. His initial drive to do what must be done, settled and certain, gave way to panic as he realised that even if he did not always feel the need, the show must go on (he increasingly thought in these euphemisms) for the sake of honour, self-respect, freedom and the future etc. Enjoying natural advantages meant that he would have to do better than copy plots straight out of *Columbo*, *Magnum* or *Miss Marple*, as no murderer had ever made it out of those reels without a police escort. Thuggery and violence, despite his hair-trigger temper, had never come naturally to him, and he suspected he would not be able to go through with an act that physically hurt Petula, in cold blood, especially if he looked her in the eye first and did not kill her straight out. The end would have to be swift, sudden and instantly conclusive. That ruled out Spider's suggestion, which owed a liberal debt to an episode of *Crimewatch* they had sat through stoned – a 'break-in' where a husband smothered his wife in her sleep under the guise of a burglary, so as to deflect police suspicion from an 'inside' job. Spider suggested Jazzy do likewise, entering through a top-floor window and stealing stuff to do full justice to the approach, whilst deflecting the finger of suspicion toward the criminal communities of Kingston-upon-Hull by 'leaving' a torn shard of a Hull City strip at the crime scene. So far as Jazzy knew no one suspected he wanted to kill his mother, so there was no suspicion to divert, and the logistical drama of smashing into a house that remained unlocked twenty-four-seven was not only unnecessarily risky, but the sort of thing only a moron would try. He did not say this to Spider, preferring to move the conversation to what he had come to think of as the 'mechanical' model.

If he were to fix the relevant parts in one of Petula's cars, which were death traps from the minute she got into them drunk on the best of nights, he would be saved from having to lay a hand on her, or witness the final smash, skid or splat. But here Jazzy remembered a book he had long ago taken to heart, *Crime and Punishment*, and the dangers of unintended consequences, namely, additional deaths that followed from the justified first. One began by putting to death the king, and ended with the head of a Danton. A car going out of control, even on the farm, might take bystanders with it, and he wanted no one's blood on his hands apart from Petula's, who he had come to see as practically responsible for her own death. This still left him with the easiest and most ignoble route of all: a firm push down the stairs. Like a car crash, a fall was a very plausible way for Petula to die all of herself, without the subject of murder being so much as raised by the coroner. His mother's legs had long lost all suppleness, and the injury at Regan's party made it impossible for her to bend her right one at all. Yet she still stumbled about in all directions drunk, scaling the steps, often by crawling, to get to her bedroom, with no thought or idea of where she was. And the getting-down, if anything, was even more perilous. One evening Jazzy had found himself at the top of the steps watching her spend the better part of twenty minutes trying to get up, comatose and completely unaware of his presence, The Heights having so many means of entry and exit that it was impossible for even a vigilant person to keep tabs on who was coming in or going out. With just the gentlest of taps, she would have gone bowling back down, breaking her neck at the bottom, waiting there for him to find her in the morning, horrified but with an all-too-plausible explanation at hand. Who wouldn't have seen it coming, once the unfortunate facts surrounding her incipient alcoholism were made more known?

Yet he did not feel *ready* for it, for in truth he still wanted time to talk to people, to bring it up in the pub, canvass opinion, and go home and have another long think about the transvaluation of all values, if not quite in those terms or that order. But what was there to think about when he already had the perfect motive matched by the ideal opportunity? It was exhausting, and to his biting disappointment he watched himself sink into the familiar cycle of tearing at the bit before hiding behind it, wanting to throw off his shackles then ask for them back, and swim intrepidly towards the light, in the hope that someone else would draw the curtains and prevent him before it was too late. Could it be that, like a long-colonised and oppressed people, he was not ready for the freedom he had for so long sought?

Disgust at what filled his mind, minute by minute, made him unusually self-critical. He did not want to admit to himself that he had become warped, mean, nasty or weird, though he could not ignore the fact that he was at the very least sick. Only part of anyone's life was about what they did; Jazzy understood that the better bit of it was to do with the qualities brought out by the endeavour, and how a person engaged with and developed these findings. Plotting the death of a family member endowed him with a shiftiness and a reflex to apologise for anything he could, be it treading on an ant or closing a door too decisively, lamentable and ascendant character traits he hoped he would be rid of once it was all over. Petula, meanwhile, incorrectly read her son's nervousness as a confused desire to apologise to her, and ask for forgiveness for being such an ungrateful shit. Her assumption, loudly broadcast in his hearing, sealed her fate – Jazzy's pride shredded by Petula telling Spider that he must man up and admit that his treatment of her had been negligent, immature and churlish: he would not find her too grand to accept his apology, so long as it was heartfelt and repeated every few weeks. Jazzy was stung in every place he could hurt; Spider looked to him as her protector and provider, and, more than anyone, believed in his ability to be more than he was. Naturally he was terrified that his indecision would destroy that, exposing him as a waffling bigmouth who lacked the ruthlessness to do as he said. In this he was most mistaken; Spider was much too kind to push and hold him to his threat as Jill might have, or judge him in any way at all, not really caring whether he killed his mother or not, so long as he was happy. As in the case of so many others, she connived in Jazzy's infantilisation, which, like his wearing shorts in winter, reinforced his image as the eternal man-boy, who like a child learning in the fear and thrall of not knowing, would never sacrifice naivety for the corrupt wisdom that would bring success. Under his salt-of-the-earth mask lay all the twisted bitterness a life could endow one with – and it was his acceptance of this lifelong deception, along with Petula's last insult, that endowed Jazzy with the strength to act, since if he could hide something so large as his true existence behind two dimensions, then he could get away with anything, even murder. He would do it: he had to before she said anything else; he *had* to.

Petula, of course, did not make it any harder for him by being nice, quite the opposite, and as the familiar cycle of rages, tepid conciliation and amnesia resumed, Jazzy noticed that he had started to observe her as a person who would no longer always be there. He *really* was going to do it. If he was a child, then his mother was a baby who did not know what she stood to lose by losing her life, in her arrogance believing there were people without whom things would not be the same, and others without whom there would be nothing at all, identifying with the latter. As such she denied death, and life for anyone else after her death, while he understood both as no more than time moving in a forward direction; individuals aged to keep abreast of life, then died to give it its due. Jazzy would be the spoke and enforcer of the great wheel of being. All roads led back to this: loving and being loved were at the heart of his well-earned existence – the house was wasted on meaningless dinner parties and gatherings, it would be different when it was his, the grounds thrown open for international seminars on orphans and land-mines, prosthetic limbs and malarial vaccines, humanity not society being the new final frontier. Jazzy gave himself until the end of the week, the month at most, and no longer. Then he would act: he had to!

Jazzy had been pondering this sort of tomorrow, when he noticed a letter that must have been shuffled under the door without his noticing. He left his joint burning on the ashtray, a giant glass hand he had swapped a box of his creatures for at a recent craft fair, and slowly rose. His face felt parched and pulled and he had no idea how long he had been sat there exploring what kind of world would be built in Petula's absence. It was a dream he fell into so often these days that it perforated all he did. The house was empty and the children and their rescue pups were out, which may not have been the case when he first sat down, whenever that had been. As he never tired of saying, the dope was getting stronger these days, and if you weren't careful, it was hard to know where you were with it. He watched the letter and giggled nervously – the writing on the card was Petula's and he was reluctant to touch it for fear of being cursed, the existence of the supernatural seeming more likely to him now than ever before.

At length he picked it up. It was an invite, an expensively pro-duced card, decorated with a herd of Rackham-like gnarly goats, asking him and Spider and the children, not individually named, to 'Sunday Family Lunch'. It was now Saturday, the lunch only a day away; what was going on? Jazzy's first thought was that they must be making up numbers, the initial choices having not replied or pulled out – Petula had certainly been complaining of something of the kind, citing ingrates and fly-by-nights. Otherwise he was stumped. His brood had never been invited en masse to the house for a formal meal before, usually eating leftovers in her kitchen on a Sunday night, when the scraps were dumped outside their front door, wrapped in tinfoil like a takeaway order. Any talk of them being part of any family was absurd. Petula's snubs, though not unwelcome (Jazzy hated dinner parties), played a reliable role in his tirades against her, and unless she was trying to make amends, it was impossible to see what she was playing at here. But perhaps that *was* what she was playing at; a last-minute attempt at redemption, or possibly a trap of a subtle kind, which could end in a fatal softening of his resolve? It was a thought that had always haunted him, that his mother could actually read his mind, and always, even as he plotted her demise, knew what was afoot.

Feeling ill, an indigestive flame lighting in his gut, Jazzy pulled open the front door and stepped outside for air. The full weight of his thinking was a difficult thing to move from one subject to the next, and he was frightened some kinesis had occurred in the Montague universe without his noticing. The wind had picked up and was howling down the chimney, as if a squad of gargoyles had flown off the battlements of Notre Dame and nested in the brickwork, slamming the front door shut like a slap across the back of his neck. Where had he put the spare keys? Jazzy stumbled down on all fours and was checking under a crumbling brick surrounded by weeds, with a view to try the watering-can next, when he noticed a car snaking its way up the drive, slowing at the bends in a way most unlike Petula.

Inside the new BMW Regan was adrift in a trance; a discombobulation of memories and meanings, most commonly experienced when falling asleep, meant her drive up from London was a sublime and sometimes hallucinatory experience, a letter dated a fortnight earlier from Mingus, that she had not the courage to open, stuffed in the glove compartment. The pressure of the easterly wind was pounding away against her little car, steering the vehicle towards the wild grassy verges, bringing her back to herself enough to spy a mystifying configuration. The paddock in which Caligula, the farm donkey, had been kept, before overdosing and expiring on a bunch of grapes some lout had fed her, was flanked by four figures in black, who had entered into it, and were advancing menacingly towards her. Pausing in unison by the new fence Jazzy had put up running parallel to the existing one, presumably to forestall Caligula coming back from the dead and kicking her way out to freedom, the figures looked up at Regan and signalled at her to watch. Then, forming a line, they each took hold of the fence with both hands, as if it were a rail that would protect them from the elements, the wind having grown ever stronger, burrowing under their clothes and peeling back their hair. They were prudent to, as no sooner had they aligned in a chain, then the gale tore into them with a new ferocity, lifting their feet and entire bodies off the ground so that all four were holding on for what seemed like dear life, the storm pummelling and blowing them about like Lowry figures in a painting by Chagall. Presently Regan could make out who they were, their heads cast backwards so she heard their upside-down screams and laughter. Herself, though younger; her mother, the same; Evita as she had never seen her; and Jazzy as he always was.

On the tempest blew, throwing them skywards like a tiger that had got hold of a box of dolls, or laundry about to be unpegged and irretrievably lost, without their once losing their grip and being carried away. Regan could tell it was a contest, who would let go first? But wouldn't it, as the ferment tore the clothes off their backs, be a relief to let go and fly? And then she saw herself cut loose, flung up into the eye of the storm, far past the black clouds, through to the stillness that lay behind them, and the others too, disappearing one by one after her, into the dark hole, until the storm subsided, and it was as if they never were.

Regan's car came off the track and thudded to a juddering halt, stalling just short of the first post, marking the start of the fence. Revving in fright, she reversed skittishly back on to the track, and set off again towards the house. To her alarm she saw

Jazzy once more, this time in his C&A dressing gown standing outside his house looking puzzled, a key dangling stupidly from what looked like a dog chain in his hand, and, making sure it was him by yelling her own name at the top of her voice, she slowed down and unwound her window to ask him, still yelling, if he was okay. There was a lack of preparation on both their faces. Regan never normally did this, Jazzy never normally replied, she never normally went into his house for a cup of tea, he never normally asked her, but all of this happened, and once inside, they sat inches away from disclosure, their mugs nearly touching, wondering who would start first.

Regan had much difficulty in taking to and accepting her surroundings; how could a member of her family live like this? It was little wonder that she and Petula had dubbed it 'The Pimple'; and that was without even being able to see in. The hurricane outside looked to have done an effective job on the interior of the bungalow too; plastic toys, mainly broken, local newspapers and bottles and plates of every kind were strewn about as though Godzilla had progressed through the habitation on his way to Tokyo. Elsewhere there was little by way of permanent ornamentation; a provisional quality to what little furniture spotted the place, contingent on whether it would still be needed tomorrow, when the next tsunami struck. Despite the overall smallness of the living area, what space there was was mismanaged; Regan noticed slightly-too-wide gaps between the television set and a large plant pot hosting a dead mangrove; a splintered magazine rack rammed with sleeveless records; and a pair of sofas collapsed so low she assumed they had been used as props in a 'Strongest Man In The World' contest, competitors doubtless awarded points for hurling themselves on the cushions until they split and the springs broke. The shabbiness of the layout was compounded by a mysterious chalky dust covering the floor, its fine particles as curled as wood shavings, which Regan was afraid she would breathe in, and be poisoned by at a later date.

Making a great play of wiping her nose, Regan sniffed her tea, able to detect cow's milk, which she believed she was allergic to, and sugar, which she could not stand. To drink the mixture, an anthropological imperative if she was to be inducted into this surly tribe, would be radically unpleasant, but refusal, confirmation that she was as shallow as Jazzy's caricature of her. The mug was also chipped, which was unsurprising as the kitchen seemed, like the bungalow itself, to be an abandoned work-in-progress. Half of the open-plan worktop area was painted a copper colour, the other half begun in a selection of blues, with no single paint winning overall control of the wall that was unfinished round the edges and sides – the job stopping well short of the ceiling at about Jazzy's shoulder-height. The colours reminded Regan of ones used in the main house, which is where the pots were most likely salvaged from, as did several other items: a wooden lavatory seat in the hallway waiting to be installed, a lonely drawing of a wild boar that had once hung in their playroom, some white goods and, lying where the children could get at them, a bronze hammer, spade and tongs that used to rest by Petula's fireplace. The impression these miscellaneous items exuded was of a haul of booty abandoned by fugitives who were in such a hurry to get away, they had forgotten to cover their tracks, and now evinced no shame in discovery. Was that, she wondered, how these people saw themselves and their home? And why bother giving the house a stupid Celtic title, if you were going to fill it full of Yorkshire crap?

Having spoken to Spider only twice, to ask her on the first occasion who she was, and on the second occasion the same question, not knowing one child of hers from the next, Regan guessed that their view of the place was closer to Jazzy's functional approach than the compact love-nest Jill had wasted her twenties trying to create; which was probably when she last entered this place, though as Regan recalled, it had seemed relatively crummy to her then too. Anyway, she had not missed much in the interim. It was much worse now, the walls smelling of the grim aftertaste of a garage sandwich, and the fetid stench of dog and man too closely entwined, lingering like a sneering challenge to her priggery. As for her brother, he looked no livelier than his cave dwelling: dematerialising hair, hard-done-by frown lines, and an unhealthy distribution of bumps and nicks, whether spots, shaving cuts, boils or signs of scurvy, she dare not ask. His broken and bent body spoke of hard work that had not made him stronger, and long hours outdoors where the elements had kept him company without sparing him any of their reputed benefits. Touched with guilt, Regan tried to avoid her brother's baby-brown eyes, helpfully facilitated by him having no wish to catch hers, and tried to picture the last time they had meaningfully engaged, without history being invoked in every alternate sentence.

She found that she could remember having seen and enjoyed virtually nothing of Jazzy for years, their lives entirely separate, if often unravelling only yards apart. The snag was that even in his absence, Jazzy was always in the air, no further than the other side of a wall or fence, repeating his droning tale of victimhood, a version of their history recited like an article of faith, whenever she was unwise enough to inquire after his health. Jazzy had his favourite incidents, and comparisons aplenty to call on: birthday treats she'd had that he hadn't, Christmas presents, holidays, new cars and a dead father, all brought out as examples of unfair treatment and parental discrimination. His upshot was always the same: his life was terrible because he laboured and strived for nothing while she, the favourite, got everything for doing nothing. The creation narrative had begun as soon as she reached her teens, first as friendly chiding, but later as an accusation, soiling her former fond regard, and before that respect, and even earlier, love-like emotions toward him. Regan had practised what she thought of as unconditional love, a concept that tripped off her adolescent imagination, remaining unconditional only up to his last chance, fourteen years before. The setting and content were unexceptional, the difference being the complacency with which Jazzy made his claims, and his ability to conduct hurt like an orchestra that would play for him alone. Jazzy had drunkenly let rip at her for being a spoilt brat and little madam in front of the new Archbishop, a personage whom she had wanted to impress with her goodness, and from that night on she had stopped trying. Time and other things to do had taken care of the rest, and now they were strangers, rapprochement too great an ordeal for either to submit to.

Regan was not the only one of Petula's children to have inherited her mother's passion for judgement. Jazzy noticed and did not care about the critical eye now cast by his sister; he would have expected nothing less from the stuck-up cow. Regan looked ill and lustreless to him. It was perfectly clear that she would like him better if he kept a clean house, bleached the bath, lasered off his tattoos and cleaned his teeth twice a day, and thus conformed to her spotless view of existence, with the germs being washed out along with the passion, spontaneity and laughter. Despite his life not exactly being awash with these things, Jazzy accepted their importance in principle, and refused to be intimidated by what he saw as 'the sisters' shared value system, which if anything manifested itself more deeply in Regan than in their mother. Regan's white skin reminded him of pristine sheets wrapped too tightly round a hard mattress, and he found it impossible to rule out a vampire latching itself to her, drinking six pints of strawberry jam before leaving the anaemic host to disgrace humanity until the next and final feed. Granted, Regan's beauty was still technically present, prim and precise, which did annoy him a bit as it pointed to the life of ease and luxury she indulged in – waxing, bath salts and what-not – but it was obvious that the spark was all but smothered. His sister was in no condition to take advantage of her advantages, as in spite of her impeccable clothing, the lemony smell emanating from behind her ears, and the fact he had still never heard her fart, she belonged in a sealed box, a doll the children would never play with. Enjoying his heady condescension, Jazzy took wary note of the dangers of relaxing around his foe. Regan had a way of drawing attention to the tolerance of her posture; the magnanimity of her sitting there with him and acknowledging a subspecies she was sometimes confused with. Her natural superiority, in essence her mother in her, held him off barrelling in hastily and going too far to be pulled back. As a consequence, Regan knew she would have to be the first to speak.

'This is cosy. It looks like you've been busy with stuff since I was last over. That's new,' she said, pointing to a Rothko print that she had last seen hung over her bed as a teenager, 'it looks really good there, with those different colours behind it.' Regan was nervous and needed her brother's help, not only to keep on talking but also to find out why she had come.

Jazzy raised an eyebrow with ironical deliberation and, lifting his chin, addressed someone who wasn't there, far at the back of the room. 'You know, the usual, no time to do anything, I've way too many jobs on, right, and way too little time to do them. I'm basically, right, on a hundred-and-seventy-two-hour week, fifty-hour day, and when I get back I have to get stuck straight into all this shit with the house. Never-ending madness, it is. You know, I'm working so hard at it, everything is so full-on I don't even know what I have done or haven't, and there's taxes and bills to sort out at the end of the day too. There's no one else to do it but *me*. I can't see the beginning or the end; it's madness.' Here Jazzy was telling the truth; he really was unable to remember where one train of thought began or what separated it from the next, which day or month they were related to, or what he was supposed to be doing when he walked out of the door in the morning, hoping rather that his work would come and find him. Haziness about everything except killing Petula, which, when done, would lift the fog and put the sun in the sky, was the order of his life. Suddenly he saw that he wanted to tell Regan about it, about this latest project that would alter her life as much as his. Was he mad? Or did he, having every reason to not go down this path, sense she would understand somehow?

Regan felt she had blundered onto the wrong track, allowing Jazzy to settle comfortably into his favoured role of the exhausted workhorse, and reel out his song of labour and woe, which was not why she had agreed to his invitation. She needed him to understand that they both must risk being open with one another, or else everything would carry on like this until they were dead.

'Shit. That doesn't sound too bright.'

'Yeah,' he continued resignedly, 'London might be booming but we see nowt of it up here, right, nothing trickles up you know, none of the brass. Here it's swings and roundabouts, one day forward two days back. It's just the way it goes for the working man, always was, always is, you know, mines shutting, shit prospects, you can see why folk go mad.' He was talking such rubbish that he hoped she wasn't listening; this conversation was making him nervous, where was he going with it? '...Yeah, shit happens and you get desperate, you know what I mean? You run out of options,' he added obliquely, 'so desperate you could see yourself doing anything to get some food on the plate, you know, to have your hope back again. To give yourself something to look forward to so you can look past all the shit and all the crap, yeah? It's been desperate. *I've* been desperate to tell the truth. Yeah, there it is.'

Had she heard something else just then? Another book waiting to be read? Regan intuited that Jazzy's heart was not in his standard litany this time, she had got him going down the old paths but he did not seem to want to go. 'I'm sorry to hear that,' she said, 'that things haven't got easier for you with time.'

'Yeah? Well so am I. So yeah, work, you know how it is, phone ringing all the time. And ever since I got that e-mail thingy, I

don't even know what half the things on the bloody computer
are for, to be brutally honest, it's been even worse. Mum uses it
all the time, fucking e-mails, I mean, Jesus, is there a technology she doesn't abuse? And the weather's just about to turn,
another fucking winter in this place with the boiler packing in
all the time... It's alright for her up there but down here, *shit*.
Everything is shit basically. Like the Tories get into power every
morning.'

'How is she?' Regan had dropped the bomb deliberately. In
the past to simply raise the subject of their mother was to invite
criticism of herself.

'She's worse than ever,' Jazzy replied sharply, and waited for
her reaction. His sister could always be relied upon to strenu-
ously defend Petula, lecturing him on how he should take better
care of her, and afford her every allowance, as she had built The
Heights in seven days and created them out of clay. His rebuke
that it was *he* who did the work, Regan knowing nothing as she
used the place as a holiday home and shag pad, had never cut
any ice. No matter how passionately he tried to set her straight,
he was always met with the same curt dismissal, followed by
the infuriating shrugging of the shoulders and yuppie neolo-
gisms like 'Deal with it,' or even worse, 'Get over it.' It had been
years since they last fought like that, there was no benefit, he
despaired of her ever seeing the light; hers was a mind that could
not be entered and tampered with, her faults and strengths too
crisscrossed and complicated to unpick. In theory, Jazzy had
always liked to believe that he was forgiving enough to allow for
a new chapter in their relationship, but only if Regan instigated
it herself through a genuine change of heart. Could that be what
was happening now?

'Really. That bad?' Regan had stopped pretending to drink her
tea and was batting her lids like an impatient lover who could
not believe the beloved had not got the message yet.

Jazzy sat bolt upright and looked at her askance. 'You *what*?

Did you hear what I just *said*? I was slagging off Mum, right? I'm saying she's *worse*-than-*ever*, got me?'

'Yes. And I said is she that bad. Worse than ever, according to you. Yes, I've got you.'

'Yeah, that's right,' said Jazzy, still not really believing what he was hearing. Regan was calm, showing no signs of tensing up for a fight.

'This is Mum I am talking about Regan, your best mate, I mean you and her, it's like Batman and Robin, "the sisters", right?'

Regan spoke over his insult: 'That must be pretty bad then. If she's worse than normal.'

'Well, knowing how you two cosy up, it's kind of surprising to hear you say that. I mean, you letting me talk the truth for once and not contradicting me.'

'But you think so, don't you? That she's entered a new phase.'

'Yeah, much worse is what I'm saying.'

'How much worse?'

'Plenty and in every way. Just the other day, she basically just came out and said she hated me over an argument about cheese, and then before that, Christ, I'd basically helped her into...'

'Go on. Please, I'm listening.'

Jazzy paused. Was it time to consult the natural suspicion that his sister's line of questioning was a set-up, she having been sent by Petula to sound him out and ensnare a full confession, which would lead to his arrest and ultimate imprisonment? History would say yes, yet he squashed the possibility with the briefest glance at her earnestly pained face. He was as certain as life exists that his sister was sincere, and her worried eyes, naked before caution, wanted him to know it. Let the ground break his fall; he believed her.

'Yeah, that's right, forget the specifics, she's worse in every way, so bad so you wouldn't believe. I've seen her at her worst before, don't get me wrong, had stuff done to me by her you wouldn't even know about, right, but this, how she's been...

I know her inside-out, is what I am saying, but what she's turning into, it's nothing like before. I mean it is, she's still the same in a way, but amplified, taken to a hundred and ten, you understand? Totally a different level. It's been hell, hell I tell you, to be near her when she lets go. Some of the things she's said about me, Spider, the kids, my Dad, even Jill and Evita, it's *horrible*.'

Regan nodded.

'Jesus, the stuff that's gone down, boozing and hating, she's become so, well, evil really. There are times when I go in and she just starts screaming at me and it's like she doesn't even know she's doing it, like she's possessed by something...'

'Her anger?'

'No, by something else, like some kind of monster's in charge. And I can't stand it. I can't bear being there hearing it.'

'You never could though. Stand it.'

'I *did* though, didn't I? I'm still here. But what I stood before wasn't this. She's got a different way about her. An evil way with her, her manner, it's so fucking dark.'

'I know she can be... nasty. I've had it happen to me too.'

'More than that, she always had it in her to be sadistic, that's all happened before, but this is new, she's pushed me over the edge, you know, beyond my limits. I'm over them now. I've never been here before, you understand, she's pushed me somewhere else.'

Jazzy felt the beginnings of tears push through, the frustration shoving them forward, 'I can't fight her in small ways anymore. If we can't *finish it*, then it's not worth doing,' he heard himself say, adding, 'we've got to finish this thing. Otherwise I can't stay in one piece anymore.'

'I think I understand,' said Regan, offering him her hand, 'I feel the same way, coming up here, not knowing why, wondering whether I ever knew why. I don't expect anything from her now, not niceness, kindness, honesty to me or to herself. I don't know what's happened to her...'

'Nothing, like I say, she's always had it in her.'

'I don't want to believe that. She's been through too much and it's changing her, I think she's going mad. She's become ill. She's even got me trying to organise her parties for her. Regan pointed at the table where Jazzy's invite lay, 'I had those printed. I don't think she can even cope with her obsessions anymore.'

'What's she ever gone through or had to cope with? Come on! She lives in paradise, does what she likes, goes where she wants, and has never had to worry or want for a thing.'

'But you yourself said she's getting worse. Let's not go back to arguing like we always have, I'm tired of that.'

'Me too, I've had my fill of it, I don't want to end up like her. And you're right in a manner, you and me, we both are. She is cracking up alright, you know, toddling round without her clothes on half-cut, off her head shouting at trees, and she's had the front gate clean off twice this year. And meaner than ever. But what's coming out, right, it isn't some disease she's contracted on holiday, it's just more of what was there already. All she's done is she's gone and lost her balance. Her intensities are out of control.'

'How do you mean?'

Jazzy pulled out his rolling apparatus enthusiastically, flattered that he had an audience for his thoughts. 'Right, the way I see it, right, is to not be mad, to be balanced, all your proportions have to be very nicely adjusted to each other. But if any one part thinks it can make the journey on its own without the others' help, it'll destroy the balance your sanity requires,' he tapped his head intently. 'Madness, like you think of it being, that's in most of us all the time, but we check it all the time to stop it getting out of hand, yeah? But Mum can't anymore, because she just doesn't want to. And because something else has got into her. She's being guided by a bad spirit.'

'What, like a ghost or a devil?'

'That's what I think after I've been at this stuff,' he said, pointing at his drug tin, 'some unhappy demon that's recognised a kindred spirit in her and is taking her over the edge with it. But,' he carried on, not wanting to alienate his new partner with too much metaphysics, 'you don't have to dig that deep to see Mum's not in control anymore. She's dangerous, to herself and us. What she did to Evita, driving her mad and away, the same's happening to me. And maybe even to you now, yeah? We can't do nothing. We can't. We have to be, right, like, *resolute* from now on. We have to take our turn to be in *charge*.'

'It's true,' said Regan, impassive, 'you sound a bit like her yourself, and why shouldn't you? I mean it as a compliment. She's always summing things up, isn't she, leading us from crisis to crisis that only she can save us from.'

'There's nothing that can stop her from carrying on like this forever unless we do something! I mean it Regan. I've thought and thought about this so much, non-stop. There is more going on in my head than there used to be, and I tell you, I keep coming back to the same thing. She's got to *go*.'

'Leave here? Me too, what's going on here has got to stop, I don't think I can last another meal myself.' Regan took another sniff of her tea, tepid, cloudy and cold now. 'If you've got any herbal, poof's tea to you, I'll have some. Otherwise could I have some hot water?'

Jazzy got up eagerly and, throwing open a cupboard, began to rummage with endearing concern, his sister metamorphosing from threat to ally, a comrade whom he would gladly protect under the threat of torture, and would be glad of a chance to prove it. His loyalties were fanatical, triggered by a surplus of care that a life of conflict had deprived him of the opportunity to share, his devotion driven by a need born of rejection that he confused with principle, the prospect of joining forces with Regan exhilaratingly liberating.

'Here, 'alf a mo'. You'll like this.'

Regan accepted the mug of microwaved fruit squash humbly, pretending to not notice the caffeine-lined rim of the Steam Fair souvenir cup. A doubt had been removed, a sceptical voice she did not hear anymore gone, and the blankness, which was simply the fear of admitting to what was what, had been filled in.

'It's so *awful*,' she said, 'because I don't know what to do about it anymore. Before I could make a hint, or stay silent, there was always a way of making Mum see herself and compromise, so if she pushed I could push back. I wasn't helpless.'

'Yeah, she understood that she could only push so far before she broke you.'

'Exactly. She did, instinctively, she had a political head like that. But I feel absolutely hopeless now, nothing I say to her works, I can't reason with her or appeal to common sense, she makes it up as she goes along. And I don't have a method or way to protect myself to keep her off me anymore. I've tried every option, being respectful, keeping my distance, and when that didn't work, being here all the time if she asks me, taking her into my confidence, even standing up for myself, but nothing makes any difference. She's too much, too much for me.'

'For sure.'

'It's only the truth. And I sit there, knowing that everything she is saying and doing, none of it's true, it's all wrong, it's all false, it's destroying her and I know that there is absolutely nothing I can do to stop it, that to try to is impossible. And then I find that I don't even have the energy to agree, even though I know disagreeing is pointless. So I'm just sort of there and not there. It's horrible, like I'm dying. It's killing me Jazzy. And she doesn't stop. The demands go on and on. I don't want to daughter as she mothered anymore.'

Regan's eyes, even when they were happy, had always looked as though they could see something sad, and for the first time Jazzy truly pitied her, the anointed one and heir to an unhappiness purer and less cluttered than his own. 'It's all survival techniques, it's alright if you think they make a difference and that things will slowly get better, but we know better than that.

Seriously Regan, you might not think it, right, but I've tried everything myself. Like you. And *nothing* works and *nothing* will change. Or if it does change, it'll change only to get even worse. We're nearly old. Our time is passing by and we've got to do something, right, before it's too late for us. This shit is urgent, no lie.'

'It's like there's this process going on,' said Regan, 'a kind of movement where everything's going faster and faster and I just know that it will all end terribly unless we can stop it somehow...'

'We can't. We're marked, all of us, and we can't get out of it. That terrible thing you mention, we either do it or we wait for it to happen to us. Do you know what I am saying?'

Regan knew what Jazzy meant but did not feel ready to speak of it yet. Instead she stood up, and he taking his cue did the same, locking in a mutual embrace, Jazzy welling up and sobbing and stopping himself and then allowing it all out again, hoping that the kids didn't barge in with the puppies as he'd have trouble explaining this one to them; Regan allowing herself to be squashed and held close, the charge of emotion agreeable and intense, if somewhat empty. She was still ice-queen enough to see that their new bond was as attributable to their mother as their old division had been, though she knew it would be a while before her brother recognised this.

'We've played her game you know,' said Jazzy, rubbing his eyes and reaching into his pocket for a lighter, 'you know, allowed ourselves to be played off against each other, letting it happen, baying for each other's blood when we should have, you know, not have let her take advantage.'

Of your natural jealously for me, Regan wanted to add, opting for the less contentious, 'I know, she doesn't mind people hating each other if it furthers her objectives, they're always free to make up later if they want. I used to think she did it by mistake but...' Regan went quiet, she had never talked about her mother like this before, but as with everything else in this exchange, her part had already been written for her, the lines simply waiting for her to realise they were there. 'Look, I don't want to just stand here and bitch her off, and then have everything go back to how it was. Let's be clear, I think I do know what you mean, what you're implying, and it isn't that she move to a new house, is it? Have you given it, you know, this thing, a lot of thought? I mean like plan what you're going to do, not just *whether* you can do it?'

'Yeah, a lot. What about you, have you?'

'Idly, not seriously, but only because I don't dare really think about it like something that I could actually do, only as sort of hypothetical dream that I want to happen. But I guess I have, yes, you know, slip something into a drink, fiddle about with her medication, I feel crazy enough to. Completely unhinged, to tell you the truth.'

'Tell me about it, you'd have to be to get into the right zone. But could you, you know, could you do it yourself. If you had to?'

'I don't know, no, not when I think about it like this, speaking normally about it. But since I came back from New York, I find that every time I think of her the only way I can stand the thought is by knowing she's going to die someday. I mean her death, it's both a surrender and an attack if you see what I mean? Oh shit, this isn't right...' Regan clutched her head.

'Are you okay?'

'No, no of course *not*! Think of what we're saying here Jasper, how could I be alright? Half of me doesn't even know what I'm talking about...' Regan sat down, lest she fall, a phalanx of nausea closing in on her, 'this is just...too crazy. I can't believe it is happening, I'm so tired, I haven't slept properly, I don't know, for literally months and months... Are we for *real*?'

Jazzy ceremoniously lifted his finger to his lips. 'Not another word, you've suffered enough, let me take this on right? I'm going to take care of it all. And look after us.'

Regan gazed up at her brother, stood over her with the murderous assurance of an underworld enforcer, and sensed his crazed excitement. And she did, she had to admit to feeling strangely safe, the wind having grown calmer, moving over the yellow stubble of the fields in gentle strokes, the howling in the chimney place now an uninhabited whispering.

'How?'

'Never you mind.'

'You're serious?'

Jazzy nodded solemnly.

'Oh.'

'Good, and not a word to anyone mind, we're into something here and...'

'I know,' Regan replied, hurrying to condemn them to a queer fate that she had no desire to understand too quickly, witness, face or explain to anyone else.

'Perfecto. Then we *get* each other then. That's the thing.'

Outside, her car looked out of place, parked where no car of hers had ever stopped before, the chrome chirruping of a jackdaw reminding her of an earlier time when she and Petula had walked down to the cottage and laughed at how ugly it was, waiting to see if their provocative cackles would draw Jazzy out into one of his amusing tirades that Petula enjoyed, and Regan secretly feared. Jazzy was no more to her than he had been when she first entered his house an hour earlier; had any of it been any more than an abrupt dream? She shuddered all over, she could see her mother's disappointed face over the dining table; you could only change sides so many times in this life: the enemy of her enemy was still her enemy; what had she *done*?

CHAPTER FOURTEEN,
late and later.

The sun had already started to stamp its way through the thin quilt of low-hanging cloud; there was not another moment for Jazzy to lose, he had spent the night awake floating on his sweat for this, sometimes thinking he had fallen asleep and experienced the relief of having done it, electric currents producing images of his face as a hammer and Petula's as the skull, the weapon chasing the object round his workshop; her screams, his tears, his screams and her tears, phantasmic companions until the alarm went and Spider, shivering in her nylon gown, winter's nip now in the air, dragged the first of the kids out of bed for school. The night before, Jazzy had calculated that it was impossible for him to remain conscious for an entire day and hold his nerve intact until nightfall, there had to be the break of sleep, or some approximation of it, so that the resolve he woke with would translate seamlessly and quickly into the deed. Little could be less suspicious than an accident in broad daylight, and with Regan in the house, who in unfeigned shock would be the one to stumble upon the corpse, he had gained a perfect and half-knowing foil. Her visit the previous afternoon was the sign he had been waiting for; his adult life had up until then been an ultimatum torn up in his face, the paper stuck to his blushing cheeks: today was the beginning of the new calendar.

Jazzy reached for the ashtray and lit the joint, a pair of crumbled Es rolled in with the baccy and skunk, a raver's rum ration. It would be just the one spliff this morning; one last compressed session of doubt, buoyed by hesitancy, blind terror, and then out the other end to life everlasting. Was it Petula he wanted to stop or the fear he felt whenever he opened his front door and skulked into the world? It wasn't too late to step off the carousel, and let the ride go on without him; he could move to another country and take the kids and Spider with him – they would always make ends meet somehow, other people did, the world was enormous and Petula would be left behind, an unreal memory that they might sometimes even look back and laugh at. Jazzy attempted to visualise where they would go, and had got as far as a couple of swings and a barn before he saw that his vision was a memory of The Heights of his childhood. He was utterly held by the place. The move would never happen, nor the laughter or looking back in mock tranquillity; he would always know that she had beaten him, and of what he could have achieved had he only the guts to stay and finish it. The fear would still be there, a killer of a different kind, living alongside him till the end of days. He had not invented this, there really were no other options or exits, and if he had not been such a good person in the first place, he would not have wasted weeks tormenting himself with ways of saving her. This was his day, the hour of the Anycock, vengeance most *justified*! He stabbed the joint out, having consumed it in four systematic inhalations, a killer whale catching its breath before going underwater again, and rolled out of bed onto the cold tiled floor. The pile of clothes he had prepared the night before, folded up on the rickety stool that doubled as something to sit on when his clothes weren't on it, lay in a bold pile; a suit of armour for the battle ahead. With the automatically repressed sensation that this might be the last thing he did with his life, Jazzy dressed, a rolled-up balaclava sat atop his head like a beanie cap going on first; next his thick walking socks and tight trunks that clung to his thighs like cycling shorts, which Spider preferred to the candy-striped boxers that made stalks of his legs, then beige combat trousers, army surplus boots, a Mickey Mouse vest (worn for luck) and donkey jacket, given to him by a veteran of the Battle of Orgreave. He was ready now, and checking his

menacing reflection in the mirror, Jazzy judged himself a suitable candidate for a coffin-bearer at an Irish Republican Army
funeral. The analogy was fitting. Movements with unrealisable
political goals gradually degenerated into criminality, obeying
a law of entropy, but in his refusal to accept he was a gangland
assassin, or idealist chasing the impossible, rather a freedom
fighter on his home turf struggling for national liberation, Jazzy
saw redemption; war called for a different kind of seriousness
to peace, for a warrior who understood that the freedom of his
people came at a blood price. By the time he had laced his boots,
his head filled with visions of himself besieging Troy, javelin in
hand, Jazzy could not have felt any better, deciding to skip kippers and porridge lest he offset his E-rush.

Clambering out of the bedroom window, somewhat unnecessarily, already completely free of his reason, Jazzy bound up the
hill, vaulting over the fence, so as to approach The Heights from
the fields and make his way round the back, a guerrilla who knew
his own land better than any invader, the frantic thrill of imaginary bullets whistling past his ears accompanying his galloping
drug-high. Crossing yet another fence, which to his annoyance
he saw he had coated in a thin line of razor-wire, dumped in the
woods by a military contractor, Jazzy felt the slack of his trousers catch and rip, wrong-footing his jump, so that he landed on
one leg turning his ankle. Grimacing in agony, but back on both
feet in an instant, Jazzy chuckled at the extent to which he still
lived in fantasy as a reflex pleasure; an embarrassing reminder
of all he was not in actual fact, his situation never so heroic as
he desired. He was a forty-four year-old would-be-murderer on a
desolate hillside in North Yorkshire with his arse hanging out of
his pants, not Che Guevara in a Bolivian Jungle leading grateful
Indians to El Dorado, but fortunately the drugs were too powerful for this to make a marked difference to his mood. The chem-
icals were throwing up all sorts of ominous shapes and shadows
in the unyielding morning light; yew trees stalking towards him

and gnarly puffs of gristle sailing through the sky like Zeppe-
lins, but nothing could extinguish the joyful emptiness that preceded his leap into the void, light and carefree, the promise that
things may not turn out as usual dazzling, if just for one day.

Jazzy sucked at his tongue, running it back and forth over his
teeth and gums, puzzled that someone had turned the music
down, before realising that he was so off his tits that keeping in
motion was all that stopped him from rolling onto the grass and
simply lying there with his feet in the air, gurning like a toxic
tramp. He had to keep moving, that was the key to landing the
plane in the right place.

Hurriedly he entered the long run of lawn that bordered the
back of the house, mown so low that it already resembled some
extinct substance; dried beds of lavender, wilting rose stalks
and overripe apples, browning and fit to explode, sucked into
a memory of the innocence he was leaving behind. Catching
himself out again, he stopped running and tried to walk, the
inclination to actually dance his way across the garden nearly
irresistible. He was far too visible, and oughtn't charge across
the garden like a rampaging barbarian, while at the same time
taking equal care to not creep in, as in the ordinary course of
things he was loud and imposing, and nothing should appear
out of the ordinary. Or was he being too cautious? After all, it
didn't matter who saw him there, he was a common enough
sight, and Petula did not deign to notice him at the politest
of times. Jazzy settled on a half-walk, half-trot, lending him
the air of a desperate comedian milking an audience for cheap
laughs, as he hobbled across the lawn out of breath, ridges of
sweat steaming off his brows.

The curtains both upstairs and down had already parted, and
he could see sharp and deliberate movements in the kitchen.
Taking a hunk of bread out of his pocket he jogged up to the
bird-table, under the guise of replenishing it, to see what the
activity heralded; faintly he could hear Petula's booming voice

carry through the glass, another passionate lecture before breakfast, he adduced. Would she be wasting her time with more talk, or the morning paper, if she knew this was the last sunrise she would ever see? Surreptitiously he shuffled nearer the window, with his back still turned to it, a moonwalk Michael Jackson would have been proud of, had Jazzy kept his balance and not fallen sideways into the flowerbed.

From his place on the ground Jazzy felt like some rodent the humans had left bait out for, the time, and not just the time, out of joint. Yes, it was his mother in full throttle alright, and on his knees again, he could make out the grave and beautiful lunacy of her face – 'After life's fitful fever, sleep well Mum,' he muttered under his breath, an autumnal dragonfly that he mistook for a fiery arrowhead blazing past his eye. Creepily and without interest, Petula's head was bent at an uncomfortable angle and she was looking right through him. She appeared hauntingly ready to embrace the routine mystery of death, her eyes half-closed in the midst of a recitation, Regan slumped at her side, Petula clasping her to her breast protectively like a refugee about to part with her child.

Hashish had always made Jazzy better at noticing things, if not talking about them, and ecstasy better at talking about them, while noticing nothing. Given his current mental condition, there were a number of unusual features to what he saw in the kitchen that made him doubt whether he observed them at all, as even by the skewed standards of The Heights, they were freakishly off-putting. Regan was pinned to her mother in her pyjamas, her face buried in Petula's naked embrace – for Petula appeared to have no clothes on, her robe piled in a heap by the windowpane, the juxtaposition of her body with Regan's, a still life that he had been called upon to paint. Except it was no painting, more of a story, the scene bald and precise, stripped to its essentials, foretelling of a cover their tragedy might one day be bound in, without any of the variables – a mug of coffee here, a bowl of fruit there – that would naturalise the view and put him at ease. Jazzy checked himself, the slalom of doubt was starting to kick in again – the fear that Regan had given him away, Petula having discarded her clothes as part of an elaborate signal to the police who would pounce from the bushes and grab him, and the underlying fear that he still did not know whether he could kill a human being, definitely not his mother, waiting for him like so many showers of shit on the filthy bathmat of his being. Or was he simply hallucinating the entire scene? To hell with it, men died in war: on.

Striding as calmly as he was able, with nothing to hide, Jazzy entered the house by way of the large glass door that led into the conservatory, and from there into her study and the main interconnecting hallway. There was a good chance that he might bump into his mother by mistake now. It was not the end of the world if he did. Jazzy was under no pressure, other than that he put himself under, to act at once. His mistake had been to try and be too exact; there could be a hundred reasons for him being in the house, and he could use any one of them to explain what he was doing there if asked. He could afford to buy his time. All he needed to do was find a corner to lie low in, or even stalk her from – he the lion and she the prey, with one giant advantage over nature: this time the deer did not know it was the food. The house was his to use as he wished, this would be a process, not a one-off hit and run, and would actually occur, he prayed, before the drugs wore off and he broke down and confessed everything to the ghost of one of the farm cats, who had been following him since he entered the house. To do it or not to do it; soon they would both know.

*

Petula gently released her daughter's head; Regan pulling away very slowly so as to not cause any unintended offence.

'Cheer up,' Petula bellowed, hoping to scare away their embarrassment, 'I'll be dead one day soon and you can tell the whole world what a monster I was. But for today, let's get those fainthearts over here for food, and then I can tell them myself. I'm good for that at least, aren't *I*?'

She sounded much more doubtful that she had a moment earlier when she had first announced her intention to address the family on the front lawn. Petula scooped up her robe and draped it gracefully over her aching shoulder; the pain in her legs had spread to every thoroughfare of her body, and she resisted the impulse to shiver. Above all, she did not want her eccentric behaviour to be construed as a mistake, and by embracing choreography and deliberate movements she may yet have succeeded in persuading her daughter she was witnessing a calculated display of strength, however bizarre. And that it would be, if Petula could only extinguish the sickening urge to confide that had burnt away at her ever since Regan flew out to New York. She knew she could go either way, let herself down or hold herself up. Survival suggested that she best stay with what she knew. The day would then go as planned. Regan would naturally comply with her request, any waverers would be winkled out and brought to The Heights for lunch at the point of a sword, her daughter could be relied on for that much, leaving her to bask in the glory of a tray full of perfectly formed meringues, and a flurry of return invitations. Which would be wonderful had these considerations not, at some point in the last few minutes, ceased to be of any importance. Under the gaze of eternity, did she actually *care* if a band of timid fools she was dimly related to came to spend a few strained hours in her company? No. Not really. Not anymore. For the moment they still feared her enough to be coerced, her position was that of a zealot who, lacking the means to convince others, could still waste her own time corralling the unwilling, but short of telling those assembled to eat her shit, and then her food, she had nothing else to offer them. She had never been magnanimous in victory, and as a consequence, had had to keep fighting the same war all over again, every day. The butcher's bill was justified because, she had always calculated, were she deprived of people she would die. But what if she no longer wanted the people? Power all along had always been too paltry a goal for one equipped with her gifts, but she had always been frightened she would lose it if she strived for something else. That self-imposed break on her development had evaporated.

'You don't believe that Mum, so please stop saying things like that, you know, that you'll be dead one day soon...'

'I didn't say *soon*, I said one day,' Petula insisted, wringing the distinction for its full meaning, 'though perhaps "soon" is what your heart desires Regan? Is it time for Mummy to die and give you some space?'

'Jesus Mum, stop talking like you're in a mad play, you're being crazy, nuts. Why do you have to go on about dying, you're not even that old yet,' Regan gabbled, immediately regretting the '*that*' and the '*yet*'. She had watched her mother pick up another aluminium sheet of pills, the days clearly marked but individual tablets torn out of order, which, next to the drawer stuffed full of assorted medical goodies Petula gorged on every day, was an overdose in waiting in any language. Even a careful person would finally end up mixing various quantities and types, and the order of both, with everything from aspirin to barbiturates hypochondriacally over-represented in Petula's stash, and her mother was not a careful person. 'Really Mum, there's just no need, you scare me when you get like this, talking about dying. It's morbid.'

'To be honest, there is, you know, there is a need,' Petula said, dry-swallowing a handful of pills she seemed to have selected on the hoof, her preferred cordial for washing them down not for Regan's eyes, and subsequent judgement. 'Everyone's too scared about coming clean about dying these days. When we grew up it was everywhere, in the air, under water, over the top; it had happened to our fathers and grandfathers when they were much younger than you. God, it was as normal as putting your uniform on or having your bum pinched. I'm not pretending to be a hero like they were, of course not, I'll admit I wanted it, dying I mean, to not happen for as long as I could put it off for, and if it wasn't going to happen tomorrow then good, because it meant I didn't have to think about it today. And it's true. I admit it. That I wanted to go on for ever and ever, like any other healthy-minded person, and wanted you to want me to *too...*'

Petula gave her daughter the chance to organically interject with a 'Hear hear,' but encountering only 'Mum, the tense you're talking in, it's a bit weird, is there something serious *wrong* with you?', she continued:

'The thing is, I didn't just want immortality for its own sake, I wanted what was *best* for the goods themselves. No, don't look as if you don't know what I'm talking about, you do, I mean the works, our art, fundamentally for this place; this house, our house, for her, look all around you,' Petula waved her hand in a self-explanatory circle – Ming plates, Venetian cabinets and an etching of Tracy Emin's hairy vagina taken in by this regal swoop – 'all these works, for *her*, because The Heights is like England. She is a *she*. I wanted to safeguard the integrity of the entire property and our lands, our whole world; I wanted what was best for these things, and I thought that the best thing for them was *me*, and then you. The whole point of afternoons like the one we have coming, and the million slogs that went before them, was, I admit it, to nourish my continued existence. Because *my* stewardship was the best guarantee this place would ever have of being properly appreciated and cultivated and added to where necessary; and to have a legacy, something to show the world that this was *us* and this is how *we* lived, yes? And to enjoy them, all this beauty, the trees, crockery, shrubbery and library, all purely for their own good, purely and for themselves, for these views to be ennobled because it was *us* gazing out at them every bloody day and no one else. But I seem to have got it wrong. Or the wrong way round. All this was just another thing to do, an excuse to get my mind off me...' Petula's jaw shook, and with some effort she continued: 'No, being scared of death is a grownup version of being scared of the dark. You have to search for the appeal of both and be prepared to take their side. Perhaps that's the thing I called to tell you.'

'I hope I die before you,' Regan lied.

'Don't, Regan. What you've seen is all you'll know and all I've told you. I'll see you later,' Petula claimed, her formidable freckly back already turned to her daughter, as she sought the corridor, her legs twitching like pillars before an earthquake.

Holding back her sobs so as to avoid impersonating an attention-seeking ghost, her legs stiff enough to snap, Petula shambled down the hallway, towards the far end of the house and store room that doubled as an indoor garage, full of old bicycles, go-carts, board games, school books, pogo sticks and tennis rackets. Beyond her beliefs, which were her own inventions, there were strange forces that she could not understand, that had withdrawn their support, and it was these that had defeated her. Her life had become no more than the shadow cast by her depression. Whereas unhappiness had always felt too much like her enemies' final vindication for her to accept, Petula saw no reason to keep from herself what she now knew to be irrevocable: soul sclerosis.

'Mediocrities of the world I absolve you all,' she quietly mithered. It was really quite surprising, she was not facing a person anymore, but drifting naturally into a world of concepts and ideas. She would have to die because she did not have a positive reason left to live, life would not do at all, and she lacked the energy to look back at this moment and deem it significant because of what she would do next. The present was neither special nor secure enough to offer the basis for future redemption.

Coughing, she noticed a speck of blood in her hand; what had she been doing to her body these past few years? She no longer gave it any thought. A good life well lived is long enough and an inauthentic life already too long. The confederate grey walls and paintings in this section of the corridor had been replaced by her memories, none of which needed to be held to the realistic standards of the present. Petula could look through the watercolours left by various talented guests and enter another world, spying the curtains she had not noticed since her honeymoon in Capri twitch in the breeze, the forecourt full of Bedouin bandsmen in Oman in the moonlight that awaited the guests on her fortieth birthday, and all three children, future enmities still unthinkable, clambering on top of one another at bath-time, their mirth and hers blowing about the place like all her remembered autumns; and as suddenly, their tainted opposite: the curtains torn down in rage, the forecourt punctuated by angry shouts and the children in tears because she could not cope with the affront of having to put on their pyjamas when there were parties she was already late for. Where was the last word? If she could just take the side of the truth and not be forced to defend her own version then she might truly surprise them at lunch, but there was too much to do and she would never get it done in time.

Ahead Petula watched Jazzy approach her with his head sloped too far into his chest to see his face, then veer sharply into the hall privy and noisily bolt the door. Didn't he have his own house to take a shit in, she thought mischievously, and then forgot all about him; dazzling spears of sunlight dropping like lightning before her, a drum banging away in the background and voices, hers and others, singing: '*Come and join our merry throng...*' Petula was ready to join them, for her nature, and the necessity to act upon it to collapse, and to simply float over the carnage in a state of grace. Forget work, the holidays had *finally* begun!

*

It was happening again; Jazzy was inside and too terrified to get out. All the horror of existence lined the corridor, every particle of the house a destabilising reminder that he ought to have brought an exorcist with him, and not a crust of bread and bottle of disinfectant. In his teens this unnecessarily spacious lavatory had been his club house, a den where he could spend many a happy hour re-reading his old 2000ADs and *Melody Makers*, safe in the smell of his own eggy excrement, his mother bounding up and down the corridor with air freshener telling him to get a move on before the guests arrived. All this, only to one day find himself lodged in a man-sized safe deposit box, hoping that his stay here would be considerably shorter than his illustrious sessions of the past. She had seen him! 'Shit, what *now*, what *now*...'

Wiping his damp palms on the surprisingly dirty floral hand towel Jazzy attempted to stem the panic and gain stock of his situation. He was too far in to clamber out and not even on the right floor – he had to be upstairs to do what he had to do, and so did she, so his current whereabouts, worse than wrong, were of no help to him unless he was prepared to alter his plan of attack, radically. One could not push someone down the stairs on the ground floor. As he weighed up this information Jazzy was at a loss as to who was actually benefitting from the feedback. His real self was left behind many decisions ago, he could not consult it for help, yet this new voice, breaking down his options into the practical language of a killer, was of little use either – he seemed to need the old him to tell the new him what do to, but the old him would open the bathroom window, crawl out and go home, and if he did that then nothing would ever work for him again.

'Focus, fuck's sake, *focus*,' he grunted under his breath. That was the issue: to stay focused, work out what had to be done, and do *it*; to terminate with extreme prejudice and never look back.

'Come on,' he muttered, 'think like a terminator...'

Winners were never victims, and it was like a victim to give up because events had unravelled in such a way as to require a Plan B. A winner would accept that everyone gets punched and know how to roll with the blows. He was in urgent need of some calm. He pulled a crumpled joint out of his pocket, one he had made just in case, and taking care to not let the smoke carry, lit it bent over the toilet bowl, with the window jarred open.

Jazzy found it easiest to think of himself back at Tianta that evening relaxing over a much bigger spliff than this one, looking back at the morning as one of his proudest, with what he had yet to do already done, than face the next few minutes as a hostile void that required praxis to fill it. The goal was already in the back of the net even though he had not taken a shot. Except it was not, and wouldn't be if he stayed there smoking drugs. And despite trying to do *something*, *nothing* still prevailed, Jazzy crushing the joint and perspiring over the sink, then retrieving it and straighten it again only to crush it once more in impotent exasperation. Fiercely he splashed cold water over his face and told himself over and over again that he would never be able to pump himself up to this point again; today was his last and only chance to grow as a person and surprise himself. But that still wasn't a strong enough team talk for what he had to do. The yellowing slits with bloodshot bullseyes he saw in the mirror were his own; the rest of his face looked like a bright-red broad bean bailing out of a triathlon. It was hopeless; he was hopeless! How long had he already wasted in here? A worryingly long time, because he had already wondered how long he had spent doing nothing a worryingly long time ago. He had to get out and do *it*, do it and let God judge him, though this was the biggest balls-up of all because he did not know whether he believed in God and a moment like this should at least be crowned by certainty; the certainty that he was doing the right thing. His mind was rejecting him, chattering away like a hundred keyboards operated by a contagion, the keys typing out the same admonition, 'You silly cunt, you silly cunt, you silly...'

Events pushed him into a snap decision. There were clippity-clop steps approaching the door again, he was not going to get Petula where he wanted her but one hard shunt onto the floor might do just as well, and if it absolutely came to it, he could always finish things off with the Encyclopaedia Britannica that had been thoughtfully left above the bog. Go, now, *yes*, do it, for God's sake *go*, for the kids and Spider, for that time Tinwood made Evita suffer, yes yes *yes*, he could hear the whistle, and it was his turn now, the light was green, it was time to jump, out to where legends are made, shrapnel flies, and Victoria Crosses grow... *go*!

Jazzy practically fell out of the bathroom, his arms and legs a wobbling jumble of conflicting commands, realising at once that his prevaricating masterplan was shot. The very reality of murder, Jazzy saw, had turned out to be another fantasy in a life of mostly good intentions gone bad; a game in which, because of his secrecy, he had had to call his own bluff, as his old self, his real self, had known all along he would do. He would never lay a finger on his mother. He was not that type of man, and nor would he be called to because it was Regan who slammed straight into him, a look of incriminating guilt spilling over her face, as she dropped a heavy jar of dissoluble sleeping pills to the floor with a sharp crack.

'What...' she began hastily.

'I... *you*?' Jazzy started and did not finish.

They were saved then, and forever, by an urgent volley of knocks on the front door, followed by a woman shrieking their names at the top of her voice.

*

Ten minutes earlier Jenny Hardfield had been busy in her kitchen – marginally, but not much, larger than the lavatory Jazzy had locked himself away in – preparing a chocolate sponge for Mingus's visit home, and a speech she would deliver to Petula when she next snubbed a greeting of hers on the track down to the village. This speech had been something of a valorous work-in-progress for many, many years now, prey to limitless revisions and changes of emphasis, new passages of freshly received offence joining those staple and long-nurtured grievances that formed its spine, the overall length at times verging on the un-performable, with a process of subtle displacement ensuring that if it ever were to find its way into the open, it ought to last not much longer than forty-five minutes, providing Petula remained silent during its hearing. To Jenny's great annoyance, on those few occasions Petula did deign to acknowledge her, it was still on her old employer's terms, and never the conversation she was preparing herself for. So even if she was insulted in some pertinent way, which she nearly always was, the necessary bridge to drive her speech over invariably failed to materialise, meaning that she was left with even more to say, if and when the fateful day of deliverance finally dawned. At times she would rehearse highlights with Seth, who characteristically made no comment beyond 'That'll get you into trouble,' and on various mutual acquaintances whose looks implied 'Rather you than me,' though after the first few years they inclined towards believing that what they were hearing was a robust form of therapy for Jenny, and not anything Petula Montague would actually find herself having to hear.

That morning, as she removed her oven gloves and turned off the radio – she loved the 'retro' stations but hated the adverts that came on every third song, tempted to defect back to the BBC – Jenny was tending towards a shorter version of her magnum opus, entertaining an idea her son had put in her head.

Mingus, who on transatlantic calls was often cast in the role of agony-uncle, knowing all the main parties and being excessively patient with matters he found elementary and risible, had, in as close to a fit of pique as he was likely to achieve, explained to his mother that her lament might be made more effective if she was to distil her injuries, and the years that suffered them, into a few simple lines, instead of the Book of bloody Revelations, because Petula had quite enough of that with Jazzy, and was probably adept at dismissing such objections with ease, if she knew what was coming, reacting only to what surprised her and not to what she could *predict*.

Jenny looked daggers; her inner voice composing a brief letter of complaint appropriate to an insurance payment that had been held up, rather than humiliation's greatest hits of the last thirty-five years, a mushy blanket of falling leaves swishing through the open window and onto her spotless floor, forming a yellow and orange quilt she had no wish to disturb yet.

Excuse me Petula, she would begin, *but don't you think it would be nice to say hello back to someone who says hello to you, even if you are in a hurry or busy with something else, and wouldn't you say hello if it was anyone else apart from me? I think you would, wouldn't you, because I see you being nice to important people all the time, and it doesn't make me feel very good about myself being made to think I'm less important than them, especially as I've always tried to be so nice to you, and so have my son and husband, even when you haven't been so careful as us in trying to be nice back. And I just think it's gone on long enough and if I don't say anything now you'll never be any nicer, so...*

It was proceeding well, Jenny thought, and she hadn't even mentioned her nuclear weapon yet – that they were moving to a new house Mingus was having built for them by the sea in Filey – or said anything about how awful it was when she had overheard Petula say she didn't want people 'like *them*' (*like them*!) in her life, ruining the happy memories Jenny associated with Mingus and Regan's childhood, where she had thought she was accepted, if made occasional fun of. The saddest part was that she could tell Petula was hurting too, as the result of her own policies, and it might be worth adding that as well, just to show she could be even-handed and that it wasn't only she who let pain get to her... Jenny stopped. She experienced a thud against the kitchen wall as though it were her skin being punctured, and heard the sound of her name being called rattle through the house, as if spoken from a dream, both noises over faster than she could register, her memory of them being loud (or was she amplifying the feeling rather than the noise?) and uncannily subdued at the same time. Jenny knew that this was of importance and that she should go out and look at what had happened, at the same time as being too scared to leave the kitchen on her own. An event had occurred, the time of preparing and waiting was over, life was very much back on again, and there was nothing she could do about it except pretend that it had not happened or admit that it had. Memories of running that boy over years earlier came back to her, how could they not, it had occurred on the very hairpin bend at which she lived so where could she go to forget? And what had she heard besides the whack of his body that night? A voice, echoing through the car, calling her name, yes, she had definitely been called again just now, by the same voice, to perform one last service, oh, she knew it, knew it and had to do *it*.

'Seth,' she cried, 'Seth, can you come here, quickly, I need your help?' Her husband had been clanging round in an upstairs room, looking for an axe handle ('Who else keeps axe handles in the spare room Seth, I mean really!' she had said, though it wasn't really a spare room, it was Mingus's old room, and she resented the way Seth stored rubbish that didn't belong there amongst the carefully preserved artefacts of the love of her life), 'Please, I need you down here love, it's an *emergency!*'

There was no answer. Taking off her apron, Jenny decided

she must be brave and bear up to it alone if she had to, and pushing the back door, which opened on to a small herb garden, she tried to avoid looking at the robe, filling with air like a parachute, and underneath it, the crumpled and naked body squashed against the wall, a bicycle lying nearby with its bent front wheel mangled, the back wheel still spinning in the air. The rider had proceeded straight down the hill at full pelt, not turned at the corner and, by choice or necessity, pivoted straight over the hedge, somersaulted, and been stopped by the kitchen wall, which is where the body, quite obviously Petula's, had ended its journey, a solitary lock of red hair having settled on one of the crushed hollyhocks.

'Christ,' whispered Jenny, 'my oh my.' So that was it. The proud city whose high walls, once thought impregnable, would stand no more, and in its place, strife, rack and ruin would rage unchecked through the land. Or the snow would melt and the little creatures would come out to play. They would find out soon enough, as there was no use pretending she was still alive.

At some point Jenny had been joined by her husband, who, scratching his nose, approaching but not getting too close to the body, inspected it mistrustfully. 'Those legs of hers couldn't bend, she wouldn't have been able to bring them up at the knee, you can't ride one of them racers if you can't peddle. Can't ride any bike if you can't peddle. Tell the truth, I'm a might surprised she could even get on, without help. Someone would have had to have lifted her. Fair go, game to the end. Not very thoughtful though, you know, to leave the house in, er, so few things.'

'She weren't on it for a *pleasure* ride Seth. Get her some of the clothes, the old ones of hers she gave me, and dress her. It's indecent as it is. They could say she was mad after all instead of saying she was ever *so* marvellous.'

'Don't you think we should wait for, er, the Police. I mean Emergency Services, love?'

'Them? Don't be daft,' laughed Jenny, going inside to fetch her coat, 'the only thing that could stop her was what did. And even then it weren't her fault. I blame the wall.'

*

Regan chose a little-known passage from Ned Wrath's posthumous notebooks to read at the funeral, which, contrary to Petula's wishes, took place at the small Baptist Church in the village, and not York Minster Cathedral:

> '*A humble born and bred race, growing up in the right conditions of outdoor as much as indoor harmony, would find it enough to merely live, in their relations to the sky, air, water, trees, and in the fact of life itself, discovering and achieving happiness, with their being suffused by wholesome ecstasy, surpassing all the pleasures that wealth, amusement, erudition, the intellect, or even a sense of art could afford, to leave all thought behind and to just be in being...*'

The pews rumbled with unease, some affected, some not, the more clued-up accusing Regan of exercising poor taste, more still consternated that they had been deprived of one last grand act to get their teeth into, Regan glad for real friends like Max Astley, who tipped his hat and bowed with a wink, as she followed the coffin out of the church into the graveyard, followed by Jazzy and Evita. Her two siblings had allowed Regan to handle everything, from the important details to the boring ones. Jazzy's immediate breakdown and confiscation of the body, lasting for six awkward hours, was fast replaced by a stately silence and an authoritative dignity that suited him, coloured a little by worrying talk about 'knowing his rights', and the hiring of a notorious local law firm that specialised in 'family' disputes and 'accident' claims. Meanwhile Evita had appeared from nowhere with twins and an earnest Paraguayan husband in tow, her smile painted-on and irremovable as she devoutly set about baking cake after cake and organising children's games for the adults, her family belonging to the Jehovah's Witnesses whose brethren, she hinted, might find their own uses for The Heights, should God be allowed to have his way. Noah was nowhere to be seen, a brief note letting his daughter understand that she was in charge now and could do whatever she pleased so long as she did not involve him, which was the most he now wished to have to do with their lives. Mindful that critics should never confer, and that if their opinion was of any use it should be all their own, all three children elected to glide past each other without conference, content to be left, for now, to enjoy these first days of freedom as best they could, before the next war started. Especially as the farm had never looked so beautiful that winter, the mildest on record, nor so full of the potential to make those that dwelt on it happy. Had this blessing now fallen to Petula's children, as her true legacy, or was the early appearance of snowdrops and daffodils marking the peace that descends on a valley between battles, its symphonious succulence no more than the prelude to the burning lake of fire all would soon be reduced to?

Moving into her mother's room, Regan grew uneasy that she might mix things up and forget the force that once was. Petula's was a personality that relied on its existence for its effect with no recourse to outside help, its strength based on the illusion of its glare; once extinguished, what trace would it leave when it was no longer there, to need or miss itself? Regan need not have entertained any doubts on that score. As the weeks passed she observed that she did not move nearer or further away from her mother, who belonged in another realm; all she had to do was switch levels. Her concern that a gulf may appear, not knowing whether the tunnel she saw as she closed her eyes led to the stars or to nothing, was baseless. Passing time, ten minutes or twenty years, could make no difference to their proximity, nor death alter their relation. Late into the night, Regan would draw open the windows to allow the nocturnal chill to advance over her bedding, and gaze out at the Thanatosphere; a silvery ring round the moon where the souls of the dead waited hopefully to be reincarnated and given another chance. She would then imagine Petula circling the cosmos in search of an opening: would they meet again?

Silently she mouthed the words, so close to becoming tears, 'I love you Mum'; then drew the covers over her shoulders and tried to forget about her.

Acknowledgements

My love and thanks to John Stubbs, whose comments on an early draft of this book were extremely helpful, and also to Georgina Garrett, Margaret Glover and Etan Ilfeld for their considered feedback. Thanks also to my editors at Repeater, Phil Jourdan, Emma Jacobs and Alex Niven; to Jan Middendorp for formatting the work; to Stephanie Rennie for the author's photograph, to Johnny Bull for the cover and Mat Osman and John Carter Cassady for the ideas that helped inspire it; and to my wife, Emma, for many happy times that outnumbered some sad ones, in the four and a half years this book took to write.

The poet Ned Wrath plagiarises selectively from John Ashbery in his essay and later from Walt Whitman for the funeral address; the rest is fiction.

Repeater Books

is dedicated to the creation of a new reality. The landscape of twenty-first-century arts and letters is faded and inert, riven by fashionable cynicism, egotistical self-reference and a nostalgia for the recent past. Repeater intends to add its voice to those movements that wish to enter history and assert control over its currents, gathering together scattered and isolated voices with those who have already called for an escape from Capitalist Realism. Our desire is to publish in every sphere and genre, combining vigorous dissent and a pragmatic willingness to succeed where messianic abstraction and quiescent co-option have stalled: abstention is not an option: we are alive and we don't agree.